Books by Tess Gerritsen

Harvest
Life Support
Bloodstream
Gravity

Published by POCKET BOOKS

TESS GERRITSEN

HARVEST
LIFE SUPPORT

POCKET BOOKS

New York   London   Toronto   Sydney

POCKET BOOKS, a division of Simon & Schuster, Inc.
1230 Avenue of the Americas, New York, NY 10020

Life Support is a work of fiction. Names, characters, places and incidents are products of the author's imagination or are used fictitiously. Any resemblance to actual events or locales or persons, living or dead, is entirely coincidental.

Harvest is a work of fiction. Names, characters, places and incidents are products of the author's imagination or are used fictitiously.

The New England Organ bank (NEOB) is a not-for-profit agency that recovers and distributes human organs and tissues for transplant. The United Network for Organ Sharing (UNOS) maintains the national transplant network under contract to the federal government and monitors compliance with national rules for organ sharing and distribution.

Both NEOB and UNOS have systems in place to prevent unlawful recovery of organs and to ensure equitable distribution of organs to recipients. It is illegal to buy or sell organs.

The use of their names and acronyms for their names in this book is for the sake of the novel's atmosphere and plot. Any other resemblance to actual events or locales or persons, living or dead, is entirely coincidental.

ISBN: 1-4165-0740-X

First Pocket Books trade paperback edition January 2005

10 9 8 7 6 5 4 3 2 1

POCKET and colophon are registered trademarks of
Simon & Schuster, Inc.

Manufactured in the United States of America

For information regarding special discounts for bulk purchases,
please contact Simon & Schuster Special Sales at 1-800-456-6798
or business@simonandschuster.com.

HARVEST

*To Jacob, my husband
and my very best friend*

Acknowledgments

A heartfelt thanks to Emily Bestler for her gentle and insightful editing; to David Bowman for sharing his expertise on the Russian mafia; to Transplant Coordinators Susan Pratt, at Penobscot Bay Medical Center, and Bruce White, at Maine Medical Center, for their invaluable insights into the organ donation process; to Patty Kahn for helping me navigate the medical library computer; to John Sargent of Rockland, Maine, for his locksmithing advice; and to Roger Pepper for faithfully sending research materials my way.

Above all, a very special thanks to Meg Ruley and Don Cleary of the Jane Rotrosen Agency. You made it happen.

1

He was small for his age, smaller than the other boys who panhandled in the underpass at Arbats-Kaya, but at eleven years old he had already done it all. He had been smoking cigarettes for four years, stealing for three and a half, and turning tricks for two. This last vocation Yakov did not much care for, but it was something Uncle Misha insisted upon. How else were they to buy bread and cigarettes? Yakov, being the smallest and blondest of Uncle Misha's boys, bore the brunt of the trade. The customers always favored the young ones, the fair ones. They did not seem to care about Yakov's missing left hand; indeed, most did not even notice his withered stump. They were too enchanted by his smallness, his blondness, his unflinching blue eyes.

Yakov longed to grow out of the trade, to earn his keep by picking pockets like the bigger boys. Every morning when he woke up in Misha's flat, and every evening before he fell asleep, he would reach up with his one good hand and grasp the head bar of his cot. He'd stretch and stretch, hoping to add another fraction of a centimeter to his height. A useless exercise, Uncle Misha advised him. Yakov was small because he came from stunted stock. The woman who'd abandoned him in Moscow seven years ago had been stunted too. Yakov could scarcely remember the woman, nor could he remember much

1

of anything else from his life before the city. He knew only what Uncle Misha told him, and he believed only half of it. At the tender age of eleven, Yakov was both diminutive and wise.

So it was with his natural skepticism that he now regarded the man and woman talking business with Uncle Misha over the dining table.

The couple had come to the flat in a large black car with dark windows. The man, named Gregor, wore a suit and tie and shoes of real leather. The woman Nadiya was a blonde dressed in a skirt and jacket of fine wool and she carried a hard-shelled valise. She was not Russian—that much was immediately evident to all four boys in the flat. She was American, perhaps, or English. She spoke in fluent but accented Russian.

While the two men conducted business over vodka, the woman's gaze wandered about the tiny flat, taking in the old army cots shoved up against the wall, the piles of dirty bedclothes, and the four boys huddled together in anxious silence. She had light gray eyes, pretty eyes, and she studied the boys each in turn. First she looked at Pyotr, the oldest at fifteen. Then she looked at Stepan, thirteen, and Aleksei, ten.

And finally, she looked at Yakov.

Yakov was accustomed to such scrutiny by adults, and he gazed back calmly. What he was not accustomed to was being so quickly passed over. Usually the adults ignored the other boys. This time it was gangly, pimply-faced Pyotr who garnered the woman's attention.

Nadiya said to Misha: "You are doing the right thing, Mikhail Isayevich. These children have no future here. We offer them such a chance!" She smiled at the boys.

Stepan, the dullard, grinned back like an idiot in love.

"You understand, they speak no English," said Uncle Misha. "Only a word, here and there."

"Children pick it up quickly. For them, it is effortless."

"They will need time to learn. The language, the food—"

"Our agency is quite familiar with transitional needs. We work with so many Russian children. Orphans, like these. They will stay, for a while, in a special school to give them time to adjust."

"And if they cannot?"

Nadiya paused. "Every so often, there are exceptions. The

ones with emotional difficulties.'' Her gaze swept the four boys. ''Is there one in particular who concerns you?''

Yakov knew that *he* was the one with the difficulties of which they spoke. The one who seldom laughed and never cried, the one Uncle Misha called his ''little stone boy.'' Yakov did not know why he never cried. The other boys, when hurt, would shed fat and sloppy tears. Yakov would simply turn his mind blank, the way the television screen turned blank late at night after the stations shut off. No transmission, no images, just that comforting white fuzz.

Uncle Misha said, ''They are all good boys. Excellent boys.''

Yakov looked at the other three boys. Pyotr had a jutting brow and shoulders perpetually hunched forward like a gorilla's. Stepan had odd ears, small and wrinkled, between which floated a walnut for a brain. Aleksei was sucking his thumb.

And I, thought Yakov, looking down at his stump of a forearm, I have only one hand. Why do they say we are excellent? Yet that was precisely what Uncle Misha kept insisting. And the woman kept nodding. These were good boys, healthy boys.

''Even their teeth are good!'' pointed out Misha. ''Not rotten at all. And look how tall my Pyotr is.''

''That one there looks undernourished.'' Gregor pointed to Yakov. ''And what happened to his hand?''

''He was born without it.''

''The radiation?''

''It does not affect him otherwise. It's just the missing hand.''

''It should pose no problem,'' said Nadiya. She rose from the chair. ''We must leave. It's time.''

''So soon?''

''We have a schedule to keep.''

''But—their clothes—''

''The agency will provide clothes. Better than what they're wearing now.''

''Is it to happen so quickly? We have no time to say goodbye?''

A ripple of irritation passed through the woman's eyes. ''A moment. We don't want to miss our connections.''

Uncle Misha looked at his boys, his four boys, related to him not by blood, nor even by love, but by mutual dependence. Mutual need. He hugged each of the boys in turn. When he came to Yakov, he held on a little longer, a little tighter. Uncle Misha smelled of onions and cigarettes, familiar smells. Good smells. But Yakov's instinct was to recoil from the closeness. He disliked being held or touched, by anyone.

"Remember your uncle," Misha whispered. "When you are rich in America. Remember how I watched over you."

"I don't want to go to America," said Yakov.

"It's for the best. For all of you."

"I want to stay with you, Uncle! I want to stay here."

"You have to go."

"Why?"

"Because I have decided." Uncle Misha grasped his shoulders and gave him a hard shake. "I have decided."

Yakov looked at the other boys, who were grinning at each other. And he thought: They are happy about this. Why am I the only one with doubts?

The woman took Yakov by the hand. "I'll bring them to the car. Gregor can finish up here with the papers."

"Uncle?" called Yakov.

But Misha had already turned away and was staring out the window.

Nadiya shepherded the four boys into the hallway and down the stairs. It was three flights to the street. All those clomping shoes, all that noisy boy energy, seemed to ricochet loudly through the empty stairwell.

They were already on the ground floor when Aleksei suddenly halted. "Wait! I forgot Shu-Shu!" he cried and went tearing back up the stairs.

"Come back here!" called Nadiya. "You can't go up there!"

"I can't leave him!" yelled Aleksei.

"Come back here *now!*"

Aleksei just kept thudding away up the steps. The woman was about to chase after him when Pyotr said, "He won't leave without Shu-Shu."

"Who the devil is Shu-Shu?" she snapped.

"His stuffed dog. He's had it forever."

She glanced up the stairwell toward the fourth floor, and in that instant Yakov saw, in her eyes, something he did not understand.

Apprehension.

She stood as though poised between pursuit and abandonment of Aleksei. When the boy came running back down the stairs with the tattered Shu-Shu clutched in his arms, the woman seemed to melt in relief against the banister.

"Got him!" crowed Aleksei, embracing the stuffed animal.

"Now we *go*," the woman said, ushering them outside.

The four boys piled into the backseat of the car. It was cramped, and Yakov had to sit halfway on Pyotr's lap.

"Can't you put your bony ass somewhere else?" grumbled Pyotr.

"Where shall I put it? In your face?"

Pyotr shoved him. He shoved back.

"Stop it!" ordered the woman from the front seat. "Behave yourselves."

"But there's not enough room back here," complained Pyotr.

"Then make room. And hush!" The woman glanced up at the building, toward the fourth floor. Toward Misha's flat.

"Why are we waiting?" asked Aleksei.

"Gregor. He's signing the papers."

"How long will it take?"

The woman sat back and stared straight ahead. "Not long."

A close call, thought Gregor as the boy Aleksei left the flat for the second time and slammed the door behind him. Had the little bastard popped in a moment later, there would be hell to pay. What was that stupid Nadiya doing, letting the brat back upstairs? He had been against using Nadiya from the start. But Reuben had insisted on a woman. People would trust a woman.

The boy's footsteps receded down the stairwell, a loud clomp-clomp followed by the thud of the building door.

Gregor turned to the pimp.

Misha was standing at the window, staring down at the street, at the car where his four boys sat. He pressed his hand to the glass, his fat fingers splayed in farewell. When he turned to face Gregor, his eyes were actually misted with tears.

But his first words were about the money. "Is it in the valise?"

"Yes," said Gregor.

"All of it?"

"Twenty thousand American dollars. Five thousand per child. You did agree to the price."

"Yes." Misha sighed and ran a hand over his face. A face whose furrows showed only too well the effect of too much vodka, too many cigarettes. "They will be adopted by proper families?"

"Nadiya will see to it. She loves children, you know. It's why she chose this work."

Misha managed a weak smile. "Perhaps she could find *me* an American family."

Gregor had to get him away from the window. He pointed to the valise, which was resting on an end table. "Go ahead. Check it if you wish."

Misha went to the valise and unsnapped the catch. Inside were stacks of American bills, bound together in neat bundles. Twenty thousand dollars, enough for all the vodka a man would need to rot his liver. How cheap it is these days to buy a man's soul, thought Gregor. On the streets of this new Russia, one could barter for anything. A crate of Israeli oranges, an American television, the pleasure of a woman's body. Opportunity everywhere, for those with the talent to mine it.

Misha stood staring down at that money, his money, but not with a look of triumph. Rather, it was a look of disgust. He closed the valise and stood with head bowed, hands resting on the hard black plastic.

Gregor stepped up behind Misha's balding head, raised the barrel of a silenced automatic, and fired two bullets into the man's brain.

Blood and gray matter spattered the far wall. Misha collapsed facedown, toppling the end table as he fell. The valise thudded onto the rug beside him.

Gregor snatched up the valise before the pooling blood could reach it. There were clumps of human tissue on the side. He went into the bathroom, used toilet paper to wipe the splatters off the plastic, and flushed away the tissue. When he walked back into the room where Misha lay, the pool of blood had already crept across the floor and was soaking into another rug.

Gregor glanced around the room to assure himself that his work here was done and that no evidence remained. He was tempted to take the bottle of vodka with him, but decided against it. Explanations would be required as to why he had

Misha's precious bottle, and Gregor had no patience for the questions of children. That was Nadiya's department.

He left the flat and went downstairs.

Nadiya and her charges were waiting in the car. She looked at him as he slid behind the wheel, the questions plain in her eyes.

"You have the papers all signed?" she asked.

"Yes. All of them."

Nadiya sat back, exhaling an audible sigh of relief. She had no nerves for this, Gregor thought as he started the car. No matter what Reuben said, the woman was a liability.

There were sounds of scuffling from the backseat. Gregor glanced in the rearview mirror and saw that the boys were shoving each other back and forth. All except the smallest one, Yakov, who was staring straight ahead. In the mirror their gazes met, and Gregor had the eerie sensation that the eyes of an adult were staring out of that child's face.

Then the boy turned and punched his neighbor in the shoulder. Suddenly the backseat was a tangle of squirming bodies and flailing limbs.

"Behave yourselves!" said Nadiya. "Can't you keep quiet? We have a long drive to Riga."

The boys calmed down. For a moment there was silence in the backseat. Then, in the rearview mirror, Gregor saw the little one, the one with the adult eyes, jab an elbow at his neighbor.

That made Gregor smile. No reason to worry, he thought. They were, after all, merely children.

2

It was midnight, and Karen Terrio was fighting to keep her eyes open. Fighting to stay on the road.

She had been driving for the better part of two days now, had left right after Aunt Dorothy's funeral, and she hadn't stopped except to pull over for a quick nap or a hamburger and coffee. Lots of coffee. Her aunt's funeral had receded to a two-day-old blur of memories. Wilting gladioli. Nameless cousins. Stale finger sandwiches. Obligations, so damn many obligations.

Now all she wanted was to go home.

She knew she should pull off again, should try to catch another quick nap before pressing onward, but she was so close, only fifty miles from Boston. At the last Dunkin' Donuts, she'd tanked up on three more cups of coffee. That had helped, a little; it had given her just enough of a buzz to get from Springfield to Sturbridge. Now the caffeine was starting to wear off, and even though she thought she was awake, every so often her head would dip in a sharp bob, and she knew she'd fallen asleep, if only for a second.

A Burger King sign beckoned from the darkness ahead. She pulled off the highway.

Inside she ordered coffee and a blueberry muffin and sat

down at a table. At this hour of night, there were only a few patrons in the dining room, all of them wearing the same pasty masks of exhaustion. Highway ghosts, thought Karen. The same tired souls who seemed to haunt every highway rest stop. It was eerily quiet in that dining room, everyone focused on trying to stay awake and get back on the road.

At the next table sat a depressed-looking woman with two small children, both of them quietly chewing on cookies. Those children, so well-behaved, so blond, made Karen think of her own daughters. It was their birthday tomorrow. Tonight, asleep in their beds, she thought, they are only a day away from being thirteen. A day further from their childhood.

When you wake up, she thought, I'll be home.

She refilled her coffee cup, snapped on a plastic cover, and walked out to her car.

Her head felt clear now. She could make it. An hour, fifty miles, and she'd be walking in her front door. She started the engine and pulled out of the parking lot.

Fifty miles, she thought. Only fifty miles.

Twenty miles away, parked behind a 7-Eleven, Vince Lawry and Chuck Servis finished off the last six-pack. They'd been going at it for four straight hours, just a little friendly competition to see who could toss back the most Buds without puking it all up again. Chuck was ahead by one. They'd lost track of the total; they'd have to figure it out in the morning when they tallied up the beer cans mounded in the backseat.

But Chuck was definitely ahead, and he was gloating about it, which pissed Vince off, because Chuck was better at every fucking thing. And this wasn't a fair contest. Vince could've gone another round, but the Bud had run out, and now Chuck was wearing that eat-shit grin of his, even though he knew it wasn't a fair contest.

Vince shoved open the car door and climbed out of the driver's seat.

"Where you going?" asked Chuck.

"T'get some more."

"You can't handle no more."

"Fuck you," said Vince, and stumbled across the parking lot toward the 7-Eleven's front door.

Chuck laughed. "You can't even walk!" he yelled out the window.

Asshole, thought Vince. What the fuck, he could walk. See, he was walking fine. He'd just stroll into the 7-Eleven and pick up two more sixes. Maybe three. Yeah, he could do three, easy. His stomach was iron, and except for having to piss every few minutes, he didn't feel the effects at all.

He tripped going in the door—goddamn high threshold, they could get sued for that—but he picked himself right up. He got three six-packs from the cooler and swaggered over to the cash register. He plunked down a twenty-dollar bill.

The clerk looked at the money and shook his head. "Can't take it," he said.

"What do you mean, can't take it?"

"Can't sell beer to an intoxicated customer."

"Are you saying I'm drunk?"

"That's right."

"Look, it's money, isn't it? You don't want my fucking money?"

"I don't wanna get sued. You just put the beer back, son, OK? Better yet, why don't you buy a cup of coffee or something? A hot dog."

"I don't want a fucking hot dog."

"Then just walk on out, boy. Go on."

Vince shoved one of the six-packs across the countertop. It slid off the edge and crashed to the floor. He was about to launch another six-pack off the counter when the clerk pulled out a gun. Vince stood staring at it, his body poised in mid-shove.

"Go on, get the hell out," said the clerk.

"OK." Vince stepped back, both hands raised in submission. "OK, I hear you."

He tripped on the damn threshold again as he went out the door.

"So where is it?" asked Chuck as Vince climbed back in the car.

"They're outta beer."

"They can't be out of beer."

"They're fucking *out*, OK?" Vince started the car and goosed the accelerator. They squealed out of the lot.

"Where we going now?" asked Chuck.

"Find another store." He squinted ahead at the darkness. "Where's the on-ramp? Gotta be around here somewhere."

"Man, give it up. No way you'll go another round without puking."

"Where's the fucking on-ramp?"

"I think you passed it."

"No, there it is." Vince veered left, tires squealing over the pavement.

"Hey," said Chuck. "Hey, I don't think—"

"Got twenty fucking bucks left to blow. They'll take it. Someone'll take it."

"Vince, you're going the wrong way!"

"What?"

Chuck yelled, "You're going the *wrong way!*"

Vince gave his head a shake and tried to focus on the road. But the lights were too bright and they were shining right in his eyes. They seemed to be getting brighter.

"Pull right!" screamed Chuck. "It's a car! Pull right!"

Vince veered right.

So did the lights.

He heard a shriek, unfamiliar, unearthly.

Not Chuck's, but his own.

Dr. Abby DiMatteo was tired, more tired than she'd ever been in her life. She had been awake for twenty-nine straight hours, if one didn't count her ten-minute nap in the X-ray lounge, and she knew her exhaustion showed. While washing her hands in the SICU sink she had glimpsed herself in the mirror and had been dismayed by the smudges of fatigue under her dark eyes, by the disarray of her hair, which now hung in a tangled black mane. It was already ten A.M., and she had not yet showered or even brushed her teeth. Breakfast had been a hard-boiled egg and a cup of sweet coffee, handed to her an hour ago by a thoughtful surgical ICU nurse. Abby would be lucky to find time for lunch, luckier still to get out of the hospital by five and home by six. Just to sink into a chair right now would be luxury.

But one did not sit during Monday morning attending rounds. Certainly not when the attending was Dr. Colin Wettig, chairman of Bayside Hospital's surgical residency program. A retired Army general, Dr. Wettig had a reputation for crisp and

11

merciless questions. Abby was terrified of the General. So were all the other surgical residents.

Eleven residents now stood in the SICU, forming a semicircle of white coats and green scrub suits. Their gazes were all trained on the residency chairman. They knew that any one of them could be ambushed with a question. To be caught without an answer was to be subjected to a prolonged session of personalized humiliation.

The group had already rounded on four postop patients, had discussed treatment plans and prognoses. Now they stood assembled beside SICU Bed 11. Abby's new admission. It was her turn to present the case.

Though she held a clipboard in her arms, she did not refer to her notes. She presented the case from memory, her gaze focused on the General's unsmiling face.

"The patient is a thirty-four-year-old Caucasian female, admitted at one this morning via the trauma service after a high-speed head-on collision on Route Ninety. She was intubated and stabilized in the field, then airlifted here. On arrival to the ER, she had evidence of multiple trauma. There were compound and depressed skull fractures, fractures of the left clavicle and humerus, and severe facial lacerations. On my initial exam, I found her to be a well-nourished white female, medium build. She was unresponsive to all stimuli with the exception of some questionable extensor posturing—"

"Questionable?" asked Dr. Wettig. "What does that mean? Did she or did she not have extensor posturing?"

Abby felt her heart hammering. Shit, he was already on her case. She swallowed and explained, "Sometimes the patient's limbs would extend on painful stimuli. Sometimes they wouldn't."

"How do you interpret that? Using the Glasgow Coma Scale for motor response?"

"Well. Since a nil response is rated a one, and extensor posturing is a two, I suppose the patient could be considered a . . . one and a half."

There was a ripple of uneasy laughter among the circle of residents.

"There is no such score as a one and a half," said Dr. Wettig.

"I'm aware of that," said Abby. "But this patient doesn't fit neatly into—"

"Just continue with your exam," he cut in.

Abby paused and glanced around at the circle of faces. Had she screwed up already? She couldn't be sure. She took a breath and continued. "Vital signs were blood pressure of ninety over sixty and pulse of a hundred. She was already intubated. She had no spontaneous respirations. Her rate was fully supported by mechanical ventilation at twenty-five breaths per minute."

"Why was a rate of twenty-five selected?"

"To keep her hyperventilated."

"Why?"

"To lower her blood carbon dioxide. That would minimize brain edema."

"Go on."

"Head exam, as I mentioned, revealed both depressed and compound skull fractures of the left parietal and temporal bones. Severe swelling and lacerations of the face made it difficult to evaluate facial fractures. Her pupils were mid-position and unreactive. Her nose and throat—"

"Oculocephalic reflexes?"

"I didn't test them."

"You didn't?"

"No, sir. I didn't want to manipulate the neck. I was concerned about possible spinal dislocation."

She saw, by his slight nod, that her answer had been acceptable.

She described the physical findings. The normal breath sounds. The unremarkable heart. The benign abdomen. Dr. Wettig did not interrupt. By the time she'd finished describing the neurologic findings, she was feeling more self-assured. Almost cocky. And why shouldn't she? She knew what the hell she'd been doing.

"So what was your impression?" asked Dr. Wettig. "Before you saw any X-ray results?"

"Based on the mid-position and unreactive pupils," said Abby, "I felt there was probable midbrain compression. Most likely from an acute subdural or epidural hematoma." She paused, and added with a quiet note of confidence, "The CT scan confirmed it. A large left-sided subdural with severe midline shift. Neurosurgery was called in. They performed an emergency evacuation of the clot.''

"So you're saying your initial impression was absolutely correct, Dr. DiMatteo?''

Abby nodded.

"Let's take a look at how things are this morning,'' said Dr. Wettig, moving to the bedside. He shone a penlight into the patient's eyes. "Pupils unresponsive,'' he said. He pressed a knuckle, hard, against the breastbone. She remained flaccid, unmoving. "No response to pain. Extensor or otherwise.''

All the other residents had edged forward, but Abby remained at the foot of the bed, her gaze focused on the patient's bandaged head. While Wettig continued his exam, tapping on tendons with a rubber hammer, flexing elbows and knees, Abby felt her attention drift away on a tide of fatigue. She kept staring at the woman's head, recently shorn of hair. The hair had been a thick brown, she remembered, clotted with blood and glass. There had been glass ground into the clothes as well. In the ER, Abby had helped cut away the blouse. It was a blue and white silk with a Donna Karan label. That last detail was what seemed to linger in Abby's memory. Not the blood or the broken bones or the shattered face. It was that label. Donna Karan. A brand she herself had once purchased. She thought of how, sometime, somewhere, this woman must once have stood in a shop, flipping through blouses, listening to the hangers squeak as they slid across the rack . . .

Dr. Wettig straightened and looked at the SICU nurse. "When was the hematoma drained?''

"She came out of Recovery about four A.M.''

"Six hours ago?''

"Yes, that would make it six hours.''

Wettig turned to Abby. "Then why has nothing changed?''

Abby stirred from her daze and saw that everyone was watching her. She looked down at the patient. Watched the chest rise and fall, rise and fall, with every wheeze of the ventilator bellows.

"There . . . may be some postop swelling,'' she said, and glanced at the monitor. "The intracranial pressure is slightly elevated at twenty millimeters.''

"Do you think that's high enough to cause pupillary changes?''

"No. But—"

"Did you examine her immediately postop?"

"No, sir. Her care was transferred to Neurosurgery Service. I spoke to their resident after surgery, and he told me—"

"I'm not asking the neurosurgery resident. I'm asking you, Dr. DiMatteo. You diagnosed a subdural hematoma. It's been evacuated. So why are her pupils still mid-position and unreactive six hours postop?"

Abby hesitated. The General watched her. So did everyone else. The humiliating silence was punctuated only by the whoosh of the ventilator.

Dr. Wettig glanced imperiously at the circle of residents. "Is there anyone here who can help Dr. DiMatteo answer the question?"

Abby's spine straightened. "I can answer the question myself," she said.

Dr. Wettig turned to her, his eyebrow raised. "Yes?"

"The . . . pupillary changes—the extensor posturing of the limbs—they were high midbrain signs. Last night I assumed it was because of the subdural hematoma, pressing downwards on the midbrain. But since the patient hasn't improved, I . . . I guess that indicates I was mistaken."

"You guess?"

She let out a breath. "I was mistaken."

"What's your diagnosis now?"

"A midbrain hemorrhage. It could be due to shearing forces. Or residual damage from the subdural hematoma. The changes might not show up yet on CT scan."

Dr. Wettig regarded her for a moment, his expression unreadable. Then he turned to the other residents. "A midbrain hemorrhage is a reasonable assumption. With a combined Glasgow Coma Scale of three"—he glanced at Abby—"and a *half*," he amended, "the prognosis is nil. The patient has no spontaneous respirations, no spontaneous movements, and she appears to have lost all brain stem reflexes. At the moment, I have no suggestions other than life support. And consideration of organ harvest." He gave Abby a curt nod. Then he moved on to the next patient.

One of the other residents gave Abby's arm a squeeze. "Hey, DiMatteo," he whispered. "Flying colors."

Wearily Abby nodded. "Thanks."

*   *   *

Chief surgical resident Dr. Vivian Chao was a legend among the other residents at Bayside Hospital. As the story went, two days into her very first rotation as an intern, her fellow intern suffered a psychotic break and had to be carted off, sobbing uncontrollably, to the loony ward. Vivian was forced to pick up the slack. For twenty-nine straight days, she was the one and only orthopedic resident on duty, around the clock. She moved her belongings into the call room and promptly lost five pounds on an unrelenting diet of cafeteria food. For twenty-nine straight days, she did not step out of the hospital front doors. On the thirtieth day her rotation ended, and she walked out to her car, only to discover that it had been towed away a week before. The parking lot attendant had assumed it was abandoned.

Four days into the next rotation, vascular surgery, Vivian's fellow intern was struck by a city bus and hospitalized with a broken pelvis. Again, someone had to take up the slack.

Vivian Chao moved right back into the hospital call room.

In the eyes of the other residents, she had thus achieved honorary manhood, a lofty status that was later acknowledged at the yearly awards dinner when she was presented with a boxed pair of steel balls.

When Abby first heard the Vivian Chao stories, she'd had a hard time reconciling that steel-balls reputation with what she saw: a laconic Chinese woman who was so petite she had to stand on a footstool to operate. Though Vivian seldom spoke during attending rounds, she could always be found standing fearlessly at the very front of the group, wearing an expression of cool dispassion.

It was with her usual air of detachment that Vivian approached Abby in the SICU that afternoon. By then Abby was moving through a sea of exhaustion, every step a struggle, every decision an act of pure will. She didn't even notice Vivian was standing beside her until the other woman said, "I hear you admitted an AB positive head trauma."

Abby looked up from the chart where she'd been recording patient progress notes. "Yes. Last night."

"Is the patient still alive?"

Abby glanced toward Bed 11's cubicle. "It depends what you mean by alive."

"Heart and lungs in good shape?"

"They're functioning."

"How old?"

"She's thirty-four. Why?"

"I've been following a medical patient on the teaching service. End-stage congestive failure. Blood type AB positive. He's been waiting for a new heart." Vivian went over to the chart rack. "Which bed?"

"Eleven."

Vivian pulled the chart out of the rack and flipped open the metal cover. Her face betrayed no emotion as she scanned the pages.

"She's not my patient anymore," said Abby. "I transferred her to Neurosurgery. They drained a subdural hematoma."

Vivian just kept reading the chart.

"She's only ten hours postop," said Abby. "It seems a little early to be talking harvest."

"No neurologic changes so far, I see."

"No. But there's a chance . . ."

"With a Glasgow Scale of three? I don't think so." Vivian slid the chart back into the rack and crossed to Bed 11.

Abby followed her.

From the cubicle doorway she stood and watched as Vivian briskly performed a physical exam. It was the same way Vivian performed in the OR, wasting no time or effort. During Abby's first year—the year of her internship—she had often observed Vivian in surgery, and she had admired those small, swift hands, had watched in awe as those delicate fingers spun perfect knots. Abby felt clumsy by comparison. She had invested hours of practice and yards and yards of thread learning to tie surgical knots on the handles of her bureau drawers. Though she could manage the mechanics competently enough, she knew she would never have Vivian Chao's magical hands.

Now, as she watched Vivian examine Karen Terrio, Abby found the efficiency of those hands profoundly chilling.

"No response to painful stimuli," Vivian observed.

"It's still early."

"Maybe. Maybe not." Vivian pulled a reflex hammer from her pocket and began tapping on tendons. "This is a stroke of luck."

"I don't see how you can call it that."

"My patient in MICU is AB positive. He's been waiting a year for a heart. This is the best match that's come up for him."

Abby looked at Karen Terrio and she remembered, once again, the blue and white blouse. She wondered what the woman had been thinking as she'd buttoned it up that last time. Mundane thoughts, perhaps. Certainly not mortal thoughts. Not thoughts of a hospital bed or IV tubes or machines pumping air into her lungs.

"I'd like to go ahead with the lymphocyte cross match. Make sure they're compatible," said Vivian. "And we might as well start HL-A typing for the other organs. The EEG's been done, hasn't it?"

"She's not on my service," said Abby. "And anyway, I think this is premature. No one's even talked to the husband about it."

"Someone's going to have to."

"She has kids. They'll need time for this to sink in."

"The organs don't have a lot of time."

"I know. I know it's got to be done. But, as I said, she's only ten hours postop."

Vivian went to the sink and washed her hands. "You aren't really expecting a miracle, are you?"

An SICU nurse appeared at the cubicle door. "The husband's back with the kids. They're waiting to visit. Will you be much longer?"

"I'm finished," said Vivian. She tossed the crumpled paper towel into the trash can and walked out.

"Can I send them in?" the nurse asked Abby.

Abby looked at Karen Terrio. In that instant she saw, with painful clarity, what a child would see gazing at that bed. "Wait," said Abby. "Not yet." She went to the bed and quickly smoothed out the blankets. She wet a paper towel in the sink and wiped away the flecks of dried mucus from the woman's cheek. She transferred the bag of urine around to the side of the bed, where it would not be so visible. Then, stepping back, she took one last look at Karen Terrio. And she realized that nothing she could do, nothing anyone could do, would lessen the pain of what was to come for those children.

She sighed and nodded to the nurse. "They can come in now."

* * *

18

By four-thirty that afternoon, Abby could barely concentrate on what she was writing, could barely keep her eyes focused. She had been on duty thirty-three and a half hours. Her afternoon rounds were completed. It was, at last, time to go home.

But as she closed the last chart, she found her gaze drawn, once again, to Bed 11. She stepped into the cubicle. There she lingered at the foot of the bed, gazing numbly at Karen Terrio. Trying to think of something else, anything else, that could be done.

She didn't hear the footsteps approaching from behind.

Only when a voice said: "Hello, gorgeous," did Abby turn and see brown-haired, blue-eyed Dr. Mark Hodell smiling at her. It was a smile meant only for Abby, a smile she'd sorely missed seeing today. On most days, Abby and Mark managed to share a quick lunch together or, at the very least, exchange a wave in passing. Today, though, they had missed seeing each other entirely, and the sight of him now gave her a quiet rush of joy. He bent to kiss her. Then, stepping back, he eyed her uncombed hair and wrinkled scrub suit. "Must've been a bad night," he murmured sympathetically. "How much sleep did you get?"

"I don't know. Half an hour."

"I heard rumors you batted a thousand with the General this morning."

She shrugged. "Let's just say he didn't use me to wipe the floor."

"That qualifies as a triumph."

She smiled. Then her gaze shifted back to Bed 11 and her smile faded. Karen Terrio was lost in all that equipment. The ventilator, the infusion pumps. The suction tubes and monitors for EKG and blood pressure and intracranial pressure. A gadget to measure every bodily function. In this new age of technology, why bother to feel for a pulse, to lay hands on a chest? What use were doctors when machines could do all the work?

"I admitted her last night," said Abby. "Thirty-four years old. A husband and two kids. Twin girls. They were here. I saw them just a little while ago. And it's strange, Mark, how they wouldn't touch her. They stood looking. Just looking at her. But they wouldn't touch her. I kept thinking, *you have*

19

to. *You have to touch her now because it could be your last chance. The last chance you'll ever have.* But they wouldn't. And I think, someday, they're going to wish . . ." She shook her head. Quickly she ran her hand across her eyes. "I hear the other guy was driving the wrong way, drunk. You know what pisses me off, Mark? And it really pisses me off. He'll survive. Right now he's sitting upstairs in the orthopedic ward, whining about a few fucking broken bones." Abby took another deep breath and with the sigh that followed, all her anger seemed to dissipate. "Jesus, I'm supposed to save lives. And here I am wishing that guy was smeared all over the highway." She turned from the bed. "It must be time to go home."

Mark ran his hand down her back, a gesture of both comfort and possession. "Come on," he said. "I'll walk you out."

They left the SICU and stepped onto the elevator. As the doors slid shut, she felt herself wobble and melt against him. At once he took her into the warm and familiar circle of his arms. It was a place where she felt safe, where she'd always felt safe.

A year ago, Mark Hodell had seemed a far from reassuring presence. Abby had been an intern. Mark had been a thoracic surgery attending—not just any attending physician, but a key surgeon on the Bayside cardiac transplant team. They'd met in the OR over a trauma case. The patient, a ten-year-old boy, had been rushed in by ambulance with an arrow protruding from his chest—the result of a sibling argument combined with a bad choice in birthday presents. Mark had already been scrubbed and gowned when Abby entered the OR. It was only her first week as an intern, and she'd been nervous, intimidated by the thought of assisting the distinguished Dr. Hodell. She'd stepped up to the table. Shyly she'd glanced at the man standing across from her. What she saw, above his mask, was a broad, intelligent forehead and a pair of beautiful blue eyes. Very direct. Very inquisitive.

Together they operated. The kid survived.

A month later, Mark asked Abby for a date. She turned him down twice. Not because she didn't *want* to go out with him, but because she didn't think she *should* go out with him.

A month went by. He asked her out again. This time temptation won out. She accepted.

Five and a half months ago, Abby moved into Mark's Cambridge home. It hadn't been easy at first, learning to live with a forty-one-year-old bachelor who'd never before shared his life—or his home—with a woman. But now, as she felt Mark holding her, supporting her, she could not imagine living with, or loving, anyone else.

"Poor baby," he murmured, his breath warm in her hair. "Brutal, isn't it?"

"I'm not cut out for this. What the hell do I think I'm doing here?"

"You're doing what you always dreamed about. That's what you told me."

"I don't even remember what the dream *was* anymore. I keep losing sight of it."

"I believe it had something to do with saving lives?"

"Right. And here I am wishing that drunk in the other car was dead." She shook her head in self-disgust.

"Abby, you're going through the worst of it now. You've got two more days on trauma. You just have to survive two more days."

"Big deal. Then I start thoracic—"

"A piece of cake in comparison. Trauma's always been the killer. Tough it out like everyone else."

She burrowed deeper into his arms. "If I switched to psychiatry, would you lose all respect for me?"

"All respect. No doubt about it."

"You're such a jerk."

Laughing, he kissed the top of her head. "Many people think it, but you're the only one allowed to say it."

They stepped off on the first floor and walked out of the hospital. It was autumn already, but Boston was sweltering in the sixth day of a late-September heat wave. As they crossed the parking lot, she could feel her last reserves of strength wilting away. By the time they reached her car, she was scarcely able to drag her feet across the pavement. This is what it does to us, she thought. It's the fire we walk through to become surgeons. The long days, the mental and emotional abuse, the hours of pushing onward while bits and pieces of our lives peel away from us. She knew it was simply a winnowing process, ruthless and necessary. Mark had survived it; so would she.

He gave her another hug, another kiss. "Sure you're safe driving home?" he asked.

"I'll just put the car on automatic pilot."

"I'll be home in an hour. Shall I pick up a pizza?"

Yawning, she slid behind the wheel. "None for me."

"Don't you want supper?"

She started the engine. "All I want tonight," she sighed, "is a bed."

3

In the night it came to her like the gentlest of whispers or the brush of fairy wings across her face: *I am dying.* That realization did not frighten Nina Voss. For weeks, through the changing shifts of three private duty nurses, through the daily visits of Dr. Morissey with his ever-higher doses of furosemide, Nina had maintained her serenity. And why should she not be serene? Her life had been rich with blessings. She had known love, and joy, and wonder. In her forty-six years she had seen the sun rise over the temples of Karnak, had wandered the twilight ruins of Delphi, and climbed the foothills of Nepal. And she had known the peace of mind that comes with the acceptance of one's place in God's universe. She was left with only two regrets in her life. One was that she had never held a child of her own.

The other was that Victor would be alone.

All night her husband had maintained his vigil at her bedside, had held her hand through the long hours of labored breaths and coughing, through the changing of the oxygen tanks and the visits of Dr. Morissey. Even in her sleep she had felt Victor's presence. Sometime near dawn, through the haze of her dreams, she heard him say: *She is so young. So very young. Can't something else, anything else, be done?*

Something! Anything! That was Victor. He did not believe in the inevitable.

But Nina did.

She opened her eyes and saw that night had finally passed, and that sunlight was shining through her bedroom window. Beyond that window was a sweeping view of her beloved Rhode Island Sound. In the days before her illness, before the cardiomyopathy had drained her strength, dawn would usually find Nina awake and dressed. She would step out onto their bedroom balcony and watch the sun rise. Even on mornings when fog cloaked the Sound, when the water seemed little more than a silvery tremor in the mist, she would stand and feel the earth tilting, the day spilling toward her. As it did today.

So many dawns have I known. I thank you, Lord, for every one of them.

"Good morning, darling," whispered Victor.

Nina focused on her husband's face smiling down at her. Some who looked at Victor Voss saw the face of authority. Some saw genius or ruthlessness. But this morning, as Nina gazed at her husband, she saw only love. And weariness.

She reached out for his hand. He took it and pressed it to his lips. "You must get some sleep, Victor," she said.

"I'm not tired."

"But I can see you are."

"No I'm not." He kissed her hand again, his lips warm against her chilled skin. They looked at each other for a moment. Oxygen hissed softly through the tubes in her nostrils. From the open window came the sound of ocean waves sluicing across the rocks.

She closed her eyes. "Remember the time . . ." Her voice faded as she paused to catch her breath.

"Which time?" he prompted gently.

"The day I . . . broke my leg . . ." She smiled.

It was the week they'd met, in Gstaad. He told her later that he'd first spotted her schussing down a double black diamond, had pursued her down the mountain, back up in the lift, and down the mountain again. That was twenty-five years ago.

Since then they had been together every day of their lives.

24

"I knew," she whispered. "In that hospital . . . when you stayed by my bed. I knew."

"Knew what, darling?"

"That you were the only one for me." She opened her eyes and smiled at him again. Only then did she see the tear trickle down his cheek. Oh, but Victor did not cry! She had never seen him cry, not once in their twenty-five years together. She had always thought of Victor as the strong one, the brave one. Now, as she looked at his face, she realized how very wrong she had been.

"Victor," she said and clasped his hand in hers. "You mustn't be afraid."

Quickly, almost angrily, he mopped his hand across his face. "I won't let this happen. I won't lose you."

"You never will."

"No. That's not enough! I want you here on this earth. With me. With *me*."

"Victor, if there's one thing . . . one thing I know . . ." She took a deep breath, a gasp for air. "It's that this time . . . we have here . . . is a very small part . . . of our existence."

She felt him stiffen with impatience, felt him withdraw. He rose from the chair and paced to the window, where he stood gazing out at the Sound. She felt the warmth of his hand fade from her skin. Felt the chill return.

"I'll take care of this, Nina," he said.

"There are things . . . in this life . . . we cannot change."

"I've already taken steps."

"But Victor . . ."

He turned and looked at her. His shoulders, framed by the window, seemed to blot out the light of dawn. "It will all be taken care of, darling," he said. "Don't you worry about a thing."

It was one of those warm and perfect evenings, the sun just setting, ice cubes clinking in glasses, perfumed ladies floating past in silk and voile. It seemed to Abby, standing in the walled garden of Dr. Bill Archer, that the air itself was magical. Clematis and roses arched across a latticed pergola. Drifts of flowers swept broad strokes of color across the expanse of lawn. The garden was the pride and joy of Marilee Archer, whose loud contralto could be heard booming out botanical names as she shepherded the other doctors' wives from flowerbed to flowerbed.

Archer, standing on the patio with highball in hand, laughed. "Marilee knows more goddamn Latin than I do."

"I took three years of it in college," said Mark. "All I remember is what I learned in medical school."

They were gathered next to the brick barbecue, Bill Archer, Mark, the General, and two surgical residents. Abby was the only woman in that circle. It was something she'd never grown accustomed to, being the lone female in a group. She might lose sight of it for a moment or two, but then she would glance around a room where surgeons were gathered, and she'd experience that familiar flash of discomfort with the realization that she was surrounded by men.

Tonight there were wives at Archer's house party, of course, but they seemed to move in a parallel universe seldom intersecting with that of their husbands. Abby, standing with the surgeons, would occasionally hear far-off snippets from the wives' conversations. Talk of damask roses, of trips to Paris, and meals savored. She would feel pulled both ways, as though she stood straddling the divide between men and women, belonging to neither universe, yet drawn to both.

It was Mark who anchored her in this circle of men. He and Bill Archer, also a thoracic surgeon, were close colleagues. Archer, chief of the cardiac transplant team, had been one of the doctors who'd recruited Mark to Bayside seven years ago. It wasn't surprising the two men got along so well. Both of them were hard-driving, athletic, and fiercely competitive. In the OR they worked together as a team, but out of the hospital, their friendly rivalry extended from the ski slopes of Vermont to the waters of Massachusetts Bay. Both men kept their J-35 sailboats moored at Marblehead Marina, and so far this season, the racing score stood at six to five, Archer's *Red Eye* versus Mark's *Gimme Shelter*. Mark planned to even the score this weekend. He'd already recruited Rob Lessing, the other second-year resident, as crew.

What was it about men and boats? wondered Abby. This was gizmo talk, men and their sailing machines, high-tech conversation fueled by testosterone. In this circle, center stage belonged to the men with graying hair. To Archer, with his silver-threaded mane. To Colin Wettig, already a distinguished gray. And to Mark, who at forty-one was just starting to turn silver at the temples.

As the conversation veered toward hull maintenance and keel design and the outrageous price of spinnakers, Abby's attention drifted. That's when she noticed two late arrivals: Dr. Aaron Levi and his wife, Elaine. Aaron, the transplant team cardiologist, was a painfully shy man. Already he had retreated with his drink to a far corner of the lawn, where he stood stoop-shouldered and silent. Elaine was glancing around in search of a conversational beachhead.

This was Abby's chance to flee the boat talk. She slipped away from Mark and went to join the Levis.

"Mrs. Levi? It's so nice to see you again."

Elaine returned a smile of recognition. "It's . . . Abby, isn't it?"

"Yes, Abby DiMatteo. I think we met at the residents' picnic."

"Oh yes, that's right. There are so many residents, I have trouble keeping you all straight. But I do remember you."

Abby laughed. "With only three women in the surgery program, we do stick out."

"It's a lot better than the old days, when there were no women at all. Which rotation are you on now?"

"I start thoracic surgery tomorrow."

"Then you'll be working with Aaron."

"If I'm lucky enough to scrub on any transplants."

"You're bound to. The team's been so busy lately. They're even getting referrals from Massachusetts General, which tickles Aaron pink." Elaine leaned toward Abby. "They turned him down for a fellowship years ago. Now they're sending *him* patients."

"The only thing Mass Gen has over Bayside is their Harvard mystique," said Abby. "You know Vivian Chao, don't you? Our chief resident?"

"Of course."

"She graduated top ten at Harvard Med. But when it came time to apply for residency, Bayside was her number one choice."

Elaine turned to her husband. "Aaron, did you hear that?"

Reluctantly he looked up from his drink. "Hear what?"

27

"Vivian Chao picked Bayside over Mass Gen. Really, Aaron, you're already at the top here. Why would you want to leave?"

"Leave?" Abby looked at Aaron, but the cardiologist was glaring at his wife. Their sudden silence was what puzzled Abby most. From across the lawn came the sound of laughter, the echoing drifts of conversation, but in this corner of the garden, nothing was said.

Aaron cleared his throat. "It's just something I've toyed with," he said. "You know. Getting away from the city. Moving to a small town. Everyone daydreams about small towns, but no one really wants to move there."

"I don't," said Elaine.

"I grew up in a small town," said Abby. "Belfast, Maine. I couldn't wait to get out."

"That's how I imagine it would be," said Elaine. "Everyone clawing to get to civilization."

"Well, it wasn't *that* bad."

"But you're not going back. Are you?"

Abby hesitated. "My parents are dead. And both my sisters have moved out of state. So I don't have any reason to go back. But I have a lot of reasons to stay here."

"It was just a fantasy," said Aaron, and he took a deep gulp of his drink. "I wasn't really thinking about it."

In the odd silence that followed, Abby heard her name called. She turned and saw Mark waving to her.

"Excuse me," she said, and crossed the lawn to join him.

"Archer's giving the tour of his inner sanctum," said Mark.

"What inner sanctum?"

"Come on. You'll see." He took her hand and led her across the terrace and into the house. They climbed the staircase to the second floor. Only once before had Abby been upstairs in the Archer house, and that was to view the oil paintings hung in the gallery.

Tonight was the first time she'd been invited into the room at the end of the hall.

Archer was already waiting inside. In a grouping of leather chairs were seated Drs. Frank Zwick and Raj Mohandas. But Abby scarcely noticed the people; it was the room itself that commanded her attention.

She was standing in a museum of antique medical instruments. In display cases were exhibited a variety of tools both fascinating and frightening. Scalpels and bloodletting basins. Leech jars. Obstetrical forceps with jaws that could crush an infant's skull. Over the fireplace hung an oil painting: the battle between Death and the Physician over the life of a young woman. A Brandenburg Concerto was playing on the stereo.

Archer turned down the volume, and the room suddenly seemed very quiet, with only the whisper of music in the background.

"Isn't Aaron coming?" asked Archer.

"He knows about it. He'll be on his way up," said Mark.

"Good." Archer smiled at Abby. "What do you think of my little collection?"

She studied the contents of a display case. "This is fascinating. I can't even tell you what some of these things are."

Archer pointed to an odd contraption of gears and pulleys. "That device over there is interesting. It was meant to generate a weak electrical current, which was applied to various parts of the body. Said to be helpful for anything from female troubles to diabetes. Funny, isn't it? The nonsense medical science would have us believe?"

Abby stopped before the oil painting and gazed at the black-robed image of Death. Doctor as hero, Doctor as conqueror, she thought. And of course the object of rescue is a woman. A beautiful woman.

The door opened.

"Here he is," said Mark. "We wondered if you'd forgotten about it, Aaron."

Aaron came into the room. He said nothing, only nodded as he sat down in a chair.

"Can I refill your drink, Abby?" said Archer, gesturing to her glass.

"I'm fine."

"Just a splash of brandy? Mark's driving, right?"

Abby smiled. "All right. Thanks."

Archer touched up Abby's drink and handed it back to her. The room had fallen strangely quiet, as though everyone was waiting for this formality to be completed. It struck her then: she was the only resident in the room. Bill Archer threw this sort of party every few months, to welcome another batch of house staff to the thoracic and trauma rotations. At this moment, there were six other surgical residents circulating downstairs in the garden. But here, in Archer's private retreat, there was only the transplant team.

And Abby.

She sat down on the couch next to Mark and sipped her drink. Already she was feeling the brandy's heat, and the warmth of this special attention. As an intern, she'd viewed these five men with awe, had felt privileged just to assist in the same OR with Archer and Mohandas. Though her relationship with Mark had brought her into their social circle, she never forgot who these men were. Nor did she forget the power they held over her career.

Archer sat down across from her. "I've been hearing some good things about you, Abby. From the General. Before he left tonight, he paid you some wonderful compliments."

"Dr. Wettig did?" Abby couldn't help a surprised laugh. "To be honest, I'm never quite sure what he thinks about my performance."

"Well, that's just the General's way. Spreading a little insecurity around in the world."

The other men laughed. Abby did too.

"I do respect Colin's judgment," said Archer. "And I know he thinks you're one of the best Level Two residents in the program. I've worked with you, so I know he's right."

Abby shifted uneasily on the couch. Mark reached for her hand and gave it a squeeze. That gesture was not missed by Archer, who smiled.

"Obviously, Mark thinks you're pretty special. And that's part of the reason we thought we should have this discussion. I know it may seem a little premature, but we're long-range planners, Abby. We think it never hurts to scout out the territory in advance."

"I'm afraid I don't quite follow you," said Abby.

Archer reached for the brandy decanter and poured himself a scant refill. "Our transplant team's interested in only the best. The best credentials, the best performance. We're always looking over the residents for fellowship material. Oh, we have a selfish motive, of course. We're grooming people for the team." He paused. "And we were wondering if you might have an interest in transplant surgery."

Abby flashed Mark a startled look. He nodded.

"It's not something you have to decide anytime soon," said Archer. "But we want you to think about it. We have the next few years to get to know each other. By then, you may not even want a fellowship. It may turn out transplant surgery's not something you're even vaguely interested in."

"But it is." She leaned forward, her face flushing with enthusiasm. "I guess I'm just . . . surprised by this. And flattered. There are so many good residents in the program. Vivian Chao, for instance."

"Yes, Vivian is good."

"I think she'll be looking for a fellowship next year."

Mohandas said, "There's no question that Dr. Chao's surgical technique is outstanding. I can think of several residents with excellent technique. But you have heard the saying? One can teach a monkey how to operate. The trick is teaching him *when* to operate."

"I think what Raj is trying to say is, we're looking for good clinical judgment," said Archer. "And a sense of teamwork. We see you as someone who works well with a team. Not at cross-purposes. That's something we insist on, Abby, teamwork. When you're sweating it out in the OR, all sorts of things can go wrong. Equipment fails. Scalpels slip. The heart gets lost in transit. We have to be able to pull together, come hell or high water. And we do."

"We help each other out, too," said Frank Zwick. "Both in the OR and outside of it."

"Absolutely," said Archer. He glanced at Aaron. "Wouldn't you agree?"

Aaron cleared his throat. "Yes, we help each other out. It's one of the benefits of joining this team."

"One of the many benefits," added Mohandas.

For a moment no one spoke. The Brandenburg Concerto played softly in the background. Archer said, "I like this part," and turned up the volume. As the sound of violins spilled from the speakers, Abby found herself gazing, once again, at Death versus the Physician. The battle for a patient's life, a patient's soul.

"You mentioned there were . . . other benefits," said Abby.

"For example," offered Mohandas, "when I completed my surgery residency, I had a number of student loans to pay off.

So that was part of my recruitment package. Bayside helped me pay off my loans.''

"Now that's something we can talk about, Abby," said Archer. "Ways we can make this attractive to you. Young surgeons nowadays, they come out of residency at thirty years old. Most of them are already married with maybe a kid or two. And they owe—what? A hundred thousand dollars in loans. They don't even own a house yet! It'll take 'em ten years just to get out of debt. By then they're forty, and worried about college for their kids!" He shook his head. "I don't know why anyone goes into medicine these days. Certainly not to make money.''

"If anything," agreed Abby, "it's a hardship."

"It doesn't have to be. That's where Bayside can help. Mark mentioned to us that you were on financial aid all the way through medical school."

"A combination of scholarships and loans. Mostly loans."

"Ouch. That sounds painful."

Abby nodded ruefully. "I'm just beginning to feel the pain."

"College loans as well?"

"Yes. My family had financial problems," Abby admitted.

"You make it sound like something to be ashamed of."

"It was more a case of . . . bad luck. My younger brother was hospitalized for a number of months and we weren't insured. But then, in the town where I grew up, a lot of people weren't insured."

"Which only confirms how hard you must have worked to beat the odds. Everyone here knows what that's like. Raj here was an immigrant, didn't speak English until he was ten. Me, I'm the first in my family to go to college. Believe me, there are no goddamn Boston Brahmins in this room. No rich daddies or handy little trust funds. We know about beating the odds because we've all done it. That's the kind of drive we're looking for in this team."

The music swelled to its finale. The last chord of trumpets and strings faded away. Archer shut off the stereo and looked at Abby.

"Anyway. It's something for you to think about," he said. "We're not making any firm offers, of course. It's more like talking about a, uh . . ." Archer grinned at Mark. "First date."

"I understand," said Abby.

"One thing you should know. You're the only resident we've approached. The only one we're really considering. It would be wise if you didn't mention this to the rest of the house staff. We don't want to stir up any jealousy."

"Of course not."

"Good." Archer looked around the room. "I think we're all in agreement about this. Right, gentlemen?"

There was a general nodding of heads.

"We have consensus," said Archer. And, smiling, he reached once again for the brandy decanter. "This is what I call a real team."

"So what do you think?" Mark asked as they drove home. Abby threw back her head and shouted deliriously. "I'm floating! God, what a night!"

"You're happy about it, huh?"

"Are you kidding? I'm terrified."

"Terrified? Of what?"

"That I'll screw up. And blow it all."

He laughed and gave her knee a squeeze. "Hey, we've worked with all the other residents, okay? We know we're recruiting the best."

"And just how much of this was your influence, Dr. Hodell?"

"Oh, I put in my two cents' worth. The others just happened to be in complete agreement."

"Right."

"It's true. Believe me, Abby, you're our number one choice. And I think you'd find it a terrific arrangement, too."

She sat back, smiling. Imagining. Until tonight, she'd had only a fuzzy notion of where she'd be working in three and a half years. Toiling in an HMO, most likely. Private practice was in its dying days; she saw no future in it, at least, not in the city of Boston. And Boston was where she wanted to stay.

Where Mark was.

"I want this so badly," she said. "I just hope I don't disappoint you all."

"Not a chance. The team knows what it wants. We're all together on this."

She fell silent for a moment. "Even Aaron Levi?" she asked.

"Aaron? Why wouldn't he be?"

"I don't know. I was talking to his wife tonight. Elaine. I got the feeling Aaron isn't very happy. Did you know he was thinking of leaving?"

"What?" Mark glanced at her in surprise.

"Something about moving to a small town."

He laughed. "It'll never happen. Elaine's a Boston girl."

"It wasn't Elaine. It was Aaron who was thinking about it."

For a while Mark drove without saying a word. "You must have misunderstood," he said at last.

She shrugged. "Maybe I did."

"Light, please," said Abby.

A nurse reached up and adjusted the overhead lamp, focusing the beam on the patient's chest. The operative site had been drawn on the skin in black marker, two tiny X's connected by a line tracing along the top of the fifth rib. It was a small chest, a small woman. Mary Allen, eighty-four years old and a widow, had been admitted to Bayside a week ago complaining of weight loss and severe headaches. A routine chest X ray had turned up an alarming find: multiple nodules in both lungs. For six days she'd been probed, scanned, and x-rayed. She'd had a bronchoscope down her throat, needles punched through her chest wall, and still the diagnosis was unclear.

Today they'd know the answer.

Dr. Wettig picked up the scalpel and stood with blade poised over the incision site. Abby waited for him to make the cut. He didn't. Instead he looked at Abby, his eyes a hard, metallic blue over the mask.

"How many open lung biopsies have you assisted on, DiMatteo?" he asked.

"Five, I think."

"You're familiar with this patient's history? Her chest films?"

"Yes, sir."

Wettig held out the scalpel. "This one's yours, Doctor."

Abby looked in surprise at the scalpel glittering in his hand. The General seldom relinquished the blade, even to his upper-level residents.

She took the scalpel, felt the weight of stainless steel settle comfortably in her grasp. With steady hands, she made her incision, stretching the skin taut as she sliced a line along the rib's upper edge. The patient was thin, almost wasted; there was scant subcutaneous fat to obscure the landmarks. Another, slightly deeper incision parted the intercostal muscles.

She was now in the pleural cavity.

She slipped a finger through the incision and could feel the surface of the lung. Soft, spongy. "Everything all right?" she asked the anesthesiologist.

"Doing fine."

"Okay, retract," said Abby.

The ribs were spread apart, widening the incision. The ventilator pumped another burst of air, and a small segment of lung tissue ballooned out of the incision. Abby clamped it, still inflated.

Again she glanced at the anesthesiologist. "Okay?"

"No problem."

Abby focused her attention on the exposed segment of lung tissue. It took only a glance to locate one of the nodules. She ran her fingers across it. "Feels pretty solid," she said. "Not good."

"No surprise," said Wettig. "She looked like a chemotherapy special on X ray. We're just confirming cell type."

"The headache? Brain metastases?"

Wettig nodded. "This one's aggressive. Eight months ago she had a normal X ray. Now she's a cancer farm."

"She's eighty-four," said one of the nurses. "At least she had a long life."

But what kind of life? wondered Abby as she resected the wedge of lung containing the nodule. Yesterday, she had met Mary Allen for the first time. She had found the woman sitting very quiet and still in her hospital room. The shades had been drawn, the bed cast in semidarkness. It was the headaches, Mary said. *The sun hurts my eyes. Only when I sleep does the pain go away. So many different kinds of pain . . .*

Please, doctor, couldn't I have a stronger sleeping pill?

Abby completed the resection and sutured the cut edge of lung. Wettig offered no comment. He merely watched her work, his gaze as chilly as ever. The silence was compliment enough;

she'd learned long ago that just to escape the General's criticism was a triumph.

At last, the chest closed, the drain tube in place, Abby stripped off her bloodied gloves and deposited them in the bin labeled CONTAMINATED.

"Now comes the hard part," she said, as the nurses wheeled the patient out of the OR. "Telling her the bad news."

"She knows," said Wettig. "They always do."

They followed the squeak of the gurney wheels to Recovery. Four postop patients in various states of consciousness occupied the curtained stalls. Mary Allen, in the last stall, was just beginning to stir. She moved her foot. Moaned. Tried to pull her hand free of the restraint.

With her stethoscope, Abby took a quick listen to the patient's lungs, then said: "Give her five milligrams of morphine, IV."

The nurse injected an IV bolus of morphine sulfate. Just enough to dull the pain, yet allow a gentle return to consciousness. Mary's groaning ceased. The tracing on the heart monitor remained steady and regular.

"Postop orders, Dr. Wettig?" the nurse asked.

There was a moment's silence. Abby glanced at Wettig, who said, "Dr. DiMatteo's in charge here." And he left the room.

The nurses looked at each other. Wettig always wrote his own postop orders. This was another vote of confidence for Abby.

She took the chart to the desk and began to write: *Transfer to 5 East, Thoracic Surgery Service. Diagnosis: Postop open lung biopsy for multiple pulmonary nodules. Condition: stable.* She wrote steadily, orders for diet, meds, activity. She reached the line for code status. Automatically she wrote: *Full code.*

Then she looked across the desk at Mary Allen, lying motionless on the gurney. Thought about what it would be like to be eighty-four years old and riddled with cancer, the days numbered, each one filled with pain. Would the patient choose a kinder, swifter death? Abby didn't know.

"Dr. DiMatteo?" It was a voice over the intercom.

"Yes?" said Abby.

"You had a call from Four East about ten minutes ago. They want you to come by."

"Neurosurg? Did they say why?"

"Something about a patient named Terrio. They want you to talk to the husband."

"Karen Terrio's not my patient any longer."

"I'm just passing the message along, Doctor."

"Okay, thanks."

Sighing, Abby rose to her feet and went to Mary Allen's gurney for one last check of the cardiac monitor, the vital signs. The pulse was running a little fast, and the patient was moving, groaning again. Still in pain.

Abby looked at the nurse. "Another two milligrams of morphine," she said.

The blip on the EKG monitor traced a slow and steady rhythm.

"Her heart's so strong," murmured Joe Terrio. "It doesn't want to give up. She doesn't want to give up."

He sat at his wife's bedside, his hand clasping hers, his gaze fixed on that green line squiggling across the oscilloscope. He looked bewildered by all the gadgetry in the room. The tubes, the monitors, the suction pump. Bewildered and afraid. He focused every ounce of attention on the EKG monitor, as though, if he could somehow master the secrets of that mysterious box, he could master everything else. He could understand why and how he had come to be sitting at the bedside of the woman he loved, the woman whose heart refused to stop beating.

It was three P.M., sixty-two hours since a drunk driver had slammed into Karen Terrio's car. She was thirty-four years old, HIV negative, cancer free, infection free. She was also braindead. In short, she was a living supermarket of healthy donor organs. Heart. Lungs. Kidneys. Pancreas. Liver. Bone. Corneas. Skin. With one terrible harvest, half a dozen different lives could be saved or changed for the better.

Abby pulled up a stool and sat down across from him. She was the only doctor who'd actually spent much time talking with Joe, so she was the one the nurses had called to speak to him now. To convince him to sign the papers and allow his wife to die. She sat quietly with him for a moment. Karen Terrio's body stretched between them, her chest rising and falling at a preselected twenty breaths per minute.

"You're right, Joe," said Abby. "Her heart is strong. It could keep going for some time. But not forever. Eventually the body knows. The body understands."

Joe looked across at her, his eyes red-rimmed with tears and sleeplessness. "Understands?"

"That the brain is dead. That there's no reason for the heart to keep beating."

"How would it know?"

"We need our brains. Not just to think and feel, but also to give the rest of our body a purpose. When that purpose is gone, the heart, the lungs, they start to fail." Abby looked at the ventilator. "The machine is breathing for her."

"I know." Joe rubbed his face with his hands. "I know, I know. I know . . ."

Abby said nothing. Joe was rocking back and forth in his chair now, his hands in his hair, his throat squeezing out little grunts and whimpers, the closest thing to sobs a man could allow himself. When he raised his head again, clumps of his hair stood up damp and stiff with tears.

He looked up at the monitor again. The one spot in the room he seemed to feel safe to stare at. "It all seems too soon."

"It isn't. There's only a certain amount of time before the organs start to go bad. Then they can't be used. And no one is helped by that, Joe."

He looked at her, across the body of his wife. "Did you bring the papers?"

"I have them."

He scarcely looked at the forms. He merely signed his name at the bottom and handed the papers back. An ICU nurse and Abby witnessed the signature. Copies of the form would go into Karen Terrio's record, to the New England Organ Bank, and Bayside's transplant coordinator files. Then the organs would be harvested.

Long after Karen Terrio was buried, bits and pieces of her would go on living. The heart that she'd once felt thudding in her chest when she'd played as a five-year-old, married as a twenty-year-old, and strained at childbirth as a twenty-one-year-old, would go on beating in the chest of a stranger. It was as close as one could come to immortality.

But it was scarcely much comfort to Joseph Terrio, who continued his silent vigil at the bedside of his wife.

* * *

Abby found Vivian Chao undressing in the OR locker room. Vivian had just emerged from four hours of emergency surgery, yet not a single blot of sweat stained the discarded scrub clothes lying on the bench beside her.

Abby said, "We have consent for the harvest."

"The papers are signed?" asked Vivian.

"Yes."

"Good. I'll order the lymphocyte cross match." Vivian reached for a fresh scrub top. She was dressed only in her bra and underpants, and every rib seemed to stand out on her frail, flat chest. Honorary manhood, thought Abby, is a state of mind, not body. "How are her vitals?" asked Vivian.

"They're holding steady."

"Have to keep her blood pressure up. Kidneys perfused. It's not every day a nice pair of AB-positive kidneys comes along." Vivian pulled on a pair of drawstring trousers and tucked in her shirt. Every movement she made was precise. Elegant.

"Will you be scrubbing in on the harvest?" asked Abby.

"If my patient gets the heart, I will. The harvest is the easy part. It's reattaching the plumbing that gets interesting." Vivian closed the locker door and snapped the padlock shut. "You have a minute? I'll introduce you to Josh."

"Josh?"

"My patient on the teaching service. He's in MICU."

They left the locker room and headed down the hall toward the elevator. Vivian made up for her short legs by her quick, almost fierce stride. "You can't judge the success of a heart transplant until you've seen the before *and* the after," said Vivian. "So I'm going to show you the before. Maybe it'll make things easier for you."

"What do you mean?"

"Your woman has a heart but no brain. My boy has a brain and practically no heart." The elevator door opened. Vivian stepped in. "Once you get past the tragedy, it all makes sense."

They rode the elevator in silence.

Of course it makes sense, thought Abby. *It makes perfect sense. Vivian sees it clearly. But I can't seem to get past the image of two little girls standing by their mother's bed. Afraid to touch her . . .*

Vivian led the way to the Medical ICU.

Joshua O'Day was asleep in Bed 4.

"He's sleeping a lot these days," whispered the nurse, a sweet-faced blonde with HANNAH LOVE, R.N. on her name tag.

"Change in meds?" asked Vivian.

"I think it's depression." Hannah shook her head and sighed. "I've been his nurse for weeks. Ever since he was admitted. He's such a terrific kid, you know? Really nice. A little goofy. But lately, all he does is sleep. Or stare at his trophies." She nodded at the bedside stand, where a display of various awards and ribbons had been lovingly arranged. One ribbon went all the way back to the third grade—an honorable mention for a Cub Scout Pinewood Derby. Abby knew about Pinewood Derbies. Like Joshua O'Day, her brother had been a Cub Scout.

Abby moved to the bedside. The boy looked much younger than she had expected. Seventeen, according to the birthdate on Hannah Love's clipboard. He could have passed for fourteen. A thicket of plastic tubes surrounded his bed, IV's and arterial and Swan-Ganz lines. The last was used to monitor pressures in the right atrium and pulmonary artery. On the screen overhead, Abby could read the right atrial pressure. It was high. The boy's heart was too weak to pump effectively, and blood had backed up in his venous system. Even without the monitor, she could have reached that conclusion by a glance at his neck veins. They were bulging.

"You're looking at Redding High School's baseball star from two years ago," said Vivian. "I'm not into the game so I don't really know how to judge his batting average. But his dad seems pretty proud of it."

"Oh, his dad *is* proud," said Hannah. "He was in here the other day with a ball and mitt. I had to kick him out when they started a game of catch." Hannah laughed. "The dad's as crazy as the kid!"

"How long has he been sick?" asked Abby.

"He hasn't been to school in a year," said Vivian. "The virus hit him about two years ago. Coxsackievirus B. Within six months, he was in congestive heart failure. He's been in the ICU for a month now, just waiting for a heart." Vivian paused. And smiled. "Right, Josh?"

The boy's eyes were open. He was looking at them as though

through layers of gauze. He blinked a few times, then smiled at Vivian. "Hey, Dr. Chao."

"I see some new ribbons on display," said Vivian.

"Oh. Those." Josh rolled his eyes. "I don't know where my mom digs those up. She keeps everything, you know. She even has this plastic bag with all my baby teeth. I think it's pretty gross."

"Josh, I brought someone along to meet you. This is Dr. DiMatteo, one of our surgical residents."

"Hello, Josh," said Abby.

It seemed to take the boy a moment to fully refocus his gaze. He didn't say anything.

"Is it okay for Dr. DiMatteo to examine you?" asked Vivian.

"Why?"

"When you get your new heart, you'll be like that crazy Road Runner on TV. We won't be able to tie you down long enough for an exam."

Josh smiled. "You're so full of it."

Abby moved to the bedside. Already, Josh had pulled up his gown and bared his chest. It was white and hairless, not a teenager's chest but a boy's. She laid her hand over his heart and felt it fluttering like bird's wings against the cage of ribs. She laid her stethoscope against it and listened to the heartbeat, the whole time aware of the boy's gaze, wary and untrusting. She had seen such looks from children who had been too long in pediatric wards, children who'd learned that every new pair of hands brings a new variety of pain. When she finally straightened and slipped her stethoscope back into her pocket, she saw the look of relief in the boy's face.

"Is that all?" he said.

"That's all." Abby smoothed down his hospital gown. "So. Who's your favorite team, Josh?"

"Who else?"

"Ah. Red Sox."

"My dad taped all their games for me. We used to go to the park together, my dad and me. When I get home, I'm going to watch 'em all. All those tapes. Three straight days of baseball . . ." He took a deep breath of oxygen-infused air and looked up at the ceiling. Softly he said, "I want to go home, Dr. Chao."

"I know," said Vivian.

"I want to see my room again. I miss my room." He swallowed, but he couldn't hold back the sob. "I want to see my room. That's all. I just want to see my room."

At once Hannah moved to his side. She gathered the boy into her arms and held him, rocked him. He was fighting not to cry, his fists clenched, his face buried in her hair. "It's okay," murmured Hannah. "Baby, you just go ahead and cry. I'm right here with you. I'm going to stay right here, Josh. As long as you need me. It's okay." Hannah's gaze met Abby's over the boy's shoulder. The tears on the nurse's face weren't Josh's, but hers.

In silence, Abby and Vivian left the room.

At the MICU nurses' station, Abby watched as Vivian signed in duplicate the order for the lymphocyte cross match between Josh O'Day's and Karen Terrio's blood.

"How soon can he go to surgery?" asked Abby.

"We could be scrubbed and ready to cut by tomorrow morning. The sooner the better. The kid's had three episodes of V. tach in just the last day. With a heart rhythm that unstable, he doesn't have much time." Vivian swiveled around to face Abby. "I'd really like that boy to see another Red Sox game. Wouldn't you?"

Vivian's expression was as calm and unreadable as ever. She might be soft as slush inside, thought Abby, but Vivian would never show it.

"Dr. Chao?" said the ward clerk.

"Yes?"

"I just called SICU about that lymphocyte cross match. They said they're already running a match against Karen Terrio."

"Great. For once my intern's on the ball."

"But Dr. Chao, the cross match isn't with Josh O'Day." Vivian turned and looked at the clerk. "What?"

"SICU says they're running it on someone else. Some private patient named Nina Voss."

"But Josh is critical! He's at the top of the list."

"All they said was the heart's going to that other patient."

Vivian shot to her feet. In three quick steps she was at the telephone, punching in a number. A moment later, Abby heard her say:

"This is Dr. Chao. I want to know who ordered that lymphocyte cross match on Karen Terrio." She listened. Then, frowning, she hung up.

"Did you get the name?" asked Abby.

"Yes."

"Who ordered it?"

"Mark Hodell."

4

Abby and Mark had made reservations that night for Casablanca, a restaurant just down the road from their Cambridge house. Though it was meant to be a celebration, to mark the six-month anniversary of their moving in together, the mood at their table was anything but cheerful.

"All I want to know," said Abby, "is who the hell is Nina Voss?"

"I told you, I don't know," said Mark. "Now can we drop the subject?"

"The boy's critical. He's coding practically twice a day. He's been on the recipient list for a year. Now an AB-positive heart finally becomes available, and you're bypassing the registry system? Giving the heart to some private patient who's still living at home?"

"We're not *giving* it away, OK? It was a clinical decision."

"Whose decision was it?"

"Aaron Levi's. He called me this afternoon. Told me that Nina Voss was being admitted tomorrow. He asked me to order the screening labs on the donor."

"That's all he told you?"

"Essentially." Mark reached for the bottle of wine and refilled his glass, sloshing burgundy onto the tablecloth. "Now can we change the subject?"

She watched him sip the wine. He wasn't looking at her, wasn't meeting her gaze.

"Who is this patient?" she asked. "How old is she?"

"I don't want to talk about it."

"You're the one taking her to surgery. You must know how old she is."

"Forty-six."

"From out of state?"

"Boston."

"I heard she was flying in from Rhode Island. That's what the nurses told me."

"She and her husband live in Newport during the summer."

"Who's her husband?"

"Some guy named Victor Voss. That's all I know about him, his name."

She paused. "How did Voss get his money?"

"Did I say anything about money?"

"A summer home in Newport? Give me a break, Mark."

He still wouldn't look at her, still wouldn't lift his gaze from that glass of wine. So many times before, she'd looked across a table at him and seen all the things that had first attracted her. The direct gaze. The forty-one years of laugh lines. The quick smile. But tonight, he wasn't even looking at her.

She said, "I didn't realize it was so easy to buy a heart."

"You're jumping to conclusions."

"Two patients need a heart. One is a poor, uninsured kid on the teaching service. The other has a summer home in Newport. So which one gets the prize? It's pretty obvious."

He reached again for the wine bottle and poured himself another glass—his third. For a man who prided himself on his temperate lifestyle, he was drinking like a lush. "Look," he said. "I spend all day in the hospital. The last thing I feel like doing is talking about it. So let's just drop the subject."

They both fell silent. The subject of Karen Terrio's heart was like a blanket snuffing out the sparks of any other conversation. *Maybe we've already said everything there is to say to each other,* she thought. Maybe they'd reached that dismal phase of a relationship when their life stories had been told and the time had come to dredge up new material. *We've been together only six months, and already the silences have started.*

She said: "That boy makes me think of Pete. Pete was a Red Sox fan."

"Who?"

"My brother."

Mark said nothing. He sat with shoulders hunched in obvious discomfort. He'd never been at ease with the subject of Pete. But then, death was not a comfortable subject for doctors. Every day we play a game of tag with that word, she thought. We say "expired" or "could not resuscitate" or "terminal event." But we seldom use that word: *died.*

"He was crazy about the Red Sox," she said. "He had all these baseball cards. He'd save his lunch money to buy them. And then he'd spend a fortune on little plastic covers to keep them safe. A five-cent cover for a one-cent piece of cardboard. I guess that's the logic of a ten-year-old for you."

Mark took a sip of wine. He sat wrapped in his discomfort, insulated against her attempts at conversation.

The celebration dinner was a bust. They ate with scarcely another word between them.

Back in the house, Mark retreated behind his stack of surgical journals. That was the way he always reacted to their disagreements—withdrawal. Damn it, *she* didn't mind a good, healthy fight. The DiMatteo family, with its three headstrong daughters and little Pete, had weathered more than its share of adolescent conflicts and sibling rivalries, but their love for each other had never been in doubt. Oh yes, Abby could deal with a healthy argument.

It was silence she couldn't stand.

In frustration she went into the kitchen and scrubbed the sink. I'm turning into my mother, she thought in disgust. I get angry and what do I do? I clean the kitchen. She wiped the stovetop, then dismantled the burners and scrubbed those as well. She had the whole damn kitchen sparkling by the time she heard Mark finally head upstairs to the bedroom.

She followed him.

In darkness they lay side by side, not touching. His silence had rubbed off on her and she could think of no way to break through it without seeming like the needy one, the weak one. But she couldn't stand it any longer.

"I hate it when you do this," she said.

"Please, Abby. I'm tired."

"So am I. We're both tired. It seems like we're always tired. But I can't go to sleep this way. And neither can you."

"All right. What do you want me to say?"

"Anything! I just want you to keep talking to me."

"I don't see the point of talking things to death."

"There are things I *need* to talk about."

"Fine. I'm listening."

"But you're doing it through a wall. I feel like I'm in confession. Talking through a grate to some guy I can't see." She sighed and stared up at the darkness. She had the sudden, dizzying sensation that she was floating free, unattached. Unconnected. "The boy's in MICU," she said. "He's only seventeen."

Mark said nothing.

"He reminds me so much of my brother. Pete was a lot younger. But there's this sort of fake courage that all boys have. That Pete had."

"It's not my decision alone," he said. "There are others involved. The whole transplant team. Aaron Levi, Bill Archer. Even Jeremiah Parr."

"Why the hospital president?"

"Parr wants our statistics to look good. And all the research shows that outpatients are more likely to survive a transplant."

"Without a transplant, Josh O'Day's not going to survive at all."

"I know it's a tragedy. But that's life."

She lay very still, stunned by his matter-of-fact tone.

He reached out to touch her hand. She pulled away.

"You could change their minds," she said. "You could talk them into—"

"It's too late. The team's decided."

"What *is* this team, anyway? God?"

There was a long silence. Quietly, Mark said: "Be careful what you say, Abby."

"You mean about the holy team?"

"The other night, at Archer's, we all meant what we said. In fact, Archer told me later that you're the best fellowship material he's seen in three years. But Archer's careful about which

47

people he recruits, and I don't blame him. We need people who'll work with us. Not against us."

"Even if I don't agree with the rest of you?"

"It's part of being on a team, Abby. We all have our points of view. But we make the decisions together. And we stick by them." He reached out again to touch her hand. This time she didn't pull away. Neither did she return his squeeze. "Come on, Abby," he said softly. "There are residents out there who'd kill for a transplant fellowship at Bayside. Here you're practically handed one on a platter. It *is* what you want, isn't it?"

"Of course it's what I want. It scares me how much I want it. The crazy thing is, I never knew I did, not until Archer raised the possibility . . ." She took a deep breath, released it in a long sigh. "I hate the way I keep wanting more. Always wanting more. There's something that keeps pulling me and pulling me. First it was getting into college, then med school. Then a surgery residency. And now, it's this fellowship. It's moved so far from where I started. When I just wanted to be a doctor . . ."

"It's not enough anymore. Is it?"

"No. I wish it was. But it isn't."

"Then don't blow it, Abby. Please. For both our sakes."

"You make it sound as if *you're* the one with everything to lose."

"I'm the one who suggested your name. I told them you're the best choice they could make." He looked at her. "I still think so."

For a moment they lay without talking, only their hands in contact. Then he reached over and caressed her hip. Not a real embrace, but an attempt at one.

It was enough. She let him take her into his arms.

The simultaneous squeal of half a dozen pocket pagers was followed by the curt announcement over the hospital speaker system:

Code Blue, MICU, Code Blue, MICU.

Abby joined the other surgical residents in a dash for the stairway. By the time she'd jogged into the MICU, a crowd of medical personnel was already thronging the area. A glance told her there were more than enough people here to deal with a Code Blue. Most of the residents were starting to drift out of the room. Abby, too, would have left.

Had she not seen that the code was in Bed 4. Joshua O'Day's cubicle.

She pushed into the knot of white coats and scrub suits. At their center lay Joshua O'Day, his frail body fully exposed to the glare of overhead lights. Hannah Love was administering chest compressions, her blond hair whipping forward with every thrust. Another nurse was frantically rummaging through the crash cart drawers, pulling out drug vials and syringes and passing them to the medical residents. Abby glanced up at the cardiac monitor screen.

Ventricular fibrillation. The pattern of a dying heart.

"Seven and a half ET tube!" a voice yelled.

Only then did Abby notice Vivian Chao crouched behind Joshua's head. Vivian already had the laryngoscope ready.

The crash cart nurse ripped the plastic cover off an ET tube and passed it to Vivian.

"Keep bagging him!" Vivian ordered.

The respiratory tech, holding an anesthesia mask to Josh's face, continued squeezing the balloonlike reservoir a few times, manually pumping oxygen into the boy's lungs.

"OK," said Vivian. "Let's intubate."

The tech pulled the mask away. Within seconds, Vivian had the ET tube in place, the oxygen connected.

"Lidocaine's in," said a nurse.

The medical resident glanced up at the monitor. "Shit. Still in V. fib. Let's have the paddles again. Two hundred joules." A nurse handed him the defibrillator paddles. He slapped them onto the chest. The placement was already marked by conductive gel pads: one paddle near the sternum, the other outside the nipple. "Everyone back."

The burst of electricity shot through Joshua O'Day's body, jolting every muscle into a simultaneous spasm. He gave a grotesque jerk and then lay still.

Everyone's gaze shot to the monitor screen.

"Still in V. fib," someone said. "Bretylium, two-fifty."

Hannah automatically resumed chest compressions. She was flushed, sweating, her expression numb with fear.

"I can take over," Abby offered.

Nodding, Hannah stepped aside.

Abby climbed onto the footstool and positioned her hands on Joshua's chest, her palm on the lower third of the sternum. His chest felt thin and brittle, as though it would crack under a few vigorous thrusts; she was almost afraid to lean against it.

She began to pump. It was a task that required no mental exertion. Just that repetitive motion of lean forward, release, lean forward, release. The alpha rhythm of CPR. She was a participant in the chaos yet she was apart from it, her mind pulling back, withdrawing. She could not bring herself to look at the boy's face, to watch as Vivian taped the ET tube in place. She could only focus on his chest, on that point of contact between his sternum and her clasped hands. Sternums were anonymous. This could be anyone's chest. An old man's. A stranger's. *Lean, release.* She concentrated. *Lean, release.*

"Everyone back again!" someone yelled.

Abby pulled away. Another jolt of the paddles, another grotesque spasm.

Ventricular fibrillation. The heart signaling that it cannot hold on.

Abby crossed her hands and placed them again on the boy's chest. Lean, release. *Come back, Joshua,* her hands were saying to him. *Come back to us.*

A new voice joined in the bedlam. "Let's try a bolus of calcium chloride. A hundred milligrams," said Aaron Levi. He was standing near the footboard, his gaze fixed on the monitor.

"But he's on digoxin," said the medical resident.

"At this point, we've got nothing to lose."

A nurse filled a syringe and handed it to the resident. "One hundred milligrams calcium chloride."

The bolus was injected into the IV line. A penny toss into the chemical wishing well.

"OK, try the paddles again," said Aaron. "Four hundred joules this time."

"Everyone back!"

Abby pulled away. The boy's limbs jerked, fell still.

"Again," said Aaron.

Another jolt. The tracing on the monitor shot straight up. As it settled back to baseline, there was a single blip—the jagged peak of a QRS complex. At once it deteriorated back to V. fib.

"One more time!" said Aaron.

The paddles were slapped on the chest. The body thrashed under the shock of 400 joules. There was a sudden hush as everyone's gaze shot to the monitor.

A QRS blipped across. Then another. And another.

"We're in sinus," said Aaron.

"I'm getting a pulse!" said a nurse. "I feel a pulse!"

"BP seventy over forty . . . up to ninety over fifty . . ."

A collective sigh seemed to wash through the room. At the foot of the bed, Hannah Love was crying unashamedly. *Welcome back, Josh,* Abby thought, her gaze blurred with tears.

Gradually the other residents filed out, but Abby couldn't bring herself to leave; she felt too drained to move on. In silence she helped the nurses gather up the used syringes and vials, all the bits of glass and plastic that are the aftermath of every Code Blue. Working beside her, Hannah Love sniffled as she wiped away the electrode paste, her washcloth stroking lovingly across Josh's chest.

It was Vivian who broke the silence.

"He could be getting that heart right now," she said. Vivian was standing by the tray table of Joshua's trophies. She picked up the Cub Scout ribbon. Pinewood Derby, third grade. "He could've gone to the OR this morning. Had the transplant by ten o'clock. If we lose him, it's your fault, Aaron." Vivian looked at Aaron Levi, whose pen had frozen in the midst of signing the code sheet.

"Dr. Chao," said Aaron quietly. "Would you care to talk about this in private?"

"I don't care who's listening! The match is perfect. I wanted Josh on the table this morning. But you wouldn't give me a decision. You just delayed. And delayed. And fucking *delayed.*" She took a deep breath and looked down at the award ribbon she was holding. "I don't know what the hell you think you're doing. Any of you."

"Until you calm down, I'm not going to discuss this with you," said Aaron. He turned and walked out.

"You are. You are going to," said Vivian, following him out of the cubicle.

Through the open doorway, Abby could hear Vivian's pursuit of Aaron across the MICU. Her angry questions. Her demands for an explanation.

Abby bent down and picked up the Pinewood Derby ribbon that Vivian had dropped on the floor. It was green—not a winner's ribbon, but merely an honorable mention for the hours spent laboring over a small block of wood, sanding it, painting it, greasing the axles, pounding in the lead fishing weights to make it tumble faster. All that effort must be rewarded. Little boys need their tender egos soothed.

Vivian came back into the cubicle. She was white-faced, silent. She stood at the foot of Josh's bed, staring down at the boy, watching his chest rise and fall with each whoosh of the ventilator.

"I'm transferring him," she said.

"What?" Abby looked at her in disbelief. "Where?"

"Massachusetts General. Transplant Service. Get Josh ready for the ambulance. I'm going to make the calls."

The two nurses didn't move. They were staring at Vivian. Hannah protested, "He's in no condition to be moved."

"If he stays here, we're going to lose him," said Vivian. *"We are going to lose him.* Are you willing to let that happen?"

Hannah looked down at the frail chest rising and falling beneath her washcloth. "No," she said. "No. I want him to live."

"Ivan Tarasoff was my professor at Harvard Med," said Vivian. "He's head of their transplant team. If our team won't do it, then Tarasoff will."

"Even if Josh survives the transfer," said Abby, "he still needs a donor heart."

"Then we'll have to get him one." Vivian looked straight at Abby. "Karen Terrio's."

That's when Abby understood exactly what she had to do. She nodded. "I'll talk to Joe Terrio now."

"It has to be in writing. Make sure he signs it."

"What about the harvest? We can't use the Bayside team."

"Tarasoff likes to send his own man for the harvest. We'll assist. We'll even deliver to his doorstep. There can't be any delay. We have to do it fast, before anyone here can stop us."

"Wait a minute," said the other nurse. "You can't authorize a transfer to Mass Gen."

"Yes I can," said Vivian. "Josh O'Day is on teaching service. Which means the chief residents are in charge. I'll take full responsibility. Just follow my orders and get him ready for ambulance transfer."

"Absolutely, Dr. Chao," said Hannah. "In fact, I'll ride with him."

"You do that." Vivian looked at Abby. "Okay, DiMatteo," she snapped. "Go get us a heart."

Ninety minutes later, Abby was scrubbing in. She completed her final rinse and, elbows bent, backed through the swinging door into OR 3.

The donor lay on the table, her pale body washed in fluorescent light. A nurse-anesthetist was changing IV bottles. No need for anesthesia on this patient; Karen Terrio could feel no pain.

Vivian, gowned and gloved, stood at one side of the table. Dr. Lim, a kidney surgeon, stood on the other. Abby had worked with Lim on previous cases. A man of few words, he was known for his swift, silent work.

"Signed and sealed?" asked Vivian.

"In triplicate. It's in the chart." She herself had typed up the directed-donation consent, a statement specifying that Karen Terrio's heart be given to Josh O'Day, age seventeen.

It was the boy's age that had swayed Joe Terrio. He'd been sitting at his wife's bedside, holding her hand, and had listened in silence as Abby told him about a seventeen-year-old boy who loved baseball. Without saying a word, Joe had signed the paper.

And then he'd kissed his wife good-bye.

Abby was helped into a sterile gown and size six and a half gloves. "Who's doing the harvest?" she asked.

"Dr. Frobisher, from Tarasoff's team. I've worked with him before," said Vivian. "He's on his way now."

"Any word about Josh?"

"Tarasoff called ten minutes ago. They've got his blood typed and crossed and an OR cleared. They're standing by." She looked down impatiently at Karen Terrio. "Jesus, I could do the heart myself. Where the hell's Frobisher?"

They waited. Ten minutes, fifteen. The intercom buzzed with a call from Tarasoff at Mass Gen. Was the harvest proceeding?

"Not yet," said Vivian. "Any minute now."

Again the intercom buzzed. "Dr. Frobisher's arrived," said the nurse. "He's scrubbing now."

Five minutes later, the OR door swung open and Frobisher pushed in, his hefty arms dripping water. "Size nine gloves," he snapped.

At once the atmosphere in the room stretched taut. No one except Vivian had ever worked with Frobisher before, and his fierce expression did not invite any conversation. With silent efficiency, the nurses helped him gown and glove.

He stepped to the table and critically eyed the prepped operative site. "Causing trouble again, Dr. Chao?" he said.

"As usual," said Vivian. She gestured to the others standing at the table. "Dr. Lim will do the kidneys. Dr. DiMatteo and I will assist as needed."

"History on this patient?"

"Head injury. Brain-dead, donor forms all signed. She's thirty-four, previously healthy, and her blood's been screened."

He picked up a scalpel and paused over the chest. "Anything else I should know?"

"Not a thing. NEOB confirms it's a perfect match. Trust me."

"I hate it when people tell me that," muttered Frobisher. "Okay, let's take a quick look at our heart, make sure it's in good shape. Then we'll move aside and let Dr. Lim do his thing first." He touched the scalpel blade to Karen Terrio's chest. In one swift slice, he cut straight down the center, exposing the breast bone. "Sternal saw."

The scrub nurse handed him the electric saw. Abby took hold of the retractor. As Frobisher cut through the sternum, Abby couldn't help turning away. She felt vaguely nauseated by the whine of the blade, the smell of bone dust, neither of which seemed to bother Frobisher, whose hands moved with swift skill. In moments he was in the chest cavity, his scalpel poised over the pericardial sac.

Cutting through the sternum had seemed an act of brute force. What lay ahead was a far more delicate task. He slit open the membrane.

At his first glance at the beating heart, he gave a soft murmur of satisfaction. Glancing across at Vivian, he asked: "Opinion, Dr. Chao?"

With almost reverential silence, Vivian reached deep into the chest cavity. She seemed to caress the heart, her fingers stroking the walls, tracing the course of each coronary artery. The organ pulsed vigorously in her hands. "It's beautiful," she said softly. Eyes shining, she looked across at Abby. "It's just the heart for Josh."

The intercom buzzed. A nurse's voice said: "Dr. Tarasoff's on the line."

"Tell him the heart looks fine," said Frobisher. "We're just starting the kidney harvest."

"He wants to talk to one of the doctors. He says it's extremely urgent."

Vivian glanced at Abby. "Go ahead and break scrub. Take the call."

Abby peeled off her gloves and went to pick up the wall phone. "Hello, Dr. Tarasoff? This is Abby DiMatteo, one of the residents. The heart looks great. We should be at your doorstep in an hour and a half."

"That may not be soon enough," answered Tarasoff. Over the line, Abby could hear a lot of background noise: a rapid-fire exchange of voices, the clank of metal instruments. Tarasoff himself sounded tense, distracted. She heard him turn away, talk to someone else. Then he was back on the line. "The boy's coded twice in the last ten minutes. Right now we've got him back in sinus rhythm. But we can't wait any longer. Either we get him on the bypass machine now or we lose him. We may lose him in any event." Again he turned from the receiver, this time to listen to someone. When he came back on line, it was only to say: "We're going to cut. Just get here, okay?"

Abby hung up and said to Vivian: "They're putting Josh on bypass. He's coded twice. They need that heart now."

"It'll take me an hour to free up the kidneys," said Dr. Lim.

"Screw the kidneys," snapped Vivian. "We go straight for the heart."

"But—"

"She's right," said Frobisher. He called to the nurse: "Iced saline! Get the Igloo ready. And someone better call an ambulance for transport."

"Shall I scrub in again?" asked Abby.

"No." Vivian reached for the retractor. "We'll be done in a few minutes. We need you for a delivery."

"What about my patients?"

"I'll cover for you. Leave your beeper at the OR desk."

One nurse began to pack an Igloo cooler with ice. Another was arranging buckets of cold saline next to the operating table. Frobisher didn't need to issue any more orders; these were cardiac nurses. They knew exactly what to do.

Already, Frobisher's scalpel was moving swiftly, freeing up the heart in preparatory dissection. The organ was still pumping, each beat squeezing oxygen-rich blood into the arteries. Now it was time to stop it, time to shut down the last vestiges of life in Karen Terrio.

Frobisher injected five hundred cc's of a high-potassium solution into the aortic root. The heart beat once. Twice.

And it stopped. It was now flaccid, its muscles paralyzed by the sudden infusion of potassium. Abby couldn't help glancing at the monitor. There was no EKG activity. Karen Terrio was finally, and clinically, dead.

A nurse poured a bucket of the iced solution into the chest cavity, quickly chilling the heart. Then Frobisher got to work, ligating, cutting.

Moments later, he lifted the heart out of the chest and slid it gently into a basin. Blood swirled in the cold saline. A nurse stepped forward, holding open a plastic bag. Frobisher gave the heart a few more swishes in the liquid, then eased the rinsed organ into the bag. More iced saline was poured in. The heart was double-bagged and placed in the Igloo.

"It's yours, DiMatteo," said Frobisher. "You ride in the ambulance. I'll follow in my car."

Abby picked up the Igloo. She was already pushing out the OR doors when she heard Vivian's voice calling after her:

"Don't drop it."

5

I'm holding Josh O'Day's life in my hands, thought Abby as she clutched the Igloo in her lap. Boston traffic, heavy as always at the noon hour, parted like magic before the flashing ambulance lights. Abby had never before ridden in an ambulance. Under other circumstances, she might have enjoyed this ride, the exhilarating experience of watching Boston drivers— the rudest in the world—finally yield the right of way. But at the moment, she was too focused on the cargo she held in her lap, too aware that every second that ticked by was another second drained from the life of Josh O'Day.

"Got yourself a live one in there, huh Doc?" said the ambulance driver. G. Furillo, according to his name tag.

"A heart," said Abby. "A nice one."

"So who's it going to?"

"Seventeen-year-old boy."

Furillo maneuvered the ambulance around a row of stalled traffic, his loose-jointed arms steering with almost casual grace. "I've done kidney runs, from the airport. But I have to tell you, this is my first heart."

"Mine too," said Abby.

"It stays good—what, five hours?"

"About that."

Furillo glanced at her and grinned. "Relax. I'll get you there with four and a half hours to spare."

"It's not the heart I'm worried about. It's the kid. Last I heard, he wasn't doing so well."

Furillo focused his gaze more intently on the traffic. "We're almost there. Five minutes, tops."

A voice crackled over the radio. "Unit Twenty-three, this is Bayside. Unit Twenty-three, this is Bayside."

Furillo picked up the microphone. "Twenty-three, Furillo."

"Twenty-three, please return to Bayside ER."

"Impossible. I'm transporting live organ to Mass Gen. Do you copy? I'm en route to Mass Gen."

"Twenty-three, your instructions are to return to Bayside immediately."

"Bayside, try another unit, okay? We have live organ on board—"

"This order is specific for Unit Twenty-three. Return immediately."

"Who's ordering this?"

"Comes direct from Dr. Aaron Levi. Do not proceed to Mass Gen. Do you copy?"

Furillo glanced at Abby. "What the hell's this all about?"

They found out, thought Abby. *Oh God, they found out. And they're trying to stop us . . .*

She looked down at the Igloo containing Karen Terrio's heart. She thought about all the months and years of living that should lie ahead for a boy of seventeen.

She said, "Don't turn around. Keep going."

"What?"

"I said, *keep going.*"

"But they're ordering me—"

"Unit Twenty-three, this is Bayside," the radio cut in. "Please respond."

"Just get me to Mass Gen!" said Abby. *"Do it."*

Furillo glanced at the radio. "Jesus H.," he said. "I don't know—"

"Okay, then let me off!" ordered Abby. "I'll walk the rest of the way!"

The radio said: "Unit Twenty-three, this is Bayside. Please respond immediately."

"Oh, fuck you," Furillo muttered to the radio.

And he stepped on the gas.

A nurse in green scrubs was waiting at the ambulance dock. As Abby stepped out carrying the Igloo, the nurse snapped: "From Bayside?"

"I have the heart."

"Follow me."

Abby had time for only a last wave of thanks to Furillo, then she was following the nurse through the ER. Moving at a near-jog, Abby caught a fast-forward view of corridors and busy hallways. They stepped into an elevator, and the nurse inserted the emergency key.

"How's the boy doing?" asked Abby.

"He's on bypass. We couldn't wait."

"He coded again?"

"He doesn't *stop* coding." The nurse glanced at the Igloo. "That's his last chance you've got there."

They stepped off the elevator, made another quick jog through a set of automatic doors, into the surgery wing.

"Here. I'll take the heart," said the nurse.

Through the suite window, Abby saw a dozen masked faces turn to look as the container was passed through the door to a circulating nurse. The Igloo was immediately opened, the heart lifted from its bed of ice.

"If you put on fresh scrubs, you can go in," said a nurse. "Women's locker room's down the hall."

"Thanks. I think I will."

By the time Abby had donned new greens, cap, and shoe covers, the team in the OR had already removed Josh O'Day's diseased heart. Abby slipped in among the throng of personnel, but found she couldn't see a thing over all those shoulders. She could hear the surgeons' conversation, though. It was relaxed, even congenial. All ORs looked alike, the same stainless steel, the same blue-green drapes and bright lights. What varied was the atmosphere for the people working in that room, and the atmosphere was determined by the senior surgeon's personality.

Judging by the easy conversation, Ivan Tarasoff was a comfortable surgeon to work with.

Abby eased around to the head of the table and stood beside the anesthesiologist. Overhead, the cardiac monitor showed a flat line. There was no heart beating in Josh's chest; the bypass machine was doing all the work. His eyelids had been taped shut to protect the corneas from drying, and his hair was covered by a paper cap. One dark tendril had escaped, curling over his forehead. *Still alive,* she thought. *You can make it, kid.*

The anesthesiologist glanced at Abby. "You from Bayside?" he whispered.

"I'm the courier. How's it going so far?"

"Touch and go for a while. But we're over the worst of it. Tarasoff's fast. He's already on the aorta." He nodded toward the chief surgeon.

Ivan Tarasoff, with his snowy eyebrows and mild gaze, was the image of everyone's favorite grandfather. His requests for a fresh suture needle, for more suction, were spoken in the same gentle tone with which one might ask for another cup of tea, please. No showmanship, no high-flying ego, just a quiet technician laboring at his job.

Abby looked up again at the monitor. Still a flat line.

Still no sign of life.

Josh O'Day's parents were crying in the waiting room, sobs mingled with laughter. Smiles all around. It was six P.M., and their ordeal was finally over.

"The new heart's working just fine," said Dr. Tarasoff. "In fact, it started beating before we expected it to. It's a good strong heart. It should last Josh for a lifetime."

"We didn't expect this," said Mr. O'Day. "All we heard was that they moved him here. That there was some kind of emergency. We thought—we thought—" He turned away, wrapped his arms around his wife. They clung together, not speaking. Not able to speak.

A nurse said, gently, "Mr. and Mrs. O'Day? If you'd like to see Josh, he's starting to wake up."

A smiling Tarasoff watched as the O'Days were led toward the Recovery Room. Then he turned and looked at Abby, his blue eyes glistening behind the wire-rim glasses. "That's why we do it," he said softly. "For moments like that."

"It was close," said Abby.

"Too damn close." He shook his head. "And I'm getting too damn old for this excitement."

They went into the surgeons' lounge, where he poured them both cups of coffee. With his cap off, his gray hair in disarray, he looked more the part of the rumpled professor than the renowned thoracic surgeon. He handed Abby a cup. "Tell Vivian to give me a little more warning next time," he said. "I get one phone call from her, and suddenly this kid's on our doorstep. *I'm* the one who almost coded."

"Vivian knew what she was doing. Sending the kid to you."

He laughed. "Vivian Chao always knows what she's doing. She was like that as a medical student."

"She's a great chief resident."

"You're in the Bayside surgery program?"

Abby nodded and sipped the hot coffee. "Second year."

"Good. Not enough women in the field. Too many macho blades. All they want to do is cut."

"That doesn't sound like a surgeon talking."

Tarasoff glanced at the other doctors gathered near the coffee pot. "A little blasphemy," he whispered, "is a healthy thing."

Abby drained her coffee and glanced at the time. "I've got to get back to Bayside. I probably shouldn't have stayed for the surgery. But I'm glad I did." She smiled at him. "Thanks, Dr. Tarasoff. For saving the boy's life."

He shook her hand. "I'm just the plumber, Dr. DiMatteo," he said. "You brought the vital part."

It was after seven when the taxi delivered Abby to Bayside's lobby entrance. As she walked in the door, the first thing she heard was her name being paged on the overhead. She picked up the in-house phone.

"This is DiMatteo," she said.

"Doctor, we've been paging you for hours," said the operator.

"Vivian Chao was supposed to cover for me. She's carrying my beeper."

"We have your beeper here at the operator's desk. Mr. Parr's the one who's been paging you."

"Jeremiah Parr?"

"His extension is five-six-six. Administration."

"It's seven o'clock. Is he still there?"

"He was there five minutes ago."

Abby hung up, her stomach fluttering with a sense of alarm. Jeremiah Parr, the hospital president, was an administrator, not a physician. She'd spoken to him only once before, at the annual welcoming picnic for new house staff. They'd shaken hands, exchanged a few pleasantries, and then Parr had moved on to greet the other residents. That brief encounter had left her with a vivid impression of a man who was unflappable. And he wore great suits.

She'd seen him since the picnic, of course. They'd smile and nod in recognition whenever they met in elevators or passed in hallways, but she doubted he remembered her name. Now he was paging her at seven o'clock in the evening.

This can't be good, she thought. *This can't be good at all.*

She picked up the phone and dialed Vivian's house. Before she spoke to Parr, she had to know what was going on. Vivian would know.

There was no answer.

Abby hung up, her sense of alarm more acute than ever. *Time to face the consequences. We made a decision; we saved a boy's life. How can they fault us for that?*

Heart thudding, she rode the elevator to the second floor.

The Administration wing was only dimly lit by a single row of fluorescent ceiling panels. Abby walked beneath the strip of light, her footsteps noiseless on the carpet. The offices on either side of her were dark, the secretaries' desks deserted. But at the far end of the hall, light was shining under a closed door. Someone was inside the conference room.

She went to the door and knocked.

It swung open. Jeremiah Parr stood gazing at her, his backlit face unreadable. Behind him, seated at the conference table, were half a dozen men. She glimpsed Bill Archer, Mark, and Mohandas. The transplant team.

"Dr. DiMatteo," said Parr.

"I'm sorry, I didn't know you were trying to reach me," said Abby. "I was out of the hospital."

"We know where you were." Parr stepped out of the room. Mark came out right behind him, both men confronting Abby in the dim hallway. They'd left the door ajar and she saw Archer rise from his chair and shut the door against her gaze.

"Come into my office," said Parr. The instant they stepped inside, he slammed the door and said, "Do you understand the damage you've done? Do you have any idea?"

Abby looked at Mark, but his face told her nothing. That's

what scared her most: that she could not see past the mask, to the man she loved.

"Josh O'Day's alive," she said. "The transplant saved his life. I can't consider that any kind of mistake."

"The mistake lies in *how* it was done," said Parr.

"We were standing over his bed. Watching him die. A boy that young shouldn't have to—"

"Abby," said Mark. "We're not questioning your instincts. They were good, of course they were good."

"What's this crap about instincts, Hodell?" snapped Parr. "They stole a goddamn heart! They knew what they were doing, and they didn't care who they dragged into it! Nurses. Ambulance drivers. Even Dr. Lim got suckered in!"

"Following the orders of her chief resident is exactly what Abby was supposed to do. And that's all she did. Obey orders."

"There have to be repercussions. Firing the chief resident isn't enough."

Fired? Vivian? Abby looked at Mark for confirmation.

"Vivian admitted everything," Mark said. "She admits that she coerced you and the nurses to go along with her."

"I hardly think Dr. DiMatteo is so easily coerced," said Parr.

"What about Lim?" said Mark. "He was in the OR too. Are you going to kick him off the staff?"

"Lim had no idea what was going on," said Parr. "He was just there to harvest the kidneys. All he knew was that Mass Gen had a recipient on the table. And there was a directed donation form in the chart." Parr turned to Abby. "Drawn up and witnessed by *you.*"

"Joe Terrio signed it willingly," said Abby. "He agreed the heart should go to the boy."

"Which means no one can be accused of organ theft," Mark pointed out. "It was perfectly legal, Parr. Vivian knew exactly which strings to pull and she pulled them. Including Abby's."

Abby started to speak, to defend Vivian, but then she saw the cautionary look in Mark's eyes. *Careful. Don't dig yourself a grave.*

"We have a patient who came in for a heart. And now we have no heart to give her. What the hell am I supposed to tell her husband? 'Sorry, Mr. Voss, but the heart got *misplaced?*'"

63

Parr turned to Abby, his face rigid with anger. "You are just a resident, Dr. DiMatteo. You took a decision into your own hands, a decision that wasn't yours to make. Voss has already found out about it. Now Bayside's going to have to pay for it. Big time."

"Come on, Parr," said Mark. "It hasn't reached that point."

"You think Victor Voss *won't* call his lawyers?"

"On what basis? There's a directed-donation consent. The heart *had* to go to the boy."

"Only because *she* coerced the husband into signing!" said Parr, pointing angrily at Abby.

"All I did was tell him about Josh O'Day," said Abby. "I told him the boy was only seventeen—"

"That alone is enough to get you fired," said Parr. He glanced at his watch. "As of seven-thirty—that's right now—you're out of the residency program."

Abby stared at him in shock. She started to protest, but found her throat had closed down, strangling the words.

"You can't do that," said Mark.

"Why not?" said Parr.

"For one thing, it's a decision for the program director. Knowing the General, I don't think he'll take to having his authority usurped. For another thing, our surgical house staff is already stretched thin. We lose Abby, that means thoracic service rotates call every other night. They'll get tired, Parr. They'll make mistakes. If you want lawyers on your doorstep, *that's* how to do it." He glanced at Abby. "You're on call tomorrow night, aren't you?"

She nodded.

"So what do we do now, Parr?" said Mark. "You know of some other second-year resident who can just step right in and take her place?"

Jeremiah Parr glared at Mark. "This is temporary. Believe me, this is only temporary." He turned to Abby. "You'll hear more about this tomorrow. Now get out of here."

On unsteady legs, Abby somehow managed to walk out of Parr's office. She felt too numb to think. She made it halfway down the hallway and stopped. Felt the numbness give way to tears. She would have broken down and cried right then and there, had it not been for Mark, who came up beside her.

"Abby." He turned her around to face him. "It's been a

battlefield here all afternoon. What the hell did you think you were doing today?''

"I was saving a boy's life. That's what I thought I was doing!'' Her voice cracked, shattered into sobs. "We saved him, Mark. It's exactly what we *should* have done. I wasn't following orders. I was following my own instincts. *Mine.''* She made an angry swipe at her tears. "If Parr wants to get back at me, then let him. I'll present the facts to any ethics committee. A seventeen-year-old boy versus some rich man's wife. I'll lay it all out, Mark. Maybe I'll still get fired. But I'll go down kicking and screaming.'' She turned and continued down the hall.

"There's another way. An easier way.''

"I can't think of one.''

"Listen to me.'' Again he caught her arm. "Let Vivian take the fall! She'll do it anyway.''

"I did more than just follow her orders.''

"Abby, take a gift when it's offered! Vivian accepted the blame. She did it to protect you and the nurses. Leave it at that.''

"And what happens to her?''

"She's already resigned. Peter Dayne's taking over as chief resident.''

"And where does Vivian go?''

"That's her concern, not Bayside's.''

"She did exactly what she should have done. She saved her patient's life. You don't fire someone for that!''

"She violated the number one rule here. And that's play with the team. This hospital can't afford loose cannons like Vivian Chao. A doctor's either with us or against us.'' He paused. "Where does that put you?''

"I don't know.'' She shook her head. Felt the tears beginning to fall again. "I don't know anymore.''

"Consider your options, Abby. Or your lack of them. Vivian's finished her five years of residency. She's already board-eligible. She could find a job, open a surgical practice. But all you've got is an internship. You get fired now, you'll never be a surgeon. What're you going to do? Spend the rest of your life doing insurance physicals? Is that what you want?''

"No.'' She took a breath and let it out in a rush of despair. "No.''

"What the hell *do* you want?"

"I know exactly what I want!" She wiped her face with a furious swipe of her hand. Took another deep breath. "I knew it today. This afternoon. When I watched Tarasoff in the OR. I saw him pick up the donor heart and it's limp, like a handful of dead meat. And there's the boy on the table. He connects the two and the heart starts beating. And suddenly there's life again ... " She paused, swallowing back another surge of tears. "That's when I knew what I wanted. I want to do what Tarasoff does." She looked at Mark. "Graft a piece of life onto kids like Josh O'Day."

Mark nodded. "Then you have to make it happen. Abby, we can still make this work. Your job. The fellowship. Everything."

"I don't see how."

"I'm the one who pushed your name for the transplant team. You're still my number one choice. I can talk to Archer and the others. If we all stick by you, Parr will have to back down."

"That's a big if."

"You can help make it happen. First, let Vivian take the blame. She was chief resident. She made a bad judgment call."

"But she didn't!"

"You saw only half the picture. You didn't see the other patient."

"What other patient?"

"Nina Voss. She was admitted at noon today. Maybe you should take a look at her now. See for yourself that the choice wasn't so clear. That it's possible you *did* make a mistake."

Abby swallowed. "Where is she?"

"Fourth floor. Medical ICU."

Even from the hallway, Abby could hear the commotion in the MICU: the cacophony of voices, the whine of a portable X-ray machine, two telephones ringing at once. The instant she walked through the doorway, she felt a hush descend on the room. Even the telephones suddenly went silent. A few of the nurses were staring at her; most were pointedly looking the other way.

"Dr. DiMatteo," said Aaron Levi. He had just emerged from Cubicle 5, and he stood staring at her with a look of barely suppressed rage. "Perhaps you should come and see this," he said.

The throng of personnel silently moved aside to let Abby approach Cubicle 5. She went to the window. Through the glass, she saw a woman lying in the bed, a fragile-looking woman with white-blond hair and a face as colorless as the sheets. An ET tube had been inserted down her throat and was hooked up to a ventilator. She was fighting the machine, her chest moving spasmodically as she tried to suck in air. The machine wasn't cooperating. Alarms buzzed as it fed her breaths at its own preset rhythm, ignoring the patient's desperate inhalations. Both the woman's hands were restrained. A medical resident was inserting an arterial line into one of the patient's wrists, piercing deep under the skin and threading a plastic catheter into the radial artery. The other wrist, tied to the bed, looked like a pincushion of IV lines and bruises. A nurse was murmuring to the patient, attempting to calm her down, but the woman, fully conscious, stared up with an expression of sheer terror. It was the look of an animal being tortured.

"That's Nina Voss," said Aaron.

Abby remained silent, stunned by the horror she saw in the woman's eyes.

"She was admitted eight hours ago. Almost from the moment she arrived, her condition deteriorated. At five o'clock she coded. Ventricular tachycardia. Twenty minutes ago, she coded again. That's why she's intubated. She was scheduled for surgery tonight. The team was ready. The OR was ready. The patient was more than ready. Then we find out the donor went to surgery hours ahead of schedule. And the heart that should have gone to this woman has been stolen. *Stolen*, Dr. DiMatteo."

Still Abby said nothing. She was transfixed by the ordeal she was witnessing in Cubicle 5. At that instant, Nina Voss's eyes lifted to hers. It was only a brief meeting of gazes, an appeal for mercy. The pain in those eyes left Abby shaken.

"We didn't know," Abby whispered. "We didn't know her condition was critical . . . "

"Do you realize what will happen now? Do you have any idea?"

"The boy—" She turned to Aaron. "The boy's alive."

"What about this woman's life?"

There was no reply Abby could make. No matter what she said, how she defended herself, she could not justify the suffering beyond that window.

She scarcely noticed the man crossing toward her from the nurses' station. Only when he said "Is this Dr. DiMatteo?" did she focus on the man's face. He was in his sixties, tall and well dressed, the sort of man whose very presence demands attention.

Quietly she answered, "I'm Abby DiMatteo." Only as she said it did she realize what she saw in the man's eyes. It was hatred, pure and poisonous. She almost backed away as the man stepped toward her, his face darkening in rage.

"So you're the other one," he said. "You and that chink doctor."

"Mr. Voss. Please," said Aaron.

"You think you can fuck around with me?" Voss yelled at Abby. "With my wife? There'll be consequences, doctor. Damn you, I'll see there are consequences!" Hands clenched, he took another step toward Abby.

"Mr. Voss," said Aaron, "Believe me, we'll deal with Dr. DiMatteo in our own way."

"I want her out of this hospital! I don't want to see her face again!"

"Mr. Voss," said Abby. "I'm so sorry. I can't tell you how sorry I am—"

"Just get her the hell *away* from me!" roared Voss.

Aaron quickly moved between them. He took Abby firmly by the arm and pulled her away from the cubicle. "You'd better leave," he said.

"If I could just talk to him—explain—"

"The best thing you can do right now is leave the ICU."

She glanced at Voss, who stood squarely in front of Cubicle 5 as though guarding his wife from attack. Never before had Abby seen such a look of hatred. No amount of talking, of explanation, could ever get past that.

Meekly she nodded to Aaron. "All right," she said softly. "I'll leave."

And she turned and walked out of the MICU.

Three hours later, Stewart Sussman pulled up at the curb on Tanner Avenue, and from his car he studied number 1451. The house was a modest cape with dark shutters and a covered front porch. A white picket fence surrounded the property. Though it was too dark for Sussman to see much of the yard, instinct told him the grass would be trim and the flowerbeds free of weeds. The faint perfume of roses hung in the air.

Sussman left his car and walked through the gate and up the porch steps to the front door. The occupants were home. The lights were on, and he could see movement through the curtained windows.

He rang the bell.

A woman answered. Tired face, tired eyes, her shoulders sagging under some terrible psychic weight. "Yes?" she said.

"I'm sorry to disturb you. My name is Stewart Sussman. I wonder if I might have a word with Joseph Terrio?"

"He'd rather not speak to anyone right now. You see, we've just had a . . . loss in the family."

"I understand, Mrs. . . ."

"Terrio. I'm Joe's mother."

"I know about your daughter-in-law, Mrs. Terrio. And I'm very, very sorry. But it's important I speak to your son. It has to do with Karen's death."

The woman hesitated only a moment. Then she said: "Excuse me," and shut the door. He could hear her call: "Joe?"

A moment later the door opened again and a man appeared, eyes red-rimmed, every movement sluggish with grief. "I'm Joe Terrio," he said.

Sussman extended his hand. "Mr. Terrio, I've been sent here by someone who's very concerned about the circumstances surrounding your wife's death."

"Circumstances?"

"She was a patient at Bayside Medical Center. Is that correct?"

"Look, I don't understand what this is all about."

"It's about your wife's medical care, Mr. Terrio. And whether any mistakes were made. Mistakes that may have proved fatal."

"Who are you?"

"I'm an attorney with Hawkes, Craig and Sussman. My specialty is medical malpractice."

"I don't need any attorney. I don't want any goddamn ambulance chaser bothering me tonight."

"Mr. Terrio—"

"Get the hell out of here." Joe started to close the door, but Sussman put out a hand to stop it.

"Mr. Terrio," Sussman said quietly. Calmly. "I have reason to believe one of Karen's doctors made an error. A terrible error. It's possible your wife didn't have to die. I can't be certain of that yet. But with your permission, I can look at the record. I càn uncover the facts. All of the facts."

Slowly Joe let the door swing open again. "Who sent you? You said somebody sent you. Who was it?"

Sussman gazed back with a look of sympathy. "A friend."

6

Never before had Abby dreaded going to work, but as she walked into Bayside Hospital that morning, she felt she was walking straight into the fire. Last night Jeremiah Parr had threatened repercussions; today she'd have to face them. But until Wettig actually stripped her of her hospital privileges, she was determined to carry on as usual with her duties. She had patients to round on and cases scheduled for the OR. Tonight she was on call. Damn it, she was going to do her job, and do it well. She owed it to her patients—and to Vivian. Only an hour ago, they had spoken on the phone, and Vivian's last words to her were: "Someone there has to speak up for the Josh O'Days. Stay with it, DiMatteo. For both of us."

The moment Abby walked into the SICU, she heard the instantaneous lowering of voices. By now, everyone must know about Josh O'Day. Though no one said a word to Abby, she could hear the nurses' quiet murmurings, could see their uneasy looks. She went to the rack and gathered her patients' charts for rounds. It took every ounce of concentration for her to complete that one task. She placed the charts in a rolling cart and wheeled it out of the station, to the cubicle of the first patient on her list. It was a relief just to step inside, away from everyone's gaze. She shut the curtains, blocking the view through the doorway, and turned to the patient.

Mary Allen lay on the bed, her eyes closed, her sticklike arms and legs drawn up in a fetal position. Mary's open lung biopsy two days ago had been followed by two brief episodes of hypotension, so she'd been kept in the SICU for close observation. According to the nurse's notes, Mary's blood pressure had remained stable for the past twenty-four hours and no abnormal cardiac rhythms had been noted. Chances were, Mary could be transferred today to an unmonitored room in the surgery ward.

Abby went to the bedside and said, "Mrs. Allen?"

The woman stirred awake. "Dr. DiMatteo," she murmured.

"How are you feeling today?"

"Not so good. It still hurts, you know."

"Where?"

"My chest. My head. Now my back. It hurts all over."

Abby saw from the chart that the nurses had been giving morphine around the clock. Obviously it wasn't enough; Abby would have to order a higher dose.

"We'll give you more medicine for the pain," said Abby. "As much as you need to keep you comfortable."

"To help me sleep, too. I can't sleep." Mary gave a sigh of profound weariness and closed her eyes. "I just want to go to sleep, doctor. And not wake up . . ."

"Mrs. Allen? Mary?"

"Couldn't you do that for me? You're my doctor. You could make it so easy. So simple."

"We can make the pain go away," said Abby.

"But you can't take away the cancer. Can you?" The eyes opened again, and regarded Abby with a look that pleaded for undiluted honesty.

"No," said Abby. "We can't take that away. The cancer's spread to too many places. We can give you chemotherapy, to slow it down. Gain some time for you."

"Time?" Mary gave a resigned laugh. "What do I need time for? To lie here another week, another month? I'd rather have it done and over with."

Abby took Mary's hand. It felt like bones wrapped in parchment, no flesh at all. "Let's take care of the pain first. If we do that, it could make everything else seem different."

In answer, Mary simply turned on her side, away from Abby. She was closing her off, shutting her out. "I suppose you want to listen to my lungs," was all she said.

They both knew the exam was merely a formality. It was a useless ceremony, the stethoscope on the chest, on the heart. Abby went through the motions anyway. She had little else to offer Mary Allen except this laying on of hands. When she was finished, her patient still lay with her back turned.

"We'll be transferring you out of the SICU," said Abby. "You can go to a room on the ward. It'll be quieter there. Not so many disturbances."

No answer. Just a deep breath, a long sigh.

Abby left the cubicle feeling more defeated, more useless than ever. There was so little she could do. An absence of pain was the best she had to offer. That, and a promise to let nature take its course.

She opened Mary's chart and wrote: "Patient expresses wish to die. Will increase morphine sulfate for pain control and change code status to Do Not Resuscitate." She wrote the transfer orders and handed them to Cecily, Mary's nurse.

"I want her kept comfortable," said Abby. "Titrate the dose to her pain. Give her as much as she needs to sleep."

"What's our upper limit?"

Abby paused, considered the fine line between comfort and unconsciousness, between sleep and coma. She said, "No upper limit. She's dying, Cecily. She wants to die. If the morphine makes it easier, then that's what we should give her. Even if it means the end comes a little sooner."

Cecily nodded, a look of unspoken agreement in her eyes.

As Abby started toward the next cubicle, she heard Cecily call out: "Dr. DiMatteo?"

Abby turned. "Yes?"

"I . . . just wanted to tell you. I think you should know that, well . . ." Nervously Cecily glanced around the SICU. She saw that some of the other nurses were watching. Waiting. Cecily cleared her throat. "I wanted you to know that we think you and Dr. Chao did the right thing. Giving the heart to Josh O'Day."

Abby blinked away an unexpected flash of tears. She whispered, "Thank you. Thank you so much."

Only then, as Abby looked around the room, did she see all the nods of approval.

"You're one of the best residents we've ever had, Dr. D.," said Cecily. "We wanted you to know that, too."

In the hush that followed, a pair of hands started clapping. Another joined in, then another. Abby stood speechless, clutching a chart to her chest, as all the SICU nurses burst out in loud and spontaneous applause. They were applauding *her*. It was a standing ovation.

"I want her off the staff and out of this hospital," said Victor Voss. "And I'll do whatever the hell it takes to accomplish that."

Jeremiah Parr had faced numerous crises during his eight-year tenure as president of Bayside Medical Center. He'd dealt with two nursing strikes, several multimillion-dollar malpractice suits, and militant Right-to-Lifers rampaging through the lobby, but never had he faced such outright fury as he saw now in the face of Victor Voss. At ten A.M., Voss, flanked by his two attorneys, had marched into Parr's office and demanded a conference. It was now close to noon and the group had expanded to include Surgical Residency Director Colin Wettig and Susan Casado, the attorney representing Bayside. Calling Susan was Parr's idea. As yet there was no talk of any legal action, but Parr couldn't be too cautious. Especially when dealing with someone as powerful as Victor Voss.

"My wife is dying," said Voss. "Do you understand? *Dying*. She may not survive another night. I lay the blame squarely on those two residents."

"Dr. DiMatteo is only in her second year," said Wettig. "She wasn't the one who made the decision. Our chief resident did. Dr. Chao is no longer in our program."

"I want Dr. DiMatteo's resignation as well."

"She hasn't offered it."

"Then find a reason to fire her."

"Dr. Wettig," said Parr, calmly. Reasonably. "We must be able to find some basis for termination."

"There's no basis at all," said Wettig, stubbornly holding

his ground. "All her evaluations have been outstanding and they're all on record. Mr. Voss, I know this is a painful situation for you. I know it's only normal to want to lay blame somewhere. But I think your anger is misdirected. The real problem lies in the shortage of organs. Thousands of people need new hearts and there are only a few to go around. Consider what would happen if we did fire Dr. DiMatteo. She could lodge an appeal. The matter would go to higher review. They look at this case and they'll ask questions. They'll ask why a seventeen-year-old boy didn't get that heart from the beginning."

There was a pause. "Jesus," murmured Parr.

"You understand what I'm saying?" said Wettig. "It looks bad. It makes the hospital look bad. This isn't the sort of thing we want to see in the newspapers. Hints of class warfare. The poor getting the short end of the stick. That's how they'll play it up. Whether or not it's true." Wettig looked questioningly around the table. No one said a thing.

Our silence speaks volumes, thought Parr.

"Of course we can't allow people to get the wrong impression," said Susan. "Outrageous as it may seem, even the appearance of human organ deals would kill us in the press."

"I'm just telling you how it looks," said Wettig.

"I don't care how it looks," said Voss. "They stole that heart."

"It was a directed donation. Mr. Terrio had every right to specify the recipient."

"My wife was guaranteed that heart."

"Guaranteed?" Wettig frowned at Parr. "Is there something I don't know about?"

"It was decided before her admission," Parr said. "The match was perfect."

"So was the boy's," countered Wettig.

Voss shot to his feet. "Let me explain something to you people. My wife is dying because of Abby DiMatteo. Now, you people don't know me very well. But let me tell you, no one screws me or my family and gets away with—"

"Mr. Voss," interjected one of his attorneys. "Perhaps we should discuss this in—"

"Goddamn it! Let me *finish!*"

"Please, Mr. Voss. This isn't in your best interests."

Voss glared at his attorney. With apparent effort, he broke off his attack and sat back down. "I want something done about Dr. DiMatteo," he said. And he looked straight at Parr.

By now Parr was sweating. God, it would be so easy just to fire that resident. Unfortunately, the General wasn't going to play ball with them. Damn these surgeons and their egos; they resented anyone else calling the shots. Why was Wettig being so stubborn about this?

"Mr. Voss," said Susan Casado in her silkiest voice. Her tame-the-savage-beast voice. "May I suggest we all take some time to think this over? Rushing into legal action is seldom the best course. In a few days, we may be able to resolve your concerns." Susan looked pointedly at Wettig.

The General just as pointedly ignored her.

"In a few days," said Voss, "my wife may be dead." He rose to his feet and regarded Parr with a look of contempt. "I don't need to think this over. I want something done about Dr. DiMatteo. And I want it done soon."

"I see the bullet," said Abby.

Mark redirected the light beam, focusing it on the posterior reaches of the thoracic cavity. Something metallic glinted back at them, then vanished behind the inflating lung.

"Sharp eyes, Abby. Since you spotted it, you want to do the honors?"

Abby took a pair of needle forceps off the instrument tray. The lungs had expanded again, blocking off her view of the cavity. "I need deflation. Just for a sec."

"You got it," said the anesthesiologist.

Abby plunged her hand deep into the thorax, following the inner curve of the ribs. As Mark gently retracted the right lung, Abby clamped the forceps tips around the metal fragment and carefully withdrew it from the cavity.

The bullet, a flattened twenty-two, clattered into the metal basin.

"No bleeding. Looks like we can close," said Abby.

"This is one lucky guy," Mark said, eyeing the probable trajectory. "Entry hole just right of the sternum. Rib must have deflected it or something. And it tumbled free along the pleural space. All he gets is a pneumothorax."

"Hope he learned his lesson," said Abby.

"What lesson?"

"Never piss off your wife."

"*She* was the shooter?"

"Hey, we've come a long way, baby."

They were closing the chest now, working together with the companionable ease of two people who know each other well. It was four P.M. Abby had been on duty since seven that morning. Already her calves ached from standing all day, and she had another twenty-four hours on duty to go. But she was on a high right now, buoyed by the success of this operation—and by the chance to operate with Mark. This was exactly how she'd pictured their future together: working hand in hand, confident of themselves and each other. Mark was a superb surgeon, swift yet meticulous. From the very first day she'd scrubbed in with him, Abby had been impressed by the comfortable atmosphere in his OR. Mark never lost his cool, never yelled at a nurse, never even raised his voice. She'd decided then that if *she* ever had to go under the knife, Mark Hodell was the one surgeon she'd want to be holding the scalpel.

Now she was working right beside him, her gloved hand brushing against his, their heads bent close. This was the man she loved, the work she loved. Just for this moment, she could forget Victor Voss and the crisis shadowing her career. Perhaps the crisis was over. No ax had yet fallen, no ominous message had been issued from Parr's office. In fact, Colin Wettig had taken her aside this morning to tell her, in his usual gruff way, that she'd received outstanding evaluations for trauma rotation.

It will all work out, she thought as she watched the patient wheeled out to Recovery. *Somehow, this will all turn out just fine.*

"Excellent job, DiMatteo," said Mark, stripping off his OR gown.

"I bet you say that to all the residents."

"Here's something I never say to the other residents." He leaned toward her and whispered: "Meet me in the call room."

"Uh . . . Dr. DiMatteo?"

Abby and Mark, both flushing, turned and looked at the circulating nurse, who'd just poked her head in the door.

77

"There's a call for you from Mr. Parr's secretary. They want to see you in Administration."

"Now?"

"They're waiting for you," said the nurse, and she left.

Abby shot Mark a look of apprehension. "Oh God. Now what?"

"Don't let 'em rattle you. I'm sure it'll be OK. Want me to come with you?"

She thought it over a moment, then shook her head. "I'm a big girl. I should be able to handle this."

"If there's any problem, page me. I'll be right there." He gave her hand a squeeze. "That's a promise."

She managed to return the thinnest of smiles. Then she pushed through the OR door and headed grimly for the elevator.

With the same feeling of dread she'd felt last night, she stepped off onto the second floor and headed up the carpeted hall to Jeremiah Parr's office. Parr's secretary directed her to the meeting room. Abby knocked on the door.

"Come in," she heard Parr say.

Taking a shaky breath, she stepped inside.

Parr rose from his seat at the conference table. Also in the room were Colin Wettig and a woman whom Abby did not recognize, a fortyish brunette in a nicely tailored blue suit. Nothing she saw in those faces gave Abby the slightest clue as to the purpose of this meeting, but every instinct told her this session would not be a pleasant one.

"Dr. DiMatteo," said Parr, "let me introduce you to Susan Casado, the hospital's corporate attorney."

An attorney? This is not good.

The two women shook hands. Ms. Casado's grip felt unnaturally warm against Abby's icy skin.

Abby took a chair next to Wettig. There was a brief silence, punctuated by the lawyer's rattling of papers and Wettig's gruff throat clearing.

Then Parr said, "Dr. DiMatteo, perhaps you could tell us what you recall about your role in the care of a Mrs. Karen Terrio."

Abby frowned. This was not at all what she'd expected. "I performed the initial evaluation on Mrs. Terrio," she said.

"Then I referred her to Neurosurgery. They took over her case."

"So how long was she under your care?"

"Officially? About two hours. More or less."

"And during those two hours, what did you do, exactly?"

"I stabilized her. Ordered the necessary labs. It would be in the medical record."

"Yes, we have a copy," said Susan Casado. She patted the chart lying on the table.

"You'll find it all documented in there," said Abby. "My admitting notes and orders."

"Everything you did?" said Susan.

"Yes. Everything."

"Do you remember anything you did that might have negatively affected the patient's course?"

"No."

"Anything you *should* have done? In retrospect?"

"No."

"I understand the patient expired."

"She'd suffered massive head trauma. A motor vehicle accident. She was declared brain-dead."

"After you cared for her."

In frustration, Abby glanced around the table. "Could someone please tell me what's going on?"

"What's going on," said Parr, "is that our insurance carrier, Vanguard Mutual—that's your carrier as well—received written notification just a few hours ago. It was hand-delivered and signed by an attorney from Hawkes, Craig and Sussman. I'm sorry to tell you this, Dr. DiMatteo, but it appears as if you—and Bayside—are about to be sued for malpractice."

The air went out of Abby's lungs in a sickening rush. She found herself gripping the table, fighting the sudden nausea rising in her stomach. She knew they were waiting for her to respond, but all she could manage was a shocked look and a disbelieving shake of her head.

"I take it you weren't expecting this," said Susan Casado.

"I . . ." Abby swallowed. "No. No."

"It's only a preliminary notification," said Susan Casado. "You understand, of course, that there are a number of formalities that lead up to any actual trial. First, the case will be reviewed by a state screening panel to determine whether or not this is, in fact, malpractice. If the panel decides there was none, this whole thing may stop right there. But the plaintiff still has the right to proceed to trial, regardless.''

"The plaintiff," murmured Abby. "Who is the plaintiff?"

"The husband. Joseph Terrio."

"There has to be a mistake. A misunderstanding—"

"Damn right there's a misunderstanding," said Wettig. Everyone looked at the General, who had, until then, sat in stony silence. "I've reviewed the record myself. Every page of it. There's no malpractice there. Dr. DiMatteo did everything she should have done."

"Then why is she the only doctor named in the lawsuit?" said Parr.

"I'm the only one?" Abby looked at the attorney. "What about Neurosurgery? The emergency room? No one else was named?"

"Just you, Doctor," said Susan. "And your employer. Bayside."

Abby sat back, stunned. "I don't believe this . . ."

"Neither do I," said Wettig. "This isn't the way it's done and we all know it. Damn lawyers usually take the shotgun approach, name every M.D. who came within a mile of the patient. There's something wrong here. Something else is going on."

"It's Victor Voss," said Abby softly.

"Voss?" Wettig gave a dismissive wave. "He has no stake in this case."

"He's out to ruin me. That's his stake." She looked around the table. "Why do you think I'm the only doctor named? Somehow Voss has gotten to Joe Terrio. Convinced him I did something wrong. If I could just talk to Joe—"

"Absolutely not," said Susan. "It would be a sign of desperation. A tip-off to the plaintiff that you know you're in trouble."

"I *am* in trouble!"

"No. Not yet. If there's really no malpractice here, it will all blow over sooner or later. Once the panel rules in your favor, chances are the other side will drop the suit."

"What if they insist on going to trial anyway?"

"It would make no sense. The legal expenses alone would—"

"Don't you see, *Voss* must be footing the bill. He doesn't care about winning or losing! He could pay an army of lawyers, just to keep me running scared. Joe Terrio may be only the first lawsuit. Victor Voss could track down every patient I've ever cared for. Convince every single one of them to file suit against me."

"And we're her employer. Which means they'll file suit against Bayside as well," said Parr. He looked ill. Almost as ill as Abby felt.

"There's got to be a way to defuse this," said Susan. "Some way to approach Mr. Voss and cool down the situation."

No one said anything. But Abby, looking at Parr's face, could read the thought going through his head: *The fastest way to cool this down is to fire you.*

She waited for the blow to fall, expected it to fall. It didn't. Parr and Susan merely exchanged glances.

Then Susan said, "We're still early in the game. We have months to maneuver. Months to plan a response. In the meantime . . ." She looked at Abby. "You'll be assigned counsel by Vanguard Mutual. I suggest you meet with their attorney as soon as possible. You may also consider hiring your own private counsel."

"Do you think I need to?"

"Yes."

Abby swallowed "I don't know how I'm going to afford to hire an attorney . . ."

"In your particular situation, Dr. DiMatteo," said Susan, "you can't afford not to."

For Abby, being on call that night was a blessing in disguise. A flurry of calls and pages kept her on the run all evening, attending to everything from a pneumothorax in the medical ICU to a postop fever in the surgical ward. There was little time for her to brood over Joe Terrio's lawsuit. But every so often, when there was a lull in the phone calls, she would find herself hovering dangerously close to tears. Of all the grieving spouses she'd comforted and counseled, Joe Terrio was the last one she'd expected to sue her. *What did I do wrong?* she wondered. *Could I have been more compassion-ate? More caring?*

Damn it, Joe, what else did you want from me?

Whatever it was, she knew she could not have given more of herself. She'd done the very best job she could have done. And for all her anguish over Karen Terrio, she was being rewarded with a slap in the face.

She was angry now, at the attorneys, at Victor Voss, even at Joe. She felt sorry for Joe Terrio, but she also felt betrayed by him. By the very man whose suffering she had so acutely felt.

At ten o'clock she was finally free to retreat to the on-call room. Too upset to read her journals, too demoralized to talk to anyone, even Mark, she lay down on the bed and stared at the ceiling. Her legs felt paralyzed, her whole body lifeless. *How the hell do I get through this night,* she wondered, *when I can't even bring myself to move from this bed?*

But move she did when, at ten-thirty, the phone rang. She sat up and reached for the receiver. "Dr. DiMatteo."

"This is the OR. Drs. Archer and Hodell need you up here."

"Now?"

"ASAP. They've got a case brewing."

"I'll be there." Abby hung up. Sighing, she ran both her hands through her hair. Any other time, any other evening, she'd already be on her feet and raring to scrub. Tonight she could barely stand the thought of facing Mark and Archer across an operating table.

Damn it, you're a surgeon, DiMatteo. So act like one!

It was self-disgust that finally propelled her to her feet and out of the call room.

She found Mark and Archer upstairs in the surgeons' lounge. They were standing by the microwave, their voices lowered in quiet conversation. She knew, just by the way their heads jerked up as she entered, that their conversation was meant to be private. But the instant they saw her, both of them smiled.

"There you are," said Archer. "All quiet in the trenches?"

"For the moment," said Abby. "I hear you two have a case coming up."

"Transplant," said Mark. "The team's coming in now. Trouble is, we can't get hold of Mohandas. A fifth-year resident's going to be standing in for him, but we may need you to assist as well. Feel up to scrubbing in?''

''On a heart transplant?'' The quick shot of adrenaline was exactly what Abby needed to shake off her depression. She gave Mark an emphatic nod. ''I'd be thrilled.''

''There's only one small problem,'' said Archer. ''The patient is Nina Voss.''

Abby stared at him. ''They found her a heart so soon?''

''We got lucky. The heart's coming in from Burlington. Victor Voss would probably have a stroke if he knew we were using you. But we're calling the shots right now. And we may need another pair of hands in that OR. On such short notice, you're the obvious choice.''

''Are you still up for it?'' asked Mark.

Abby didn't even hesitate. ''Absolutely,'' she said.

''OK,'' said Archer. ''Looks like we got our assistant.'' He nodded to Mark. ''Meet you both in OR three. Twenty minutes.''

At eleven-thirty P.M., they got the call from the thoracic surgeon at Wilcox Memorial Hospital in Burlington, Vermont. The donor harvest was completed; the organ appeared to be in excellent shape and was being rushed to the airport. Preserved at four degrees centigrade, its beating temporarily paralyzed by a concentrated potassium flush, the heart could be kept viable for only four to five hours. Without blood flow to the coronary arteries, every minute that passed—ischemic time—could result in the death of a few more myocardial cells. The longer the ischemic time, the less likely the heart would function in Nina Voss's chest.

The flight, by emergency charter, was expected to take a maximum of an hour and a half.

By midnight, the Bayside Hospital transplant team was assembled and dressed in surgical greens.. Along with Bill Archer, Mark, and anesthesiologist Frank Zwick, there was a small army of support staff: nurses, a perfusion technician, cardiologist Aaron Levi, and Abby.

Nina Voss was wheeled to OR 3.

At one-thirty, the call came in from Logan International: the plane had landed safely.

That was the cue for the surgeons to head to the scrub area.

As Abby washed her hands at the sink, she could look through the window into OR 3, where the rest of the transplant team was already busy with preparations. The nurses were laying out instrument trays and tearing open packets of sterile drapes. The perfusionist was recalibrating the cabinetlike bypass machine. A fifth-year resident, already scrubbed in, stood by waiting to prep the surgical site.

On the operating table, at the center of a tangle of EKG wires and IV lines, lay Nina Voss. She seemed oblivious to the activity around her. Dr. Zwick stood at Nina's head, murmuring to her gently as he injected a bolus of pentobarb into her IV line. Her eyelids flickered shut. Zwick placed the mask over her mouth and nose. With the ambubag he pumped a few breaths of oxygen in quick succession, then removed the mask.

The next step had to be performed swiftly. The patient was unconscious now, unable to breathe on her own. Tilting her head back, Zwick slipped a curved laryngoscope blade into her throat, located the vocal cords, and inserted the plastic endotracheal tube. An air-inflated cuff would keep the tube in place in her trachea. Zwick connected the tube to the ventilator and her chest began to rise and fall with the whoosh of the bellows. The intubation had taken less than thirty seconds.

The operating lights were turned on and directed at the table. Bathed in that brilliant glow, Nina seemed unearthly. Spectral. A nurse pulled off the sheet draping Nina's body and exposed the torso, the ribs arching beneath pale skin, the breasts small, almost shrunken. The resident proceeded to disinfect the operative site, painting broad strokes of iodine across the skin.

The OR doors banged open as Mark, Archer, and Abby, freshly scrubbed, walked in with hands held up, elbows dripping water. They were greeted with sterile towels, gowns, and gloves. By the time everyone was fully garbed, Nina Voss had been prepped and draped.

Archer moved to the operating table. "Is it here yet?" he asked.

"Still waiting for it," said a nurse.

"It's only a twenty-minute drive from Logan."

"Maybe they got caught in a traffic jam."

"At two in the morning?"

"Jesus," said Mark. "That's all we need now. An accident."

Archer peered up at the monitors. "Happened at Mayo. Had a kidney flown in all the way from Texas. Right out of the airport, ambulance hits a truck. Organ gets squashed. Perfectly matched one, too."

"You're kidding," said Zwick.

"Hey, would I kid about a kidney?"

The fifth-year resident glanced up at the wall clock. "We're going on three hours since harvest."

"Wait. Just wait," said Archer.

The phone rang. Everyone's head swiveled to watch as the nurse answered it. Seconds later she hung up and announced: "It's downstairs. The courier's on his way up from the ER."

"OK," snapped Archer. "Let's cut."

From where Abby stood, she caught only a slanted glimpse of the procedure, and even then her view was intermittent, cut off by Mark's shoulder. Archer and Mark were working swiftly and in concert, making a midline sternotomy incision, exposing fascia, then bone.

The wall intercom buzzed. "Dr. Mapes from the harvest team is here with a special delivery," came the message from the OR front desk.

"We're cannulating," said Mark. "Have him join the fun."

Abby glanced toward the OR door. Through the viewing window, she could see the scrub area beyond, where a man stood waiting. Beside him, on a gurney, was a small Igloo cooler. The same sort of cooler in which she'd transported Karen Terrio's heart.

"He'll be in," said the desk nurse. "As soon as he changes clothes."

Moments later, Dr. Mapes entered, now wearing greens. He was a small man with an almost Neanderthal brow and a nose that jutted out like a hawk's beak under the surgical mask.

"Welcome to Boston," said Archer, glancing up at the visitor. "I'm Bill Archer. This is Mark Hodell."

"Leonard Mapes. I scrubbed with Dr. Nicholls at Wilcox."

"Good flight, Len?"

"Could've used a beverage service."

Archer cracked a smile, visible even through his mask. "So what'd you bring us for Christmas, Len?"

"Nice one. I think you'll be pleased."

"Let me finish cannulating and I'll take a look."

Cannulation of the ascending aorta was the first step to connecting the patient to the bypass machine. That squat box, under control of the perfusion technician, would temporarily assume the job of the heart and lungs, collecting venous blood, replenishing its oxygen, and pumping it back into the patient's aorta.

Archer, using silk sutures, sewed two concentric "purse strings" in the wall of the ascending aorta. With a scalpel tip he made a tiny stab in the vessel. Bright blood spurted out. Swiftly he inserted the arterial cannula into the incision and tightened the purse strings. The bleeding slowed to an ooze, then stopped as he sewed the cannula tip in place. The other end of the cannula was connected to the bypass machine's arterial line.

Mark, with Abby retracting, was already starting on the venous cannulation.

"OK," said Archer, moving from the table. "Let's unwrap our present."

A nurse unpacked the Igloo cooler and lifted out the organ, wrapped in two ordinary plastic bags. She untwisted the ties and slid the naked organ into a basin of sterile saline.

Gently Archer lifted the chilled heart from its bath. "Nice excision job," he noted. "You guys did good work."

"Thanks," said Mapes.

Archer ran his gloved finger over the surface. "Arteries soft and smooth. Clean as a whistle."

"Seems a bit on the small side, doesn't it?" said Abby, glancing across the table. "How big was the donor?"

"Forty-four kilograms," said Dr. Mapes.

Abby frowned. "Adult?"

"An adolescent, previously healthy. A boy."

Abby caught the flicker of distress in Archer's eyes. She remembered then that he had two teenage sons. Gently he lay the organ back in its bath of chilled saline.

"We won't let this one go to waste," he said. And he turned his attention back to Nina.

By then, Mark and Abby were already finishing up the

venous cannulation. Two Tygon tubes fitted with metal baskets at the end were inserted through stab wounds in the right atria, and secured by purse-string sutures. Venous blood would be collected by these cannulae and directed to the pump-oxygenator.

Working together now, Archer and Mark snared shut the inferior and superior venae cavae, cutting off return blood to the heart.

"Cross-clamping aorta," announced Mark as he closed off the ascending aorta.

The heart, cut off from both venous inflow and arterial outflow, was now a useless sac. Nina Voss's circulation was under the complete control of the perfusionist and her magical machine. Also under her control was the body temperature. By chilling the fluids, the body could be slowly cooled down to twenty-five degrees centigrade—profound hypothermia. This would preserve the newly implanted myocardial cells and lessen the body's oxygen consumption.

Zwick turned off the ventilator. The rhythmic wheeze of the bellows ceased. There was no need to pump air into the lungs when the bypass machine was doing the work.

Transplantation could now proceed.

Archer cut the aorta and pulmonary arteries. Blood gushed out into the chest, spilled onto the floor. At once a nurse threw a towel down to soak up the mess. Archer kept working, oblivious to the sweat beading his forehead, to the lights burning down. Next he transected the atria. More blood, darker, splashed Archer's gown. He reached elbow-deep into the chest cavity. Nina Voss's sick heart, pale and flabby, was now lifted away and dropped into a basin. What remained was a gaping hollow.

Abby glanced up at the monitor screen and felt an automatic rush of alarm at the flat EKG line. Of course there was no tracing. There was no heart. In fact, all the classic signs of life had ceased. The lungs were still. The heart was gone. Yet the patient still lived.

Mark lifted the donor heart from the basin and lowered it into the chest. "Some folks call this procedure a glorified plumbing job," he said, rotating the heart to match up the left atrial chambers. "They think it's like stitching together a stuffed animal or something. But you let your attention slip for a minute, and before you realize it, you're sewing the heart in backwards.''

The fifth-year resident laughed.

"Not funny. It's happened.''

"Saline,'' said Archer, and a nurse poured a basin of chilled saline over the heart to keep it cold under the lights.

"A hundred things can go wrong,'' said Mark, his suture needle taking deep, almost savage bites into the left atrium. "Drug reaction. Anesthetic disasters. And damn it, the surgeon always gets the blame.''

"Lot of blood pooling in here,'' said Archer. "Suction, Abby.''

The hiss of the suction machine gave way to a tense silence as the surgeons worked more quickly now. There was only the whir of the pump-oxygenator and the click of the needle clamps as the serrated jaws snapped shut with each new stitch. Despite Abby's repeated suctioning, blood kept soaking into the drapes and dribbling onto the floor. The towels at their feet were saturated. The surgeons kicked them aside and new towels were thrown down.

Archer snipped away the suture needle. "Right atrial anastomosis done.''

"Perfusion catheter,'' said Mark.

A nurse handed him the catheter. He introduced it into the left atrium and infused four-degree-centigrade saline. The flood of chilled liquid cooled down the ventricle and flushed out any air pockets inside.

"Okeydoke,'' said Archer, repositioning the heart to sew the aortic anastomosis. "Let's hook up these pipes.''

Mark glanced up at the wall clock. "Look at that. We're ahead of schedule, folks. What a team.''

The intercom buzzed. It was the OR desk nurse. "Mr. Voss wants to know how his wife is doing.''

"Fine,'' called Archer. "No problems.''

"How much longer, do you think?''

"An hour. Tell him to hang in there.''

The intercom shut off. Archer glanced across at Mark. "He rubs me the wrong way.''

"Voss?''

"Likes to be in control.''

"No kidding.''

Archer's suture needle curved in and out of the glistening aortic wall. "But then, I guess if I had his money, I'd call the shots too."

"Where does his money come from?" asked the fifth-year resident.

Archer glanced at him in surprise. "You don't know about Victor Voss? VMI International? Everything from chemicals to robotics."

"Is that what the V stands for in VMI?"

"You got it." Archer tied off and snipped the last suture. "Aorta done. Cross clamp off."

"Perfusion catheter coming out," said Mark, and turned to Abby. "Get those two pacing wires ready for insertion."

Archer picked up a fresh suture needle from the tray and began the pulmonary anastomosis. He was just tying off when he noticed the organ balling up. "Look at that!" he said. "Ice cold and already a spontaneous contraction. This baby's rarin' to go."

"Pacing wires on," said Mark.

"Isuprel infusion going in," said Zwick. "Two micrograms."

They watched and waited for the Isuprel to take effect, for the heart to repeat the contraction.

It lay inert as a limp sac.

"Come on," said Archer. "Don't let me down."

"Defibrillator?" asked a nurse.

"No, give it a chance."

Slowly the heart tightened into a fist-sized knot, then fell flaccid.

Zwick said, "Increasing Isuprel to three mics."

There was one more contraction. Then nothing.

"Go on," said Archer. "Flog it a little more."

"Four mics," said Zwick, dialing up the IV infusion.

The heart tightened, relaxed. Contracted, relaxed.

Zwick glanced up at the monitor. QRS spikes were now tracing across the screen. "Rate's up to fifty. Sixty-four. Seventy . . ."

"Titrate to one-ten," said Mark.

"That's what I'm doing," said Zwick, adjusting the Isuprel.

Archer said to the circulation nurse: "Get on the intercom, will you? Tell Recovery we're about to close."

"Rate's one-ten," said Zwick.

"OK," said Mark. "Let's take her off bypass. Get those cannulae out."

Zwick flipped on the ventilator. Everyone in the room seemed to exhale a simultaneous sigh of relief.

"Let's just hope she and this heart get along," said Mark.

"We know how close the HL-A match is?" asked Archer. He turned around to look at Dr. Mapes.

There was no one standing behind him.

Abby had been so focused on the operation, she hadn't noticed the man had left.

"He walked out twenty minutes ago," one of the nurses said.

"Just like that?"

"Maybe he had a plane to catch," she said.

"Didn't even get a chance to shake his hand," said Archer. He turned back to the patient on the table. "OK. Let's close."

7

Nadiya had had enough. All the whining, all the demands, all the pent-up boy energy that regularly erupted into swearing and shoving, had sucked away her strength. That, and now the seasickness. Gregor, the big ape, was sick as well, as were most of the boys. On the roughest days, when the ship's hull pounded like a hammer on the anvil of the North Sea, they all lay groaning in their bunks, the sounds and smells of their wretchedness penetrating even to the decks above. On such days, the mess hall below remained dark and half-deserted, the passageways were empty, and the ship was like some great and moaning ghost vessel, guided by the hands of a spirit crew.

Yakov had never had such a good time.

Unstricken by even the faintest twinge of nausea, he roamed freely throughout the ship. No one stopped him. Indeed, the crew seemed to enjoy his presence. He would visit Koubichev in the engine room, and in that noisy hell of grinding pistons and diesel fumes, the two of them played chess. Sometimes, Yakov even won. When he got hungry, Yakov would wander into the galley where Lubi, the cook, would offer him tea and beet soup and medivnyk, the fragrant spiced honey cake from his native Ukraine. Lubi never said much. "More?" and "Enough, eh?" was the extent of his conversation. The food he served was eloquence enough. Then there was the dusty cargo hold to explore, and the radio room with its dials and knobs, and the deck with its tarp-covered lifeboats to hide in. The only place he could not wander was the far aft section. He could not find any passage to get in there.

His favorite place of all was the bridge. Captain Dibrov and the navigator would greet Yakov with indulgent smiles and allow him to sit at the chart table. There he'd trace with the index finger of his one hand the course they had already sailed. From the port of Riga, down the Baltic Sea, through the channel past Malmö and Copenhagen, around the top of Denmark, and across the North Sea with its stepping stones of oil platforms with names like Montrose and Forties and Piper. The North Sea was bigger than he'd imagined. It was not just a little puddle of blue, the way it seemed on the chart. It was two days of water. And soon, the navigator told him, they'd be crossing an even bigger sea, the Atlantic Ocean.

"They won't live that long," Yakov predicted.

"Who won't?"

"Nadiya and the other boys."

"Of course they will," said the navigator. "Everyone gets sick in the North Sea. After a while their stomachs settle. It has to do with the inner ear."

"What does the ear have to do with the stomach?"

"It senses motion. Too much motion makes it confused."

"How?"

"I don't really understand it. But that's how it works."

"I'm not sick. Is there something different about my inner ear?"

"You must be a born sailor."

Yakov looked down at the stump of his left arm and shook his head. "I don't think so."

The navigator smiled. "You have a good brain. Brains are far more important. You will need them, where you're going."

"Why?"

"In America, if you're clever, you can become rich. You want to be rich, don't you?"

"I don't know."

Both the navigator and the captain laughed.

"Maybe the boy doesn't have any brains after all," said the captain.

Yakov looked at them without smiling.

"It was just a joke," said the navigator.

"I know."

"Why don't you ever laugh, boy? I never see you laugh."

"I never feel like it."

The captain snorted. "Lucky little bastard's going to some rich family in America. And he doesn't feel like laughing? What's wrong with him?"

Yakov shrugged and looked back at the chart. "I don't cry, either."

Aleksei was curled up on the lower bunk, clutching Shu-Shu to his chest. He was startled awake as Yakov sat down on the mattress.

"Aren't you ever going to get up?" asked Yakov.

Aleksei closed his eyes. "I'm sick."

"Lubi made lamb dumplings for supper. I ate nine of them."

"Don't talk about it."

"Aren't you hungry?"

"Of course I'm hungry. But I'm too sick to eat."

Yakov sighed and looked around the cabin. There were eight bunk beds in the room, and six of them were occupied by boys too ill to play. Yakov had already visited the adjoining quarters and found the other boys equally incapacitated. Would it be this way all across the Atlantic?

"It's all because of your inner ear," said Yakov.

"What are you talking about?" moaned Aleksei.

"Your ear. It's making your stomach sick."

"My ears are fine."

"You've been sick four days now. You've got to get up and eat."

"Oh, leave me alone."

Yakov grabbed Shu-Shu and yanked it away.

"Give him back!" wailed Aleksei.

"Come and get him."

"Just give him back!"

"First you get up. Come on." Yakov scurried away from the

bunk as Aleksei made a futile swipe for the stuffed dog. "You'll feel better if you're out of bed."

Aleksei sat up. For a moment he huddled at the edge of his mattress, his head swaying with every tilt of the ship. Suddenly he clapped his hand to his mouth, lurched to his feet, and scrambled across the cabin. He vomited into the sink. Groaning, he crawled back into his bunk.

Solemnly, Yakov handed back Shu-Shu.

Aleksei hugged the stuffed dog against his chest. "I told you I was sick. Now go away."

Yakov left the boys' quarters and wandered into the corridor. At Nadiya's stateroom door, he knocked. There was no answer. He moved on to Gregor's stateroom and knocked again.

"Who is it?" came a growl.

"It's me. Yakov. Are you still sick as well?"

"Get the fuck away from my door."

Yakov left. He wandered around the ship for a while, but Lubi had retired for the night. The captain and the navigator were too busy to talk to him. As usual, Yakov was on his own.

He went down to visit Koubichev in the engine room.

They set up the chessboard. Yakov drew the first move, pawn to king four.

"Have you ever been to America?" Yakov asked over the rumble of the pistons.

"Twice," said Koubichev, moving his queen's pawn forward.

"Did you like it there?"

"Wouldn't know. They always order us confined to quarters as soon as we get into port. I never see a fucking thing."

"Why does the captain order this?"

"The captain doesn't. It's those people in the aft cabin."

"What people? I've never seen them."

"No one ever does."

"Then how do you know they're there?"

"Ask Lubi. He cooks for them. Someone's eating the food he sends up. Now are you going to move a piece or what?"

With great concentration, Yakov advanced another pawn. "Why don't you just leave the ship when we get there?" he asked.

"Why would I?"

"To stay in America and get rich."

Koubichev grunted. "They pay me enough. I can't complain."

"How much do they pay you?"

"You're too nosy."

"Is it a lot?"

"It's more than I used to make. More than a lot of men make. And just to go back and forth, back and forth across this damned Atlantic."

Yakov moved out his queen. "So it's a good job? To be a ship's engineer?"

"That's a stupid move, bringing out your queen. Why did you make it?"

"I'm trying new things out. Should I be a ship's engineer some day?"

"No."

"But you get paid a lot."

"It's only because I work for the Sigayev Company. They pay very well."

"Why?"

"I keep my mouth shut."

"Why?"

"How the hell should I know?" Koubichev reached across the board. "My knight takes your queen. See, I told you it was a stupid move."

"It was an experiment," said Yakov.

"Well, I hope you learned something from it."

A few days later, on the bridge, Yakov asked the navigator: "What's the Sigayev Company?"

The navigator shot him a look of surprise. "How did you hear that name?"

"Koubichev told me."

"He shouldn't have."

"So you don't talk about it either," said Yakov.

"That's right."

For a moment, Yakov didn't say anything. He watched the navigator fuss with his electronics equipment. There was a small screen where little numbers kept flashing, and the navigator would write the numbers in a book, then look in his chart.

"Where are we?" asked Yakov.

"Here." The navigator pointed to a tiny X on the chart. It was in the middle of the ocean.

"How do you know?"

"By the numbers. I read them on the screen. The latitude and longitude. See?"

"You have to be very clever to be a navigator, don't you?"

"Not so clever, really." The man was moving two plastic rulers across the chart now. They were connected by hinges, and he'd clack them together as he slid them to the compass rose at the edge of the chart.

"Are you doing something illegal?" asked Yakov.

"What?"

"Is that why you're not supposed to talk about it?"

The navigator sighed. "My only responsibility is to guide this ship from Riga to Boston and back to Riga."

"Do you always carry orphans?"

"No. Usually we carry cargo. Crates. I don't ask what's in them. I don't ask questions, period."

"So you could be doing something illegal."

The navigator laughed. "You are a little devil, aren't you?" He began to write again in his notebook, recording numbers in neat columns.

The boy watched him for a while in silence. Then he said, "Do you think anyone will adopt me?"

"Of course someone will."

"Even with this?" Yakov raised his stump of an arm.

The navigator looked at him, and Yakov recognized the flicker of pity in the man's eyes. "I know for a fact someone will adopt you," he said.

"How do you know?"

"Someone's paid for your passage, haven't they? Arranged for your papers."

"I've never seen my papers. Have you?"

"It's none of my business. My only job is to get this ship to Boston." He waved Yakov aside. "Why don't you go back to the other boys? Go on."

"They're still not feeling well."

"Well, go play somewhere else."

Reluctantly Yakov left the bridge and went out on deck. He was the only one there. He stood by the rail and stared down at the water splintering before the bow. He thought of the fish swimming somewhere below in their gray and turbid world, and suddenly he found he couldn't breathe; the image of swirling water was suffocating. Yet he didn't move. He stayed at the rail, gripping it with his one hand, letting the panicky thoughts of cold, deep water wash through him. Fear was something he had not felt in a very long time.

He was feeling it now.

8

She had had the same dream two nights in a row. The nurses told her it was because of all the medications she'd been taking. The methylprednisolone and the cyclosporine and the pain pills. The chemicals were scrambling her brain. And after days of hospitalization, of course she'd be having bad dreams. Everyone did. It was nothing to worry about. The dreams would, eventually, fade away.

But that morning, as Nina Voss lay in her ICU bed, the tears fresh in her eyes, she knew the dream would not go away, would never go away. It was part of her now. Just as this heart was part of her.

Softly, she touched her hand to the bandages on her chest. It had been two days since the operation, and though the soreness was just starting to ease, it still awakened her at night, a reminder of the gift she'd received. It was a good, strong heart. She had known that within a day of the surgery. During the long months of her illness, she'd forgotten what it was like to have a strong heart. To walk without gasping for air. To feel the blood pump, warm and vital, to her muscles. To look down at her own fingers and marvel at the rosy flush of her capillaries. She had lived so long waiting for death, accepting death, that life itself had become foreign to her.

But now she could see it in her own hands. Could feel it in her fingertips.

And in the beating of this new heart.

It did not yet feel as if it belonged to her. Perhaps it never would.

As a child, she would often inherit her older sister's clothing, Caroline's good wool sweaters, her scarcely worn party dresses. Although the garments had unquestionably passed to Nina's ownership, she had never stopped thinking of them as her sister's. In her mind, they would always be *Caroline's* dresses, *Caroline's* skirts.

And whose heart are you? she thought, her hand gently touching her chest.

At noon, Victor came to sit by her bed.

"I had the dream again," she told him. "The one about the boy. It was so clear to me this time! When I woke up, I couldn't stop crying."

"It's the steroids, darling," said Victor. "They warned you about that side effect."

"I think it means something. Don't you see? I have this part of him inside me. A part that's still alive. I can feel him . . ."

"That nurse should never have told you it was a boy's."

"I asked her."

"Still, she shouldn't have told you. It does no one any good to release that information. Not you. Not the boy."

"No," she said softly. "Not the boy. But the family—if there's a family—"

"I'm sure they don't wish to be reminded. Think about it, Nina. It's a strictly confidential process. There's a reason for it."

"Would it be so bad? To send the family a thank-you letter? It would be completely anonymous. Just a simple—"

"No, Nina. Absolutely not."

Nina sank back quietly on the pillows. She was being foolish again. Victor was right. Victor was always right.

"You're looking wonderful today, darling," he said. "Have you been up in a chair yet?"

"Twice," said Nina. Suddenly the room seemed very, very cold to her. She looked away and shivered.

* * *

Pete was sitting in a chair by Abby's bed, looking at her. He wore his blue Cub Scout uniform, the one with all the little patches sewn on the sleeves and the plastic beads dangling from the breast pocket, one bead for each achievement. He was not wearing his cap. Where is his cap? she wondered. And then she remembered that it was lost, that she and her sisters had searched and searched the roadside but had not found it anywhere near the mangled remains of his bicycle.

He had not visited in a long time, not since the night she'd left for college. When he did visit, it was always the same. He would sit looking at her, not speaking.

She said, "Where have you been, Pete? Why did you come if you're not going to say anything?"

He just sat watching her, his eyes silent, his lips unmoving. The collar of his blue shirt was starched and stiff, just the way their mother had pressed it for the burial. He turned and looked toward another room. A musical note seemed to be calling to him; he was starting to shimmer, like water that has been stirred.

She said, "What did you come to tell me?"

The waters were churning now, beaten to a froth by all those musical notes. Another bell-like jangle led to total disintegration. There was only darkness.

And the ringing telephone.

Abby reached for the receiver. "DiMatteo," she said.

"This is the SICU. I think maybe you'd better come down."

"What's happening?"

"It's Mrs. Voss in Bed Fifteen. The transplan.. She's running a fever, thirty-eight point six."

"What about her other vitals?"

"BP's a hundred over seventy. Pulse is ninety-six."

"I'll be there." Abby hung up and switched on the lamp. It was two A.M. The chair by her bed was empty. No Pete. Groaning, she climbed out of bed and stumbled across the room to the sink, where she splashed cold water on her face. Its temperature didn't even register. She felt the water as though through anesthesia. Wake up, wake up, she told herself. You have to know what the hell you're doing. A postop fever. A three-day-old transplant. First step, check the wound. Examine the lungs, the abdomen. Order a chest X ray and cultures.

And keep your cool.

She couldn't afford to make any mistakes. Not now, and certainly not with this patient.

Every morning for the past three days, she'd walked into Bayside not knowing if she still had a job. And every afternoon at five o'clock she'd heaved a sigh of relief that she'd survived another twenty-four hours. With each day that passed, the crisis seemed a little dimmer and Parr's threats more remote. She knew she had Wettig on her side, and Mark as well. With their help maybe—just maybe—she'd keep her job. She didn't want to give Parr any reason to question her performance as a doctor, so she'd been especially meticulous at work, had checked and rechecked every lab result, every physical finding. And she'd been careful to steer clear of Nina Voss's hospital room. Another angry encounter with Victor Voss was the last thing she needed.

But now Nina Voss was running a fever and Abby was the resident on the spot. She couldn't avoid this; she had a job to do.

She pulled on her tennis shoes and left the on-call room.

Late at night, a hospital is a surreal place. Hallways stretch empty, the lights are too bright, and through tired eyes, all those white walls seem to curve and sway like moving tunnels. She was weaving through one of those tunnels now, her body still numb, her brain still struggling to function. Only her heart had fully responded to the crisis; it was pounding.

She turned a corner, into the SICU.

The lights were dimmed for the night—modern technology's concession to the diurnal needs of human patients. In the gloom of the nurses' station, the electrical patterns of sixteen patients' hearts traced across sixteen screens. A glance at Screen 15 confirmed that Mrs. Voss's pulse was running fast. A rate of 100.

The monitor nurse picked up the ringing telephone, then said: "Dr. Levi's on the line. He wants to talk to the on-call resident."

"I'll take it," said Abby, reaching for the receiver. "Hello, Dr. Levi? This is Abby DiMatteo."

There was a silence. "You're on call tonight?" he said, and she heard a distinct note of dismay in his voice. She understood at once the reason for it. Abby was the last person he wanted to lay hands on Nina Voss. But tonight there was no alternative; she was the senior resident on call.

She said: "I was just about to examine Mrs. Voss. She's running a fever."

"Yes, they told me about it." Again there was a pause.

She plunged into that void, determined to keep their conversation purely professional. "I'll do the usual fever workup," she said. "I'll examine her. Order a CBC and cultures, urine, and chest X ray. As soon as I have the results I'll call you back."

"All right," he finally said. "I'll be waiting for your call."

Abby donned an isolation gown and stepped into Nina Voss's cubicle. A single lamp had been left on, and it shone dimly above the bed. Under that soft cone of light, Nina Voss's hair was a silvery streak across the pillow. Her eyelids were shut, her hands crossed over her body in a strange semblance of holy repose. The princess in the sepulchre, thought Abby.

She moved to the side of the bed and said softly: "Mrs. Voss?"

Nina opened her eyes. Slowly her gaze focused on Abby. "Yes?"

"I'm Dr. DiMatteo," said Abby. "I'm one of the surgical residents." She saw the flicker of recognition in the other woman's eyes. *She knows my name,* thought Abby. *She knows who I am.* The grave robber. The body thief.

Nina Voss said nothing, merely looked at her with those fathomless eyes.

"You have a fever," explained Abby. "We need to find out why. How are you feeling, Mrs. Voss?"

"I'm . . . tired. That's all," whispered Nina. "Just tired."

"I'll have to check your incision." Abby turned up the lights and gently peeled the bandages off the chest wound. The incision looked clean, no redness, no swelling. She pulled out her stethoscope and moved on to the rest of the fever workup. She heard the normal rush of air in and out of the lungs. Felt the abdomen. Peered into the ears, nose, and throat. She found nothing alarming, nothing that would cause a fever. Through it all, Nina remained silent, her gaze following Abby's every move.

At last Abby straightened and said: "Everything seems to be fine. But there must be a reason for the fever. We'll be getting a chest X ray and collecting three different blood samples for cultures." She smiled apologetically. "I'm afraid you're not going to get much sleep tonight."

Nina shook her head. "I don't sleep much, anyway. All the dreams. So many dreams . . . "

"Bad dreams?"

Nina took in a breath, slowly let it out. "About the boy."

"Which boy, Mrs. Voss?"

"This boy." Softly she touched her hand to her chest. "They told me it was a boy's. I don't even know his name. Or how he died. All I know is, this was a boy's." She looked at Abby. "It was. Wasn't it?"

Abby nodded. "That's what I heard in the operating room."

"You were there?"

"I assisted Dr. Hodell."

A small smile formed on Nina's lips. "Strange. That you should be there, after . . ." Her voice faded.

Neither one of them spoke for a moment, Abby silenced by guilt, Nina Voss by . . . what? The irony of this meeting? Abby dimmed the lights. Once again the cubicle took on its sepulchral gloom.

"Mrs. Voss," said Abby. "What happened a few days ago. The other heart, the first heart . . ." She looked away, unable to meet the other woman's gaze. "There was a boy. Seventeen. Boys that age, they want cars or girlfriends. But this boy, all he wanted was to go home. Nothing else, just to go home." She sighed. "In the end, I couldn't let it happen. I didn't know you, Mrs. Voss. You weren't the one lying in that bed. He was. And I had to make a choice." She blinked, felt tears wet her lashes.

"He lived?"

"Yes. He lived."

Nina nodded. Again she touched her own chest. She seemed to be conferring with her heart. Listening, communicating. She said, "This boy. This boy's alive, too. I'm so aware of his heart. Every beat. Some people believe that the heart is where the soul lives. Maybe that's what his parents believe. I think about them, too. And how hard it must be. I never had a son. I never had a child." She closed her hand into a fist, pressed it against the bandages. "Don't you think it would be a comfort, to know that some part of him is still alive? If it was my son,

I'd want to know. I'd want to know." She was crying now, the tears a sparkling trickle down her temple.

Abby reached for the woman's hand and was startled by the force of Nina's grasp, the skin feverish, the fingers tight with need. Nina was looking up at her, a gaze that seemed to shine with its own strange fire. *If I had known you then,* thought Abby, *If I had watched you dying in one bed and Josh O'Day in another, which one of you would I have chosen?*

I don't know.

Above the bed, a line skipped across the green glow of the oscilloscope. The heart of an unknown boy, beating a hundred times a minute, pumping fevered blood through a stranger's veins.

Abby, holding Nina's hand, could feel the throb of a pulse. A slow, steady pulse.

Not Nina's, but her own.

It took twenty minutes for the X-ray tech to arrive and shoot the portable chest film, and another fifteen minutes before Abby had the developed X ray in hand. She clipped it to the SICU viewing box and examined it for signs of pneumonia. She saw none.

It was three A.M. She called Aaron Levi's house.

Aaron's wife answered, her voice husky with sleep. "Hello?"

"Elaine, this is Abby DiMatteo. I'm sorry to bother you at this hour. May I speak with Aaron?"

"He left for the hospital."

"How long ago?"

"Uh . . . it was just after the second phone call. Isn't he there?"

"I haven't seen him," said Abby.

There was a silence on the other end of the line. "He left home an hour ago," said Elaine. "He should be there."

"I'll page his beeper. Don't worry about it, Elaine." Abby hung up, then dialed Aaron's beeper and waited for the phone to ring.

By three-fifteen, he still hadn't answered.

"Dr. D.?" said Sheila, Nina Voss's nurse. "The last blood culture's been drawn. Is there anything else you want to order?"

What have I missed? thought Abby. She leaned forward against the desk and massaged her temples, struggling to stay awake. Think. A postop fever. Where was the infection coming from? What had she overlooked?

"What about the organ?" said Sheila.

Abby looked up. "The heart?"

"It was just something that occurred to me. But I guess it's not very likely . . ."

"What are you thinking, Sheila?"

The nurse hesitated. "I've never seen it happen here. But before I came to Bayside, I used to work with a renal transplant service in Mayo. I remember we had this patient. A kidney recipient with postop fevers. We didn't figure out what his infection was until after he died. It turned out to be fungal. Later they tracked down the donor record and found out the donor's blood cultures were positive, but the results didn't come back until a week after the kidney was harvested. By then it was too late for the recipient. Our patient."

Abby thought it over for a moment. She looked at the bank of monitors, at the heart tracing of Bed 15 dancing across the screen.

"Where's the donor information kept?" asked Abby.

"It would be in the transplant coordinator's office downstairs. The nursing supervisor has the key."

"Could you ask her to get the file for me?"

Abby reopened Nina Voss's chart. She turned to the New England Organ Bank donor form—the sheet that had accompanied the heart from Vermont. Recorded there was the ABO blood type, HIV status, syphilis antibody titers, and a long list of other lab screens for various viral infections. The donor was not identified.

Fifteen minutes later, the phone rang. It was the nursing supervisor, calling for Abby.

"I can't find the donor file," she said.

"Isn't it under Nina Voss's name?"

"They're filed under the recipient's medical record number. There's nothing here under Mrs. Voss's number."

"Could it be misfiled?"

"I've looked in all the kidney and liver transplant files too. And I double-checked that record number. Are you sure it isn't somewhere up in the SICU?"

"I'll ask them to look. Thanks." Abby hung up and sighed. Missing paperwork. It was the last thing she felt like dealing with at this time of the morning. She looked at the SICU records shelf, where files from current patients' previous hospitalizations were kept. If the missing file was buried somewhere in *that*, she could be searching for an hour.

Or she could call the donor hospital directly. They could pull the record, tell her the donor's medical history and lab tests.

Directory assistance gave her the number for Wilcox Memorial. She dialed the number and asked for the nursing supervisor.

A moment later a woman answered: "Gail DeLeon speaking."

"This is Dr. DiMatteo calling from Bayside Hospital in Boston," said Abby. "We have a heart transplant recipient here who's running a postop fever. We know the donor heart came from your OR. I need a little more information on the donor's medical history. I wonder if you might know the patient's name."

"The organ harvest was done here?"

"Yes. Three days ago. The donor was a boy. An adolescent."

"Let me check the OR log. I'll call you back."

Ten minutes later, she did—not with an answer but with a question: "Are you sure you have the right hospital, doctor?"

Abby glanced down at Nina's chart. "It says right here. Donor hospital was Wilcox Memorial. Burlington, Vermont."

"Well, that's us. But I don't see a harvest on the log."

"Can you check your OR schedule? The date would have been . . ." Abby looked at the form. "September twenty-fourth. The harvest would've been done sometime around midnight."

"Hold on."

Over the receiver, Abby heard the sound of turning pages and the nurse's intermittent throat clearing. The voice came back. "Hello?"

"I'm here," said Abby.

"I've checked the schedule for September twenty-third, twenty-fourth, and twenty-fifth. There are a couple of appendectomies, a cholecystectomy, and two cesareans. But there's no organ harvest anywhere."

"There has to be. We got the heart."

"We're not the ones who sent it."

Abby scanned the OR nurses' notes and saw the notation: *0105: Dr. Leonard Mapes arrived from Wilcox Memorial.* She said, "One of the surgeons who scrubbed on the harvest was Dr. Leonard Mapes. That's the same guy who delivered it."

"We don't have any Dr. Mapes on our staff."

"He's a thoracic surgeon—"

"Look, there's no Dr. Mapes here. In fact, I don't know of any Dr. Mapes practicing anywhere in Burlington. I don't know where you're getting your info, doctor, but it's obviously wrong. Maybe you should check again."

"But—"

"Try another hospital."

Slowly Abby hung up.

For a long time she sat staring at the phone. She thought about Victor Voss and his money, about all the things that money could buy. She thought about the amazing confluence of events that had granted Nina Voss a new heart. A matched heart.

She reached, once again, for the telephone.

9

"You're overreacting," said Mark, flipping through Nina Voss's SICU chart. "There has to be a reasonable explanation for all of this."

"I'd like to know what it is," said Abby.

"It was a good excision. The heart came packed right, delivered right. And there *were* donor papers."

"Which now seem to be missing."

"The transplant coordinator will be in at nine. We can ask her about the papers then. I'm sure they're around somewhere."

"Mark, there's one more thing. I called the donor hospital. There's no surgeon named Leonard Mapes practicing there. In fact, there's no such surgeon practicing in Burlington." She paused. Softly she said, "Do we really know where that heart came from?"

Mark said nothing. He seemed too dazed, too tired to be thinking straight. It was four-fifteen. After Abby's phone call, he'd dragged himself out of bed and driven to Bayside. Postop fevers required immediate attention, and although he trusted Abby's findings, he had wanted to see the patient for himself. Now Mark sat in the gloom of the SICU, struggling to make sense of the paperwork in Nina Voss's chart. A bank of heart monitors faced him on the countertop, and three bright green lines traced across the reflection in his glasses. In the semidarkness nurses moved like shadows and spoke in hushed voices.

Mark closed the chart. Sighing, he pulled off his glasses and rubbed his eyes. "This fever. What the hell is causing the fever? That's what really concerns me."

"Could it be an infection passed from the donor?"

"Unlikely. I've never seen it happen with a heart."

"But we don't know anything about the donor. Or his medical history. We don't even know which hospital that heart came from."

"Abby, you're going off the deep end here. I know Archer spoke on the phone to the harvesting surgeon. I also know there were papers. They came in this brown envelope."

"I remember seeing it."

"All right. Then we saw the same thing."

"Where's the envelope now?"

"Hey, I was the one operating, OK? I'm up to my elbows in blood. I can't keep track of some goddamn envelope."

"Why is there all this secrecy about the donor, anyway? We don't have records. We don't know his name."

"That's standard procedure. Donor records are confidential. They're always kept separate from the recipient's chart. Otherwise you'd have families contacting each other. The donor side would expect undying gratitude, the recipient side would either resent it or feel guilty. It leads to one giant emotional mess." He sank back in his chair. "We're wasting time on this issue. It'll all be resolved in a few hours. So let's concentrate on the fever."

"All right. But if there's any question about this, New England Organ Bank wants to discuss it with you."

"How did NEOB get involved?"

"I called them. They have this twenty-four-hour line. I told them you or Archer would get back to them."

"Archer can handle it. He'll be here any minute."

"He's coming in?"

"He's worried about the fever. And we can't seem to get hold of Aaron. Have you paged him again?"

"Three times. No answer. Elaine told me he was driving in."

"Well, I know he got here. I just saw his car down in the parking lot. Maybe he got busy on the medical floor." Mark flipped through Nina Voss's chart to the order sheets. "I'm going to move on this without him."

Abby glanced toward Nina Voss's cubicle. The patient's eyes were closed, her chest rising and falling with the gentle rhythm of sleep.

"I'm starting antibiotics," said Mark. "Broad-spectrum."

"What infection are you treating?"

"I don't know. It's just a temporary bridge until the cultures come back. As immunosuppressed as she is, we can't take a chance she's infected somewhere." In frustration, Mark rose from the chair and walked over to the cubicle window. He stood there a moment, staring in at Nina Voss. The sight of her seemed to calm him. Abby came to stand beside him. They were very close, almost touching each other, and yet separated by the gulf of this crisis. On the other side of the window, Nina Voss slept peacefully.

"It could be a drug reaction," said Abby. "She's on so many things. Any one of them could cause a fever."

"That's a possibility. But not likely on steroids and cyclosporine."

"I couldn't find any source of infection. Anywhere."

"She's immunosuppressed. We miss something, she's dead." He turned to pick up the chart. "I'm starting the bug juice."

At six A.M. the first dose of IV Azactam was dripping into Nina's vein. A stat infectious disease consult was requested, and at seven-fifteen the consultant, Dr. Moore, arrived. He concurred with Mark's decision. A fever in an immunosuppressed patient was too dangerous to go untreated.

At eight o'clock, a second antibiotic, piperacillin, was infused.

By then Abby was making morning SICU rounds, her wheeled cart piled six-deep with charts. It had been a bad call night—just one hour of sleep before that two A.M. phone call, and not a moment's rest since then. Fueled by two cups of coffee and a view of the end in sight, she pushed her cart along the row of cubicles, thinking: *Four hours and I'm out of here. Only four more hours until noon.* She passed by Bed 15, and she glanced through the cubicle window.

Nina was awake. She saw Abby and weakly managed a beckoning wave.

Abby left her charts by the door, donned an isolation gown, and stepped into the cubicle.

"Good morning, Dr. DiMatteo," murmured Nina. "I'm afraid you didn't get much sleep because of me."

Abby smiled. "That's okay. I slept last week. How are you feeling?"

"Like quite the center of attention." Nina glanced up at the bottle of IV antibiotics hanging over the bed. "Is that the cure?"

"We hope so. You're getting a combination of piperacillin and Azactam. Broad-spectrum antibiotics. If you have an infection, that should take care of it."

"And if this isn't an infection?"

"Then the fever won't respond. And we'll try something else."

"So you don't really know what's causing this."

Abby paused. "No," she admitted. "We don't. It's more of an educated shot in the dark."

Nina nodded. "I thought you'd tell the truth. Dr. Archer wouldn't, you know. He was here this morning, and he kept telling me not to worry. That everything was taken care of. He never admitted he didn't know." Nina gave a soft laugh, as though the fever, the antibiotics, all these tubes and machines were part of some whimsical illusion.

"I'm sure he didn't want to worry you," said Abby.

"But the truth doesn't scare me. Really it doesn't. Doctors don't tell the truth often enough." She looked straight at Abby. "We both know that."

Abby found her gaze shifting automatically to the monitors. She saw that all the lines tracing across the screen were in the normal ranges. Pulse. Blood pressure. Right atrial pressure. It was pure habit, that focus on the numbers. Machines didn't pose difficult questions, didn't expect painfully truthful answers.

She heard Nina say, softly: "Victor."

Abby turned. Only then, as she faced the doorway, did she realize Victor Voss had just stepped into the cubicle.

"Get out," he said. "Get out of my wife's room."

"I was only checking on her."

"I said, get *out!*" He took a step toward her and grabbed a handful of the isolation gown.

Reflexively Abby resisted, pulling free. The cubicle was so tiny there was no more room to back away, no space to retreat to.

He lunged at her. This time he caught hold of her arm with a grip that was meant to hurt.

"Victor, don't!" said Nina.

Abby gave a cry of pain as she was wrenched forward. He thrust her out of the cubicle. The force of his shove sent her backward against the wheeled cart. She felt herself falling as the cart slid away. She landed hard on her buttocks. The cart, still rolling, slammed against a counter and charts thudded to the floor. Abby, stunned by the impact, looked up to see Victor Voss standing over her. He was breathing hard, not from exertion but from fury.

"Don't you go near my wife again," he said. "Do you hear me, doctor? *Do you hear me?*" Voss turned his gaze to the shocked personnel standing around the SICU. "I don't want this woman near my wife. I want that written in the chart and posted on the door. I want it done now." He gave Abby one last look of disgust, then he walked into his wife's cubicle and yanked the curtain across the window.

Two of the nurses hurried over to help Abby to her feet.

"I'm okay," said Abby, waving them away. "I'm fine."

"He's crazy," one of the nurses whispered. "We should report him to Security."

"No, don't," said Abby. "Let's not make things worse."

"But that was assault! You could press charges."

"I just want to forget about it, okay?" Abby went over to the cart. Her charts were on the floor, loose pages and lab slips scattered everywhere. Face burning, she gathered up all the papers and set them back in the cart. By then she was fighting to hold back tears. *I can't cry,* she thought. *Not here. I won't cry.* She looked up.

Everyone was watching her.

She left the cart right where it was and walked out of the SICU.

Mark found her three hours later, in the cafeteria. She was

sitting at a corner table, hunched over a cup of tea and a blueberry muffin. The muffin had only one bite taken out of it, and the teabag had been left soaking so long the water was black as coffee.

Mark pulled out a chair across from her and sat down. "Voss was the one who threw the tantrum, Abby. Not you."

"I'm just the one who landed on her butt in front of everyone."

"He shoved you. That's something you can use. Leverage against any more of those nutty lawsuits."

"You mean I charge him with assault?"

"Something like that."

She shook her head. "I don't want to think about Victor Voss. I don't want to have anything to do with him."

"There were half a dozen witnesses. They saw him push you."

"Mark, let's forget the whole thing." She picked up the muffin, took an unenthusiastic bite, and put it back down again. She sat staring at it, desperately wanting to change the subject.

Finally she said, "Did Aaron agree about starting antibiotics?"

"I haven't seen Aaron all day."

She looked up, frowning. "I thought he was here."

"I beeped him but he never answered."

"Did you call his home?"

"I got the housekeeper. Elaine left for the weekend, visiting their kid at Dartmouth." Mark shrugged. "It's Saturday. This isn't Aaron's weekend to make rounds anyway. He probably decided to take a vacation from all of us."

"A vacation," Abby sighed and rubbed her face. "God, that's what I want. A beach and a few palm trees and a piña colada."

"Sounds good to me, too." Reaching across the table, he took her hand. "Mind if I join you?"

"You don't even like piña coladas."

"But I like beaches and palm trees. And you." He gave her hand a squeeze. That was just what she needed at that moment. His touch. It felt as solid and dependable as the man himself.

He leaned across the table. Right there, in the cafeteria, he kissed her. "Look at us. Creating another public spectacle," he whispered. "You'd better go home, before we get everyone's attention."

She glanced at her watch. It was twelve o'clock, and a Saturday. The weekend, at last, had begun.

He walked her out of the cafeteria and across the hospital lobby. As they pushed through the front doors he said, "I almost forgot to tell you. Archer called Wilcox Memorial and spoke to some thoracic surgeon named Tim Nicholls. Turns out Nicholls assisted on the harvest. He confirmed the patient was theirs. And that Dr. Mapes did the excision."

"Then why isn't Mapes listed on the Wilcox staff?"

"Because Mapes was flown in by private jet from Houston. We knew nothing about it. Apparently, Mr. Voss didn't trust just any Yankee surgeon to do the job. So he had a specialist flown in."

"All the way from Texas?"

"With his money, Voss could've flown in the whole Baylor team."

"So the harvest *was* done at Wilcox Memorial."

"Nicholls says he was there. Whatever nurse you spoke to last night must've been looking at the wrong log sheet. If you'd like me to call and confirm it again—"

"No, just forget it. It all seems so stupid now. I don't know what I was thinking." She sighed and looked across at her car, parked in its usual spot at the far end of the lot. Outer Siberia, the residents called their assigned parking area. Then again, slave labor was lucky to get assigned parking at all. "I'll see you at home," she said. "If I'm still awake."

He put his arms around her, tipped her head back, and kissed her, one tired body clinging to another. "Careful driving home," he whispered. "I love you."

She walked across the lot, dazed by fatigue and by the sound of those three words still echoing in her head.

I love you.

She stopped and looked back to wave at him, but he had already vanished through the lobby doors.

"I love you too," she said, and smiled.

She turned to her car, her keys already out of her purse. Only then did she notice that the lock button was up. Jesus, what an idiot. She'd left the car unlocked all night.

She opened the door.

At the first foul whiff of air, she backed away, gagging on the stench. And repulsed by the sight of what lay on the front seat.

Loops of rotting intestine were coiled around the gear shift and one end hung like a grotesque streamer from the bottom of the steering wheel. A hacked-up mass of unidentifiable tissue was smeared across the passenger seat. And on the driver's side, propped up against the cushion, was a single bloody organ.

A heart.

The address was in Dorchester, a rundown neighborhood in southeast Boston. He parked across the street and eyed the boxy house, the weedy lawn. There was a kid of about twelve bouncing a basketball in the driveway, every so often flinging it at a hoop over the garage, and missing every time. No athletic scholarship for that one. Judging by the junker of a car parked in the garage and the general shabbiness of the home, a scholarship would certainly come in handy.

He got out of his car and crossed the street. As he walked up the driveway, the boy suddenly fell still. Hugging the ball to his chest, he eyed the visitor with obvious suspicion.

"I'm looking for the Flynt residence."

"Yeah," said the boy. "This is it."

"Are your parents at home?"

"My dad is. Why?"

"Maybe you could let him know he has a visitor."

"Who are you?"

He handed the boy his business card. The boy read it with only vague interest, then tried to hand it back.

"No, keep it. Show it to your father."

"You mean right now?"

"If he's not busy."

"Yeah. Okay." The boy went into the house, the screen door slapping shut behind him.

A moment later a man came to the door, big-bellied, unsmiling. "You looking for me?"

"Mr. Flynt, my name is Stewart Sussman. I'm with the law firm of Hawkes, Craig and Sussman."

"Yeah?"

"I understand you were a patient at Bayside Medical Center six months ago."

"I was in an accident. Other guy's fault."

"You had your spleen removed. Is that correct?"

"How do you know all this?"

"I'm here in your best interests, Mr. Flynt. You had major surgery, did you not?"

"They said I coulda died. I guess that makes it major."

"Was one of your doctors a woman resident named Abigail DiMatteo?"

"Yeah. She saw me every day. Real nice lady."

"Did she or any of the other doctors tell you the consequences of having your spleen removed?"

"They said I could have bad infections if I'm not careful."

"Fatal infections. Did they say that?"

"Uh . . . maybe."

"Did they mention anything about an accidental nick during surgery?"

"What?"

"A scalpel slipping, cutting the spleen. Causing a lot of bleeding."

"No." The man was leaning toward him now, with a look of intense worry. "Did something like that happen to me?"

"We'd like to confirm the facts. All we need is your consent to obtain your medical record."

"Why?"

"It would be in your interest, Mr. Flynt, to know if the loss of your spleen was, in fact, due to surgical error. If a mistake was made, then you've suffered unnecessary damage. And you should be compensated."

Mr. Flynt said nothing. He looked at the boy, who was listening to the conversation. Probably understanding none of it. Then he looked at the pen that was being offered to him.

"By compensation, Mr. Flynt," said the attorney, "I was referring to money."

The man took the pen and signed his name.

Back in his car, Sussman slipped the signed records request

form in his briefcase and reached once again for the list. There were four more names, four more signatures to obtain. He should have no problem. Greed and retribution were a powerful combination.

He crossed off the name *Flynt, Harold*, and started the car.

10

"It was a pig's heart. They probably left it in my car the night before, where it baked all day in the heat. I still can't get rid of the smell."

"The man is mindfucking you," said Vivian Chao. "I say you should fuck him right back."

Abby and Vivian pushed through the front doors and crossed the lobby to the elevators. It was Sunday noon at Massachusetts General, and the public elevator was already crammed tight with visitors and get-well balloons bobbing overhead. The doors slid shut and the scent of carnations was instantly overpowering.

"We don't have any proof," murmured Abby. "We can't be sure he's the one doing this."

"Who else would it be? Look what he's done already. Manufacturing lawsuits. Shoving you in public. I'm telling you, DiMatteo, it's time to press charges. Assault. Terroristic threatening."

"The problem is, I understand why he's doing it. He's upset. His wife's having a rocky postop course."

"Do I detect a note of guilt?"

Abby sighed. "It's hard not to feel guilty every time I pass her bed."

They stepped off the elevator onto the fourth floor and headed up the hall toward the cardiac surgery wing.

"He has the money to make your life hell for a very long time," said Vivian. "You've got one lawsuit against you already. There'll probably be more."

"I think there already are. Medical Records told me they've had six more chart requests from Hawkes, Craig and Sussman. That's the law firm representing Joe Terrio."

Vivian stopped and stared at her. "Jesus. You're going to be in court for the rest of your natural life."

"Or until I resign. Like you."

Vivian began walking again, her stride as fierce as ever. The little Asian Amazon, afraid of nothing.

"How come *you* aren't fucking back?" said Abby.

"I'm trying to. The problem is, the man we're up against is Victor Voss. When I mentioned that name to my attorney, she turned a few shades whiter. Which is an amazing feat for a black woman."

"What was her advice?"

"To walk away from it. And call myself lucky that I'm already a board-eligible surgeon. At least I can find another job. Or open up my own practice."

"Voss scares her that much?"

"She wouldn't admit it, but yes. He scares a lot of people. I'm in no position to fight, anyway. I was the one in charge, so it's my head that rolls. We stole a heart, DiMatteo. There's no way around that. If it had been anyone else but Victor Voss, we might have gotten away with it. Now it's costing me." She looked at Abby. "But not as much as it could cost you."

"At least I still have my job."

"For how long? You're only a second-year resident. You've got to start fighting back, Abby. Don't let him ruin you. You're too good a doctor to be forced out."

Abby shook her head. "Sometimes I wonder if it was all worth it."

"Worth it?" Vivian stopped outside Room 417. "Take a look. You tell me." She knocked on the door, then stepped into the room.

The boy was sitting up in bed, fussing with a TV remote. If not for the Red Sox cap on his head, Abby might not have recognized Josh O'Day, so transformed was his appearance by the rosy flush of health. At his first glimpse of Vivian, he grinned hugely.

"Hey, Dr. *Chao!*" he whooped. "Geez, I wondered if you were *ever* coming to see me."

"I did come by," said Vivian. "Twice. But you were always asleep." She shook her head in mock disgust. "Typical lazy teenager."

They both laughed. There was a brief silence. Then, almost shyly, Josh opened his arms for a hug.

For a moment Vivian didn't move. It was as if she didn't know how to respond. Then she suddenly snapped free of some invisible restraint and stepped toward him. The embrace was brief and clumsy. Vivian seemed almost relieved when it was over.

"So how are you?" she asked.

"Real good. Hey, didja see?" He pointed to the TV. "My dad brought me all those baseball tapes. But we can't figure out how to hook up the VCR. You know how to do it?"

"I'd probably blow up the TV."

"And you're a doctor?"

"Okay. Next time you need surgery, buster, you call a TV repairman." She nodded toward Abby. "You remember Dr. DiMatteo, don't you?"

Josh looked uncertainly at Abby. "I think so. I mean . . ." He shrugged. "I forgot some things, you know? Things that happened last week. It's almost like I got dumb or something."

"That's nothing to worry about," said Vivian. "When your heart stops, Josh, you don't get enough blood to your brain. You can forget a few things." She touched his shoulder. It was not the sort of thing Vivian Chao would normally do. But there she was, actually making contact. "At least you didn't forget me," she said. And added with a laugh, "Though you may have tried."

Josh looked down at the bedspread. "Dr. Chao," he said softly, "I don't ever want to forget you."

Neither one spoke for a moment. They seemed frozen by embarrassment in that awkward pose, Vivian's hand on the boy's shoulder. The boy looking downward, his face hidden under the bill of his cap.

Abby had to turn away and focus on something else. The trophies. They were all there, all the ribbons and plaques, arranged on the nightstand. No longer an altar to a dying boy, but a celebration of life. Of rebirth.

There was a knock on the door and a woman called out: "Joshie?"

"Hey, Mom," said Josh.

The door swung open and the room was invaded by parents and siblings and aunts and uncles, sweeping in with them a forest of helium balloons and the smell of McDonald's fries. They swarmed around the bed, assaulted Josh with hugs and kisses and exclamations of "Look at him!" "He looks so good." "Doesn't he look good?" Josh bore it all with an expression of sheepish delight. He didn't seem to notice that Vivian had slipped away from his bedside, to make room for the noisy army of O'Days.

"Josh, honey, we brought Uncle Harry from Newbury. He knows all about VCRs. He can hook it up, can't you, Harry?"

"Oh, sure. I do all my neighbors' VCRs."

"Did you bring the right wires, Harry? You sure you got all the wires you need?"

"You think I'd forget the wires?"

"Look, Josh. Three extra-large orders of fries. It's okay, isn't it? Dr. Tarasoff didn't say you couldn't have fries?"

"Mom, we forgot the camera! I was gonna take a picture of Josh's scar."

"You don't want a picture of his scar."

"My teacher said it'd be cool."

"Your teacher's too old to use words like cool. No pictures of scars. That's an invasion of privacy."

"Hey Josh, you need any help eating those fries?"

"So Harry, you think you can hook it up?"

"Gee, I don't know. This is a pretty old TV . . ."

Vivian had managed at last to sidle around to where Abby was standing. There was another knock on the door, and a fresh spurt of relatives pushed into the room, with more cries of "He looks so good!" "Doesn't he look good?" Through the crowd of O'Days, Abby caught a fleeting glimpse of Josh. He was looking their way. He gave them a helpless smile, a wave.

Quietly Abby and Vivian left the room. They stood in the hallway, listening to the voices beyond the door. And Vivian said, "So, Abby. To the question of *Was it worth it?*, that's your answer."

* * *

At the nurses' station, they asked to speak to Dr. Ivan Tarasoff. The ward clerk suggested they look in the surgeons' lounge. That's exactly where Abby and Vivian found him, sipping coffee and scribbling in his charts. With his drooping glasses and tweed jacket, Dr. Tarasoff looked more like some puttering English gentleman than the renowned cardiac surgeon.

"We just saw Josh," said Vivian.

Tarasoff looked up from his coffee-splattered notes. "And what do you think, Dr. Chao?"

"I think you do good work. The kid looks fantastic."

"He has a little postcode amnesia. Otherwise, he's bounced back the way kids always do. He'll be out of here in a week. If the nurses don't kick him out sooner." Tarasoff closed the chart and looked at Vivian. His smile faded. "I have a very big bone to pick with you, Doctor."

"Me?"

"You know what I'm talking about. That other transplant patient at Bayside. When you shipped us the boy, you didn't tell me the whole story. Then I find out the heart was already assigned."

"It wasn't. There was a directed-donation consent."

"Obtained through a certain amount of subterfuge." He frowned over his glasses at Abby. "Your administrator, Mr. Parr, told me all the details. So did Mr. Voss's attorney."

Vivian and Abby glanced at each other.

"His attorney?" said Vivian.

"That's right." Tarasoff's gaze shifted back to Vivian. "Were you *trying* to get me sued?"

"I was trying to save the boy."

"You withheld information."

"And now he's alive and well."

"I'm only going to say it once. Don't ever do anything like this again."

Vivian seemed about to reply, but then thought better of it. Instead she gave a solemn nod. It was her deferential Asian act, eyes downcast, head dipping in a faint bow.

Tarasoff didn't buy it. He regarded her with a look of mild vexation. Then, unexpectedly, he laughed. Turning back to his charts, he said: "I should have expelled you from Harvard. When I had the chance."

"Ready about. Hard a lee!" Mark yelled, and shoved the tiller.

The bow of *Gimme Shelter* turned into the wind, sails crackling, ropes lashing the deck. Raj Mohandas scurried across to the starboard winch and began cranking the jib sheet. With a loud *whap,* the sail filled, and *Gimme Shelter* heeled to starboard, sending off a clatter of soft drink cans in the cabin below.

"Upwind rail, Abby!" Mark yelled. "Get to the upwind rail!"

Abby scrambled across the deck to the port side, where she clung to the lifeline and offered up another fervent vow of *never again.* What was it about men and their boats? she wondered. What was it about the sea that made them yell?

They were *all* yelling, all four of them, Mark and Mohandas and Mohandas's eighteen-year-old son Hank, and Pete Jaegly, a third-year resident. Yelling about sheets that needed tightening and spinnaker poles and wasted wind puffs. They were yelling about Archer's boat, *Red Eye,* which was gaining on them. And, every so often, they would yell at Abby. She actually had a role in this race, a role known politely as *ballast.* Dead weight. A job that could be performed by sandbags. Abby was a sandbag with legs. They'd yell and she'd run across to the opposite rail, where, with some regularity, she'd throw up. The men weren't throwing up. They were too busy scampering around in their expensive boat shoes and yelling.

"Coming up on the mark! One more tack. Ready about!"

Mohandas and Jaegly resumed their frantic deck dance.

"Hard a lee!"

Gimme Shelter turned through the wind and heeled to port. Abby scrambled to the other side. Sails flapped, ropes thrashed. Mohandas cranked the winch, the muscles of his brown arm rippling with each turn of the handle.

"She's coming up on us!" Hank called.

Behind them, *Red Eye* had gained another half boat length. They could hear Archer yelling at *his* crew, exhorting them to *Come up, come up!*

Gimme Shelter rounded the buoy and started her downwind course. Jaegly struggled with the spinnaker pole. Hank pulled down the jib.

Abby was throwing up over the side.

"Shit, he's right on our tail!" yelled Mark. "Get the fucking spinnaker up! Go, go, *go!*"

Jaegly and Hank hoisted the spinnaker. The wind filled it with a thunderous *whomp* and *Gimme Shelter* suddenly surged ahead.

"That's it, baby!" Mark whooped. "Baby, baby, here we go!"

"Look," said Jaegly, pointing aft. "What the hell's happening?"

Abby managed to raise her head and look back, toward Archer's boat.

Red Eye was no longer in pursuit. It had turned around near the buoy and was now heading back to port.

"They've started their motor," said Mark.

"Think they're conceding defeat?"

"Archer? Not a chance."

"So why're they going back?"

"I guess we'd better find out. Get the spinnaker down." Mark started the engine. "We're heading back too."

Thank you, God! thought Abby.

Her nausea was already subsiding by the time they motored into the marina. *Red Eye* was tied up at the dock and her crew was busy folding up sails and coiling ropes.

"Ahoy *Red Eye!*" yelled Mark as they glided past. "What's going on?"

Archer waved his cellular phone. "Got a call from Marilee! She told us to come in. It's something serious. She's waiting for us in the yacht club."

"Okay. Meet you at the bar," said Mark. He looked at his own crew. "Let's tie up. We'll have a drink and take her back out again."

"You'll have to do it without your ballast," said Abby. "I'm jumping ship."

Mark glanced at her in surprise. "Already?"

"Didn't you see me hanging over the side? I wasn't admiring the scenery."

"Poor Abby! I'll make it up to you, okay? Promise. Champagne. Flowers. Restaurant of your choice."

"Just get me off this goddamn boat."

Laughing, he steered toward the dock. "Aye aye, first mate."

As *Gimme Shelter* glided alongside the visitor's dock, Mohandas and Hank stepped onto the pier and tied fast the bow and stern lines. Abby was off the boat in a flash. Even the dock seemed to be swaying.

"Just leave her rigged," said Mark. "Until we find out what's up with Archer."

"He's probably got the party started already," said Mohandas.

Oh Lord, Abby thought as she and Mark walked up the pier, his arm slung possessively around her shoulder. More boat talk coming up. Tanned men standing around with their gin and tonics and their polo shirts and their booming laughter.

They went inside the club, stepping from sunlight into shadow. The first thing she noticed was the silence. She saw Marilee standing at the bar with a drink in her hand. Saw Archer sitting by himself at a table, no drink, just a paper coaster in front of him. *Red Eye*'s crew was gathered around the bar, no one moving, no one saying a thing. The only sound in the room was the clatter of ice cubes in Marilee's glass as she lifted the drink to her lips, took a sip, and set it back down again on the counter.

Mark said, "Is something wrong?"

Marilee looked up and blinked, as if noticing Mark for the first time. Then she looked back down at the counter. At her drink.

"They found Aaron," she said.

It was the grinding of the Stryker bone saw that usually did it; that or the smell. This one smelled pretty bad.

Homicide Detective Bernard Katzka glanced across the autopsy table and saw that the stench had gotten to Lundquist. His younger partner was turned partially away from the table, gloved hand cupped over his nose and mouth, his movie-star good looks twisted into a squint of nausea. Lundquist had not yet developed the stomach for autopsies; most cops never did. While the cutting open of dead bodies was not Katzka's favorite spectator sport, over the years he had trained himself to view the procedure as an intellectual exercise, to focus not on the humanity of the victim but on the purely organic nature of death. He had seen bodies cooked in fires, bodies scraped off the pavement after twenty-story free falls, bodies shot or stabbed or both, bodies gnawed by rodents. Except for the children, which always upset him, one body was like any other on the table, a specimen stripped, examined, and cataloged. To view them any other way was to invite nightmares.

Bernard Katzka was forty-four years old and a widower. Three years ago, he had watched his wife die of cancer. Katzka had already lived his worst nightmare.

He focused impassively on the body now being autopsied. The corpse was a fifty-four-year-old white male, married with two college-aged children, a cardiologist by profession. His identity had been confirmed by fingerprints as well as visual ID by the widow. The experience must have been profoundly upsetting to her. Viewing the corpse of a loved one is difficult enough. When that loved one has been hanging by the neck for two days in a warm and unventilated room, the sight would be truly horrifying.

The widow, he'd been told, had fainted dead away on the morgue floor.

And no wonder, thought Katzka, looking down at the corpse of Aaron Levi. The face was a bloodless white; its arterial supply had been cut off by the pressure of the leather belt looped around the neck. The protruding tongue was a scaly black, its mucous surface dried out by two days' exposure to air. The eyelids were only partially closed. The slitted openings revealed scleral hemorrhages that had turned the whites of the eyes a frightening blood-red. Below the neck, where the belt had imprinted its ligature mark, the skin showed the classic pattern of dependent pooling, a bruiselike discoloration of the lower legs and arms as well as pinpoint hemorrhages, called Tardieu spots, where vessels had ruptured. All of this was consistent with death by hanging. The only visible injury, aside from the ligature marks around the neck, was a coin-shaped bruise on the left shoulder.

Dr. Rowbotham and his assistant, both gowned, gloved, and wearing protective goggles, completed the thoraco-abdominal incision. It was Y-shaped with two diagonal incisions starting at the shoulders and joining at the lower end of the sternum, then a vertical slice down the abdomen to the pubic bone. Rowbotham had served thirty-two years with the ME's office, and very little seemed to surprise or excite him. If anything, he looked slightly bored as he cut into the body. He was dictating in his usual monotone as his foot clicked on and off the recording pedal. Now he lifted off the triangular shield of rib and breastbone and exposed the pleural cavity.

"Take a look, Slug," he said to Katzka. The nickname had nothing to do with Katzka's appearance, which was average in every way. Rather, it was a reflection of Katzka's unflappable nature. Among his fellow cops, the running joke was that if you shot Bernard Katzka on a Monday, he might react by Friday. But only if he was pissed.

Katzka leaned forward to peer inside the chest cavity, his expression every bit as flat as Rowbotham's. "I don't see anything unusual."

"Exactly. Maybe a little pleural congestion. Probably due to capillary leakage from hypoxia. But it's all consistent with asphyxiation."

"So I guess we're out of here, huh?" said Lundquist. Already he was sidling away from the table, away from the smell, impatient to get on to other things. He was like all the other young bucks, eager to cut to the chase. Any chase. Suicide by hanging was not something he wanted to waste his time on.

Katzka did not move from the table.

"We really need to watch the rest of this, Slug?" asked Lundquist.

"They're just starting."

"It's a suicide."

"This one feels different to me."

"The findings are classic. You just heard it."

"He got out of bed in the middle of the night. He got up, got dressed, and climbed in his car. Think about it. Getting out of your nice warm bed to go hang yourself on the top floor of a hospital."

Lundquist glanced at the body, then looked away again.

By now Rowbotham and his assistant had severed the trachea and the great vessels and were removing the heart and lungs in one floppy bundle. Rowbotham dropped them onto a hanging scale. The steel cradle bounced a few times, squeaking with the weight of the organs.

"It's your only chance to view it," said Rowbotham, his scalpel now at work on the spleen. "We finish up here, and it goes straight to burial. Family request."

"Any particular reason?" asked Lundquist.

"Jewish. You know, quick interment. All the organs have to be returned to the body." Rowbotham dropped the spleen onto the scale and watched as the indicator needle quivered, then came to a rest.

Lundquist yanked off his autopsy gown, revealing shoulders bulky with muscle. It was all those hours in the gym, pumping and sweating. He had restless energy and he was showing it now. Always on to bigger and better things, that was Lundquist. Katzka still had to work on him, and the lesson today ought to be the fallibility of first impressions—not an easy thing to get across to a young cop who had all that confidence, all those good looks. That and a full head of hair.

Rowbotham continued with the disembowelment. He cut free the intestines, pulling out what seemed like endless loops of bowel. The liver, pancreas, and stomach were removed in a single mass. Finally, the kidneys and bladder were dissected out and dropped onto that squeaky scale. Another weight was called out, recorded. A few more mutterings into the tape recorder. What was left was a gaping cavity.

Now Rowbotham circled around to the corpse's head. He made an incision behind one ear and cut straight across the back of the scalp. He peeled the scalp forward in one flap, doubling it over the face. Then he peeled the other flap back over the neck, exposing the base of the skull. He picked up the oscillating saw. His expression twisted into a grimace as the bone dust began to fly. No one was talking at this point. The saw was too noisy, and the procedure had turned sickening. Cutting into a chest and abdomen, though grotesque, was somehow impersonal. Like butchering a cow. But peeling a man's scalp over his face was mutilating the most human, the most personal aspect of a corpse.

Lundquist, looking a little green, suddenly sat down in a chair by the sink and dropped his head in his hands. Many a cop had made use of that particular chair.

Rowbotham put down the saw and removed the skull cap. Now he freed up the brain for removal. He cut the optic nerves and severed the blood vessels and spinal cord. Then, gingerly, he lifted the brain out in one quivering mass. "Nothing unusual," he said, and slid it into a pail of formalin.

"Now we get down to the nitty-gritty. The neck."

Everything that had come before this was merely preliminary to this stage. The removal of viscera and brain had allowed drainage of fluids out the cranial and chest cavities. The neck dissection could proceed with a minimum of obscuring blood and fluids.

The belt ligature had been removed from the neck early in the autopsy. Rowbotham now examined the furrow left behind on the skin.

"Your classic inverted V shape," he noted aloud. "See here, Slug, you've got parallel ligature marks which match the edges of the belt. And at the back here, you see this?"

"Looks like a mark from the buckle."

"Right. No surprises so far." Rowbotham picked up his scalpel and began the neck dissection.

By now Lundquist had recovered and was back at the table, looking a little humble. Nausea, thought Katzka, was so satisfyingly democratic. It brought down even muscle-bound cops with full heads of hair.

Rowbotham's blade had already sliced through the skin of the anterior neck. He cut deeper, exposing the pearly white superior horns of the thyroid cartilage.

"No fractures. You've got some hemorrhage over here, in the strap muscles. But the thyroid cartilage and hyoid bone both seem intact."

"Meaning?"

"Not a thing. Hanging doesn't necessarily cause much internal neck damage. Death results purely from interruption of the blood supply to the brain. All that's needed is compression of the carotid arteries. It's a relatively painless way to kill yourself."

"You seem pretty sure it's suicide."

"The only other possibility is accidental. Autoerotic asphyxiation. But you say there was no evidence of that."

Lundquist said, "His cock was still zipped up. Didn't look like he'd been jerking off."

"So we're talking suicide. Homicidal hanging is almost unheard of. If someone was strangled first, you'd see a different ligature pattern. Not this inverted V. And forcing a man's head in a noose, well, that would almost certainly leave other injuries. He'd fight back."

"There's that bruise on the upper arm."

Rowbotham shrugged. "He could have hurt himself in any number of ways."

"What if he was drugged and unconscious before he was hanged?"

"We'll do a tox screen, Slug, just to make you happy."

Lundquist cut in with a laugh, "And we do have to keep Slug happy." He moved away from the table. "It's four o'clock. You coming, Slug?"

"I'd like to see the rest of the neck dissection."

"Whatever turns you on. I say we just call it a suicide and leave it."

"I would. Except for the lights."

"What lights?" said Rowbotham, his eyes finally registering interest behind the protective goggles.

"Slug's hung up on the lights in that room," said Lundquist.

"Dr. Levi was found hanging in an unused patient room of the hospital," explained Katzka. "The workman who found the body was almost certain the lights were off."

"Go on," said Rowbotham.

"Well, your time-of-death finding correlates with what we think happened—that Dr. Levi died very early Saturday morning. Well before sunrise. Which means he either hung himself in the dark. Or someone else turned off the lights."

"Or the workman didn't remember what the fuck he saw," said Lundquist. "The guy was puking his guts into the toilet. You think he'd remember if the light switch was up or down?"

"It's just a detail that concerns me."

Lundquist laughed. "Doesn't bother me," he said, and tossed his gown into the laundry bag.

It was nearly six o'clock that evening when Katzka pulled his Volvo into a parking space at Bayside Hospital. He got out, walked into the lobby, and took the elevator to the thirteenth floor. That was as far as it would take him without a pass key. He had to leave the elevator and climb the emergency stairwell to reach the top level.

The first thing he noticed as he emerged from the stairwell was the silence. The sense of emptiness. For months, this area had been undergoing renovations. No construction workers had come in today, but their equipment was everywhere. The air smelled of sawdust and fresh paint . . . and something else. An odor he recognized from the autopsy room. Death. Decay. He walked past ladders and a Makita saw, and turned the corner.

Halfway down the next corridor, yellow police tape was plastered across one of the doorways. He ducked under the tape and pushed through the closed door.

In this room, the renovations had been completed. There was new wallpaper, custom cabinetry, and a floor-to-ceiling window with a view over the city. A penthouse hospital suite for that special patient with a bottomless wallet. He went into the bathroom and flicked on the wall switch. More luxury. A marble vanity, brass fixtures, a mirror with cosmetic lighting. A thronelike toilet. He turned off the lights and walked back out of the bathroom.

He went to the closet.

This was where Dr. Aaron Levi had been found hanging. One end of the leather belt had been tied to the closet dowel. The other end had been looped around Levi's neck. Apparently, he had simply let his legs go limp, causing the belt to tighten around his throat, cutting off carotid blood flow to the brain. If he had changed his mind at the last moment, all he had to do was set his feet back on the floor, stand up, and loosen the belt. But he had not done so. He had hung there for the five to ten seconds it had taken for consciousness to fade.

Thirty-six hours later, on a Sunday afternoon, one of the workmen had come into this room to finish grouting the bathtub. He had not planned on finding a dead body.

Katzka crossed to the window. There he stood looking over the city of Boston. Dr. Aaron Levi, he thought, what could've gone so wrong in your life?

A cardiologist. A wife, a nice home, a Lexus. Two kids, grown and in college. For one irrational moment, Katzka felt a flash of rage at Aaron Levi. What the hell had *he* known about despair and hopelessness? What possible reason did he have to end his life? Coward. Coward. Katzka turned away from the window, shaken by his own anger. By his disgust at anyone who chose such an end. And why *this* end? Why hang yourself in this lonely room where no one might find you for days?

There were other ways to commit suicide. Levi was a doctor. He had access to narcotics, barbiturates, any number of drugs that could be ingested in fatal doses. Katzka knew exactly how much phenobarb it took to end a life. He had made it his business to know. Once, he had counted out the right number of pills, calculated for his own body weight. He had laid them on his dining room table, had contemplated the freedom they represented. An end to grief, to despair. An easy but irreversible way out, once his affairs were in order. But the time had never been quite right. He had too many responsibilities to take care of first. Annie's funeral arrangements. Paying off her hospital bills. Then there'd been a trial that required his testimony, then a double homicide in Roxbury, and the last eight car payments to complete, and then a triple homicide in Brookline, and another trial requiring his testimony.

In the end, Slug Katzka had simply been too busy to kill himself.

Now it was three years later and Annie was buried and those phenobarb pills had long since been disposed of. He never thought about suicide these days. Every so often, though, he'd think about the pills lying on his dining room table, and he would wonder why he had ever been tempted. How he had ever come so close to surrender. He had no sympathy for the Slug of three years ago. Nor did he have sympathy for anyone else with a bottle of pills and a terminal case of self-pity.

And what was your reason, Dr. Levi?

He looked at that glowing view of Boston, and he thought about how it must have been in the last hour of Aaron Levi's life. He tried to imagine climbing out of bed at three in the morning. Driving to the hospital. Riding the elevator to the thirteenth floor and then climbing the last flight of steps to the fourteenth. Walking into this room. Tying the belt over the closet dowel and slipping your head into the loop.

Katzka frowned.

He crossed to the light switch and flipped it up. The lights came on. They worked just fine. So who had turned them off? Aaron Levi? The workman who'd found the body?

Someone else?

Details, thought Katzka. It was the details that drove him crazy.

11

"I can't believe it," Elaine kept saying. "I just can't believe it." She was not crying, had sat dry-eyed through the burial, a fact that greatly disturbed her mother-in-law, Judith, who had wept loudly and unashamedly while the Kaddish was recited over the grave. Judith's pain was as public as the ceremonial slash in her blouse, a symbol of a heart cut by grief. Elaine had not slashed her blouse. Elaine had not shed tears. She now sat in a chair in her living room, a plate of canapés on her lap, and she said, again: "I can't believe he's gone."

"You didn't cover the mirrors," Judith said. "You should cover them. All the mirrors in your house."

"Do what you want," said Elaine.

Judith left the room in search of sheets for the mirrors. A moment later, all the guests gathered in the living room could hear Judith opening and closing closets upstairs.

"It must be a Jewish thing," whispered Marilee Archer as she passed another tray of finger sandwiches to Abby.

Abby took an olive sandwich and passed the tray along. It moved from hand to hand down a succession of guests. No one was really eating. A polite nibble, a sip of soda, was all that anyone seemed to have stomach for. Abby didn't feel much like eating either. Or talking. At least two dozen people were in the room, seated solemnly on couches and chairs or standing around in small groups, but no one was saying much.

Upstairs, a toilet flushed. Judith, of course. Elaine gave a little wince of embarrassment. Here and there, subdued smiles appeared among the guests. Behind the couch where Abby was seated, someone began to talk about how late autumn was this year. It was October already, and the leaves were just beginning to turn. The silence, at last, had been breached. Now new conversations stirred to life, murmurings about fall gardens and how do you like Dartmouth? and wasn't it warm for October? Elaine sat at the center of it all, not conversing, but obviously relieved that others were.

The sandwich platter had made its rounds and now came back, empty, to Abby. "I'll refill it," she said to Marilee, and she rose from the couch and went into the kitchen. There she found the marble countertops covered with platters of food. No one would go hungry today. She was unwrapping a tray of smoked salmon when she looked out the kitchen window and noticed Archer, Raj Mohandas, and Frank Zwick standing outside on the flagstone terrace. They were talking, shaking their heads. Leave it to the men to retreat, she thought. Men had no patience for grieving widows or long silences; they left that ordeal to their wives in the house. They'd even brought a bottle of scotch outside with them. It sat on the umbrella table, positioned for easy refills. Zwick reached around for the bottle and poured a splash into his glass. As he recapped the bottle, he caught sight of Abby. He said something to Archer. Now Archer and Mohandas were looking at her as well. They all nodded and gave a quick wave. Then the three men crossed the terrace and walked away, into the garden.

"So much food. I don't know what I'm going to do with all of it," said Elaine. Abby hadn't noticed that she had come into the kitchen. Elaine stood gazing at the countertop and shaking her head. "I told the caterer forty people, and this is what she brings me. It's not like a wedding. Everyone eats at a wedding. But no one eats much after a funeral." Elaine looked down at one of the trays and picked up a radish, carved into a tiny rosette. "Isn't it pretty, how they do it? So much work for something you just put in your mouth." She set it back down again and stood there, not talking, admiring in silence that radish rosette.

"I'm so sorry, Elaine," said Abby. "If only there was something I could say to make it easier."

"I just wish I could understand. He never said anything. Never told me he . . ." She swallowed and shook her head. She carried the platter of food to the refrigerator, slid it onto a shelf, and shut the door. Turning, she looked at Abby. "You spoke to him that night. Was there anything you talked about—anything he might have said . . ."

"We discussed one of our patients. Aaron wanted to make sure I was doing all the right things."

"That's all you talked about?"

"Just the patient. Aaron didn't seem any different to me. Just concerned. Elaine, I never imagined he would . . ." Abby fell silent.

Elaine's gaze drifted to another platter. To the garnish of green onions, the leaves slitted and curled into lacy puffs. "Did you ever hear anything about Aaron that . . . you wouldn't want to tell me?"

"What do you mean?"

"Were there ever rumors about other women?"

"Never." Abby shook her head. And said again, with more emphasis, "Never."

Elaine nodded, but seemed to take little comfort from Abby's reassurance. "I never really thought it was a woman," she said. She picked up another tray and carried it to the refrigerator. When she'd closed the door she said, "My mother-in-law blames me. She thinks it must be something I did. A lot of people must be wondering."

"No one makes another person commit suicide."

"There was no warning. Nothing at all. Oh, I know he wasn't happy about his job. He kept talking about leaving Boston. Or quitting medicine entirely."

"Why was he so unhappy?"

"He wouldn't talk about it. When he had his own practice in Natick, we'd talk about his work all the time. Then the offer came in from Bayside, and it was too good to refuse. But after we moved here, it was as if I didn't know him anymore. He'd come home and sit down like a zombie in front of that damn computer. Playing video games all evening. Sometimes, late at night, I'd wake up and hear those weird beeps and clicks. And it was Aaron, sitting up all alone, playing some game." She shook her head and stared down at the countertop. At yet another platter of untouched food. "You're one of the last people who spoke to him. Isn't there anything you remember?"

Abby gazed out the kitchen window, trying to piece together that last conversation with Aaron. She could think of nothing to distinguish it from any other late-night phone call. They all seemed to blur together, a chorus of monotonous voices demanding action from her tired brain.

Outside, the three men were returning from their garden walk. She watched them cross the terrace to the kitchen door. Zwick was carrying the bottle of scotch, now half-empty. They entered the house and nodded to her in greeting.

"Nice little garden," said Archer. "You should go out and take a tour, Abby."

"I'd like to," she said. "Elaine, maybe you'd come out and show me . . ." She paused.

There was no one standing by the refrigerator. She glanced around the kitchen, saw the platters of food on the counter and an open carton of plastic wrap, a glassy sheet hanging out and fluttering in the air.

Elaine had left the room.

A woman was praying by Mary Allen's bed. She had been sitting there for the last half hour, head bowed, hands clasped together as she murmured aloud to the good Lord Jesus, imploring him to rain down miracles upon the mortal shell of Mary Allen. Heal her, strengthen her, purify her body and her unclean soul so that she might finally accept His word in all its glory.

"Excuse me," said Abby. "I'm sorry to intrude, but I need to examine Mrs. Allen."

The woman kept praying. Perhaps she had not heard her. Abby was about to repeat the request, when the woman at last said, "Amen," and raised her head. She had unsmiling eyes and dull brown hair with the first streaks of gray. She regarded Abby with a look of irritation.

"I'm Dr. DiMatteo," said Abby. "I'm taking care of Mrs. Allen."

"So am I," the woman said, rising to her feet. She made no attempt to shake hands with Abby, but stood with arms cradling the Bible to her chest. "I'm Brenda Hainey. Mary's niece."

"I didn't know Mary had a niece. I'm glad you're able to visit."

"I only heard about her illness two days ago. No one bothered to call me." Her tone of voice implied that this oversight was somehow Abby's fault.

"We were under the impression Mary had no close relatives."

"I don't know why. But I'm here now." Brenda looked at her aunt. "And she'll be fine."

Except for the fact she's dying, thought Abby. She moved to the bedside and said softly: "Mrs. Allen?"

Mary opened her eyes. "I'm awake, Dr. D. Just resting."

"How are you feeling today?"

"Still nauseated."

"It could be a side effect of the morphine. We'll give you something to settle your stomach."

Brenda interjected: "She's getting morphine?"

"For the pain."

"Aren't there other ways to relieve her pain?"

Abby turned to the niece. "Mrs. Hainey, could you leave the room please? I need to examine your aunt."

"It's Miss Hainey," said Brenda. "And I'm sure Aunt Mary would rather have me stay."

"I still have to ask you to leave."

Brenda glanced at her aunt, obviously expecting a protest. Mary Allen stared straight ahead, silent.

Brenda clutched the Bible tighter. "I'll be right outside, Aunt Mary."

"Dear Lord," whispered Mary, as the door shut behind Brenda. "This must be my punishment."

"Are you referring to your niece?"

Mary's tired gaze focused on Abby. "Do you think my soul needs saving?"

"I'd say that's entirely up to you. And no one else." Abby took out her stethoscope. "Can I listen to your lungs?"

Obediently Mary sat up and lifted her hospital gown.

Her breath sounds were muffled. By tapping down Mary's back, Abby could hear the change between liquid and air, could tell that more fluid had accumulated in the chest since the last time she'd examined her.

Abby straightened. "How's your breathing?"

"It's fine."

"We may need to drain some more fluid pretty soon. Or insert another chest tube."

"Why?"

"To make your breathing easier. To keep you comfortable."

"Is that the only reason?"

"Comfort is a very important reason, Mrs. Allen."

Mary sank back on the pillows. "Then I'll let you know when I need it," she whispered.

When Abby emerged from the room, she found Brenda Hainey waiting right outside the door. "Your aunt would like to sleep for a while," said Abby. "Maybe you could come back some other time."

"There's a matter I need to discuss with you, Doctor."

"Yes?"

"I was just checking with the nurse. About that morphine. Is it really necessary?"

"I think your aunt would say so."

"It's making her drowsy. All she does is sleep."

"We're trying to keep her as pain free as possible. The cancer's spread everywhere. Her bones, her brain. It's the worst kind of pain imaginable. The kindest thing we can do for her is to help her go with a minimum of discomfort."

"What do you mean, help her go?"

"She's dying. There's nothing we can do to change that."

"You used those words. *Help her go.* Is that what the morphine's for?"

"It's what she wants and needs right now."

"I've confronted this sort of issue before, Doctor. With other relatives. I happen to know for a fact it's not legal to medically assist a suicide."

Abby felt her face flush with anger. Fighting to control it, she said as calmly as she could manage: "You misunderstand me. All we're trying to do is keep your aunt comfortable."

"There are other ways to do it."

"Such as?"

"Calling on higher sources of help."

"Are you referring to prayer?"

"Why not? It's helped me through difficult times."

"You're certainly welcome to pray for your aunt. But if I recall, there's nothing against morphine in the Bible."

Brenda's face went rigid. Her retort was cut off by the sound of Abby's beeper.

"Excuse me," said Abby coolly, and she walked away, leaving the conversation unfinished. A good thing, too; she'd been on the verge of saying something really sarcastic. Something like: *While you're praying to your God, why don't you ask Him for a cure?* That would surely have pissed off Brenda. With Joe Terrio's lawsuit lurking on the horizon, and Victor Voss determined to get her fired, the last thing she needed was another complaint lodged against her.

She picked up a phone in the nurses' station and dialed the number on her beeper readout.

A woman's voice answered: "Information Desk."

"This is Dr. DiMatteo. You paged me?"

"Yes, Doctor. There's a Bernard Katzka standing here at the desk. He's wondering if you could meet him here in the lobby."

"I don't know anyone by that name. I'm sort of busy up here. Could you ask him what his business is?"

There was a background murmur of conversation. When the woman came back on, her voice sounded oddly reticent. "Dr. DiMatteo?"

"Yes."

"He's a policeman."

The man in the lobby looked vaguely familiar. He was in his mid-forties, medium height, medium build, with the sort of face that was neither handsome nor homely and not particularly memorable. His hair, a dark brown, was starting to thin at the top, a fact he made no effort to conceal the way some men did with a sideways combing of camouflaging strands. As she approached him, she had the impression that he recognized her as well. His gaze had, in fact, singled her out the moment she stepped off the elevator.

"Dr. DiMatteo," he said. "I'm Detective Bernard Katzka. Homicide."

Just hearing that word startled her. What was this all about? They shook hands. Only then, as she met his gaze, did she remember where she'd seen him. The cemetery. Aaron Levi's funeral. He'd been standing slightly apart from everyone, a silent figure in a dark suit. During the service, their gazes had intersected. She'd understood none of the Hebrew being recited, and her attention had wandered to the other mourners. That's when she'd become aware that someone else was scanning the gathering. They had looked at each other, only for a second, and then he'd looked away. At the time, she'd registered almost no impression of the man. Looking up at his face now, she found herself focusing on his eyes, which were a calm, unflinching gray. If not for the intelligence of those eyes, one might never notice Bernard Katzka.

She said, "Are you a friend of the Levi family?"

"No."

"I saw you at the cemetery. Or am I mistaken?"

"I was there."

She paused, waiting for an explanation, but all he said was, "Is there somewhere we can talk?"

"Can I ask what this is all about?"

"Dr. Levi's death."

She glanced at the lobby doors. The sun was shining and she had not been outside all day.

"There's a little courtyard with a few benches," she said. "Why don't we go out there?"

It was warm outside, a perfect October afternoon. The courtyard garden was in its chrysanthemum phase, the circular bed planted with blooms of rust, orange, and yellow. At the center a fountain poured out a quietly comforting trickle of water. They sat down on one of the wooden benches. A pair of nurses occupying the other bench rose and walked back toward the building, leaving Abby and the detective alone. For a moment nothing was said. The silence made Abby uneasy, but it did not appear to disturb her companion in the least. He seemed accustomed to long silences.

"Elaine Levi gave me your name," he said. "She suggested I talk to you."

"Why?"

"You spoke to Dr. Levi early Saturday morning. Is that correct?"

"Yes. On the phone."

"Do you remember what time that was?"

"Around two A.M., I guess. I was at the hospital."

"He made the call?"

"Well, he called the SICU and asked to speak to the upper-level resident. I happened to be it that night."

"Why was he calling?"

"About a patient. She was running a postop fever, and Aaron wanted to discuss a plan of action. Which labs we should order, which X rays. Do you mind telling me what this is all about?"

"I'm trying to establish the chronology of events. So Dr. Levi called the SICU at two A.M. and you came on the line."

"That's right."

"Did you talk to him again? After that two A.M. call?"

"No."

"Did you try to call him?"

"Yes, but he'd already left the house. I spoke to Elaine."

"What time was that?"

"I don't know. Maybe three o'clock, three-fifteen. I wasn't paying a lot of attention to the clock."

"You didn't call his house any other time that morning?"

"No. I tried paging his beeper several times, but he never answered. I knew he was somewhere in the building, because his car was in the parking lot."

"What time did you see it there?"

"I didn't. My boyfriend—Dr. Hodell—he saw it when he drove in around four A.M. Look, why is Homicide investigating this?"

He ignored her question. "Elaine Levi says there was a call around two-fifteen. Her husband answered the phone. A few minutes later he got dressed and left the house. Do you know anything about that call?"

"No. It could have been one of the nurses. Doesn't Elaine know?"

"Her husband took the phone into the bathroom. She didn't hear the conversation."

"It wasn't me. I spoke to Aaron only once. Now I'd really like to know why you're asking me these questions. This can't possibly be a routine thing you do."

"No. It's not routine."

Abby's beeper went off. She recognized the number on the

readout. It was the residency office—not an emergency, but she was getting fed up with this conversation anyway. She rose to her feet. "Detective, I've got work to do. Patients to see. I don't have time to answer a lot of vague questions."

"My questions are quite specific. I'm trying to establish who made calls at what time that morning. And what was said during those calls."

"Why?"

"It may have a bearing on Dr. Levi's death."

"Are you saying someone talked him into hanging himself?"

"I'd just like to know who did talk to him."

"Can't you pull it off the phone company computer or something? Don't they keep records?"

"The two-fifteen call to Dr. Levi was made from Bayside Hospital."

"So it could have been a nurse."

"Or anyone else in the building."

"Is that your theory? That someone from Bayside called Aaron and told him something so upsetting that he killed himself?"

"We're considering possibilities other than suicide."

She stared at him. He had said it so quietly, she wondered if she had understood him correctly. Slowly she sank back down on the bench. Neither one spoke for a moment.

A nurse pushed a woman in a wheelchair across the courtyard. The pair lingered by the flower bed, admiring the chrysanthemums, then moved on. The only sound in the courtyard was the musical splash of the fountain.

"Are you saying he might have been murdered?" said Abby.

He didn't answer immediately. And she couldn't tell, looking at his face, what his answer might be. He sat motionless, revealing nothing by his posture, his hands, his expression.

"*Did* Aaron hang himself?" she asked.

"The autopsy findings were consistent with asphyxia."

"That's what you'd expect. It sounds like a suicide."

"It very well could be."

"Then why aren't *you* convinced?"

He hesitated. For the first time she saw uncertainty in his eyes, and she knew he was weighing his next words. This was the sort of man who made no move without considering all the ramifications. The sort of man for whom spontaneity itself was a planned action.

He said, "Two days before he died, Dr. Levi brought home a brand new computer."

"That's all? That's the basis for your questions?"

"He used it to do several things. First, he made plane reservations for two to St. Lucia in the Caribbean. Leaving around Christmas time. Also, he sent E-mail to his son at Dartmouth, discussing plans for Thanksgiving break. Think about it, Doctor. Two days before committing suicide, this man is making plans for the future. He has a nice vacation on the beach to look forward to. But at two-fifteen A.M., he climbs out of his bed and drives to the hospital. Takes an elevator, then the stairwell, to a deserted floor. Ties a belt to the closet dowel, loops the other end around his neck, and simply lets his legs go limp. Consciousness wouldn't fade at once. There would be five, maybe ten seconds left to change his mind. He has a wife, kids, and a beach on St. Lucia to look forward to. But he chooses to die. Alone, and in the dark." Katzka's gaze held hers. "Think about it."

Abby swallowed. "I'm not sure I want to."

"I have."

She looked at his quiet gray eyes and she wondered: What other nightmarish things do you think about? What kind of man chooses a job that requires such terrible visions?

"We know Dr. Levi's car was found in its usual parking spot here at the hospital. We don't know why he drove here. Or why he left the house at all. Except for that two-fifteen caller, you're the last person we know of who spoke to Dr. Levi. Did he say anything about leaving for the hospital?"

"He was concerned about our patient. He might have decided to come in and see to the problem himself."

"As opposed to letting you deal with it?"

"I'm a second-year resident, Detective Katzka, not the attending physician. Aaron was the transplant team internist."

"I understood he was a cardiologist."

"He was also an internist. When there was a medical problem, like a fever, the nurses would usually contact him. And he'd call in other consultants if he needed them."

"During that phone call, did he say he was coming into the hospital?"

"No. It was just a game plan discussion. I told him what I was going to do. That I'd examine the patient and order some blood work and X rays. He approved."

"That was it?"

"That was the extent of our conversation."

"Did anything he say strike you as not quite right?"

Again she thought about it. And she remembered that initial pause in their phone conversation. And how dismayed Aaron had sounded when she'd first come on the line.

"Dr. DiMatteo?"

She looked up at Katzka. Though he'd said her name quietly, his expression had taken on new alertness.

"Do you remember something?" he asked.

"I remember he didn't sound very happy that I was the resident on duty."

"Why not?"

"Because of the particular patient involved. Her husband and I—we'd had a conflict. A serious one." She looked away, feeling a little queasy at the thought of Victor Voss. "I'm sure Aaron would've preferred that I stay miles away from Mrs. Voss."

Katzka's silence made her look up again.

"Mrs. *Victor* Voss?" he said.

"Yes. You know the name?"

Katzka sat back, exhaling softly. "I know he founded VMI International. What surgery did his wife have?"

"A heart transplant. She's doing much better now. The fever resolved after a few days of antibiotics."

Katzka was staring at the fountain, where sprays of sunlit water sparkled like gold chain. Abruptly he rose to his feet.

"Thank you for your time, Dr. DiMatteo," he said. "I may call you again."

She started to reply "Any time," but he had already turned and was swiftly walking away. The man had gone from absolute motionlessness to the speed of sound. Amazing.

Her beeper chirped. It was the residency office again. She silenced it. When she looked up, Katzka was nowhere in sight. The magical disappearing cop. Still puzzling over his questions, she returned to the lobby and picked up the house phone.

A secretary answered her call. "Residency office."

"This is Abby DiMatteo. You paged me?"

"Oh, yes. Two things. You had an outside call from Helen Lewis at New England Organ Bank. She wanted to know if you ever got an answer to your question about that transplant. You didn't answer your page, so she hung up."

"If she calls again, let her know my question's already been answered. What was the second thing?"

"You have a certified letter up here. I signed for it. I hope that's okay."

"Certified?"

"It was delivered a few minutes ago. I thought you'd want to know."

"Who sent it?"

There was a sound of shuffling papers. Then, "It's from Hawkes, Craig and Sussman. Attorneys at Law."

Abby's stomach went into free fall. "I'll be right there," she said, and hung up. The Terrio lawsuit again. The wheels of justice would surely grind her to dust. Her hands were sweating as she rode the elevator to the administrative floor. *Dr. DiMatteo, known for her calmness in the OR, is a nervous wreck.*

The residency office secretary was on the telephone. She saw Abby and pointed at the mail cubicles.

There was one envelope in Abby's slot. *Hawkes, Craig and Sussman* was printed in the upper left-hand corner. She ripped it open.

At first she didn't understand what she was reading. Then she focused on the plaintiff's name, and the meaning at last sank in. Her stomach had ended its free fall. It had crashed. This letter wasn't about Karen Terrio at all. It was about another patient, a Michael Freeman. An alcoholic, he had unexpectedly ruptured a swollen blood vessel in his esophagus and bled to death in his hospital room. Abby had been the intern on his case. She remembered it as a shockingly gruesome end. Now Michael Freeman's wife was suing, and she had retained Hawkes, Craig and Sussman to represent her. Abby was the defendant. The only defendant named in the lawsuit.

"Dr. DiMatteo? Are you all right?"

Abby suddenly realized that she was leaning against the mail cubicles and that the room wasn't quite steady. The secretary was frowning at her.

"I'm . . . fine," said Abby. "I'm okay."

By the time Abby made it out of the room, she was in full

retreat. She fled straight to the on-call room, locked herself inside, and sat down on the bed. Then she unfolded the letter and read it again. And again.

Two lawsuits in two weeks. Vivian was right. Abby would be in court for the rest of her natural life.

She knew she should call her attorney, but she couldn't bring herself to deal with that right now. So she remained sitting on the bed, staring at that letter on her lap. Thinking about all the years, all the work it had taken, just to get to this point in her career. She thought about the nights she'd fallen asleep on her books while everyone else in the dorm was out on dates. The weekends she'd worked double shifts as a hospital phlebotomist, drawing tubes and tubes of blood to earn her tuition. She thought about the hundred and twenty thousand dollars in student loans she still had to pay off. The dinners of peanut butter sandwiches. The movies and concerts and plays she had never seen.

And she thought about Pete, who'd been the reason for it all. The brother she'd wanted to save, and hadn't been able to. Most of all, she thought of Pete, eternally ten years old.

Victor Voss was winning. He'd said he would destroy her and that was exactly what he was going to do.

Fight back. It was time to fight back. Only she couldn't think of any way to do it. She wasn't clever enough. The letter burned like acid in her hands. She thought and thought about how to stop him, but she had nothing with which to fight back except that shove he'd given her in the SICU. A charge of assault and battery. It was not enough, not nearly enough to stop him.

Fight back. You have to think of a way.

The beeper went off. It was a page from the surgical ward. She was in no mood to take any goddamn calls. She reached for the phone and stabbed in the numbers. "DiMatteo," she snapped.

"Doctor, we're having a problem here with Mary Allen's niece."

"What is it?"

"We're trying to give the four o'clock morphine dose, but Brenda won't let us. Maybe you could—"

"I'm on my way." Abby slammed the receiver down. Fuck Brenda, she thought, shoving the attorney's letter in her pocket.

She used the stairwell, running the two flights down. By the time she emerged on the ward she was breathing hard, not from exertion, but from rage. She stormed straight into Mary Allen's room.

Two nurses were inside, talking with Brenda. Mary Allen was awake in bed, but she looked too weak and in pain to contribute a word.

"She's doped up enough as it is," Brenda was saying. "Look at her. She can't even talk to me."

"Maybe she doesn't want to talk to you," said Abby.

The nurses turned to Abby with expressions of relief. The voice of authority had arrived.

"Please leave the room, Miss Hainey," said Abby.

"The morphine isn't necessary."

"I'll determine that. Now leave the room."

"She hasn't got much time left. She needs all her faculties."

"For what?"

"To fully accept the Lord. If she dies before accepting Him—"

Abby held her hand out to the nurse. "Give me the morphine. I'll administer it."

At once the syringe was handed to her. Abby stepped over to the IV line. As she uncapped the needle, she saw Mary Allen's weak nod of gratitude.

"You give her that dope and I'll call an attorney," said Brenda.

"Do that," said Abby. She slipped the needle into the IV injection port. She was just pushing the plunger when Brenda surged forward and pulled the catheter out of her aunt's arm. Blood dribbled from the puncture site onto the floor. Those bright red drops spattering the linoleum were the final outrage.

A nurse clapped gauze to Mary Allen's arm. Abby turned to Brenda and said: "Get out of this room."

"You left me no choice, Doctor."

"*Get out!*"

Brenda's eyes widened. She took a step backward.

"Do you want me to call Security to throw you out?" Abby was yelling now, moving toward Brenda, who continued to back away into the hall. "I don't want you anywhere near my patient! I don't want you harassing her with your Bible bullshit!"

147

"I'm her relative!"

"I don't give a fuck who you are!"

Brenda's jaw dropped open. Without another word she spun around and walked away.

"Dr. DiMatteo, can I speak to you?"

Abby turned and saw the nursing supervisor, Georgina Speer.

"That was very inappropriate, Doctor. We don't speak to the public that way."

"She just pulled the IV out of my patient's arm!"

"There are better ways to handle it. Call Security. Call for any assistance. But profanity is definitely not the way we do it in this hospital. Do you understand?"

Abby took a deep breath. "I understand," she said. And added, in a whisper, "I'm sorry."

After she'd restarted Mary Allen's IV, Abby retreated to the on-call room and lay listlessly on the bed. Staring up at the ceiling, she wondered: What the hell is wrong with me? She'd never lost control like that before, never even come close to cursing at a patient or relative. I'm going crazy, she thought. The stress is finally breaking me. Maybe I'm not fit to be a doctor.

Her beeper went off. God, would they never leave her alone? What she'd give to go a whole day, a whole week, without being beeped or phoned or harassed. It was the hospital operator paging her. She picked up the phone and dialed zero.

"Outside call for you, Doctor," said the operator. "Let me put it through." There were a few transfer clicks, then a woman said:

"Dr. Abby DiMatteo?"

"Speaking."

"This is Helen Lewis at New England Organ Bank. You left a message last Saturday about a heart donor. We expected someone at Bayside to call back, but no one did. So I thought I should check back."

"I'm sorry. I should have called you, but things have been crazy around here. It turns out it was just a misunderstanding."

"Well that makes it easy. Since I couldn't find the information anyway. If you have any other questions, just give me a—"

"Excuse me," Abby cut in. "What did you just say?"

"I couldn't find the information."

"Why not?"

"The data you requested isn't in our system."

For a solid ten seconds Abby was silent. Then she asked, slowly, "Are you absolutely certain it's not there?"

"I've searched our computer files. On the date you gave for the harvest, we have no record of a heart donor. Anywhere in Vermont."

12

"Here it is," said Colin Wettig, laying open the *Directory of Medical Specialists*. "Timothy Nicholls. B.A., University of Vermont. M.D., Tufts. Residency, Massachusetts General. Specialty: Thoracic Surgery. Affiliated with Wilcox Memorial, Burlington, Vermont." He slid the book onto the conference table for anyone in the room to look at. "So there really is a thoracic surgeon named Tim Nicholls practicing in Burlington. He's not some figment of Archer's imagination."

"When I spoke to him on Saturday," said Archer, "Nicholls claimed he was there at the harvest. And he said it took place at Wilcox Memorial. Unfortunately, I haven't been able to find anyone else who was in the OR with him. And now I can't get hold of Nicholls. His office staff tells me he's taken a prolonged leave of absence. I don't know what's going on, Jeremiah, but I sure as hell wish we'd had nothing to do with it. Because it's starting to smell pretty rotten."

Jeremiah Parr shifted uneasily in his chair and glanced at attorney Susan Casado. He didn't bother to look at Abby, who was sitting at the far end of the table, next to the transplant coordinator, Donna Toth. Maybe he didn't *want* to look at her. Abby, after all, was the one who had brought this mess to everyone's attention. The one who had initiated this meeting.

"What exactly *is* going on here?" Parr asked.

Archer said, "I think Victor Voss arranged to keep the donor out of the registry system. To shunt the heart directly to his wife."

"Could he do that?"

"Given enough money—probably."

"And he certainly has the money," said Susan. "I just saw the latest list in *Kiplinger's*. The fifty wealthiest people in America. He's moved up to number fourteen."

"Maybe you'd better explain to me how donor assignments are *supposed* to work," said Parr. "Because I don't understand how this happened."

Archer looked at the transplant coordinator. "Donna usually handles it. Why don't we let her explain?"

Donna Toth nodded. "The system's pretty straightforward," she said. "We have both a regional and a national waiting list of patients needing organs. The national system's the United Network for Organ Sharing, or UNOS for short. The regional list is maintained by New England Organ Bank. Both systems rank patients in order of need. The list has nothing to do with wealth, race, or social status. Only how critical their conditions are." She opened a folder and took out a sheet of paper. She passed it to Parr. "That's what the latest regional list looks like. I had it faxed over from the NEOB office in Brookline. As you can see, it gives each patient's medical status, organ required, the nearest transplant center, and the phone number to contact, which is usually the transplant coordinator's."

"What're these other notations here?"

"Clinical information. Minimum and maximum height and weight acceptable for the donor. Whether the patient's had any previous transplants, which would make cross matching more difficult because of antibodies."

"You said this list is in order of need?"

"That's right. The number one name is the most critical."

"Where was Mrs. Voss?"

"On the day she received her transplant, she was number three on the AB blood type list."

"What happened to the first two names?"

"I checked with NEOB. Both names were reclassified as Code Eights a few days later. Permanently inactive and off the list."

151

"Meaning they died?" Susan Casado asked softly.

Donna nodded. "They never got their transplants."

"Jesus," groaned Parr. "So Mrs. Voss got a heart that should have gone to someone else."

"That seems to be what happened. We don't know how it was arranged."

"How did *we* get notified of the donor?" asked Susan.

"A phone call," said Donna. "That's how it usually happens. The transplant coordinator at the donor hospital handles it. He or she will check the latest NEOB waiting list and call the contact number for the first patient on the list."

"So you were called by Wilcox Memorial's transplant coordinator?"

"Yes. I've spoken to him before on the phone, about other donors. So I had no reason to question this particular donation."

Archer shook his head. "I don't know how Voss managed this. Every step of the way, it looked legal and aboveboard to us. Someone at Wilcox obviously got paid off. My bet is, it's their transplant coordinator. So Voss's wife gets the heart. And Bayside gets suckered into a cash-for-organs arrangement. And we don't have any of the donor paperwork to double-check this."

"It's still missing?" asked Parr.

"I haven't been able to find it," said Donna. "The donor records aren't anywhere in my office."

Victor Voss, thought Abby. *Somehow, he's made the papers disappear.*

"The worst part," said Wettig, "is the kidneys."

Parr frowned at the General. "What?"

"His wife didn't need the kidneys," said Wettig. "Or the pancreas or the liver. So what happened to those? If they never made it to the registry?"

"They must have gotten dumped," said Archer.

"Right. That's three, four lives that could have been saved. And got tossed instead."

There was a ballet of shaking heads, dismayed expressions.

"What are we going to do about this?" said Abby.

Her question was met with a momentary silence.

"I'm not sure what we should do," said Parr. He looked at the attorney. "Are we obligated to follow up on this?"

"Ethically, yes," said Susan. "However, there's a conse-quence, if we report this. I can think of several consequences, in fact. First, there's no way we can keep this from the press. A cash-for-organs deal, especially involving Victor Voss, is a juicy story. Second, we're going to be, in a sense, breaching patient confidentiality. That's not going to sit well with a cer-tain segment of our patient population."

Wettig snorted. "Meaning the bloody rich ones."

"The ones who keep this hospital alive," corrected Parr.

"Exactly." Susan continued. "If they hear that Bayside spurred the investigation of someone like Victor Voss, they're not going to trust us to keep *their* records private. We could lose all our private-pay transplant referrals. Finally, what if this somehow gets turned around? Made to look like we were *part* of the conspiracy? We'd lose our credibility as a transplant center. If it turns out Voss really did keep that donor out of the registry system, we'll be tainted as well."

Abby glanced at Archer, who looked stunned by the possi-bility. This could destroy the Bayside transplant program. It could destroy the team.

"How much of this has already gotten out?" asked Parr. He looked, at last, at Abby. "What did you tell NEOB about this, Dr. DiMatteo?"

"When I spoke to Helen Lewis, I wasn't sure what was going on. Neither of us were. We were just trying to figure out why the donor hadn't been entered in their system. That's how we left it. Unresolved. Immediately after the call, I told Archer and Dr. Wettig about it."

"And Hodell. You must have told Hodell."

"I haven't spoken to Mark yet. He's been in surgery all day."

Parr sighed with relief. "All right. So it's just in this room. And all Mrs. Lewis knows is that you're not sure what hap-pened."

"Correct."

Susan Casado shared Parr's look of relief. "We've still got a shot at damage control. I think what needs to be done now is, Dr. Archer should call NEOB. Reassure Mrs. Lewis that we've cleared up the misunderstanding. Chances are, she'll leave it at that. We'll continue to make inquiries, but discreetly. We should try reaching Dr. Nicholls again. He might be able to clear things up.''

''No one seems to know when Nicholls is coming back from his leave of absence,'' said Archer.

''What about the other surgeon?'' asked Susan. ''The guy from Texas?''

''Mapes? I haven't tried calling him yet.''

''Someone should.''

Parr cut in: ''I disagree. I don't think we should be contacting anyone else about this.''

''Your reason, Jeremiah?''

''The less we know about it, the less involved we'll be in this mess. We should stay miles away from it. Tell Helen Lewis that it was a directed donation. And that's why it never went through NEOB. Then let's just move on.''

''In other words,'' said Wettig, ''stick our goddamn heads in the sand.''

''See no evil, hear no evil.'' Parr glanced around the table. He seemed to take the lack of response as a sign of general assent. ''Needless to say, we don't talk about it outside this room.''

Abby couldn't hold her silence. ''The problem is,'' she said, ''the evil doesn't go away. Whether or not we hear about it or see it, it's still *there*.''

''Bayside's the innocent party,'' said Parr. ''We shouldn't have to suffer. And we certainly shouldn't expose ourselves to unfair scrutiny.''

''What about the ethical obligations? This could happen again.''

''I really doubt Mrs. Voss will be needing another heart any time soon. It's an isolated incident, Dr. DiMatteo. A desperate husband bent the rules to save his wife. It's done with. We just need to install safeguards to ensure it doesn't happen again.'' Parr looked at Archer. ''Can we do that?''

Archer nodded. ''We're damn well going to have to.''

''What happens to Victor Voss?'' said Abby. By the silence that followed, she knew the answer: nothing would happen to him. Nothing ever happened to men like Victor Voss. He could beat the system and buy a heart, buy a surgeon, buy an entire hospital. And he could buy lawyers, too, a whole army of them, enough to turn a lowly surgical resident's dreams into scorched earth.

She said, "He's out to ruin me. I thought it would ease up after his wife's transplant, but it hasn't. He's dumped offal in my car. He's initiated two lawsuits, with more on the way, I'm sure of it. It's hard for me to see no evil, hear no evil, when he's resorting to tactics like those."

"Can you prove it's Voss doing these things?" asked Susan.

"Who else would it be?"

"Dr. DiMatteo," said Parr, "this hospital's reputation is on the line. We need everyone to be on the same team, everyone to pull together. Including you. This is your hospital too."

"What if it all comes out anyway? What if it hits the front page of the *Globe?* Bayside's going to be accused of a coverup. And this'll blow up in all your faces."

"That's why it can't leave this room," said Parr.

"It could get out anyway." She lifted her chin. "It probably will."

Parr and Susan exchanged nervous glances.

Susan said: "That's a risk we'll have to take."

Abby stripped off her OR gown, tossed it in the laundry hamper, and pushed through the double doors. It was nearly midnight. The patient, a stabbing victim, was now in Recovery, the postop orders were being written by the intern, and the ER had nothing coming down the pike. All was quiet in the trenches.

She wasn't sure she welcomed the lull. It gave her too much time to brood over what had been said at that afternoon meeting.

My one chance to fight back, she thought, and I can't. Not if I'm going to be a team player. Not if I'm going to keep Bayside's interests at heart.

And her own interests as well. That she was still considered part of the team was a good sign. It meant she had a chance of staying on here, a chance of actually completing her residency. It came down to a deal with the devil. Keep her mouth shut, and hang on to the dream. If Victor Voss would let her.

If her conscience would let her.

Several times that evening, she'd been on the verge of picking up the phone and calling Helen Lewis. That's all it would take, one phone call, to get NEOB into the picture. One phone call to expose Victor Voss. Now, as she headed back to the on-call room, she was still mulling over what she should do. She unlocked the door and stepped inside.

It was the fragrance she noticed first, even before she turned on the lights. The perfume of roses and lilies. She switched on the lamp and stared in wonder at the vase of flowers on the desk.

A rustle of sheets drew her gaze to the bed. "Mark?" she said.

He came awake with a start. For a moment he seemed unsure of where he was. Then he saw her and smiled. "Happy birthday."

"God. I completely forgot."

"I didn't," he said.

She went to the bed and sat down beside him. He'd fallen asleep in his surgical scrubs and when she bent down to kiss him, she could smell that familiar on-call scent of Betadine and fatigue. "Ouch. You need a shave."

"I need another kiss."

She smiled and obliged him. "How long have you been here?"

"What time is it?"

"Midnight."

"Two hours."

"You've been waiting here since ten?"

"I didn't actually plan it this way. I guess I just fell asleep." He moved aside to make room for her on the narrow mattress. She pulled off her shoes and lay down beside him. At once she felt comforted by the warmth of the bed, and of the man. She thought of telling him about the meeting this afternoon, about the second lawsuit, but she didn't want to talk about any of it. All she wanted was to be held.

"Sorry I forgot the cake," he said.

"I can't believe I forgot my own birthday. Maybe I wanted to forget it. Twenty-eight already."

Laughing, he wrapped an arm around her. "Such a decrepit old lady."

"I *feel* old. Especially tonight."

"Yeah, well then, I feel ancient." He kissed her, softly, on the ear. "And I'm not getting any younger. So maybe now's the time."

"Time for what?"

"To do what I should have done months ago."

"Which is?"

He turned her toward him and cupped her face in his hand. "Ask you to marry me."

She stared at him, unable to say a word, but so filled with happiness she knew the answer must be plain in her eyes. She was suddenly, joyfully, aware of his every aspect. His hand warming her cheek. His face, tired and no longer young, but far more dear to her because of that.

"I knew, a couple of nights ago, that this was what I wanted," he said. "You were on call. And there I was at home, eating dinner out of a carton. I went up to bed, and I saw your things on the dresser. Your hairbrush. Jewelry box. That bra that you never seem to put away." Softly he laughed. So did she. "Anyway, that's when I knew. I never want to live anywhere without your stuff lying on my dresser. I don't think I could. Not anymore."

"Oh, Mark."

"The crazy thing is, you're hardly ever home. And when you are home, I'm not. We sort of wave to each other in the hallways. Or hold hands in the elevator if we're lucky. What matters to me is knowing that, when I do go home, I see your things on that dresser. I know you've been there, or you will be there. And that's enough."

Through tears, she saw him smile. And she felt his heart thudding as though in fear.

"So what do you think, Dr. D.?" he whispered. "Can we fit a wedding into our tight schedules?"

Her answer was half sob, half laughter. "Yes. Yes, yes, *yes!*" And rising up, she rolled on top of him, her arms thrown around his neck, her mouth finding his. They were both laughing, kissing, while the mattress springs gave horrible squeaks. The bed was far too small; they'd never be able to sleep in it together.

But for the purpose of lovemaking, it suited just fine.

She had been beautiful once. Sometimes, when Mary Allen looked at her own hands and saw the wrinkles and brown stains of age, she would wonder with a start: Whose hands are these? A stranger's, certainly; an old woman's. Not my hands, not pretty Mary Hatcher's. Then the flash of confusion would pass, and she'd look around the hospital room and realize she'd been dreaming again. Not a true dream that came with true sleep, but a sort of mist that drifted through her brain and lingered there, even into wakefulness. It was the morphine. She was grateful for the morphine. It took away her pain and it opened some secret gate in her mind, allowing images to flow in, images of a remembered life, almost over now. She had heard life described as a circle, a returning to the point of one's beginning, but her own life did not seem nearly so organized. Rather, it was like a tapestry of unruly threads, some broken, some raveled, none of them straight and true.

But woven with so many, many colors.

She closed her eyes and that secret gate swung open. A path to the sea. Hedges of beach roses, pink and sweet smelling. Warm sand swallowing up her toes. Waves tumbling in from the bay. The luxury of hands skimming lotion down her body.

Geoffrey's hands.

The gate swung wider, and he stepped in, a memory fully rendered. Not as he was, on that beach, but as she'd first seen him, in his uniform, dark hair ruffled, his face turning toward her in mid-laugh. Their first look at each other. It had been on a Boston street. She was carrying a sack of groceries, looking every inch the efficient young housewife on her way home to cook her husband his evening meal. Her dress had been an exceedingly ugly shade of brown; it was wartime, and one had to make do with what was available in the shops. She had not done up her hair, and the wind was whipping it into a witch's mane. She thought she looked quite hideous. But there was that young man, smiling at her, his gaze following her as she passed him on the sidewalk.

The next day, he would be there again, and they would look at each other, not strangers this time, but something more.

Geoffrey. Another lost thread. Not one that merely frayed and weakened until it broke, like her husband, but one that had been ripped too early from the tapestry, tearing an empty furrow that ran all the way down to the final weaving.

She heard a door swing open. A real door. Heard footsteps. Softly they approached her bed.

Suspended in her morphine daze, she had to struggle just to open her eyes. When at last she did, she found the room was dark except for one small circle of light hovering nearby. It was the light she tried to focus on. It danced like a firefly, then steadied to a single bright pinpoint on her bedsheet. She focused harder and made out a patch of darkness that had materialized by her bed. Something not quite solid, not quite real. She wondered if this, too, was a morphine dream. Some unwelcome memory come through the gate to haunt her. She heard the sheets slither aside and felt a hand grasp her arm with a touch that was cold and rubbery.

Her breath come out in a rush of fear. This was not a dream. This was real. *Real.* The hand was here to lead her somewhere, to take her away.

In panic she thrashed, managed to pull free from that grip.

A voice said, softly: "It's all right, Mary. It's all right. It's just time for you to sleep."

Mary fell still. "Who are you?"

"I'm taking care of you tonight."

"Is it already time for my medicine?"

"Yes. It's time."

Mary saw the penlight playing, once again, on her arm. Her IV. She watched as the gloved hand produced a syringe. The plastic cap was removed and something glittered in the thin beam of light. A needle.

Mary felt a fresh stirring of alarm. Gloves. Why were the hands wearing gloves?

She said, "I want to see my nurse. Please call my nurse."

"There's no need." The needle tip pierced the IV injection port. The plunger began its slow and steady descent. Mary felt a warmth flush through her vein and then up her arm. She realized that the syringe was very full, that the plunger was taking far longer than usual to deliver its dose of painless oblivion. Not right, she thought, as the syringe emptied its contents into her vein. Something is not right.

"I want my nurse," she said. She managed to lift her head and call out, weakly, "Nurse! Please! I need—"

A gloved hand closed over her mouth. It shoved her head back to the pillow with such force Mary felt as though her neck had snapped. She reached up to pry away the hand, but could not. It was clamped too tightly over her mouth, muffling her cries. She thrashed, felt the IV rip loose, felt the disconnected tubing dribbling saline. Still the hand would not release her mouth. By now the liquid warmth had spread from her arm to her chest and was rushing toward her brain. She tried to move her legs and found she couldn't.

Found, suddenly, that she didn't care.

The hand slid away from her face.

She was running. She was a girl again, her hair long and brown and flying around her shoulders. The sand was warm under her bare feet, and the air smelled of beach roses and the sea.

The gate hung wide open before her.

The ringing telephone pulled Abby from a place that was both warm and safe. She stirred awake and found an arm wrapped around her waist. Mark's. Somehow, despite the small bed, they'd managed to fall asleep together. Gently she disentangled herself from his embrace and reached for the ringing telephone.

"DiMatteo."

"Dr. D., this is Charlotte on Four West. Mrs. Allen just expired. The interns are all busy at the moment, so we wondered if you could come down and pronounce the patient."

"Right. I'll be there." Abby hung up and lay back down on the bed for a moment, allowing herself the luxury of slowly coming awake. Mrs. Allen. Dead. It had happened sooner than she'd expected. She felt relieved that the ordeal was finally over, and guilty that she should experience such relief at all. At three in the morning, a patient's death seems less a tragedy and more a nuisance, just another reason for lost sleep.

Abby sat up on the side of the bed and pulled on her shoes. Mark was snoring softly, oblivious to ringing telephones. Smiling, she leaned over and gave him a kiss. "I do," she whispered in his ear. And she left the room.

Charlotte met her at the Four West nurses' station. Together they walked to Mary's room, at the far end of the hall.

"We found her at two A.M. rounds. I checked her at midnight, and she was sleeping, so it happened sometime after that. At least she went peacefully."

"Have you called the family?"

"I called the niece. The one listed in the chart. I told her she didn't have to come in, but she insisted. She's on her way now. We've been cleaning things up for the visit."

"Cleaning?"

"Mary must have pulled her IV out. There was saline and blood spilled on the floor." Charlotte opened the door to the patient's room, and they both entered.

By the light of a bedside lamp, Mary Allen lay in a serene pose of sleep, her arms at her sides, the bedsheets neatly folded back across her chest. But she was not sleeping, and that was readily apparent. Her eyelids hung partially open. A washcloth had been rolled up and placed under her chin to prop up the sagging jaw. Relatives paying their last respects did not want to stare into a loved one's gaping mouth.

Abby's task took only moments. She placed her fingers on the carotid artery. No pulse. She lifted the gown and lay her stethoscope on the chest. She listened for ten seconds. No respirations, no heartbeat. She shone a penlight into the eyes. Pupils mid-position and fixed. A pronouncement of death was merely a matter of paperwork. The nurses had already recognized the obvious; Abby's role was simply to confirm the nurses' findings and record the event in the chart. It was one of those responsibilities they never explained to you in medical school. Newly minted interns, asked to pronounce their first dead patient, often had no idea what they were supposed to do. Some made impromptu speeches. Or called for a Bible, thus earning an exalted place in the nurses' annals of Stupid Doctor stories.

A death in a hospital is not an occasion for a speech, but for signatures and paperwork. Abby picked up Mary Allen's chart and completed the task. She wrote: "No spontaneous respirations or pulse. Auscultation reveals no heart sounds. Pupils fixed and mid-position. Patient pronounced expired at 0305." She closed the chart and turned to leave.

Brenda Hainey was standing in the doorway.

"I'm sorry, Miss Hainey," said Abby. "Your aunt passed away in her sleep."

"When did it happen?"

"Sometime after midnight. I'm sure she was comfortable."

"Was anyone with her when it happened?"

"There were nurses on duty in the ward."

"But no one was here. In the room?"

Abby hesitated. Decided that the truth was always the best answer. "No, she was alone. I'm sure it happened in her sleep. It was a peaceful way to go." She stepped away from the bed. "You can stay with her for a while, if you want. I'll ask the nurses to give you some privacy." She started past Brenda, toward the door.

"Why was nothing done to save her?"

Abby turned back to look at her. "Nothing could be done."

"You can shock a heart, can't you? Start it up again?"

"Under certain circumstances."

"Did you do that?"

"No."

"Why not? Because she was too old to save?"

"Age had nothing to do with it. She had terminal cancer."

"She came into the hospital only two weeks ago. That's what she told me."

"She was already very sick."

"I think you people made her sicker."

By now Abby's stomach was churning. She was tired, she wanted to go back to bed, and this woman wouldn't let her. Abuse heaped on abuse. But she had to take it. She had to stay calm.

"There was nothing we could do," Abby repeated.

"Why wasn't her heart shocked, at least?"

"She was a no-code. That means we don't shock her. And we don't put her on a breathing machine. It was your aunt's request, and we honored it. So should you, Miss Hainey." She left before Brenda could say anything else. Before *she* could say anything she regretted.

She found Mark still asleep in the on-call room. She crawled in bed, turned on her side with her back to his chest, and pulled his arm over her waist. She tried to burrow back into that safe, warm haven of unconsciousness, but she kept seeing Mary Allen, the washcloth stuffed under her sagging chin, the eyelids drooping over glassy corneas. A body in its first stages of decay. She realized she knew almost nothing at all about Mary Allen's life, what she had thought, whom she had loved. Abby was her doctor, and all she knew about Mary Allen was the way she had died. Asleep, in her bed.

No, not quite. Sometime before her death, Mary had pulled out her IV. The nurses had found blood and saline on the floor.

Had Mary been agitated? Confused? What had induced her to tug the line out of her vein?

It was one more detail about Mary Allen that she would never know.

Mark sighed and nestled closer to her. She took his hand and clasped it to her chest. To her heart. *I do.* She smiled, in spite of the sadness. It was the beginning of a new life, hers and Mark's. Mary Allen's was over, and theirs was about to start. The death of an elderly patient was a sad thing, but here, in the hospital, was where lives passed on.

And where new lives began.

It was ten A.M. when the taxi dropped Brenda Hainey off at her house in Chelsea. She had not eaten breakfast, had not slept since that call from the hospital, but she felt neither tired nor hungry. If anything, she felt immensely serene.

She had prayed at her aunt's bedside until five A.M., when the nurses had come to take the body to the morgue. She had left the hospital intending to come straight home, but during the taxi ride, she had been troubled by a sense of unfinished business. It had to do with Aunt Mary's soul, and where it might be at this moment in its cosmic journey. If, indeed, it was in transit at all. It could be stuck somewhere, like an elevator between floors. Whether it was headed upward or downward, Brenda could not be certain, and that was what troubled her.

Aunt Mary had not made things easy for herself. She had not joined in prayer, had not asked Him for forgiveness, had not even glanced at the Bible Brenda had left at her bedside. Aunt Mary had been entirely too indifferent, Brenda thought. One could not be indifferent in such a situation.

Brenda had seen it before, in other dying friends and relatives, that mindless serenity as the end approached. She was the only one who dared address the salvation of their souls, the only one who seemed at all concerned about which way their elevator might be heading. And a good thing she was concerned. So concerned, in fact, she had made it her business to know who in the family might be seriously ailing. Wherever they were in the country, she would go to them, stay with them until the end. It had become her calling, and there were those who considered her the family saint because of it. She was too modest to accept such a title. No, she was simply doing His bidding, as any good servant would do.

In Aunt Mary's case, though, she had failed. Death had come too soon, before her aunt had accepted Him into her heart. That was why, as the taxi pulled away from Bayside Hospital at five forty-five A.M., Brenda had felt such a sense of failure. Her aunt was dead, her soul beyond salvation. She, Brenda, had not been persuasive enough. If Aunt Mary had lived only another day, perhaps there would have been time.

The taxi passed a church. It was an Episcopal church, not Brenda's denomination, but it was a church all the same.

"Stop," she'd ordered the driver. "I want to get off here."

And so, at six A.M., Brenda had found herself sitting in a pew at St. Andrew's. She sat there for two and a half hours, her head bent, her lips moving silently. Praying for Aunt Mary, praying that the woman's sins, whatever they might be, would be forgiven. That her aunt's soul would no longer be stuck between floors and that the elevator she was riding would be heading not down, but up. When at last Brenda raised her head, it was eight-thirty. The church was still empty. Morning light was cascading down in a mosaic of blues and golds through the stained glass windows. As she focused on the altar, she saw the shape of Christ's head emblazoned there. It was just the projected figure from the window, she knew that, but it seemed at that moment to be a sign. A sign that her prayers had been answered.

Aunt Mary was saved.

Brenda had risen from the bench feeling light-headed with hunger, but joyous. Another soul turned to the light, and all because of her efforts. How fortunate that He had listened!

She'd left St. Andrew's feeling wondrously buoyant, as though there were little cloud slippers on her feet. Outside, she found a taxi that just happened to be idling at the curb, waiting for her. Another sign.

She rode home in a trance of contentment.

Climbing the steps to her front porch, she looked forward to a quiet breakfast and then a long and deserved nap. Even His servants needed rest. She unlocked the door.

A scattering of mail lay on the floor, deposited that morning through the door slot. Bills and church newsletters and appeals for donations. So many needy people in the world! Brenda gathered up the mail and shuffled through the stack as she went into the kitchen. At the very bottom of the pile, she found an envelope with her name on it. That's all that was written there, just her name. No return address.

She broke the seal and unfolded the enclosed slip of paper. There was one typewritten line:

Your aunt did not die a natural death.

It was signed: A friend.

The stack of mail slipped from Brenda's grasp, the bills and newsletters scattering across the kitchen floor. She sank into a chair. She was no longer hungry, no longer serene.

She heard a cawing outside her window. She looked up and saw a crow perched on a nearby tree branch, its yellow eye staring straight at her.

It was another sign.

13

Frank Zwick glanced up from the patient on the operating table and said, "I understand congratulations are in order."

Abby, her hands dripping from the obligatory ten-minute scrub, had just walked into the OR to find Zwick and the two nurses grinning at her.

"I never thought that one would get hooked. Not in a million years," said the scrub nurse, handing Abby a towel. "Just goes to show you, bachelorhood *is* a curable illness. When did he pop the question, Dr. D.?"

Abby slipped her arms into the sterile gown and snapped on gloves. "Two days ago."

"You kept it a secret for two whole days?"

Abby laughed. "I wanted to make sure he wasn't going to suddenly change his mind." *And he hasn't. If anything, we're more sure of each other than ever before.* Smiling, she moved to the table. The patient, already anesthetized, lay with chest exposed and skin stained a yellow-brown from Betadine. It was to be a simple thoracotomy, a wedge resection of a peripheral pulmonary nodule. Her hands moved through the preop routine with the ease of one who's done it many times before. She lay down sterile cloths. Fastened clamps. Lay down the blue drapes and fastened more clamps.

"So when's the big day?" asked Zwick.

"We're still talking about it." In fact, she and Mark had done little *but* talk about it. How big a wedding? Whom to invite. Outdoors or indoors? Only one thing had been decided for certain. Their honeymoon would be spent on a beach. Any beach, as long as there were palm trees in the vicinity.

She could feel her smile broadening at the prospect of warm sand and blue water. And Mark.

"I bet Mark's thinking *boat,*" said Zwick. "That's where he'll want to get married."

"Not the boat."

"Uh-oh. That sounds definite."

She finished draping the patient and looked up as Mark, freshly scrubbed, pushed through the doors. He donned gown and gloves and took his place across the table from her.

They grinned at each other. Then she picked up the scalpel.

The intercom buzzed. A voice over the speaker said, "Is Dr. DiMatteo in there?"

"Yes she is," said the circulating nurse.

"Could you have her break scrub and come out?"

"They're just about to open. Can't this wait till later?"

There was a pause. Then: "Mr. Parr needs her out of the OR."

"Tell him we're in surgery!" said Mark.

"He knows that. We need Dr. DiMatteo out here," repeated the intercom. "Now."

Mark looked at Abby. "Go ahead. I'll have them call one of the interns to assist."

Abby backed away from the table and nervously stripped off her gown. Something was wrong. Parr wouldn't pull her out of surgery unless there was some kind of crisis.

Her heart was already racing as she pushed through the OR doors and walked to the front desk.

Jeremiah Parr was standing there. Beside him were two hospital security guards and the nursing supervisor. No one was smiling.

"Dr. DiMatteo," said Parr, "could you come with us?"

Abby looked at the guards. They had fanned out to either side of her. The nursing supervisor, too, had shifted position, taking a step back.

"What's this all about?" said Abby. "Where are we going?"

"Your locker."

"I don't understand."

"It's just a routine check, Doctor."

There's nothing routine about this. Flanked by the two guards, Abby had no choice but to follow Parr up the hall to the women's locker room. The nursing supervisor went in first, to clear the area of personnel. Then she beckoned Parr and the others inside.

"Your locker is number seventy-two?" said Parr.

"Yes."

"Could you open it please?"

Abby reached for the combination padlock. She made one spin of the dial, then stopped and turned to Parr. "I want to know what this is all about first."

"It's just a check."

"I think I'm a little beyond the stage of high school locker inspections. What are you looking for?"

"Just *open the locker.*"

Abby glanced at the guards, then at the nursing supervisor. They were watching her with heightened suspicion. She thought: I can't win this one. If I refuse to open it, they'll think I'm hiding something. The best way to defuse this crazy situation was to cooperate.

She reached for the lock, spun the combination, and tugged it open.

Parr stepped closer. So did the guards. They were standing right beside him as she swung open the locker door.

Inside were her street clothes, her stethoscope, her purse, a flowered toilet bag for on-call nights, and the long white coat she used for attending rounds. They wanted cooperation, she'd damn well give them cooperation. She unzipped the flowered bag and held it open for everyone to see. It was a show and tell of intimate feminine toiletries. Toothbrush and tampons and Midol. One of the male guards flushed. He'd gotten his thrill for the day. She zipped up the bag and opened her purse. No surprises in there either. A wallet, checkbook, car keys, more tampons. Women and their specialized plumbing. The guards were looking uncomfortable now, and a little sheepish.

Abby was starting to enjoy this.

She put the purse back in the locker and took the white coat off the hook. The instant she did, she knew there was something different about it. It was heavier. She reached into the pocket and felt something cylindrical and smooth. A glass vial. She took it out and stared at the label.

Morphine sulfate. The vial was almost empty.

"Dr. DiMatteo," said Parr, "please give that to me."

She looked up at him. Slowly she shook her head. "I don't know what it's doing there."

"Give me the vial."

Too stunned to think of an alternative action, she simply handed it to him. "I don't know how it got there," she said. "I've never seen it before."

Parr handed the vial to the nursing supervisor. Then he turned to the guards. "Please escort Dr. DiMatteo to my office."

"This is bullshit," said Mark. "Someone set her up and we all know it."

"We don't know any such thing," said Parr.

"It's part of the same pattern of harassment! The lawsuits. The bloody organs in her car. And now this."

"This is entirely different, Dr. Hodell. This is a dead patient." Parr looked at Abby. "Dr. DiMatteo, why don't you just tell us the truth and make things easier for all of us?"

A confession was what he wanted. A clean and simple admission of guilt. Abby glanced around the table, at Parr and Susan Casado and the nursing supervisor. The only person she couldn't look at was Mark. She was afraid to look at him, afraid to see any doubt in his eyes.

She said, "I told you, I don't know anything about it. I don't know how the morphine got in my locker. I don't know how Mary Allen died."

"You pronounced her death," said Parr. "Two nights ago."

"The nurses found her. She'd already expired."

"That was the night you were on call."

"Yes."

"You were in the hospital all night."

"Of course. That's what being on call *means.*"

"So you were here on the very night Mrs. Allen expired of a morphine OD. And today we find this in your locker." He set the vial on the table where it sat, center stage, on the gleaming mahogany surface. "A controlled substance. Just the fact it's in your possession is serious enough."

Abby stared at Parr. "You just said Mrs. Allen died of a morphine OD. How do you know that?"

"A postmortem drug level. It was sky-high."

"She was on a therapeutic dose, titrated to comfort."

"I have the report right here. It came back this morning. Four-tenths milligram per liter. A level of two-tenths is considered fatal."

"Let me see that," said Mark.

"Certainly."

Mark scanned the lab slip. "Why would anyone order a postmortem morphine level? She was a terminal cancer patient."

"It was ordered. That's all you need to know."

"I need to know a hell of a lot more."

Parr looked at Susan Casado, who said: "There was reason to suspect this was not a natural death."

"What reason?"

"That's not the point of this—"

"*What* reason?"

Susan released a sharp breath. "One of Mrs. Allen's relatives asked us to look into it. She received some kind of note implying the death was suspicious. We notified Dr. Wettig, of course, and he ordered an autopsy."

Mark handed Abby the lab slip. She stared at it, recognizing the indecipherable scrawl on the line *Ordering Physician*. It was, indeed, the General's signature. He'd ordered a quantitative drug screen at eleven A.M. yesterday morning. Eight hours after Mary Allen's death.

"I had nothing to do with this," said Abby. "I don't know how she got all this morphine. It could be a lab error. A nursing error—"

"I can speak for my staff," said the nursing supervisor. "We follow strict controls on narcotics administration. You all know that. There's no nursing error here."

"Then what you're saying," said Mark, "is that the patient was deliberately overdosed."

There was a long silence. Parr said, "Yes."

"This is ridiculous! I was *with* Abby that night, in the call room!"

"All night?" said Susan.

"Yes. It was her birthday, and we, uh . . ." Mark cleared his throat and glanced at Abby. *We slept together* was what they were both thinking. "We celebrated," he said.

"You were together the whole time?" said Parr.

Mark hesitated. He doesn't really know, thought Abby. He'd slept through all her phone calls, hadn't even stirred when she'd left to pronounce Mrs. Allen at three o'clock, nor when she'd left again to restart an IV at four. He was about to lie for her, and she knew that it wouldn't work because Mark had no idea what she'd done that night. Parr did. He had it from the nurses. From the notes and orders she'd written, each one recorded with the time.

She said, "Mark was in the call room with me. But he slept all night." She looked at him. *We have to stick to the truth. It's the only thing that'll save me.*

"What about you, Dr. DiMatteo?" said Parr. "Did you stay in the room?"

"I was called to the wards several times. But you know that already, don't you?"

Parr nodded.

"You think you know everything!" said Mark. "So tell me this. Why would she do it? Why would she kill her own patient?"

"It's no secret she has sympathies with the euthanasia movement," said Susan Casado.

Abby stared at her. *"What?"*

"We've spoken with the nurses. On one occasion, Dr. DiMatteo was heard to say, quote"—Susan flipped through the pages of a yellow legal pad—"'If the morphine makes it easier, then that's what we should give her. Even if it makes the end come sooner.' Unquote." Susan looked at Abby. "You did say that, didn't you?"

"That had nothing to do with euthanasia! I was talking about pain control! About keeping a patient comfortable."

"So you did say it?"

"Maybe I did! I don't remember."

"Then there was the exchange with Mrs. Allen's niece, Brenda Hainey. It was witnessed by several nurses, as well as

Mrs. Speer here.'' She nodded toward the nursing supervisor. And again she glanced at her legal pad. ''It was an argument. Brenda Hainey felt her aunt was getting too much morphine. And Dr. DiMatteo disagreed. To the point of using obscenities.''

It was a charge Abby couldn't deny. She *had* argued with Brenda. She *had* used an obscenity. It was all crashing in on her now, wave after giant wave. She felt unable to breathe, unable to move, as the waves just kept slamming her down.

There was a knock and Dr. Wettig walked in and carefully shut the door behind him. He didn't say anything for a moment. He just stood at the end of the table and looked at Abby. She waited for the next wave to crash.

''She says she knows nothing about it,'' said Parr.

''I'm not surprised,'' Wettig said. ''You really don't know anything about this, do you, DiMatteo?''

Abby met the General's gaze. It had never been easy for her to look directly at those flat blue eyes. She saw too much power there, and it was power over her future. But she was looking straight at him now, determined to make him see that she had nothing to hide.

''I didn't kill my patient,'' she said. ''I swear it.''

''That's what I thought you'd say.'' Wettig reached in his lab coat pocket and produced a combination padlock. He set it down with a thud on the table.

''What's this?'' said Parr.

''It's from Dr. DiMatteo's locker. In the last half hour, I've become something of an expert on combination padlocks. I called a locksmith. He says it's a spring-loaded model, a piece of cake to get open. One sharp blow is all it takes. And it'll snap open. Also, there's a code on the back. Any registered locksmith can use that code to obtain the combination.''

Parr glanced at the lock, then gave a dismissive shrug. ''That doesn't prove anything. We're still left with a dead patient. And *that.*'' He pointed to the vial of morphine.

''What's wrong with you people?'' said Mark. ''Can't you see what's happening here? An anonymous note. Morphine conveniently planted in her locker. Someone's setting her up.''

''To what purpose?'' said Susan.

"To discredit her. Get her fired."

Parr snorted. "You're suggesting someone actually murdered a patient just to ruin Dr. DiMatteo's career?"

Mark started to answer, then seemed to think better of it. It was an absurd theory and they all knew it.

"You have to agree, Dr. Hodell, that a conspiracy is pretty far-fetched," said Susan.

"Not as far-fetched as what's already happened to me," said Abby. "Look at what Victor Voss has already done. He's mentally unstable. He assaulted me in the SICU. Putting bloody organs in my car is something only a sick mind would think of. And then there are the lawsuits—two of them already. And that's just the beginning."

There was a silence. Susan glanced at Parr. "Doesn't she know?"

"Apparently not."

"Know *what?*" said Abby.

"We got a call from Hawkes, Craig and Sussman just after lunch," said Susan. "The lawsuits against you have been dropped. Both of them."

Abby reeled back in her chair. "I don't understand," she murmured. "What is he doing? What is Voss doing?"

"If Victor Voss *was* trying to harass you, it appears he's stopped. This has nothing to do with Voss."

"Then how else do we explain this?" said Mark.

"Look at the evidence." Susan pointed to the vial.

"There are no witnesses, nothing to link that particular vial with the patient's death."

"Nevertheless, I think we can all draw the same conclusion."

The silence was suffocating. Abby saw that no one was looking at her, not even Mark.

At last Wettig spoke. "What do you propose to do, Parr? Call in the police? Turn this mess into a media circus?"

Parr hesitated. "It would be premature . . ."

"You either make your accusations stick, or you withdraw them. Anything else would be unfair to Dr. DiMatteo."

"My God, General. Let's keep the police out of this," said Mark.

"If you people want to call this murder, then the police

should be involved,'' said Wettig. "Call in a few reporters as well, put your PR people to work. They could use a little excitement. Get it all out in the open, that's the best policy.'' He looked directly at Parr. *"If* you're going to call this murder.''

It was a dare.

Parr was the one to back down. He cleared his throat and said to Susan, "We can't be absolutely certain that's what it is.''

"You'd better be certain it's murder,'' said Wettig. "You'd better be *damn* certain. Before you call the police.''

"The matter's still being looked into,'' said Susan. "We have to interview a few more nurses on that ward. Find out if there's something we've missed.''

"You do that,'' said Wettig.

There was another pause. No one was looking at Abby. She had faded from view, the invisible woman no one wanted to acknowledge.

They all seemed startled when Abby spoke. She scarcely recognized her own voice; it sounded like a stranger's, calm and steady. "I'd like to return to my patients now. If I may,'' she said.

Wettig nodded. "Go ahead.''

"Wait,'' said Parr. "She can't go back to her duties.''

"You haven't proved anything,'' said Abby, rising from her chair. "The General's right. Either you make the charges stick, or you withdraw them.''

"We have one charge that's indisputable,'' said Susan. "Illegal possession of a controlled substance. We don't know how you obtained the morphine, Doctor, but the fact you had it in your locker is serious enough.'' She looked at Parr. "We don't have a choice. The potential for liability is sky-high. If something goes wrong with *any* of her patients, and people find out we knew about this morphine business, we're dead.'' She turned to Wettig. "So's the reputation of your residency program, General.''

Susan's warning had its intended effect. Liability was something they all worried about. Wettig, like every other doctor, dreaded lawyers and lawsuits. This time, he didn't argue.

"What does this mean?" said Abby. "Am I being fired?"

Parr rose to his feet, a signal that the meeting was over, the decision now made. "Dr. DiMatteo, until further notice, you're on suspension. You're not to go on the wards. You're not to go anywhere near a patient. Do you understand?"

She understood. She understood perfectly.

14

Yakov had not dreamed of his mother in years, had scarcely thought of her in months, so he was bewildered when, on his thirteenth day at sea, he awakened with a memory of her so vivid he could almost smell her scent still lingering in the air. His last glimpse of her, as the dream faded, was her smile. A wisp of blond hair tracing her cheek. Green eyes that seemed to be looking through him, beyond him, as though *he* were the one who was not real, not flesh. Her face was so instantly familiar to him that he knew this must surely be his mother. Over the years he had tried hard to remember her, but her face had never quite come to him. Yakov had no photographs, no mementos. But somehow, through the years, he must have carried the memory of her face stored like a seed in the dark but fertile soil of his mind. Last night, it had finally blossomed.

He remembered her, and she was beautiful.

That afternoon, the sea turned flat as glass and the sky darkened to the same cold gray as the water. Standing on the deck, looking over the railing, Yakov could not tell where the sea ended and the sky began. They were adrift in a giant gray fishbowl. He'd heard the cook say there was bad weather ahead, that by tomorrow no one would be keeping down much more than bread and soup. Today, though, the sea was calm, the air heavy and metallic with the taste of rain. Yakov was finally able to coax Aleksei from his bunk to go exploring.

The first place Yakov took him was Hell. The engine room. They wandered for a while in the clanking darkness until Aleksei complained the smell of fuel was making him sick. Aleksei had the stomach of a baby—always puking. So Yakov took him up to the bridge, where the captain was too busy to talk to them. So was the navigator. Yakov could not even demonstrate his special status as a regular and accepted visitor.

Next they headed to the galley, but the cook was in a cranky mood and did not offer them even a slice of bread. He had a meal to prepare for the aft passengers, the people no one ever saw. They were a demanding pair, he complained, requiring far too much of his time and attention. He grumbled as he set two glasses and a wine bottle on a tray and slid it into the dumbwaiter. He pressed a button and sent it whirring upward, to their private quarters. Then he turned back to the stove, where a pan was sizzling and pots were steaming. He lifted one of the pot lids, releasing the fragrance of butter and onions. He stirred the contents with a wooden spoon.

"Onions have to be cooked slowly," he said. "It makes them sweet as milk. It takes patience to cook well, but no one has patience these days. Everyone wants things done at once. Stick it in the microwave! Might as well eat old leather." He closed the pot lid, then lifted the lid to the frying pan. Browning inside were six tiny birds, each one no bigger than a boy's fist. "Like morsels from heaven," he said.

"Those are the smallest chickens I've ever seen," marveled Aleksei.

The cook laughed. "They're quail, idiot."

"Why do we never eat quail?"

"Because you're not in the aft cabin." The cook arranged the steaming birds on a platter and drizzled them with chopped parsley. Then he stepped back, his face red and sweating as he admired his creation. "This they cannot complain about," he said, and slid the platter into the dumbwaiter, which by then had returned empty.

"I'm hungry," said Yakov.

"You're always hungry. Go, cut yourself a slice of bread. The loaf is stale, but you can toast it."

The two boys rummaged in drawers for the bread knife. The cook was right; the loaf was dry and stale. Holding down the loaf with the stump of his left arm, Yakov sawed off two slices and carried them across to the toaster.

"Look what you're doing to my floor!" said the cook. "Dropping crumbs all over. Pick them up."

"You pick them up," Yakov told Aleksei.

"You dropped them. I didn't."

"I'm making the toast."

"But I didn't drop the crumbs."

"All right then. I'll just throw away your slice."

"*Someone* pick them up!" roared the cook.

Aleksei instantly dropped to his knees and picked up the crumbs.

Yakov slid the first piece of bread into the toaster. A furry ball of gray suddenly popped out of one of the slots and leaped to the floor.

"A mouse!" shrieked Aleksei. "There's a mouse!"

The gray ball was scampering around Aleksei's dancing feet now, chased in one direction by Yakov, then in the other direction by the cook who threw a pot lid at it for good measure. The mouse skittered halfway up Aleksei's leg, eliciting such a scream of terror it immediately changed course. It dropped back to the floor and shot off, vanishing under a cabinet.

Something was burning on the stove. Cursing, the cook ran to turn off the flame. He cursed some more as he scraped blackened onions from the pot, the onions he'd been so tenderly nursing along in butter. "A mouse in my kitchen! And look at this! Ruined. I'll have to start over again. Bloody fucking mouse."

"He was in the toaster," said Yakov. Suddenly he felt a little sick. He thought about that mouse crawling, scratching around inside.

"Probably left it full of his shit," said the cook. "Bloody mouse."

Yakov cautiously peered into the toaster. No more mice, but lots of mysterious brown specks.

He slid the toaster toward the sink, intending to dump out the crumbs.

The cook gave a shout. "Hey! Are you stupid? What are you doing?"

"I'm cleaning out the toaster."

"There's water in that sink! And look, the thing is still plugged in. If you put that in there and you touch the water, you're dead. Didn't anyone ever teach you that?"

"Uncle Misha never had a toaster."

"It's not just toasters. It's anything that plugs in, anything with an electric cord. You're as stupid as all the others." He waved his arms, shoving them toward the door. "Go on, get out of here, both of you. You're a nuisance."

"But I'm hungry," said Yakov.

"You wait for supper like everyone else." He threw a fresh slab of butter into a saucepan. Glancing at Yakov, he barked: "Go!"

The boys left.

They played on deck for a while, until they grew chilled. They tried the bridge again, but were shooed from there as well. Sheer boredom took them, at last, to the one place in the boat where Yakov knew they would bother no one, and no one would bother them. It was his secret place, and he'd meant to show it to Aleksei only as a reward, and only if Aleksei could manage, for once, not to be a crybaby. He had found it on his third day of exploring, when he had spotted the closed door in the engine room corridor. He had opened that door and found it led to a stairwell shaft.

Wonderland.

The shaft soared three levels. A circular staircase spiraled up and up, and leading off the second level was a flimsy steel walkway that clattered and shook if you jumped up and down on it. The blue door leading aft from the walkway was always kept locked. Yakov had stopped even bothering to try it.

They climbed up to the top level. There, with the floor a dizzying drop below them, it was easy to scare Aleksei with a few noisy jumps.

"Stop it!" Aleksei cried. "You're making it move!"

"That's the ride. The Wonderland ride. Don't you like it?"

"I don't want to take a ride!"

"You never want to do anything." Yakov would have kept jumping up and down, shaking the walkway, but Aleksei was on the verge of hysteria. He had one hand clenched around the railing, the other hugging Shu-Shu.

"I want to go back down," Aleksei whimpered.

"Oh, all right."

They went down the staircase, setting off lovely clatters. At the bottom they played for a while under the steps. Aleksei found some old rope and tied one end to the lowest walkway railing. He used it to swing back and forth like the ape man. It was only a foot off the ground; not very exciting.

Then Yakov showed him the empty crate, the one he'd found shoved into a nook under the stairs. They crawled inside. There they lay in darkness among the wood shavings and listened to the engines rumble in Hell. The sea felt very close here, a great, dark cradle that rocked the hull of the ship.

"This is my secret place," said Yakov. "You can't tell anyone about it. Swear to me you won't tell."

"Why should I? It's a disgusting place. It's cold and wet. And I bet there are mice in here somewhere. We're probably lying right now in mouse shit."

"There's no mouse shit in here."

"How do you know? You can't see anything."

"If you don't like it, you can get out. Go on." Yakov gave him a kick through the wood shavings. Stupid Aleksei. He should have known better than to bring him here. Anyone who carried a filthy stuffed dog everywhere could not be expected to enjoy adventures. "Go on! You're no fun anyway."

"I don't know the way back."

"You think I'm going to show you?"

"You brought me here. You have to bring me back."

"Well I'm not going to."

"You bring me back or I tell everyone about your stupid secret place. Disgusting place, full of mouse shit." Aleksei was climbing out of the crate now, kicking up shavings in Yakov's face. "Bring me back now or—"

"Shut *up,*" said Yakov. He grabbed Aleksei by the shirt and yanked him backward. Both boys tumbled together into the shavings.

"You asshole," said Aleksei.

"Listen. *Listen!*"

"What?"

Somewhere above, a door squealed and clanged shut. The walkway was rattling now, the sound of every footstep shattering to a thousand echoes in the stairway shaft.

Yakov crawled to the opening and peered out of the crate at

the walkway above. Someone was knocking at the blue door. A moment later the door opened, and he caught a glimpse of blond hair as the woman vanished inside. The door closed behind her.

Yakov retreated back into the crate. "It's just Nadiya."

"Is she still out there?"

"No, she went in the blue door."

"What's in there?"

"I don't know."

"I thought you were the great explorer."

"And you're the great asshole." Yakov gave another kick, but only succeeded in tossing up a puff of shavings. "It's always locked. Someone's living in there."

"How do you know?"

"Because Nadiya knocked, and they let her in."

Aleksei retreated deeper into the crate, having changed his mind about venturing out quite yet. He whispered: "It's the quail people."

Yakov thought of the tray with the wine bottle and the two glasses, the onions sizzling in butter, the six tiny birds blanketed in gravy. His stomach suddenly gave a rumble.

"Listen to this," said Yakov. "I can make really sick noises with my stomach." He sucked in and thrust out his belly. Anyone else would have been impressed by the symphony of gurgles.

Aleksei just said, "That's disgusting."

"Everything's disgusting to you. What's wrong with you, anyway?"

"I don't like disgusting things."

"You used to like them."

"Well, I don't anymore."

"It's because of that Nadiya. She's turned you all soft and gooey. You're sweet on her."

"Am not."

"Are too."

"Am *not!*" Aleksei threw a handful of shavings, catching Yakov full in the face. Suddenly both boys were grappling, rolling against one side of the crate, then the other, cursing, kicking. There was not much room to move, so they could not really hurt each other. Then Aleksei lost Shu-Shu somewhere in the shavings and began scrabbling around in the darkness, searching for his dog. Yakov was tired of fighting anyway.

So they both stopped.

For a while they rested side by side, Aleksei clutching Shu-Shu, Yakov trying to coax new and more repulsive sounds from his stomach. Soon he tired of even that. They lay immobilized by boredom, by the sleep-inducing rumble of the engines, and by the sway of the sea.

Aleksei said, "I'm not sweet on her."

"I don't care if you are."

"But the other boys like her. Haven't you noticed how they talk about her?" Aleksei paused. And added: "I like the way she smells. Women smell different. They smell soft."

"Soft doesn't make a smell."

"Yes it does. You smell a woman like that, and you know, when you touch her, she'll be soft. You just know it." Aleksei stroked Shu-Shu. Yakov could hear his hand skimming the tattered fabric.

"My mother smelled that way," said Aleksei.

Yakov remembered his dream. The woman, the smile. The wisp of blond hair tracing across a cheek. Yes, Aleksei was right. In his dream, his mother had indeed worn the scent of softness.

"It sounds stupid," said Aleksei. "But I remember that. Some things I still remember about her."

Yakov stretched, and his feet touched the other end of the crate. Have I grown? he wondered. If only. If only I could grow big enough to kick my feet right through that wall.

"Don't you ever think about your mother?" asked Aleksei.

"No."

"You wouldn't remember her anyway."

"I remember she was a beauty. She had green eyes."

"How would you know? Uncle Misha says you were a baby when she left."

"I was four. That's not a baby."

"I was six when my mother left and I hardly remember anything."

"I'm telling you, she had green eyes."

"So she had green eyes. So what?"

The clang of a door made them both fall silent. Yakov squirmed over to the crate opening and looked up. It was

Nadiya again. She'd just come out of the blue door and was crossing the walkway. She vanished through the forward hatch.

"I don't like her," said Yakov.

"I do. I wish she was *my* mother."

"She doesn't even like children."

"She told Uncle Misha she dedicates her life to us."

"You believe that?"

"Why would she say it if it isn't true?"

Yakov tried to think of an answer, but could not come up with one. Even if he had, it would make no difference to Aleksei. Stupid Aleksei. Stupid everyone. Nadiya had them all fooled. Eleven boys, and each and every one of them was in love with her. They fought to sit beside her at supper. They watched her, studied her, sniffed at her like puppies. At night, in their bunks, they whispered about Nadiya this and Nadiya that. What foods she preferred, what she'd eaten at lunch. They speculated about everything from how old she was to what undergarments she wore under her gray skirts. They discussed whether or not Gregor, whom everyone despised, was her lover, and unanimously decided he was not. They pooled their knowledge about feminine anatomy, the older boys explaining, in lurid detail, the function of tampons and how and where they are inserted, thus transforming forever the way the younger boys would view women—as creatures with dark and mysterious holes. This only increased their fascination with Nadiya.

Yakov shared that fascination, but his was not adoration. He was afraid of her.

It was all because of the blood tests.

On their fourth day at sea, when the boys were still puking and moaning in their bunks, Gregor and Nadiya had come around carrying a tray of needles and tubes. It will be only a small prick, they'd said, a small tube of blood to confirm you are healthy. No one will adopt you if they cannot be assured you are healthy. The pair had moved from boy to boy, weaving a bit from the rough sea, the glass tubes clattering on the tray. Nadiya had looked sick, on the verge of throwing up. Gregor had been the one to draw the blood. At each bunk they'd asked the boy his name and fitted him with a plastic bracelet on which they'd written a number. Then Gregor tied a giant rubber band around the boy's arm and slapped the skin a few times, to make the vein swell. Some of the boys cried, and Nadiya had to hold their hand and comfort them while Gregor drew the blood.

Yakov was the only boy whom she was unable to comfort. No matter how she tried, she could not make him hold still. He did not want that needle in his arm, and he had given Gregor a kick to emphasize the point. That's when the real Nadiya took over. She pinned Yakov's one arm to the bed, holding it there with a grasp that pinched and twisted at the same time. As Gregor drew the blood, she had kept her gaze fixed on Yakov, had spoken quietly, even sweetly to him as the needle pierced his skin and the blood streamed into the tube. Everyone else in that room, listening to Nadiya's voice, heard only murmured words of reassurance. But Yakov, staring into those pale eyes of hers, saw something entirely different.

Afterward, he had gnawed off his plastic bracelet.

Aleksei still wore his. Number 307. His certification of good health.

"Do you think she has children of her own?" asked Aleksei.

Yakov gave a shudder. "I hope not," he said, and crawled to the crate opening. He looked up and saw the deserted walkway and the empty stairway, coiling above like a serpent's skeleton. The blue door, as always, was shut.

Brushing off the wood shavings, he scrambled out of their hiding place. "I'm hungry," he said.

As the cook had predicted, that gray and oppressive afternoon was soon followed by heavy seas—not a severe storm, but rough enough to confine the passengers, both children and adults, to their cabins. And that was precisely where Aleksei intended to stay. All the coaxing in the world would not budge him from his bunk. It was cold and wet outside, and the floor was rocking, and he had no interest in poking around the dark, damp corners that seemed to fascinate Yakov so. Aleksei liked it in his bed. He liked the coziness of a blanket pulled up around his shoulders, liked the drafts of warmth that puffed at his face when he turned or wiggled, liked the smell of Shu-Shu sleeping beside him on the pillow.

All morning, Yakov tried to drag Aleksei out of bed, to tempt him with another visit to Wonderland. Finally he gave up and went off on his own. He came back once or twice to see if

Aleksei had changed his mind, but Aleksei slept all afternoon, through supper, and straight into the evening.

In the night, Yakov awakened and sensed at once that something was different. At first he could not decide what it was. Perhaps just the passing of the storm? He could feel the ship had steadied. Then he realized it was the engines that had changed. That ceaseless rumble had muffled to a soft growl.

He crawled out of his bunk and went to give Aleksei a shake. "Wake up," he whispered.

"Go away."

"Listen. We've stopped moving."

"I don't care."

"I'm going up to take a look. Come with me."

"I'm sleeping."

"You've been sleeping a whole day and night. Don't you want to see land? We must be near land. Why would the ship stop in the middle of the ocean?" Yakov bent closer to Aleksei, his whispers softly enticing. "Maybe we can see the lights. America. You'll miss it unless you come with me."

Aleksei sighed, stirred a bit, not quite certain what he wanted to do.

Yakov threw out the ultimate lure. "I saved a potato from supper," he said. "I'll give it to you. But only if you come up with me."

Aleksei had missed supper, and lunch as well. A potato would be heaven. "All right, all right." Aleksei sat up and began buckling on his shoes. "Where's the potato?"

"First we go up."

"You're an asshole, Yakov."

They tiptoed past the double bunks of sleeping boys and climbed the stairway, to the deck.

Outside, a soft wind was blowing. They looked over the railing, straining for a view of city lights, but the stars met only a black and formless horizon.

"I don't see anything," said Aleksei. "Give me my potato."

Yakov produced the treasure from his pocket. Aleksei squatted down and devoured it right there, cold, like a wild animal.

Yakov turned and looked up toward the bridge. He could see the greenish glow of the radar screen through the window, and the silhouette of a man standing watch. The navigator. What did he see from that lonely perch of his?

Aleksei had finished his potato. Now he stood up and said: "I'm going to bed."

"We can look for more food in the galley."

"I don't want to see another mouse." Aleksei began to feel his way across the deck. "Besides, I'm cold."

"I'm not cold."

"Then *you* stay out here."

They had just reached the stairway when they heard a series of sharp thuds. Suddenly the deck was ablaze with light. Both boys froze, blinking at the unexpected glare.

Yakov grabbed Aleksei's hand and tugged him under the bridge stairway, where they crouched, peering out between the steps. They heard voices and saw two men walk into the circle of floodlights. Both men were wearing white overalls. Together they bent down and gave something a tug. There was a scrape of metal as some kind of cover was forced aside. It revealed a new light, this one blue. It shone at the center of the floodlit circle, like the forbidding iris of an eye.

"Bloody mechanics," one of the men said. "They'll never get this repaired."

Both men straightened and looked up at the sky. Toward the distant growl of thunder.

Yakov, too, looked up. The thunder was moving closer. No longer just a growl, it deepened to a rhythmic *whup-whup*. The two men retreated from the floodlights. The sound drew right overhead, churning the night like a tornado.

Aleksei clapped his hands over his ears and shrank deeper into the shadows. Yakov did not. He watched, unflinching, as the helicopter descended into the wash of light and touched down on the deck.

One of the men in overalls reappeared, running bent at the waist. He swung open the helicopter door. Yakov could not see what was inside; the stairway post was blocking his direct view. He eased out from the shadows, moving out onto the deck just far enough to see around the post. He caught a glimpse of the pilot and one passenger—a man.

"Hey!" came a shout from overhead. "You! Boy!"

Yakov glanced straight up and saw the navigator peering down at him from the bridge deck.

"What are you doing down there? You come up here right now, before you get hurt! Come on!"

The man in overalls had spotted the boys too, and was crossing toward them. He did not look pleased.

Yakov scurried up the stairway. Aleksei, in a panic, was right on his heels.

"Don't you know enough to stay off the main deck when a chopper's landing?" yelled the navigator. He gave Aleksei a whack on the rump and pulled them inside, into the wheelhouse. He pointed to two chairs. "Sit. Both of you."

"We were just watching," said Yakov.

"You two are supposed to be in bed."

"I *was* in bed," whimpered Aleksei. "He made me come out."

"Do you know what a chopper rotor can do to a boy's head? Do you?" The navigator slashed a hand across Aleksei's skinny neck. "Just like that. Your head goes flying straight off. And blood shoots everywhere. Quite spectacular. You think I'm joking, don't you? Believe me, I don't go down there when the chopper comes. I stay the hell away. But if you want your stupid heads sliced off, be my guests. Go on."

Aleksei sobbed, "I *wanted* to stay in bed!"

The roar of the helicopter made them all turn to look. They watched as it lifted into the sky, the rotor wash whipping the overalls of the two men standing on deck. It make a slow ninety-degree turn, then veered off, to be swallowed by the night. Only a soft rumble lingered, fading away like retreating thunder.

"Where does it go?" asked Yakov.

"You think they tell me?" said the navigator. "They just call me when it's coming in for a pickup and I turn the bow into the wind. That's all." He reached for one of the panel switches and flicked it.

The floodlights were instantly extinguished. The main deck vanished into darkness.

Yakov pressed close to the bridge window. The chopper rumble was gone now. In every direction stretched the blackness of the sea.

Aleksei was still crying.

"Stop it now," said the navigator. He gave Aleksei a scolding slap on the shoulder. "A boy your age, acting like a woman."

"But what does it come for? The helicopter?" asked Yakov.

"I told you. A pickup."

"What does it pick up?"

"I don't ask. I just do what they tell me."

"Who?"

"The passengers in the aft cabin." He tugged Yakov away from the window and gave him a push toward the door. "Go back to your bunks. Can't you see I have work to do?"

Yakov was following Aleksei to the door when his gaze lit on the radar screen. So many times before, he'd stared at that screen, transfixed by the hypnotic sweep of the line tracing its three-hundred-sixty-degree arc. Now he stood before it again, watching the line circle around and around. He saw it at once, a small white sliver at the edge of the screen.

"Is it another ship?" Yakov asked. "There, on the radar." He pointed to the sliver, which suddenly pulsed whiter as the line swept over it.

"What else would it be? Get out of here."

The boys went outside and clattered down the bridge stairway to the main deck. Yakov glanced up and saw, against the green glow of the bridge window, the navigator's silhouette. Watching. Always watching.

And he said: "Now I know where the helicopter goes."

Pyotr and Valentin were not at breakfast. By then the news of their departure during the night had already spread to Yakov's cabin, so when he sat down at the table that morning and faced the row of boys sitting across from him, he knew the reason for their silence. They did not understand, any of them, why Pyotr and Valentin should be the first to leave the ship, the first to be chosen. Pyotr, they'd all thought from the start, would be among the leftovers, or would be consigned to some unlikely family who favored idiot children. Valentin, who'd joined the group in Riga, had been clever enough, handsome enough, but he had a secret perversion known to the younger boys. After the lights went out at night, he would crawl into their bunks without his underwear, would whisper: "Feel that? Feel how big I am?" And he would grab their hands and force them to touch him.

But Valentin was gone now, he and Pyotr. Gone to new parents who'd chosen them, Nadiya said.

The rest of them were the leftovers.

In the afternoon, Yakov and Aleksei climbed to the deck and stretched out on the spot where the helicopter had landed. They lay gazing up at the hard blue glare of the sky. No clouds, no helicopters. The deck was warm and, like two kittens on a radiator, they began to feel drowsy.

"I've been thinking," said Yakov, his eyes closed against the sun. "If my mother is alive, I don't want to be adopted."

"She's not."

"She could be."

"Why didn't she come back for you, then?"

"Maybe she's looking for me right now. And here I am, in the middle of the sea where no one can find me. Except with radar. I'm going to tell Nadiya to take me back. I don't want a new mother."

"I do," said Aleksei. He was quiet for a moment. Then he said, "Do you think there's something wrong with me?"

Yakov laughed. "You mean besides the fact you're retarded?"

When Aleksei didn't answer, Yakov squinted up at his friend and was puzzled to see the boy had his hands over his face, and his shoulders were shaking.

"Hey," said Yakov. "Are you crying?"

"No."

"You are, aren't you?"

"No."

"You're such a baby. I didn't mean it. You're not retarded."

Aleksei had folded into a ball of arms and legs. He was crying all right. Though he didn't make a sound, Yakov could see his chest spasmodically sucking in gulps of air. Yakov didn't know what to make of this or what to say. A fresh insult was what automatically came to mind. *Stupid girl. Crybaby.* But then he thought better of it. He had never seen Aleksei this way, and he felt a little guilty, a little scared. It was just a joke. Why couldn't Aleksei see it was a joke?

"Let's go down and swing on the rope," said Yakov. He gave Aleksei a poke in the ribs.

Aleksei lashed back with an angry shove and jumped up, his face red and wet.

"What's the matter with you anyway?" said Yakov.

"Why did they choose that stupid Pyotr instead of me?"

"They didn't choose me either," said Yakov.

"But there's nothing wrong with *me!*" cried Aleksei. He ran from the deck.

Yakov sat very still. He looked down at the stump of his left arm. And he said, "There's nothing wrong with me either."

"Knight to bishop three," said Koubichev, the engineer.

"You always do that. Don't you ever try anything new?"

"I believe in the tried and true. It's beaten you every time. Your move. Don't take all day."

Yakov rotated the chessboard and studied it first from one angle, then another. He got on his knees and peered down the row of pawns. Imagined black-armored soldiers standing in formation, awaiting orders.

"What the hell are you doing now?" said Koubichev.

"Did you ever notice the queen has a beard?"

"What?"

"She has a beard. Look."

Koubichev grunted. "That's just her neck ruffle. Now will you make your move?"

Yakov set the queen back on the board and reached for a knight. He set it down, picked it up. Set it down in a different place and again picked it up. All around them rumbled the engines of Hell.

Koubichev was no longer watching. He'd opened a magazine and was flipping through the pages, eyeing a succession of glamorous faces. The one hundred most beautiful women in America. Every so often he'd grunt and say, "You call *that* beautiful?" or "I wouldn't let my dog fuck that one."

Yakov picked up the queen again and set her down on bishop four. "There."

Koubichev regarded Yakov's latest move with a snort. "Why do you always repeat the same mistake? Moving your queen out too early?" He tossed the magazine down and leaned forward to move his pawn. That's when Yakov spotted the face on the magazine page. It was a woman. Blond hair, with one wisp curling over the cheek. A melancholy smile. Eyes that seemed to be gazing not at you, but beyond you.

"It's my mother," said Yakov.

"What?"

"It's her. It's my *mother!*" He lunged for the magazine, knocking against the crate that served for a table. The chessboard toppled. Pawns and bishops and knights flew in every direction.

Koubichev snatched the magazine out of reach. "What the hell is wrong with you?"

"Give it to me!" screamed Yakov. He was clawing at the man's arm now, frantic to claim his mother's photo. "Give it!"

"You crazy boy, it's not your mother!"

"It is! I remember her face! She looked like that, just like that!"

"Stop scratching me. Get away, do you hear?"

"Give it to me!"

"All right, all right. Here, I'll show you. It's not your mother." Koubichev slapped the magazine down on the crate. "See?"

Yakov stared at the face. Every detail was exactly as he'd dreamed it. The way the head was tilted, the way her skin dimpled near the corners of her mouth. Even the way the light fell on her hair. He said, "It's her. I've seen her face."

"Everyone's seen her face." Koubichev pointed to the name on the photo. "Michelle Pfeiffer. She's an actress. American. Not even the name is Russian."

"But I know her! I had a dream about her!"

Koubichev laughed. "You and every other horny boy." He glanced around at the scattered chess pieces. "Look at this mess. We'll be lucky to find all the pawns. Come on, you knocked it over. Now pick them up."

Yakov didn't move. He stood staring at the woman, remembering the way she had smiled at him.

Koubichev, grumbling, dropped to his hands and knees and began to crawl about, retrieving chess pieces from underneath machinery. "You've probably seen her face somewhere. The TV, or maybe some magazine, and you forgot about it. Then you have a dream about her, that's all." He set two bishops and a queen on the board, then heaved himself back onto the chair. His face was flushed, his barrel chest panting heavily. He tapped his head. "The brain is a mysterious thing. It takes real life and spins it into dreams, and we can't tell what's made up and what's real. Sometimes I have this dream where I'm sitting at a table with all this wonderful food, everything I could want to eat. Then I wake up and I'm still on this fucking boat.'' He reached for the magazine and tore out the page with Michelle Pfeiffer. ''Here. It's yours.''

Yakov took the page but didn't say anything. He just held it. Looked at it.

''If you want to pretend that's your mother, go ahead. A boy could do worse. Now pick up the pieces. Hey! Hey, boy! Where do you think you're going?''

Yakov, still clutching the page, fled Hell.

Up on deck he stood at the rail, his face to the sea. The page was wrinkled now, flapping and crackling in the wind. He looked at it, saw that he'd been holding it so tightly a crease now cut across those half-smiling lips.

He grasped one corner with his teeth and ripped the page in two. It was not enough. Not enough. He was breathing hard, close to crying, but no sound came out. He ripped the page again and again, using his teeth like an animal tearing at real flesh, letting the pieces fly off into the wind.

When he'd finished, he was still holding on to one scrap of the page. It was an eye. Just beneath it, pinched by his fingers, was a star-shaped crease. Like the sparkle of a single teardrop.

He threw the scrap over the rail and watched it flutter away and fall into the sea.

15

She was in her late forties, with the thin, dry face of a woman who had long ago lost her estrogenic glow. In Bernard Katzka's opinion, that alone did not make a woman unattractive. A woman's appeal lay not in the luster of her skin and hair, but in what was revealed by her eyes. In that regard, he had met a number of fascinating seventy-year-olds, among them his maiden aunt Margaret, whom he'd grown particularly close to since Annie's death. That Katzka actually looked forward to his weekly coffee chats with Aunt Margaret would probably bewilder his partner, Lundquist. Lundquist was of the masculine school that believed women were not worth a second glance once they'd crossed the menopausal finish line. No doubt it was all rooted in biology. Males mustn't waste their energy or sperm on a nonreproductive female. No wonder Lundquist had looked so relieved when Katzka agreed to interview Brenda Hainey. Lundquist considered postmenopausal women to be Bernard Katzka's forte, by which he meant Katzka was the one detective in Homicide who had the patience and fortitude to hear them out.

And this was precisely what Katzka had been doing for the last fifteen minutes, listening patiently to Brenda Hainey's bizarre charges. She was not easy to follow. The woman mingled the mystical with the concrete, in the same breath telling him

193

about signs from heaven and syringes of morphine. He might have been amused by the quirky nature of this encounter if the woman had been likable, but Brenda Hainey was not. There was no warmth in her blue eyes. She was angry, and angry people were not attractive.

"I've spoken to the hospital about this," she said. "I went straight to their president, Mr. Parr. He promised he'd investigate, but that was five days ago, and so far I've heard nothing. I call every day. His office tells me they're still looking into it. Well, today I decided enough was enough. So I called your people. And *they* tried to put me off too, tried to make me talk to some rookie police officer first. Well I believe in going straight to the highest authority. I do it all the time, every morning when I pray. In this case, the highest authority would be *you*."

Katzka suppressed a smile.

"I've seen your name in the newspaper," Brenda said. "In connection with that dead doctor from Bayside."

"You're referring to Dr. Levi?"

"Yes. I thought, since you already know about the goings-on in that hospital, you're the one I should speak to."

Katzka almost sighed, but caught himself. He knew she would take it for what it was, an expression of weariness. He said, "May I see the note?"

She pulled a folded paper from her purse and handed it to him. It had one typewritten line: *Your aunt did not die a natural death. A friend.*

"Was there an envelope?"

This, too, she produced. On it was typed the name *Brenda Hainey*. The flap had been sealed, then torn open.

"Do you know who might have sent this?" he asked.

"I have no idea. Maybe one of the nurses. Someone who knew enough to tell me."

"You say your aunt had terminal cancer. She could have died of natural causes."

"Then why send me that note? Someone knew differently. Someone wants this looked into. *I* want it looked into."

"Where is your aunt's body now?"

"Garden of Peace Mortuary. The hospital shipped it out pretty quick, if you ask me."

"Whose decision was that? It must have been next of kin."

"My aunt left instructions before she died. That's what the hospital told me, anyway."

"Have you spoken to your aunt's doctors? Perhaps they can clear this up."

"I'd prefer not to speak to them."

"Why not?"

"Given the situation, I'm not sure I trust them."

"I see." Now Katzka did sigh. He picked up his pen and flipped to a fresh page in his notebook. "Why don't you give me the names of all your aunt's doctors."

"The physician in charge was Dr. Colin Wettig. But the one who really seemed to be making all the decisions was that resident of his. I think she's the one you should look at."

"Her name?"

"Dr. DiMatteo."

Katzka glanced up in surprise. "Abigail DiMatteo?"

There was a brief silence. Katzka could see consternation clearly written on Brenda's face.

She said, cautiously, "You know her."

"I've spoken to her. On another matter."

"It won't affect your judgment on this case, will it?"

"Not at all."

"Are you certain?" She challenged him with a gaze he found irritating. He was not easily irritated, and he had to ask himself now why this woman so annoyed him.

Lundquist chose that moment to walk past the desk, and he flashed what could only be characterized as a sympathetic smirk. Lundquist should have interviewed this woman. It would have been good for him, an exercise in polite restraint, which Lundquist needed to develop.

Katzka said: "I always try to be objective, Miss Hainey."

"Then you should take a close look at Dr. DiMatteo."

"Why her in particular?"

"She's the one who wanted my aunt dead."

Brenda's charges struck Katzka as improbable. Still, there was the matter of that note and who had sent it. One possibility was that Brenda had sent it to herself; stranger things had been done by people hungry for attention. That was easier for him to believe than what she was claiming had happened: that Mary Allen had been murdered by her doctors. Katzka had spent weeks watching his wife slowly die in the hospital, so he was well acquainted with cancer wards. He had witnessed the compassion of nurses, the dedication of oncologists. They knew when to keep fighting for a patient's life. They also knew when the fight was lost, when the suffering outweighed the benefits of one more day, one more week, of life. There had been times toward the end when Katzka had wanted desperately to ease Annie across the final threshold. Had the doctors suggested such a move, he would have agreed to it. But they never had. Cancer killed quickly enough; which doctor would risk his professional future to hurry along a patient's death? Even if Mary Allen's doctors had made such a move, could one truly consider it homicide?

It was with reluctance that he drove to Bayside Hospital that afternoon after Brenda Hainey's visit. He was obligated to make a few inquiries. At the hospital's public information office, he confirmed that Mary Allen had indeed expired on the date Brenda said she had, and that the diagnosis had been undifferentiated metastatic carcinoma. The clerk could give him no other information. Dr. Wettig, the attending, was in surgery and unavailable for the afternoon. So Katzka picked up the phone and paged Abby DiMatteo.

A moment later she called back.

"This is Detective Katzka," he said. "We spoke last week."

"Yes, I remember."

"I have some questions on an unrelated matter. Where can I meet you?"

"I'm in the medical library. Is this going to take a long time?"

"It shouldn't."

He heard a sigh. Then a reluctant: "Okay. The library's on the second floor, administrative wing."

In Katzka's experience, the average person—provided he or she was not a suspect—enjoyed talking to homicide cops. People were curious about murder, about police work. He'd been astonished by the questions they asked *him,* even the sweetest-faced old ladies, everyone longing to hear the details, the bloodier the better. Dr. DiMatteo, however, had sounded genuinely unwilling to speak to him. He wondered why.

He found the hospital library tucked between data processing and the financial office. Inside were a few aisles of bookshelves, a librarian's desk, and a half dozen study carrels along one wall. Dr. DiMatteo was standing beside the photocopier, positioning a surgical journal on the plate. She'd already collated a number of papers into piles, and had stacked them on a nearby desk. It surprised him to see her performing such a clerical task. He was also surprised to see her dressed in a skirt and blouse rather than the scrub clothes he'd assumed was the uniform of all surgical residents. From the first day he'd met Abby DiMatteo, he'd thought her an attractive woman. Now, seeing her in a flattering skirt, with all that black hair hanging loose about her shoulders, he decided she was really quite stunning.

She looked up and gave a nod. That's when he noticed something else different about her today. She seemed nervous, even a little wary.

"I'm almost finished," she said. "I have one more article to copy."

"Not on duty today?"

"Excuse me?"

"I thought surgeons lived in scrub suits."

She placed another page on the Xerox machine and hit the Copy button. "I'm not scheduled for the OR today. So I'm doing a literature search. Dr. Wettig needs these for a conference." She stared down at the copier, as though the flashing light, the machine's whir, required all her concentration. When the last pages rolled out, she took them to the table, where the other stacks lay waiting, and sat down. He pulled out the chair across from her. She picked up a stapler, then set it back down again.

Still not looking at him, she asked: "Have there been new developments?"

"In regard to Dr. Levi, no."

"I wish I could think of something new to tell you. But I can't." She gathered up a few pages and stapled them together with a sharp snap of the wrist.

"I'm not here about Dr. Levi," he said. "This is about a different matter. A patient of yours."

"Oh?" She picked up another stack of papers and slid it between the stapler teeth. "Which patient are we talking about?"

"A Mrs. Mary Allen."

Her hand paused for a second in midair. Then it came down, hard, on the stapler.

"Do you remember her?" he asked.

"Yes."

"I understand she died last week. Here, at Bayside."

"That's right."

"Can you confirm that her diagnosis was metastatic undifferentiated carcinoma?"

"Yes."

"And was she in the terminal stages?"

"Yes."

"Then her death was expected?"

There was a hesitation. It was just long enough to notch up his alertness.

She said, slowly, "I would say it was expected."

He was watching her more closely, and she seemed to know it. He didn't say anything for a moment. Silence, in his experience, was far more unnerving. Quietly he asked: "Was her death in any way unusual?"

At last she looked up at him. He realized she was sitting absolutely still. Almost rigid.

"In what way unusual?" she asked.

"The circumstances. The manner in which she expired."

"Can I ask why you're pursuing this?"

"A relative of Mrs. Allen's came to us with some concerns."

"Are we talking about Brenda Hainey? The niece?"

"Yes. She thinks her aunt died of causes unrelated to her disease."

"And you're trying to turn this into a homicide?"

"I'm trying to determine if there's anything worth investigating. Is there?"

She didn't answer.

"Brenda Hainey received an anonymous note. It claimed that Mary Allen didn't die of natural causes. Do you have any reason, any reason at all, to think there might be substance to that?"

He could have predicted several likely responses. She might have laughed and said this was all ridiculous. She might have told him that Brenda Hainey was crazy. Or she might show puzzlement, even a flash of anger, that she was being subjected to these questions. Any one of those reactions would have been appropriate. What he did not expect was her actual response.

She stared at him with a face suddenly drained white. And she said softly: "I refuse to answer any more questions, Detective Katzka."

Seconds after the policeman left the library, Abby reached in panic for the nearest telephone and paged Mark. To her relief, he immediately answered her call.

"That detective was here again," she whispered. "Mark, they know about Mary Allen. Brenda's been talking to them. And this cop's asking questions about how she died."

"You didn't tell him anything, did you?"

"No, I—" She took a deep breath. The sigh that followed was close to a sob. "I didn't know what to say. Mark, I think I gave it away. I'm scared and I think he knows it."

"Abby, listen. This is important. You didn't tell him about the morphine in your locker, did you?"

"I wanted to. Jesus, Mark, I was ready to spill my guts. Maybe I should. If I just came out and told him everything—"

"*Don't.*"

"Isn't it better to just tell him? He'll find out anyway. Sooner or later, he'll dig it all up. I'm sure he will." She let out another breath, and felt the first flash of tears sting her eyes. She was going to be sobbing in a minute, right here in the library, where anyone could see her. "I don't see any way around it. I have to go to the police."

"What if they don't believe you? They take one look at the circumstantial evidence, that morphine in your locker, and they'll jump to the obvious conclusion."

"So what am I supposed to do? Wait for them to arrest me? I can't stand this. I can't." Her voice faltered. In a whisper she repeated, "I can't."

"So far the police have nothing. I won't tell them a thing. Neither will Wettig or Parr, I'm sure of it. They don't want this out in the open any more than you do. Just hold on, Abby. Wettig's doing everything he can to get you reinstated."

It took her a moment to regain her composure. When at last she spoke again, her voice was quiet but steady. "Mark, what if Mary Allen *was* murdered? Then there *should* be an investigation. We should bring this to the police ourselves."

"Is that what you really want to do?"

"I don't know. I keep thinking it's what we *ought* to do. That we're obligated. Morally and ethically."

"It's your decision. But I want you to think long and hard about the consequences."

She already had. She'd thought about the publicity. The possibility of arrest. She'd gone back and forth on this, knowing what she *should* do, yet afraid to take action. *I'm a coward. My patient's dead, maybe murdered, and all I can worry about is saving my own goddamn skin.*

The hospital librarian walked into the room, wheeling a squeaky cart of books. She sat down at her desk and began stamping the inside covers. *Whap. Whap.*

"Abby," said Mark. "Before you do anything, *think.*"

"I'll talk to you later. I've got to go now." She hung up and went back to the table, where she sat down and stared at the stack of photocopied journal articles. This was the extent of her work today. This was what she'd spent all morning doing, collecting this pile of paper. She was a physician who could no longer practice, a surgeon banished from the OR. The nurses and house staff didn't know what to make of it all. She was sure the rumors were already swirling thick and furious. This morning, when she'd walked through the wards looking for Dr. Wettig, the nurses had all turned to look at her. What are they saying behind my back? she wondered.

She was afraid to find out.

The *whap, whap* had ceased. She realized the librarian had stopped stamping her book covers and was now eyeing Abby. *Like everyone else in this hospital, she, too, is wondering about me.*

Flushing, Abby gathered up her papers and carried them to the librarian's desk.

"How many copies?"

"They're all for Dr. Wettig. You can charge them to the residency office."

"I need to know the exact count for the copier log. It's our standing policy."

Abby set the stack of papers down and began counting pages. She should have known the librarian would insist. This woman had been at Bayside forever, and she'd never failed to inform each new crop of interns that, in this room, things were done *her* way. Abby was getting angry now, at this librarian, at the hospital, at the mess her life had become. She finished counting the last article.

"Two hundred fourteen pages," she said, and slapped it down on the pile. The name *Aaron Levi, M.D.*, seemed to jump out at her from the top page. The article's title was "Comparison of Cardiac Transplant Survival Rates Between Critically Ill and Outpatient Recipients." The authors were Aaron, Rajiv Mohandas, and Lawrence Kunstler. She stared at Aaron's name, shaken by the unexpected reminder of his death.

The librarian, too, noticed Aaron's name and she shook her head. "It's hard to believe Dr. Levi's gone."

"I know what you mean," Abby murmured.

"And to see both those names on the same article." The woman shook her head.

"Excuse me?"

"Dr. Kunstler and Dr. Levi."

"I'm afraid I don't know Dr. Kunstler."

"Oh, he was here before you came." The librarian closed the copier log and primly slid it back onto her bookshelf. "It must have happened six years ago, at least."

"What happened six years ago?"

"It was just like that Charles Stuart case. You know, the man who jumped off the Tobin Bridge. That's where Dr. Kunstler jumped."

Abby focused again on the article. On the two names at the top of the page. "He killed himself?"

The librarian nodded. "Just like Dr. Levi."

The clatter of Mah-Jongg tiles being stirred on the dining table was too loud to talk over. Vivian shut the kitchen door and went back to the sink, where she'd set the colander of bean sprouts. She resumed snapping off the shriveled tails and throwing the tops into a bowl. Abby didn't know anyone bothered to snap off bean sprout roots. Only the goddamn nitpicky Chinese, Vivian told her. The Chinese spent hours laboring over some dish that's devoured in minutes. And who noticed the tails, anyway? Vivian's grandmother did. And her grandmother's friends did. Put a dish of bean sprouts with the tails still attached in front of those ladies, and they'd all wrinkle their noses. So here was the obedient granddaughter, the gifted surgeon soon to be opening her own practice, concentrating on the weighty task of snapping sprouts. She did it swiftly, efficiently, every movement vintage Vivian. The whole time she listened to Abby's story, those graceful hands of hers never fell still.

"Jesus," Vivian kept murmuring. "Jesus, you are screwed."

In the next room the clatter of tiles had stopped, the new round of play begun. Every so often, through the buzz of gossip, there'd be a clunk as someone tossed a tile into the center.

"What do you think I should do?" said Abby.

"Either way, DiMatteo, he's got you."

"That's why I'm talking to *you*. You've been screwed by Victor Voss. You know what he's capable of."

"Yeah." Vivian sighed. "I know too well."

"Do you think I should go to the police? Or should I ride this out and hope they don't dig any deeper?"

"What does Mark think?"

"He thinks I should keep my mouth shut."

"I agree with him. Call it my inherent distrust of authority. You must have more faith in the police than I do, if you're thinking of turning yourself in and hoping for the best." Vivian reached for a dish towel and dried her hands. She looked at Abby. "Do you really think your patient was murdered?"

"How else do I explain that morphine level?"

"She was already getting it. And probably tolerant enough to need sky-high levels just to stay comfortable. Maybe the doses finally accumulated."

"Only if she got an extra dose. Accidentally or intentionally."

"Just to set you up?"

"No one ever checks morphine levels on terminal cancer patients! Someone wanted to make sure her murder didn't slip by unnoticed. Someone who knew it *was* murder. And sent that note to Brenda Hainey."

"How do we know Victor Voss did it?"

"He's the one who wants me out of Bayside."

"Is he the only one?"

Abby stared at Vivian. And wondered: *Who else wants me out?*

In the dining room, the thunderous clatter of mah-jongg tiles signaled the end of another round. The noise startled Abby. She began to pace the kitchen. Past the rice cooker burbling on the counter, past the stove where steam wafted, spicy and exotic, from cooking pots. "This is crazy. I can't believe anyone else would do this, just to get me fired."

"Jeremiah Parr's got his own neck to save. And Voss is probably breathing down it right this minute. Think about it. The hospital board is packed with Voss's rich buddies. They could have Parr fired. Unless he fires *you* first. Hey, you're not paranoid, DiMatteo. People really *are* out to get you."

Abby sank into a chair at the kitchen table. The noise from the game in the next room was giving her a headache. That and all the old-lady chatter. This house was full of noise, visitors talking Cantonese at a near shout, friendly conversation raised to argument pitch. How could Vivian stand having her grandmother live with her? The din alone would drive Abby crazy.

"It still all comes back to Victor Voss," said Abby. "One way or the other, he'll have his revenge."

"Then why did he drop those lawsuits? That part doesn't make sense. He sends steamrollers coming right at you. Then suddenly, they all stop."

"Instead of being sued by everyone, I'm accused of murder. What a wonderful alternative."

"But you do see that it doesn't make sense? Voss probably paid a lot to get those lawsuits rolling. He wouldn't just drop them. Not unless he was concerned about some possible consequence. A countersuit, for instance. Were you planning something like that?"

"I discussed it with my lawyer, but he advised against it."

"So why *did* Voss drop the lawsuits?"

It didn't make sense to Abby, either.

She considered that question all the way home, driving back from Vivian's house in Melrose. It was late afternoon, and the traffic was heavy as usual on Route 1. Though it was drizzling outside, she kept her window open. The stench of rotting pig organs still lingered in her car. She didn't think the smell would ever disappear. It would always linger, a permanent reminder of Victor Voss's rage.

The Tobin Bridge was coming up—the place where Lawrence Kunstler had chosen to end his life. She slowed down. Perhaps it was a morbid compulsion that made her glance sideways, toward the water, as she drove onto the bridge. Under dreary skies, the river looked black, its surface stippled by wind. Drowning was not a death she would choose. The panic, the thrashing limbs. Throat closing against the rush of cold water. She wondered if Kunstler had been conscious after he hit the water. Or whether he had struggled against the current. She wondered, too, about Aaron. Two doctors, two suicides. She'd forgotten to ask Vivian about Kunstler. If he had died only six years ago, Vivian might have heard of him.

Abby's gaze was so drawn to the water, she didn't notice that the car in front of her had slowed down, that traffic had backed up from the toll booth. When she glanced up at the road, she saw that the car in front was stopped dead.

Abby slammed on the brakes. An instant later, she was jolted by a rear-end thump. She glanced in the mirror and saw the woman behind her shaking her head apologetically. For the moment, traffic on the bridge was going nowhere. Abby stepped out of her car and ran back to survey the damage.

The other woman got out as well. She stood by nervously as Abby inspected the rear bumper.

"It looks okay," said Abby. "No harm done."

"I'm sorry, I guess I wasn't paying attention."

Abby glanced at the woman's car, and saw that her front bumper was equally undamaged.

"This is embarrassing," the woman said. "I was so busy watching that tailgater behind me." She pointed at a maroon van idling behind her car. "Then *I* go and bump someone."

A horn honked. Traffic was moving again. Abby returned to her car and continued across. As she drove past the toll booth, she couldn't help one last backward glance at the bridge, where Lawrence Kunstler had made his fatal leap. *They knew each other, Aaron and Kunstler. They worked together. They wrote that article together.*

That thought kept going around in her mind as she navigated the streets back to Cambridge.

Two doctors on the same transplant team. And both of them commit suicide.

She wondered if Kunstler had left a widow. Wondered if Mrs. Kunstler had been just as bewildered as Elaine Levi was.

She looped around the Harvard Common. As she veered off onto Brattle Street, she happened to glance in the rearview mirror.

A maroon van was behind her. It, too, drove onto Brattle.

She drove another block, past Willard Street, and looked again at the mirror. The van was still there. Was it the tailgater from the bridge? She hadn't given that van more than a glance at the time, and all she'd taken in was its color. She didn't know why seeing it now made her feel uneasy. Maybe it was that recent crossing of the bridge, and that glimpse of the water. The reminder of Kunstler's death. Of Aaron's death.

On impulse, she turned left, onto Mercer.

So did the van.

She turned left again, onto Camden, then right onto Auburn. She kept glancing in the mirror, waiting for, almost expecting, the van to come into view. Only when she'd reached Brattle Street again, and the van hadn't reappeared, did she allow herself a sigh of relief. What a nervous Nellie.

She drove straight home and pulled into the driveway. Mark wasn't back yet. That didn't surprise her. Despite drizzly skies, he'd planned to take *Gimme Shelter* out for another round-the-buoy race against Archer. Bad weather, he'd told her, was no excuse not to sail, and short of a hurricane, the race would go on.

She stepped into the house. It was gloomy inside, the afternoon light gray and watery through the windows. She crossed to the tabletop lamp and was about to switch it on when she heard the low growl of a car on Brewster Street. She looked out the window.

A maroon van was moving past the house. As it approached her driveway, it slowed to a crawl, as though the driver was taking a long, careful look at Abby's car.

Lock the doors. Lock the doors.

She ran to the front door, turned the dead bolt, and slid the chain into place.

The back door. Was it locked?

She ran down the hall and through the kitchen. No dead bolt, just a button lock. She grabbed a chair and slid it against the door, propping it under the knob.

She ran back to the living room and, standing behind the curtain, she peeked outside.

The van was gone.

She looked in both directions, straining for a view toward each corner, but saw only empty street, slick with drizzle.

She left the curtains open and the lights off. Sitting in the dark living room, she stared out the windows and waited for the van to reappear. Wondered if she should call the police. With what complaint? No one had threatened her. She sat there for close to an hour, watching the street, hoping that Mark would come home.

The van didn't appear. Neither did Mark.

Come home. Get off your goddamn boat and come home.

She thought of him out on the bay, sails snapping overhead, boom slamming across in the wind. And the water, turbid and churning under gray skies. Like the river had been. The river where Kunstler died.

She picked up the phone and dialed Vivian. The clamor of the Chao household came through the line in a lively blast of noise. Over the sounds of laughter and shouted Cantonese, Vivian said: "I'm having trouble hearing you. Can you say that again?"

"There was another doctor on the transplant team who died six years ago. Did you know him?"

Vivian's answer came back in a shout. "Yeah. But I don't think it was that long ago. More like four years."

"Do you have any idea why he committed suicide?"

"It wasn't a suicide."

"What?"

"Look, can you hold on a minute? I'm going to change extensions."

Abby heard the receiver clunk down and had to endure what seemed like an endless wait before Vivian picked up the extension. "Okay, Grandma! You can hang up!" she yelled. The chatter of Cantonese was abruptly cut off.

"What do you mean, it wasn't a suicide?" Abby said.

"It was an accident. There was some defect in his furnace and carbon monoxide collected in the house. It killed his wife and baby girl, too."

"Wait. Wait a minute. I'm talking about a guy named Lawrence Kunstler."

"I don't know anyone named Kunstler. That must have happened before I got to Bayside."

"Who are *you* talking about?"

"An anesthesiologist. The one before they hired Zwick. I'm blocking on his name right now ... Hennessy. That's the name."

"He was on the transplant team?"

"Yeah. A young guy, right out of fellowship. He wasn't here very long. I remember he was thinking about moving back West when it happened."

"Are you sure it was an accident?"

"What else would it be?"

Abby stared out the window at the empty street and said nothing.

"Abby, is something wrong?"

"Someone was following me today. A van."

"Come on."

"Mark isn't home yet. It's almost dark and he should be home by now. I keep thinking about Aaron. And Lawrence Kunstler. He jumped off the Tobin Bridge. And now you're telling me about Hennessy. That's three, Vivian."

"Two suicides and an accident."

"That's more than you'd expect in one hospital."

"Statistical cluster? Or maybe there's something about working for Bayside that's really, really depressing." Vivian's attempt at humor fell flat and she knew it. After a pause she said, "Do you honestly think someone was following you?"

"What did you tell me? *You're not paranoid. Someone's really out to get you.*"

"I was referring to Victor Voss. Or Parr. They have reasons to harass you. But to follow you around in a van? And what does it have to do with Aaron or the other two guys?"

"I don't know." Abby drew her legs up on the chair and hugged herself for warmth. For self-protection. "But I'm getting scared. I keep thinking about Aaron. I told you what that detective said—that Aaron's death may not be a suicide."

"Does he have any evidence?"

"If he did, he certainly wouldn't tell me."

"He might tell Elaine."

Of course. The widow. The one who'd want to know, who'd demand to know.

After she hung up, Abby looked up Elaine Levi's phone number. Then she sat gathering the nerve to actually make the call. It was now dark outside, and the drizzle had turned to a steady rain. Mark still wasn't home. She shut the curtains and turned on the lights. All of them. She needed brightness and warmth.

She picked up the phone and dialed Elaine.

It rang four times. She cleared her throat, preparing to leave a message on the inevitable answering machine. Then she heard three piercing tones, followed by a recording: "The number you have dialed is no longer in service. Please check your listing and dial again . . ."

Abby redialed, painstakingly confirming each number as she punched it in.

Four rings were followed by the same piercing tones. "The number you have dialed is no longer in service . . ."

She hung up and stared at the phone as if it had betrayed her. Why had Elaine changed her number? Who was she trying to avoid?

Outside, a car splashed through the rain. Abby ran to the window and peered through a crack in the curtains. A BMW was pulling into the driveway.

She offered up a silent prayer of thanks.

Mark was home.

16

Mark refilled his wine glass. "Sure, I knew them both," he said. "I knew Larry Kunstler better than Hennessy. Hennessy wasn't with us very long. But Larry was one of the guys who recruited me here, straight from my fellowship. He was an okay guy." Mark set the wine bottle down on the table. "A really nice guy."

The maître d' swept past, escorting a flamboyantly dressed woman to a nearby table, where she was greeted with a noisy chorus of "There you are, darling," and "Love your dress!" Their high-pitched gaiety at that particular moment struck Abby as vulgar. Even obscene. She wished she and Mark had stayed home. But he had wanted to eat out. They had so few free evenings together, and they hadn't properly celebrated their engagement. He had ordered wine, had made the toast, and now he was finishing off the bottle—something he seemed to be doing more and more these days. She watched him drain the last of the wine, and she thought: All the stress of my legal problems is affecting Mark as well.

"Why didn't you ever tell me about them?" she asked.

"It never came up."

"I would think *someone* would mention them. Especially after Aaron died. The team loses three colleagues in six years, and no one says a thing. It's almost as if you're all afraid to talk about it.''

"It's a pretty depressing thing to talk about. We try not to bring up the subject, especially around Marilee. She knew Hennessy's wife. She even arranged her baby shower.''

"The baby who died?''

Mark nodded. "It was a shock when it happened. A whole family, just like that. Marilee went a little hysterical when she heard about it.''

"It was definitely an accident?''

"They'd bought the house a few months before. They never got the chance to replace the old furnace. Yes, it was an accident.''

"But Kunstler's death wasn't.''

Mark sighed. "No. Larry's was not an accident.''

"Why do you think he did it?''

"Why did Aaron do it? Why does anyone commit suicide? We can come up with half a dozen possible reasons, but the truth is, Abby, we don't know. We never know. And we never understand. We look at the big picture and say, *things get better. They always get better.* Somehow, Larry lost that perspective. He couldn't see the long range anymore. And that's when people fall apart. When they lose all sight of the future.'' He took a sip of wine, than another, but he seemed to have lost any enjoyment in its taste. Or in the food.

They skipped dessert and left the restaurant, both of them silent and depressed.

Mark drove through thickening fog and intermittent rain. The whisk of the windshield wipers filled in for conversation. *That's when people fall apart,* Mark had said. *When they lose all sight of the future.*

Staring at the mist, she thought: *I'm reaching that point. I can't see it anymore. I can't see what's going to happen to me. Or even to us.*

Mark said, softly: "I want to show you something, Abby. I want to know what you think about it. Maybe you'll think I'm just crazy. Or maybe you'll be wild about the idea.''

"What idea?''

"It's something I've been dreaming about. For a long time, now.''

They drove north, out of Boston, kept driving through Revere and Lynn and Swampscott. At Marblehead Marina, he parked the car and said, "She's right there. At the end of the pier."

She was a yacht.

Abby stood shivering and bewildered on the dock as Mark paced up and down the boat's length. His voice was animated now, more animated than it had been all evening, his arms gesturing with enthusiasm.

"She's a cruiser," he said. "Forty-eight feet, fully equipped, everything we'd need. Brand new sails, new nav equipment. Hell, she's hardly been used. She could take us anywhere we'd want to go. The Caribbean. The Pacific. You're looking at freedom, Abby!" He stood on the dock, arm raised as if in salute to the boat. "Absolute freedom!"

She shook her head. "I don't understand."

"It's a way out! Fuck the city. Fuck the hospital. We buy this boat. Then we bail out of here and *go.*"

"Where?"

"Anywhere."

"I don't want to go anywhere."

"There's no reason to stay. Not now."

"Yes there is. For *me* there is. I can't just pack up and leave! I've got three years left, Mark. I have to finish them now, or I'll never be a surgeon."

"I *am* one, Abby. I'm what *you* want to be. What you *think* you want to be. And I'm telling you, *it's not worth it.*"

"I've worked so hard. I'm not going to give up now."

"What about *me?*"

She stared at him. And realized that, of course, this *was* all about him. The boat, the escape to freedom. The soon-to-be-married man, suddenly seized with the urge to run away from home. It was a metaphor that perhaps even he did not understand.

"I want to do this, Abby," he said. He went to her, his eyes glittering. Feverish. "I put in an offer, on this boat. That's why I got home so late. I was meeting with the broker."

"You made an offer without telling me? Without even calling me?"

"I know it sounds crazy—"

"How can we afford this thing? I'm way over my head in debt! It'll take me years to pay back my student loans. And you're buying a *boat?*"

"We can take out a mortgage. It's like buying a second home."

"This isn't a home."

"It's still an investment."

"It's not what I'd invest my money in."

"I'm not spending *your* money."

She took a step back and stared at him. "You're right," she said quietly. "It's not my money at all."

"Abby." He groaned. "Jesus, Abby—"

The rain was starting to fall again, cold and numbing against her face. She walked back to the car and climbed inside.

He got into the car as well. For a moment, neither one of them spoke. The only sound was the rain on the roof.

He said, quietly, "I'll withdraw the offer."

"That's not what I want."

"What do you want?"

"I thought we'd be sharing more. I don't mean the money. I don't care about that. What hurts is that you think of it as *your* money. Is that how it's going to be? Yours or mine? Should we call in the lawyers now and draw up the prenuptial agreement? Divide up the furniture and the kids?"

"You don't understand," he said, and she heard a strange and unexpected note of desperation in his voice. He started the car.

They drove halfway home without speaking.

Then Abby said: "Maybe we should rethink the engagement. Maybe getting married isn't really what you want, Mark."

"Is it what you want?"

She looked out the window and sighed. "I don't know," she murmured. "I don't know anymore."

It was the truth. She didn't.

Tragedy Claims Family of Three

While Dr. Alan Hennessy and his family slept through the night, a killer was creeping up the basement steps. Deadly carbon monoxide gas, produced by a faulty furnace, is blamed for the New Year's Day deaths of thirty-four-year-old Hennessy, his wife Gail, thirty-three, and their six-month-old daughter Linda. Their bodies were discovered late that afternoon by friends who'd been invited to the house for dinner . . .

Abby repositioned the microfiche, and photos of Hennessy and his wife appeared on the screen, his face pudgy and serious, hers seemingly snapped in mid-laugh. There was no photo of the baby. Perhaps the *Globe* thought all six-month-old babies looked alike anyway.

Abby changed microfiches to a date three and a half years before the Hennessy deaths. She found the article she was looking for on the front page of the Metro section.

Body of Missing Physician
Recovered from Inner Harbor

A body found floating Tuesday in Boston Harbor was identified today as Dr. Lawrence Kunstler, a local thoracic surgeon. Dr. Kunstler's car was found abandoned last week in the southbound Tobin Bridge breakdown lane. Police are speculating that his death was a suicide. No witnesses, however, have come forward, and the investigation remains open . . .

Abby centered Kunstler's photograph on the microfilm screen. It was a blandly formal pose, complete with white coat and stethoscope, Dr. Kunstler gazing directly at the camera.

And now, directly at her.

Why did you do it? Why did you jump? she wondered. And she couldn't suppress the afterthought: *Or did you?*

The one advantage of being relieved of ward duties was that Abby could skip out for the whole afternoon and no one at Bayside would notice, or even care. So when she walked out of the Boston Public Library and into the bustle of Copley Square, she felt a sense of both emptiness and relief that she didn't have to return to the hospital. The afternoon, if she so desired, was hers.

She decided to drive to Elaine's house.

For the past few days, she'd been asking around for Elaine's new phone number. Neither Marilee Archer nor any of the other transplant team wives had even known that Elaine's number had been changed.

Now, with the images of Kunstler and Hennessy still painfully sharp in her mind, she headed west on Route 9, to Newton. Talking to Elaine was not something she looked forward to, but over the last few days, whenever she thought about Kunstler and Hennessy, she couldn't help thinking about Aaron as well. She remembered the day of his funeral, and how no one had even mentioned the two previous deaths. Any other group of people would have found it an unavoidable topic. Someone would normally have remarked, *This makes number three.* Or *Why is Bayside so unlucky?* Or *Do you think there's a common factor here?* But no one had said a thing. Not even Elaine, who must have known about Kunstler and Hennessy.

Not even Mark.

If he kept this from me, what else hasn't he told me?

She pulled into Elaine's driveway and sat there for a moment, her head in her hands, trying to shake off her depression. But the pall remained. *It's all falling apart for me,* she thought. *My job. And now I'm losing Mark. The worst part about it is, I don't have any idea why it's happening.*

Ever since the night she'd brought up the subject of Kunstler and Hennessy, everything had changed between her and Mark. They lived in the same house and slept in the same bed, but their interactions had become purely automatic. Like the sex. In the dark, with her eyes closed, she could have been making love to anyone.

She looked up at the house. And thought: *Maybe Elaine knows something.*

She got out of the car and climbed the steps to the front door. There she noticed the newspapers, two of them, still rolled up and lying on the porch. They were a week old and already yellowed. Why hadn't Elaine picked them up?

She rang the doorbell. When no one answered, she tried knocking, then rang again. And again. She could hear the bell echoing inside the house, followed by silence. No footsteps, no voices. She looked down at the two newspapers and knew that something was wrong.

The front door was locked; she left the porch and circled around the side of the house, to the back garden. A stone path trailed off into curving beds of well-tended azaleas and hydrangeas. The lawn looked recently mown, the hedges clipped, but the flagstone patio seemed disconcertingly empty. Then she remembered the furniture, the umbrella table and chairs that she'd seen here the afternoon of the funeral. They were gone.

The kitchen door was locked, but just off the patio was a sliding glass door that hadn't been latched. Abby gave it a tug and it glided open. She called: "Elaine?" and stepped inside.

The room was vacant. Furniture, rugs—it was all gone, even the pictures. She stared in bewilderment at the blank walls, at the floor where the missing rug had left a darker rectangle on the sun-faded wood. She went into the living room, her footsteps echoing in the bare rooms. The house was swept clean, vacant except for a few advertisement postcards lying just inside the front door mail slot. She picked one up and saw it was addressed to Occupant.

She went into the kitchen. Even the refrigerator was empty, the surfaces wiped down and smelling of disinfectant. The wall telephone had no dial tone.

She walked outside and stood in the driveway, feeling completely disoriented. Only two weeks ago she had been inside this very house. She had sat on the living room couch and eaten canapés and eyed the Levi family photos over the fireplace. Now she wondered if she'd hallucinated the whole scene.

Still in a daze, she got in her car and backed out of the driveway. She drove on automatic pilot, scarcely paying attention to the road, her mind focused on Elaine's bizarre disappearance. Where would she go? To uproot her life so abruptly after Aaron's death didn't seem rational. Rather, it seemed like something one did out of panic.

Suddenly uneasy, she glanced in the rearview mirror. She'd made it a habit to check the mirror, ever since Saturday, when she'd first glimpsed the maroon van.

There was a dark green Volvo driving behind her. Hadn't it been parked outside Elaine's house? She couldn't be sure. She hadn't really been paying attention.

The Volvo blinked its lights on and off.

She accelerated.

The Volvo did too.

She turned right, onto a major thoroughfare. Ahead stretched a suburban strip of gas stations and mini-malls. *Witnesses. Lots of witnesses.* Yet the Volvo was still right behind her, still blinking its lights.

She'd had enough of being pursued, enough of being frightened. To hell with this. If he wanted to harass her, she'd turn the tables and confront *him.*

She swerved into the parking lot of a shopping mall. He followed her. One glance outside told her there were plenty of people around, shoppers pushing carts, drivers searching for parking spots. Here was the place to do it.

She slammed on the brakes.

The Volvo screeched to a halt inches from her rear bumper.

She scrambled out of her car and ran back to the Volvo. Furiously she rapped at the driver's window. "Open up, damn you! *Open up!*"

The driver rolled down his window and looked out at her. Then he removed his sunglasses. "Dr. DiMatteo?" said Bernard Katzka. "I thought it was you."

"Why have you been following me?"

"I saw you drive away from the house."

"No, *before.* Why did you follow me before?"

"When?"

"Saturday. The van."

He shook his head. "I don't know about any van."

She backed away. "Forget it. Just quit tailing me, okay?"

"I was trying to get you to pull over. Didn't you see me flash my lights?"

"I didn't know it was you."

"Mind telling me what you were doing at Dr. Levi's house?"

"I stopped by to see Elaine. I didn't know she'd moved."

"Why don't you pull into that parking space? I'd like to

talk to you. Or are you going to refuse to answer questions again?"

"That depends on what you're going to ask me."

"It's about Dr. Levi."

"That's all we're going to talk about? Just Aaron?"

He nodded.

She thought about it. And decided that questions could go both ways. That even the close-mouthed Detective Katzka might be induced to give out information.

She glanced toward the mall. "I see a doughnut shop over there. Why don't we go in and have a cup of coffee?"

Cops and doughnuts. The association had become an urban joke, reinforced in the public's mind by every overweight cop, by every patrol car ever parked outside a Dunkin' Donuts. Bernard Katzka, however, did not appear to be a doughnut fan; he ordered only a cup of black coffee, which he sipped without any apparent pleasure. Katzka did not strike Abby as the sort of man who indulged in much of anything that was pleasurable, sinful, or even remotely unnecessary.

His first question came right to the point. "Why were you at the house?"

"I came to see Elaine. I wanted to talk to her."

"About what?"

"Personal matters."

"It was my impression that you two were just acquaintances."

"Did she tell you that?"

He ignored her question. "Is that how you'd characterize the relationship?"

She let out a breath. "Yes, I guess so. We know each other through Aaron. That's all."

"So why did you come to see her?"

Again she took a deep breath. And realized she was probably clueing him in to her own nervousness. "Some strange things have happened to me lately. I wanted to talk to Elaine about it."

"What things?"

"Someone was following me last Saturday. A maroon van.

I spotted it on the Tobin Bridge. Then I saw it again, when I got home.''

"Anything else?''

"Isn't that upsetting enough?'' She looked straight at him. "It scared me.''

He regarded her in silence, as though trying to decide if it really was fear he was seeing in her face. "What does this have to do with Mrs. Levi?''

"You're the one who got me wondering about Aaron. About whether he really committed suicide. Then I found out two other Bayside doctors have died.''

Katzka's frown told her this was news to him.

"Six and a half years ago,'' she said, "there was a Dr. Lawrence Kunstler. A thoracic surgeon. He jumped off the Tobin Bridge.''

Katzka said nothing, but he had shifted forward, almost imperceptibly, in his chair.

"Then three years ago, there was an anesthesiologist,'' continued Abby. "A Dr. Hennessy. He and his wife and baby died of carbon monoxide poisoning. They called it an accident. A broken furnace.''

"Unfortunately, that kind of accident happens every winter.''

"And then there's Aaron. That makes three. All of them were on the transplant team. Doesn't that seem like a terribly unlucky coincidence to you?''

"What are you formulating here? That someone's stalking the transplant team? Killing them off one by one?''

"I'm just pointing out a pattern here. You're the policeman. You should investigate it.''

Katzka sat back. "How is it you got involved in all this?''

"My boyfriend's on the team. Mark doesn't admit it, but I think he's worried. I think the whole team's worried, and they're wondering who's going to be next. But they never talk about it. The way people never talk about plane crashes when they're standing at the boarding gate.''

"So you're worried about your boyfriend's safety?''

"Yes,'' she said simply, leaving out the larger truth: that she was doing this because she wanted Mark back. All of him. She didn't understand what had happened between them, but she knew their relationship was crumbling. And it had all started to deteriorate the night she'd mentioned Kunstler and Hennessy. None of this she shared with Katzka, because it was all based on feelings. Instinct. Katzka was the kind of man who worked with more tangible coinage.

Obviously, he'd expected her to say more. When she remained silent, he asked: "Is there anything else you want to tell me? About anything at all?"

He's talking about Mary Allen, she thought with a flash of panic. Looking at him, she had the overwhelming urge to tell him everything. Here, now. Instead she quickly avoided his gaze. And responded with a question of her own.

"Why were you watching Elaine's house?" she asked. "That's what you're doing, isn't it?"

"I was talking to the next-door neighbor. When I came out, I saw you pull out of the driveway."

"You're questioning Elaine's neighbors?"

"It's routine."

"I don't think so."

Almost against her will, her gaze lifted to his. His gray eyes admitted nothing, gave nothing away.

"Why are you still investigating a suicide?"

"The widow packs up and leaves practically overnight, with no forwarding address. That's unusual."

"You're not saying Elaine's guilty of anything, are you?"

"No. I think she's scared."

"Of what?"

"Do you know, Dr. DiMatteo?"

She found she could not look away, found there was something about the quiet intensity of his eyes that held her transfixed. She felt a brief and completely unexpected flicker of attraction, and she had no idea why this man, of all people, should inspire it.

"No," she said. "I have no idea what Elaine's running from."

"Maybe you can help me answer another question, then."

"Which is?"

"How did Aaron Levi accumulate all his wealth?"

She shook her head. "He wasn't particularly wealthy, as far as I knew. A cardiologist earns maybe two hundred thousand, tops. And he was sending a lot of that to his two kids in college.''

"Was there family money?"

"You mean like an inheritance?" She shrugged. "I heard Aaron's father was an appliance repairman."

Katzka sat back, thinking. He wasn't looking at her now, but was staring at his coffee cup. There was a depth of concentration to this man that intrigued her. He could drop out of a conversation just like that, leaving her feeling abandoned.

"Detective, how much wealth are we talking about?"

He looked up at her. "Three million dollars."

Stunned, Abby could only stare at him.

"After Mrs. Levi vanished," he said, "I thought I should take a closer look at the family finances. So I spoke to their CPA. He told me that shortly after Dr. Levi died, Elaine discovered her husband had a Cayman Islands bank account. An account she'd known nothing about. She asked the CPA how to access the money. And then, without warning, she skipped town." Katzka gave her a questioning look.

"I have no idea how Aaron got that much money," she murmured.

"Neither does his accountant."

They were silent a moment. Abby reached for her coffee and found it had gone cold. So had she.

She asked, softly: "Do you know where Elaine is?"

"We have an idea."

"Can you tell me?"

He shook his head. "At the moment, Dr. DiMatteo," he said, "I don't think she wants to be found."

Three million dollars. How had Aaron Levi accumulated three million dollars?

All the way home, she considered that question. She couldn't see how a cardiologist would be able to do it. Not with two kids in private universities and a wife with expensive taste in antiques. And why had he hidden his wealth? The Cayman Islands was where people stashed their money when they wanted it kept out of sight of the IRS. But even Elaine had not known about the account until after Aaron's death. What a shock it must have been to go through her dead husband's papers. To discover that he'd been hiding a fortune from her.

Three million dollars.

She pulled into the driveway. Found herself surveying the neighborhood for a maroon van. It was getting to be a habit, that quick glance up and down the street.

She walked in the front door and stepped over the usual pile of afternoon mail. Most of it was professional journals, two of everything for the two doctors in the house. She gathered them all up and lugged them into the kitchen. On the table she began sorting everything into two piles. His junk, her junk. His life, her life. Nothing here worth a second glance.

It was four o'clock. Tonight, she decided, she'd cook a nice dinner. Serve it with candlelight and wine. Why not? She was now a lady of leisure. While Bayside took its sweet time deciding her future as a surgeon, she could stay busy fixing things up between her and Mark with romantic dinners and feminine coddling. Lose the career but keep the man.

Shit, DiMatteo. You're starting to sound desperate.

She scooped up her half of the junk mail, carried it to the trash can, and stepped on the pop-up-lid pedal. Just as the mail was tumbling in, she glimpsed a large brown envelope stuffed at the bottom. The word *yachts,* printed in bold letters in the return address, caught her eye. She dug out the envelope and brushed off the coffee grounds and egg shells.

At the top left was printed:

East Wind Yachts
Sales and Service
Marblehead Marina

It had been sent to Mark. But it was not addressed to their Brewster Street house. It had been sent to a P.O. box.

She looked again at the words: *East Wind Yachts Sales and Service.*

She left the kitchen and went to Mark's desk in the living room. The bottom drawer, where he kept his files, was locked, but she knew where the key was. She'd heard him plunk it into the pencil cup. She found the key and opened the drawer.

Inside were all his household files. Insurance papers, mortgage papers, car papers. She found a tab with *Boat* written on it. There was a folder for *Gimme Shelter,* his J-35. There was also a second folder. It looked new. On the tab was written *H-48.*

She pulled out the H-48 file. It was a sales contract from East Wind Yachts. *H-48* was an abbreviation for the boat's design. A Hinckley yacht, forty-eight feet long.

She sank into a chair, feeling sick. *You kept it a secret,* she thought. *You told me you'd withdraw the offer. Then you bought it anyway. It's your money, all right. I guess this makes it perfectly clear.*

Her gaze moved to the bottom of the page. To the terms of sale.

Moments later, she walked out of the house.

"Cash for organs. Is it possible?"

In the midst of stirring cream into his coffee, Dr. Ivan Tarasoff stopped and glanced at Vivian. "Do you have any proof this is going on?"

"Not yet. We're just asking you if it's possible. And if so, how could it be done?"

Dr. Tarasoff sank back on the couch and sipped his coffee as he thought it over. It was four forty-five, and except for the occasional scrub-suited resident passing through to the adjoining locker room, the Mass Gen surgeons' lounge was quiet. Tarasoff, who'd come out of the OR only twenty minutes ago, still had a dusting of glove talc on his hands and a surgical mask dangling around his neck. Watching him, Abby was comforted, once again, by the image of her grandfather. The gentle blue eyes, the silver hair. The quiet voice. *The voice of ultimate authority,* she thought, *belongs to the man who never has to raise it.*

"There've been rumors, of course," said Tarasoff. "Every time a celebrity gets an organ, people wonder if money was involved. But there's never been any proof. Only suspicions."

"What rumors have you heard?"

"That one can buy a higher place on the waiting list. I myself have never seen it happen."

"I have," said Abby.

Tarasoff looked at her. "When?"

"Two weeks ago. Mrs. Victor Voss. She was third on the

waiting list and she got a heart. The two people at the top of the list later died.''

''UNOS wouldn't allow that. Or NEOB. They have strict guidelines.''

''NEOB didn't know about it. In fact, they have no record of the donor in their system.''

Tarasoff shook his head. ''This is hard to believe. If the heart didn't come through UNOS or NEOB, where did it come from?''

''We think Voss paid to keep it out of the system. So it could go to his wife,'' said Vivian.

''This is what we know so far,'' said Abby. ''Hours before Mrs. Voss's transplant, Bayside's transplant coordinator got a call from Wilcox Memorial in Burlington that they had a donor. The heart was harvested and flown to Boston. It arrived in our OR around one A.M., delivered by some doctor named Mapes. The donor papers came with it, but somehow they got misplaced. No one's seen them since. I looked up the name Mapes in the Surgery section of the *Directory of Medical Specialists*. There's no such surgeon.''

''Then who did the harvest?''

''We think it was a surgeon named Tim Nicholls. His name *is* listed in the *Directory,* so we know he does exist. According to his CV, he trained a few years at Mass Gen. Do you remember him?''

''Nicholls,'' murmured Tarasoff. He shook his head. ''When was he here?''

''Nineteen years ago.''

''I'd have to check the residency records.''

''We're thinking this is what happened,'' said Vivian. ''Mrs. Voss needed a heart, and her husband had the money to pay for it. Somehow the word went out. Grapevine, underground, I don't know how. Tim Nicholls happened to have a donor. So he funneled the heart directly to Bayside, bypassing NEOB. And various people got paid off. Including some of the Bayside staff.''

Tarasoff looked horrified. ''It's possible,'' he said. ''You're right, it could happen that way.''

The lounge door suddenly swung open and two residents walked in, laughing, as they headed for the coffee pot. They seemed to take forever as they fussed with the cream and sugar. At last they left the room.

Tarasoff was still looking stunned. "I've referred patients to Bayside myself. We're talking about one of the top transplant centers in the country. Why would they go outside the registry? Risk getting into trouble with NEOB and UNOS?"

"The answer's obvious," said Vivian. "Money."

Again they fell silent when another surgeon walked into the lounge, his scrub top soaked with sweat. He gave a grunt of exhaustion and sank into one of the easy chairs. Leaning back, he closed his eyes.

Softly Abby said to Tarasoff: "We need you to look up the residency file on Tim Nicholls. Find out what you can about him. Tell us if he really did train here. Or if his CV's a complete fabrication."

"I'll just call him myself. Put the questions to him directly."

"No, don't. We're not sure yet how far this reaches."

"Dr. DiMatteo, I believe in being blunt. If there's a shadow organ procurement network out there, I want to know about it."

"So do we. But we have to be very careful, Dr. Tarasoff." Abby glanced uneasily at the dozing surgeon in the chair. She lowered her voice to a whisper. "In the last six years, three Bayside doctors have died. Two suicides and an accident. All of them were on our transplant team."

She saw, from the look of shock on his face, that her warning had had its intended effect. "You're trying to scare me," he said. "Aren't you?"

Abby nodded. "You should be scared. We all should."

Outside, in the parking lot, Abby and Vivian stood together under a gray, drizzling sky. They had arrived in their separate cars, and now it was time to go their own ways. The days were growing so short now; only five o'clock, and already the light was fading. Shivering, Abby pulled her slicker tighter and glanced around the lot. No maroon vans.

"We don't have enough," said Vivian. "We can't force an investigation yet. And if we tried, Victor Voss could just cover his tracks."

"Nina Voss wasn't the first one. I think Bayside's done this before. Aaron died with three million dollars in his account. He must have been getting payoffs for some time.''

''You think he got second thoughts?''

''I know he was trying to get out of Bayside. Out of Boston. Maybe they wouldn't let him go.''

''That could be what happened to Kunstler and Hennessy.''

Abby released a deep breath. Again she glanced around the lot, searching for the van. ''I'm afraid that's exactly what happened to them.''

''We need other names, other transplants. Or more donor information.''

''All the information about donors is locked up in the transplant coordinator's office. I'd have to break in and steal it. If it's even there. Remember how they misplaced the donor papers on Nina Voss?''

''Okay, so we go at it from the recipient side.''

''Medical Records?''

Vivian nodded. ''Let's find out the names of who got transplanted. And where they were on the waiting list when it happened.''

''We'll need NEOB's help.''

''Right. But first we need names and dates.''

Abby nodded. ''I can do that.''

''I'd help you out, but Bayside won't let me in its doors anymore. They think I'm their worst nightmare.''

''You and me both.''

Vivian grinned, as if it was something to be proud of. She seemed small, almost childlike in her oversize raincoat. Such a fragile-looking ally. But while her size didn't inspire much confidence, her gaze did. It was direct and uncompromising. And it saw too much.

''Okay, Abby,'' sighed Vivian. ''Now tell me about Mark. And why we're keeping this from him.''

Abby released a deep breath. The answer spilled out in a rush of anguish. ''I think he's part of it.''

''Mark?''

Abby nodded. And looked up at the drizzling sky. ''He wants out of Bayside. He's been talking about sailing away. Escape. Just like Aaron did before he died.''

''You think Mark's been taking payoffs?''

"A few days ago, he bought a boat. I don't mean just a boat. A *yacht.*"

"He's always been crazy about boats."

"This one cost half a million dollars."

Vivian said nothing.

"Here's the worst part," whispered Abby. "He paid in cash."

17

The Medical Records file room was in the hospital basement, just down the hall from Pathology and the morgue. It was a department well known to every physician at Bayside. This was where doctors signed off on charts, dictated discharge summaries, and initialed lab reports and verbal orders. The room was furnished with comfortable chairs and tables, and to accommodate the often erratic work hours of its physicians, the department stayed open until nine P.M. every night.

It was six that evening when Abby walked into Medical Records. As she'd expected, the room was nearly deserted for the dinner hour. The only other physician was a haggard-looking intern, his desk piled high with delinquent charts.

Heart pounding, Abby approached the clerk's desk and smiled. "I'm compiling statistics for Dr. Wettig. He's doing a study on heart transplant morbidity. Could you pull up a list on your computer? The names and record numbers of all heart transplants done here in the last two years."

"For a records search like that, we need a request form from the department."

"They've all gone home by now. Could I get that form to you some other time? I'd like to have this ready for him by the morning. You know how the General is."

The clerk laughed. Yes, she knew exactly how the General was. She sat down at her keyboard and called up the Search screen. Under Diagnosis, she typed in *Cardiac Transplant*, then the years to be searched. She hit the Enter button.

One by one, a list of names and record numbers began to appear. Abby watched, mesmerized by what she saw scrolling down the screen. The clerk hit Print. Seconds later, the list rolled out of the printer. She handed the page to Abby.

There were twenty-nine names on the list. The last one was Nina Voss.

"Could I have the first ten charts?" Abby asked. "I might as well start working on this tonight."

The clerk vanished into the file room. A moment later she reemerged hugging a bulky armful of files. "These are only the first two. I'll get you the rest."

Abby lugged the charts to a desk. They landed with a heavy thud. Every heart transplant patient generated reams and reams of documentation, and these two were no different. She opened the first folder to the patient information sheet.

The name was Gerald Luray, age fifty-four. Source of payment was private insurance. Home address was in Worcester, Massachusetts. She didn't know how relevant any of this information was, so she copied it all down onto a yellow legal pad. She also copied the date and time of transplant and the names of the doctors in attendance. She recognized all the names: Aaron Levi, Bill Archer, Frank Zwick, Rajiv Mohandas. *And Mark.* As expected, there was no donor information anywhere in the chart. That was always kept separate from recipient records. However, among the nurses' notes, she found written: "0830—Harvest reported complete. Donor heart now enroute from Norwalk, Connecticut. Patient wheeled to OR for prep . . ."

Abby wrote: 0830. Harvest in Norwalk, Conn.

The records clerk wheeled a cart to Abby's desk, deposited five more charts, and went back for more.

Abby worked straight through the supper hour. She didn't stop to eat, didn't allow herself even a break, except to call Mark to tell him she'd be home late.

By closing time, she was starving.

She stopped at a McDonald's on the way home and ordered a Big Mac and giant fries and a vanilla shake. Cholesterol to feed the brain. She ate it all while sitting in a corner booth, keeping an eye on the dining room. At that hour, the other patrons were mostly the postmovie crowd, teenagers on dates, and here and there a few depressed-looking bachelors. No one even seemed to notice she was there. She finished every last french fry, then left.

Before she started the car, she made a quick survey of the parking lot. No van.

At ten-fifteen, she arrived home to find that Mark was already in bed and the lights were out. She was relieved that she would not have to answer any questions. She undressed in the dark and climbed under the covers, but she didn't touch him. She was almost afraid to touch him.

When he suddenly stirred and reached out to her, she felt her whole body go rigid.

"I missed you tonight," he murmured. He turned her face to his and gave her a long and intimate kiss. His hand slid down to her waist and caressed her hip. Stroked along her thigh. She didn't move; she felt as frozen as a mannequin, unable to respond or resist. She lay with her eyes closed, her pulse roaring in her ears, as he pulled her into his arms. As he slid inside her.

Who am I making love to? she wondered as he thrust again and again, their hips colliding with brutish force.

Then it was over, and he was sliding out of her.

"I love you," he whispered.

It was a long time later, after he'd fallen asleep, that she whispered her answer.

"I love you too."

At seven-forty A.M. she was back in Medical Records. Several of the desks were now occupied by physicians cleaning up paperwork before making their morning rounds. Abby requested five more charts. Quickly she took notes, gave the charts back to the clerk, and left.

She spent the morning in the medical library, looking up more articles for Dr. Wettig. It wasn't until late that afternoon when she returned to Medical Records.

She requested ten more charts.

*   *   *

229

Vivian finished off the last slice of pizza. It was her fourth slice, and where she put it all was a mystery to Abby. That elfin body consumed calories like a fat-burning furnace. Since they'd sat down in the booth at Gianelli's, Abby had eaten only a few bites, and even those were an effort.

Vivian wiped her hands on a napkin. "So Mark still doesn't know?"

"I haven't said a thing to him. I guess I'm afraid to."

"How can you stand it? Living in the same house and not talking?"

"We talk. We just don't talk about *this*." Abby touched the sheaf of notes on the table—the notes she'd been carrying around all day. She'd been careful to keep them where Mark wouldn't find them. Last night, when she'd returned home after McDonald's, she had hidden the notes under the couch. Lately it seemed she'd been hiding so many things from him, and she didn't know how long she could keep it up.

"Abby, you've got to talk to him about this eventually."

"Not yet. Not until I know."

"You're not afraid of *Mark,* are you?"

"I'm afraid he'll deny everything. And I'll have no way of knowing if he's telling the truth." She ran her hands through her hair. "God, it's like reality's completely shifted on me. I used to think I was standing on such solid ground. If I wanted something badly enough, I just worked like hell for it. Now I can't decide what to do, which move to make. All the things I counted on aren't there for me anymore."

"Meaning Mark."

Wearily, Abby rubbed her face. "Especially Mark."

"You look awful, Abby."

"I haven't been sleeping very well. I've got so many things to think about. Not just Mark. But also that business with Mary Allen. I keep waiting for Detective Katzka to show up on my doorstep with his handcuffs."

"You think he suspects you?"

"I think he's too bright not to."

"You haven't heard anything from him. Maybe he'll let it slide. Maybe you're giving him too much credit."

Abby thought of Bernard Katzka's calm gray eyes. And she said, "He's a hard man to read. But I think Katzka's not only smart, he's persistent. I'm scared of him. And weirdly enough, fascinated by him too.''

Vivian sat back. "Interesting. The prey intrigued by her hunter.''

"Sometimes I just want to call Katzka and blurt out everything. Get it all over with.'' Abby dropped her head in her hands. "I'm so tired, I wish I could run away somewhere. Sleep for a whole week.''

"Maybe you should move out of Mark's house. I've got an extra bedroom. And my grandmother's leaving.''

"I thought she was a permanent houseguest.''

"She makes the rounds of all her grandkids. Right now I've got a cousin in Concord who's bracing herself for *the visit*.''

Abby shook her head. "I don't know what to do. The thing is, I love Mark. I don't trust him anymore, but I love him. At the same time, I know that what we're doing could ruin him.''

"It could also save his life.''

Abby looked miserably at Vivian. "I save his life. But I destroy his career. He may not thank me much for that.''

"Aaron would have thanked you. Kunstler would have. Certainly Hennessy's wife and baby would have thanked you.''

Abby said nothing.

"How certain are you that Mark's involved?''

"I'm *not* certain. That's what makes this so hard. *Wanting* to believe in him. And not having any evidence to tell me one way or the other.'' She touched her notes. "I've looked at twenty-five files so far. Some of the transplants go back to two years ago. Mark's name is on every one of them.''

"So is Archer's. And Aaron's. That doesn't tell us anything. What else have you learned?''

"All the records look pretty much the same. Nothing to distinguish one from any other.''

"Okay, what about the donors?''

"That's where things get a little interesting.'' Abby glanced around the restaurant. Then she leaned toward Vivian. "Not all of the charts mention which city the donor organ comes from. But a number of them do. And there seems to be a cluster. Four of them came from Burlington, Vermont.''

"Wilcox Memorial?''

"I don't know. The hospital was never specified in the nurses' notes. But I find it interesting that a relatively small town like Burlington ends up with so many brain-dead people.''

Vivian's gaze met hers in a stunned look. ''There's something really wrong here. We were hypothesizing nothing more than a shadow referral network. Donors who are simply kept out of the registry system. But that doesn't explain a cluster of donors in one town. Unless . . .''

''Unless donors are being generated.''

They fell silent.

Burlington is a university town, thought Abby. *Full of young, healthy college students. With young, healthy hearts.*

''Can I have the dates on those four Burlington harvests?'' said Vivian.

''I have them right here. Why?''

''I'm going to check them against the Burlington obituaries. Find out who died on those dates. Maybe we can identify the names of the four donors. And find out how they ended up brain-dead.''

''Not all obits list the cause of death.''

''Then we may have to go to the death certificates. Which means a trip to Burlington for one of us. A place I've been dying to visit. *Not.''* Vivian's tone of voice was almost breezy. That warrior woman bravado again; she had the act down pat. But this time it wasn't enough to hide the note of apprehension.

''Are you sure you want to do this?'' said Abby.

''If we don't, then Victor Voss wins. And the losers are going to be people like Josh O'Day.'' She paused. And asked, quietly: ''Is this what *you* want to do, Abby?''

Abby dropped her head in her hands. ''I don't think I have a choice any longer.''

Mark's car was in the driveway.

Abby pulled up behind it and turned off her engine. For a long time she simply sat there, scraping up the energy to get out of the car, to walk into the house. To face him.

At last she stepped out of the car and walked in the front door.

He was in the living room, watching the late night news. As soon as she came in, he clicked off the TV. ''How is Vivian doing these days?'' he asked.

''She's fine. Landed right back on her feet. She's buying into a practice in Wakefield." Abby hung up her coat in the closet. "And how was your day?"

"We got a dissecting aorta. He bled out sixteen units just like that. I didn't get out till seven."

"Did he make it?"

"No. We ended up losing him."

"That's too bad. I'm sorry." She shut the closet door. "I'm kind of tired. I think I'll go up and take a bath."

"Abby?"

She paused and looked at him. They were separated by the width of the living room. But the gulf between them seemed miles wider.

"What's happened to you?" he asked. "What's wrong?"

"You know what's wrong. I'm worried about my job."

"I'm talking about us. Something's wrong with *us.*"

She didn't say anything.

"I hardly see you anymore. You're at Vivian's more than you are here. When you are home, you act like you're somewhere else."

"I'm preoccupied, that's all. Can't you understand why?"

He sank back, suddenly looking very tired. "I have to know, Abby. Are you seeing someone else?"

She stared at him. Of all the things Mark might say to her, this was the last thing she'd expected. She almost felt like laughing at the trivial nature of his suspicions. *If only it were that simple. If only our problems were the same as every other couple's.*

"There's no one else," she said. "Believe me."

"Then why aren't you talking to me anymore?"

"I'm talking to you now."

"This isn't talking! This is *me* trying to get the old Abby back. Somewhere along the way I've lost her. I've lost *you.*" He shook his head and looked away. "I just want you back again."

She went to the couch and sat down beside him. Not close enough to touch, but close enough to feel connected, if only distantly.

"Talk to me, Abby. Please." He looked at her, and suddenly it was the old Mark she saw. The same face that had smiled at her across the operating table. The face she loved. "Please," he repeated, softly. He took her hand and she didn't pull away.

She let him take her into his arms. But even there, where she'd once felt safe, she could not relax. She lay stiff and uneasy against his chest.

"Tell me," he said. "What's wrong between us?"

She closed her eyes against the sting of fresh tears. "Nothing's wrong," she said.

She felt his arms go very still around her. Without even looking at his face, she knew that he could tell she was, once again, lying.

At seven-thirty the next morning, Abby pulled into her parking space at Bayside Hospital.

She sat in her car for a moment, eyeing the wet pavement, the steady drizzle. Only mid-October, she thought, and already this dreary foretaste of winter. She had not slept well last night. In fact, she could not remember the last good night's sleep she'd had. How long could a person hold up without sleep? How long before fatigue led to psychosis? Glancing in the rearview mirror, she scarcely recognized the haggard stranger staring back at her. In two weeks it seemed she had aged ten years. At this rate she'd be hitting menopause by November.

A flash of maroon in the mirror caught her eye.

She snapped her head around just in time to see a van retreating behind the next aisle of cars. She waited for another glimpse of it. It didn't reappear.

Quickly she stepped outside and began to walk toward the hospital. The weight of her briefcase felt like an anchor weighing her down. Off to her right, a car engine suddenly roared to life. She whirled, expecting to see the van, but it was a station wagon pulling out of a space.

Her heart was slamming against her chest. It didn't calm down until she was inside the building. She took the stairs down to the basement and walked into Medical Records. This would be her final visit; she was down to the last four names on the list.

She lay the request slip on the counter and said, "Excuse me, may I have these charts please?"

The clerk turned to face her. Perhaps Abby was only imagining it, but the woman seemed to freeze momentarily. They had dealt with each other before, and the clerk usually seemed friendly enough. Today she wasn't even smiling.

"I need these four charts," said Abby.

The clerk looked at the request slip. "I'm sorry, Dr. DiMatteo. I can't get these files for you."

"Why not?"

"They're not available."

"But you haven't even checked."

"I've been told not to release any more files to you. It's Dr. Wettig's orders. He said if you came in, we're to refer you to his office immediately."

Abby felt the blood drain from her face. She said nothing.

"He said he never authorized any chart search." The clerk's tone of voice was plainly accusatory. *You lied to us, Dr. DiMatteo.*

Abby had no answer. It seemed to her the room had suddenly fallen silent. She turned and saw that three other doctors were in the room, and they were all watching her.

She walked out of Medical Records.

Her first impulse was to leave the building. To avoid the inevitable confrontation with Wettig and just drive away. To keep driving until this was a thousand miles behind her. She wondered how long it would take to reach Florida and the beach and palm trees. She'd never been to Florida. She'd never done so many things other people had done. She could do them all now if she'd just walk out of this goddamn hospital, climb in her car, and say: *Fuck it. You win. You all win.*

But she didn't walk out of the building. She stepped into the basement elevator and punched Two.

On that short ride to the administrative floor, several things became instantly clear to her. The first was that she was too stubborn or too stupid to run. The second was that a beach was not really what she wanted. What she wanted was her dream back.

She got out of the elevator and walked up the carpeted hall. The residency office was around the corner, past Jeremiah Parr's suite. As she walked past Parr's secretary, she saw the woman sit up sharply and reach for the phone.

Abby turned the corner and walked into the residency office. There were two men standing by the secretary's desk, neither of whom Abby had ever seen before. The secretary looked up at Abby with that same stunned expression that had flashed across the face of Parr's secretary, and blurted: "Oh! Dr. DiMatteo—"

"I need to see Dr. Wettig," said Abby.

The two men turned to look at her. In the next instant, Abby was startled by a flash of light. She flinched away as the light went off again and again. A camera flashbulb.

"What are you doing?" she demanded.

"Doctor, would you care to comment on the death of Mary Allen?" one of the men said.

"What?"

"She was your patient, wasn't she?"

"Who the hell are you?"

"Gary Starke, *Boston Herald*. Is it true you're an advocate of euthanasia? We know you've made statements to that effect."

"I never said anything of the—"

"Why were you relieved of your ward duties?"

Abby took a step back. "Get away from me. I'm not talking to you."

"Dr. DiMatteo—"

Abby turned to flee the office. She almost collided with Jeremiah Parr, who'd just walked in the door.

"I want you reporters out of my hospital *now*," Parr snapped. Then he turned to Abby. "Doctor, come with me."

Abby followed Parr out of the room. They walked swiftly down the hall and into his office. He shut the door and turned to look at her.

"The *Herald* started calling half an hour ago," he said. "Then the *Globe* called, followed by about half a dozen other newspapers. It hasn't let up since."

"Did Brenda Hainey tell them?"

"I don't think it was her. They seemed to know about the morphine. And the vial in your locker. Things she didn't know."

She shook her head. "How?"

"Somehow it leaked out." Parr sank into the chair behind his desk. "This is going to kill us. A criminal investigation. Police swarming up and down the halls."

The police. Of course. By now it's leaked out to them as well.

Abby stared at Parr. Her throat felt too parched to produce a single word. She wondered if *he* was the source of the leak, then decided it was unlikely. This scandal would hurt him, too.

There was a sharp rap on the door, and Dr. Wettig walked in. "What the hell do I do about those reporters?" he said.

"You'll have to prepare a statement, General. Susan Casado's on her way over. She'll help you with the wording. Until then, no one talks to anyone."

Wettig gave a curt nod. Then his gaze focused on Abby. "May I see your briefcase, Dr. DiMatteo?"

"Why?"

"You know why. You had no authority to search those patient records. They are private and confidential. I'm ordering you to turn over all the notes you took."

She did nothing. Said nothing.

"I hardly think an additional charge of theft is going to help your case."

"Theft?"

"Any information you gleaned from that illegal chart search was stolen. Give me the briefcase. *Give it to me.*"

Wordlessly she handed it to him. She watched him open it. Watched him shuffle through the papers and remove her notes. She could do nothing except hang her head in defeat. Once again they had beaten her. They had made the preemptive strike, and she hadn't been prepared. She should have known better. She should have stashed the notes before coming up here. But she'd been too focused on what she would say, how she would explain herself to Wettig.

He shut the briefcase and handed it back to her. "Is that everything?" he asked.

She could only nod.

Wettig regarded her for a moment in silence. Then he shook his head. "You would have made a fine surgeon, DiMatteo. But I think it's time to recognize the fact you need help. I'm recommending you seek psychiatric evaluation. And I'm releasing you from the residency program, effective today." To her surprise, she heard a note of genuine regret in his voice when he added, quietly: "I'm sorry."

18

Detective Lundquist was a handsome blond, the ideal Teutonic specimen. He had interviewed Abby for two hours now, asking his questions while pacing around the cramped interview room. If it was a tactic designed to make her feel threatened, then it was working. In the small Maine town where Abby grew up, cops were the guys who waved at you from their cars, who walked cheerfully around town with keys clinking on their belts, and who handed out citizenship awards at high school graduations. They were not people you were supposed to be afraid of.

Abby was afraid of Lundquist. She'd been afraid of him from the moment he'd walked into the room and set a tape recorder on the table. She'd been even more afraid when he'd pulled out a card from his suit pocket and read her her rights. *She* was the one who'd walked into the police station of her own volition. She had asked to speak to Detective Katzka. Instead they had sent in Lundquist, and he had questioned her with the barely restrained aggression of an arresting officer.

The door opened, and at last Bernard Katzka walked into the room. To finally see someone she knew should have been a relief to Abby, but Katzka's impassive face offered no reassurance whatsoever. He stood across the table from her, regarding her with a weary expression.

"I understand you haven't called an attorney," he said. "Do you wish to call one now?"

"Am I under arrest?" she asked.

"Not at the moment."

"Then I'm free to go at any time?"

He paused and looked at Lundquist, who shrugged. "This is only a preliminary investigation."

"Do you think I need an attorney, Detective?"

Again Katzka hesitated. "That's really your decision, Dr. DiMatteo."

"Look, I walked in here on my own. I did it because I *wanted* to talk to you. To tell you what happened. I've willingly answered all this man's questions. If you're putting me under arrest, then yes, I'll call an attorney. But I want to make it clear from the start that it's not because I've done anything wrong." She looked Katzka in the eye. "So I guess my answer is, I don't need an attorney."

Again Lundquist and Katzka exchanged glances, their meaning unclear to her. Then Lundquist said, "She's all yours, Slug," and he moved off into a corner.

Katzka sat down at the table.

"I suppose you're going to ask all the same questions he did," said Abby.

"I missed the beginning. But I think I've already heard most of your answers."

He nodded at the mirror in the far wall. It was a viewing window, she realized. He'd been listening to the session with Lundquist. She wondered how many others were standing behind that glass, watching her. It made her feel exposed. Violated. She shifted her chair, turning her face away from the mirror, and found she was now gazing directly at Katzka.

"So what are *you* going to ask me?"

"You said you think someone is setting you up. Can you tell us who?"

"I thought it was Victor Voss. Now I'm not so sure."

"Do you have other enemies?"

"Obviously I do."

"Someone who dislikes you enough to murder your patient? Just to set you up?"

"Maybe it wasn't murder. That morphine level was never confirmed."

"It has been. Mrs. Allen was exhumed a few days ago, at the request of Brenda Hainey. The medical examiner ran the quantitative test this morning."

Abby absorbed his information in silence. She could hear the tape recorder, still whirring. She sank back in her chair. There was no question now. Mrs. Allen had died of an OD.

"A few days ago, Dr. DiMatteo, you told me you were being followed by a purple van."

"Maroon," she whispered. "It was a maroon van. I saw it again, today."

"Did you get a license number?"

"It was never close enough."

"Let me see if I understand this correctly. Someone administers a morphine overdose to your patient, Mrs. Allen. Then he—or she—plants a vial of morphine in your locker. And now you're being followed around town by a van. And you think these incidents were all engineered by Victor Voss?"

"That's what I thought. But maybe it's someone else."

Katzka sat back and regarded her. His look of weariness had spread to his shoulders, which were now slumped forward.

"Tell us about the transplants again."

"I've already told you everything."

"I'm not entirely clear how it's connected to this case."

She took a deep breath. She'd gone over this already with Lundquist, had told him the whole story of Josh O'Day and the suspicious circumstances of Nina Voss's transplant. Judging by Lundquist's disinterested response, it had been a waste of time. Now she was expected to repeat the story, and it would be a waste of more time. Defeated, she closed her eyes. "I'd like a drink of water."

Lundquist left the room. While he was gone, neither she nor Katzka said a word. She just sat with her eyes closed, wishing it were all over. But it would never be over. She would be in this room for eternity, answering the same questions forever. Maybe she should have called an attorney after all. Maybe she should just walk out. Katzka had told her she was not under arrest. Not yet.

Lundquist returned with a paper cup of water. She drank it down in a few gulps and set the empty cup on the table.

"What about the heart transplants, Doctor?" prodded Katzka.

She sighed. "I think that's how Aaron got his three million dollars. By finding donor hearts for rich recipients who didn't want to wait their turn on the list."

"The list?"

She nodded. "In this country alone, we have over five thousand people who need heart transplants. A lot of them are going to die because there's a shortage of donor hearts. Donors have to be young and in previously good health—which means the vast majority of donors are trauma victims with brain death. And there aren't enough of those to go around."

"So who decides which patient gets a heart?"

"There's a computerized registry. Our regional system is run by New England Organ Bank. They're absolutely democratic. You're prioritized according to your condition. Not your wealth. Which means if you're way down the list, you have a long wait. Now let's say you're rich, and you're worried you'll die before they find you a heart. Obviously, you'll be tempted to go outside the system to get an organ."

"Can it be done?"

"It would have to involve a shadow matchmaking service. A way to keep potential donors out of the system and funnel their hearts directly to wealthy patients. Or there's even a worse possibility."

"Which is?"

"They're generating new donors."

"You mean *killing* people?" said Lundquist. "Then where are all the dead bodies? The missing persons reports?"

"I didn't say that's what's happening. I'm just telling you how it could be done." She paused. "I think Aaron Levi was part of it. That might explain his three million dollars."

Katzka's expression had scarcely changed. His impassivity was beginning to irritate her.

She said, more animated now: "Don't you see? It makes sense to me now, why those lawsuits against me were dropped. They probably hoped I'd stop asking questions. But I didn't stop. I just kept asking more and more. And now they *have* to discredit me, because I can blow the whistle on them. I could ruin everything."

"So why don't they just kill you?" It was Lundquist asking the question in a plainly skeptical tone of voice.

She paused. "I don't know. Maybe they don't think I know enough yet. Or they're afraid of how it'd look. So soon after Aaron's death."

"This is very creative," said Lundquist, and he laughed.

Katzka lifted his hand in a terse gesture to Lundquist to shut up. "Dr. DiMatteo," he said, "I'll be honest with you. This is not coming across as a likely scenario."

"It's the only one I can think of."

"Can I offer one?" said Lundquist. "One that makes perfect sense?" He stepped toward the table, his gaze on Abby. "Your patient Mary Allen was suffering. Maybe she asked you to help her over the edge. Maybe you thought it was the humane thing to do. And it *was* humane. Something any caring physician would consider doing. So you slipped her an extra dose of morphine. Problem is, one of the nurses saw you do it. And she sends an anonymous note to Mary Allen's niece. Suddenly you're in trouble, and all because you were trying to be humane. Now you're looking at charges of homicide. Prison time. It's all getting pretty scary, isn't it? So you cobble together a conspiracy theory. One that can't be proved—or disproved. Doesn't that make more sense, Doctor? It makes more sense to me."

"But that's not what happened."

"What did happen?"

"I told you. I've told you everything—"

"Did you kill Mary Allen?"

"No." She leaned forward, her hands clenched in fists on the table. "I did not kill my patient."

Lundquist looked at Katzka. "She's not a very good liar, is she?" he said, and he walked out of the room.

For a moment neither Abby nor Katzka spoke.

Then she asked, softly, "Am I under arrest now?"

"No. You can leave." He rose to his feet.

So did she. They stood looking at each other as though neither one of them had quite decided that the interview was over.

"Why am I being released?" she asked.

"Pending further investigation."

"Do you think I'm guilty?"

He hesitated. She knew it was not a question he should answer, yet he seemed to be struggling for some measure of honesty in his reply. In the end, he chose to avoid the question entirely.

"Dr. Hodell's been waiting for you," he said. "You'll find him at the front desk." He turned to open the door. "I'll be talking to you again, Dr. DiMatteo," he said, and left the room.

She walked down the hall and into the waiting area.

Mark was standing there. "Abby?" he said softly.

She let him take her into his arms, but her body registered his touch with a strange sense of numbness. Detachment. As if she herself were floating above them both, observing from a distance two strangers embracing, kissing.

And from across that same distance, she heard him say: "Let's go home."

Through the security partition, Bernard Katzka watched the couple walk toward the door, observing how closely Hodell held the woman. It was not something a cop saw every day. Affection. Love. More often it was couples wrangling away, bruised faces, cut lips, fingers pointed in accusation. Or it was pure lust. Lust he saw all the time. It was out in full view, as blatant as the whores walking the streets of Boston's Combat Zone. Katzka himself was not immune to it, to that occasional need for a woman's body.

But love was something he had not felt in a long time. And at that moment, he envied Mark Hodell.

"Hey, Slug!" someone called. "Call on line three."

Katzka reached for the telephone. "Detective Katzka," he said.

"This is the ME's office. Hold for Dr. Rowbotham, please."

As Katzka waited, his gaze shifted back toward the waiting area, and he saw that Abby DiMatteo and Hodell were gone. The couple with everything, he thought. Looks. Money. High-powered careers. Would a woman in her enviable position risk it all, just to ease the pain of a dying patient?

Rowbotham came on the line. "Slug?"

"Yeah. What's up?"

"A surprise."

243

"Good or bad?"

"Let's just call it unexpected. I have the tissue GC-MS results back on Dr. Levi."

GC-MS, or gas chromatography-mass spectrometry, was a method used by the crime lab for identification of drugs and toxins.

"I thought you already ruled out everything," said Katzka.

"We ruled out the usual drugs. Narcotics, barbs. But that was using immunoassay and thin-layer chromatography. This is a doctor we're talking about, so I figured we couldn't go with just the usual screen. I also checked for fentanyl, phencyclidine, some of the volatiles. I came up with a positive in the muscle tissue. Succinylcholine."

"What's that?"

"It's a neuromuscular blocking agent. Competes with the body's neurotransmitter, acetylcholine. The effect is sort of like d-tubocurarine."

"Curare?"

"Right, but succinylcholine has a different chemical mechanism. It's used in the OR all the time. To immobilize muscles for surgery. Allow easier ventilation."

"Are you saying he was paralyzed?"

"Completely helpless. The worst part of it is, he would've been conscious, but unable to struggle." Rowbotham paused. "It's a terrible way to die, Slug."

"How is the drug administered?"

"Injection."

"We didn't see any needle marks on the body."

"It could have been in the scalp. Hidden in the hair. It's just a pinprick we're talking about. We could easily have missed it with all the postmortem skin changes."

Katzka thought it over for a moment. And he remembered something Abby DiMatteo had told him only a few days ago, something he hadn't completely followed up on.

He said, "Could you look up two old autopsy reports for me? One would be from about six years ago. A jumper off the Tobin Bridge. The name was Lawrence Kunstler."

"Spell it for me. . . . Okay, got it. And the next name?"

"Dr. Hennessy. I'm not sure about his first name. That one was three years ago. Accidental carbon monoxide poisoning. The whole family died as well."

"I think I remember that one. There was a baby."

"That's the one. I'll see if I can't get exhumation orders rolling."

"What are you looking for, Slug?"

"I don't know. Something that might've been missed before. Something we might pick up now."

"In a corpse that's been dead six years?" Rowbotham's laugh was plainly skeptical. "You must be turning into an optimist."

"More flowers, Mrs. Voss. They were just delivered. Do you want them in here? Or shall I put them in the parlor?"

"Bring them in here, please." Sitting in a chair by her favorite window, Nina watched the maid carry the vase into the bedroom and set it down on a night table. Now she was fussing with the arrangement, moving stems around, and the fragrance of sage and phlox wafted toward Nina.

"Put them here, next to me."

"Of course, ma'am." The maid moved the vase to the small tea table beside Nina's chair. She had to make room for it by taking away another vase of Oriental lilies. "They're not your usual flowers, are they?" the maid said, and her tone of voice was not entirely approving as she regarded the usurping vase.

"No." Nina smiled at the unruly arrangement. Already her gardener's eye had picked out and identified each splash of color. Russian sage and pink phlox. Purple coneflowers and yellow heliopsis. And daisies. Lots and lots of daisies. Such common, undistinguished flowers. How did one find daisies so late in the season?

She brushed her hand across the blossoms and inhaled the scents of late summer, the remembered fragrance of the garden she had been too ill to tend. Now summer was gone, and their house in Newport was closed for the winter. How she disliked this time of year! The fading of the garden. The return to Boston, to this house with its gold-leafed ceilings and carved doorways and bathrooms of Carrara marble. She found all the dark wood oppressive. Their summer home was blessed with light and warm breezes and the smell of the sea. But this house made her think of winter. She picked out a daisy and breathed in its pungent scent.

"Wouldn't you rather have the lilies next to you?" the maid asked. "They smell so lovely."

"They were giving me a headache. Who are these flowers from?"

The maid pulled off the tiny envelope taped to the vase and opened the flap. " 'To Mrs. Voss. A speedy recovery. Joy.' That's all it says."

Nina frowned. "I don't know anyone named Joy."

"Maybe it'll come to you. Would you like to go back to bed now? Mr. Voss says you should rest."

"I've had enough of lying in bed."

"But Mr. Voss says—"

"I'll go to bed later. I'd like to sit here for a while. By myself."

The maid hesitated. Then, with a nod, she reluctantly left the room.

At last, thought Nina. *At last I'm alone.*

For the past week, ever since she'd left the hospital, she had been surrounded by people. Private duty nurses and doctors and maids. And Victor. Most of all, Victor, hovering at her bedside. Reading aloud all her get-well cards, screening all her phone calls. Protecting her, insulating her. Imprisoning her in this house.

All because he loved her. Perhaps he loved her too much.

Wearily she leaned back in the chair and found herself staring at the portrait hanging on the opposite wall. It was her portrait, painted soon after their marriage. Victor had commissioned it, had even chosen which gown she should wear, a long mauve silk patterned faintly with roses. In the painting she was standing under a vine-covered arbor, a single white rose clutched in one hand, her other hand dangling awkwardly at her side. Her smile was shy, uncertain, as though she were thinking to herself: *I am only standing in for someone else.*

Now, as she studied that portrait of her younger self, she realized how little she'd changed since that day she'd posed as a young bride in the garden. The years had altered her physically, of course. She'd lost her robust good health. In so many ways, though, she was unchanged. Still shy, still awkward. Still the woman Victor Voss had claimed as his possession.

She heard his footsteps and looked up as he came into the bedroom.

"Louisa told me you were still up," he said. "You should be taking your nap."

"I'm fine, Victor."

"You don't look strong enough yet."

"It's been three and a half weeks. Dr. Archer says his other patients are already walking on treadmills by now."

"You're not like any other patient. I think you should take a nap."

She met his gaze. Firmly she said: "I'm going to sit here, Victor. I want to look out the window."

"Nina, I'm only thinking of what's best for you."

But she had already turned away from him, and was staring down at the park. At the trees, their fall brilliance fading to winter brown. "I'd like to go for a drive."

"It's too soon."

". . . to the park. The river. Anywhere, just away from this house."

"You're not listening to me, Nina."

She sighed. And said, sadly, "You're the one who's not listening."

There was a silence. "What are these?" he said, pointing to the vase of flowers by her chair.

"They just arrived."

"Who sent them?"

She shrugged. "Someone named Joy."

"You can pick these kinds of flowers at the roadside."

"That's why they're called wildflowers."

He lifted the vase and carried it to a table in a far corner. Then he brought the Oriental lilies back and set them beside her. "At least these aren't weeds," he said, and left the room.

She stared at the lilies. They *were* beautiful. Exotic and perfect. Their cloying fragrance sickened her.

She blinked away an unexpected film of tears and focused on the tiny envelope lying on the table. The one that had come with the wildflowers.

Joy. Who was Joy?

She opened the flap and took out the enclosed card. Only

then did she notice that something was written on the back of the card.

Some doctors always tell the truth, it said.

And beneath that was a phone number.

Abby was home alone when Nina Voss called at five P.M.

"Is this Dr. DiMatteo?" said a soft voice. "The one who always tells the truth?"

"Mrs. Voss? You got my flowers."

"Yes, thank you. And I got your rather odd note."

"I've tried every other way to contact you. Letters. Phone calls."

"I've been home over a week."

"But you haven't been available."

There was a pause. Then a quiet, "I see."

She has no idea how isolated she's been, thought Abby. *No idea how her husband has cut her off from the outside.*

"Is anyone else listening to this?" asked Abby.

"I'm alone in my room. What is this all about?"

"I have to see you, Mrs. Voss. And it has to be without your husband's knowledge. Can you arrange it?"

"First tell me why."

"It's not an easy thing to say over the phone."

"I won't meet with you until you tell me."

Abby hesitated. "It's about your heart. The one you got at Bayside."

"Yes?"

"No one seems to know whose heart it was. Or where it came from." She paused. And asked quietly: "Do you know, Mrs. Voss?"

The silence that followed was broken only by the sound of Nina's breathing, rapid and irregular.

"Mrs. Voss?"

"I have to go."

"Wait. When can I see you?"

"Tomorrow."

"How? Where?"

There was another pause. Just before the line went dead, Nina said: "I'll find a way."

* * *

The rain beat a relentless tattoo on the striped awning over Abby's head. For forty minutes now she had been standing in front of Cellucci's Grocery, shivering beneath the narrow overhang of canvas. A succession of delivery trucks had pulled up to unload, the men wheeling in dollies and cartons. Snapple and Frito-Lay and Winston cigarettes. Little Debbie had a snack for you.

At four-twenty the rain began coming down harder, swirling with the wind. Gusts of it angled under the awning, splattering her shoes. Her feet were freezing. An hour had passed; Nina Voss was not going to show up.

Abby flinched as a Progresso Foods truck suddenly roared away from the curb, spewing exhaust. When she looked up again, she saw that a black limousine had stopped across the street. The driver's window rolled down a few inches and a man called: "Dr. DiMatteo? Come into the car."

She hesitated. The windows were too darkly tinted for Abby to see inside, but she could make out the silhouette of a single rear-seat passenger.

"We haven't much time," urged the driver.

She crossed the street, head bent under the beating rain, and opened the rear door. Blinking water from her eyes, she focused on the backseat passenger. What she saw dismayed her.

In the gloom of the car, Nina Voss looked pale and shrunken. Her skin was a powdery white. "Please get in, Doctor," said Nina.

Abby slid in beside her and shut the door. The limousine pulled away from the curb and glided noiselessly into the stream of traffic.

Nina was so completely bundled up in a black coat and scarf that her face seemed to be floating, bodyless, in the car's shadows. This was not the picture of a recovering transplant patient. Abby remembered Josh O'Day's ruddy face, remembered his liveliness, his laughter.

Nina Voss looked like a talking corpse.

"I'm sorry we're late," said Nina. "We had a problem leaving the house."

"Does your husband know you're meeting me?"

"No." Nina sat back, her face almost swallowed up in all that black wool. "I've learned, over the years, that one doesn't tell Victor certain things. The real secret of a happy marriage, Dr. DiMatteo, is silence.''

''That hardly sounds like a happy marriage.''

''It is. Strangely enough.'' Nina smiled and looked out the window. The watery light cast distorted shadows on her face. ''Men have to be protected from so many things. Most of all from themselves. That's why they need us, you know. The funny thing is, they'll never admit it. They think they're taking care of *us*. And all the time, we know the truth.'' She turned to Abby, and her smile faded. ''Now I need to know. What has Victor done?''

''I was hoping you could tell me.''

''You said it had to do with my heart.'' Nina touched her hand to her chest. In the gloom of the car, her gesture seemed almost religious. Father, Son, Holy Ghost. ''What do you know about it?''

''I know your heart didn't come through normal channels. Almost all transplant organs are matched to recipients through a central registry. Yours wasn't. According to the organ bank, you never got a heart at all.''

Nina's hand, still resting on her chest, had squeezed into a tense white ball. ''Then where did this one come from?''

''I don't know. Do you?''

The corpselike face stared at her in silence.

''I think your husband knows,'' said Abby.

''How would he?''

''He bought it.''

''People can't just buy hearts.''

''With enough money, people can buy anything.''

Nina said nothing. By her silence, she admitted her acceptance of that fundamental truth. *Money can buy anything.*

The limousine turned onto Embankment Road. They were driving west along the Charles River. Its surface was gray and stippled by falling rain.

Nina asked, ''How did you learn about this?''

''Lately I seem to have a lot of free time on my hands. It's amazing what you can accomplish when you find yourself suddenly unemployed. In just the last few days, I've found out a lot of things. Not just about your transplant, but about others as well. And the more I learn, Mrs. Voss, the more scared I get.''

"Why come to me about this? Why not go to the authorities?"

"Haven't you heard? I have a new nickname these days. *Dr. Hemlock.* They're saying I kill my patients with kindness. None of it's true, of course, but people are always ready to believe the worst." Wearily Abby gazed out at the river. "I have no job. No credibility. And no proof."

"What do you have?"

Abby looked at her. "I know the truth."

The limousine dipped through a puddle. The spray of water drummed the underside of the car. They had veered away from the river and the road to the Back Bay Fens now curved ahead of them.

"At ten P.M. on the night of your transplant," said Abby, "Bayside Hospital got a call that a donor had been found in Burlington, Vermont. Three hours later, the heart was delivered to our OR. The harvest was supposedly done at Wilcox Memorial Hospital, by a surgeon named Timothy Nicholls. Your transplant was performed, and there was nothing out of the ordinary about it. In so many ways, it was like every other transplant done at Bayside." She paused. "With one major difference. No one knows where your donor heart came from."

"You said it came from Burlington."

"I said it supposedly did. But Dr. Nicholls has vanished. He may be hiding. Or he may be dead. And Wilcox Memorial denies any knowledge of a harvest on that night."

Nina had retreated into silence. She seemed to be shrinking away into the woolen coat.

"You weren't the first one," said Abby.

The white face stared back with a numb expression. "There were others?"

"At least four. I've seen the records from the past two years. It always happened the same way. Bayside would get a call from Burlington that there's a donor. The heart is delivered to our OR sometime after midnight. The transplant's done, and it's all routine. But something's wrong with this picture. We're talking about four hearts, four dead people. A friend and I have searched the Burlington obituaries for those dates. None of the donors appear."

"Then where are the hearts coming from?"

Abby paused. Meeting Nina's disbelieving gaze, she said, "I don't know."

The limousine had looped north and was once again skirting the Charles River. They were heading back toward Beacon Hill.

"I have no proof," said Abby. "I can't get through to New England Organ Bank, or anyone else. They all know I'm under investigation. They think of me as the crazy lady. That's why I came to you. That night we met in the ICU, I thought: *There's a woman I'd want as a friend.*" She paused. "I need your help, Mrs. Voss."

For a long time, Nina said nothing. She was not looking at Abby, but was staring straight ahead, her face white as bleached bone. At last she seemed to come to a decision. She released a deep breath and said, "I'm going to drop you off now. Would this corner be all right?"

"Mrs. Voss, your husband bought that heart. If he did it, so can other people. We don't know who the donors are! We don't know how they're getting them—"

"*Here,*" Nina said to the driver.

The limousine pulled over to the curb.

"Please get out," said Nina.

Abby didn't move. She sat for a moment, not speaking. The rain tapped monotonously on the roof.

"Please," whispered Nina.

"I thought I could trust you. I thought . . ." Slowly Abby shook her head. "Good-bye, Mrs. Voss."

A hand touched her arm. Abby glanced back, into the other woman's haunted eyes.

"I love my husband," said Nina. "And he loves me."

"Does that make it right?"

Nina didn't answer.

Abby climbed out and shut the door. The limousine drove away. As she watched the car glide into the dusk, she thought: I'll never see her again.

Then, shoulders slumped, she turned and walked away through the rain.

"Home now, Mrs. Voss?" The chauffeur's voice, flat and tinny through the speaker phone, startled Nina from her trance.

"Yes," she said. "Take me home."

She wrapped herself tighter in her cocoon of black wool and stared at the rain streaking across her window. She thought of what she would say to Victor. And what she would not, could not, say. *This is what has become of our love,* she thought. *Secrets upon secrets. And he is keeping the most terrible secret of all.*

She lowered her head and began to cry, for Victor, and for what had happened to their marriage. She wept for herself as well, because she knew what had to be done, and she was afraid.

The rain streamed like tears down the window. And the limousine carried her home, to Victor.

19

Shu-Shu needed a bath. The older boys had been saying this for days, had even threatened to toss Shu-Shu into the sea if Aleksei did not give her a good cleaning. She stinks, they said, and no wonder, with all your snot on her. Aleksei did not think Shu-Shu stank. He liked the way she smelled. She had not been washed, ever, and each scent she wore was like a different memory. The smell of gravy, which he'd spilled on the tail, reminded him of last night's supper, when Nadiya had served him double portions of everything. (And smiled at him, too!) The odor of cigarettes was Uncle Misha's smell, gruff but warm. The sour beet smell was from last Easter morning, when they had laughed and eaten boiled eggs and he had spilled soup on Shu-Shu's head. And if he closed his eyes and inhaled deeply, he could sometimes detect another scent, fainter, but still there after all the years. It was not something he could classify as sour or sweet. Rather, he recognized it by the feelings it stirred in him. By the smell it brought to his heart. It was the smell of his babyhood. The smell of being caressed and sung to and loved.

Hugging Shu-Shu, Aleksei burrowed deeper under his blanket. I'll never let them give you a bath, he thought.

Anyway, there weren't so many of *them* left to torment him.

Five days ago, another boat had appeared through the fog, and had drifted alongside them. While all the boys had scrambled to the rail to watch, Nadiya and Gregor had walked back and forth, calling out name after name. *Nikolai Alekseyenko! Pavel Prebrazhensky!* There were whoops of triumph, fists punched in the air as each name was called. *Yes! I have been chosen!*

Later, the ones not chosen, the ones left behind, remained huddled at the rail, watching in silence as the motor launch carried the chosen boys to the other ship.

"Where do they go?" Aleksei asked.

"To families in the West," Nadiya answered. "Now come away from the rail. It's getting cold up here."

The boys didn't move. After a while Nadiya didn't seem to care if they stayed up on deck or not, and she left to go below.

"Families in the West must be stupid," said Yakov.

Aleksei turned to look at him. Yakov was staring fiercely out to sea, his chin jutted out like someone hungry for a fight. "You think everyone's stupid," said Aleksei.

"They are. Everyone on this boat is."

"That means you too."

Yakov didn't answer. He simply clutched the rail with his one hand, his gaze directed at the other ship as it glided back into the fog. Then he walked away.

Over the next few days, Aleksei scarcely saw him.

Tonight, as usual, Yakov had disappeared right after supper. He was probably in his stupid Wonderland, Aleksei thought. Hiding out in that crate with all the mouse turds.

Aleksei pulled the blanket over his head. And that was how he fell asleep, curled up in his bunk with dirty Shu-Shu cradled against his face.

A hand shook him. A voice called softly in the night: "Aleksei. Aleksei."

"Mommy," he said.

"Aleksei, it's time to wake up. I have a surprise for you."

Slowly he drifted up through layers of sleep, surfacing into darkness. The hand was still shaking him. He recognized Nadiya's scent.

"It's time to go," she whispered.

"Where am I going?"

"You must get ready to meet your new mother."

"Is she here?"

"I'll take you to her, Aleksei. Out of all the boys, you've been chosen. You're very lucky. Now come. But be quiet."

Aleksei sat up. He was not quite awake yet, not quite certain if he was dreaming. Nadiya reached up and helped him off the bunk.

"Shu-Shu," he said.

Nadiya put the dog in his arms. "Of course you can bring your Shu-Shu." She took his hand. She had never held his hand before. The sudden rush of happiness shook him fully awake. He was holding her hand and they were walking together, to meet his mother. It was dark and he was scared of the dark, but Nadiya would see to it that nothing happened to him. He remembered, somehow he remembered: *This is how it feels to hold your mother's hand.*

They left the cabin and walked down a dimly lit corridor. He was stumbling through a joyous daze, not paying attention to where they were going, because Nadiya was taking care of everything. They turned down another corridor. This one he did not recognize. They pushed through a door.

Into Wonderland.

The steel walkway stretched before them. Beyond it stood the blue door.

Aleksei stopped.

"What is it?" asked Nadiya.

"I don't want to go in there."

"But you have to."

"There are people living there."

"Aleksei, don't be difficult." Nadiya gripped his hand more firmly. "This is where you must go."

"Why?"

Suddenly she seemed to understand that a different tactic was called for. She crouched down so that they were eye to eye, and took him firmly by the shoulders. "Do you want to ruin everything? Do you want to make her angry? She expects an obedient little boy, and now you are being very disagreeable."

His lips trembled. He tried so hard not to cry, because he knew how much adults hated children's tears. But the tears were starting to fall anyway, and now he'd probably ruined everything. Just as Nadiya had said he would. He was always ruining everything.

"Nothing is settled yet," said Nadiya. "She can still choose another boy. Is that what you want?"

Aleksei sobbed. "No."

"Then why aren't you behaving?"

"I'm afraid of the quail people."

"What? You are ridiculous. I wouldn't be surprised if *no one* ever wanted you." She straightened and snatched his hand again. *"Come."*

Aleksei looked at the blue door. He whispered: "Carry me."

"You're too big. You'll hurt my back."

"Please carry me."

"You have to walk, Aleksei. Now hurry, or we'll be late." She put her arm around him.

He began to walk, only because she was there beside him, hugging him close. The way he was hugging Shu-Shu close. As long as they held each other, the three of them, nothing bad would happen.

Nadiya knocked at the blue door.

It swung open.

Yakov heard them on the walkway above. Aleksei's whining. Nadiya's impatient coaxing. He crawled to the edge of the crate and cautiously peered up at them. They were crossing to the blue door now. A moment later, they vanished through it.

Why does Aleksei get to go in there, and not me?

Yakov slipped out of the crate and up the stairs to the blue door. He tried to open it, but as always, it was locked.

Defeated, he went back to his crate. It was quite a comfortable hiding place now. Over the last week, he had scavenged a blanket, a flashlight, and a number of magazines with naked ladies in them. He had also lifted a lighter and a pack of cigarettes from Koubichev. Sometimes Yakov would smoke one, but there were so few cigarettes, he was careful to save them. Once he'd accidentally set the shavings on fire. That had been exciting. Most of the time, though, he just liked having the cigarettes around, liked holding the pack, reading and re-reading the label under the beam of the flashlight.

That's what he'd been doing when he'd heard Aleksei and Nadiya on the walkway.

Now he waited for them to come back out of the blue door. It was taking a long time. What were they doing in there?

Yakov threw the cigarettes down. It wasn't fair.

He looked at a few pictures in the magazines. Practiced flicking the lighter on and off. Then he decided he was sleepy. He curled up in the blanket and dozed off.

Sometime later, he was awakened by a rumbling sound. At first he thought something was wrong with the ship's engines, then he realized the sound was growing louder, and that it was not coming from Hell, but from the deck above.

It was a helicopter.

Gregor tied the twist top and set the plastic bag in the cooler. He handed it to Nadiya. "Well, take it."

At first she didn't seem to hear. Then she looked at him, her face drained white, and he thought: *The bitch can't handle it.* "It needs ice. Go on, do it." He shoved the cooler toward her.

She seemed to recoil in horror. Then, breathing deeply, she took it, carried it across the room, and set it on the countertop. She began scooping ice into the cooler. He noticed that her legs were not quite steady. The first time around was always a shock to the system. Even Gregor had had his queasy moments the first time. Nadiya would get over it.

He turned to the operating table. The anesthetist had already zipped up the shroud and was now gathering up the bloodied drapes. The surgeon had made no move to help. Instead, he was slumped back against the counter, as though trying to catch his breath. Gregor regarded him with distaste. There was something especially disgusting about a doctor who let himself get so grotesquely fat. The surgeon did not look well tonight. He had wheezed his way through the entire procedure, and his hands had seemed more tremulous than usual.

"My head hurts," the surgeon groaned.

"You've been drinking too much. Probably got yourself a fucking hangover." Gregor moved to the table and grasped one end of the shroud. Together, he and the anesthetist lifted their burden and slid it onto the gurney. Next, Gregor picked up the pile of dirty clothes and set those on the gurney as well. He almost overlooked the stuffed dog. It was lying on the floor, the ratty fur soaked with blood. He tossed it on top of the dirty clothes, then he and the anesthetist wheeled the gurney to the disposal chute. They opened the hatch and deposited the shroud, the clothes, and the dog into the chute.

The surgeon moaned. "This is the worst fucking headache . . ."

Gregor ignored him. He stripped off his gloves and went to the sink to wash his hands. One never knew what one might pick up handling those filthy clothes. Lice, perhaps. He scrubbed as thoroughly as a doctor preparing to operate.

There was a loud crash, the clatter of falling metal instruments. Gregor turned.

The surgeon was lying on the floor, his face bright red, his limbs jerking like a puppet gone out of control.

Nadiya and the anesthetist stood frozen in horror.

"What's wrong with him?" demanded Gregor.

"I don't know!" said the anesthetist.

"Well do something about it!"

The anesthetist knelt beside the convulsing man and made a few helpless attempts to revive him. He loosened the man's surgical gown, clapped an oxygen mask on his face. The convulsions were worse now, the arms flapping like goose wings.

"Hold the mask on for me!" said the anesthetist. "I'm going to give him an injection!"

Gregor knelt at the man's head and took hold of the mask. The surgeon's face felt repulsive, doughy and oily. Spittle had dribbled out of his mouth, turning the oxygen mask slippery. His skin was beginning to turn blue. Gregor knew then, looking at the darkening cyanosis, that their efforts were futile.

Moments later, the man was dead.

For a long time, the three of them stood around staring at the corpse. It seemed to have ballooned even larger and more grotesque. The stomach was distended and the fleshy folds of the face had spread out like a boneless jellyfish.

"What the fuck do we do now?" said the anesthetist.

"We need another surgeon," Gregor said.

"You can't exactly pull one out of the sea. We'll have to head into port sooner than planned."

"Or transfer the live cargo . . ." Gregor suddenly glanced upward. So did Nadiya and the anesthetist. They all heard it now: the *whup-whup* of the helicopter. He looked at the cooler on the countertop. "Is it ready?"

"I packed it with ice," said Nadiya.

"Go, then. Bring it up to them." Gregor looked back down

at the carcass of the dead surgeon. He gave it a kick of disgust. "We'll take care of the whale."

The blue eye was shining on deck.

From his hiding place under the bridge stairway, Yakov had watched the blue light flare on first, followed by the surrounding circle of white lights. They were all blazing now, so brightly he could not look directly at them. Instead he looked up at the sky, at the helicopter hovering overhead. It descended from the darkness, and Yakov closed his eyes as the wash of the rotors whipped his face. When he opened his eyes again, he saw that the helicopter had landed.

The door swung open, but no one emerged. It was waiting for someone to board.

Yakov crept forward so that he was gazing through the gap between two steps, straight at the helicopter. *Lucky Aleksei,* he thought. *Aleksei must be leaving tonight.*

He heard the clang of a door shutting and a figure appeared at the edge of the lit circle. It was Nadiya. She crossed the deck, her body bent forward at the waist, her ass sticking in the air. She was scared those rotors would chop off her stupid head. She leaned inside the helicopter door, her ass still poking out as she spoke to the pilot. Then she backed out and retreated to the edge of the lights.

A moment later, the helicopter lifted off.

The lights shut off, plunging the deck into darkness.

Yakov eased around the stairway to watch as the helicopter rose. He saw the tail swing away like a giant pendulum on a string. Then the craft thundered away, swooping low over the water, and vanished into the night.

A hand grabbed Yakov's arm. He gave a cry as he was yanked backward and spun around.

"What the fuck are you doing up here?" said Gregor.

"Nothing!"

"What did you see?"

"Just a helicopter—"

"*What did you see?*"

Yakov only stared at him, too terrified to answer.

Nadiya had heard their voices. Now she crossed the deck toward them. "What is it?"

"The boy's been watching again. I thought you locked the cabin."

"I did. He must have slipped out earlier." She looked at Yakov. "It's always *him*. I can't watch him every second."

"I've had enough of this one anyway." Gregor gave Yakov's arm a jerk, pulling him toward the stairway hatch. "He can't go back with the others." He turned to open the hatch.

Yakov kicked him in the back of the knee.

Gregor shrieked, releasing his grip.

Yakov ran. He heard Nadiya's shouts, heard footsteps pounding after him. Then more footsteps, clanging down the bridge stairway. He darted forward, toward the bow. Too late, he realized he had run straight onto the landing deck.

There was a loud *clank,* and the deck lights flared on.

Yakov was trapped in the very center of their brilliance. Shielding his eyes, he stumbled blindly away from the sounds of pursuit. But they were all around him now, moving in. Grabbing his shirt. He flailed.

Someone slapped him across the face. The blow sent Yakov sprawling. He tried to crawl away, but his legs were kicked out from under him.

"That's enough!" said Nadiya. "You don't want to kill him!"

"Little motherfucker," Gregor grunted.

Yakov was yanked up by the hair. Gregor shoved him forward across the deck, toward the stairwell hatch. Yakov kept stumbling, only to be dragged back up again by the hair. He couldn't see where they were going. He knew only that they were going down some steps, moving along a corridor. Gregor was cursing the whole way. He was also limping a little, which gave Yakov some small measure of satisfaction.

A door swung open and Yakov was tossed over the threshold.

"You can rot in there for a while," said Gregor. And he slammed the door shut.

Yakov heard the latch close. Heard footsteps fade away. He was alone in the darkness.

He drew his knees to his chest and lay hugging himself. A strange trembling seized his body, and he tried to stop it but couldn't. He could hear his own teeth chattering, not from the cold, but from some quaking deep in his soul. He closed his

261

eyes and was confronted with the images of what he'd seen tonight. Nadiya crossing the deck, gliding, floating through an unearthly field of light. The helicopter door open and waiting. Now Nadiya bending over, reaching out as she hands something to the pilot.

A box.

Yakov drew his legs more tightly to his chest, but the trembling didn't ease.

Whimpering, he put his thumb in his mouth and began to suck.

20

For Abby, mornings were the worst. She would awaken feeling that first sleepy flush of anticipation for the day ahead. Then suddenly she'd remember: *I have nowhere to go.* That realization would strike as cruelly as any physical blow. She would lie in bed, listening to Mark getting dressed. She'd hear him moving around in the still-dark bedroom, and she would feel so engulfed by depression she could not say a word to him. They shared a house and a bed, yet they'd scarcely spoken to each other in days. *This is how love dies,* thought Abby, hearing him walk out the front door. *Not with angry words, but with silence.*

When Abby was twelve years old, her father was laid off from his job at the tannery. For weeks afterward, he'd drive away each morning, as though heading for work as usual. Abby never found out where he went, or what he did. Till the day he died, he never told her. All Abby knew was that her father was terrified of staying home and confronting his own failure. So he'd continued the charade, fleeing the house every morning.

Just as Abby was doing today.

She left the car at home and walked instead, blocks and blocks, not really caring where she went. Last night the weather had turned cold, and by the time she finally stopped in at a bagel shop, her face was numb. She bought coffee and a sesame seed bagel and slid into one of the booths. She'd taken only two bites when she happened to glance at the man at the next table. He was reading a *Boston Herald*.

Abby's photo was on the front page.

She felt like crawling out the door. Furtively she glanced around the café, half expecting everyone to be looking at her, but no one was.

She bolted out of the booth, tossed her bagel in the trash, and walked out. Her appetite was gone. At a newsstand a block away, she purchased a copy of the *Herald* and huddled shivering in a doorway while she scanned the article.

Rigors of Surgical Training
May Have Led to Tragedy

By all accounts, Dr. Abigail DiMatteo was an outstanding resident—one of the best at Bayside Medical Center, according to Department Chairman Dr. Colin Wettig. But sometime in the last few months, soon after Dr. DiMatteo entered her second year in the program, things began to go terribly wrong . . .

Abby had to stop reading; her breaths were coming too hard and fast. It took her a few moments to calm down enough to finish the article. When she finally did, she felt truly sick.

The reporter had included everything. The lawsuits. Mary Allen's death. The shouting match with Brenda. None of it was deniable. All the elements, taken together, painted the picture of an unstable, even dangerous personality. It fed right into the public's secret horror of being at the mercy of a deranged physician.

I can't believe it's me they're writing about.

Even if she managed to retain her medical license, even if she finished a residency, an article like this would follow her forever. So would the doubts. No patient in his right mind would go under the knife of a psychopath.

She didn't know how long she walked around with that newspaper clutched in her hand. When she finally came to a halt, she was standing on the Harvard University Common, and her ears were aching from the cold. She realized it was already well past lunchtime. She'd been walking around all morning, and now half the day was gone. She didn't know where to go next. Everyone else on the Common—students with backpacks, shaggy professors in tweeds—seemed to have a destination. But not her.

She looked down again, at the newspaper. The photograph they'd used of her was from the residency directory, a shot taken when she was an intern. She'd smiled straight at the camera, her face fresh and eager, the look of a young woman ready and willing to work for her dream.

She threw the newspaper into the nearest trash receptacle and walked home, thinking: *Fight back. I have to fight back.*

But she and Vivian had run out of leads. Yesterday, Vivian had flown to Burlington. When she'd called Abby last night, it had been with bad news: Tim Nicholls's practice had closed down, and no one knew where he was. Dead end. Also, Wilcox Memorial had no records of any harvests on those four dates. Another dead end. Finally, Vivian had checked with the local police and had found no records of missing persons or unidentified bodies with their hearts cut out. Final dead end.

They've covered their tracks. We'll never beat them.

As soon as she stepped in the front door, she saw the answering machine was blinking. It was a message from Vivian to call back. She'd left a Burlington number. Abby dialed the number, but got no answer, so she hung up.

Next she called NEOB, but as usual, they wouldn't put her through to Helen Lewis. No one, it seemed, wanted to hear the latest theories of the psychopathic Dr. DiMatteo. She didn't know who else to call. She ran through the list of all the people she knew at Bayside. Dr. Wettig. Mark. Mohandas and Zwick. Susan Casado. Jeremiah Parr. She didn't trust any of them. *Any* of them.

She'd just picked up the phone to try calling Vivian again when she happened to glance out the window. Parked at the far end of the street was a maroon van.

You bastard. This time you're mine!

She ran to the hall closet and pulled out the binoculars.

Focusing from the window, she could just make out the license plate.

I got you, she thought in triumph. *I got you.*

She grabbed the phone and dialed Katzka. It struck her then, as she was waiting for him to come on the line, how strange it was that *he* should be the one she'd call. Maybe it was an automatic response. You need help, you call a cop. And he was the only cop she knew.

"Detective Katzka," he said in his usual flat and business-like voice.

"The van is back!" she blurted.

"Excuse me?"

"This is Abby DiMatteo. The van that was following me—it's parked right outside my house. The license number's five-three-nine, TDV. Massachusetts plate."

There was a pause as he wrote it down. "You live on Brewster Street, right?"

"Yes. Please send someone right away. I don't know what he's going to do."

"Just sit tight and keep the doors locked. Got that?"

"Okay." She let out a nervous breath. "Okay."

She knew the doors were already locked, but she rechecked them anyway. Everything was secure. She returned to the living room and sat near the curtain, every so often glancing outside to make sure the van was still there. She wanted it to stay right where it was. She wanted to see the driver's reaction when the cops arrived.

Fifteen minutes later, a familiar green Volvo drove by and pulled over at the curb, right across the street from the van. She hadn't expected Katzka himself to show up, but there he was, stepping out of his car. At her first glimpse of him, she felt an overwhelming sense of relief. He'll know what to do, she thought. Katzka was clever enough to deal with anything.

He crossed the street and slowly approached the van.

Abby pressed closer to the window, her heart suddenly pounding. She wondered if Katzka's pulse was racing as fast as hers was. He moved with almost casual grace toward the driver's door. Only as he shifted, turning slightly toward Abby, did she notice that he'd drawn his gun. She hadn't even seen him reach for it.

She was almost afraid to watch now. Afraid for *him.*

He edged forward and glanced in the window. Apparently he saw nothing suspicious. He circled around to the rear of the van and peered through the back window. Then he reholstered his gun and looked up and down the street.

At a nearby house, the front door suddenly swung open and a man in gray overalls stormed down the porch steps, yelling and waving. Katzka responded with his trademark unflappability and produced his badge. The other man took a look at it and handed it back. Then he took out his wallet and showed *his* ID.

For a while the two men stood talking, gesturing every so often toward the van and the house. At last the man in the overalls went back inside.

Katzka walked toward Abby's.

She let him in the front door. "What happened?"

"Nothing."

"Who's the driver? Why's he been following me?"

"He says he has no idea what you're talking about."

She followed him into the living room. "I'm not blind! I've seen that van here before. On this street."

"The driver says he's never been here before."

"Who *is* the driver, anyway?"

Katzka pulled out his notebook. "John Doherty, age thirty-six, Massachusetts resident. Licensed plumber. He says this is the first call he's ever made to Brewster Street. The van is registered to Back Bay Plumbing. And it's full of tools." He closed his notebook and slid it into his coat pocket. Then he regarded her with his usual detachment.

"I was so sure," she murmured. "I was so sure it was the same one."

"You still insist there was a van?"

"Yes, godammit!" she snapped. "There *was* a van!"

He reacted to her outburst with a slightly raised eyebrow. She forced herself to take a deep breath. A burst of temper was the last thing this man would respond to. He was all logic, all reason. Mr. Spock with a badge.

She said, more calmly now, "I am not imagining things. And I'm not making them up."

"If you think you see the van again, get the license number."

"If I *think* I see it?"

"I'll call Back Bay Plumbing, to confirm Doherty's information. But I really do believe he's just a plumber." Katzka glanced toward her living room. The phone was ringing. "Aren't you going to answer it?"

"Please don't leave. Not yet. I have a few things to tell you."

He had already reached for the doorknob. Now he paused, watching as she picked up the phone.

"Hello?" she said.

A woman's voice responded softly, "Dr. DiMatteo?"

Instantly Abby's gaze shot to Katzka's. He seemed to understand, just from her glance, that this call was important. "Mrs. Voss?" said Abby.

"I've learned something," said Nina. "I don't know what it means. If it means anything at all."

Katzka moved to Abby's side. He had done it so quickly, so quietly, she'd barely registered his approach. He bent his head toward the receiver to listen in.

"What did you find out?" said Abby.

"I made some calls. To the bank, and to our accountant. On September twenty-third, Victor transferred funds to a company called the Amity Corporation. In Boston."

"You're sure about that date?"

"Yes."

September twenty-third, thought Abby. One day before Nina Voss's transplant.

"What do you know about Amity?" asked Abby.

"Nothing. Victor's never mentioned the name. With a transaction this large, he'd normally discuss it . . ." There was a silence. Abby heard voices in the background, then the sounds of frantic shuffling. Nina's voice came back on. Tenser. Softer. "I have to get off the phone."

"You said it was a large transaction. How large?"

For a moment there was no reply. Abby thought perhaps Nina had already hung up. Then she heard the whispered answer.

"Five million," said Nina. "He transferred five million dollars."

Nina hung up the telephone. She heard Victor's footsteps, but she did not look up as he came into the bedroom.

"Who were you talking to?" he asked.

"Cynthia. I called to thank her for the flowers."

"Which flowers were those again?"

"The orchids."

He glanced at the vase on the dresser. "Oh, yes. Very nice."

"Cynthia says they're going to Greece next spring. I guess they're tired of the Caribbean." How easily she lied to him. When had it started? When had they stopped speaking the truth to each other?

He sat down beside her on the bed. She felt him studying her. "When you're all better," he said, "maybe we'll go back to Greece. Maybe we'll even go with Cynthia and Robert. Wouldn't you like that?"

She nodded and looked down at the bedspread. At her hands, the fingers bony and wasting away. *But I am never getting better. We both know that.*

She slid her legs out from under the covers. "I have to use the bathroom," she said.

"Shall I help you?"

"No. I'm fine." Rising to her feet, she felt a brief spell of light-headedness. Lately she'd been having the spells often, whenever she stood up or exerted herself in even the slightest way. She said nothing about it to Victor, but just waited for the feeling to pass. Then she continued slowly into the bathroom.

She heard him pick up the telephone.

Only when she'd shut the bathroom door did she suddenly realize her mistake. The last number she'd called was still in the phone's memory system. All Victor had to do was press Redial, and he would know she'd lied to him. It was just the sort of thing Victor would do. He'd learn she hadn't called Cynthia. He'd find out, somehow he'd find out, that it was Abby DiMatteo she'd called.

Nina stood with her back pressed to the bathroom door, listening. She heard him hang up the phone again. Heard him say, "Nina?"

Another wave of light-headedness hit her. She dropped her head, fighting the darkness that was beginning to cloud her vision. Her legs seemed to melt away beneath her. She felt herself sliding downward.

He rattled the door. "Nina, I need to speak to you."

"Victor," she whispered, but knew he couldn't hear her. No one could hear her.

She lay on the bathroom floor, too weak to move, too weak to call out to him.

She felt her heart flutter like a butterfly's wings in her chest.

"This has to be the wrong place," said Abby.

She and Katzka were parked on a run-down street in Roxbury. It was a neighborhood of barred storefronts and businesses on the verge of collapse. The only apparently thriving enterprise was a bodybuilding gym a few doors down. Through the gym's open windows, they could hear the clank of weights and occasional masculine laughter. Adjacent to the gym was an unoccupied building with a FOR LEASE sign. And next to that was the Amity building, a four-story brownstone. Over the entrance hung the sign:

Amity Medical Supplies
Sales and Service

Behind the barred front windows was a tired-looking display of company products: Crutches and canes. Oxygen tanks. Foam mattress pads to prevent bedsores. Bedside commodes. A mannequin wearing a nurse's uniform and cap straight out of the sixties.

Abby gazed across the street at the shabby display window and said, "This can't be the right Amity."

"It's the only listing in the phone book," said Katzka.

"Why would he transfer five million dollars to *this* business?"

"It could be just one branch of a larger corporation. Maybe he saw an investment opportunity."

She shook her head. "The timing's all wrong. Put yourself in Victor Voss's place. His wife is dying. He's desperate to get her the operation she needs. He's not going to be thinking about his investments."

"It depends how much he cares about his wife."

"He cares a lot."

"How do you know?"

She looked at him. "I know."

He regarded her in that quiet way of his. How strange, she

thought, that his gaze no longer made her feel uncomfortable.

He opened his door. "I'll see what I can find out."

"What are you going to do?"

"Look around. Ask a few questions."

"I'll go in with you."

"No, you stay in the car." He started to step out, but she pulled him back.

"Look," she said. "I'm the one with everything to lose. I've already lost my job. I'm losing my license. And now people are calling me a murderer or a psychotic or both. It's *my* life they've fucked up. This could be my one chance to fight back."

"Then let's not screw it up, okay? Someone in there could recognize you. That would certainly tip them off. Do you want to risk that?"

She sank back. Katzka was right. Goddamn it, he was right. He hadn't wanted her to come along on this ride in the first place, but she'd insisted. She'd told him she could drive here on her own, with or without him. So here she was, and she couldn't even walk into the building. She couldn't even fight her own battles anymore. They'd taken that away from her, too. She sat shaking her head, angry about her own impotence. Angry at Katzka for having pointed it out.

He said, "Lock the doors." And he stepped out of the car.

She watched him cross the street, watched him walk into the shabby entrance. She could picture what he'd find inside. Depressing displays of wheelchairs and emesis basins. Racks of nurses' uniforms under dustcovers of yellowing plastic. Boxes of orthopedic shoes. She could imagine every detail because she had been in shops just like it when she'd purchased her first set of uniforms.

Five minutes passed. Then ten.

Katzka, Katzka. What are you doing in there?

He'd said he was going to ask questions, that he would try not to tip them off. She trusted his judgment. The average homicide cop, she decided, was probably smarter than the average surgeon. But maybe not smarter than the average internist. That was the running joke among hospital house staff: the stupidity of surgeons. Internists relied on their brains, surgeons on their precious hands. If an internist is in an elevator and the door starts to shut prematurely, he'll stick in his hand to stop it. A surgeon will stick in his head. Ha, ha.

Twenty minutes had gone by. It was after five now, and the anemic sunshine had already faded to a gloomy dusk. Through the window crack, she could hear the continual whoosh of cars on Martin Luther King Boulevard. Rush hour. Up the street, two men with biceps of heroic proportions came out of the gym and lumbered to their cars.

She kept watching the entrance, waiting for Katzka to emerge.

It was five-twenty.

The traffic was beginning to thicken even on this street. Through the flow of cars, she caught only intermittent glimpses of the front entrance. Then, suddenly, there was a gap in the traffic and she was looking straight across the street as a man emerged from the side door of the Amity building. He paused on the sidewalk and glanced at his watch. When he looked up again, Abby felt her heart kick into a gallop. She recognized that face. The grotesquely heavy brow. The hawklike nose.

It was Dr. Mapes. The courier who'd delivered Nina Voss's donor heart to the operating room.

Mapes began walking. Halfway up the street, he stopped at a blue Trans Am parked at the curb. He took out a set of car keys.

Abby looked back at the Amity building, hoping, praying for Katzka to appear. *Come on, come on. I'm going to lose Mapes!* She looked back at the Trans Am. Mapes had climbed inside now, and was fastening his seat belt. He started the engine. Easing slightly away from the curb, he waited for a break in the traffic.

Abby cast a frantic glance down at the ignition and saw that Katzka had left his keys dangling there.

This could be her one chance. Her only chance.

The blue Trans Am pulled into the street.

There was no time left to think it over.

Abby scrambled into the driver's seat and started Katzka's car. She lurched into traffic, eliciting a screech of tires and an angry honk from another car behind her.

A block ahead, Mapes glided through the intersection just as the light turned red.

Abby squealed to a stop. There were four cars between her and the intersection and no way to get around them. By the time the light turned green again, Mapes could be blocks away. She sat counting the seconds, cursing Boston traffic lights and Boston drivers and her own indecision. If only she'd pulled away from the curb earlier! The Trans Am was barely in view now, just a glint of blue in a river of cars. What the hell was wrong with this light?

At last it turned green, but still no one was moving. The driver in front must be asleep at the wheel. Abby leaned on her horn, releasing a deafening blast. The cars ahead of her finally began to move. She stepped on the accelerator, then let up on it.

Someone was pounding at the side of her car.

Glancing right, she saw Katzka running alongside the passenger door. She braked and hit the lock-release button.

He yanked open the door. "What the hell are you doing?"

"Get in."

"No, first you pull over—"

"Get the fuck in!"

He blinked in surprise. And got in.

At once she goosed the accelerator, and they shot through the intersection. Two blocks ahead, a flash of blue streaked rightward. The Trans Am was turning onto Cottage Street. If she didn't stay right on his tail, she could lose him in the traffic coming up. She swerved left across a double line, raced past three cars in a row, and screeched back into her lane just in time. She heard Katzka snap on his seat belt. Good. Because this could be one hell of a wild ride. They turned onto Cottage.

"Are you going to tell me?" he said.

"He came out the side door of the Amity building. The guy in the blue car."

"Who is he?"

"The organ courier. He said his name was Mapes." She spotted another break in traffic, made another passing swoop into the left lane, then back again.

Katzka said, "I think I should drive."

"He's heading into the traffic circle. Now which way? Which way's he going..."

The Trans Am looped around the circle, then cut away east.

"He's heading for the expressway," said Katzka.

"Then so are we." Abby entered the traffic circle and peeled off after the Trans Am.

Katzka had guessed correctly. Mapes was heading onto the expressway ramp. She followed him, her heart ramming her chest, her hands slick on the steering wheel. Here's where she could lose him. The expressway at five-thirty was like a bumper car ride at sixty miles an hour, every driver a maniac intent on getting home. She merged into traffic and spotted Mapes way ahead, switching to the left lane.

She tried to make the same lane change, only to find a truck muscling in, refusing to yield. Abby signaled, nudged closer to his lane. The truck only tightened the gap. This had turned into a dangerous game of chicken now, Abby veering toward the truck, the truck holding fast. She was too pumped up on adrenaline to be afraid, too intent on keeping up with Mapes. Behind the wheel, she had transformed into some other woman, a desperate, foul-mouthed stranger she scarcely recognized. She was fighting back at them, and it felt good. It felt powerful. Abby DiMatteo on fucking testosterone.

She floored the accelerator and shot left, right in front of the truck.

"Jesus Christ!" yelled Katzka. "Are you trying to get us killed?"

"I don't give a shit. I want this guy."

"Are you like this in the OR?"

"Oh, yeah. I'm a real fucking terror. Haven't you heard?"

"Remind me not to get sick."

"Now what's he doing?"

Up ahead the Trans Am had switched lanes again. It peeled to the right, onto the turnoff for the Callahan Tunnel.

"*Shit*," said Abby, cutting right as well. She shot across two lanes and they entered the cavelike gloom of the tunnel. Graffiti whipped past. Concrete walls echoed back the grinding of tires over pavement, the whoosh-whoosh of cars slicing the air. Their reemergence into the gray light of dusk was a shock to their eyes.

The Trans Am left the expressway. Abby followed.

They were in East Boston now, the gateway to Logan International Airport. That must be where Mapes was headed, she thought. The airport.

She was surprised when, instead, he rattled across a railroad track and worked his way west, away from the airport. He headed into a maze of streets.

Abby slowed down, gave him some space. That surge of adrenaline she'd felt during the frantic chase on the expressway was fading. The Trans Am wasn't going to get away from her in this neighborhood. Now her challenge was to avoid being noticed.

They were heading along the wharves of Boston's Inner Harbor. Behind a chain-link fence, rows and rows of unused ship's containers were stacked three deep like giant Legos. And beyond the container yard was the industrial waterfront. Against the setting sun loomed the silhouettes of loading cranes and ships in port. The Trans Am turned left, drove through an open gate and into the container yard.

Abby pulled up beside the fence and parked. Peering through a gap between a forklift and a container, she saw the Trans Am drive to the foot of the pier and stop. Mapes got out of his car. He strode onto the dock, where a ship was moored. It looked like a small freighter—a two-hundred footer, she estimated.

Mapes gave a shout. After a moment, a man appeared on deck and waved him aboard. Mapes climbed the gangplank and disappeared into the vessel.

"Why did he come here?" she said. "Why a boat?"

"Are you sure it's the same man?"

"If it isn't, then Mapes has a double working at Amity." She paused, suddenly remembering where Katzka had just spent the last half hour. "What did you find out about the place, anyway?"

"You mean before I noticed someone stealing my car?" He shrugged. "It looked like what it's supposed to be. A medical supply business. I told them I needed a hospital bed for my wife, and they demonstrated some of the latest models."

"How many people in the building?"

"I saw three. One guy in the showroom. Two on the second floor handling phone orders. None of them looked very happy to be working there."

"What about the upper two floors?"

"Warehouse space, I assume. There's really nothing about that building worth pursuing."

She looked past the fence, at the blue Trans Am. "You could

subpoena their financial records. Find out where Voss's five million dollars went to.''

"We have no basis on which to subpoena any records.''

"How much evidence do you need? I *know* that was the courier! I know what these people are doing.''

"Your testimony isn't going to sway any judge. Certainly not under the circumstances.'' His answer was honest—brutally so. "I'm sorry, Abby. But you know as well as I do that you have a whopping credibility problem.''

She felt herself closing off against him, withdrawing in anger. "You're absolutely right,'' she shot back "Who'd believe me? It's just the psychotic Dr. DiMatteo, babbling nonsense again.''

He didn't respond to that self-pitying statement. In the silence that followed, she regretted having said it. The sound of her own voice, wounded and sarcastic, seemed to hang between them.

They said nothing for a while. Overhead a jet screamed, the shadow of its wings swooping past like a raptor's. It climbed, glittering in the last light of the setting sun. Only as the jet's roar faded away did Katzka speak again.

"It's not that I don't believe you," he said.

She looked at him. "No one else does. Why would you?''

"Because of Dr. Levi. And the way he died.'' He gazed straight ahead at the darkening road. "It wasn't the way people usually kill themselves. In a room where no one will find you for days. We don't like to think of our bodies decomposing. We want to be found before the maggots get to us. Before we're black and bloated. While we can still be recognized as human. Then there were all the plans he'd made. The trip to the Caribbean. Thanksgiving with his son. He was looking ahead, expecting a future.'' Katzka glanced sideways, at a streetlamp that had just flickered on in the gathering dusk. "Finally there's his wife, Elaine. I often have to talk to surviving spouses. Some of them are shocked, some of them grieving. Some of them are just plain relieved. I'm a widower myself. I remember, after my wife died, that it was all I could manage just to crawl out of bed every morning. But what does Elaine Levi do? She calls a moving company, packs up her furniture, and leaves town. It's not the act of a grieving spouse. It's what someone does when they're guilty. Or they're scared.''

Abby nodded. It's what she'd thought as well. That Elaine was afraid.

"Then you told me about Kunstler and Hennessy,'' he said. "And suddenly I'm not looking at a single death. I'm dealing with a series of them. And Aaron Levi's is beginning to look less and less like a suicide.''

Another jet took off, the scream of its engines making conversation impossible. It banked left, skimming the evening mist now gathering over the harbor. Even after the jet had vanished into the western sky, Abby could still hear the roar in her ears.

"Dr. Levi didn't hang himself,'' said Katzka.

Abby frowned at him. "I thought the autopsy was confirmatory.''

"We found something on toxicology. We got the results back just last week from the crime lab.''

"Something turned up?''

"In his muscle tissue. They found traces of succinylcholine.''

She stared at him. *Succinylcholine.* It was used every day by anesthesiologists to induce muscle relaxation during surgery. In the OR, it was a vitally useful drug. Outside the OR, its administration would cause the most horrible of deaths. Complete paralysis in a fully conscious subject. Though awake and aware, one would be unable to move or breathe. Like drowning in a sea of air.

She swallowed, her throat suddenly dry. "It wasn't a suicide.''

"No.''

She took a breath and slowly let it out. For a moment she was too horrified to speak. She didn't dare even consider what Aaron's death must have been like. She looked through the fence, toward the pier. Evening fog was forming over the harbor and starting to drift in wispy fingers across the waterfront. Mapes had not reappeared. The freighter loomed, black and silent in the fading light.

"I want to know what's on that boat,'' she said. "I want to know why he's gone there.'' She reached for the door.

He stopped her. "Not yet."

"When?"

"Let's drive up a block and pull over. We can wait there." He glanced at the sky, then at the fog thickening over the water. "It'll be dark soon."

21

"How long has it been?"

"Only about an hour," said Katzka.

Abby hugged herself and shivered. The evening had turned even colder, and inside the car, their breaths fogged the windows. In the mist outside, the distant streetlamp gave off a sulfurous yellow glow.

"Interesting you should put it that way. *Only an hour.* To me it feels like all night."

"It's a matter of perspective. I've put in a lot of time in surveillance. Early in my career."

Katzka as a young man—she couldn't picture that, couldn't imagine him as a fresh-faced rookie. "What made you become a policeman?" she asked.

He shrugged, a blip of shadow in the gloom of the car. "It suited me."

"I guess that explains everything."

"What made you become a doctor?"

She wiped a streak across the fogged windshield and stared out at the boxy canyons formed by ships' containers. "I don't quite know how to answer that."

"Is it such a difficult question?"

"The answer's complicated."

279

"So it wasn't something simple. Like for the good of humanity."

Now it was her turn to shrug. "Humanity will scarcely notice my absence."

"You go to school for eight years. You train for another five years. It has to be a pretty compelling reason."

The window had fogged up again. She wiped her hand across it and the condensation felt strangely warm against her skin. "I guess, if I had to give you a reason, it would be my brother. When he was ten years old, he had to be hospitalized. I spent a lot of time watching his doctors. Seeing how they worked."

Katzka waited for her to elaborate. When she didn't, he said softly, "Your brother didn't live?"

She shook her head. "It was a long time ago." She looked down at the moisture glistening on her hand. Warm as tears, she thought. And for one precarious moment she thought she might shed real tears. She was glad Katzka remained silent; she did not feel up to answering any more questions, not up to reviving the images of the ER, of Pete lying on a gurney, the blood splashed on his brand new tennis shoes. How small those shoes had seemed, far too small for a ten-year-old boy. And then there'd been the months of watching him lie in a coma, his flesh shrinking away, his limbs contracting into a permanent self-embrace. The night he'd died, Abby had lifted him from the bed and had sat rocking him in her arms. He'd felt weightless, and as fragile as an infant.

She told Katzka none of this, yet she sensed he understood all he needed to know. Communication by empathy. It was not a talent she'd suspected he possessed. But then, there were so many things about Katzka that she found surprising.

He looked out at the night. And he said: "I think it's dark enough."

They stepped out of the car and walked through the open gate, into the container yard. The freighter loomed in the mist. The only light aboard the vessel was a weirdly greenish glow from one of the lower portholes. Otherwise the ship seemed abandoned. They walked onto the pier, passing a tower of empty crates stacked on a loading pallet.

At the ship's gangplank they paused, listening to the slap of water on the hull, to the myriad groans of steel and cable. The shriek of another jet taking off startled them both. Abby glanced up at the sky, and as she watched the jet's lights lift away she had the disorienting sensation that she was the one moving through space and time. She almost reached out to Katzka for a steadying grip. *How did I end up standing on this pier, with this man?* she wondered. *What strange chain of events has brought me to this unexpected moment in my life?*

Katzka touched her arm, his contact warm and solid. "I'm going to look around on board." He stepped onto the gangplank. He'd taken only a few paces toward the vessel when he halted and glanced back up the pier.

A pair of headlights had just swung through the gate. The vehicle was now rolling toward them, across the container yard. It was a van.

Abby had no chance to duck for cover behind the crates. The headlights' beams had already caught her, trapped at the end of the pier.

The van skidded to a halt. Shielding her eyes against the glare, Abby could see almost nothing, but she heard doors open and slam shut. Heard footsteps crunching across the gravel as the men moved in to cut off any escape.

Katzka materialized right beside her. She hadn't even heard him scramble off the gangplank, but suddenly there he was, stepping between her and the van. "Okay, just back off," he said. "We're not here to cause any trouble."

The two men, silhouetted by the headlights, hesitated only a second. Then they began to advance.

"Let us by!" Katzka said.

Abby's view of the men was partially blocked by Katzka's back. She didn't see what happened next. All she knew was that he suddenly dropped to a crouch, that there was a simultaneous crack of gunfire and the zing of something ricocheting off the concrete pier behind her.

She and Katzka lunged at the same time for the cover of the crates. He shoved her head to the ground as more gunfire rang out, chunking out splinters of wood.

Katzka returned fire. Three quick blasts.

There was a tattoo of retreating footsteps. A terse exchange of voices.

Then the sound of the van being started, the engine revving and tires spitting up gravel.

Abby raised her head to look. To her horror she saw the van

was rolling toward them, bearing down on the crates like a battering ram.

Katzka took aim and fired. Four bursts that shattered the windshield.

The van bumped crazily onto the pier, swerved right, then left, a battering ram gone out of control.

Katzka fired two last, desperate blasts.

The van kept coming.

Abby registered a blinding glimpse of headlights. Then she flung herself off the pier and hurtled into pitch darkness.

The plunge into icy water was shocking. She sputtered back to the surface, choking on brine and spilled diesel fuel, her limbs flailing at the black water. She heard men shouting on the pier above, then a thunderous splash. Water boiled up and washed over her head. She surfaced again, coughing. At the end of the pier the water seemed to be glowing a phosphorescent green. The van. It was sliding under the surface, its headlights casting two watery beams of light. As it sank, the greenish glow faded to black.

Katzka. Where was Katzka?

She whirled around in the water, stroking as she scanned the blackness. The surface was still churning, wavelets slapping her face, and she was struggling to see through the sting of salt in her eyes.

She heard a soft splash and a head popped out of the brine a few feet away. Treading water, Katzka glanced in her direction, and saw that she was holding her own. Then he looked up, at the sound of more voices—from the ship? There were two men, maybe three, their footsteps thudding up and down the pier. They were yelling to each other, but their shouts seemed garbled and unintelligible.

Not English, thought Abby, but she could not identify the language.

Overhead a light appeared, the beam cutting through the mist and slowly skimming the water.

Katzka dove. So did Abby. She swam as far as her breath would carry her, away from the pier, toward the blackness of open water. Again and again she came up, gasped in a breath, then dove again. When she resurfaced a fifth time, she was treading in darkness.

There were now two lights moving on the pier, the beams

scanning the mist like a pair of relentless eyes. She heard the splash of water somewhere close, and then a quick intake of breath, and she knew Katzka had surfaced nearby.

"Lost my gun," he panted.

"What the hell's going on?"

"Just keep swimming. The next pier."

The night suddenly lit up with shocking brilliance. The freighter had turned on its deck lights, illuminating every detail on the pier. There was one man on the gangplank, and one crouching at the pier's edge with a searchlight. Towering beside them was a third man, his rifle aimed at the water.

"*Go*," said Katzka.

Abby dove, clawing her way through liquid blackness. She'd never been a good swimmer. Deep water scared her. Now she was swimming through water so dark it might as well be bottomless. She came up for another breath, but could not seem to get enough air, no matter how deeply she gasped.

"Abby, keep moving!" urged Katzka. "Just get to that next pier!"

Abby glanced back toward the freighter. She saw that the searchlights were tracing an ever-larger circle on the water. That the beam was flitting toward them.

She slipped, once again, underwater.

By the time she and Katzka finally clambered out onto land, Abby could barely move her limbs. She crawled up rocks slippery with oil and seaweed. Crouching in the darkness, the barnacles biting into her knees, she vomited into the water.

Katzka took her arm, steadied her. She was shaking so hard from exertion she thought she might shatter were it not for his grip.

At last there was nothing left in her stomach. Weakly she raised her head.

"Better?" he whispered.

"I'm freezing."

"Then let's get someplace warm." He glanced up at the pier, looming above them. "I think we can make it up those pilings. Come on."

Together they scrambled up the rocks, slipping and sliding on moss and seaweed. Katzka made it up onto the pier first, then he reached down and hauled her up after him. They rose to a crouch.

The searchlight sliced through the mist, trapping them in its glare.

A bullet ricocheted off the concrete right behind Abby.

"Move!" said Katzka.

They sprinted away. The searchlight pursued them, the beam zigzagging through the darkness. They were off the concrete pier now, running toward the container yard. Bullets spat up gravel all around them. Ahead loomed the containers, stacked up in a giant maze of shadows. They ducked down the nearest row, heard bullets pinging on metal. Then the gunfire ceased.

Abby slowed down to catch her breath. She was still exhausted from the swim, still weak from retching up seawater. And now she was shaking so hard her feet were stumbling.

Voices drew near. They seemed to come from two directions at once.

Katzka grabbed her hand and pulled her deeper into the maze of containers.

They ran to the end of the row, turned left, and kept running. Then both of them halted.

At the far end of the row, a light winked.

They're in front of us!

Katzka veered right, turned down another row. Stacked containers towered on both sides of them like the walls of a chasm. They heard voices and corrected course again. By now they'd made so many turns, Abby couldn't tell if they were moving in circles, couldn't tell if they'd fled this way seconds earlier.

A light danced ahead of them.

They halted, spun around to retrace their steps. And saw another flashlight beam winking. It swept back and forth, moving toward them.

They're ahead of us. And behind us.

In panic she stumbled backward. Reaching out to steady herself, she felt the cleft between two containers. The gap was barely wide enough to fit into.

The flashlight beam winked closer.

Grabbing Katzka's arm, she squeezed into the opening, pulling him after her. Deeper and deeper she wormed, through a filigree of cobwebs, until she bumped up against the wall of an adjacent container. No way forward. They were trapped here, wedged tightly into a space narrower than a coffin.

The crunch of footsteps on gravel approached.

Katzka's hand reached out to grip hers, but his touch did nothing to ease her panic. Her heart was slamming against her chest. The footsteps drew closer.

She heard voices, now—one man hailing another, then a second man answering in some unrecognizable tongue. Or was it the blood roaring through her ears that made their words seem garbled beyond comprehension?

A light danced past the cleft opening. The two men were standing close by, conversing in puzzled tones. They had only to shine their flashlights into the gap, and they'd spot their prey in the crevice. Someone kicked at the ground and gravel skittered and clanged against the container.

Abby closed her eyes, too terrified to look. She didn't want to be watching when that beam of light flooded into their hiding place. Katzka's grip tightened around her hand. Her limbs were rigid with tension, her breath coming in short, shallow gasps. She heard another scrape of shoes across the ground, another skittering of gravel.

Then the footsteps moved away.

Abby didn't dare move. She wasn't sure she *could* move; her legs felt locked in position. *Years from now,* she thought, *they'll find me standing here, my skeleton frozen stiff in terror.*

It was Katzka who made the first move. He eased toward the opening and was about to poke his head out for a look when they heard a soft *whick.* A light flared and went out. Someone had lit a match. Katzka went dead still. The smell of cigarette smoke wafted through the darkness.

Somewhere, faintly, a man was calling.

The cigarette smoker grunted out a reply, and then his footsteps faded away.

Katzka didn't move.

They remained frozen, hands clasped together, neither one daring to whisper a word. Twice they heard their pursuers pass by; both times, the men moved on.

There was a distant rumble, like the growl of thunder somewhere over the horizon.

Then, for a long time, they heard nothing.

It was hours later when they finally emerged from their hiding place. They crept down the row of containers and stopped to scan the waterfront. The night had turned unnervingly silent. The mist had lifted, and overhead, stars twinkled faintly in a sky washed by city lights.

The next pier was dark. They saw no men, no lights, not even the glow of a porthole. There was only the long low silhouette of the concrete pier jutting out, and the sparkle of moonlight on the water.

The freighter was gone.

22

The alarm on the heart monitor was going crazy, squealing as the line traced a chaotic dance of death across the screen.

"Mr. Voss." A nurse grasped Victor's arm, tried to pull him away from Nina's bed. "The doctors need room to work."

"I'm not leaving her."

"Mr. Voss, they can't do their job if you're here!"

Victor shook off the woman's hand with a violence that made her cringe, as though struck. He remained standing at the end of his wife's bed, gripping the footrail so tightly his knuckles looked like exposed bone.

"Back!" came a command. "Everyone back!"

"Mr. Voss!" It was Dr. Archer speaking now, his voice slicing through the bedlam. "We need to shock your wife's heart! You have to move away from the bed *now.*"

Victor released the footrail and stepped back.

The shock was delivered. It coursed through Nina's body in a single, barbaric jolt. She was too small, too fragile to be abused this way! Enraged, he took a step forward, ready to snatch the paddles away. Then he stopped.

On the monitor above the bed, the jagged line had transformed to a calmly rhythmic series of blips. He heard someone release a sigh, and felt his own breath escape in a single rush.

"Systolic's sixty. Up to sixty-five . . ."

"Rhythm seems to be holding."

"Up to seventy-five systolic."

"Okay, turn down that IV."

"She's moving her arm. Can we get a wrist restraint over here?"

Victor pushed past the nurses to Nina's side. No one tried to stop him. He took her hand and pressed it to his lips. And he tasted, on her skin, the salt of his own tears.

Stay with me. Please, please, stay with me.

"Mr. Voss?" The voice seemed to call to him from across a long distance. Turning, he focused on Dr. Archer's face.

"Can we step outside?" said Archer.

Victor shook his head.

"She's all right for the moment," said Archer. "All these people are taking good care of her. We'll be just outside the room. I need to speak to you. Now."

At last Victor nodded. Tenderly he lay down Nina's hand and followed Archer out of the cubicle.

They stood together in a quiet corner of the ICU. The lights had been dimmed for the evening, and against the bank of green screens, the silhouette of the monitor nurse sat silent and motionless.

"The transplant's been postponed," said Archer. "There was a problem with the harvest."

"What do you mean?"

"It couldn't be done tonight. We'll have to reschedule for tomorrow."

Victor looked at his wife's cubicle. Through the uncurtained window, he could see her head moving. She was waking up. She needed him at her side.

He said, "Nothing can go wrong tomorrow night."

"It won't."

"That's what you told me after the first transplant."

"Organ rejection is something we can't always stop. No matter how hard we try to prevent it, it happens."

"How do I know it won't happen again? With a second heart?"

"I can't make promises. But at this point, Mr. Voss, we don't have an alternative. Cyclosporine's failed. And she had an anaphylactic reaction to OKT-3. There's nothing left except another transplant.''

"It *will* be done tomorrow?"

Archer nodded. "We'll make sure it's done tomorrow."

Nina was not yet fully conscious when Victor returned to her bedside. So many times before, he had watched her as she slept. Over the years he had taken note of the changes in her face. The delicate lines that had formed at the corners of her mouth. The gradual sagging of the jawline. The new whisper of white in her hair. Each and every change he had mourned, because it reminded him that their journey together was but a temporary passage through a cold and lonely eternity.

And yet, because it was *her* face, each and every change he had loved.

It was hours later when she opened her eyes. At first he did not realize she was awake. He was sitting in a chair by her bed, his shoulders slumped with fatigue, when something made him raise his head and turn to her.

She was looking at him. She opened her hand in a silent request for his touch. He grasped it, kissed it.

"Everything," she whispered, "will be all right."

He smiled. "Yes. Yes, of course it will."

"I've been lucky, Victor. So very lucky . . ."

"We both have."

"But now you have to learn to let me go."

Victor's smile faded. He shook his head. "Don't say that."

"You have so much ahead of you."

"What about *us?*" He was grasping her hand in both of his now, like a man trying to hold on to water as it trickles away. "You and I, Nina, we're not like everyone else! We always used to say that to each other. Don't you remember? How we were different. We were special. And nothing could ever happen to us?"

"But something has, Victor," she murmured. "Something has happened to me."

"And *I will take care of it.*"

She said nothing, only shook her head sadly.

It seemed to Victor that the last thing he saw, as Nina's eyelids closed again, was a look of quiet defiance. He gazed down at her hand, the one he'd been holding so possessively. And he saw that it was closed, in a fist.

*   *   *

It was nearly midnight when Detective Lundquist dropped off an exhausted Abby at her front door. She saw that Mark's car was not parked in the driveway. When she stepped inside the house, she could feel its emptiness as clearly as one senses a chasm yawning at one's feet. He's had an emergency at the hospital, she thought. It was not unusual for him to leave the house late at night, called into Bayside to tend to a gunshot wound or a stabbing. She tried to visualize him as she had seen him so many times before in the OR, his face masked in blue, his gaze focused downward, but she could not seem to come up with the image. It was as though the memory, the old reality, had been erased.

She went to the answering machine, hoping he'd left a voice memo on the recorder. All she found were two phone messages. Both were from Vivian, and the number she'd left had an out-of-state area code. She was still in Burlington. It was too late now to call her back. She'd try in the morning.

Upstairs, she stripped off her wet clothes, threw them in the washing machine, and stepped into the shower. She noticed the tiles were dry; Mark hadn't used the shower tonight. Had he even been home?

As the hot water beat down on her shoulders, she stood with her eyes closed, thinking. Dreading what she'd have to say to Mark. This was why she had returned to his house tonight. The time had come to confront him, to demand answers. The uncertainty had become unbearable.

After she got out of the shower, she sat down on the bed and called in a page for Mark. She was startled when the phone rang almost immediately.

"Abby?" It wasn't Mark, but Katzka. "Just checking to see if you're okay. I called a little while ago and there was no answer."

"I was in the shower. I'm fine, Katzka. I'm just waiting for Mark to get home."

A pause. "You're by yourself?"

His note of concern brought a faint smile to her lips. Scratch that armor of his, and you'd find a real man under there after all.

"I locked all the doors and windows," she said. "Just like you told me." Over the phone, she could hear a background buzz of voices, along with the squeal of a police radio, and she could picture him standing on that dock, the blue emergency lights flashing on his face. "What's happening over there?" she asked.

"We're waiting for the divers. The equipment's already in position."

"You really think the driver's still trapped in the van?"

"I'm afraid so." He sighed, and it was a sound of such profound weariness, she gave a murmur of concern.

"You should go home, Katzka. You need a hot shower and some chicken soup. That's my prescription."

He laughed. It was a surprising sound, one she'd never heard from him before. "Now if I could just find a pharmacy to fill it." Someone spoke to him. It sounded like another cop, asking about bullet trajectories. Katzka turned to answer the man, then he came back on the line. "I have to go. You sure you're okay there? You wouldn't rather stay in a hotel?"

"I'll be fine."

"Okay." Again, she heard Katzka sigh. "But I want you to call a locksmith in the morning. Have him install dead bolts on all the doors. Especially if you're going to be spending a lot of nights home alone."

"I'll do that."

There was a brief silence. He had pressing matters to attend to, yet he seemed reluctant to hang up. At last he said, "I'll check back with you in the morning."

"Thanks, Katzka." She hung up.

Again she paged Mark. Then she lay down on the bed and waited for him to call back. He didn't.

As the hours passed, she tried to calm her growing fears by tallying up all the possible reasons he wasn't answering. He could be asleep in one of the hospital call rooms. His beeper could be broken. He could be scrubbed and unavailable in the OR.

Or he could be dead. Like Aaron Levi. Like Kunstler and Hennessy.

She paged him again. And again.

At three A.M., the phone finally rang. In an instant she was wide awake and reaching for the receiver.

"Abby, it's me." Mark's voice crackled on the wire, as though he were calling from across a long distance.

"I've been paging you for hours," she said. "Where are you?"

"I'm in the car, heading to the hospital right now." He paused. "Abby, we need to talk. Things have ... changed."

She said, softly: "Between us, you mean."

"No. No, this has nothing to do with you. It never did. It has to do with *me*. You just got sucked into it, Abby. I tried to get them to back off, but now they've taken it too far."

"*Who* has?"

"The team."

She was afraid to ask the next question, but she had no choice now. "All of you? You're all involved?"

"Not anymore." The connection briefly faded, and she heard what sounded like the whoosh of traffic. His voice regained its volume. "Mohandas and I came to a decision tonight. That's where I've been, at his house. We've been talking, comparing notes. Abby, we're putting our heads on the block. But we decided it's time to end this. We can't do it any longer. We're going to blow this thing wide open, Mohandas and me. And fuck everyone else. Fuck Bayside." He paused, his voice suddenly breaking. "I've been a coward. I'm sorry."

She closed her eyes. "You knew. All this time you knew."

"I knew *some* of it—not all. I had no idea how far Archer was taking it. I didn't *want* to know. Then you started asking all those questions. And I couldn't hide from the truth any longer ..." He released a deep breath and whispered, "This is going to ruin me, Abby."

She still had her eyes closed. She could see him in the darkness of his car, one hand on the wheel, the other gripping the cellular phone. Could imagine the misery on his face. And the courage; most of all, the courage.

"I love you," he whispered.

"Come home, Mark. Please."

"Not yet. I'm meeting Mohandas at the hospital. We're going to get those donor records."

"Do you know where they're kept?"

"We have an idea. With just two of us, it could take us a while to search all the files. If you helped us out, we might be able to get through them by morning."

She sat up in bed. "I won't be getting much sleep tonight anyway. Where are you meeting Mohandas?"

"Medical Records. He has the key." Mark hesitated. "Are you sure you want to be in on this, Abby?"

"I want to be wherever *you* are. We'll do this together. Okay?"

"Okay," he said softly. "See you soon."

Five minutes later, Abby walked out the front door and climbed into her car.

The streets of West Cambridge were deserted. She turned onto Memorial Drive, skirting the Charles River as she headed southeast, toward the River Street bridge. It was three-fifteen A.M., but she could not remember feeling so awake. So alive.

At last we're going to beat them! she thought. *And we're going to do it together. The way we should have done it from the start.*

She crossed the bridge and headed onto the ramp for the turnpike. There were few cars traveling at that hour, and she merged easily with sparse eastbound traffic.

Three and a half miles later, the turnpike came to an end. She changed lanes, preparing to turn off onto the Southeast Expressway ramp. As she curved onto it, she suddenly became aware of a pair of headlights bearing down on her.

She accelerated, merging onto the southbound expressway.

The headlights pulled closer, high beams glaring off her rearview mirror. How long had they been behind her? She had no idea. But they were zooming in now like twin bats out of hell.

She sped up.

So did the other car. Suddenly it swooped left into the next lane. It pulled up beside her until they were almost neck and neck.

She glanced sideways. Saw the other car's window roll down. Glimpsed the silhouette of a man in the right passenger seat.

In panic, she floored the accelerator.

Too late she spotted the car stalled ahead of her. She slammed on the brakes. Her car spun and caromed off the concrete barrier. Suddenly the world tilted sideways. Then everything was tumbling over and over. She saw darkness and light. Darkness, light.

Darkness.

* * *

". . . repeat, this is Mobile Unit Forty-one. Our ETA is three minutes. Copy?"

"Copy, Forty-one. How're the vitals?"

"Systolic holding at ninety-five. Pulse one ten. We've got normal saline going in one peripheral line. Hey, looks like she's starting to move."

"Keep her immobilized."

"We've got her in a collar and a spinal board."

"Okay, we're ready and waiting for you."

"See you in a minute, Bayside . . ."

. . . Light.

And pain. Short, sharp explosions of it in her head.

She tried to scream, but no sound came out. She tried to turn away from that piercing light, but her neck seemed trapped in a chokehold. She thought if she could just escape that light and burrow back into darkness, the pain would go away. With all her strength she twisted, straining to break free of the paralysis that had seized her limbs.

"Abby. Abby, hold still!" a voice commanded. "I have to look in your eyes."

She twisted the other way, felt restraints chafing her wrists, her ankles. And she realized that it was not paralysis that prevented her movement. She was tied down, all four limbs strapped to the gurney.

"Abby, it's Dr. Wettig. Look at me. Look at the light. Come on, open your eyes. *Open.*"

She opened her eyes, forced herself to keep them open, even though the beam of his penlight felt like a blade piercing straight through her skull.

"Follow the light. Come on. That's good, Abby. Okay, both pupils are reactive. EOMs are normal." The penlight, mercifully, shut off. "I still want that CT."

Abby could make out shapes now. She could see the shadow of Dr. Wettig's head against the diffuse brightness of the overhead lights. There were other heads moving around on the periphery of her vision, and a white privacy curtain billowing like a cloud off in the distance. Pain pricked her left arm; she gave a jerk.

"Easy, Abby." It was a woman's voice, soft, soothing. "I

have to draw some blood. Hold very still. I have a lot of tubes to collect.''

Now a third voice: "Dr. Wettig, X ray's ready for her.''

"In a minute," said Wettig. "I want a bigger-bore IV in. Sixteen gauge. Come on, people.''

Abby felt another stab, this time in her right arm. The pain drove straight through her confusion and brought her mind into startling focus. She knew exactly where she was. She couldn't recall how she'd arrived, but she knew this was Bayside Emergency Room, and that something terrible must have happened.

"Mark," she said, and tried to sit up. "Where's Mark?''

"Don't move! We'll lose this IV!''

A hand closed over her elbow, pinning her arm to the gurney. The grasp was too firm to be gentle. They were all hurting her, stabbing her with their needles, holding her down like some captive animal.

"Mark!" she cried.

"Abby, listen to me." It was Wettig again, his voice low and impatient. "We're trying to reach Mark. I'm sure he'll be here soon. Right now, you have to cooperate or we can't help you. Do you understand? Abby, do you understand?''

She stared up at his face and she went very still. So many times before, as a resident, she had felt intimidated by his flat blue eyes. Now, strapped down and helpless under that gaze, she felt more than intimidated. She felt truly, deeply frightened. She glanced around the room, seeking a friendly face, but everyone was too busy attending to IVs and blood tubes and vital signs.

She heard the curtain whisk open, felt a lurch as the gurney began to move. Now the ceiling was rushing past in a flashing succession of lights, and she knew they were taking her deeper into the hospital. Into the heart of the enemy. She didn't even try to struggle; the restraints were impossible to fight. *Think,* she thought. *I have to think.*

They turned the corner, into X ray. Now another face, a man's, appeared over her gurney. The CT technician. Friend or enemy? She couldn't tell anymore. They moved her onto the table and buckled straps across her chest and hips.

"Hold very still," the tech commanded, "or we'll have to do this all over again.''

As the scanner slid over her head, she felt a sudden rush of claustrophobia. She remembered how other patients had described CT scans: *like having your head jammed into a pencil sharpener.* Abby closed her eyes. Machinery clicked and whirred around her head. She tried to think, to remember the accident.

She remembered getting into her car. Driving onto the turnpike. Then her memory tape had a gap. Retrograde amnesia; the accident itself was a complete blank. But the events leading up to it were slowly coming back into focus.

By the time the scan was completed, she'd managed to piece together enough memory fragments to understand what she had to do next. If she wanted to stay alive.

She was quietly cooperative as the CT technician transferred her back onto the gurney—so cooperative, in fact, that he left off the wrist restraints and buckled on only the chest strap. Then he wheeled her into the X ray anteroom.

"The ER's coming to get you," he said. "If you need me, just call. I'm right in the next room."

Through the open doorway she could hear him talking on the telephone.

"Yeah, this is CT. We're all done here. Dr. Blaise is looking over the scan now. You want to come get her?"

Abby reached up and quietly unbuckled the chest strap. As she sat up, she felt the room begin to whirl. She pressed her hands to her temples and everything seemed to settle back into focus.

The IV.

She ripped the tape off her arm, wincing at the sting, and pulled out the catheter. Saline dribbled out of the tubing, onto the floor. She ignored the saline, concentrating instead on stopping the flow of blood from her vein. A sixteen-gauge puncture is a big hole. Though she taped over it tightly, it continued to ooze. She couldn't worry about that now. They were coming to get her.

She climbed off the gurney, her bare feet landing in a pool of saline. In the next room, the tech was cleaning up the CT table. She could hear the rattle of tissue paper, the clang of a trash can.

She took a lab coat off the door hook and pulled it on over her hospital gown. Just that effort seemed to drain her. She was struggling to think, to see through a white haze of pain as she moved to the door. Her legs felt sluggish, as though she were wading through quicksand. She pushed into the hallway.

It was empty.

Still slogging through quicksand, she moved up the corridor, reaching out every so often to steady herself against the wall. She turned a corner. At the far end of the hallway was an emergency exit. She struggled toward it, thinking: If I can just reach that door, I'll be safe.

Somewhere behind her, from what seemed like a great distance, she heard voices. The sound of hurrying footsteps.

She lunged against the emergency exit bar and pushed out, into the night. Alarm bells started ringing. At once she began to run, fleeing in panic into the darkness. She stumbled off the curb into the parking lot. Broken glass and gravel cut into her bare feet. She had no plan of escape, no destination in mind; she knew only that she had to get away from Bayside.

There were voices behind her. A shout.

Glancing back, she saw three security guards run out the ER entrance.

She ducked behind a car—too late. They had spotted her.

She lurched to her feet and began to run again. Her legs still didn't work right. She was stumbling as she dodged between parked cars.

Her pursuers' footsteps pounded closer, moving in from two directions at once.

She turned left, between two parked cars.

They surrounded her. One guard grabbed her left arm, another her right. She kicked, punched. Tried to bite them.

But now there were three of them, and they were dragging her back to the Emergency Room. Back to Dr. Wettig.

"They'll kill me!" 'she screamed. "Let me go! They're going to kill me!"

"No one's going to hurt you, lady."

"You don't understand. *You don't understand!*"

The ER doors whisked open. She was swept inside, into the light, and lifted onto a gurney. Strapped down, even as she kicked and thrashed.

Dr. Wettig's face appeared, white and taut above hers. "Five milligrams Haldol IM," he snapped.

"No!" shrieked Abby. *"No!"*

"Come on, I want it given *stat.*"

A nurse materialized, syringe in hand. She uncapped the needle.

Abby lurched, trying to buck free of the restraints.

"Hold her down," said Wettig. "Goddamn it, can we get her immobilized here?"

Hands clamped over her wrists. She was twisted sideways, her right buttock bared.

"Please," begged Abby, looking up at the nurse. "Don't let him hurt me. Don't let him."

She felt the icy lick of alcohol, then the prick of the needle plunging into her buttock.

"Please," she whispered. But she knew it was already too late.

"It will be all right," said the nurse. And she smiled at Abby. "Everything will be all right."

23

"No skid marks on the pier," said Detective Carrier. "The windshield's shattered. And the driver's got what looked to me like a bullet hole over the right eye. You know the drill, Slug. I'm sorry, but we're going to need your gun."

Katzka nodded. And he gazed, wearily, down at the water. "Tell the diver he'll find my gun right about there. Unless the current's moved it."

"You think you fired off eight rounds?"

"Maybe more. I know I started with a full clip."

Carrier nodded, then he gave Katzka a pat on the shoulder. "Go home. You look like shit warmed over, Slug."

"As good as that?" said Katzka. And he walked back up the pier, through the gathering of crime lab personnel. The van had been pulled out of the water hours before, and it now sat at the edge of the container yard. Streamers of seaweed had snagged on the axle. Because of the air in the tires, the van had turned over underwater, and its roof had sunk into the bottom ooze. The windshield was caked with mud. They'd already traced its registration to Bayside Hospital, Operations and Facilities. According to the Facilities manager, the van was one of three owned and operated by the hospital for the purpose of shuttling supplies and personnel to outlying clinics. The manager had

not noticed any of his vans were missing until the police had
called him an hour ago.

The driver's door now hung open, and a photographer was
leaning inside, shooting pictures of the dashboard. The body
had been removed half an hour ago. His driver's license had
identified him as Oleg Boravoy, age thirty-nine, a resident of
Newark, New Jersey. They were still awaiting further information.

Katzka knew better than to approach the vehicle. His actions
were being called into question, and he had to keep his distance
from the evidence. He crossed the container yard to where his
own car was parked, outside the fence, and slid inside. Groaning, he dropped his face in his hands. At two A.M. he'd gone
home to shower and catch a few hours of sleep. Shortly after
sunrise, he'd been back on the pier. *I'm too old for this,* he
thought, *too old by at least a decade.* All this running around
and shooting in the dark was for the young lions, not for a
middle-aged cop. And he was feeling very middle-aged.

Someone tapped on his window. He looked up and saw it
was Lundquist. Katzka rolled down the glass.

"Hey, Slug. You okay?"

"I'm going home to get some sleep."

"Yeah, well before you do, I thought you'd want to hear
about the driver."

"We have something back?"

"They ran the name Oleg Boravoy through the computer.
Bingo, he's in there. Russian immigrant, came here in eighty-
nine. Last known residence Newark, New Jersey. Three arrests,
no convictions."

"What charges?"

"Kidnapping and extortion. The charges never stick because
the witnesses keep disappearing." Lundquist leaned forward,
his voice dropping to a murmur. "You ran into some really bad
shit last night. The Newark cops say Boravoy's Russian mafia."

"How sure are they?"

"They ought to know. New Jersey's where Russian mafia
has its home base. Slug, those guys make the Colombians look
like the fucking Rotary Club. They don't just make a hit. They
chop off your fingers and toes first, for the fun of it."

Katzka frowned, remembering the panic of last night. Treading water in the darkness as men ran on the pier above, shouting words in a language he didn't understand. He was having visions now of dismembered fingers and toes, of Boston streets littered with random body parts. Which made him think of scalpels. Operating rooms.

"What's Boravoy's connection to Bayside?" he asked.

"We don't know."

"He was driving their vehicle."

"And the van's full of medical supplies," said Lundquist. "Couple thousand dollars' worth. Maybe we're talking black market. Boravoy could have partners at Bayside siphoning off drugs and supplies. And you just caught him delivering the goods to their freighter."

"What about that freighter? You talk to the harbormaster?"

"The ship's owned by some New Jersey firm called the Sigayev Company. Panamanian registry. Her last known port of call was Riga."

"Where's that?"

"Latvia. I think it's some breakaway Russian republic."

The Russians again, thought Katzka. If this was indeed Russian mafia, then they were dealing with criminals known for pure and bloody viciousness. With every legitimate wave of immigrants rode a shadow wave of predators, criminal networks that followed their countrymen to the land of opportunity. The land of easy prey.

He thought of Abby DiMatteo, and his anxiety suddenly sharpened. He hadn't spoken to her since that one A.M. phone call. Just an hour ago, he'd been about to call her again. But as he was dialing her number, he'd realized that his pulse had quickened. And he'd recognized that sign for what it was. Anticipation. A joyful, aching, completely irrational eagerness to hear her voice. They were feelings he had not experienced in years, and he understood, only too painfully, what they meant.

He had quickly disconnected. And had spent the last hour in a deepening depression.

He gazed off toward the pier. By now the ship could be a hundred miles out to sea. Even if they located it, there would be a jurisdiction problem.

He said to Lundquist, "I want anything there is on the Sigayev Company. I want any links to Amity and to Bayside Hospital."

"On my list, Slug."

Katzka started his car. He looked at Lundquist. "Your brother still in the Coast Guard?"

"No. But he's got buddies who're still in."

"Run this by them. See if they've boarded that freighter lately."

"Doubt it. If she just sailed in from Riga." Lundquist paused, glancing up. Detective Carrier was crossing toward them, waving.

"Hey, Slug," said Carrier. "Did you get the message about Dr. DiMatteo?"

Instantly Katzka turned off the engine. But he couldn't shut off the sudden roar of his own pulse. He stared at Carrier, expecting the worst.

"There's been an accident."

A lunch cart rattled down the hallway. Abby woke up with a start and found she was lying in sheets damp with sweat. Her heart was still pounding from the nightmare. She tried to turn in bed, but found she couldn't; her hands were tied down, her wrists sore from chafing. And she realized that she had not been dreaming at all. This *was* the nightmare, and it was one from which she could not wake up.

With a sob of frustration she sank back against the pillow and stared at the ceiling. She heard the creak of a chair. She turned her head.

Katzka was sitting by the window. In the glare of midday, his unshaven face looked older and wearier than she had ever seen him before.

"I asked them to take off the restraints," he said. "But they told me you'd pulled out a few too many IVs." He rose and came to her bedside. There he stood gazing down at her. "Welcome back, Abby. You're a very lucky young lady."

"I don't remember what happened."

"You had an accident. Your car rolled over on the Southeast Expressway."

"Was there anyone else . . ."

He shook his head. "No one else was hurt. But your car was pretty much totaled." There was a silence. She realized he was no longer looking at her. He was looking somewhere at her pillow instead.

"Katzka?" she asked softly. "Was it my fault?"

Reluctantly he nodded. "Based on the skid marks, it appears you were traveling at a high rate of speed. You must have braked to avoid a vehicle stalled in your lane. Your car veered into a highway barrier. And rolled over, across two lanes."

She closed her eyes. "Oh my God."

Again there was a pause. "I guess you haven't heard the rest," he said. "I spoke to the investigating officer. I'm afraid they found a shattered container of vodka in your car."

She opened her eyes and stared at him. "That's impossible."

"Abby, you can't remember what happened. Last night, on the pier, was a traumatic experience. Maybe you felt the need to unwind. To have a few drinks at home."

"I'd remember *that!* I'd remember if I'd been drinking—"

"Look, what's important right now is—"

"*This* is important! Can't you see, Katzka? They're setting me up again!"

He rubbed his hand over his eyes, the unfocused gesture of a man struggling to stay awake. "I'm sorry, Abby," he murmured. "I know this can't be an easy thing for you to acknowledge. But Dr. Wettig just showed me your blood alcohol level. They drew it last night in the ER. It was point two-one."

He wasn't facing her now, but was gazing blankly out the window, as though just the act of looking at her had taken too much out of him. She could not even turn her body to confront him face to face; the restraints wouldn't allow it. She gave a violent yank on her bonds, and the pain that stung her chafed wrists almost brought tears to her eyes. She was not going to cry. Damn it, she was not going to cry.

She closed her eyes and concentrated on channeling her rage. It was all she had left, the only weapon with which she could fight back. They had taken everything else away from her. They had taken even Katzka.

She said, slowly: "I was not drinking. You have to believe me. I was not drunk."

"Can you tell me where you were going at three in the morning?"

"I was coming here, to Bayside. I remember that much. Mark called me, and I was coming to . . ." She stopped. "Has he been here? Why isn't he here?"

His silence was chilling. She turned her head to look at him, but could not see his face.

"Katzka?"

"Mark Hodell hasn't been answering his pages."

"What?"

"His car's not in the hospital parking lot. No one seems to know where he is."

She tried to speak, but her throat felt as if it had swollen shut, and the only sound that came out was a whispered: "No."

"It's too early to draw any conclusions, Abby. His pager may be broken. We don't know anything yet."

But Abby knew. She knew with a certainty that was both immediate and shattering. Her whole body suddenly felt numb. Lifeless. She didn't realize she was crying, didn't even feel the tears sliding down until Katzka rose, tissue in hand, and gently wiped her cheek.

"I'm sorry," he murmured. He brushed her hair off her face, and just for a moment, his hand lingered there, fingers resting protectively on her forehead. He said, more softly, "I'm so sorry."

"Find him for me," she whispered. "Please. Please, find him for me."

"I will."

A moment later she heard him walk out of the room. Only then did she realize he had untied the restraints. She was free to leave the bed, to walk out of the room. But she didn't.

She turned her face into the pillow and wept.

At noon a nurse came in to remove the IV and to leave a lunch tray. Abby didn't even look at the food. The tray was later removed, untouched.

At two o'clock, Dr. Wettig walked in. He stood by her bed, flipping through the pages of her chart, making clucking sounds as he reviewed the lab results. At last he looked down at her. "Dr. DiMatteo?"

She didn't answer him.

"Detective Katzka tells me you deny drinking any alcohol last night," he said.

She said nothing.

Wettig sighed. "The first step toward recovery is acknowledging you have a problem. Now, I should have been more aware. I should have realized what you were struggling with all this time. But now it's all out in the open. It's time to deal with the problem.''

She looked up at him. "What would be the point?'' she said dully.

"The point is, you have some sort of future worth salvaging. A DUI is a serious setback, but you're an intelligent woman. There will be other careers open to you besides medicine.''

Her response was silence. The loss of her career felt almost insignificant at that moment, compared to the greater grief she felt over Mark's vanishing.

"I've asked Dr. O'Connor to evaluate you,'' said Wettig. "He'll be in sometime this evening.''

"I don't need a psychiatrist.''

"I think you do, Abby. I think you need a lot of help. You have to get beyond these delusions of persecution. I'm not going to approve your release until O'Connor clears it. He may decide to transfer you to the Psychiatry Unit. That's his call. We can't have you hurting yourself, the way you tried to last night. We're all very concerned about you, Abby. *I'm* concerned about you. That's why I'm ordering a psychiatric evaluation. It's for your own good, believe me.''

She looked straight up at him. "Fuck you, General.''

To her immense satisfaction, he flinched and stepped away from the bed. He slapped the chart shut. "I'll check in on you later, Dr. DiMatteo,'' he said, and left the room.

For a long time she stared at the ceiling. Only moments ago, before Wettig had walked in, she had felt too weary to fight. Now every muscle had tensed and her stomach was in turmoil. Her hands ached. She looked down and realized they were knotted into fists.

Fuck all of you.

She sat up. The dizziness lasted only a few seconds, then passed. She'd been lying in bed too long. It was time to get moving. To regain control of her life.

She crossed the room and opened the door a crack.

A nurse looked up from her desk and stared directly at Abby. Her name tag said W. SORIANO, R.N. "Do you need something?''

"Uh, no,'' said Abby, and quickly retreated back behind her closed door.

Shit. Shit, they were keeping her a prisoner.

In bare feet she paced a circle around the room, trying to plan her next move. She couldn't think about Mark right now. If she did, she'd just curl up in bed again, crying. That's what they wanted her to do, what they expected her to do.

She went to the chair by the window and sat down to think. She considered the moves open to her, but couldn't come up with any. Last night, Mark had said Mohandas was on their side, but now Mark was missing. She wasn't going to trust Mohandas. She wasn't going to trust anyone in this hospital.

She went to the nightstand and picked up the phone. There was a dial tone. She called Vivian's number, and got a recording. Then she remembered that Vivian was still in Burlington.

She called her own home, punched in her access code, and listened to the messages from her answering machine. There had been another call from Vivian, and by the tone of her voice, the call had been urgent. She'd left a Burlington number.

Abby dialed it.

This time Vivian answered. "You barely caught me. I was just about to check out of here."

"You're coming home?"

"I've got a six o'clock flight to Logan. Listen, this trip has been nothing but a wild goose chase. There were no harvests done in Burlington."

"How do you know?"

"I checked the airport here. And every other airstrip in the area. On the nights of those transplants, there were no midnight flights logged out of here to Boston. Not a single dinky plane. Burlington's just a cover for them. And Tim Nicholls provided the official paperwork."

"And now Nicholls has vanished."

"Or they got rid of him."

They both fell momentarily silent. Then Abby said, softly: "Mark's missing."

"What?"

"No one knows where he is. Detective Katzka says they can't find his car. And Mark doesn't answer his pages." She paused, her throat closing over.

"Oh, Abby. Abby . . ." Vivian's voice faltered.

In the brief silence, Abby heard a click on the line. She was gripping the receiver so tightly her fingers ached.

"Vivian?" she said.

There was another click. And then the line went dead.

She hung up and tried to call again, but there was no dial tone. She tried the operator, tried hanging up again and again. Still no dial tone.

The hospital had disconnected her telephone.

Katzka stood on the narrow walkway of the Tobin Bridge and stared down at the water far below. From the west ran the Mystic River, on its way to join the waters of the Chelsea River before flowing out to Boston Harbor and the sea. It was a long drop, thought Katzka, imagining the force with which a body would impact on that water. Almost certainly a fatal drop.

Turning, he gazed past the late afternoon traffic whizzing by and focused on the downriver side of the bridge. He traced the hypothetical sequence of events that would follow a body's plunge. The corpse would be carried by the current into the harbor. At first, it would drift along below the water's surface, perhaps scraping across the bottom silt. Eventually the body's internal gases would expand. This would happen over a time span of hours to days. It depended on the water temperature and the speed with which the gas-forming bacteria multiplied in the rotting intestines. At a certain point, the corpse would float to the surface.

That's when it would be found. In a day or two. Bloated and unrecognizable.

Katzka turned to the patrolman standing beside him. He had to shout over the sound of traffic. "What time did you notice the car?"

"Around five A.M. It was pulled over in the northbound breakdown lane. Right over there." He pointed across the lanes of whizzing cars. "Nice green BMW. I stopped right away."

"You didn't see anyone near the BMW?"

"No, sir. It looked abandoned. I called in the license number and confirmed it wasn't reported stolen. I figured maybe the driver had engine trouble and left to get help. It was a hazard to traffic, sitting there. So I called the tow truck."

"No keys in the car? No note?"

"No, sir. Nothing. It was clean as a whistle inside."

Katzka looked back down at the water. He wondered how deep the river was at this point, and how fast the current was moving.

"I did try calling Dr. Hodell's home, but no one answered," said the patrolman. "I didn't know at the time that he was missing."

Katzka said nothing. He just kept gazing down at the river, thinking about Abby, wondering what he should tell her. She had looked so heartbreakingly fragile in that hospital bed, and he couldn't bear the thought of inflicting any more blows. Any more pain.

I won't tell her. Not yet, he decided. *Not until we find a body.*

The patrolman looked down at the river, too. "Jesus. Do you think he jumped?"

"If he's down there," said Katzka, "it wasn't because he jumped."

The phones had been ringing all day, two LPNs had called in sick, and charge nurse Wendy Soriano had missed lunch. She was in no mood to be pulling a double shift. Yet here she was at three thirty P.M., facing the prospect of another eight hours on duty.

Her kids had already called twice. *Mommy, Jeffy's hitting me again. Mommy, what time is Daddy coming home? Mommy, can we use the microwave? We promise we won't burn the house down.* Mommy, Mommy, Mommy

Why didn't they ever bother Daddy at work?

Because Daddy's job is so much more fucking important.

Wendy dropped her head in her hands and stared down at the stack of charts flagged with doctors' orders. The residents loved to write orders. They breezed in with their fancy Cross pens and scribbled such earthshattering instructions as: "Milk of magnesia for constipation," or "bedrails up at night." Then they presented the flagged charts to the nurses like God passing instructions to Moses. *Thou shalt not tolerate constipation.*

With a sigh, Wendy reached for the first chart.

The phone rang. It better not be the kids again, she thought. Not another *Mommy he's hitting me* call. She answered it with an irritated: "Six East, Wendy."

"This is Dr. Wettig."

"Oh." Automatically she sat up straight. One didn't slouch when speaking to Dr. Wettig. Even if it was on the phone. "Yes, Doctor?"

"I want to follow up that blood alcohol level on Dr. DiMatteo. And I want it sent out to MedMark Labs."

"Not our lab?"

"No. Route it directly to MedMark."

"Certainly, Doctor," said Wendy, scribbling down the order. It was an unusual request, but one didn't question the General.

"How's she doing?" he asked.

"A little restless."

"Has she tried to leave?"

"No. She hasn't even come out of the room."

"Good. Make sure she stays there. And absolutely no visitors. That includes all medical personnel, except for the ones I specify in my orders."

"Yes, Dr. Wettig."

Wendy hung up and stared at her desk. During that call, three more flagged charts had been deposited there. Damn. She'd be taking off order sheets all evening. Suddenly she felt dizzy from hunger. She still hadn't had lunch, hadn't even had a break in hours.

She glanced around, and saw two LPNs chatting in the hallway. Was she the only person working her butt off here?

She tore off the order for the blood alcohol level and deposited it in the lab tech's box. As she rose from the desk, the phone began to ring. She ignored it; after all, that's what ward clerks were for.

She walked away to the sound of two lines jangling.

For once, someone else could answer the damn phone.

The vampire was back, carrying her tray of blood tubes and lab slips and needles. "I'm sorry, Dr. DiMatteo. But I need to stick you again."

Abby, standing at the window, merely glanced at the phlebotomist. Then she turned back to the view. "This hospital's sucked all the blood I have to give," she said, and stared at the dreary view beyond the window. In the parking lot below, nurses scurried for the hospital doors, hair flying, raincoats flapping in the wind. In the east, clouds had gathered, black and threatening. Will the skies never clear? wondered Abby.

Behind her came the clatter of glass tubes. "Doctor, I really do have to get this blood."

"I don't need any more tests."

"But Dr. Wettig ordered it." The phlebotomist added, with a quiet note of desperation, "Please don't make things hard for me."

Abby turned and looked at the woman. She seemed very young. Abby was reminded of herself at some long-ago time. A time when she, too, was terrified of Wettig, of doing the wrong thing, of losing all she'd worked for. She was afraid of none of these things now. But this woman was.

Sighing, Abby went to the bed and sat down.

The phlebotomist set her blood tray on the bedside table and began opening sterile packets containing gauze, a disposable needle, and a Vacutainer syringe. Judging by the number of filled blood tubes in her tray, she had already gone through the motions dozens of times today. There were only a few empty slots remaining.

"Okay, which arm would you prefer?"

Abby held out her left arm and watched impassively as the rubber tourniquet was tucked into place with a snap. She made a fist. The antecubital vein swelled into view, bruised by all the earlier venipunctures. As the needle pierced her skin, Abby turned away. She looked, instead, at the phlebotomist's tray, at all the neatly labeled tubes of blood. A vampire's candy box.

Suddenly she focused on one specimen in particular, a purple-topped tube with the label facing toward her. She stared at the name.

VOSS, NINA
SICU BED 8

"There we go," said the vampire, withdrawing the needle. "Can you hold that gauze in place?"

Abby looked up. "What?"

"Hold the gauze while I get you a Band-Aid."

Automatically Abby pressed the gauze to her arm. She looked back at the tube containing Nina Voss's blood. The attending physician's name was just visible, at the corner of the label. *Dr. Archer.*

Nina Voss is back in the hospital, thought Abby. *Back on cardiothoracic service.*

The phlebotomist left.

Abby paced over to the window and stared out at the darkening clouds. Scraps of paper were flying around the parking lot. The window rattled, buffeted by a fresh gust of wind.

Something has gone wrong with the new heart.

She should have realized that days ago, when they'd met in the limousine. She remembered Nina's appearance in the gloom of the car. The pale face, the bluish tinge of her lips. Even then, her transplant was already failing.

Abby went to the closet. There she found a bulging plastic bag labeled PATIENT BELONGINGS. It contained her shoes, her blood-stained slacks, and her purse. Her wallet was missing; it was probably locked up in the hospital safe. A thorough search of the purse turned up a few loose nickels and dimes in the bottom. She would need every last one.

She zipped on the slacks, tucked in her hospital gown top, and stepped into the shoes. Then she went to the door and peeked out.

Nurse Soriano wasn't at the desk. However, two other nurses were in the station, one talking on the phone, another bent over paperwork. Neither was looking in Abby's direction.

She glanced down the hall and saw the cart with the evening meal trays come rattling into the ward, pushed by an elderly volunteer in pink. The cart came to a stop in front of the nurses' desk. The volunteer pulled out two meal trays and carried them into a nearby patient room.

That's when Abby slipped out into the hall. The meal cart blocked the nurses' view as Abby walked calmly past their desk and out of the ward.

She couldn't risk being spotted on the elevators; she headed straight for the stairwell.

Six flights up she emerged on the twelfth floor. Straight ahead was the OR wing; around the corner was the SICU. From the linen cart in the OR hallway, she picked up a surgical gown, a flowered cap, and shoe covers. Completely garbed in blue like everyone else, she just might pass unnoticed.

She turned the corner and walked into the SICU.

Inside she found chaos. The patient in Bed 2 was coding. Judging by the tensely staccato voices and by all the personnel frantically pressing into the cubicle, the resuscitation was not going well. No one even glanced in Abby's direction as she walked past the monitor station and crossed to Cubicle 8.

She paused outside the viewing window just long enough to confirm that it was, indeed, Nina Voss in the bed. Then she pushed into the cubicle. The door swung shut behind her, muffling the voices of the code team. She pulled the curtains over the window, to shut off all view of the room, and turned to the bed.

Nina was sleeping, serenely unaware of the frantic activity going on beyond her closed door. She seemed to have shrunk since Abby had last seen her, like a candle slowly being consumed by the flame of her illness. The body beneath those sheets looked as small as a child's.

Abby picked up the nurses' clipboard hanging at the foot of the bed. In a glance she took in all the parameters recorded there. The rising pulmonary wedge pressure. The slowly falling cardiac output. The upward titration of dobutamine in a futile attempt to boost cardiac performance.

Abby hung the clipboard back on the hook. As she straightened, she saw that Nina's eyes were open and staring at her.

"Hello, Mrs. Voss," said Abby.

Nina smiled and murmured, "It's the doctor who always tells the truth."

"How are you feeling?"

"Content." Nina sighed. "I am content."

Abby moved to her bedside. They looked at each other, neither one speaking.

Then Nina said, "You don't have to tell me. I already know."

"Know what, Mrs. Voss?"

"That it's almost over." Nina closed her eyes and took a deep breath.

Abby took the other woman's hand. "I never got the chance to thank you. For trying to help me."

"It was Victor I was trying to help."

"I don't understand."

"He's like that man in the Greek myth. The one who went into Hades to bring back his wife."

"Orpheus."

"Yes. Victor is like Orpheus. He wants to bring me back. He doesn't care what it takes. What it costs." She opened her eyes and her gaze was startlingly clear. "In the end," she whispered, "it will cost him too much."

They were not speaking of money. Abby understood that at once. They were speaking of souls.

The cubicle door suddenly opened. Abby turned to see a nurse staring at her in surprise.

"Oh! Dr. DiMatteo, what are you . . ." She glanced at the closed curtains, then her gaze swiftly assessed all the monitors and IV lines. *Checking for signs of sabotage.*

"I haven't touched anything," said Abby.

"Would you please leave?"

"I was only visiting. I heard she was back in SICU and—"

"Mrs. Voss needs her rest." The nurse opened the door and swiftly ushered Abby out of the cubicle. "Didn't you see the NO VISITORS sign? She's scheduled for surgery tonight. She can't be disturbed."

"What surgery?"

"The retransplant. They found a donor."

Abby stared at the closed door to Cubicle 8. She asked, softly, "Does Mrs. Voss know?"

"What?"

"Did she sign the consent form for surgery?"

"Her husband's already signed it for her. Now please leave *immediately.*"

Without another word, Abby turned and walked out of the unit. She didn't know if anyone noticed her departure; she just kept walking down the hall until she'd reached the elevators. The door opened; the car was filled with people. She stepped inside and quickly turned her back to the other passengers and faced the door.

They found a donor, she thought, as the elevator descended. *Somehow they found a donor. Tonight, Nina Voss will have a new heart.*

By the time the car reached the lobby, she had already worked out the sequence of events that would be taking place tonight. She had read the records of other Bayside transplants; she knew what was going to happen. Sometime around midnight, they would wheel Nina into the OR, where Archer's team would prep and drape her. There they would wait for the call. And at that precise moment, a different surgical team in a different OR would already be gathered around another patient. They would reach for scalpels and begin to slice skin and

313

muscle. Bone saws would grind. Ribs would be lifted, exposing the treasure within. A living, beating heart.

The harvest would be swift and clean.

Tonight, she thought, *it will happen just the way it has before.*

The elevator door opened. She stepped out, head bowed, eyes focused on the floor. She walked out the front doors and into a driving wind.

Two blocks away, cold and shaking, she ducked into a phone booth. Using her precious cache of nickels and dimes, she called Katzka's number.

He wasn't at his desk. The policeman who answered the extension offered to take a message.

"This is Abby DiMatteo," she said. "I have to talk to him now! Doesn't he have a pager or something?"

"Let me transfer you to the operator."

She heard two transfer clicks, then the operator came on. "I'll have Dispatch radio his car now," she said.

A moment later, the operator came back on. "I'm sorry, we're still waiting for Detective Katzka to respond. Can he reach you at your current number?"

"Yes. I mean, I don't know. I'll try calling him later." Abby hung up. She was out of coins, out of phone calls.

She turned and looked out the phone booth, and saw scraps of newspapers tumbling by. She didn't want to step out into that wind again, but she didn't know what else to do.

There was one more person she could call.

Half the phone book had been torn away. With a sense of futility, she flipped through the white pages anyway. She was startled to actually find the listing: *I. Tarasoff.*

Her hands were shaking as she dialed collect. *Please talk to me. Please take my call.*

After four rings she heard his gentle "Hello?" She could hear chinaware clattering, the sounds of a dinner table being set, the sweet strains of classical music. Then: "Yes, I'll accept the charges."

She was so relieved, her words spilled out in a rush. "I didn't know who else to call! I can't reach Vivian. And no one else will listen to me. *You* have to go to the police. *Make* them listen!"

"Now slow down, Abby. Tell me what's happening."

She took a deep breath. Felt her heart thudding with the need to share her burden. "Nina Voss is getting a second transplant tonight," she said. "Dr. Tarasoff, I think I know how it works. They don't fly the hearts in from somewhere else. The harvests are done right *here*. In *Boston*."

"Where? Which hospital?"

Her gaze suddenly focused on a car moving slowly up the street. She held her breath until the car continued around the corner and vanished.

"Abby?"

"Yes. I'm still here."

"Now Abby, I understand from Mr. Parr that you've been under a great strain lately. Isn't it possible this is—"

"Listen. Please listen to me!" She closed her eyes, forcing herself to stay calm. To sound rational. He must not have any doubts at all about her sanity. "Vivian called me today from Burlington. She found out there weren't any harvests done there. The organs didn't come from Vermont."

"Then where are the harvests done?"

"I'm not entirely sure. But I'm guessing they're done in a building in Roxbury. Amity Medical Supplies. The police have to get there before midnight. Before the harvest can be done."

"I don't know if I can convince them."

"You *have* to! There's a Detective Katzka, in Homicide. If we can reach him, I think he'll listen to us. Dr. Tarasoff, this isn't just an organ matchmaking service. They're generating donors. They're *killing* people."

In the background, Abby heard a woman call out: "Ivan, aren't you going to eat your dinner? It's getting cold."

"I'll have to skip it, dear," said Tarasoff. "There's been an emergency . . ." His voice came back on the line, soft and urgent. "I don't think I need to tell you that this whole thing scares me, Abby."

"It scares the hell out of me, too."

"Then let's just drive straight to the police. Drop it in *their* laps. It's too dangerous for us to handle."

"Agreed. One hundred percent."

"We'll do it together. The bigger the chorus, the more convincing our message."

She hesitated. "I'm afraid that having me along may hurt the cause."

"I don't know all the details, Abby. *You* do."

"Okay," she said, after a pause. "Okay. We'll go together. Could you come and get me? I'm freezing. And I'm scared."

"Where are you?"

She glanced out the phone booth window. Two blocks away, the lights of the hospital towers seemed to pulsate in the blowing darkness. "I'm in a phone booth. I don't know which street it's on. I'm a few blocks west of Bayside."

"I'll find you."

"Dr. Tarasoff?"

"Yes?"

"Please," she whispered. "Hurry."

24

As Vivian Chao's plane touched down at Logan International, she felt her anxiety tighten another notch. It wasn't the flight that had rattled her. Vivian was a fearless flyer, able to sleep soundly through even the worst turbulence. No, what was worrying her now, as the plane pulled up at the gate and as she gathered her carry-on from the overhead bin, was that last phone conversation with Abby. The abrupt disconnection. The fact that Abby had never called back.

Vivian had tried calling Abby at home, but there'd been no answer. Thinking about it during the flight, she'd realized that she didn't know where Abby had been calling from. Their connection had been severed too quickly for her to find out.

Lugging her carry-on, she walked off the plane and into the terminal. She was startled to find a huge crowd waiting at the gate. There was a forest of bright balloons and mobs of teenagers holding up signs that read *Welcome home, Dave!* and *Atta Boy* and *Local Hero!* Whoever Dave was, he had an adoring public. She heard cheers, and glancing back, she saw a grinning young man stride out of the elevated walkway right behind her. The crowd surged forward, practically swallowing up Vivian in their eagerness to greet Dave, the local

317

hero. Vivian had to navigate through a crush of squealing kids.

Kids, hell. They all towered over her by at least a head.

It took good old quarterback drive to shove her way through. By the time she emerged from the mob, she was pushing ahead with so much momentum, she practically bowled over a man standing on the periphery. She muttered a quick apology and kept walking. It took her a few paces to realize he hadn't said a word in exchange.

Her first stop was the restroom. All this anxiety was putting the squeeze on her bladder. She ducked inside to use the toilet and came back out.

That's when she saw the man again—the one she'd bumped into only moments ago. He was standing by the gift shop across from the women's restroom. He appeared to be reading a newspaper. She knew it was him because the collar of his raincoat was turned under. When she'd collided with him earlier, that inside-out flap was what her eyes had focused on.

She continued walking, toward baggage claim.

It was during that long hike past an endless succession of airline gates that her brain finally clicked on. Why was the man waiting at her gate unless he was there to meet someone? And if he *had* met a passenger, why was he now by himself?

She stopped at a newsstand, randomly picked up a magazine, and took it to the cashier. As the woman rang up the purchase, Vivian shifted just enough to cast a furtive glance around her.

The man was standing by a do-it yourself flight insurance counter. He seemed to be reading the instructions.

Okay, Chao, so he's following you. Maybe it's a case of love at first sight. Maybe he took one look at you and decided he couldn't let you walk out of his life.

As she paid for the magazine, she could feel her heart hammering. *Think. Why is he following you?*

That one was easy. The phone call from Abby. If anyone had been listening in, they'd know that Vivian was arriving at Logan on a six P.M. flight from Burlington. Just before the call was disconnected, she'd heard clicks on the line.

She decided to hang around the newsstand shop for a while. She browsed among the paperbacks, her eyes scanning the covers, her mind racing. The man probably didn't have a weapon on him; he would have had to bring it through the security check. As long as she didn't leave the airport's secured area, she should be safe.

Cautiously she peered over the paperback shelf.

The man wasn't there.

She came out of the shop and glanced around. There was no sign of him anywhere.

You are such an idiot. No one's following you.

She continued walking, past the security check and down the steps to baggage claim.

The suitcases from the Burlington flight were just rolling onto the carousel. She spotted her red Samsonite sliding down the ramp. She was about to push closer when she spotted the man in the raincoat. He was standing near the terminal exit, reading his newspaper.

At once she looked away, her pulse battering her throat. He was waiting for her to pick up her luggage. To walk past him out that exit, into the night.

Her red Samsonite made another revolution.

She took a deep breath and edged into the crowd of passengers waiting for their baggage. Her Samsonite was coming past again. She didn't pick it up but casually followed it around as it made its slow circle. When she was standing on the other side of the carousel, the crowd blocked her view of the man in the raincoat.

She dropped her carry-on bag and ran.

There were two carousels ahead of her, both of them unused at the moment. She sprinted past them, then darted out the far exit doors.

She emerged into the windblown night. Off to her left she heard a commotion. The man in the raincoat had just pushed his way out of the other exit. A second man came out a few steps behind him. One of them pointed at Vivian and barked out something incomprehensible.

Vivian took off, fleeing up the sidewalk. She knew the men were chasing her; she could hear the thud of a luggage cart toppling and the angry shouts of a porter.

There was a *pop,* and she felt something flick through her hair.

A bullet.

Her heart was banging, her lungs gasping in air thick with bus fumes.

She saw a doorway ahead. She ducked in it and raced for the nearest escalator. The moving stairs were going the wrong way. She ran up them two at a time. As she reached the upper level, she heard another *pop*. This time pain sliced her temple, and she felt a dribble of warmth on her cheek.

The American Airlines ticket counter was straight ahead. It was fully manned, a line of people snaking in front of it.

She heard footsteps pounding on the escalator behind her. Heard one of the men shouting words she couldn't understand.

She sprinted for the ticket counter, bowled over a man and a suitcase dolly, and leaped onto the countertop. Her momentum carried her straight over. She landed on the other side, her body slamming against the luggage loading belt.

Four astonished airline reps were staring down at her.

Her legs were shaking as she rose to her feet. Cautiously she peered across the countertop. She saw only a crowd of stunned bystanders. The men had vanished.

Vivian looked at the reps, who were still frozen in place. "Well, aren't you going to call Security?"

Wordlessly, one of the women reached for the phone.

"And while you're at it," said Vivian, "dial nine-one-one."

A dark Mercedes crawled along the road and came to a stop beside the phone booth. Abby could just make out the driver's profile, backlit by the lights of a passing car. It was Tarasoff.

She ran to the passenger door and climbed inside. "Thank God you're here."

"You must be freezing. Why don't you take my coat? It's on the back seat."

"Please, just go! Let's get out of here."

As Tarasoff pulled away from the curb, she glanced back to see if anyone was following them. The road behind them was dark.

"Do you see any cars?" he asked.

"No. I think we're okay."

Tarasoff released a shaky breath. "I'm not very good at this. I don't even like to watch crime shows."

"You're doing fine. Just get us to the police station. We can call Vivian to meet us there."

Tarasoff glanced nervously in the rearview mirror. "I think I just saw a car."

"What?" Abby looked back, but saw nothing.

"I'm going to turn here. Let's see what happens."

"Go ahead. I'll keep watching."

As they rounded the corner, Abby kept her gaze focused on the road behind them. She saw no headlights, no other cars at all. Only when they slowed to a stop did she turn and face forward. "What's wrong?"

"Nothing's wrong." Tarasoff cut the headlights.

"Why are you . . ." Abby's words froze in her throat.

Tarasoff had just pressed the lock release button.

She glanced right in panic as her door swung open. A gust of wind swept in. Suddenly hands reached in and she was being dragged out into the night. Her hair fell across her eyes, obscuring her vision. She fought blindly against her captors but could not succeed in loosening their grips. Her hands were yanked behind her back and the wrists bound together. Her mouth was taped. Then she was lifted and thrust into the trunk of a nearby car.

The hood slammed shut, trapping her in darkness.

They were moving.

She rolled onto her back and kicked upward. Again and again she slammed her feet against the trunk lid, kicking until her thighs ached, until she could scarcely lift her legs. It was useless; no one could hear her.

Exhausted, she curled up on her side and forced herself to think.

Tarasoff. How is Tarasoff involved?

Slowly the puzzle came together, piece by piece. Lying in the cramped darkness, with the road rumbling beneath her, she began to understand. Tarasoff was chief of one of the most respected cardiac transplant teams on the East Coast. His reputation attracted desperately ill patients from around the world, patients with the wherewithal to go to any surgeon they chose. They demanded the best, and they could afford to pay for it.

What they could not buy, what the system would never allow them to buy, was what they needed to stay alive: hearts. Human hearts.

That's what the Bayside transplant team could provide. She

remembered what Tarasoff had once said: *"I refer patients to Bayside all the time."*

He was Bayside's go-between. He was their matchmaker.

She felt the car brake and turn. The tires rolled across gravel, then stopped. There was a distant roar, a sound she recognized as a jet taking off. She knew exactly where they were.

The trunk hood opened. She was lifted out, into a buffeting wind that smelled of diesel fuel and the sea. They half-carried, half-dragged her down the pier and up the gangplank. Her screams were muffled by the tape over her mouth and lost in the thunder of the jet's takeoff. She caught only a glimpse of the freighter deck, of shifting blackness and geometric shadows, and then she was dragged below, down steps that rattled and clanged. One flight, then another.

A door screeched open and she was thrust inside, into darkness. Her hands were still bound behind her back; she could not break her fall. Her chin slammed to the metal floor and the impact was blinding. She was too stunned to move, to utter even a whimper as pain drove like a stake through her skull.

Another set of footsteps clanged down the stairway. Dimly she heard Tarasoff say: "At least it's not a total waste. Take the tape off her mouth. We can't have her suffocating."

She rolled onto her back and struggled to focus. She could make out Tarasoff's silhouette, standing in the faintly lit doorway. She flinched as one of the men bent down and ripped off the tape.

"Why?" she whispered. It was the only question she could think of. *"Why?"*

The silhouette gave a faint shrug, as though her question was irrelevant. The other two men backed out of the room. They were preparing to shut her inside.

"Is it the money?" she cried. "Is it that simple an answer?"

"Money means nothing," Tarasoff said, "if it can't buy you what you need."

"Like a heart?"

"Like the life of your own child. Or your own wife, your own sister or brother. You, of all people, should understand that, Dr. DiMatteo. We know all about little Pete and his accident. Only ten years old, wasn't he? We know you've lived through your own private tragedy. Think, doctor, what would you have given to have saved your brother's life?''

She said nothing. By her silence, he knew her answer.

"Wouldn't you have given anything? Done everything?''

Yes, she thought, and that admission took no reflection at all. *Yes.*

"Imagine what it's like,'' he said, "to watch your own child dying. To have all the money in the world and know that she still has to wait her turn in line. Behind the alcoholics and the drug abusers. And the mentally incompetent. And the welfare cheats who haven't worked a single day in their lives.'' He paused. And said, softly, "Imagine.''

The door swung shut. The latch squealed into place.

She was lying in pitch darkness. She heard the rattle of the stairway as the three men climbed back to deck level, heard the faint thud of a hatch closing. Then, for a time, she heard only the wind and the groan of the ship straining at its lines.

Imagine.

She closed her eyes and tried not to think of Pete. But there he was standing in front of her, proudly dressed in his Cub Scout uniform. She thought of what he'd said when he was five: that Abby was the only girl he wanted to marry. And she thought of how upset he'd been to learn that he could not marry his own sister . . .

What would I have done to save you? Anything. Everything.

In the darkness, something rustled.

Abby froze. She heard it again, the barest whisper of movement. *Rats.*

She squirmed away from the sound and managed to rise up onto her knees. She could see nothing, could only imagine giant rodents scurrying on the floor all around her. She struggled to her feet.

There was a soft *click.*

The sudden flare of light flooded her retinas. She jerked backward. A bare bulb swung overhead, clinking softly against the dangling pull-chain.

It was not a rat she had heard moving in the darkness. It was a boy.

They stared at each other, neither one of them saying a word. Though he stood very still, she could see the wariness in his eyes. His legs, thin and bare beneath shorts, were tensed for flight. But there was nowhere to run.

He looked about ten, very pale and very blond, his hair almost silver under the swaying lightbulb. She noticed a bluish smudge on his cheek, and realized with a sudden start of outrage that the smudge was not dirt, but a bruise. His deep-set eyes were like two more bruises in his white face.

She took a step toward him. At once he backed away. "I won't hurt you," she said. "I just want to talk to you."

A frown flickered across his forehead. He shook his head. "I promise. I won't hurt you."

The boy said something, but his answer was incomprehensible to her. Now it was her turn to frown and shake her head.

They looked at each other in shared bewilderment.

Suddenly they both glanced upward. The ship's engines had just started up.

Abby tensed, listening to the rattle of chain, the squeal of hydraulics. Moments later, she felt the rocking of the hull as it cut through the water. They had left the dock and were now under way.

Even if I get out of these bonds, out of this room, there's nowhere for me to run.

In despair, she looked back at the boy.

He was no longer paying any attention to the sound of the engines. Instead, his gaze had dropped to her waist. Slowly he edged sideways and stared at her bound wrists, tucked close to her back. He looked down at his own arm. Only then did Abby see that his left hand was missing, that his forearm ended in a stump. He had held it close to his body, concealing the deformity from her view. Now he seemed to be studying it.

He looked back at her and spoke again.

"I can't understand what you're saying," she said.

He repeated himself, this time with an edge of petulance in his voice. Why *couldn't* she understand? What was wrong with her?

She simply shook her head.

They regarded each other in mutual frustration. Then the boy lifted his chin. She realized that he had come to some sort of decision. He circled around to her back and tugged at her wrists, trying to loosen the bonds with his one hand. The cord was too tightly knotted. Now he knelt on the floor behind her. She felt the nip of his teeth, the heat of his breath against her skin. As the lightbulb swayed overhead, he began to gnaw, like a small but determined mouse, at her bonds.

"I'm sorry, but visiting hours are over," said a nurse. "Wait, you can't go in there. Stop!"

Katzka and Vivian walked straight past the nurses' desk and pushed into Room 621. "Where's Abby?" demanded Katzka.

Dr. Colin Wettig turned to look at them. "Dr. DiMatteo is missing."

"You told me she'd be watched here," said Katzka. "You assured me nothing could happen to her."

"She *was* watched. No one came in here without my express orders."

"Then what happened to her?"

"That's a question you'll have to ask Dr. DiMatteo."

It was Wettig's flat voice that angered Katzka. That and the emotionless gaze. Here was a man who revealed nothing, a man in control. Staring at Wettig's unreadable face, Katzka suddenly recognized himself, and the revelation was startling.

"She was under *your* care, doctor. What've you people done with her?"

"I don't like your implications."

Katzka crossed the room, grabbed the lapels of Wettig's lab coat, and shoved him backward against the wall. "Goddamn you," he said, *"Where did you take her?"*

Wettig's blue eyes at last betrayed a flicker of fear. "I told you, I don't know where she is! The nurses called me at six-thirty to tell me she was gone. We've alerted Security. They've already searched the hospital but they can't find her."

"You know where she is, don't you?"

Wettig shook his head.

"Don't you?" Katzka gave him another shove.

"I don't know!" gasped Wettig.

Vivian stepped forward and tried to pull them apart. "Stop it! You're choking him! Katzka, let him *go!"*

Abruptly Katzka released Wettig. The older man swayed backward against the wall, breathing heavily. "I thought, given her delusional state, she'd be safer in the hospital." Wettig straightened and rubbed his neck where the collar of the lab coat had left a bright red strangulation mark. Katzka stared at the mark, shocked by the evidence of his own violence.

"I didn't realize," said Wettig, "that she might be telling the truth after all." Wettig pulled a slip of paper from his pocket and handed it to Vivian. "The nurses just gave that to me."

"What is it?" said Katzka.

Vivian frowned. "This is Abby's blood alcohol level. It says here it's zero."

"I had it redrawn this afternoon and sent to an independent lab," Wettig explained. "She kept insisting she hadn't been intoxicated. I thought, if I could confront her with undeniable evidence, that I could break through her denial . . ."

"This result is from an outside lab?"

Wettig nodded. "Completely independent of Bayside."

"You told me her alcohol was point two-one."

"That was the one done at four A.M. in Bayside's lab."

Vivian said, "The half-life of blood alcohol ranges anywhere from two to fourteen hours. If it was that high at four A.M., then this test should show at least a trace left."

"But there's no alcohol in her system," said Katzka.

"Which tells me that either her liver is amazingly fast at metabolizing it," said Wettig, "or Bayside's lab made a mistake."

"Is that what you're calling it?" said Katzka. "A mistake?"

Wettig said nothing. He looked drained. And very old. He sat down on the rumpled bed. "I didn't realize . . . didn't want to consider the possibility . . ."

"That Abby was telling the truth?" said Vivian.

Wettig shook his head. "My God," he murmured. "This hospital should be shut down. If what she's been saying is true."

Katzka felt Vivian's gaze. He looked at her.

She said, softly: "Now do you have any doubts?"

For hours the boy had slept in her arms, his breath puffing out warm whispers against her neck. He lay limp, arms and legs askew, the way children do when they are deeply, trustingly asleep. He had been shivering when she'd first embraced him. She'd massaged his bare legs, and it was like rubbing cold, dry sticks. Eventually his shaking had stopped, and as his breathing slowed, she'd felt that flush of warmth that children give off when they finally fall asleep.

She, too, slept for a while.

When she woke up, the wind was blowing harder. She could hear it in the groaning of the ship. Overhead, the bare lightbulb swayed back and forth.

The boy whimpered and stirred. There was something touching about the smell of young boys, she thought, like the scent of warm grass. Something about the sweet androgyny of their bodies. She remembered how her brother Pete had felt, sagging against her shoulder as he slept in the backseat of the family car. For miles and miles, while their father drove, Abby had felt the gentle drumming of Pete's heart. Just as she was feeling this boy's heart now, beating in its cagelike chest.

He gave a soft moan and shuddered awake. Looking up at her, recognition slowly dawned in his eyes.

"Ah-bee," he whispered.

She nodded. "That's right. Abby. You remembered." Smiling, she stroked his face, her finger tracing across the bruise. "And you're . . . Yakov."

He nodded.

They both smiled.

Outside, the wind groaned and Abby felt the floor rock beneath them. Shadows swayed across the boy's face. He was watching her with an almost hungry look.

"Yakov," she said again. She brushed her mouth across one silky blond eyebrow. When she lifted her head, she felt the wetness on her lips. Not the boy's tears, but hers. She turned her face against her shoulder to wipe away the tears. When she looked back at him, she saw he was still watching her with that strange, rapt silence of his.

"I'm right here," she murmured. And, smiling, she brushed her fingers through his hair.

After a while his eyelids drifted shut and his body relaxed once again into the trusting limpness of sleep.

"So much for the search warrant," said Lundquist, and he kicked the door. It flew open and banged against the wall. Cautiously he edged into the room and froze. "What the fuck is all this?"

Katzka flipped on the wall switch.

Both men blinked as light flooded their eyes. It shone down with blinding intensity from three overhead lamps. Everywhere Katzka looked, he saw gleaming surfaces. Stainless steel cabinets. Instrument trays and IV poles. Monitors studded with knobs and switches.

In the center of the room was an operating table.

Katzka approached the table and stared down at the straps hanging from the sides. Two for the wrists, two for the ankles, two longer straps for the waist and chest.

His gaze moved to the anesthesia cart set up at the head of the table. He went to it and slid open the top drawer. Inside lay a row of glass syringes and needles capped in plastic.

"What the hell is this doing here?" said Lundquist.

Katzka closed the drawer and opened the next one. Inside he saw small glass vials. He took one out. *Potassium chloride.* It was half empty. "This equipment's been used," he said.

"This is bizarre. What kind of surgery were they doing up here?"

Katzka looked at the table again. At the straps. Suddenly he thought of Abby, her wrists tied down on the bed, tears trickling down her face. The memory was so painful he gave his head a shake to dispel the image. Fear was making it hard for him to think. If he couldn't think, he couldn't help her. He couldn't save her. Abruptly he moved away from the table.

"Slug?" Lundquist was eyeing him in puzzlement. "You okay?"

"Yeah." Katzka turned and walked out the door. "I'm fine."

Back outside on the sidewalk, he stood in the gusting wind and looked up at the Amity building. From street level, one saw nothing unusual about it. It was just another run-down building on a run-down street. Dirty brownstone facade, windows with air conditioners jutting out. When he had been inside it the day before, he had seen only what he'd expected to see. What he was supposed to see. The dingy showroom, the battered desks piled high with supply catalogs. A few salesmen listlessly talking on telephones. He had not seen the top floor, had never suspected that a single elevator ride would bring him to that room.

To that table with its straps.

Less than an hour ago, Lundquist had traced the building's

ownership to the Sigayev Company—the same New Jersey company to which the freighter was registered. That Russian mafia connection again. How deep into Bayside did it reach? Or were the Russians merely allied with someone inside the hospital? A trading partner, perhaps, in black market goods?

Lundquist's beeper chirped. He glanced at the readout, and reached into the car for the cellular phone.

Katzka remained in front of the building, his thoughts shifting back to Abby and where he should look next. Every room of the hospital had already been searched. So had the parking lot and the surrounding areas. It appeared that Abby had left the hospital on her own. Where would she go? Whom would she have called? It would have been someone she trusted.

"Slug!"

Katzka turned to see Lundquist waving the telephone. "Who's on the line?"

"The Coast Guard. They've got a chopper waiting for us."

Footsteps clanged on the stairway.

Abby's head snapped up. In her arms, Yakov slept on, unaware. Her heart was thundering so hard she thought it would surely wake him, but he didn't stir.

The door swung open. Tarasoff, flanked by two men, stood looking in at her. "It's time to go."

"Where?" she said.

"Only a short walk." Tarasoff glanced at Yakov. "Wake him up. He comes too."

Abby hugged Yakov closer. "Not the boy," she said.

"Especially the boy."

She shook her head. "Why?"

"He's AB positive. The only AB we happen to have in stock at the moment."

She stared at Tarasoff. Then she looked down at Yakov, his face flushed with sleep. Through his thin chest she could feel the beating of his heart. *Nina Voss,* she thought. *Nina Voss is AB positive . . .*

One of the men grabbed her arm and hauled her to her feet. She lost her grip on the boy; he tumbled to the floor where he lay blinking in confusion. The other man gave Yakov a sharp prod with his foot and barked a command in Russian.

The boy sleepily stumbled to his feet.

Tarasoff led the way. Down a dim corridor, then through a locked hatch. Up a staircase and through another hatch, to a steel walkway. Straight ahead was a blue door. Tarasoff started toward it, the walkway rattling under his weight.

Suddenly the boy balked. He twisted free and started to run back the way they'd come. One of the men snagged him by the shirt. Yakov spun around and sank his teeth into the man's arm. Howling in pain, the man slapped Yakov across the face. The impact was so brutal it sent the boy sprawling.

"Stop it!" screamed Abby.

The man jerked Yakov to his feet and gave him another slap. Now the boy stumbled toward Abby. At once she swept him up into her arms. Yakov clung to her, sobbing into her shoulder. The man moved toward her, as though to separate them.

"You stay the fuck away from him!" Abby yelled.

Yakov was shaking, whimpering incomprehensibly. She pressed her lips to his hair and whispered: "Sweetheart, I'm with you. I'm right here with you."

The boy raised his head. Looking into his terrified eyes, she thought: *He knows what's going to happen to us.*

She was shoved forward, across the walkway, and through the blue door.

They passed into a different world.

The corridor beyond was paneled in bleached wood, the floor was white linoleum. Overhead glowed a haze of softly diffused light. Their footsteps echoed as they walked past a spiral staircase and turned a corner. At the end of the passage was a wide door.

The boy was shaking even harder now. And he was getting heavy. She set him down on his feet and cupped his face in her hand. Just for a second their gazes met, and what could not be communicated in words was now shared in that single look. She took Yakov's hand and gave it a squeeze. Together they walked toward the door. One man was in front of them, one behind them. Tarasoff was in the lead. As he unlocked the door, Abby shifted her weight forward, every muscle tensing for the next move. Already she had released Yakov's hand.

Tarasoff pushed the door and it swung open, revealing a room of stark white.

Abby lunged. Her shoulder slammed into the man in front of

her, shoving him against Tarasoff, who stumbled across the threshold to his knees.

"You bastards!" yelled Abby, flailing at them. *"You bastards!"*

The man behind her tried to seize her arms. She twisted around and swung at his face, her fist connecting in a satisfying thud. She spied a flash of movement. It was Yakov, darting away and vanishing around the corner. Now the man she'd shoved was on his feet again, coming at her from the other direction. Together the two men trapped her between them and lifted her from the floor. She didn't stop fighting and thrashing as they carried her through the doorway into the white room.

"You've got to control her!" said Tarasoff.

"The boy—"

"Forget the boy! He can't go anywhere. Get her up on the table!"

"She won't hold still!"

"Bastards!" Abby screamed, kicking one leg free.

She heard Tarasoff fumbling in cabinets. He snapped: "Give me her arm! I need to get at her arm!"

Tarasoff approached, syringe in hand. Abby cried out as the needle plunged in. She twisted, but couldn't break free. She twisted again, and this time her limbs barely responded. She was having trouble seeing now. Her eyelids wouldn't stay open. Her voice came out barely a sigh. She tried to scream, but could not even draw the next breath.

What is wrong with me? Why can't I move?

"Get her in the next room!" said Tarasoff. "We have to intubate now or we're going to lose her."

The men carried her into the adjoining room and slid her onto a table. Lights came on overhead, searingly bright. Though fully awake, fully aware, she could not move a muscle. But she could feel everything. The straps tightening around her wrists and ankles. The pressure of Tarasoff's hand on her forehead, tipping her head back. The cold steel blade of the laryngoscope sliding into her throat. Her shriek of horror echoed only in her head; no sound came out. She felt the plastic ET tube snaking down her throat, gagging, suffocating her as it moved past her vocal cords and into her trachea. She could not turn away, could not even fight for air. The tube was taped to her face and connected to an ambubag. Tarasoff squeezed the bag and Abby's chest rose and fell in three quick, lifesaving breaths. Now he took off the ambubag and connected the ET tube to a ventilator. The machine took over, pumping air into her lungs at regular intervals.

"Now go get the boy!" snapped Tarasoff. "No, not both of you. I need someone to assist."

One of the men left. The other stepped closer to the table.

"Fasten that chest strap," said Tarasoff. "The succinylcholine will wear off in another minute or two. We can't have her thrashing around while I start the IV."

Succinylcholine. This is how Aaron died. Unable to struggle. Unable to breathe.

Already the drug's effect was starting to fade. She could feel her chest muscles begin to spasm against the insult of that tube. And she could raise her eyelids now, could see the face of the man standing above her. He was cutting away her clothes, his gaze flickering with interest as he bared her breasts, then her abdomen.

Tarasoff started the IV in her arm. As he straightened, he saw that Abby's eyes were fully open now and staring at him. He read the question in her gaze.

"A healthy liver," he said, "is not something we can take for granted. There's a gentleman in Connecticut who's been waiting over a year for a donor." Tarasoff reached for a second IV bag and he hung it on the pole. Then he looked at her. "He was delighted to hear we've finally found a match."

All that blood they drew from me in the ER, she thought. *They used it for tissue typing.*

He continued with his tasks. Connecting the second bag to the line. Drawing medications into syringes. She could only look at him mutely as the ventilator pumped air into her lungs. Her muscle function was beginning to return. Already she could wiggle her fingers, could shrug her shoulders. A drop of perspiration slid down her temple. She was sweating with the effort to move. To regain control of her body. A clock on the wall read eleven-fifteen.

Tarasoff had finished laying out the tray of syringes. He heard the sound of the door open and shut again, and he turned. "The boy's loose," he said. "They're still hunting him down. So we'll take the liver first."

Footsteps approached the table. Another face came into view and stared down at Abby.

So many times before she had looked across the operating table at that face. So many times before, she had seen those eyes smiling at her above a surgical mask. They were not smiling now.

No, she sobbed, but the only sound that came out was the soft rush of air through the ET tube. *No* . . .

It was Mark.

25

Gregor knew that the only way out of the ship's aft section was through the blue door, and it was locked. The boy must have gone up the spiral staircase.

Gregor peered up at the steps, but he saw only curving shadows. He began to climb, the flimsy staircase ringing with his weight. His arm still throbbed where the boy had bit him. The little bastard. This one had caused trouble from the start.

He reached the next level and stepped off the staircase, onto thick carpet. He was now in the living quarters of the surgeon and the surgeon's assistant. To the aft were two private cabins with a shared head and a shower. At the forward end was a well-appointed saloon. The only way out of this section was back down the staircase. The boy was trapped.

Gregor headed aft first.

The first cabin he came to was the dead surgeon's. It stank of tobacco. He flicked on the light and saw an unmade bed, a locker with the door hanging open, a desk with an overflowing ashtray. He crossed to the locker. Inside he found clothes reeking of smoke, an empty vodka bottle, and a secret stash of pornographic magazines. No boy.

Gregor next searched the surgical assistant's cabin. It was far more orderly, the bed made, the clothes in the locker neatly pressed. No boy in here either.

He glanced in the head, then started toward the saloon. Before he reached it, he heard the noise. It was a muffled whine.

He entered the saloon and turned on the lights. Quickly his gaze swept the room, taking in the couch, the dining table and chairs, and the television set with its stack of videotapes. Where was the boy? He circled the room, then stopped, staring at the forward wall.

The dumbwaiter.

He ran to it and pried open the doors. All he saw were cables. He slapped the Up button, and the cables began to move, groaning as they lifted their burden. Gregor leaned forward, ready to snatch hold of the boy.

Instead he found himself staring at the empty dumbwaiter. The boy had already escaped into the galley.

Gregor headed back down the staircase. This was not a catastrophe. The galley was already secured. Gregor had started padlocking it every night, after discovering that the crew was sneaking food out of the pantry. The boy was still trapped.

Gregor pushed through the blue door and started across the walkway.

"I'm sorry, Abby," said Mark. "I never thought it would go this far."

Please, she thought. *Please don't do this . . .*

"If there was any other way . . ." He shook his head. "You pushed it too hard. And then I couldn't stop you. I couldn't control you."

A tear slid from her eye and trickled into her hair. Just for an instant, she saw a flash of pain in his face. He turned away.

"It's time to gown up," said Tarasoff. "Will you do the honors?" He held out a syringe to Mark. "Pentobarb. We want to be humane about this, after all."

Mark hesitated. Then he took the syringe and turned to the IV pole. He uncapped the needle and poked it into the injection port. Again he hesitated. He looked at Abby.

I loved you, she thought. *I loved you so much.*

He pushed the plunger.

The lights began to dim. She saw his face waver, then fade into a deepening pool of gray.

I loved you.
I loved you . . .

The galley door was locked.

Yakov tugged again and again at the knob, but the door would not budge. What now? The dumbwaiter again? He scurried back to it and pressed the button. Nothing happened.

Frantically he glanced around the galley, considering all the possible hiding places. The pantry. The cupboards. The walk-in refrigerator. All of them offered only temporary concealment. Eventually the men would look in all those places. Eventually they would find him.

He would have to make it difficult for them.

He looked up at the lights. There were three bare bulbs shining overhead. He ran to the cupboard and plucked out a heavy ceramic coffee cup. He threw it at the nearest light.

The bulb shattered and went dark.

He fished out more cups. Three throws and the second bulb shattered.

He was about to aim at the last bulb when his gaze suddenly fell on the cook's radio. It was set in its usual place on top of the cupboard. His gaze followed the radio's extension cord as it trailed down to the countertop, where the toaster sat.

Yakov glanced at the stove and spotted an empty soup pot. He dragged the pot off the burner and carried it to the sink. He turned on the faucet.

A radio was playing at full volume.

Gregor pushed open the galley door and stepped inside. Music blasted away in the darkness. Drums and electric guitars. He felt for the wall switch and flicked it on. No lights. He tried it a few more times, but nothing happened. He took a step forward and his leather sole crunched on glass.

The little bastard's smashed out the lights. He's going to try to slip by me in the dark.

Gregor pushed the door shut. By the light of a match, he inserted his key in the lock and turned the deadbolt. No escape now. The match went out.

He turned to the darkness. "Come on, boy!" he yelled. "Nothing's going to happen to you!"

He heard only the radio blaring away, drowning out any

other noise. He moved toward the sound, then paused to light another match. The radio was sitting on the countertop, right in front of him. As he switched off the music, he noticed the meat cleaver lying on the countertop. Beside it lay scraps of what looked like brown rubber.

So he's got his hands on the cook's knives, has he?

The match flickered out.

Gregor took out his gun and called out: "Boy?"

Only then did he notice that his feet were wet.

He lit a third match and looked down.

He was standing in a pool of water. Already it had soaked into his leather shoes, certainly ruining them. Where was the water coming from? In the wavering light of the flame, he scanned the area around his feet and saw that the water had spread halfway across the floor. Then he saw the extension cord, the end sliced off, one coil glistening at the edge of the pool. In bewilderment he scanned the length of the cord as it snaked across the floor and looped upward, to a chair.

Just before his match flickered out, the last image that Gregor registered was the faint gleam of blond hair, and the figure of the boy, his arm stretched toward the wall socket.

The end of the cord was dangling from his hand.

Tarasoff held out the scalpel. "You make the first incision," he said, and saw the look of dismay in the other man's eyes. *You have no choice, Hodell,* he thought. *You're the one who tried to recruit her into the fold. You're the one who made the mistake. Now you have to correct it.*

Hodell took the scalpel. They had not even begun to operate, and already sweat had broken out on his forehead. He paused, the blade poised over the exposed abdomen. They both knew this was a test—perhaps the ultimate one.

Go ahead. Archer did his part by taking care of Mary Allen. Just as Zwick did with Aaron Levi. Now it's your turn. Prove you're still part of the team, still one of us. Cut open the woman you once made love to.

Do it.

Mark shifted the scalpel in his hand, as though trying to get a better grip. Then he took a breath and pressed the blade to the skin.

Do it.

Mark sliced. A long, curving incision. The skin parted and a line of blood welled up and dribbled onto the surgical drapes.

Tarasoff relaxed. Hodell was not going to be a problem after all. He had, in fact, passed the point of no return years ago, as a surgical fellow. A night of heavy drinking, a few snorts of cocaine. The next morning, a strange bed, and a pretty nursing student strangled to death on the pillow beside him. And Hodell with no memory of what had really happened. It was all very persuasive.

And there'd been the money to cement the recruitment.

The carrot and the stick. It worked almost every time. It had worked with Archer and Zwick and Mohandas. And with Aaron Levi too—for a while. Theirs had been a closed society, meticulous about guarding their secrets. And their profits. No one else at Bayside, not Colin Wettig, not even Jeremiah Parr, could even begin to guess how much money had changed hands. It was enough money to buy the very best doctors, the very best team—a team Tarasoff had created. The Russians merely supplied the parts and, when necessary, the brute force. In the OR, it was the team that performed the miracles.

Money alone had not been enough to keep Aaron Levi in their fold. But Hodell was still theirs. He was proving it now with every slice of his scalpel.

Tarasoff assisted, positioning retractors, clamping bleeders. It was a pleasure to work with such young and healthy tissue. The woman was in excellent condition. She had a minimum of subcutaneous fat and her abdominal muscles were flat and tight—so tight that their assistant, standing at the head of the table, had to infuse more succinylcholine to relax them for easier retraction.

The scalpel blade penetrated the muscle layer. They were in the abdominal cavity now. Tarasoff widened the retractors. Beneath a thin veil of peritoneal tissue glistened the liver and loops of small intestine. All of it healthy, so healthy! The human organism was a beautiful sight to behold.

The lights flickered and almost went off altogether.

"What's going on?" said Hodell.

They both looked up at the lamps. The lights brightened again to full intensity.

"Just a glitch," said Tarasoff. "I can still hear the generator."

"This is not an optimal setup. A rocking ship. The power going off—"

"It's a temporary arrangement. Until we find a replacement for the Amity building." He nodded at the surgical site. "Proceed."

Hodell raised his scalpel and paused. He'd been trained as a thoracic surgeon; a liver resection was a procedure he'd performed only a few times before. Perhaps he needed extra guidance.

Or perhaps the reality of what he was doing was starting to sink in.

"Is there a problem?" Tarasoff asked.

"No." Mark swallowed. Once again he began to cut, but his hand was shaking. He lifted the scalpel and took a few deep breaths.

"We haven't a lot of time, Dr. Hodell. There's another donor to harvest."

"It's just . . . isn't it hot in here?"

"I hadn't noticed. Proceed."

Hodell nodded. Gripping the scalpel, he was about to make another incision when he suddenly froze.

Tarasoff heard a sound behind him—the sigh of the door as it whished shut.

Mark, staring straight ahead, lifted his scalpel.

The explosion seemed to punch him in the face. Hodell's head snapped backward. Blood and bone fragments sprayed across the table.

Tarasoff spun around to look at the door, and he caught a glimpse of blond hair and the boy's white face.

The gun fired a second time.

The shot went wild, the bullet shattering a glass door in the supply cabinet. Shards rained onto the floor.

The anesthetist ducked for cover behind the ventilator.

Tarasoff backed away, his gaze never leaving the gun. It was Gregor's gun, compact enough, light enough, for even a child to hold. But the hand clutching that gun was shaking too hard now to shoot straight. *He's only a boy,* thought Tarasoff. A frightened boy whose aim kept wavering indecisively between the anesthetist and Tarasoff.

Tarasoff glanced sideways at the instrument tray, and he spotted the syringe of succinylcholine. It still contained more than enough to subdue the child. Slowly he edged sideways, stepping over Hodell's body and through the spreading pool of blood. Then the gun swung back toward him, and he froze.

The boy was crying now, his breath coming in quick, tearful gasps.

"It's all right," soothed Tarasoff. And he smiled. "Don't be afraid. I'm only helping your friend. Making her well again. She's very sick. Don't you know that? She needs a doctor."

The boy's gaze focused on the table. On the woman. He took a step forward, then another. His breath suddenly escaped in a high, keening wail. He did not hear the anesthetist slip past him and flee from the room. Nor did he seem to hear the faint rumble of the helicopter. It was approaching, preparing to land for the pickup.

Tarasoff took the syringe from the tray. Quietly he moved closer to the table.

The boy lifted his head and his cry rose to a despairing shriek.

Tarasoff raised the syringe.

At that instant the boy looked up at him. And it was no longer fear, but rage that shone in the boy's eyes as he aimed Gregor's gun.

And fired one last time.

26

The boy would not leave her bedside. From the moment the nurses had wheeled her out of Recovery and into the SICU, he had stayed right beside her, a pale little ghost haunting her bed. Twice the nurses had taken him by the hand and led him out of the cubicle. Twice the boy had found his way back in again. Now he stood gripping the siderail, his gaze silently pleading with her to wake up. At least he was no longer hysterical, the way he'd been when Katzka had come across him on the ship. He'd found the boy leaning over Abby's butchered body, sobbing, imploring her to live. Katzka had not understood a word of what the boy was saying. But he'd understood perfectly his panic. His despair.

There was a tapping on the cubicle window. Turning, Katzka saw Vivian Chao motioning to him. He opened the door and joined her outside the cubicle.

"That kid can't stay here all night," she said. "He's getting in their way. Plus, he doesn't look very clean."

"Every time they try to take him away, he starts screaming."

"Can't you talk to him?"

"I don't know any Russian. Do you?"

"We're still waiting for the hospital translator. Why don't you exert some male authority? Just pull him out."

"Give the boy some time with her, okay?" Katzka turned and gazed through the window at the bed. And he found himself struggling to shake off the superimposed image that would haunt him for the rest of his days: Abby lying on the table, her abdomen slit open, her intestines glistening under the OR lights. The boy whimpering, cradling her face. And on the floor, lying in a lake of their own blood, the two men—Hodell already dead, Tarasoff unconscious and bleeding but still alive. Like everyone else aboard that freighter, Tarasoff had been taken into custody.

Soon there would be more arrests. The investigation was just beginning. Even now, federal authorities were closing in on the Sigayev Company. Based on what the freighter's crew had already told them, the scope of the organ-selling operation was wider—and far more horrifying—than Katzka could have imagined.

He blinked and refocused on the here and now: Abby, lying on the other side of that window, her abdomen swathed in bandages. Her chest rising and falling. The monitor tracing the steady rhythm of her heart. Just for an instant, he felt the same flash of panic he'd experienced on the ship, when Abby's heartbeat had started skipping wildly across the monitor. When he'd thought he was about to lose her, and the chopper bringing Vivian and Wettig to the ship had still been miles away. He touched the glass and found himself blinking again. And again.

Behind him, Vivian said softly, "Katzka, she'll be okay. The General and I do good work."

Katzka nodded. Without a word, he slipped back into the cubicle.

The boy looked up at him, his gaze as moist as Katzka's. "Ah-bee," he whispered.

"Yeah, kid. That's her name." Katzka smiled.

They both looked at the bed. A long time seemed to pass. The silence was broken only by the soft and steady beep of the cardiac monitor. They stood side by side, sharing a vigil over this woman whom neither of them knew well, but about whom they already cared so deeply.

At last Katzka held out his hand. "Come on. You need your sleep, son. And so does she."

The boy hesitated. For a moment he studied Katzka. Then, reluctantly, he took the offered hand.

They walked together through the SICU, the boy's plastic shoes scuffling across the linoleum. Without warning, the boy slowed down.

"What is it?" said Katzka.

The boy had paused outside another cubicle. Katzka, too, looked through the glass.

Beyond the window, a silver-haired man sat in a chair by the patient's bed. His head was bowed in his hands, his whole body was quaking with silent sobs. *There are things even Victor Voss cannot buy,* thought Katzka. *Now he's about to lose everything. His wife. His freedom.* Katzka looked at the woman lying in the bed. Her face was as white and fragile-looking as porcelain. Her eyes, half-opened, had the dull sheen of impending death.

The boy pressed closer to the glass.

In that instant, as he leaned forward, the woman's eyes seemed to register one last flicker of life. She focused on the boy. Slowly her lips curved into a silent smile. And then she closed her eyes.

Katzka murmured, "It's time to go."

The boy looked up. Firmly, he shook his head. As Katzka watched in helpless silence, the boy turned and walked back into Abby's cubicle.

Suddenly Katzka felt weary beyond belief. He looked at Victor Voss, a ruined man who now sat with his body crumpled forward in despair. He looked at the woman in the bed, her soul slipping away even as he watched. And he thought: *So little time. We have so little time on this earth with the people we love.*

He sighed. Then he, too, turned and walked into Abby's cubicle.

And took his place beside the boy.

LIFE SUPPORT

To Jacob, Adam, and Josh—
the guys in my life

ACKNOWLEDGMENTS

With many thanks to:

Emily Bestler, who can make any book shine

Ross Davis, M.D., neurosurgeon and Renaissance man

Jack Young, who cheerfully answers my oddest questions

Patty Kahn, for all her research assistance

Jane Berkey and Don Cleary, my navigators in the publishing world

And most of all, to Meg Ruley, who always points me in the right direction. And then walks me there.

1

A scalpel is a beautiful thing.

Dr. Stanley Mackie had never noticed this before, but as he stood with head bowed beneath the OR lamps, he suddenly found himself marveling at how the light reflected with diamondlike brilliance off the blade. It was a work of art, that razor sharp lunula of stainless steel. So beautiful, in fact, that he scarcely dared to pick it up for fear he would somehow tarnish its magic. In its surface he saw a rainbow of colors, light fractured to its purest elements.

"Dr. Mackie? Is something wrong?"

He looked up and saw the scrub nurse frowning at him over her surgical mask. He had never before noticed how green her eyes were. He seemed to be seeing, really seeing, so many things for the very first time. The creamy texture of the nurse's skin. The vein coursing along her temple. The mole just above her eyebrow.

Or *was* it a mole? He stared. It was moving, crawling like a many-legged insect toward the corner of her eye. . . .

"Stan?" Dr. Rudman, the anesthesiologist, was speaking now, his voice slicing through Mackie's dismay. "Are you all right?"

Mackie gave his head a shake. The insect vanished. It was a mole again, just a tiny fleck of black pigment on the nurse's pale skin. He took a deep breath and picked up the scalpel from the instrument tray. He looked down at the woman lying on the table.

The overhead light had already been focused on the patient's lower abdomen. Blue surgical drapes were clamped in place, framing a rectangle of exposed skin. It was a nice flat belly with a bikini line connecting the twin flares of the hip bones—a surprising sight to behold in this season of snowstorms and winter white faces. What a shame he would have to cut into it. An appendectomy scar would certainly mar any future Caribbean tans.

He placed the tip of the blade on the skin, centering his incision on McBurney's point, halfway between the navel and the protrusion of the right hip bone. The approximate location of the appendix. With scalpel poised to cut, he suddenly paused.

His hand was shaking.

He didn't understand it. This had never happened before. Stanley Mackie had always possessed rock steady hands. Now it took enormous effort just to maintain his grip on the handle. He swallowed and lifted the blade from the skin. *Easy. Take a few deep breaths. This will pass.*

"Stan?"

Mackie looked up and saw that Dr. Rudman was frowning. So were the two nurses. Mackie could read the questions in their eyes, the same questions that people had been whispering about him for weeks. *Is old Dr. Mackie competent? At the age of seventy-four, should he still be allowed to operate?*

He ignored their looks. He had already defended himself before the Quality Assurance Committee, had explained, to their satisfaction, the circumstances of his last patient's death. Surgery, after all, was not a risk-free proposition. When too much blood pools in the abdomen, it's easy to confuse one's landmarks, to make the wrong slice.

The committee, in their wisdom, had absolved him of blame.

Nevertheless, doubts had seeped into the minds of the hospital staff. He could see it in the nurses' expressions, in Dr. Rudman's frown. All those eyes watching him. Suddenly he sensed other eyes as well. He caught a fleeting glimpse of dozens of eyeballs floating in the air, all of them staring at him.

He blinked, and the terrible vision was gone.

My glasses, he thought. *I will have to get my glasses checked.*

A drop of sweat slid down his cheek. He tightened his grip on the scalpel handle. This was just a simple appendectomy, a procedure a lowly surgical intern could pull off. Surely he could manage this, even with shaking hands.

He focused on the patient's abdomen, on that flat belly with its golden tan. Jennifer Halsey, age thirty-six. A visitor from out of state, she had awakened this morning in her Boston motel room suffering from right lower quadrant pain. With the pain growing worse, she had driven through a blinding snowstorm to the ER at Wicklin Hospital, and had been referred to the surgeon on call for the day: Mackie. She knew nothing about the rumors concerning his competence, nothing about the lies and whispers that were slowly destroying his practice. She was merely a woman in pain who needed her inflamed appendix removed.

He pressed the blade to Jennifer's skin. His hand had steadied. He could do it. Of course he could do it. He made the incision, a smooth, clean slice. The scrub nurse assisted, sponging up blood, handing him hemostats. He cut deeper, through the yellow subcutaneous fat, pausing every so often to cauterize a bleeder. *No problem. Everything's going to be fine.* He would get in, remove the appendix, and get out again. Then he would go home for the afternoon. Maybe a little rest was all he needed to clear his head.

He slit through the glistening peritoneum, into the abdominal cavity. "Retract," he said.

The scrub nurse took hold of the stainless steel retractors and gently tugged open the wound.

Mackie reached into the gap and felt the intestines, warm and slippery, squirm around his gloved hand. What a wondrous sensation, to be cradled in the heat of the human body. It was like being welcomed back into the womb. He exposed the appendix. One glance at the red and swollen tissue told him his diagnosis had been correct; the appendix would have to come out. He reached for the scalpel.

Only as he focused once again on the incision did he realize that something was not quite right.

There was far too much intestine crowded into the abdomen, twice as much as there should be. Far more than the woman needed. This wouldn't do. He tugged on a loop of small bowel, felt it glide, warm and slick, across his gloved hands. With the scalpel, he sliced off the excess length and set the dripping coil on the tray. There, he thought. That was much neater.

The scrub nurse was staring at him, her eyes wide over the surgical mask. "What are you *doing?*" she cried.

"Too much intestine," he answered calmly. "Can't have that." He reached into the abdomen and grasped another loop of bowel. No need for all this excess tissue. It only obscured his view of things.

"Dr. Mackie, no!"

He sliced. Blood pulsed out in a hot, arcing spray from the severed coil.

4

The nurse grabbed his gloved hand. He shook it off, outraged that a mere nurse would dare interrupt the procedure.

"Get me another scrub nurse," he commanded. "I need suction. Have to clear away all this blood."

"Stop him! Help me stop him—"

With his free hand, Mackie reached for the suction catheter and plunged the tip into the abdomen. Blood gurgled up the tube and poured into the reservoir.

Another hand grasped his gown and pulled him away from the table. It was Dr. Rudman. Mackie tried to shake him off, but Rudman wouldn't let go.

"Put down the scalpel, Stan."

"She has to be cleaned out. There's too much intestine."

"Put it down!"

Struggling free, Mackie swung around to confront Rudman. He'd forgotten he was still holding the scalpel. The blade slashed across the other man's neck.

Rudman screamed and clapped his hand to his throat.

Mackie backed away, staring at the blood seeping out between Rudman's fingers. "Not my fault," he said. "It's not my fault!"

A nurse yelled into the intercom: "Send Security! He's going crazy in here! We need Security STAT!"

Mackie stumbled backward, through slippery pools of blood. Rudman's blood. Jennifer Halsey's blood. A spreading lake of it. He turned and bolted from the room.

They were chasing him.

He fled down the hallway, running in blind panic, lost in a maze of corridors. Where was he? Why did nothing seem familiar? Then, straight ahead, he saw the window, and beyond it, the swirling snow. *Snow.* That cold, white lace would purify him, would cleanse this blood from his hands.

Behind him, footsteps pounded closer. Someone shouted, *"Halt!"*

5

Mackie took three running steps and leaped toward the rectangle of light.

Glass shattered into a million diamonds. Then the cold air whistled past him and everything was white. A beautiful, crystalline white.

And he was falling.

2

It was a scorching day outside, but the driver had the air conditioner going full blast, and Molly Picker was feeling chilled as she rode in the backseat of the car. The cold air blowing out the vent by her knees seemed to knife straight up her miniskirt. She leaned forward and rapped on the Plexiglas partition.

"Excuse me?" she said. "Hey, mister? Could you turn down that air conditioner? Mister?" She rapped again.

The driver didn't seem to hear her. Or maybe he was ignoring her. All she saw was the back of his blond head.

Shivering, she crossed her bare arms over her chest and scooted sideways, away from that vent. Staring out the car window, she watched the streets of Boston glide by. She didn't recognize this neighborhood at all, but she knew they were headed south. That's what the last sign had said, Washington Street, South. Now she looked out at boxy buildings and barred windows, at clumps of men sitting on front stoops, their faces glossed with sweat. Not even June, and already the temperature was in the eighties. Molly could read the day's heat just by looking at the people on the street. The languid slump of their shoulders, their slow-motion shuffle down the sidewalks. Molly enjoyed looking at people. Mostly she looked at women because she found them so much more interesting. She would study their dresses and wonder why some wore black in the heat of summer, why the fat ones with big butts chose bright stretch pants, why nobody wore hats these days. She would study how the pretty ones walked, their hips swaying ever so slightly, their feet perched, perfectly balanced, on high heels. She wondered what secrets pretty women knew that she didn't. What lessons their mamas had passed along to them, lessons that Molly had somehow missed. She would gaze long and hard at their faces, hoping for divine insight into what makes a woman beautiful. What special magic they possessed that she, Molly Picker, did not have.

The car stopped at a red light. A woman in platform heels was standing on the corner, one hip jutted out. Like Molly, a hooker, but older—maybe eighteen, with lustrous black hair that tumbled all over her bronzy shoulders. Black hair would be nice, thought Molly wistfully. It made a statement. It was not an in-between color, like Molly's limp hair, which was neither blond nor brown and made no statement at all. The car window was darkly tinted, and the black-haired girl couldn't see Molly staring at her. But she seemed to sense it, because she slowly pivoted on her platform heels to face the car.

She was not so pretty after all.

Molly sat back, feeling oddly disappointed.

The car turned left and continued southeast. They were far from Molly's neighborhood now, heading into territory that was both unfamiliar and threatening. The heat had driven people out of their apartments and they sat fanning themselves in shady doorways. Their gazes followed the car as it passed by. They knew it did not belong in this neighborhood. Just as Molly knew she did not belong here. Where was Romy sending her?

He hadn't given her any address. Usually a scrawled street number was thrust in her hand, and she was responsible for scrounging up her own taxi. This time, though, there'd been a car waiting at the curb for her. A nice car, too, with no telltale stains on the backseat, no stinky wads of tissue paper stuffed in the ashtray. It was all so clean. She'd never ridden in a car this clean.

The driver turned left, onto a narrow street. No people were sitting outside on the sidewalk here. But she knew they were watching her. She could feel it. She dug in her purse, fished out a cigarette, and lit up. She'd taken only two drags when a disembodied voice suddenly said: "Please put it out."

Molly glanced around, startled. "What?"

"I said, put it out. We don't allow smoking in the car."

Flushing with guilt, she quickly stubbed out the cigarette in the ashtray. Then she noticed the tiny speaker mounted in the partition.

"Hello? Can you hear me?" she said.

No reply.

"If you can, could you turn down the air conditioner? I'm freezing back here. Hello? Mister driver?"

The blast of cold air shut off.

"*Thank* you," she said. And added under her breath: "Asshole."

She found the electric switch for the window and rolled it down a crack. The smell of summer in the city wafted in, hot and sulfurish. She didn't mind the heat. It felt like home. Like all the damp and sweaty summers of her childhood in Beaufort. Damn, she wanted a cigarette. But she didn't feel like arguing with that tinny little box.

The car rolled to a stop. The voice from the speaker said: "This is the address. You can get out now."

"What, here?"

"The building's right in front of you."

Molly peered out at the four-story brownstone. The first-floor windows were boarded up. Broken glass glittered on the sidewalk. "You've got to be kidding," she said.

"The front door's open. Go up two flights to the third floor. It'll be the last door on your right. No need to knock, just walk right in."

"Romy didn't say nothing about this."

"Romy said you'd cooperate."

"Yeah, well—"

"It's just part of the fantasy, Molly."

"What fantasy?"

"The client's. You know how it is."

Molly gave a deep sigh and stared out at the building again. Clients and their fantasies. So what was this guy's dream fuck? Doing it among the rats and cockroaches? A little danger, a little grunge to notch up the excitement? Why did clients' fantasies never match her own? A clean hotel room, a Jacuzzi. Richard Gere and Pretty Woman sipping champagne.

"He's waiting."

"Yeah, I'm going, I'm going." Molly shoved open the car door and stepped out onto the curb. "You're gonna wait for me, right?"

"I'll be right here."

She faced the building and took a deep breath. Then she climbed the steps and pushed into the entrance.

It was as bad inside as it looked on the outside. Graffiti all over the walls, the hallway littered with newspapers and a rusty box spring. Someone had trashed the place good.

She started up the stairs. The building was eerily silent,

and the clatter of her shoes echoed in the stairwell. When she reached the second floor, her palms were sweaty.

This felt wrong. All wrong.

She paused on the landing and gazed toward the third floor. *What the hell did you get me into, Romy? Who is this client, anyway?*

She wiped her damp palms on her blouse. Then she took another breath and ascended the next flight of stairs. In the third-floor hallway, she stopped outside the last door on the right. She heard a humming sound from the room beyond—an air conditioner? She opened the door.

Cool air spilled out. She stepped inside and was amazed to find herself in a room with pristine white walls. In the center was some sort of doctor's exam table, padded in maroon vinyl. Overhead hung an enormous lamp. There was no other furniture. Not even a chair.

"Hello, Molly."

She spun around, searching for the man who'd just said her name. There was no one else in the room. "Where are you?" she demanded.

"There's nothing to be afraid of. I'm just a little shy. First I'd like to get a look at you."

Molly focused on a mirror, mounted in the far wall. "You're back there, aren't you? Is that some kinda one-way glass?"

"Very good."

"So what do you want me to do?"

"Talk to me."

"Is that all?"

"There'll be more."

Naturally. There was always more. She walked, almost casually, to the mirror. He'd said he was shy. That made her feel better. More in control. She stood with one hand propped on her miniskirted hip. "Okay. If you want to talk, mister, it's your money."

"How old are you, Molly?"

"Sixteen."

"Are your periods regular?"

"What?"

"Your menstrual periods."

She gave a laugh. "I don't believe this."

"Answer the question."

"Yeah. They're sorta regular."

"And your last period was two weeks ago?"

"How do you know *that?*" she demanded. Then, shaking her head, she muttered, "Oh. Romy told you." Romy would know, of course. He always knew when his girls were on the rag.

"Are you healthy, Molly?"

She glared at the mirror. "Don't I look healthy?"

"No blood diseases? Hepatitis? HIV?"

"I'm clean. You won't catch anything, if that's what worries you."

"Syphilis? Clap?"

"Look," she snapped. "Do you want to get laid or not?"

There was a silence. Then the voice said, softly: "Take off your clothes."

This was more like it. This was what she expected.

She stepped closer to the mirror, so close her breath intermittently steamed the glass. He would want to watch every detail. They always did. She reached up and began to unbutton her blouse. She did it slowly, drawing out the performance. As the fabric parted she let her thoughts go blank, felt herself withdrawing into some safe mental closet where men did not exist. She was moving her hips, swaying to imagined music. The blouse slid off her shoulders to the floor. Her breasts were exposed now, her nipples dimpling in the room's chill. She closed her eyes. Somehow that made it better. *Let's get this over with*, she thought. *Just screw him and get out of here.*

She unzipped her skirt and stepped out of it. Then she peeled off her panties. All this she did with her eyes closed. Romy had told her she had a good body. That if she used it right, no one would even notice how plain her face was. She was using that body now, dancing to a rhythm only she could hear.

"That's fine," the man said. "You can stop dancing."

She opened her eyes and stared at the mirror in bewilderment. She saw her own reflection there. Limp brown hair. Breasts small but pointed. Hips as narrow as a boy's. When she'd been dancing with her eyes closed, she had been acting out a part. Now she confronted her own image. Her real self. She couldn't help crossing her arms over her naked chest.

"Go to the table," he said.

"What?"

"The exam table. Lie down on it."

"Sure. If that's what turns you on."

"That's what turns me on."

To each his own. She climbed onto the table. The burgundy vinyl was cold against her bare buttocks. She lay down and waited for something to happen.

A door opened, and she heard footsteps. She stared as the man approached the foot of the table and loomed above her. He was garbed entirely in green. All she could see of his face was his eyes, a cold steel blue. They were gazing at her over a surgical mask.

She sat up in alarm.

"Lie down," he commanded.

"What the hell do you think you're doing?"

"I said, lie *down*."

"Man, I'm getting out of here—"

He grabbed her arm. Only then did she notice he was wearing gloves. "Look, I won't hurt you," he said, his voice softer. Gentler. "Don't you understand? *This* is my fantasy."

"You mean—playing doctor?"

13

"Yes."

"I'm supposed to be your patient?"

"Yes. Does that scare you?"

She sat thinking about it. Remembering all the other fantasies she'd endured on behalf of clients. This one, in the scheme of things, seemed relatively tame.

"All right," she sighed, and lay back down.

He slid out the stirrups and extended the footrests so they jutted out from the end of the table. "Come on, Molly," he said. "Surely you know what to do with your feet."

"Do I have to?"

"I'm the doctor. Remember?"

She stared at his masked face, wondering what lay behind that rectangle of cloth. A perfectly ordinary man, no doubt. They were all *so* ordinary. It was their fantasies that repulsed her. Frightened her.

Reluctantly she raised her legs and positioned her feet in the stirrups.

He released the foot of the table and it swung down on hinges. She was lying with her thighs spread wide apart, her exposed bottom practically hanging off the table's edge. She displayed herself to men all the time, but there was something horribly vulnerable about this position. Those bright lights shining down between her legs. Her utter nakedness against the exam table. And the man, whose gaze was focused with clinical detachment on her most intimate anatomy.

He looped a Velcro strap around her ankle.

"Hey," she said. "I don't like being tied down."

"I like it," he murmured, fastening the other strap. "I like my girls this way."

She flinched as he inserted his gloved fingers. He leaned toward her, his gaze narrowed in concentration as his fingers probed deeper. She closed her eyes and tried to detach her thoughts from what was happening between her legs, but the sensations were difficult to ignore. Like a rodent burrowing deep inside her. He had one hand pressed down on top of her abdomen, and the fingers of his other hand were moving inside. Somehow this seemed a worse violation than any mere fuck, and she wanted it over and done with. *Is this turning you on, creep?* she wondered. *Are you stiff yet? When are you going to get on with it?*

He withdrew his hand. She gave a shudder of relief. Opening her eyes, she saw that he was not looking at her anymore. His gaze was focused instead on something beyond her field of vision. He nodded.

Only then did she realize there was someone else in the room.

A rubber mask was clamped over her mouth and nose. She tried to twist away, but her head was pressed hard against the table. She reached up, frantically clawing at the edges of the anesthesia mask. At once her hands were yanked away, and her wrists firmly and efficiently tied down. She gasped in a breath of acrid-smelling gas, felt it sear her throat. Her chest rebelled in a spasm of coughing. She bucked harder, but the mask would not go away. She took another breath; she could not help it. Now all sensation was draining from her limbs. The lights seemed dimmer. Bright white fading to gray.

To black.

She heard a voice say, "Draw the blood now."

But the words meant nothing to her. Nothing at all.

"Man, oh man, what a mess you've made."

It was Romy's voice—that much she could figure out. But she could not seem to make sense of anything else. Where she was. Where she'd been.

Why her head ached and her throat felt so dry.

"Come on, Molly Wolly. Open your eyes."

15

She groaned. Just the rumble of her own voice made her head vibrate.

"Open your fuckin' eyes, Molly. You're stinking up the whole room."

She rolled onto her back. Light filtered, blood red, through her eyelids. She struggled to open them, to focus on Romy's face.

He was staring down at her with an expression of disgust in his dark eyes. His black hair was slicked back and shiny with pomade. It reflected light like a brass helmet. Sophie was there too, her face slightly sneering, her arms crossed over her balloon breasts. It made Molly even more miserable to see Sophie and Romy standing so close together, like the old lovers they were. Maybe still were. That horse-faced Sophie was always hanging around, trying to cut Molly out. And now she'd come into Molly's room, trespassing where she had no right to be.

Outraged, Molly tried to sit up, but her vision blanked out and she collapsed back on the bed. "I feel sick," she said.

"You've *been* sick," said Romy. "Now go get cleaned up. Sophie'll help you."

"I don't want her to touch me. Get her out of here."

Sophie gave a snort. "Miss Titless, I wouldn't hang around your pukey room anyway," she said and walked out.

Molly groaned. "I don't remember what happened, Romy."

"Nothing happened. You came back and went to bed. And threw up all over your pillow."

Again she struggled to sit up. He didn't help her, or even touch her. She smelled that bad. Already he was heading for the door, leaving her to clean up her own filthy sheets.

"Romy," she said.

"Yeah?"

"How did I get here?"

16

He laughed. "Geez, you really did get wasted, didn't you?" And he left the room.

For a long time she sat on the side of the bed, trying to remember the last few hours. Trying to shake off her residual wooziness.

There had been a client—that much she remembered. A man all in green. A room with a giant mirror. And there had been a table.

But she couldn't remember the sex. Maybe she had blocked it out. Maybe it had been so disgusting an experience she'd shoved it into her subconscious, the way she'd successfully blocked out so much of her childhood. Only occasionally did she allow a wisp of a childhood memory to return. The good memories, mostly; she did have a few good memories of her years growing up in Beaufort, and she could conjure them up at will. Or suppress them at will.

But the events of this afternoon, she could hardly remember at all.

God, she stank. She looked down at her blouse and saw it was stained with vomit. The buttons had been done up wrong, and bare skin showed through an unfastened gap.

She began to strip. She peeled off the miniskirt, unbuttoned the blouse, and tossed them in a pile on the floor. Then she stumbled to the shower and turned on the water.

Cold. She wanted it cold.

Standing under the sputtering faucet, she felt her head begin to clear. As it did, another memory flickered into focus. The man in green, towering above her. Staring down at her. And the straps, pinching her wrists and ankles.

She looked down at her hands and saw the bruises, like circular cuff marks around her wrists. He had tied her down—not so unusual. Men and their crazy games.

Then her gaze focused on another bruise, in the crook of her left arm. It was so faint she'd almost missed the small

17

blue circle. In the very center of the bruise, like the point of a bull's eye, was a single puncture mark.

She struggled to remember a needle, but she could not. All she remembered was the man in the surgeon's mask.

And the table.

Cold water dribbled down her shoulders. Shivering, Molly stared at the needle mark and she wondered what else she'd forgotten.

3

A nurse's voice called to her from the wall intercom: "Dr. Harper, we need you out here."

Toby Harper awakened with a start to find that she had fallen asleep at her desk, with a stack of medical journals as her pillow. Reluctantly she raised her head, squinting against the light from the reading lamp. The brass desktop clock said 4:49 A.M. Had she really slept for almost forty minutes? It seemed as if she'd laid her head down just a moment ago. The words of the journal article she'd been reading had begun to blur, and she'd thought she'd allow her eyes a short rest. That was all she'd intended, just a moment's respite from dull writing and painfully small print. The journal was still open to the article she'd been trying to absorb, the page now crinkled with the imprint of her face. "A randomized controlled study comparing the effectiveness of lamivudine and zidovudine in the treatment of HIV patients with less than 500 CD4+ cells per cubic centimeter." She closed the journal. God. No wonder she'd fallen asleep.

There was a knock on the door, and Maudeen poked her head into the doctor's room. Ex-army major Maudeen Collins had a voice like a megaphone—not at all what one expected from a five-foot-two-inch pixie. "Toby? You weren't asleep, were you?"

"I guess I dozed off. What've you got out there?"

"Sore toe."

"At this hour?"

"Patient ran out of Colchicine and he thinks his gout's acting up."

Toby groaned. "Jesus. Why don't these crazy patients ever plan ahead?"

"They think we're just an all-night pharmacy. Look, we're still doing his paperwork. So why don't you take your time?"

"I'll be right out."

After Maudeen left, Toby allowed herself a moment to fully wake up. She wanted to sound halfway intelligent when she spoke to the patient. She rose from the desk and crossed to the sink. She'd been on duty for ten hours now, and so far it had been an uneventful shift. That was the nice part about working in a quiet suburb like Newton. There were often long periods when absolutely nothing happened in the Springer Hospital ER, periods when Toby could stretch out on the doctor's bed and take a nap, if she was so inclined. She knew the other ER doctors took naps, but Toby usually resisted the temptation. She was paid to work the twelve-hour night shift, and it seemed unprofessional to spend any of those hours in a state of unconsciousness.

So much for professionalism, she thought, staring at herself in the mirror. She'd fallen asleep on the job, and she could see the aftereffects in her face. Her green eyes were puffy. Newsprint from the medical journal had smudged words on her cheek. Her expensive salon haircut looked as though it had been whipped up by an eggbeater, and her hair stuck out in short blond spikes. This was the precise and elegant Dr. Harper as she really was—not so elegant after all.

In disgust Toby turned on the faucet and vigorously scrubbed the newsprint from her face. She splashed water on her hair as well, and combed it back with her fingers. So much for expensive haircuts. At least she no longer looked like a fuzzy blond dandelion. There was nothing she could do about the puffy eyes or the lines of exhaustion. At the age of thirty-eight, Toby couldn't bounce back from an all-nighter the way she did as a twenty-five-year-old medical student.

She left the room and walked down the hall to the ER.

No one was there. The front desk was unmanned, the waiting room deserted. "Hello?" she called.

"Dr. Harper?" answered a voice over the intercom.

"Where is everyone?"

"We're in the staff room. Could you come back here?"

"Don't I have a patient to see?"

"We have a problem. We need you *now.*"

Problem? Toby didn't like the sound of that word. At once her pulse kicked into high gear. She hurried toward the staff room and pushed open the door.

A camera flashbulb went off. She froze in place as a chorus of voices began to sing:

"Happy birthday to you! Happy birthday to you . . ."

Toby looked up at the red and green streamers fluttering overhead. Then she looked at the cake, glittering with lit candles—dozens of them. As the last notes of "Happy Birthday" faded away, she covered her face with her hand and groaned. "I don't believe this. I completely forgot."

"Well we didn't," said Maudeen, snapping off another picture with her Instamatic. "You're seventeen, right?"

"I wish. Who's the joker who put on a zillion candles?"

Morty, the lab tech, raised his pudgy hand. "Hey, no one told me when to stop."

"See, Morty wanted to test our sprinkler system—"

"Actually, this is a pulmonary function test," said Val, the other ER nurse. "In order to pass, Toby, you have to blow 'em all out with a single breath."

"And if I don't?"

"Then we're gonna *intubate!*"

"C'mon, Toby. Make a wish!" urged Maudeen. "And make him tall, dark, and handsome."

"At my age, I'd settle for short, fat, and rich."

Arlo, the security guard, piped up: "Hey! I've got two out of three qualifications!"

"You've also got a wife," shot back Maudeen.

"Go, Tobe! Make a wish!"

"Yeah, make a wish!"

Toby sat down in front of the cake. The other four gathered around her, giggling and jostling like rowdy kids. They were her second family, related to her not by blood but by years of shared crises in the Emergency Room. The Nanny Brigade was what Arlo called the night ER team. Maudeen and Val and the lady doc. God help the male patient who came in with a urologic complaint.

A wish, thought Toby. *What do I wish for? Where do I start?* She took a breath and blew. All the candles puffed out to a burst of applause.

"Way to go," said Val, and she began plucking out the candles. Suddenly she glanced at the window. So did everyone else.

A Newton police car, blue lights flashing, had just pulled into the ER parking lot.

"We got a customer," said Maudeen.

"Okay," sighed Val, "the ladies gotta go to work. Don't you boys eat all the cake while we're gone."

Arlo leaned toward Morty and whispered, "Aw, those girls are always on a diet anyway. . . ."

Toby led the charge down the hall. The three women reached the front desk just as the automatic ER doors whisked open.

A young cop poked his head inside. "Hey, we got this old guy out in the car. Found him wandering in the park. You ladies wanna take a look at him?"

Toby followed the cop outside, into the parking lot. "Is he hurt?"

"Doesn't seem to be. But he's pretty confused. I didn't smell alcohol, so I'm thinking maybe Alzheimer's. Or diabetic shock."

Great, thought Toby. A cop who thinks he's a doctor. "Is he fully conscious?" she asked.

"Yeah. We got him in the backseat." The cop opened the rear door of the patrol car.

The man was completely nude. He sat curled into a ball of thin arms and legs, his bald head bobbing back and forth. He was muttering to himself, but she could not quite make out what he was saying. Something about having to get ready for bed.

"Found him on a park bench," said the other cop, who looked even younger than his partner. "He was wearing his underwear then, but he took it off in the car. We found the rest of his clothes in the park. They're on the front seat."

"Okay, we'd better get him inside." Toby nodded to Val, who already had a wheelchair waiting.

"C'mon, buddy," the cop urged. "These nice ladies are gonna take care of you."

The man hugged himself tighter and began to rock on his skinny buttocks. "Can't find my pajamas . . ."

"We'll get you some pajamas," said Toby. "You come inside with us, sir. We'll give you a ride in this chair."

Slowly the old man turned and focused on her. "But I don't know you."

"I'm Dr. Harper. Why don't you let me help you out of the car?" She held out her hand to him.

He studied it, as though he'd never seen a hand before. At last he reached for it. She slipped her arm around his waist and helped him out of the car. It was like lifting a bundle of dry twigs. Val scurried forward with the wheelchair just as the man's legs seemed to buckle beneath him. They strapped him into the chair and set his bare feet on the footrests. Then Val wheeled him through the ER doors. Toby and one of the baby-faced cops followed a few paces behind.

"Any history?" Toby asked him.

"No, Ma'am. He couldn't give us any. Didn't seem like he'd hurt himself or anything."

"Does he have any ID?"

"There's a wallet in his pants pocket."

"Okay, we'll need to contact his next of kin and find out if he has any medical problems."

"I'll get his things out of the car."

Toby walked into the exam room.

Maudeen and Val had already put the patient on the gurney and were now tying his wrist restraints to the siderails. He was still babbling about his pajamas and making half-hearted attempts to sit up. Except for a sheet discreetly draped across his groin, he was naked. Spasms of gooseflesh intermittently stippled his bare chest and arms.

"He says his name is Harry," said Maudeen, slipping a blood pressure cuff around the man's arm. "No wedding ring. No obvious bruises. Smells like he could use a bath."

"Harry," said Toby. "Do you hurt anywhere? Are you in any pain?"

"Turn off the lights. I want to go to bed."

"Harry—"

"Can't sleep with those damn lights on."

"Blood pressure one fifty over eighty," said Maudeen. "Pulse is a hundred and regular." She reached for the electronic thermometer. "C'mon, sweetie. Put this in your mouth."

"I'm not hungry."

"You don't eat it, dear. I'm going to take your temperature."

Toby stood back for a moment and just watched the man. He was moving all four limbs, and although he was on the thin side, he seemed adequately nourished, his muscles lean and wiry. It was his hygiene that bothered her. He had at least a week's worth of gray beard stubbling his face, and his fingernails were dirty and unclipped. Maudeen was right about that smell. Harry definitely needed a bath.

The electronic thermometer beeped. Maudeen took it out of the man's mouth and frowned at the reading. "Thirty seven point nine. You feel okay, hon?"

"Where are my pajamas?"

"Boy, you do have a one-track mind."

Toby shone a penlight in the man's mouth and saw the gleam of gold crowns—five of them. You could tell a lot about a patient's socioeconomic status just by looking at the teeth. Fillings and gold crowns meant middle class or better. Rotten teeth and gum disease said *empty bank account.* Or a morbid fear of dentists. She smelled no alcohol on his breath, no fruity odors that would indicate diabetic ketosis.

She began her physical exam at his head. Running her fingers across his scalp, she detected no obvious fractures or lumps. With her penlight she tested his pupillary reactions. Normal. So were his extraocular movements and gag reflex. All the cranial nerves seemed intact.

"Why don't you go away," he said. "I want to sleep."

"Did you hurt yourself, Harry?"

"Can't find my damn pajamas. Did you take my pajamas?"

25

Toby looked at Maudeen. "Okay, let's get some bloods cooking. CBC, lytes, glucose STAT. Couple of extra red tops for an SMA and tox screen. We'll probably have to cath him for a urine."

"Gotcha." Maudeen already had the tourniquet and Vacutainer syringe ready. While Val immobilized the man's arm, Maudeen drew the blood. The patient scarcely seemed to feel the needle going in.

"All right, honey," said Maudeen, applying a bandage to the puncture site. "You're a very good patient."

"You know where I put my pajamas?"

"I'm gonna get you a fresh set, right now. You just wait." Maudeen gathered up the blood tubes. "I'll send these up under John Doe."

"His name's Harry Slotkin," said one of the cops. He had returned from the patrol car and now stood in the doorway, holding up Harry's trousers. "Checked his wallet. According to the ID, he's seventy-two years old and he lives at 119 Titwillow Lane. That's right up the road, in that new Brant Hill development."

"Next of kin?"

"There's an emergency contact here. Someone named Daniel Slotkin. It's a Boston phone number."

"I'll give him a call," said Val. She left the room, sliding the privacy curtains shut behind her.

Toby was left alone with the patient. She resumed the physical exam. She listened to the heart and lungs, felt the abdomen, tapped on tendons. She poked and prodded and squeezed, and found nothing out of the ordinary. Perhaps this is just Alzheimer's, she thought, standing back to study the patient. She knew the signs of Alzheimer's all too well: the crumbling memory, the nocturnal wanderings. The personality fracturing, breaking off a piece at a time. Darkness was distressing for these patients. As daylight faded, so did their visual links to reality. Perhaps Harry Slotkin was a victim of sundowning—the nighttime psychosis so common to Alzheimer's patients.

Toby picked up the ER clipboard and began to write, using the cryptic code of medical shorthand. VSS for vital signs stable. PERRL for pupils equal, round, and reactive to light.

"Toby?" called Val through the curtain. "I've got Mr. Slotkin's son on the phone."

"Coming," said Toby. She turned to pull aside the curtain. She didn't realize an instrument stand was right on the other side. She knocked against the tray; a steel emesis basin fell off and clanged loudly to the floor.

As Toby bent down to pick it up, she heard another noise behind her—a strange, rhythmic rattling. She looked at the gurney.

Harry Slotkin's right leg was jerking back and forth.

Is he having a seizure?

"Mr. Slotkin!" said Toby. "Look at me. Harry, look at me!"

The man's gaze focused on her face. He was still conscious, still able to follow commands. Though his lips moved, silently forming words, no sound came out.

The jerking suddenly stopped, and the leg lay still.

"Harry?"

"I'm so tired," he said.

"What just happened, Harry? Were you trying to move your leg?"

He closed his eyes and sighed. "Turn off the lights."

Toby frowned at him. Had it been a seizure? Or merely an attempt to free his restrained ankle? He seemed calm enough now, both legs lying motionless.

She stepped through the privacy curtain and went to the nurses' desk.

"The son's on line three," said Val.

Toby picked up the receiver. "Hello, Mr. Slotkin? This is

27

Dr. Harper at Springer Hospital. Your father was brought to our ER a short time ago. He doesn't seem to be hurt, but he—"

"What's wrong with him?"

Toby paused, surprised by the sharpness of Daniel Slotkin's response. Was it irritation or fear that she heard in his voice? She answered calmly, "He was found in a park and brought here by the police. He's agitated and confused. I can't find any focal neurologic problems. Does your father have a history of Alzheimer's? Or any medical problems?"

"No. No, he's never been sick."

"And there's no history of dementia?"

"My father is sharper than I am."

"When did you last see him?"

"I don't know. A few months ago, I guess."

Toby absorbed that information in silence. If Daniel Slotkin resided in Boston, then he lived less than twenty miles away. Certainly not a distance that would explain such infrequent contact between father and son.

As though sensing her unspoken question, Daniel Slotkin added: "My father leads a very busy life. Golf. Daily poker at the country club. It's not always easy for us to get together."

"He was mentally sharp a few months ago?"

"Let's put it this way. The last time I saw my father, he gave me a lecture on investment strategies. Everything from stock options to the price of soybeans. It went over *my* head."

"Is he on any medications?"

"Not that I know of."

"Do you know the name of his doctor?"

"He goes to a specialist in that private clinic at Brant Hill, where he lives. I think the doctor's name is Wallenberg. Look, just how confused *is* my father?"

"The police found him on a park bench. He'd taken off his clothes."

There was a long silence. "Jesus."

"I can't find any injuries. Since you say there's no history of dementia, there must be something acute going on. Maybe a small stroke. Or a metabolic problem."

"Metabolic?"

"An abnormal blood sugar, for instance. Or a low sodium level. They can both cause confusion."

She heard the man exhale deeply, a sound of weariness. And maybe frustration. It was five in the morning. To be awakened at such an hour, to face such a crisis, would exhaust anyone.

"It would be helpful if you came in," said Toby. "He might find a familiar face comforting."

The man was silent.

"Mr. Slotkin?"

He sighed. "I guess I'll have to."

"If there's someone else in the family who can do it—"

"No, there's no one else. Anyway, he'll expect me to show up. To make sure everything's done right."

As Toby hung up, Daniel Slotkin's last words struck her as faintly threatening: *To make sure everything's done right.* And why *wouldn't* she do everything right?

She picked up the telephone and left a message with the Brant Hill Clinic answering service, telling them their patient Harry Slotkin was in the ER, confused and disoriented. Then she punched in the beeper for the Springer Hospital X-ray tech.

A moment later, the tech called back from home, his voice groggy with sleep. "This is Vince. You beeped me?"

"This is Dr. Harper in the ER. We need you to come in and do a STAT CT head scan."

"What's the patient's name?"

"Harry Slotkin. Seventy-two-year-old man with new-onset confusion."

"Right. I'll be there in ten minutes."

Toby hung up and stared at her notes. *What have I over-looked?* she wondered. *What else should I be searching for?* She reviewed all the possible causes of new-onset dementia. Strokes. Tumors. Intracranial bleeds. Infections.

She glanced again at the vital signs. Maudeen had recorded an oral temperature of 37.9 degrees centigrade. Not quite a fever, but not quite normal, either. Harry would need a spinal tap—but not until the CT scan was done. If there was a mass in his skull, a spinal tap could lead to a catastrophic shift in pressure on the brain.

The wail of a siren made her glance up.

"Now what?" said Maudeen.

Toby shot to her feet and was already waiting at the ER entrance when the ambulance pulled up with a loud *whoop.* The vehicle's rear door flew open.

"We got a code in progress!" the driver yelled.

Everyone scrambled to unload the stretcher. Toby caught a quick glimpse of an obese woman, her face pale and limp-jawed. An ET tube was already taped in place.

"We lost her pressure en route—thought we'd better stop here instead of going on to Hahnemann—"

"What's the history?" snapped Toby.

"Found on the floor. Had an MI six weeks ago. Husband says she's on Digoxin—"

They rushed the patient through the ER doors, the driver pumping clumsily on the chest as the stretcher careened up the hall and swerved into the trauma room. Val hit the light switch. Overhead lamps flooded on, blindingly bright.

"Okay, you all got a grip? She's a big one. Watch that IV! One, two, three, *move!*" yelled Maudeen.

In one smooth transfer, four pairs of hands slid the patient off the ambulance stretcher and onto the treatment table. No one had to be told what to do. Despite the seeming confusion of a Code Blue, there was order in chaos. The driver resumed chest compressions. The other EMT continued bagging the lungs, pumping in oxygen. Maudeen and Val scrambled around the table untangling IV lines and connecting EKG wires to the cardiac monitor.

"We've got sinus rhythm," said Toby, glancing at the screen. "Stop compressions for a second."

The driver stopped pumping on the chest.

"I'm barely getting a pulse," said Val.

"Turn up that IV," said Toby. "We got any pressure yet?"

Val glanced up from the arm cuff. "Fifty over zip. Dopamine drip?"

"Go for it. Resume compressions."

The driver crossed his hands over the sternum and began to pump again. Maudeen scurried to the code cart and pulled out drug ampules and syringes.

Toby slapped her stethoscope on the chest and listened to the right lung field, then the left. She heard distinct breath sounds on both sides. That told her the ET tube was properly positioned and the lungs were filling with air. "Hold compressions," she said and slid the stethoscope over to the heart.

She could barely hear it beating.

Glancing up again at the monitor, she saw a fast sinus rhythm tracing across the screen. The heart's electrical system was intact. Why didn't the woman have a pulse? Either the patient was in shock from blood loss. Or . . .

Toby focused on the neck, and the answer instantly became apparent to her. The woman's obesity had obscured the fact that her jugular veins were bulging.

"You said she had an MI six weeks ago?" Toby asked.

"Yeah," the driver grunted out as he resumed chest compressions. "That's what the husband said."

"Any other meds besides Digoxin?"

"There was a big bottle of aspirin on the nightstand. I think she's arthritic."

That's it, thought Toby. "Maudeen, get me a fifty cc syringe and a cardiac needle."

"Gotcha."

"And toss me some gloves and a Betadine wipe!"

The packet flew toward her. Toby caught it in midair and ripped it open. "Stop compressions," she ordered.

The driver stepped back.

Toby gave the skin a quick swab of Betadine, then she pulled on the gloves and reached for the 50-cc syringe. She glanced one last time at the monitor. The rhythm was still a rapid sinus. She took a deep breath. "Okay. Let's see if this helps . . ." Using the bony protrusion of the xiphoid process as her landmark, she pierced the skin and angled the needle tip straight toward the heart. She could feel her own pulse hammering as she slowly advanced the needle. At the same time she was pulling back on the plunger, exerting gentle negative pressure.

A flash of blood shot into the syringe.

She stopped right where she was. Her hands were absolutely steady. *God, let the needle be in the right place.* She pulled back on the plunger, gradually suctioning blood into the syringe. Twenty cc's. Thirty. Thirty-five . . .

"Blood pressure?" she called out, and heard the rapid *whiff, whiff* of the cuff being inflated.

"Yes! I'm getting one!" said Val. "Eighty over fifty!"

"I guess we know what we've got now," said Toby. "We need a surgeon. Maudeen, get Dr. Carey on the line. Tell him we've got a pericardial tamponade."

"From the MI?" asked the ambulance driver.

"Plus she's on high-dose aspirin, so she's prone to bleeding. She probably ruptured a hole in her myocardium." Surrounded by blood in the closed sac of the pericardium, the heart would be unable to expand. Unable to pump.

The syringe was full. Toby withdrew the needle.

"Pressure's up to ninety-five," said Val.

Maudeen hung up the wall phone. "Dr. Carey's coming in now. So's his team. He says to keep her stabilized."

"Easier said than done," muttered Toby, her fingers probing for a pulse. She could feel one, but it remained thready. "She's probably reaccumulating. I'll need another syringe and needle pretty quick. Can we get her typed and crossed? And let's get a STAT CBC and lytes while we're at it."

Maudeen pulled out a fistful of blood tubes. "Eight units?"

"At least. Whole blood if we can get it. And send down some fresh frozen plasma."

"Pressure's falling to eighty-five," said Val.

"Shit. We'll need to do it again."

Toby ripped open a packet with a fresh syringe and tossed the wrapping aside. Already the floor was piling up with the debris of paper and plastic that accumulated during every code. *How many times will I have to repeat this?* she wondered as she positioned the needle. *Get your butt over here, Carey. I can't save this woman on my own . . .*

Toby wasn't sure Dr. Carey could save the patient either. If the woman *had* blown a hole in her ventricular wall, then she needed more than just a thoracic surgeon—she needed a full cardiac bypass team. Springer Hospital was a small suburban facility, perfectly capable of dealing with cesareans or simple gallbladder resections, but it was unequipped to deal with major surgery. Ambulance teams transporting serious trauma victims would normally bypass Springer Hospital and head straight for one of the larger medical centers like Brigham or Mass General.

This morning, though, the ambulance had unknowingly delivered a surgical crisis right to Toby's doorstep. And she didn't have the training—or the staff—to save this woman's life.

The second syringe was already filled with blood. Another fifty cc's of it—and it didn't clot.

"Pressure's going down again," said Val. "Eighty—"

"Doc, she's in V-tach!" one of the EMTs cut in.

Toby's gaze shot to the monitor. The rhythm had deteriorated to the jagged pattern of ventricular tachycardia. The heart was using only two of its four chambers now, beating too fast to be efficient.

"Defibrillator pads!" snapped Toby. "We'll go with three hundred joules."

Maudeen hit the charge button on the defibrillator. The needle climbed to three hundred watt-seconds.

Toby slapped two pads on the patient's chest. Coated with gel, the pads ensured electrical contact with the skin. She positioned the paddles. "Back!" she said, and squeezed the discharge button.

The patient thrashed, all her muscles jerking simultaneously as the current shot through her body.

Toby glanced at the monitor. "Okay, we're back in sinus—"

"No pulse. I've got no pulse," said Val.

"Resume CPR!" said Toby. "Hand me another syringe."

Even as she opened the packet and twisted on the pericardiocentesis needle, Toby knew they were losing the fight. She could suction out liters of blood, but more would accumulate, compressing the heart. *Just keep her alive until the surgeon gets here,* thought Toby, and the words became her mantra. *Keep her alive. Keep her alive . . .*

"Back in V-Tach!" said Val.

"Charge to three hundred. Get a lidocaine bolus in—"

The wall phone rang. Maudeen answered it. A moment later she called out: "Morty's having trouble crossmatching that blood I sent up! The patient's B negative!"

Shit. What else can go wrong? Toby slapped the paddles on the chest. "Everyone back!"

Again the woman's body jerked. Again the rhythm settled back into rapid sinus.

"Getting a pulse," said Val.

"Push that lidocaine *now.* Where's our fresh frozen plasma?"

"Morty's working on it," said Maudeen.

Toby glanced at the clock. They'd been coding the patient for nearly twenty minutes. It seemed like hours. Surrounded by chaos, with the phone ringing and everyone talking at once, she felt a sudden flash of disorientation. Inside the gloves, her hands were sweating, and the rubber was clammy against her skin. The crisis was spiralling out of her control. . . .

Control was the word Toby lived by. She strove to keep her life in order, her ER in order. Now this code was falling apart under her command, and there was nothing she could do to salvage it. She wasn't trained to crack a chest, to sew up a ruptured ventricle.

She looked at the woman's face. It was mottled, the flabby jowls deepening to purple. Even as she watched, she knew the brain cells were starving. Dying.

The ambulance driver, exhausted from chest compressions, switched places with his fellow EMT. A fresh pair of hands began pumping.

On the monitor, the heart tracing deteriorated to a jaggedly chaotic line. Ventricular fibrillation. A fatal rhythm.

The team responded with the usual strategies. More boluses of antiarrhythmics. Lidocaine. Bretylium. Higher and higher jolts from the paddles. In desperation Toby withdrew another fifty cc's of blood from the pericardium.

The heart tracing flattened out to a meandering line.

Toby glanced around at the other faces. They all knew it was over.

"All right." Toby released a deep breath, and her voice sounded chillingly calm. "Let's call it. What time?"

"Six-eleven," said Maudeen.

We kept her going forty-five minutes, thought Toby. That's the best we could do. The best anyone could do.

The EMT stepped back. So did everyone else. It was almost a reflex, that physical retreat, those few seconds of respectful silence.

The door banged open and Dr. Carey, the thoracic surgeon, made his usual dramatic entrance. "Where's the tamponade?" he snapped.

"She just expired," said Toby.

"What? Didn't you stabilize her?"

"We tried. We couldn't keep her going."

"Well, how long did you code her?"

"Believe me," said Toby. "It was long enough." She pushed past him and walked out of the room.

At the nurses' desk she sat down to gather her thoughts for a moment before filling out the ER sheet. She could hear Dr. Carey in the trauma room, his voice raised in complaint. They'd dragged him out of bed at five-thirty in the morning, and for what? A patient who couldn't be stabilized? Couldn't they *think* first before they ruined his night's sleep? Didn't they know he had a full day in the OR coming up?

Why are surgeons such assholes? Toby wondered, and she dropped her head in her hands. God, would the night never end? She had one more hour to go. . . .

Through the fatigue clouding her brain, she heard the whoosh of the ER doors swinging open. "Excuse me," said a voice. "I'm here to see my father."

Toby looked up at the man standing across from her. Thin-faced, unsmiling, he regarded her with an almost bitter tilt to his mouth.

Toby rose from the chair. "Are you Mr. Slotkin?"

"Yes."

"I'm Dr. Toby Harper." She held out her hand.

He shook it automatically, without any warmth. Even the touch of his skin was cold. Though he had to be at least thirty years younger than his father, the man's resemblance to Harry Slotkin was immediately obvious. Daniel Slotkin's face had the same sharply cut angles, the same narrow slash of a brow. But this man's eyes were different. They were small and dark and unhappy.

"We're still evaluating your father," she said. "I haven't seen any of his labs come back yet."

He glanced around the ER and made a sound of impatience. "I need to be back in the city by eight. Can I see him now?"

"Of course." She left the desk and led him to Harry Slotkin's room. Pushing open the door, she saw that the room was empty. "They must have him in X-ray. Let me call over and see if he's done."

Slotkin followed her back to the front desk and stood watching her as she picked up the phone. His gaze made her uneasy. She turned away from him and dialed.

"X-ray," answered Vince.

"This is Dr. Harper. How's the scan coming?"

"Haven't done it yet. I'm still getting things set up here."

"The patient's son wants to see him. I'll send him over."

"The patient isn't here."

"What?"

"I haven't gotten him in here yet. He's still in the ER."

"But I just checked the room. He's not . . ." Toby paused. Daniel Slotkin was listening, and he'd heard the dismay in her voice.

"Is there a problem?" asked Vince.

"No. No problem." Toby hung up. She looked at Slotkin. "Excuse me," she said, and headed up the hall to exam room three. She pushed open the door. There was no Harry Slotkin. But the gurney was there, and the sheet they'd used to cover him was lying crumpled on the floor.

Someone must have put him on a different gurney, moved him to a different room.

Toby crossed the hall to exam room four and shoved aside the curtain.

No Harry Slotkin.

She could feel her heart thudding as she moved down the hall to exam room two. The lights were off. No one would have put the patient in a dark room. Nevertheless she flicked on the wall switch.

Another empty gurney.

"Don't you people know where you put my father?" snapped Daniel Slotkin, who had followed her into the hall.

Pointedly ignoring his question, she stepped into the trauma room and yanked the curtain shut behind her. "Where's Mr. Slotkin?" Toby whispered to the nurse.

"The old guy?" asked Maudeen. "Didn't Vince take him to X-ray?"

"He says he never got him. But I can't find the man. And the son's right outside."

"Did you look in room three?"

"I looked in *all* the rooms!"

Maudeen and Val glanced at each other.

"We'd better check the hallways," said Maudeen, and she and Val hurried out into the corridor.

Toby was left behind to deal with the son.

"Where is he?" demanded Slotkin.

"We're trying to locate him."

"I thought he was supposed to be in your ER."

"There's been some kind of mix-up—"

"Is he or isn't he here?"

"Mr. Slotkin, why don't you have a seat in the waiting room? I'll bring you a cup of coffee—"

"I don't want a cup of coffee. My father's having some kind of medical crisis. And now you can't find him?"

"The nurses are checking X-ray."

"I thought you just called X-ray!"

"Please, if you'll just have a seat in the waiting room, we'll find out exactly what . . ." Toby's voice trailed off as she caught sight of the two nurses hurrying back toward her.

"We called Morty," said Val. "He and Arlo are checking the parking lot."

"You didn't find him?"

"He can't have gone far."

Toby felt the blood slide from her cheeks. She was afraid to look at Daniel Slotkin. Afraid to meet his gaze. But she couldn't shut out the sound of his anger.

"What is going on around here?" he demanded.

The two nurses said nothing. Both of them looked at Toby. Both of them knew that in the ER, the doctor was the captain of the ship. The one on whose shoulders rested ultimate responsibility. Ultimate blame.

"Where is my father?"

Slowly Toby turned to Daniel Slotkin. Her answer came out in barely a whisper. "I don't know."

It was dark, and his feet hurt, and he knew he had to get home. The trouble was, he could not remember *how* to get home. Harry Slotkin could not even remember how he'd come to be stumbling down this deserted street He thought about stopping at one of the houses along the way to ask for help, but all the windows he passed were dark. Were he to knock at one of those doors and beg for help, there would be questions and bright lights and he would almost certainly be humiliated. Harry was a proud man. He was not a man to ask for anyone's assistance. Nor did he volunteer assistance to others—not even to his own son. He'd always believed that charity, in the long run, was crippling, and he had not wanted to raise a cripple. *Strength is independence. Independence is strength.*

Somehow, he would find his own way home.

If only the angel would reappear.

She had come to him in that place of horrors, where he'd been put on a cold table and lights had blinded his eyes, the place where strangers had poked him with needles and jabbed him with their probing fingers. Then the angel had appeared. She hadn't hurt him at all. Instead she had smiled at him as she untied his hands and feet, and she had whispered: "Go, Harry! Before they come back for you."

Now he was free. He'd escaped, good for him!

He continued down the street of dark and silent houses, searching for some familiar landmark. Anything to tell him where he was.

I must have gotten turned around, he thought. *Went out for a walk and lost my way.*

Pain suddenly bit into his foot. He looked down and halted in amazement.

Beneath the glow of a streetlamp, he saw that he was wearing no shoes. Or socks, either. He stared at his bare feet. At his bare legs. At his penis, hanging limp and shriveled and utterly pitiful.

I'm not wearing any clothes!

In panic he glanced around to see if anyone was looking at him. The street was deserted.

Cupping his hands over his genitals, he fled the streetlamp, seeking the cover of darkness. When had he lost his clothes? He couldn't remember. He squatted down on the cold, clipped lawn of a front yard and tried to think, but panic had crowded out all memories of what had happened earlier that night. He began to whimper, soft little grunts and sobs as he rocked back and forth on his bare feet.

I want to go home. Please, oh please, if I could just wake up in my own bed . . .

He was hugging himself now, so lost in despair that he didn't notice the headlights rounding the far corner. Only when the van braked to a stop right beside him did Harry realize he'd been spotted. He clasped his arms tighter, curling into a shivering self-embrace.

A voice called softly through the darkness. "Harry?"

He didn't raise his head. He was afraid to unfold his body,

afraid to reveal his humiliating state of undress. He tried to squeeze himself into a tighter and tighter ball.

"Harry, I've come to take you home."

Slowly he raised his head. He could not make out the face of the driver, but the voice was one he knew. Or thought he knew.

"Step into the van, Harry."

He rocked back and forth on his heels and felt the wet grass brush against his bare buttocks. His voice rose in a high, thin wail. "But I have no clothes!"

"You have clothes at home. A whole closet of suits. Remember?" There was a soft clunk, the whine of metal sliding across metal.

Harry looked up and saw that the van door was open. Darkness gaped beyond. The silhouette of a man was standing beside the vehicle. The man extended his hand in a gesture of invitation.

"Come, Harry," he whispered. "Let's go home."

4

How hard can it be to find a naked man?

Toby sat in her car, squinting out at the hospital parking lot. It was already midmorning, and the sunlight seemed excruciatingly bright to her night-accustomed eyes. When had the sun come up? She hadn't seen it rise, hadn't enjoyed a single free moment to glance outside, and the daylight was a shock to her retinas. That's what came of choosing the graveyard shift. She was transforming into a creature of the night.

She sighed and started up the Mercedes. At last it was time to go home, time to leave behind the night's disasters.

But as she drove away from Springer Hospital, she was unable to shake off her gloom. Within the span of a single hour, she had lost two patients. She felt certain that the woman's death had been unavoidable, that there was nothing she could have done to save her.

Harry Slotkin was a different matter. Toby had left a confused patient unattended for nearly an hour. She was the last person to lay eyes on Harry, and try as she might, she could not remember whether she had restrained his wrists before she left the room. *I must have left him untied. It's the only way he could have escaped. It's my fault. Harry was my fault.*

Even if it *hadn't* been her fault, she was still the captain of the team, the person ultimately responsible. Now somewhere, an old man was wandering, naked and confused.

She slowed the car. Though she knew the police had already searched this area, she scanned the streets, hoping for a glimpse of her fugitive patient. Newton was a relatively safe suburb of Boston, and the neighborhood she was now driving through had the look of wealth. She turned onto a tree-lined residential street and saw well-kept houses, trimmed hedges, driveways fronted by iron gates. Not the sort of neighborhood where an old man would be assaulted. Perhaps someone had taken him in. Perhaps, right at this moment, Harry was sitting in a cozy kitchen, being fed breakfast.

Where are you, Harry?

She circled the neighborhood, trying to picture these streets from Harry's point of view. It would have been dark, confusing, cold without his clothes. Where did he think he was going?

Home. He would try to find his way home to Brant Hill.

Twice she had to stop and ask for directions. When at last she came to the turnoff for Brant Hill Road, she almost drove right past it. There were no signs; the road was marked only by two stone pillars flanking the entrance. Between them, the gate hung open. She pulled to a stop between the pillars and saw that two letters were scrolled into the gate's cast iron design, an elegantly baroque *B* and *H*. Beyond the pillars, the road twisted away and vanished behind deciduous trees. So this is Harry's neighborhood, she thought.

She drove through the open gate, onto Brant Hill Road.

Though the road was newly paved, the maple and oak trees flanking it were fully mature. Some of the leaves were tinged with the first blazing hues of fall. Already September, she thought; when had the summer gone by? She followed the curving road, glancing at the trees on either side, noting the heavy undergrowth and all the shadowy places that might conceal a body. Had the police searched that shrubbery? If Harry had wandered this way in the dark, he might have gotten lost in those bushes. She would call the Newton police, suggest they take a closer look at this road.

Up ahead, the trees suddenly thinned, giving way to a panorama that was so unexpected Toby braked to a sudden stop. At the side of the road was a sign in green and gold.

BRANT HILL
RESIDENTS AND GUESTS ONLY

Beyond the sign stretched a landscape that might have been lifted from a lush painting of English countryside. She saw gently rolling fields of manicured grass, a topiary garden with fanciful animals, and autumn-tinged stands of birch and maple. Glistening like a jewel was a pond with wild irises. A pair of swans glided serenely among water lilies. Beyond the pond was a "village," an elegant cluster of homes, each with its own picket-fenced garden. The primary mode of transportation seemed to be golf carts with green and white awnings. The carts were everywhere, parked in driveways or gliding along village paths. Toby also spotted a few rolling about on the golf course, shuttling players from green to green.

She focused on the pond, suddenly wondering how deep the water was, and whether a man could drown in it. At night, in the dark, a confused man might walk straight into that water.

She continued driving down the road, toward the village. Fifty yards later, she saw a turnoff to the right, and another sign.

BRANT HILL CLINIC
AND RESIDENTIAL CARE FACILITY

She took the turnoff.

The road twisted through evergreen forest, to emerge suddenly and unexpectedly into a parking lot. A three-story building loomed ahead. To one side of it, construction on a new wing was about to start. Through the mesh fence ringing the side, she saw the foundation pit had already been dug. At the edge of the pit, a circle of men in hardhats stood conferring over blueprints.

Toby parked in the visitors' lot and walked into the clinic building.

The whisper of classical music greeted her. Toby paused, impressed by her surroundings. This was not your usual waiting room. The couches were buttery leather, and original oil paintings hung on the walls. She looked down at the array of magazines. *Architectural Digest. Town & Country.* No *Popular Mechanics* on this coffee table.

"May I help you?" A woman in a pink nurse's uniform smiled from behind the reception window.

Toby approached her. "I'm Dr. Harper from Springer Hospital. I examined one of your patients in the ER last night. I've been trying to contact the patient's physician for more medical history, but I can't seem to reach him."

"Which doctor?"

"Dr. Carl Wallenberg."

"Oh, he's away at a medical conference. He'll be back in clinic on Monday."

"May I look at the patient's record? It might clear up a few medical questions for me."

45

"I'm sorry, but we can't release records without authorization from the patient."

"The patient's unable to give consent. Couldn't I talk to one of your other clinic doctors?"

"Let me pull the chart first." The nurse crossed to a filing cabinet. "The last name?"

"Slotkin."

The nurse slid out a drawer and flicked through the folders. "Harold or Agnes Slotkin?"

Toby paused. "There's an Agnes Slotkin? Is she related to Harry?"

The nurse glanced at the chart. "She's his wife."

Why didn't Harry's son tell me there was a wife? she wondered. She reached in her purse and found a pen. "Could you give me the wife's phone number? I really need to speak to her about Harry."

"There's no phone in her room. You can just take that elevator there."

"Where?"

"Agnes Slotkin is right upstairs in the skilled nursing facility. Room three four one."

Toby knocked at the door. "Mrs. Slotkin?" she called. There was no answer. She stepped into the room.

Inside a radio was playing softly, its station tuned to a classical program. White curtains hung at the window, and through the gauzy fabric, the morning sunlight shone in with a softly diffuse glow. On the nightstand roses in a vase shed pink petals. The woman in the bed lay unaware of any of this. Not the flowers nor the sunlight nor the presence of a visitor in her room.

Toby approached the bed. "Agnes?"

The woman didn't stir. She was lying on her left side, facing the door. Her eyes were half-open but unfocused, her body positioned by pillows propped behind her back. Her arms were curled into a fetal self-embrace. Above the bed, a bag of creamy white liquid dripped into a feeding tube that snaked into the woman's nostril. Though the linens looked clean, an odor hung in the air, undisguised by the scent of roses. It was the smell of the stroke ward, of talcum powder and urine and Ensure. The smell of a body slowly involuting.

Toby reached for the woman's hand. Gently she tugged the arm straight. The elbow extended with only slight resistance. No permanent contractures had set in; the nursing staff had been diligent with the passive range-of-motion exercises. Toby lay the hand down, noting the plumpness of the flesh. Despite her comatose state, the patient had been kept well nourished, well hydrated.

Toby focused on the slack face and wondered if those eyes were looking at her. Could the woman see anything, comprehend anything?

"Hello, Mrs. Slotkin," she murmured. "My name is Toby."

"Agnes can't answer you," a voice said behind her. "But I do believe she can hear you."

Startled, Toby turned to face the man who'd just spoken. He was standing in the doorway—in truth, he *filled* the doorway, a giant of a man with a broad black face and a gleaming wedge of a nose. It was a nice face, she thought, because he had kind eyes. He was wearing a white doctor's coat, and he held a medical chart.

Smiling, he extended his hand. His arm was so long the wrist poked out beyond the sleeve's edge. Did they make lab coats large enough for a man this size? she wondered.

"Dr. Robbie Brace," he said. "I'm Mrs. Slotkin's doc. Are you a relative?"

"No." Toby shook the man's hand, felt it engulf hers like a warm brown glove. "I'm an ER doc at Springer Hospital, down the road. Toby Harper."

"Professional call?"

"In a way. I was hoping Mrs. Slotkin could tell me about her husband's medical history."

"Is something wrong with Mr. Slotkin?"

"He was brought into the ER last night, confused and disoriented. Before I could finish my workup, Harry left the hospital. Now we can't find him, and I have no idea what was wrong with him. Would you know his history?"

"I just take care of nursing home inpatients. You might check with the doctors in the outpatient clinic downstairs."

"Harry's a patient of Dr. Wallenberg's. But Wallenberg's out of town. And the clinic won't release records to me without his approval."

Robbie Brace shrugged. "That's the standing policy here."

"Do you know Harry? Is there some medical problem I should be aware of?"

"I only know Mr. Slotkin in passing. I see him when he comes to visit Agnes."

"So you have spoken to Harry."

"Yeah, we'd say hello, that's all. I've only been working here a month, and I'm still trying to put names to faces."

"Do you have the authority to release Harry's records to me?"

He shook his head. "Only Dr. Wallenberg can, and he requires a patient's written consent before he'll release any information."

"But this could affect his patient's medical care."

He frowned. "Didn't you say Harry walked out of your ER?"

"Well yes, he did—"

"So he's not really your patient anymore, is he?"

Toby paused, unable to contradict that statement. Harry *had* walked out of her ER. He *had* left her care. She had no pressing reason to demand his records.

She looked down at the woman in the bed. "I guess Mrs. Slotkin can't tell me anything, either."

"I'm afraid Agnes doesn't talk at all."

"Was it a stroke?"

"Subarachnoid hemorrhage. According to her chart, she's been here a year. Seems to remain in a vegetative state. But every so often, she'll sort of look at me. Don't you, Agnes?" he said. "Don't you look at me, honey?"

The woman in the bed didn't stir, didn't even flutter an eyelash.

He moved to the bedside and began to examine his patient, his black hands a startling contrast against the woman's pallor. With his stethoscope he listened to her heart and lungs, and checked her abdomen for bowel sounds. He shone a light in her pupils. He extended her limbs, checking for resistance to range of motion. Finally he rolled her toward him and examined the skin on her back and buttocks. No bedsores. Gently he repositioned her against the pillows and folded the sheet over her chest.

"Lookin' good, Agnes," he murmured, patting her on the shoulder. "You have yourself a nice day."

Toby followed him out of the room, feeling like a midget tagging at a giant's heels. "She's in good condition for someone who's been vegetative for a year."

He opened the chart and scribbled his progress note. "Well, of course. We give genuine Rolls-Royce care."

"At Rolls-Royce prices?"

Brace glanced up from the chart, the first hint of a grin on his lips. "Let's just say, we don't have any Medicaid patients."

"They're all private pay?"

"They can afford it. We've got some pretty wealthy residents."

"Is this place exclusively for retirees?"

"No, we have a few active professionals who've bought into Brant Hill just to guarantee that their future needs are taken care of. We provide housing, meals, medical care.

Long-term care, if it becomes necessary. You probably saw we're already expanding the nursing home."

"I also noticed a very nice golf course."

"Along with tennis courts, a movie theater, and an indoor pool." He closed the chart and grinned at her. "Sorta makes you want to retire early, doesn't it?"

"I don't think I could afford to retire here."

"I'll let you in on a secret: neither one of us could." He glanced at his watch. "It was nice meeting you, Dr. Harper. If you'll excuse me, I've got a lot of patients to see."

"Is there any way I could find out more about Harry?"

"Dr. Wallenberg's back on Monday. You can talk to him then."

"I'd like to know *now* what I was dealing with. It's really bothering me. Couldn't you review the outpatient record? Call me if you find anything relevant?" She scribbled her home phone number on a business card and handed it to him.

Reluctantly, he took the card. "I'll see what I can do," was all he said. Then he turned and walked into a patient's room, leaving Toby standing alone in the hallway.

She turned from the closed door and sighed. She'd done her best to track down the information, but Brant Hill wasn't cooperating. Now hunger and fatigue were dragging her down, and she could feel her body issuing demands. *Food. Sleep. Now.* In slow motion, legs sluggish, she began to walk toward the elevators. Halfway there, she halted.

Someone was screaming.

It came from one of the patient rooms at the end of the hall—not a cry of pain, but of fear.

As Toby ran toward the screams, she heard other voices spilling into the hallway behind her, heard footsteps following at a run. Toby reached the room ahead of everyone else and shoved open the door.

At first all she saw was the elderly man crouching on hands and knees on the bed. He was naked below the waist, and his wrinkled buttocks were bobbing up and down in a doglike mating dance.

Then Toby saw the trapped woman underneath him, her frail body almost hidden among the tangle of blankets and sheets.

"Get him off me! Please get him off me!" the woman cried.

Toby grabbed the man's arm and tried to drag him away. He responded with a shove so powerful it sent Toby sprawling backward to the floor. A nurse ran into the room.

"Mr. Hackett, stop it! *Stop it!*" The nurse tried to pull the man away, but she too was flung aside.

Toby scrambled back to her feet. "You grab one arm, I'll get the other!" she said, circling around to the far side of the bed. Together, she and the nurse took hold of the man's arms. Even as he was dragged off the woman, he kept thrusting like a grotesque sexual robot without an off switch. The woman on the bed curled up into a fetal position and began to cry as she hugged herself among the blankets.

Suddenly the man twisted, elbowing Toby under the chin. The jab slammed her jaw shut, ramming a bolt of pain straight through her skull, She saw a burst of white and almost released him, but sheer rage kept her holding on. He lashed out at her again. They were grappling like animals now, and she could smell his sweat, could feel every muscle in his body straining against her. The nurse lost her footing and stumbled, releasing her grip. The old man reached behind Toby's head and grabbed a fistful of her hair. He was thrusting at *her* now, his erect penis stabbing at her hip. Disgust and fury boiled up in her throat. She tensed her thigh, preparing to knee him in the groin.

Then her target was gone. The man was lifted away by a pair of huge black hands. Robbie Brace hauled the man halfway across the room and barked to the nurse: "Get me some Haldol! Five milligrams IM STAT!"

The nurse ran from the room. She came back a moment later, syringe in hand.

"C'mon, I can't hold him forever," said Brace.

"Let me get at his butt—"

"Do it, do it!"

"But he keeps squirming away—"

"Man, this guy's strong. What've you been feeding him?"

"He's a protocol patient—plus he's got Alzheimer's—I can't get at him!"

Brace shifted his grip, turning the man's rear end toward the nurse. She pinched a fold of bare buttock and stabbed it with the needle. The old man shrieked. Bucking, he yanked away from Brace. In a blur of motion, he grabbed a water glass from the nightstand and swung it at the doctor's face.

The glass shattered against Brace's temple.

Toby lunged, catching the old man's wrist before he could swing again. Viciously she twisted his hand and the broken shard tumbled from his grasp.

Brace wrapped giant arms around the man's shoulders and yelled, "Give him the rest of the Haldol!"

Again the nurse jabbed the needle into the man's buttock and squeezed the plunger. "It's all in! God, I hope this works better than the Mellaril."

"This guy's on Mellaril?"

"Around the clock. I *told* Dr. Wallenberg it wasn't holding him. These Alzheimer's patients need to be watched every second or they—" The nurse took in a sharp breath. "Dr. Brace, you're bleeding!"

Toby glanced up and was alarmed to see blood trickling down Brace's cheek and splattering his white coat. The broken glass had sliced open the skin on his temple.

"We have to stop that bleeding," said Toby. "It's obvious you'll need stitches."

"First let me get this guy into a nice tight Posey restraint. Come on, sir. Let's get you back to your room."

The old man let fly a glob of spit. "Nigger! Let me go!"

"Oh man," said Brace. "You're trying to get on my good side, aren't you?"

"Don't like niggers."

"Yeah, you and everyone else," said Brace, sounding more tired than angry. He half-dragged, half-marched the old man out of the room and into the hall. "Buddy, it looks like you've earned yourself a date with a straitjacket."

"Ouch. Don't make me look like Frankenstein's monster, okay?"

Gently Toby emptied the syringe of Xylocaine and withdrew the needle. She had injected local anesthetic along both edges of Robbie's laceration and now she gave the skin a gentle prick. "Feel that?"

"Nope. It's numb."

"Are you sure you wouldn't rather have a plastic surgeon stitch you up?"

"You're an ER doc. Don't you do this all the time?"

"Yes, but if you're concerned about the cosmetic result—"

"Why would I be? I'm already so damn ugly. A scar will be an improvement."

"Well, it'll give your face character," she said and reached for the needle forceps and suture. She'd found all the supplies she needed in the well-stocked treatment room. Like everything else at Brant Hill, the equipment was spanking new and top of the line. The table where Robbie Brace lay could be adjusted to a wide variety of positions, which made it convenient for treating anything from scalp wounds to hemorrhoids. The overhead lights were bright enough for surgery. And in the corner, ready for emergencies, was the cardiac crash cart, a state-of-the-art model, of course.

She swabbed the wound again with Betadine and poked the curved suture needle through the edges of the laceration. Robbie Brace lay on his side, perfectly still. Most patients would have closed their eyes, but he kept his wide open and staring at the opposite wall. Though his size was intimidating, his eyes seemed to neutralize any threat. They were a soft brown, the lashes thick as a child's.

She took another stitch and drew the suture through his skin. "The old guy cut pretty deep," she said. "You're lucky he missed your eye."

"I think he was trying for my throat."

"And he's on round-the-clock sedation?" She shook her head. "You'd better double the dose and keep him locked up."

"He usually is. We keep the Alzheimer's patients in a separate ward, where we can control their movements. I guess Mr. Hackett slipped out. And you know, sometimes those old guys can't handle the libido. The self-control's gone, but the body's still willing."

Toby snipped off the needle and tied the last stitch. The wound was closed now, and she began wiping the site with alcohol. "What protocol is he on?" she asked.

"Hm?"

"The nurse said Mr. Hackett was on some kind of protocol."

"Oh. It's something Wallenberg's testing. Hormone injections in elderly men."

"For what purpose?"

"The fountain of youth, what else? We've got a wealthy clientele, and most of them want to live forever. They're all eager to volunteer for the latest treatment fad." He sat up on the side of the table and gave his head a shake, as though to dispel a sudden rush of dizziness. Toby thought with sudden panic: The bigger they are, the harder they fall. And the harder they are to pick up off the floor.

"Lie back down," she said. "You got up too fast."

"I'm fine. I've gotta get back to work."

"No, you sit there, okay? Or you'll fall and I'll just have to stitch up the other side of your face."

"Another scar," he grunted. "More character."

54

"You're already a character, Dr. Brace."

He smiled, but his gaze looked a little unfocused. Warily she watched him for a moment, ready to catch him if he passed out, but he managed to stay upright.

"So tell me more about the protocol," she said. "Which hormones is Wallenberg injecting?"

"It's a cocktail. Growth hormone. Testosterone. DHEA. A few others. There's plenty of research to back it all up."

"I know growth hormone increases muscle mass in the elderly. But I haven't seen many studies using it in combination."

"It makes sense though, doesn't it? As you get older, your pituitary starts to fade out. Doesn't produce all those juicy young hormones. The theory is, that's the reason we age. Our hormones conk out."

"So Wallenberg replaces them."

"It seems to be having *some* effect. Look at Mr. Hackett. Plenty of get up and go."

"Too much. Why're you giving hormones to an Alzheimer's patient? He can't give consent."

"He probably gave consent years ago, while he was still competent."

"The study's been going on that long?"

"Wallenberg's research dates back to '92. Check out the *Index Medicus*. You'll see his name pop up on a dozen published papers. Everyone working in geriatrics knows Wallenberg's name." Gingerly he lowered himself from the table. After a moment, he nodded. "Steady as a rock. So when do these stitches come out?"

"Five days."

"And when do I get the bill?"

She smiled. "No bill. Just do me a favor."

"Uh, oh."

"Look up Harry Slotkin's medical record. Call me if

there's anything I should know. If there's anything I might have missed."

"You think you might have missed something?"

"I don't know. But I hate screwing up, I really do. Harry may be lucid enough to find his way back to Brant Hill. Maybe even to his wife's room. Keep an eye out for him."

"I'll tell the nurses."

"He shouldn't be hard to miss." She reached for her purse. "He's not wearing a stitch of clothes."

Toby pulled into her driveway, parked next to Bryan's Honda, and turned off the engine. She didn't climb out of her car but simply sat there for a moment, listening to the *tick-tick* of the engine cooling off, enjoying these quiet moments, undisturbed by the demands of others. So many, many demands. She took a deep breath and leaned back against the neck rest. It was nine-thirty, a quiet hour in this neighborhood of suburban professionals. Couples had left for work, the kids were packed off to school or day care, and houses stood empty, awaiting the arrival of domestics who would vacuum and scrub and then vanish, leaving behind their telltale scent of lemon wax. It was a safe neighborhood of well-tended homes, not the most elegant section of Newton, but it satisfied Toby's need for some sort of order in her life. After the unpredictability of a shift in the ER, a manicured lawn had its attractions.

Down the street, a leaf blower suddenly roared to life. Her moment of silence had ended. The yard service trucks had begun their daily invasion of the neighborhood.

Reluctantly she stepped out of the Mercedes and climbed the porch steps.

Bryan, her mother's hired companion, was already waiting at the front door, arms crossed, eyes narrowed in reproval. He was jockey size, a trim young man in miniature, but he presented an imposing barrier.

"Your mama's been bouncing off the walls this morning," he said. "You shouldn't do this to her."

"Didn't you tell her I'd be late getting home?"

"Doesn't do any good. You know she can't understand. She expects you home early, and when you don't get here, she does her thing at the windows. You know, back and forth, back and forth, watching for your car."

"I'm sorry, Bryan. It couldn't be helped." Toby walked past him, into the house and set her purse down on the hall table. She took her time hanging up her jacket, thinking: *Don't get annoyed. Don't lose your temper. You need him. Mom needs him.*

"It doesn't matter to me if you're two hours late," he said. "I get paid. I get paid a lot, thank you very much. But your mama, poor thing, she doesn't get it."

"We had some problems at work."

"She wouldn't touch her breakfast. So now she's got a plate of cold eggs."

Toby shut the closet door, hard. *"I will make her another breakfast."*

There was a silence.

She stood with her back to him, her hand still pressed to the closet, thinking: I didn't mean to sound so angry. But I'm tired. I'm so very tired.

"Well," said Bryan, and in that one word he communicated everything. Hurt. Withdrawal.

She turned to face him. They had known each other for two years now, yet they had never gone beyond the relationship of employer-employee, had never crossed that barrier into real friendship. She'd never visited his house, had never met Noel, the man with whom he lived. Yet she realized, at that moment, that she had come to depend on Bryan more than she depended on anyone else. *He* was the one who kept her life sane, and she couldn't afford to lose him.

She said, "I'm sorry. I just can't handle another crisis right now. I've had a really shitty night."

"What happened?"

"We lost two patients. In one hour. And I'm feeling pretty awful about it. I didn't mean to take it out on you."

He gave a slight nod, a grudging acceptance of her apology.

"And how was your night?" she asked.

"She slept all the way through. I just took her out to the garden. That always seems to quiet her down."

"I hope she hasn't picked all the lettuce."

"I hate to break this to you, but your lettuce went to seed a month ago."

All right, so I'm a failure as a gardener too, thought Toby as she headed through the kitchen to the back door. Every year, with high hopes, she started a vegetable patch. She would plant rows of lettuce and zucchini and green beans, would successfully nurture them along to seedling stage. Then, inevitably, her life would get too busy and she'd neglect the garden. The lettuce would bolt, and the beans would hang yellow and woody from the vines. In disgust she'd yank it all out and promise herself a better garden next year, knowing that the next year would produce only another crop of zucchinis as inedible as baseball bats.

She stepped outside into the yard. At first she didn't see her mother. The summer flower garden had grown into a weedy jungle of chin-high flowers and vines. There had always been a pleasant randomness to this garden, as though the beds had been dug with no plan in mind, but rather had been expanded by the original gardener's whim, season by season. When Toby had bought the house eight years ago, she'd planned to tear out the more unruly plants, to ruthlessly enforce some form of horticultural discipline. It was Ellen who'd talked her out of it, Ellen who'd explained that, in the garden, disorder was to be cherished.

Now Toby stood by the back door, surveying a yard so

overgrown she could not even see the brick pathway. Something rustled among the flower stalks, and a straw hat bobbed into view. It was Ellen, crawling on her knees in the dirt.

"Mom, I'm home."

The straw hat tipped up, revealing Ellen Harper's round, sunburned face. She saw her daughter and waved, something dangling from her hand. As Toby crossed the yard and stepped through the tangle of vines, her mother rose to her feet, and Toby saw that she was clutching a fistful of dandelions. It was one of the ironies of Ellen's illness that although she had forgotten so many things—how to cook, how to bathe herself—she had not forgotten, would probably never forget, how to distinguish a weed from a flower.

"Bryan says you haven't eaten yet," said Toby.

"No, I think I did. Didn't I?"

"Well, I'm going to make some breakfast. Why don't you come inside and eat with me?"

"But I have so much work to do." Sighing, Ellen looked around at the flower beds. "I never seem to get it all done. You see these things here? These bad things?" She waved the limp plants she was holding.

"Those are dandelions."

"Yes. Well, these things are taking over. If I don't pull them up, they'll get into those purple things over there. What do you call them . . ."

"The purple flowers? I really don't know, Mom."

"Anyway, there's only so much room, then things have to be cleaned out. It's a fight for more room. I have so much work, and I never have enough time." She gazed around the garden, her cheeks ruddy from the sun. *So much to do, never enough time.* That was Ellen's mantra, a recurrent loop of words that remained intact while the rest of her memory disintegrated. Why had that particular phrase persisted in

Ellen's mind? Had her life as a widowed mother of two girls been so stamped by the pressures of time, of tasks undone?

Ellen dropped back to her knees and began rooting around in the dirt again. For what, Toby didn't know; perhaps more of those hated dandelions. Toby looked up and saw that the sky was cloudless, the day pleasantly warm. Ellen would be fine out here, unsupervised. The gate was locked, and she seemed content. This was their routine during the summertime. Toby would make her mother a sandwich and leave it on the kitchen countertop, and then she would go to bed. At four in the afternoon, she'd wake up, and she and Ellen would eat supper together.

She heard the rattle of Bryan's car driving away. At six-thirty he would be back to stay with Ellen for the night. And Toby would leave, once again, for her usual shift at the hospital.

So much to do, never enough time. It was becoming Toby's mantra as well. Like mother, like daughter, never enough time.

She took a deep breath and slowly released it. The adrenaline from this morning's crisis had worn off, and now she felt the fatigue weighing down on her like so many stones on her shoulders. She knew she should go straight up to bed, but she couldn't seem to move. Instead she stood watching her mother, thinking how young Ellen looked, not elderly at all, but more like a round-faced girl in a floppy hat. A girl happily making mud pies in the garden.

I'm the mother now, thought Toby. And like any mother, she was suddenly aware of how quickly time passed, moments passed.

She knelt down beside her mother in the dirt.

Ellen looked sideways at her, a trace of bewilderment in her light blue eyes. "Do you need something, dear?" she asked.

"No, Mom. I just thought I'd help you pull a few weeds."

"Oh." Ellen smiled and lifted a dirt-stained hand to stroke back a tendril of hair off Toby's cheek. "Are you certain you know which ones to pull?"

"Why don't you show me?"

"Here." Gently, Ellen guided Toby's hand to a clump of green. "You can start with these."

And, side by side, mother and daughter knelt in the dirt and began to pull dandelions.

5

Angus Parmenter turned up the speed on the treadmill and felt the moving belt give a little jerk under his feet. He accelerated his stride to a brisk six miles per hour. His pulse sped up as well; he could see it on the digital readout, mounted on the treadmill handgrips. 112. 116. 120. Had to get that heart rate up, the blood flowing. *Push yourself! Oxygen in, oxygen out. Get those muscles pumping.*

On the movie screen mounted in front of him, the "boredom-buster" video played scenes from the cobbled streets of a Greek village. But his gaze remained focused on the digital readout. He watched his pulse climb to 130. At last, target heart rate. He would try to keep it there for the next twenty minutes, give himself a good aerobic workout. Then he would cool down, letting his pulse gradually drop to a hundred, then eighty, then down to his usual resting pulse of sixty-eight. After that, it was time for a session on the

Nautilus, an upper-body workout, and afterward he'd hit the showers. By then it would be time for lunch, a low-fat, high-protein, high-roughage meal served in the country club dining room. With the meal would come a few of his daily pills: vitamin E, vitamin C, zinc, selenium. An arsenal of magic remedies to keep the years at bay.

It all seemed to be working. At eighty-two years old, Angus Parmenter had never felt better in his life. And he was enjoying the fruits of his labors. He had worked hard for his fortune, harder than any of these whining kids would ever work in *their* lives. He had money, and he intended to live long enough to spend it, every last goddamn penny. Let the next generation earn their own fortunes. This was *his* time to play.

After lunch, there'd be a round of golf with Phil Dorr and Jim Bigelow, his friendly rivals. Then he had the option of riding the Brant Hill van into the city. Tonight they were planning a trip to the Wang Center for a performance of *Cats*. He'd probably skip that one. All those ladies might go wild over singing kitty cats, but not him; he'd seen the show on Broadway, and once was more than enough.

He heard the stationary bicycle begin to whir beside him and he glanced sideways. Jim Bigelow was frantically pedaling away.

Angus nodded. "Hey, Jim."

"Hello, Angus."

For a moment they sweated side by side, too focused on their exercise to speak. On the screen ahead, the video changed from a Greek village to a muddy road in a rain forest. Angus's heart rate remained steady at 130 beats per minute.

"Have you heard anything yet?" asked Bigelow over the whir of his bicycle. "About Harry?"

"Nope."

"I saw them . . . the police . . . they're dragging the

63

pond." Bigelow was panting, having trouble talking and pedaling at the same time. His own fault, thought Angus. Bigelow liked his desserts, and he came to the gym only once a week. He hated exercise, hated healthy foods. At seventy-six, Bigelow looked his age.

"I heard . . . at breakfast . . . they haven't found him yet. . . ." Bigelow leaned forward, his face a bright pink from exertion.

"That's the last I heard, too," said Angus.

"Funny. Not like Harry."

"No, it's not."

"Wasn't acting right . . . over the weekend. Did you notice?"

"What do you mean?"

"Had his shirt inside out. Socks didn't match. Not like Harry at all."

Angus kept his gaze straight ahead on the video screen. Jungle saplings parted before him. A boa constrictor slithered on a tree branch overhead.

"And did you notice . . . his hands?" panted Bigelow.

"What about them?"

"They were shaking. Last week."

Angus said nothing. He gripped the treadmill bar and concentrated on his stride. *Walk, walk. Pump those calves, keep them firm and young.*

"Funniest damn thing," said Bigelow. "This business about Harry. You don't suppose . . ."

"I don't suppose anything, Jim. Let's just hope he turns up."

"Yeah." Bigelow stopped pedaling. He sat catching his breath and staring at the video screen, where a tropical rainstorm was now pounding the jungle ferns. "Trouble is," he said quietly, "I don't expect he will turn up all right. It's been two days."

Angus abruptly switched off the treadmill. Forget the cooldown. He'd move straight to the upper body workout.

He slung his towel over his shoulder and crossed the room to the Nautilus. To his annoyance, Bigelow got off the bike and followed him.

Ignoring Bigelow, Angus sat down on the bench and started with his latissimus dorsi workout.

"Angus," said Bigelow, "Doesn't it worry you?"

"There's nothing we can do about it, Jim. The police are looking."

"No, I mean doesn't it remind you of . . ." Bigelow's voice dropped to a murmur. "What happened to Stan Mackie?"

Angus went still, his hands gripping the Nautilus pulleys. "That happened months ago."

"Yes, but it was the same thing. Remember how he showed up with his fly unzipped? And then he forgot Phil's name. You don't forget the name of your best friend."

"Phil's quite forgettable."

"I can't believe you're so flippant about this. First we lose Stan. And now Harry. What if—" Bigelow paused and glanced around the gym, as though afraid someone else might be listening. "What if something's going wrong? What if we're all getting sick?"

"Stan's death was a suicide."

"That's what they *say*. But people don't go jumping out of windows for no reason."

"Did you know Stan well enough to say he didn't have a reason?"

Bigelow looked down. "No . . ."

"Well, then." Angus resumed working at the pulleys. *Pull, release. Pull, release. Keep those muscles young . . .*

Bigelow sighed. "I can't help wondering. I never felt right about it. Maybe this is some sort of . . . I don't know. Divine consequence. Maybe it's what we deserve."

"Don't be so Catholic, Jim! You're always waiting for a lightning bolt to hit you. It's been a year and a half, and I've never felt better in my life." He stretched out his leg. "Look at my quadriceps! See the muscle definition? It wasn't there two years ago."

"My quadriceps hasn't improved any," Bigelow noted glumly.

"That's because you're not working at it. And you worry too damn much."

"Yes, I suppose I do." Bigelow sighed and looped his towel around his neck. It made him look like some old tortoise poking its head out of its shell. "Are we still on for this afternoon?"

"Phil hasn't said otherwise."

"Right. Then see you at the first tee."

Angus watched his friend lumber out of the gym. Bigelow was looking old, and no wonder; he'd spent only ten minutes on the bike, hardly an aerobic workout. Some people just couldn't commit to their own health. Instead they wasted their energy worrying about things they could do nothing about.

His latissimus dorsi muscles were burning with that pleasant ache of a thorough workout. He released the pulleys and rested for a moment. Looking around the gym, he saw that all the other machines were in use, mostly by women, the granny set in their sweat suits and tennis shoes. A few of the ladies glanced his way, flashing him the come-hither look he found so ridiculous in women their age. They were far too old for his taste. A woman of, say, fifty might be more to his liking. But only if she was slim and fit enough to keep up with him, in every way.

It was time to work on the pectorals.

He reached up for the appropriate arm grips and was about to make the first squeeze when he noticed that something was wrong with the machine. The right-hand grip seemed to be vibrating.

He released his hold and stared at the grip. It was perfectly still, no vibrations at all. Then he looked down, and felt a sudden chill. *What is going on?*

His right hand was shaking.

Molly Picker raised her head from the toilet and pulled the flush lever. There was nothing left in her stomach; she'd thrown it all up. Pepsi, Fritos, and Lucky Charms. Dizzy, she sat down on the floor, leaned her back against the bathroom wall, and listened to the water whoosh down the pipes. Three weeks, she thought. I been sick for three weeks now.

She dragged herself to her feet and stumbled back to bed. Curling up on the lumpy mattress, she fell quickly and deeply asleep.

At noon, she woke up when Romy walked into her room. He didn't bother to knock first; he sat down on the bed and gave her a shake. "Hey, Molly Wolly. Still got the ol' stomach bug?"

Groaning, she looked at him. Romy reminded her of a reptile, his hair all slicked back and shiny, his eyes so dark you couldn't see the pupils. Lizard man. But the hand stroking her hair was gentle—an aspect of Romy she hadn't seen in such a very long time. He gave her a smile. "Not so good today, huh?"

"I threw up again. I can't stop throwing up."

"Yeah, well, I finally got you something for that." He placed a bottle of pills on the nightstand. It had a label with handwritten instructions: *Take one pill every eight hours for nausea.* Romy went into the bathroom, filled a glass with water, and returned to Molly's bed. He opened the bottle, shook a pill out, and helped her sit up. "Down the hatch," he said.

She frowned at the pill. "What is this?"

"Medicine."

"Where'd you get it?"

"It's okay. It's what the doctor ordered."

"What doctor?"

"Here I'm trying to be nice, trying to make you feel better, and you talk back. I don't really give a shit if you take the pill or not."

She turned away and felt his hand pressing against her back, tightening into a fist. Then, unexpectedly, he relaxed and began to rub her back in warm, coaxing strokes.

"C'mon, Moll. You know I look out for you. Always have, always will."

She gave a bitter laugh. "Like that makes me special."

"You are. You're my special babe. My own best girl." He slid his hand under her shirt and stroked across her skin. "You been so prickly lately. Didn't feel like showing you no favors. But you know I'm always watching out for you, Molly lollipop." He tasted her earlobe and murmured: "Yum."

"So what's in the pill?"

"I told you. It's so you'll stop puking and start eating again. A growing girl's gotta eat." His lips slid down her neck, to graze her shoulder. "If you don't eat, pretty soon I'll have to bring you to some hospital. You want to wind up in a hospital? Bunch of strange doctors?"

"I don't want to see no doctors." She regarded the pill in her hand and felt a sudden sense of wonder, not about the pill, but about Romy. He hadn't been this sweet to her in months, hadn't paid her much attention at all. Not like before, when she *had* been his special girl. When they'd spent nights together in bed, watching MTV, eating ice cream, drinking beer. When he was the only one who'd touch her. Who was *allowed* to touch her. Before everything between them had changed.

He was smiling, not his usual small, mean smile, but one that actually touched his eyes.

She swallowed the pill and washed it down with a sip of water.

"That's my girl." He eased her back down to the pillow and tucked her in. "You go to sleep now."

"Stay with me, Romy."

"I got things to do, babe." He stood up. "Business."

"I have to tell you something. I think I know why I been sick—"

"We'll talk about it later, okay?" He gave her a pat on the head and left the room.

Molly stared at the ceiling. *Three weeks is too long for the stomach flu,* she thought. She placed her hands on her belly and imagined she could already feel the swelling there. *When did I mess up? Which guy pumped in a live one?* She was always careful, always carried her own rubbers, had learned to apply them with the silky strokes of foreplay. She wasn't stupid; she knew a girl could get sick out there.

Now she really *was* sick, and she couldn't remember when she'd made the mistake.

Romy would blame *her.*

Rising from the bed, she felt light-headed. It was the hunger. These days she was always hungry, even when she felt nauseated. As she dressed, she munched on some more Fritos. The salt tasted good. She could have devoured handfuls, but there were only a few chips left. She tore the bag open and licked the crumbs, then saw herself in the mirror, her lips crusted with salt, and she was so disgusted by the image she tossed the bag into the rubbish and left her room.

It was only one-fifteen, and there was no action coming down yet. She saw Sophie up the street, leaning in a doorway as she chugged from a Pepsi can. Sophie was all butt and no brains. Determined to ignore her, Molly walked right past, her eyes focused straight ahead.

"If it isn't Miss Titless," said Sophie.

"Bigger the tits, smaller the brain."

"Then girl, you must have one *hell* of a big brain."

Molly kept walking, quickening her pace to escape

Sophie's whinnying laughter. She didn't stop walking until she'd reached the phone booth two blocks away. She searched the tattered copy of the Yellow Pages, then slipped a quarter into the slot and dialed.

A voice answered: "Abortion Counseling."

"I need to talk to someone," said Molly. "I'm pregnant."

A black car glided to a stop at the curb. Romy got into the backseat and shut the door.

The driver didn't turn to look at him; he never did. Most of the time Romy found himself staring at the back of the man's head, a narrow head with white-blond hair. You didn't see that color of hair very often, not on a guy. Romy wondered if the bitches went for it. But the way he figured it, bitches didn't really care if you had any hair on your head, as long as you had money in your wallet.

Romy's wallet was feeling pretty thin these days.

He looked around at the car, admiring it as he always did, yet resentful of the fact the guy in the driver's seat was the man on top in more ways than one. Didn't need to know the man's name or what he did; you could *smell* his superiority like you could smell the fact these seats were leather. To a guy like him, Romulus Bell was just a scrap of litter that had blown into the car and would soon be ejected. Not worth a backward glance.

Romy looked at the man's exposed neck and thought how easy it'd be to turn the tables. If he wanted to. That made him feel better.

"You have something to tell me?" the driver said.

"Yeah. I got another one knocked up."

"Are you certain?"

"Hey, I know my girls, inside and out. I know it before they do. I been right every other time, haven't I?"

"So you have."

"What about the money? I'm supposed to get my money."

"There's a problem."

"What problem?"

The driver reached up and adjusted the rearview mirror. "Annie Parini didn't show up for her appointment this morning."

Romy stiffened, his hand gripping the seat in front of him. "What?"

"I couldn't find her. She wasn't waiting on the Common as we agreed."

"She was there. I walked her there myself."

"Then she must have left before I arrived."

The stupid bitch, he thought. How could you keep a business going when the bitches were always going against him, always screwing things up? Bitches had no brains. And now they were making *him* look bad.

"Where is Annie Parini, Mr. Bell?"

"I'll find her."

"Do it soon. We can't let her go more than another month." The man waved his hand. "You can get out of the car now."

"What about my money?"

"There's no payment today."

"But I told you, I got another one knocked up."

"This time we want delivery first. The last week of October. And don't lose the merchandise. Now get out, Mr. Bell."

"I need—"

"Get out."

Romy climbed out and slammed the door. At once the car drove away, leaving him staring after it in fury.

He began to walk up Tremont Street, his agitation mounting with every step. He knew where Annie Parini hung out; he knew he could find her, and he would.

The words of the driver kept playing in his head. *This time, don't lose the merchandise.*

* * *

71

The phone rang, waking Toby from a sleep so deep she felt as if she was surfacing through layers of mud. She fumbled for the receiver and knocked it off its cradle. It thudded to the floor. As she rolled over in bed to retrieve the phone, she caught sight of the bedside clock. It was twelve noon—for her, the equivalent of the middle of the night. The receiver had tumbled onto the other side of the nightstand. She used the cord to haul it back up.

"Hello?"

"Dr. Harper? It's Robbie Brace."

She lay in a stupor, struggling to remember who this man was and why his voice sounded familiar.

"Brant Hill Nursing Home?" he said. "We met two days ago. You asked me about Harry Slotkin."

"Oh. Yes." She sat up, her mind suddenly swept clear of sleep. "Thanks for calling."

"I'm afraid there's not much to report. I have Mr. Slotkin's clinic chart in front of me and I see a clean bill of health."

"There's nothing at all?'

"Nothing that would explain his illness. Physical exam's unremarkable. Labs look good . . ." Over the receiver, Toby could hear the rustle of pages being turned. "He had a full endocrine panel, totally normal."

"When was this?"

"A month ago. So whatever you saw in the ER must've been fairly acute."

She closed her eyes and felt her stomach knotting up again with tension. "Have you heard anything new?" she asked.

"They dragged the pond this morning. Haven't found him. Which is good, I guess."

Yes. It means he could still be alive.

"Anyway, that's all I have to report."

"Thank you," she said, and hung up. She knew she should try to fall back to sleep. She was scheduled for another shift tonight, and she'd had only four hours of rest. But Robbie Brace's call had left her agitated.

The phone rang again.

She grabbed the receiver and said, "Dr. Brace?"

The voice on the other end sounded startled. "Uh, no. This is Paul." Paul Hawkins was chief of Springer ER. Officially he was her boss; unofficially, he was a sympathetic ear and one of her few close friends on the medical staff.

"Sorry, Paul," she said. "I thought you were someone else calling back. What's up?"

"We have a problem here. We need you to come in this afternoon."

"But I got off just a few hours ago. I'm scheduled for another shift tonight."

"This isn't for a shift. It's for a meeting with Administration. Ellis Corcoran's asked for it."

In the hierarchy of doctors at Springer Hospital, Corcoran, chief of the Med-Surg staff, was at the top of the authority pyramid. Paul Hawkins, and every other department chief, answered to Corcoran.

Toby sat up. "What's this meeting all about?"

"A couple of things."

"Harry Slotkin?"

A pause. "Partly. There are other issues they want to discuss."

"They? Who else is going to be there?"

"Dr. Carey. Administration. They have questions about what happened that night."

"I told you what happened."

"Yes, and I've tried to explain it to them. But Doug Carey's got some goddamn bee in his bonnet. He's complained to Corcoran."

She groaned. "You know what this is really about, Paul? It has nothing to do with Harry Slotkin. It's about the Freitas

73

boy. The one who died a few months ago. Carey's trying to get back at me."

"This is an entirely separate issue."

"No it's not. Carey screwed up and the kid died. I called him on it."

"You didn't just call him on a mistake. You got him *sued* for it."

"The boy's family asked for my opinion. Was I supposed to lie to them? Anyway, he *should* have been sued. Leaving a kid with a splenic rupture on an unmonitored floor? I'm the one who had to code the poor kid."

"All right, so he screwed up. But you could've been more discreet with your opinions."

And therein lay the real problem. Toby had not been discreet.

It had been the sort of code every doctor dreads: a dying child. The parents shrieking in the hallway. During her struggle to revive the boy, Toby had blurted out in frustration: *"Why isn't this boy in the ICU?"*

The parents had heard it. Eventually, the lawyers heard it too.

"Toby, right now we have to focus on the issue at hand. The meeting's scheduled for two o'clock this afternoon. They weren't going to invite you, but I insisted."

"Why wasn't I invited? Is this a secret lynching?"

"Just try to get here, okay?"

She hung up and glanced at the clock. It was already twelve-thirty; she couldn't leave until she found someone to stay with her mother. Immediately she picked up the phone again and called Bryan. She heard it ring four times, and then the answering machine picked up. *Hi, this is Noel! And this is Bryan! We're absolutely dying to hear from you, so leave a message . . .*

She hit the disconnect button and dialed another number—her sister's. *Please be home. For once, Vickie, please be there for me* . . .

"Hello?"

"It's me," said Toby, releasing a sigh of relief.

"Can you hold on a minute? I've got something on the stove . . ."

Toby heard the receiver clunk down, and the rattle of a pot lid. Then Vickie came back on the line.

"Sorry. Steve's partners are coming for dinner tonight and I'm trying out this new dessert—"

"Vickie, I'm up against a wall. I need you to watch Mom for a few hours."

"You mean . . . *now?*" Vickie's laugh was sharp and incredulous.

"I've got an emergency meeting at the hospital. I'll drop her off with you and pick her up again as soon as the meeting's over."

"Toby, I've got company coming tonight. I'm cooking, the house still needs to be cleaned, and the kids're coming home from school."

"Mom's no trouble, really. She'll keep herself busy in the backyard."

"I can't have her wandering in the yard! We just put in new grass—"

"Then set her in front of the TV. I've got to leave now or I'm not going to make it."

"Toby—"

She slammed the receiver down. She didn't have the time or patience to argue; Vickie's house was half an hour's drive away.

She found Ellen outside, happily mucking around in the compost heap.

"Mom," said Toby. "We have to go to Vickie's house."

Ellen straightened, and Toby was dismayed to see her

mother's hands were filthy, her dress soiled. There was no time to get her bathed and changed. Vickie would pitch a fit.

"Let's get in the car," urged Toby. "We have to hurry."

"We shouldn't bother Vickie, you know."

"You haven't seen her in weeks."

"She's busy. Vickie is a very busy girl. I don't want to bother her."

"Mom, we have to leave now."

"You go. I'll just stay home."

"It's only for a few hours. Then we'll come right back."

"No, I think I'll just tidy up here in the garden." Ellen squatted down and thrust her trowel deep into the black mound of compost.

"Mom, we have to *go!*" In frustration, Toby grabbed her mother's arm, and hauled her back to her feet so abruptly Ellen gave a gasp of shock.

"You're hurting me!" Ellen wailed.

Instantly Toby released her. Ellen took a step backward, rubbing her arm as she stared in bewilderment at her daughter.

It was Ellen's silence, and the glimmer of tears in her eyes, that cut straight to Toby's heart.

"Mom." Toby shook her head, sick with shame. "I'm sorry. I'm really sorry. I just need you to cooperate with me right now. Please."

Ellen looked down at her hat, which had fallen and now lay on the grass, the straw brim trembling in the wind. Slowly she bent down to retrieve it, then straightened, hugging the hat to her chest. In a gesture of sorrow, she lowered her head and nodded. Then she walked to the garden gate and stood waiting for Toby to open it.

On the drive to Vickie's, Toby tried to make up with Ellen. With forced cheerfulness she talked about what they would do this weekend. They'd put up another rose trellis against the house and plant a bush of New Dawn, or perhaps Blaze. Ellen did love red roses. They would spread compost and plan a bulb garden. They would eat fresh tomato sandwiches and drink lemonade. There was so much to look forward to!

Ellen stared at the hat in her lap and said nothing.

They pulled into Vickie's driveway, and Toby steeled herself for the ordeal to come. Vickie, of course, would make a noisy deal about just how big an imposition this was. Vickie and all her responsibilities! A faculty position in the biology department at Bentley College. A snooty executive husband whose favorite word was *me*. A son and daughter, both in sullen adolescence. Lucky Toby, single and childless! Of course she was the obvious one to take care of Mom.

What else would I do with my life?

Toby helped Ellen out of the car and up the front steps to the house. The door swung open and Vickie appeared, her face flushed with annoyance.

"Toby, this is the *worst* possible time."

"For both of us, believe me. I'll try to pick her up as soon as I can." Toby urged her mother forward. "Go on, Mom. Have a nice visit."

"I'm cooking," said Vickie. "I can't watch her—"

"She'll be fine. Sit her in front of the TV. She likes the Nickelodeon channel."

Vickie frowned at Ellen's dress. "What happened to her clothes? She's filthy. Mom, is something wrong with your arm? Why're you rubbing it?"

"Hurts." Ellen shook her head sadly. "Toby got mad at me."

Toby felt her face redden. "I had to get her into the car. She wouldn't leave the garden. That's why she's so dirty."

"Well, I can't have her looking like *that*. I have company coming at six!"

"I promise, I'll be back before then." Toby gave Ellen a kiss on the cheek. "See you later, Mom. You listen to Vickie."

Without a backward glance, Ellen walked into the house. *She's punishing me,* thought Toby. *Making me feel guilty for having lost my temper.*

77

"Toby," said Vickie, following her down the front steps to the car. "I need more warning next time. Isn't this what we pay Bryan for?"

"Not available. Your kids'll be home soon. They can watch her."

"They don't want to!"

"Then try *paying* them. Your kids certainly seem to value the almighty buck." Toby slammed the car door shut and started the engine. *Why the hell did I say that?* she thought as she drove away. *I have to cool down. I have to get back in control and get ready for this meeting.* But she'd already blown it with Vickie. Now her sister was pissed at her, and so was Ellen. Maybe the whole goddamn world was pissed at her.

She had the sudden impulse to step on the gas and keep driving, to leave this all behind. Find a new identity, a new town, a new life. The one she had now was a mess, and she didn't know whose fault that was. Certainly not all hers; she was simply trying to do the best she could.

It was 2:10 when she pulled into a parking stall at Springer Hospital. She had no time to collect her thoughts; the meeting was already under way, and she didn't want Doug Carey shooting off his mouth in her absence. If he was going to attack her, she wanted to be there to defend herself. She hurried straight to the administrative wing on the second floor and stepped into the conference room.

Inside, all conversation ceased.

Glancing around the table, she saw friendly faces among the six people sitting there. Paul Hawkins. Maudeen and Val. Toby sat down in the chair next to Val, and across from Paul, who gave her a silent nod of greeting. If she had to stare at someone, it might as well be at a good-looking man. She barely glanced at Dr. Carey, who was at the far end of the table, but his hostile presence was impossible to ignore. A small man—in more ways than one—Carey compensated for his short stature by a ramrod posture and a gaze that was threateningly direct. A mean little Chihuahua. At that moment he was looking straight at Toby.

She ignored Carey and focused instead on Ellis Corcoran, the chief of the Med-Surg staff. She didn't know Corcoran very well; she wondered if anyone at Springer did. It was hard to get past his Yankee reserve. He seldom showed emotion, and he was showing none now. Neither did the hospital administrator, Ira Beckett, who sat with bulging abdomen crammed up against the table. The silence went on a little too long for comfort. Her palms were damp; under the table, she wiped her hands on her slacks.

Ira Beckett spoke. "You were telling us, Ms. Collins?"

Maudeen cleared her throat. "I was trying to explain to you that everything happened at once. We had that code in the trauma room. That took all our attention. We figured Mr. Slotkin was stable enough—"

"So you ignored him?" said Carey.

"We didn't ignore him."

"How long *did* you leave him unattended?" asked Beckett.

Maudeen glanced at Toby with a silent plea of *help me out here.*

"I was the last one to see Mr. Slotkin," Toby said. "That was around five, five-fifteen. It was sometime after six when I realized he was gone."

"So you left him unattended for almost an hour?"

"He was waiting for a CT scan. We'd already called in the X-ray tech. There was nothing else we were doing for him at that point. We still don't know how he managed to leave the room."

"Because you people didn't keep an eye on him," said Carey. "You didn't even have him restrained."

"He *was* restrained," said Val. "Both ankles and wrists!"

"Then he must be some kind of Houdini. Nobody gets out

of four-point restraints. Or did someone forget to tie the straps down?"

Neither nurse spoke; they were both staring at the table.

"Dr. Harper?" said Beckett. "You said you were the last one to see Mr. Slotkin. Were his restraints tied?"

She swallowed. "I don't know."

Paul frowned at her across the table. "You told me they were."

"I *thought* they were. I mean, I assumed I tied them. But it was such a confusing shift. Now I'm—I'm not so sure. If he was tied down, it seems impossible that he could have escaped."

"At least we're finally being honest about this," said Carey.

"I've never *not* been honest!" she shot back. "If I screw up, at least *I* admit it."

Paul cut in, "Toby—"

"Sometimes we're juggling half a dozen crises at once. We don't remember every single detail of what goes wrong during a shift!"

"You see, Paul?" said Carey. "This is what I'm talking about. I run into this defensiveness all the time. And it's *always* the night shift."

"You're the only one who seems to complain," said Paul.

"I can name half a dozen other docs who've had problems. We get called in at all hours of the night to admit patients who don't need to be admitted. It's a judgment problem."

"Which patients are you referring to?" asked Toby.

"I don't have the names in front of me now."

"Then you get the names. If you're going to question my judgment, I want specifics."

Corcoran sighed. "We're getting off the subject."

"No, this *is* the subject," said Carey. "The competence of Paul's ER staff. Do you know what was going on in the ER that night? They were having a goddamn birthday party! I went into the staff room for a cup of coffee and they had streamers hanging all over the place! A cake and a bunch of burned candles. *That's* probably what happened. They were so busy partying in the back room, they didn't bother to—"

"That is a bunch of *crap*," said Toby.

"There *was* a party, wasn't there?" said Carey.

"Earlier in the shift, yes. But it didn't distract us from our jobs. Once that tamponade case came in, we were up to our asses in alligators. She required all our attention."

"And you lost her too," said Carey.

His comment felt like a slap, and heat flooded Toby's cheeks. The worst part of it was, he was right. She *had* lost the patient. Her shift *had* turned into a disaster—and a very public one. New patients had walked into the waiting room to hear an angry monologue by Harry Slotkin's son. Then an ambulance had pulled up with a chest pain, and the police had arrived—two squad cars called in to help search for the missing patient. The first law of physics had taken over as Toby's tightly regulated ER had devolved into a state of chaos.

She leaned forward, her hands pressed to the table, her gaze not on Carey, but on Paul. "We didn't have the backup to deal with a tamponade. That patient belonged in a trauma center. We kept her alive as long as we could. I doubt even the wonderful Dr. Carey could have saved her, either."

"You called me way too late in the game to do anything," said Carey.

"We called you as soon as we realized she had a tamponade."

"And how long did it take you to realize that?"

"Within minutes of her arrival."

"According to the ambulance record, the patient arrived at five-twenty. You didn't call me until five-forty-five."

"No, we called you earlier." She glanced at Maudeen and Val, who both nodded in agreement.

81

"It's not in the code record," said Carey.

"Who had time to take any notes? We were scrambling to save her life!"

Corcoran cut in: "Everybody, *please!* We're not here to get in a fistfight. We need to talk about how to handle this new crisis."

"What new crisis?" said Toby.

Everyone looked at her in surprise.

"I didn't get a chance to tell you," said Paul. "I just heard about it myself. Some newspaper's picked up the story. Something along the lines of 'Forgotten patient vanishes from ER.' A reporter called a little while ago, asking for details."

"What makes this newsworthy?"

"It's like that surgeon cutting off the wrong leg. People want to hear about things that go wrong in hospitals."

"But who told the newspapers?" She looked around the table, and just for an instant, her gaze met Carey's. He looked away.

"Maybe the Slotkin family told them," said Beckett. "Maybe they're laying the groundwork for a lawsuit. We really don't know *how* the newspaper got word of it."

Carey said, with a quiet note of venom, "Screwups do get noticed."

"Yours usually manage to get buried," said Toby.

"*Please,*" said Corcoran. "If the patient's found unharmed, then we'll be okay. But it's going on two days now, and as far as I know, there's been no sighting. We're just going to have to hope they find him alive and well."

"A reporter's already called the ER twice this morning," said Maudeen.

"No one talked to him, I hope?"

"No. In fact the nurses hung up on him."

Paul gave a rueful laugh. "Well, that's one way of handling the press."

Corcoran said, "If they can just find the man, we might squeeze through this without any damages. Unfortunately, these Alzheimer's patients can wander for miles."

"He's not an Alzheimer's," said Toby. "The medical history wasn't consistent with that."

"But you said he was confused."

"I don't know why. I didn't find anything focal when I examined him. All the blood work came back normal. Unfortunately, we never got the CT scan. I wish I could tell you his diagnosis, but I never finished the workup." She paused. "I *did* wonder, though, if he might be having seizures."

"Did you witness one?"

"I noticed his leg jerking. I couldn't tell if it was a voluntary movement or not."

"Oh, God." Paul sank back in his chair. "Let's hope he doesn't wander onto some highway, or near a body of water. He could be in trouble."

Corcoran nodded. "So could we."

After the meeting ended, Paul asked Toby to join him in the hospital cafeteria. It was three o'clock and the food line had closed down an hour ago, so they resorted to the vending machines, which were stocked with crackers and chips and a never-ending supply of coffee as strong as battery acid. The cafeteria was deserted, and they had the choice of any table in the room, but Paul crossed to the corner table, farthest from the doorway. Farthest from any listening ears.

He sat down without looking at her. "This isn't easy for me," he said.

She took one sip of coffee, then set the cup down with careful concentration. He was still focused not on her but on the tabletop. Neutral territory. It was not like Paul to avoid her gaze. Over the years they'd settled into a comfortable, plainspoken friendship. As with all friendships between men

83

and women, there were, of course, the small dishonesties between them. She would never admit how strongly attracted she was to him, because it served no purpose, and she liked his wife, Elizabeth, too well. But in almost every other way, she and Paul could be honest with each other. So it hurt her now, to see him staring down at the table, because it made her wonder when he had stopped being entirely truthful.

"I'm glad you were there," he said. "I wanted you to see what I'm up against."

"You mean Doug Carey?"

"It's not just Carey. Toby, I've been asked to attend the Springer board meeting next Thursday. I know this business is going to come up. Carey has friends on that board. And he's out for blood."

"He has been for months, ever since the Freitas boy died."

"Well, this is the payback he's been waiting for. Now the Slotkin case is out in the open, and the hospital board's primed to hear all of Carey's complaints about you."

"Do you think his complaints are valid?"

"If I did, Toby, you wouldn't be on my staff. I mean that."

"The problem is," she sighed, "I'm afraid I did screw up this time. I don't see how Harry Slotkin could have escaped with his restraints tied down. Which means I must have left him untied. I just can't remember . . ." Her eyes felt gritty from lack of sleep, and the coffee was churning in her stomach. Now I'm losing *my* memory, she thought. Is this the first sign of Alzheimer's disease? Is this the beginning of the end for me as well? "I keep thinking about my mother," she said. "About how I'd feel if *she* was lost somewhere on the streets. How angry I'd be at the people responsible. I got careless and I put a helpless old guy in danger. Harry Slotkin's family has every right to come after me with their lawyers. I'm just waiting for it to happen."

It was Paul's silence that made her look up.

He said, quietly, "I guess now's the time to tell you."

"What?"

"The family's asked for a copy of the ER record. The request came through their attorney's office this morning."

She said nothing. The churning in her stomach had turned to nausea.

"It doesn't mean they're going to sue," said Paul. "For one thing, the family hardly needs the money. And the circumstances may prove too embarrassing to air. A father wandering naked in the park—"

"If Harry's found dead, I'm sure they *will* sue." She dropped her head in her hands. "Oh, God. It's my second lawsuit in three years."

"The last suit was a crock, Toby. You beat it."

"I won't beat this one."

"Slotkin's seventy-two years old—not much of a life span left. That could lessen the monetary damages."

"Seventy-two is young! He could still have years ahead of him."

"But he was obviously sick in the ER. If they find his body, if they can show he already had a terminal illness, it'll work to your advantage in court."

She rubbed her face. "That's the last place I want to end up. In court."

"Let's worry about that if and when it happens. Right now, we've got other political issues brewing. We know the news has already reached the media, and they love nightmare stories about doctors. If the hospital board starts to feel any pressure from the public, they'll be on *my* back to take action. I'll do everything I can to protect you. But Toby, I can be replaced, too." He paused. "Mike Esterhaus has already expressed interest in being ER chief."

"He'd be a disaster."

"He'd be a yes-man. He wouldn't fight them the way I do.

85

Every time they try to cut another RN from our staff, I scream bloody murder. Mike will politely bend right over."

For the first time it occurred to her: *I'm taking Paul down with me.*

"The one thing we have to hope for," he said, "is that they find the patient. That will defuse this crisis. No more media interest, no threat of a lawsuit. He has to be found—alive and well."

"Which gets less and less likely every hour."

They sat in silence, their coffee growing cold, their friendship strained to its weakest point. This is why doctors should never marry each other, she thought. Tonight, Paul will go home to Elizabeth, whose work has nothing to do with medicine. They'll have none of these tensions hanging between them, no shared worries about Doug Carey or lawsuits or hospital boards to ruin their supper. Elizabeth will help him escape this crisis, at least for an evening.

And whose help do I have?

6

No rubber chicken tonight, observed Dr. Robbie Brace
as a waitress set a plate before him. He looked down at
the rack of spring lamb and new potatoes and glazed baby
vegetables. Everything looked tender and so very young.
As his knife sliced through the meat, he thought: The privileged prefer to dine on babies. But he did not feel particularly privileged tonight, despite the fact he sat at a
candlelit table, a flute of champagne beside his plate. He
glanced at his wife, Greta, sitting beside him and saw her
pale forehead etched with a frown. He suspected that frown
had nothing to do with the quality of her meal; her request for a vegetarian plate had been graciously filled, and
the food was artistically presented. As she gazed around
at the two dozen other tables in the banquet room, perhaps she was taking note of what her husband had already
observed: They'd been seated at the table farthest from

87

the dais. Banished to a corner where they'd be scarcely noticed.

Half the chairs at their table were vacant, and the other three chairs were occupied by nursing home administrators and an extremely deaf Brant Hill investor. Theirs was the Siberia of tables. Scanning the room, he saw that all the other physicians were seated in better locations. Dr. Chris Olshank—who'd been hired the same week Robbie was—rated a table far closer to the dais. *Maybe it means nothing. Maybe it's just a screwup in the seating arrangements.* But he could not help noting the essential difference between Chris Olshank and himself.

Olshank was white.

Man, you're just screwing around with your own head.

He took a swallow of champagne, drinking it down in a resentful gulp, the whole time intensely aware that he was the only black male guest at the banquet. There were two black women at another table, but he was the only black man. It was something he never failed to take stock of, something that was always in the forefront of his consciousness whenever he walked into a room full of people. How many were white, how many Asian, how many black? Too many, one way or the other, made him uneasy, as though it violated some privately acceptable racial quota. Even now, as a doctor, he couldn't get away from that painful awareness of his own skin color. The M.D. after his name had changed nothing.

Greta reached for him, her hand small and pale against his blackness. "You're not eating."

"Sure I am." He looked at her plate of vegetables. "How's the rabbit food?"

"Very good, as a matter of fact. Have a taste." She slipped a forkful of garlicky potatoes into his mouth. "Nice, isn't it? And better for your arteries than that poor lamb is."

"Once a carnivore—"

"Yes, always a carnivore. But I keep hoping you'll see the light."

At last he smiled, reflecting on the beauty of his own wife. Greta had more than just eye-of-the-beholder beauty; one saw fire and intelligence in her face. Though she seemed oblivious to her effect on the opposite sex, Brace was painfully aware of how other men looked at her. Aware, too, of how they looked at *him*, a black man married to a redhead. Envy, resentment, puzzlement—he saw it in men's eyes as they glanced between husband and wife, between black and white.

A tap on the microphone drew their attention. Brace looked up and saw that Kenneth Foley, the CEO of Brant Hill, was standing behind the podium.

The lights dimmed and a slide appeared on the projector screen over Foley's head. It was the Brant Hill logo, a curly baroque *B* intertwined with an *H,* and beneath it the words:

WHERE LIVING WELL IS THE BEST REWARD.

"That is a disgusting slogan," whispered Greta. "Why don't they just say, *Where the rich folk live?*"

Brace gave her knee a squeeze of warning. He agreed with her, of course, but one didn't spout off Socialist opinions in the presence of the mink and diamonds set.

At the podium, Foley began his presentation. "Six years ago, Brant Hill was only a concept. Not a unique concept, of course; across the country, as Americans grow older, retirement communities are springing up in every state. What makes Brant Hill unique isn't the concept. It's the *execution*. It's the degree to which we carry out the *dream*."

A new slide flashed onto the screen: a photograph of the Brant Hill common, with the swan pond in the foreground and the rolling hills of the golf course stretching into a soft shroud of mist.

"We know that the *dream* has nothing to do with a comfortable old age followed by a comfortable death. The dream has to do with *life*. With beginnings, not endings. *That* is what we offer our clients. We've made the dream a reality. And look how far we've come! Brant Hill, Newton, is expanding. Brant Hill, La Jolla, is sold out. Last month we started construction on our third development, in Naples, Florida, and already, seventy-five percent of those unbuilt units have been sold. And tonight, on the sixth anniversary of our first groundbreaking, I'm here to announce the most *exciting* news of all." He paused, and on the screen above him, the Brant Hill logo reappeared on a background of royal blue. "At eight A.M. tomorrow," he said, "we will be making our initial public offering of stock. I think you all understand what *that* means."

Money, thought Brace as he heard the murmurs of excitement in the room. A fortune for the initial investors. And for Brant Hill itself, it meant an infusion of cash that would spur construction of new developments in other states. No wonder there was champagne on the table; as of tomorrow morning, half the people in this room were going to be even more wealthy than they already were.

The audience burst out in applause.

Greta did not, which Robbie noted with some discomfort. The old stereotype about stubborn redheads held true for his wife. She was sitting with arms folded, her chin jutting out, the very picture of a pissed-off Socialist.

More slides appeared on-screen, reflecting a changing collage of colors on Greta's face. Photos of La Jolla's Brant Hill, designed as a cluster of Mediterranean-style villas overlooking the Pacific. A photo of the health club in Newton, where a dozen aging women in snazzy warm-up suits danced aerobics. A shot of Newton's fifth green, with two men posing beside their canopied golf cart. Then a photo of residents dining in the country club restaurant, a bottle of champagne chilling in a silver ice bucket.

Where the rich folk live.

Brace shifted in his chair, uncomfortably attuned to what Greta must be thinking of all this. Taking care of rich folk was not what he'd planned for his life's work when he'd been a medical student. But then, he hadn't anticipated the pressures of student loans or a home mortgage or saving for their kid's college fund. He hadn't imagined he would be forced to sell out.

Greta uncrossed her legs, and as her thigh brushed against his, he felt an unexpected dart of anger that she couldn't see his side of this. She was the wife; she could hang on to *her* principles. He was the one who had to keep their family fed and housed. And where was the sin in taking care of the rich? Like everyone else, the rich got sick, they needed doctors, they needed compassion.

They paid their bills.

He crossed his arms, withdrawing both physically and emotionally from Greta, and stared at the projector screen. So this was Ken Foley's real purpose for the dinner—to drum up excitement about the initial public offering, to fire up demand for the new stock. Foley's speech was intended for a far wider audience of investors than was now in this room. Already, Brant Hill must be showing up on radar screens of brokerage firms across the country. Every word he said tonight would be piped straight to the business media.

A new slide appeared, an artist's rendition of the new nursing home wing now under construction. Yesterday the concrete foundation had been poured, and next week excavation started on yet a second addition. They were building as fast as they could, yet the demand would only keep growing.

Foley had described the product; now he explained the market for it. The next slide was a bar graph representing the growth of the elderly population in the United States, the surge of baby boomers progressing into old age like a pig swallowed and digested as it moves through a snake. The me-generation was graduating from skis to walkers. Here's our target population, Foley said, his laser pointer circling the statistical pig in the snake. Our future clients. By the year 2005, boomers will start retiring, and Brant Hill is just the sort of development they'll turn to. We're talking growth—and extraordinary returns on your investment. Boomers will be looking toward an exciting new phase in their lives. They don't want worries about sickness or infirmity. Many of them will have money saved up—a lot of it. They'll be getting old, but they don't want to *feel* old.

And who does? thought Brace. Which one of us doesn't look in the mirror and feel a sense of dismay that the face staring back is too old to be *me*?

Dessert and coffee finally arrived at their wilderness table. Greta, tasting artificial something-or-other in the whipped topping, didn't eat hers. Brace ate both their desserts in a depressing orgy of calories. He had his mouth full of whipped cream when he heard his name spoken over the microphone.

Greta gave him a nudge. "Stand up," she whispered. "They're introducing the new doctors."

Brace shot to his feet, accidentally flicking a glob of cream across the front of his suit. He stood for only a second, fumbling with a napkin as he waved to the audience, then quickly sank back into his chair. The other three new doctors rose to their feet, waving as they were introduced, no one else wearing whipped cream on their clothes, no one else tight-faced with embarrassment. *I graduated second highest in my med school class,* he thought. *I was voted intern of the year. I did it against all odds, and without a penny of help from my family. And I am sitting here feeling like a goddamn imbecile.*

Under the table, Greta touched his knee. "The air's too

rich in here," she whispered. "I think I'm choking on the gold dust."

"Do you want to leave?"

"Do you?"

He looked at the dais, where Foley was still talking about money. Returns on investment, growth of the retiree market. There's gold in them thar old folks.

He threw his napkin on the table. "We're outta here."

Angus Parmenter was not feeling well, not feeling well at all. Since Thursday the trembling in his right hand had come and gone twice. He found that if he concentrated, he could suppress it, but it took great effort, and it left his arm aching. Both times the twitching stopped of its own accord. For the last two days, it had not recurred at all, and he'd managed to convince himself the attacks meant nothing. Too much coffee, perhaps. Or too much time at the Nautilus machine, overexerting those arm muscles. He had stopped using the Nautilus, and the movement had not returned, which was a good sign.

But now something *else* was wrong.

He had noticed it upon awakening from his afternoon nap. It was dark, and he had switched on the lamp and looked around at his bedroom. All the furniture seemed tilted. When had that happened? Had he moved things around today? He couldn't recall. But there was the nightstand, way beyond arm's reach. It was tottering on its edge, ready to fall. He stared at it, trying to understand why it didn't topple over, why the glass of water set on top of it was not sliding to the floor.

He turned and looked at the window. It, too, had shifted position. It was now far in the distance, a receding square at the end of a long tunnel.

He stepped out of bed and immediately swayed. *Was that an earthquake?* The floor seemed to roll like swells on the open sea. He stumbled one way, then the other, and finally caught himself on the dresser. There he paused, clinging to the edge, trying to regain his sense of balance. He felt something dribble onto his foot. He looked down and saw that the carpet was wet, and he smelled the warm, sour odor of urine. Who the hell had peed in his bedroom?

He heard a chiming. The notes seemed to float around the room, like tiny black balloons. Church bells? A clock? No, someone was ringing the doorbell.

He staggered out of the bedroom, holding on to the walls, doorways, anything he could cling to. The hallway seemed to elongate, the door gliding away from his outstretched hand. Suddenly his fingers closed around the knob. With a grunt of triumph, he yanked open the door.

In astonishment he stared at the two midgets standing on his front porch.

"Go away," he said.

The midgets stared at him and made mewing sounds.

Angus started to swing the door shut but couldn't get it to close. A woman had appeared and was holding it open.

"What are you doing, Dad? Why aren't you dressed?"

"Go. Get out of my house."

"Dad!" The woman was forcing her way in now.

"Get out!" said Angus. "Leave me alone!" He turned and staggered up the hall, trying to flee the woman and the two midgets. But they pursued him, the midgets whimpering, the woman yelling: "What's wrong? What's wrong with you?"

He tripped on the carpet. What happened next went by gracefully, like a slow dance underwater. He felt his body flying forward, gliding. Felt his arms stretching out like wings as he soared through liquid air.

He did not even feel the impact.

"Dad! Oh my God."

Those damn midgets were screeching and pawing at his head. Now the woman crouched over him. She turned him over on his back.

"Dad, are you hurt?"

"I can fly," he whispered.

She looked at the midgets. "Get the telephone. Call nine one one. *Go!*"

Angus moved his arm, flapping it like a wing.

"Hold still, Dad. We're getting an ambulance."

I can fly! He was floating. Gliding. *I can fly.*

"I've never seen him like this. He doesn't recognize me, and he doesn't seem to know his own grandchildren. I didn't know what else to do, so I called the ambulance." The woman shot an anxious glance into the exam room, where the nurses were trying to take Angus Parmenter's vital signs. "It's a stroke or something. Isn't it?"

"I'll be able to tell more after I examine him," said Toby.

"But does it sound like a stroke?"

"It's possible." Toby gave the woman's arm a squeeze. "Why don't you sit in the waiting room, Mrs. Lacy? I'll be out to talk to you as soon as I know more."

Edith Lacy nodded. Hugging herself, she went into the waiting area and sank onto the couch between her two daughters. The three of them hugged one another, arms forming a warm and compact universe.

Toby turned and entered the exam room.

Angus Parmenter was strapped down on the gurney in four-point restraints, babbling something about strangers in his house. For an eighty-two-year-old man, his limbs were taut and surprisingly muscular. He was dressed only in his undershirt. That's the way his daughter had found him, naked from the waist down.

Maudeen peeled off the blood pressure cuff and slid it neatly into the wall basket. "Vitals are fine. One thirty over seventy. Pulse is ninety-four and regular."

"Temp?"

"Thirty-eight degrees," said Val.

Toby stood by the man's head and tried to engage his attention. "Mr. Parmenter? Angus? I'm Dr. Harper."

" . . . came right into my house . . . wouldn't leave me alone . . ."

"Angus, did you fall down? Did you hurt yourself?"

" . . . goddamn midgets, came to steal my money. Everyone's after my money."

Maudeen shook her head. "I can't get a word of history out of him."

"The daughter says he's been healthy. No recent illnesses." Toby shone her penlight into the man's eyes. Both pupils constricted. "She spoke to him on the phone only two weeks ago and he sounded fine. Angus! Angus, what happened to you?"

" . . . always trying to take my damn money . . ."

"We have a one-track mind," sighed Toby, flicking off the penlight. She continued her exam, searching first for evidence of head trauma, then moving on to her exam of the cranial nerves. She found no localizing signs, nothing to pinpoint the cause of the man's confusion. The daughter had described a staggering gait. Had the man suffered a stroke of the cerebellum? That would affect coordination.

She unstrapped his right wrist. "Angus, can you touch my finger?" She held her hand in front of his face. "Reach up and touch my finger."

"You're too far away," he said.

"It's right here, right in front of you. Come on, try and touch it."

He raised his arm. It wobbled in midair, like a dancing cobra.

The phone rang. Maudeen reached for the receiver.

Angus Parmenter's arm began to twitch, a violently rhythmic shaking that rattled the gurney.

"What's he doing?" said Val. "Is he having a seizure?"

"Angus!" Toby grasped the man's face and stared straight

at him. He wasn't looking at her; he was gazing at his own arm.

"Can you talk, Angus?"

"There it goes again," he said.

"What? You mean the shaking?"

"That hand—whose hand is that?"

"It's *your* hand."

The shaking suddenly ceased. The arm flopped down like a deadweight onto the gurney. Angus closed his eyes. "There now," he said. "All better."

"Toby?" It was Maudeen, turning from the telephone. "There's a Dr. Wallenberg on the line. He wants to talk to you."

Toby took the receiver. "Dr. Wallenberg? This is Toby Harper. I'm the ER doctor on duty tonight."

"You have my patient there."

"You mean Mr. Parmenter?"

"I just got beeped about the ambulance transfer. What happened?"

"He was found confused at home. Right now he's awake and the vitals are stable. But he's got ataxia, and he's disoriented times three. He doesn't even recognize his own daughter."

"How long has he been there?"

"The ambulance brought him in around nine."

Wallenberg was silent for a moment. In the background, Toby heard the sound of laughter and voices. A party.

"I'll be there in an hour. Just keep him stable till I arrive."

"Dr. Wallenberg—"

The line had already gone dead.

She turned to the patient. He was lying very still, his eyes focused intently on the ceiling. Now his gaze shifted, first right, then left, as though he were watching a slow-motion tennis match.

"Let's get this man a STAT CT scan," said Toby. "And we'll need some bloods drawn."

Val pulled a fistful of glass tubes out of the drawer. "The usual? CBC and SMA?"

"Add a drug screen. He seems to be hallucinating."

"I'll call X-ray," said Maudeen, reaching once again for the phone.

"Ladies," said Toby. "One more thing."

Both nurses looked at her.

"Whatever happens tonight, we're *not* going to leave this guy alone, not for a second. Not till he's transferred out of our ER."

Val and Maudeen nodded.

Toby took hold of Angus Parmenter's unrestrained hand and tied it firmly to the gurney siderail.

"Here come the cuts," said the CT tech.

Toby stared at the computer screen as the pixels formed the first image, an oval with different shades of gray. She was looking at a cross section of Angus Parmenter's brain. Thousands of X-ray beams directed at his cranium had been analyzed by computer, and the different densities of bone and fluid and brain matter had produced this image. The skull appeared as a thick white rim, like the rind of a fruit. Inside the rind, the brain showed up as grayish pulp, indented by black wormlike sulci.

A succession of images materialized on the screen, each one a slightly different cut of the patient's cranium. She saw the anterior horns, two black ovals filled with cerebrospinal fluid. The caudate nuclei. The thalamus. There appeared to be no anatomical shifts, no asymmetry. No evidence of blood leakage into any part of the brain.

"I don't see anything acute," Toby said. "What do you think?"

Vince was not a physician, but he'd seen far more CT

scans as an X-ray tech than Toby had. He frowned at the screen as a fresh cut appeared. "Wait," he said. "That shot looks a little funny."

"What?"

"Right there." He pointed to a smudge at the center. "That's the sella turcica. See how it's not very clearly demarcated on this edge?"

"Could it be patient movement?"

"No, the rest of the shot's perfectly clean. He didn't move." Vince picked up the phone and dialed the radiologist at home. "Hi, Dr. Ritter? Are the cuts coming across okay on your computer? Great. Dr. Harper and I are looking at them right now. We're wondering about that last cut"—he typed on the keyboard, and the image reverted back to the previous screen—"that slice right there, see it? What do you think about the sella turcica?"

As Vince conferred with Dr. Ritter, Toby bent closer to the screen. What Vince had spotted was a very subtle change—so subtle she herself would have missed it. The sella turcica was a tiny pocket of thin bone housing the pituitary gland at the base of the brain. The gland itself was vital; the hormones it produced controlled a wide variety of functions, from fertility to childhood growth to the daily sleep-wake cycle. Could that tiny erosion of the sella turcica be the cause of the patient's symptoms?

"Okay, I'll do the coronal thin slices," said Vince. "Anything else you want me to do?"

"Let me talk to Ritter," said Toby. She took the receiver. "Hi, George, this is Toby. What do you think about that sella?"

"Not much," said Ritter. She heard the squeak of his chair—probably leather. George Ritter liked his luxuries. She could imagine him ensconced in his study, surrounded by the latest in computer technology. "In a man this age, pituitary adenomas aren't uncommon. Twenty percent of eighty-year-olds have them."

"Big enough to erode the sella?"

"Well, no. This one's gotten a little large. What's his endocrine status?"

"I haven't checked it. He just came in the ER with acute confusion. Could this be the cause?"

"Not unless the adenoma's produced a secondary metabolic abnormality. Have you checked the electrolytes?"

"They've been drawn. We're waiting for results."

"If those are normal, and the endocrine status is okay, I think you're going to have to look for some other reason for his confusion. This is too small a tumor to exert much anatomical pressure. I've asked Vince to do some thin-slice cuts on the coronal plane. That should define it a little better. You'll probably want to send the patient out for an MRI, too. Who's admitting him?"

"Dr. Wallenberg."

There was a silence. "This is a Brant Hill patient?"

"Yes."

Ritter gave an irritated sigh. "I wish you'd told me this earlier."

"Why?"

"I don't read X rays on Brant Hill patients. They use their own radiologist to interpret all their films. Which means I won't get paid for this."

"I'm sorry, I didn't know that. Since when did this arrangement start?"

"Springer signed a subcontract agreement with them a month ago. Their patients aren't supposed to go through the ER. The Brant Hill docs admit directly to the wards. How did this patient end up with you?"

"The daughter panicked and called nine one one. Wallenberg's on his way in now."

"Okay. Then let Wallenberg decide what to do about the coronal slices. I'm going to bed."

Toby hung up and looked at Vince. "Why didn't you tell me Brant Hill had a closed referral system?"

Vince gave her a sheepish look. "You didn't tell me this was a Brant Hill patient."

"Don't they trust our radiology staff?"

"Our hospital techs shoot the films, but the Brant Hill radiologist interprets them. I guess they're trying to keep the professional fees within their group."

Hospital politics again, she thought. Everyone fighting for the same shrinking health care dollar.

She rose and looked through the viewing window into the CT scan room. The patient was still lying on the table, his eyes closed, his lips moving silently. The twitching of his right hand had not recurred. Nevertheless, he would need an EEG to rule out seizures. And probably a lumbar puncture. Wearily she leaned against the glass, trying to think of what she might have missed, what she could not afford to miss.

Ever since Harry Slotkin had vanished from her ER two weeks ago, she knew her performance was under scrutiny by the hospital board, and she had been even more compulsively thorough than usual. Every afternoon, she'd wake up wondering if this was the day they'd find Harry Slotkin's body, if this was the day her name would once again be thrust into the public eye. The initial news coverage had been painful enough. The week of Harry's disappearance, the tale of the missing patient had aired on all the local television stations. She'd managed to ride out that storm, and now it was old news, probably forgotten by the general public. But the minute they find Harry's body, she thought, it will once again be a hot story. And I'll be in the hot seat, battling both lawyers and reporters.

Behind her, a door opened and a voice said: "Is that my patient on the table?"

Toby turned and was startled to see a strikingly tall man in a tuxedo. He glanced at Vince, his gaze quickly taking in the CT tech, and just as quickly dismissing him. Then he strode to the viewing window and stared through the glass at Angus Parmenter. "I didn't ask for a CT. Who ordered it?"

"I did," said Toby.

Now Wallenberg focused on *her,* as though finally realizing she was worth his attention. He was no older than forty, yet he regarded her with an expression of clear superiority. Perhaps it was the tuxedo; a man who looked as if he'd stepped off the pages of *GQ* had every reason to feel superior. He reminded Toby of a young lion, his brown hair perfectly clipped and swept back like a mane, his eyes like amber, alert and not particularly friendly. "Are you Dr. Harper?"

"Yes. I wanted to save you some time on the workup. I thought I'd order the CT."

"Next time, let me order my own tests."

"But it seemed more efficient to get it done now."

The amber eyes narrowed. He seemed about to make a retort, then thought better of it. Instead he simply nodded and turned to Vince. "Please get my patient back on the gurney. He's being admitted to the third floor, medical wing." He started to leave the room.

"Dr. Wallenberg," said Toby. "Did you want to hear the results of your patient's CT scan?"

"Was there anything to report?"

"A small erosion of the sella turcica. It appears he has a pituitary adenoma growing."

"Was there anything else?"

"No, but you'll probably want to order thin-slice tomography. Since he's already lying on the CT table—"

"It won't be necessary. Just get him upstairs and I'll write the admitting orders."

"What about the lesion? I know the adenoma's not an emergency, but it may require surgical removal."

With a sigh of impatience he turned to face her. "I am *fully* aware of the adenoma, Dr. Harper. I've been following it for two years now. Thin-slice tomography would be a waste of money. But *thank* you for your suggestion." He walked out of the room.

"Geez," muttered Vince. "Who shoved the pole up *his* ass?"

Toby looked through the viewing window at Angus Parmenter, who was still babbling quietly to himself. She didn't agree with Wallenberg; she thought further X-ray studies were indicated. But the patient was no longer her responsibility.

She looked at Vince. "Come on. Let's get him on the gurney."

7

The sign on the door was stenciled in soft blue on gray: PRENATAL COUNSELING. Molly could hear the sound of a telephone ringing in the room beyond, and she hesitated in the hallway, her hand clutching the knob as she listened to the faint murmur of a woman's voice beyond the closed door.

She took a breath and walked in.

The receptionist didn't see her at first; she was too busy talking on the phone. Afraid to interrupt this very busy woman, Molly stood on the other side of the desk, waiting to be noticed. At last the receptionist hung up and looked at her. "Can I help you?"

"Um, I'm supposed to talk to someone . . ."

"Are you Molly Picker?"

"Yeah." Molly gave a relieved nod. They were expecting her. "That's me."

The receptionist smiled, the sort of smile that starts off at the mouth, but then gets no further. "I'm Linda. We spoke on the phone. Why don't we go in the other room?"

Molly glanced around the reception area. "Am I gonna see a nurse or something? 'Cause maybe I'm s'posed to pee first."

"No, today we're just going to talk, Molly. The rest room's out in the hall if you need to use it right away."

"I guess I can wait."

She followed the woman into the adjoining room. It was a small office with a desk and two chairs. On one wall was a giant poster of a pregnant woman's belly, drawn as if that belly were sliced right down the middle, so you could see the baby resting inside, its chubby little arms and legs curled up, its eyes closed in sleep. On the desk was a plastic model of a pregnant womb, a 3-D puzzle that could be taken apart layer by layer, belly, womb, and then baby. There was also a big picture book open to a drawing of an empty baby stroller, which seemed like a strange image to display.

"Why don't you have a seat?" Linda said. "Would you like a cup of tea? A glass of apple juice?"

"No, Ma'am."

"Are you sure? It's really no trouble."

"I'm not thirsty, thank you, Ma'am."

Linda sat down across from Molly so that the two of them were looking directly at each other. The woman's smile had changed to an expression of concern. She had light blue eyes that, with a little makeup, might have been pretty were they not staring from a face that was so bland and humorless. Nothing about this woman—not her suburban housewife perm or her high-necked dress or her tight little mouth—set Molly at ease. She might as well be from another planet, for all the ways they were different. She knew the other woman sensed that difference as well, could see it by the way Linda sat behind her desk, her shoulders squared, her bony hands folded before her. Molly suddenly felt the need to tug down the hem of her skirt, to cross her arms over her chest. And she felt a twinge of something she hadn't felt in a long time.

She felt ashamed.

"Now," said Linda. "Tell me about your situation, Molly."

"My, uh, situation?"

"You said on the phone you're pregnant. Are you having symptoms?"

"Yes, Ma'am. I think so."

"Can you tell me what they are?"

"I, uh . . ." Molly looked down at her lap. The short skirt was riding up her thighs. She squirmed a little in her chair. "In the morning, I'm sick to my stomach. I gotta pee all the time. And I haven't had my monthly in a while."

"How long since your last period?"

Molly shrugged. "I'm not real sure. I think it was back in May."

"That's over four months ago. Didn't it worry you, being so late?"

"Well, I didn't really keep track, you know. And then I got that stomach flu and I thought that's why I was late. And also, I—I guess I didn't want to think about it. About what it might mean. You know how it is."

Linda obviously didn't know. She just kept looking at Molly with those pinched eyes. "Are you married?"

Molly gave a startled laugh. "No, Ma'am."

"But you did have . . . sex." The word came out like a throat clearing, a low, choked sound.

Molly fidgeted in her chair. "Well, yeah," she answered. "I've had sex."

"Unprotected?"

"You mean like do I use rubbers? Yeah, sure. But I guess I . . . had an accident."

Again, the woman made that throat-clearing sound. She folded her hands on the desk. "Molly, do you know what your baby looks like right now?"

Molly shook her head.

"You do understand it *is* a baby you're carrying?" The woman slid the picture book toward Molly and flipped to a page near the beginning. She pointed to an illustration, a miniature baby all wrapped around itself in a small fleshy ball. "At four months, this is what he looks like. He has a little face and little hands and feet. See how perfect he is already? He's a real baby. Isn't he cute?"

Molly shifted uneasily.

"Do you have a name for him yet? You should give him a name, don't you think? Because you're going to start feeling him move around inside you real soon, and you can't just call him *hey you.* Do you know the father's name?"

"No, Ma'am."

"Well, what was *your* daddy's name?"

Molly swallowed. "William," she whispered. "My daddy's name is William."

"Now that's a nice name! Why don't we call the baby Willie? Of course, if it's a little girl, we'd have to change it." She smiled. "There are so many nice names for girls these days! You could even name her after yourself."

Molly looked at her in bewilderment. Softly she asked: "Why're you doing this to me?"

"Doing what, Molly?"

"What you're doing . . ."

"I'm trying to offer you a choice. The only choice. You've got a baby in there. A four-month-old fetus. The Good Lord has given you a sacred responsibility."

"But, Ma'am, it wasn't the Good Lord who fucked me."

The woman gasped, her hand flying to her throat.

Molly squirmed in her chair. "I think maybe I should go—"

"No. No, I'm only trying to lay out the options for you— all of them. You do have choices, Molly, and don't let anyone tell you differently. You can choose life for that baby. For little Willie."

107

"Please don't call him that." Molly stood up.

So did Linda. "He has a name. He is a *person.* I can put you in touch with an adoption agency. There are people who want your baby—thousands of families just waiting for one. It's time to think about someone besides yourself."

"But I gotta think about myself," whispered Molly. "'Cause no one else does." She walked out of the office, out of the building.

In a phone booth she found a Boston directory. In the Yellow Pages was a listing for a Planned Parenthood clinic, on the other side of town.

I've gotta think about myself. Because no one else does. No one ever has.

She rode the bus, transferring twice, and got off a block away from her destination.

There was a crowd of people standing on the sidewalk. Molly could hear them chanting, but she couldn't understand the words. It was just a noisy chorus of voices, rhythmically punching the air. Two cops stood off to the side, arms crossed, looking bored.

Molly halted, uncertain whether to approach. The crowd suddenly turned its attention to the street, where a car had just pulled up at the curb. Two women emerged from the building and moved swiftly, defiantly, through the gathering. They helped a frightened-looking woman out of the car's passenger seat. Locking arms around her, they started back toward the building.

The two cops finally moved into action, pushing into the fray, trying to clear a path for the three women.

A man yelled: "This is what they do to babies in that building!" and he threw a jar down on the sidewalk.

Glass shattered. Blood splashed across the pavement in a bright, shocking spray of crimson.

The crowd began to chant: "*Baby killers. Baby killers. Baby killers.*"

The three women, heads ducked, blindly followed the cop up the steps and into the building. The door slammed shut.

Molly felt a tug on her arm, and a man shoved a brochure in her hand.

"Join us in the fight, sister," he said.

Molly looked down at the brochure she was holding. It was a printed photo of a smiling child with wispy blond hair. *We are all God's angels,* it said.

"We need new soldiers," the man said. "It's the only way to combat Satan. We'd welcome you." He reached out to her, fingers bony as a skeleton's.

Molly fled in tears.

She caught a bus back to her own neighborhood.

It was nearly five when she climbed the stairs to her room. She was so tired she could barely move her legs, could barely drag herself up that last flight of stairs.

A moment after she'd flopped onto her bed, Romy shoved open the door and walked in. "Where you been?"

"For a walk."

He gave her bed a kick. "You're not doing a little on the side, are you? I got my eye on you, girl. I'm keeping track."

"Leave me alone. I want to sleep."

"You fucking around on your own time? That what you been doing?"

"Get *out* of my room." With her foot, she shoved him off the bed.

Bad mistake. Romy grabbed her wrist and twisted it so savagely she thought she could feel her bones snapping.

"Stop it!" she screamed. "You're breaking my arm—"

"And you're forgetting who you are, Molly Wolly. Who I am. Don't like it when you go off without telling me where you are."

"Let me go. C'mon, Romy. Please stop hurting me."

With a grunt of disgust he released her. He crossed to the old rattan dresser where she'd left her purse. Turning the purse upside down, he emptied the contents on the floor. From her wallet he pulled out eleven dollars—all the money she had. If she'd been turning tricks on the side, she sure wasn't getting paid for it. As he stuffed the bills in his pocket, he suddenly noticed the brochure—the one with the picture of the little blond child. *We are all God's angels.*

He snatched it up and laughed. "What's this angel shit?"

"It's nothing."

"Where'd you get it?"

She shrugged. "Some guy gave it to me."

"Who?"

"I don't know his name. It was over by the Planned Parenthood. There was a whole bunch of crazy people out on the street, yelling and shoving folks."

"So what were *you* doing there?"

"Nothing. I wasn't doing nothing."

He crossed back to her bed and grabbed her under the chin. Softly he said, "You didn't go and do something without telling me?"

"What do you mean?"

"No one *touches* you without my permission. You got that?" His fingers dug into her face and suddenly she felt afraid. Romy was speaking softly, and when he got quiet was when he got mean. She'd seen the bruises he left on other girls' faces. The bloody gaps where their teeth had been. "Thought we got that straight a long time ago."

The pressure of his fingers brought tears to her eyes. She whispered, "Yeah. Yeah, I . . ." She closed her eyes, steeling herself for the blow. "Romy, I messed up. I think I'm pregnant."

To her surprise the blow never came. Instead he released her and made a sound almost like a chuckle. She didn't dare look at him but kept her head bowed in supplication.

"I don't know how it happened," she said. "I was scared to

tell you. I figured I'd just, you know, take care of it. And then I wouldn't have to tell you nothing."

His hand came down on her head, but the contact was gentle. A caress. "Now you know that's not the way we do things. You know I take care of you. Gotta learn to *trust* me, Molly Wolly. Gotta learn to *confide* in me." His fingers slid down her cheek, soft as a tickle. "I know a doctor."

She stiffened.

"I'll take care of it, Moll, just like I take care of everything else. So don't you go making other arrangements. You got that?"

She nodded.

After he left the room, she slowly unfolded her limbs and let out a deep sigh. She'd gotten off easy this time. Only now, after the encounter was over, did she realize how close she'd come to getting hurt. You didn't go against Romy, not if you wanted to hold on to your teeth.

She was hungry again; she was always hungry. She reached under the bed for the bag of Fritos, then remembered she'd eaten them all that morning. She got up and rooted around the room for something else to eat.

Her gaze fell on the picture of the blond baby. The brochure was lying on the floor, where Romy had tossed it.

We are all God's angels.

She picked up the brochure and studied the baby's face. Was it a girl or a boy? She couldn't tell. She didn't know much about babies, hadn't been around one in years, not since she was a girl. She had only a vague recollection of holding her younger sister on her lap. She remembered the crackle of plastic pants over Lily's diaper, the sweet powdery smell of her skin. How Lily had no neck, just that soft little hump between her shoulders.

She lay down and placed her hands on her belly, felt her own womb, firm as an orange, bulging under the skin. She thought of the drawing in Linda's picture book—the baby with the perfect fingers and toes. A Polly Pocket baby you could hold in one hand.

We are all God's angels.

She closed her eyes and thought wearily: *What about me? You forgot me, God.*

Toby stripped off her gloves and tossed them in the rubbish can. "All stitched up. Now you'll have something to show the other kids at school."

The boy finally got up the nerve to look at his elbow. He'd had his eyes closed tight, had not dared even a single peek while Toby was suturing. Now he stared in awe at the nubbins of blue nylon thread. "Wow. How many stitches?"

"Five."

"Is that a lot?"

"It's five too many. Maybe you should retire the old skateboard."

"Nah. I'd just bang myself up some other way." He sat up and slid off the treatment table. Immediately he swayed sideways.

"Uh oh," said Maudeen. She scooped him up under the arms and lowered him into a chair. "You're moving too fast, kid." She shoved the boy's head between his knees and rolled her eyes at Toby. Teenagers. All brag and no backbone. This one would probably strut into school tomorrow morning and proudly wave his new battle scar. He wouldn't bother to mention the part about nearly fainting into a nurse's arms.

The intercom buzzed. It was Val. "Dr. Harper, they've got a Code Blue up on Three West!"

Toby shot to her feet. "I'm on my way."

She jogged up the hall toward the stairwell, bypassing the elevator. She could make it faster on her own two feet.

Two flights up, she emerged in the Three West corridor

and spotted a nurse wheeling a crash cart through a doorway. Toby followed her into the patient's room.

Two ward nurses were already at the bedside, one holding a mask to the patient's face and bagging oxygen into the lungs, the other nurse administering chest compressions. The nurse with the crash cart pulled out EKG leads and slapped contact pads onto the patient's chest.

"What happened?" said Toby.

The nurse pumping on the chest answered. "Found him seizing. Then he went flaccid—stopped breathing—" Her words came out in rhythmic bursts as she leaned forward, released. "Dr. Wallenberg's on his way."

Wallenberg? Toby glanced at the patient's head. She hadn't recognized him because the oxygen mask had obscured her view of the face. "Is this Mr. Parmenter?"

"Hasn't been doing so well the last few days. I tried to get him transferred to the ICU this morning."

Toby squeezed around to the head of the bed. "Get those EKG leads on. I'll put the airway in. Number seven ET tube."

The crash cart nurse passed her the laryngoscope and ripped open the ET tube packet.

Toby crouched down by the patient's head. "Okay, let's do it."

The oxygen mask was removed. Tilting the head back, Toby slid the laryngoscope blade into the patient's throat. At once she identified the vocal cords and slid the plastic ET tube into place. The oxygen line was reconnected, and the nurse resumed bagging.

"I've got a tracing," said the crash cart nurse. "Looks like V. fib."

"Charge to a hundred joules. Hand me the defib paddles! And get a lidocaine bolus ready—a hundred milligrams."

It was too many orders at once, and the crash cart nurse was looking overwhelmed. In the ER, every task would have

113

been done in the blink of an eye, without a doctor uttering a single word. Now Toby wished she'd brought Maudeen upstairs with her.

Toby placed the paddles on the chest. "Back!" she ordered and pressed the discharge buttons.

A hundred joules of electricity coursed through Angus Parmenter's body.

Everyone's gaze snapped to the monitor.

The heart tracing shot straight up, then slid back to baseline. A blip appeared, the narrow peak of a QRS complex. Then another, and another.

"*Yes!*" said Toby. She reached down to feel the carotid. There was a pulse, faint but definitely present.

"Someone call ICU," said Toby. "We'll need a bed."

"I'm getting a BP—eighty-five systolic—"

"Can we draw some stat electrolytes? And hand me a blood gas syringe."

"Here, Doc."

Toby uncapped the blood gas needle. She didn't waste her time on the wrist searching for the radial artery; she went straight for the femoral. Piercing the groin, she angled the needle toward the pulse. A flash of bright red blood told her she'd found her target. She collected 3 cc's in the syringe, then handed it to a nurse.

"Okay. Okay." Applying pressure to the groin puncture, Toby took a deep breath and allowed herself a precious moment to review the situation. They had a patent airway, a heart rhythm, and an adequate blood pressure. They were doing all right. Now she could address the question: Why had the patient coded?

"You said he was seizing before he lost his blood pressure?" she asked.

A nurse answered, "I'm pretty sure it was a seizure. I found him on my ten o'clock med rounds. His arm was jerking and he was unresponsive. We have a standing order to give him IV Valium as needed, and I was getting the dose ready when he stopped breathing."

"IV Valium? Did Wallenberg order that?"

"For the seizures."

"How many has he had?"

"Since he was admitted? Maybe six. About once a day. It's usually his right arm that's affected. He's been having trouble with his balance, too."

Toby frowned at the patient. She had a sudden, vivid memory of Harry Slotkin's jerking leg. "What's their diagnosis? Do they know?"

"He's still being worked up. They've had a neurology consult, but I don't think he's figured out the problem yet."

"He's been here a whole week and they have no idea?"

"Well, nobody's told *me*." The RN glanced at the other nurses, and they all shook their heads.

They heard Wallenberg's voice before they realized he had walked into the room. "What's the status here?" he said. "Have you got him stabilized?"

Toby turned to face him. As their gazes met, she thought she saw a flash of dismay in his eyes. It was just as quickly gone.

"He was in V. fib," said Toby. "Preceded by a seizure and respiratory arrest. We cardioverted him, and he's now in sinus rhythm. We're waiting for an ICU bed."

Wallenberg nodded and automatically reached for the patient's chart. Was he avoiding her gaze? She watched him flip through the pages and couldn't help envying his unflappability. His elegance. Not a hair out of place, not one unseemly crease in his white coat. Toby, dressed in her usual baggy scrubs, felt like something dragged up from the dirty clothes hamper.

"I understand he's had a number of seizures," said Toby.

"We're not certain they are seizures. The EEG didn't confirm it." He set down the chart and gazed at the cardiac mon-

115

itor, where a normal sinus rhythm continued to trace across the oscilloscope. "It looks like everything's under control. I can take over from here, thank you."

"Have you ruled out toxins? Infectious agents?"

"We've had a neurology consult."

"Has he looked specifically for those things?"

Wallenberg shot her a puzzled look. "Why?"

"Because Harry Slotkin presented in exactly the same way. He had focal seizures. Acute onset of confusion—"

"Confusion, unfortunately, is something that happens in this age group. I hardly think it's something you can catch like the common cold."

"But they both lived at Brant Hill. They both presented with the same clinical picture. Maybe there's a common toxin involved."

"Which toxin? Can you be specific?"

"No, but a neurologist might be able to narrow it down."

"We have a neurologist on the case."

"Does he have a diagnosis?"

"Do you, Dr. Harper?"

She paused, startled by his hostile tone. She glanced at the nurses, but they studiously avoided her gaze.

"Dr. Harper?" A nurse's aide poked her head in the doorway. "ER's on the line. They have a patient downstairs. Headache."

"Tell them I'll be right down." Toby turned back to Wallenberg, but he had put on his stethoscope, effectively cutting off any further discussion. In frustration, she left the room.

As she descended the stairwell, she kept reminding herself that Angus Parmenter was not her patient, not her concern. Dr. Wallenberg specialized in geriatrics; surely he was better qualified to manage the patient's care than she was.

But she could not stop fretting over it.

For the next eight hours she attended to the usual night-shift parade of ailments, the chest pains and the stomachaches and the babies with fevers. But every so often there would be a lull in the pace and her thoughts would snap right back to Angus Parmenter.

And to Harry Slotkin, who had not yet been found. It had been over three weeks since his disappearance. Last night the temperature had dropped into the thirties, and she had sat up thinking about the cold, had imagined what it would be like to wander naked in that wind. She knew it was just another way of punishing herself. Harry Slotkin was not suffering on that cold night. He was, almost certainly, dead.

At dawn, the ER waiting room finally emptied out, and Toby retreated to the doctor's room. Over the desk was a bookshelf of medical texts. She perused the titles, then pulled out a neurology textbook. In the index, she looked up *Confusion.* There were over twenty entries, and the different diagnoses included everything from fevers to alcoholic DT's. She scanned the subheadings: *Metabolic. Infectious. Degenerative. Neoplastic. Congenital.*

She decided that *Confusion* was too broad a term; she needed something more specific, a physical sign or a lab test that would point her to the right diagnosis. She remembered Harry Slotkin's leg, thrashing on the gurney. And she remembered what the nurse had said about Mr. Parmenter's jerking arm. Seizures? According to Wallenberg, the EEG had ruled that out.

Toby closed the textbook and rose, groaning, to her feet. She needed to review Mr. Parmenter's chart. There might be some abnormal lab test, some physical finding that had not been pursued.

It was seven o'clock; her shift was finally over.

She rode the elevator to the fourth floor and walked into the ICU. At the nurses' station seven EKG tracings fluttered across monitor screens. A nurse sat staring at them as though hypnotized.

"Which bed is Mr. Parmenter in?" asked Toby.

The nurse seemed to shake herself out of her trance. "Parmenter? I don't know that name."

"He was transferred here last night from Three West."

"We didn't get any transfers. We got that MI you sent us from the ER."

"No, Parmenter was a post–Code Blue."

"Oh, I remember. They canceled that transfer."

"Why?"

"You'd have to ask Three West."

Toby took the stairwell down to the third floor. The nursing station was deserted and the telephone was blinking on hold. She went to the chart rack and scanned the names but couldn't find Parmenter. With mounting frustration, she went up the hall to the patient's room and pushed open the door.

She froze, stunned by what she saw.

Morning light shone through the window, its hard glare focused on the bed where Angus Parmenter lay. His eyes were half open. His face was bluish white, the jaw sagging limply to his chest. All the IVs and monitor lines had been disconnected. He was quite obviously dead.

She heard a door whish open and turned to see a nurse wheeling a medication cart out of the patient's room across the hall. "What happened?" Toby asked her. "When did Mr. Parmenter expire?"

"It was about an hour ago."

"Why wasn't I called for the code?"

"Dr. Wallenberg was here on the ward. He decided not to code him."

"I thought the patient was being moved to the ICU."

"They canceled the transfer. Dr. Wallenberg called the daughter, and they both agreed it didn't make sense to move the patient. Or use extraordinary measures. So they let him go."

It was a decision with which Toby could not argue; Angus Parmenter had been eighty-two years old and comatose for a week, with little hope of recovery.

She had one more question to ask: "Has the family given permission for the autopsy?"

The nurse looked up from her medication cart. "They're not doing an autopsy."

"But there has to be an autopsy."

"The funeral arrangements are all made. The mortuary's coming to pick up the body."

"Where's the chart?"

"The ward clerk's already broken it down. We're just waiting for Dr. Wallenberg to fill out the death certificate."

"So he's still in the hospital?"

"I believe so. He's seeing a consult on the surgery floor."

Toby went straight to the nurses' station. The ward clerk was away from her desk, but she'd left the loose pages from Mr. Parmenter's chart on the countertop. Quickly Toby flipped to the last progress note and read Dr. Wallenberg's final entry.

Family notified. Respirations ceased—nurses unable to detect pulse. On exam, no heartbeat noted on auscultation. Pupils midposition and fixed. Pronounced dead 0558.

There was no mention of an autopsy, no speculation about the underlying illness.

The squeak of rolling wheels made her glance up as two hospital orderlies came out of the elevator, pushing a gurney. They wheeled it toward room 341.

"Wait," said Toby. "Are you here for Mr. Parmenter?"

"Yeah."

"Hold on. Don't take him *anywhere* yet."

"The hearse is already on its way over."

"The body stays where it is. I have to talk to the family."

"But—"

"Just *wait*." Toby picked up the phone and paged Wallenberg to Three West. There was no answer. The orderlies stood waiting in the hallway, glancing at each other, shrugging. Again she picked up the phone and this time she called the patient's daughter, whose number was listed in the chart. It rang six times. She hung up, her frustration now at a boil, and saw that the orderlies had wheeled the gurney into the patient's room.

She ran after them. "I told you, the patient *stays*."

"Ma'am, we were ordered to pick him up and bring him downstairs."

"There's been a mistake, I know it. Dr. Wallenberg's still in the hospital. Just wait until I can talk to him about this."

"Talk to me about what, Dr. Harper?"

Toby turned. Wallenberg stood in the doorway.

"An autopsy," she said.

He stepped into the room, letting the door slowly whoosh shut behind him. "Are you the one who paged me?"

"Yes. They're taking the body to the mortuary. I told them to wait until you could arrange for the autopsy."

"There's no need for an autopsy."

"You don't know why he coded. You don't know why he became confused."

"A stroke is the most likely cause."

"The CT scan didn't show a stroke."

"The CT may have been done too early. And you wouldn't necessarily see a brain stem infarct."

"You're guessing, Dr. Wallenberg."

"What would you have me do? Order a head scan on a dead patient?"

The orderlies were watching the heated exchange with fascination, their gazes bouncing back and forth. Now the men's eyes were focused on Toby, waiting for her answer.

She said, "Harry Slotkin presented with identical symptoms. Acute onset of confusion and what appeared to be focal seizures. Both these men lived at Brant Hill. Both of them were previously healthy."

"Men in that age group are prone to strokes."

"But there could be something else going on. Only an autopsy can determine that. Is there some reason you're opposed to one?"

Wallenberg flushed, his anger so apparent Toby almost took a step backward. They eyed each other for a moment, then he seemed to regain his composure.

"There'll be no autopsy," he said, "because the daughter has refused. And I'm honoring her wishes."

"Maybe she doesn't understand how important this is. If I spoke to her—"

"Don't even think about it, Dr. Harper. You'd be invading her privacy." He turned to the orderlies, his dominance fully reasserted. "You can bring him downstairs now." He shot a last dismissive glance at Toby, then he left the room.

In silence Toby watched as the orderlies wheeled the gurney toward the bed and braked it in place.

"One, two, three, move."

They slid the corpse onto the gurney and secured it in place with a chest strap. It was not for safety but for aesthetics. Gurneys could be bumped, ramps could be steep, and one didn't want dead bodies accidentally tumbling onto floors. Above the corpse, a false mattress pad was clamped into place, then a long sheet draped over the whole contraption. A casual observer passing it in the hall would think it was merely an empty stretcher.

They wheeled the body out of the room.

Toby stood alone, listening to the receding squeak of the wheels. She thought of what would happen next. Downstairs, in the morgue, there would be paperwork to complete, authorization forms and releases to be signed. Then the deceased would be loaded into a hearse and transported to the mortuary, where the body fluids would be drained and replaced with embalming fluid.

Or would it be a cremation? she wondered. A fiery reduction to carbon ash and trace elements, leaving behind no answers?

This was her last chance to learn Angus Parmenter's diagnosis. And maybe Harry Slotkin's diagnosis as well. She picked up the phone and once again called the patient's daughter.

This time a voice answered with a soft "Hello?"

"Mrs. Lacy? This is Dr. Harper. We met last week, in the Emergency Room."

"Yes. I remember."

"I'm very sorry about your father. I just learned the news."

The woman gave a sigh, more a sound of weariness than of grief. "We were expecting it, I suppose. And to be perfectly honest, it's something of a . . . well, a relief. That sounds awful. But after a week of watching him . . . like that . . ." Again she sighed. "He wouldn't have wanted to live that way."

"Believe me, none of us would." Toby hesitated, searching for the right words. "Mrs. Lacy, I know this is a bad time to talk to you about this, but there's really no other time to do it. Dr. Wallenberg told me you didn't want an autopsy. I understand how hard it is for the family to give permission for something like this. But I really feel, in this case, it's vital. We don't know what your father died of, and it may turn out to be—"

"I didn't object to an autopsy."

"But Dr. Wallenberg said you refused one."

"We never discussed it."

Toby paused. *Why did Wallenberg lie to me?* She said, "May I have your permission for an autopsy, then?"

Mrs. Lacy hesitated only a few seconds. Softly she said: "If you think one is necessary. Yes."

Toby hung up. She started to call the Pathology Department next, then decided against it. Even with the family's permission, no Springer pathologist would perform the postmortem—not when the attending physician objected.

Why is Wallenberg so determined to avoid an autopsy? What is he afraid they'll find?

She looked at the telephone. *Decide. You have to decide now.* She picked it up and dialed directory assistance. "City of Boston," she said. "The office of the medical examiner."

It took a moment to obtain the phone number, another few moments to get through to the right extension. While she waited, she could picture the progress of Angus Parmenter's body toward the morgue. The ride down the elevator. The door whishing open to the basement level. The corridor with its groaning water pipes.

"Medical examiner's office. This is Stella."

Toby snapped to attention. "I'm Dr. Harper at Springer Hospital in Newton. May I speak to the chief medical examiner?"

"Dr. Rowbotham is on vacation, but I can connect you with our deputy chief, Dr. Dvorak."

"Yes, please."

There were a few clicks, and then a man's voice, flat and weary, said: "This is Dr. Dvorak."

"I have a patient who just expired," she said. "I think an autopsy is indicated."

"May I ask why?"

"He was admitted here a week ago. I saw him in the ER when he came in by ambulance—"

"Were there traumatic injuries?"

"No. He was confused, disoriented. There were cerebellar signs. Early this morning he had a respiratory arrest and died."

"Do you suspect foul play of any kind?"

"Not really, but—"

"Then your own hospital pathologist can certainly perform the autopsy. You don't have to report a death to our office unless the patient dies within twenty-four hours of being admitted."

"Yes, I realize it's not your usual coroner's case. But the attending physician refuses to order a postmortem, which means our pathologist won't do it. That's why I'm calling you. The family has already agreed to it."

She heard a long sigh and the shuffle of papers, could almost see the man at his desk, tired and overworked, surrounded by countless reminders of death. A joyless profession, she thought, and Dr. Dvorak had the voice of an unhappy man.

He said, "Dr. Harper, I don't think you're quite clear on the role of our office here. Unless there's a question of foul play or public health—"

"This *could* be a public health issue."

"How so?"

"It's the second case I've seen in my ER this month. Two elderly men, both presenting with acute confusion, cerebellar signs, and focal seizures. And here's what troubles me: these two patients lived in the same retirement complex. They drank the same water, ate in the same dining room. They probably knew each other."

Dr. Dvorak said nothing.

"I don't know what we're dealing with here," said Toby. "It could be anything from viral meningitis to garden pesticides. I would hate to overlook a preventable illness. Especially if other people are at risk."

"You say there were two patients."

"Yes. The first one was in my ER three weeks ago."

"Then the autopsy on that first patient should provide your answers."

"There was no autopsy on the first patient. He vanished from the hospital. His body's never been recovered."

The man's silence gave way to a soft exhalation. When he spoke again, she could hear the new undertone of interest. "You said you're at Springer Hospital? What's the patient's name?"

"Angus Parmenter."

"And is the body still there?"

"I'll make sure it is," she said.

She ran four flights down the stairwell and emerged in the basement. One of the overhead fluorescents was flickering like a strobe light, and her legs seemed to move in a jerky click-click-click of freeze frames as she hurried down the hall to a door labeled: AUTHORIZED PERSONNEL ONLY. She stepped into the morgue.

The lights were on, and a radio on the attendant's desk was playing, but there was no one in the anteroom.

Toby entered the autopsy lab. The stainless steel table was empty. Next she checked the cold room, the refrigerated locker where bodies were stored prior to autopsy. A chill vapor, faintly malodorous, swirled out of the locker. The smell of dead meat. She flipped on the light and saw two gurneys. She went to the first one and unzipped the shroud, revealing the face of an elderly woman, eyes open, the sclerae shockingly red from hemorrhages. Shuddering, she closed the shroud and went to the second gurney. It was a large corpse, and a foul odor rose up as she slid the zipper open. At her first sight of the man's face, she jerked away, fighting nausea. The flesh of the corpse's right cheek had melted away.

Necrotizing streptococcus, she thought, the flesh devoured by bacteria.

"This area is off limits," a voice said.

Turning, she saw the morgue attendant. "I'm looking for Angus Parmenter. Where is he?"

"They wheeled him out to the loading bay."

"They're taking him already?"

"The hearse just arrived."

"Shit," she muttered and dashed out of the morgue.

A quick jog down the hall brought her to the loading bay doors. She pushed through, and the morning sunlight caught her full in the face. Blinking against the glare, she quickly took in the situation: the orderly, standing by the empty gurney. The hearse, as it pulled away. She dashed past the orderly and ran alongside the moving hearse, rapping at the driver's window.

"Stop. Stop the car!"

The driver braked and rolled down his window. "What is it?"

"You can't take the body."

"It's been authorized. The hospital released it."

"It's going to the medical examiner."

"No one told me. As far as I know, the family's already made arrangements with the mortuary."

"This is now a medical examiner's case. You can check with Dr. Dvorak at the ME's office."

The driver glanced back at the loading bay, where the orderly stood watching in puzzlement. "Gee, I don't know . . ."

"Look, I'll take full responsibility," she said. "Now back up. We have to unload the body."

The driver shrugged. "Whatever you say," he muttered and shifted into reverse. "But someonez's gonna catch hell for this. And I sure hope it isn't me."

8

Lisa was flirting with him again. It was one of the daily irritations that Dr. Daniel Dvorak had learned to tolerate: his female assistant's eyelash-batting glances through the protective goggles, her insatiable curiosity about his private life, and her obvious frustration that he chose to ignore her advances. He didn't understand why she should find him so interesting; he suspected her attraction to him was nothing more than the challenge of a silent man.

An older man, he admitted to himself with resignation as he eyed his youthful assistant. Lisa had no wrinkles, no gray hairs, no sagging epidermis. At twenty-six she was, in the immortal words of his own teenage son, a blond babe. And what does my boy call *me* behind my back? he wondered. Old fart? Fuddy duddy? To a fourteen-year-old like Patrick, forty-five must seem as distant as the next ice age.

But we're all closer to death than we realize, thought

Dvorak, gazing at the naked body on the morgue table. The overhead lights shone down, harsh and unforgiving, emphasizing every wrinkle and mole on the corpse's skin. The gray hairs on the chest. The black seborrheic keratoses on the neck. The inevitable changes of aging. Even blond and buff Lisa would someday have liver spots.

"Looks like we have an outdoorsman," he commented, running a gloved finger across a rough patch of skin on the corpse's forehead. "Actinic keratoses. He has sun damage here."

"But pretty nice pectorals for an old guy." Lisa, of course, noticed such details. She was a health club addict, had started the gym craze two years ago, and her quest for physical perfection had reached the point where she talked incessantly about abs and lats and reps. It was the code of the muscle obsessed, who seemed to prefer one-syllable words. Often Dvorak would see Lisa glancing at her own reflection in the mirror over the sink. Was the hair perfect? Did that blond forelock curl just so? Was the tan holding, or would she need another twenty minutes on her apartment rooftop? Dvorak found her youthful preoccupation with good looks both amusing and bewildering.

Dvorak seldom looked in a mirror anymore, and that was only to shave. When he did look at himself, he was always surprised to see that his hair was now as much silver as black. He could see the passage of years in his face, the deepening lines around his eyes, the permanent frown etched between his eyebrows. He also saw how tired and drawn he'd become. He'd lost weight since his divorce three years ago, had lost even more weight since his son, Patrick, had left for boarding school two months ago. As layers of his personal life had peeled away, so had the pounds.

This morning, Lisa had commented on his new gauntness. *Lookin' good these days, Doc!* she'd chirped, which only confirmed how blind the young were. Dvorak didn't think he looked good. When he looked in the mirror, what he saw was a candidate for Prozac.

This autopsy was not going to improve his mood.

He said to Lisa, "Let's turn him over. I want to examine his back first."

Together they log-rolled the corpse sideways. Dvorak redirected the light and observed dependent mottling, consistent with the postmortem pooling of blood, as well as pale areas on the buttocks where the weight of the body had compressed the soft tissues. He pressed a gloved finger against the bruiselike discoloration. It blanched.

"Livor mortis not fixed," he noted. "We've got an abrasion here, over the right scapula. But nothing impressive."

They rolled the corpse onto its back again.

"He's in complete rigor mortis," said Lisa.

Dvorak glanced at the medical record. "Time of death recorded at five-fifty-eight. It's consistent."

"What about those bruises on the wrists?"

"Looks like restraints." Dvorak flipped through the record again and saw the nurse's note: *Patient remains agitated and in four-point restraints*. If only all his postmortems came with the circumstances of death so well documented. When a body was wheeled into his autopsy room, he felt fortunate just to have a positive identification, even more fortunate if the body was both intact and free of odors. To deal with the worst odors, he and his assistants donned protective suits and oxygen units. Today, though, they were working with standard gloves and goggles, on a cadaver that had already been screened in the hospital for HIV and hepatitis. While autopsies were never pleasant, this one would be relatively benign. And probably unrewarding.

He redirected the light straight down on the table. The corpse had pincushion arms—typical for a hospital death. Dvorak counted four different puncture sites on the left upper extremity, five on the right. There was also a needle puncture wound in the right groin—probably from an arterial blood gas draw. This patient had not gone peacefully into that good night.

He picked up the scalpel and made his Y incision. Lifting the sternum in one piece, he exposed both the chest and abdominal cavities to view.

The organs looked unremarkable.

He began to remove them, dictating his findings as he worked.

"This is the body of a well-nourished white male, age eighty-two . . ." He paused. That age couldn't be right. He flipped to the front of the chart and checked the birth date. The age was correct.

"I would've guessed sixty-five," said Lisa.

"It says here, eighty-two."

"Could that be a mistake?"

Dvorak studied the corpse's face. The variability of aging was a matter of both genetics and lifestyle. He had seen eighty-year-old women who could pass for sixty. He had also seen a thirty-five-year-old alcoholic who'd appeared ancient. Perhaps Angus Parmenter was merely the beneficiary of youthful genes.

"I'll confirm the age later," he said, and continued dictating. "Decedent expired today at five-fifty-eight in Springer Hospital, Newton, Massachusetts, where he was admitted as a patient seven days ago." Once again, he picked up the scalpel.

Dvorak had gone through these motions so many times before that much of it was automatic for him. He severed the esophagus and trachea, as well as the great vessels, and removed the heart and lungs. Lisa slid them onto the scale and called out the weights, then placed the heart on the cutting board. Dvorak sliced along the coronary vessels.

"I don't think we have an MI," he said. "Coronaries look pretty clean."

He resected the spleen, then the small intestine. The seemingly endless coils of bowel felt chill and slippery. The stomach, pancreas, and liver were resected in one block. He saw no signs of peritonitis, nor did he detect the odor of anaerobic bacteria. The joys of working on a fresh corpse. No foul smells, only the butcher-shop scent of blood.

On the cutting board, he sliced open the stomach and found it was empty.

"Hospital food must've sucked," said Lisa.

"He wasn't able to eat, according to the record."

So far, Dvorak had seen nothing on gross inspection that would point to the cause of death.

He circled around to the cadaver's head, made his incision, then folded the scalp forward over the face like a rubber mask. Lisa had the Stryker saw ready. Neither of them spoke as the saw whined, opening up the skull.

Dvorak lifted off the cap of bone. The brain looked like a mass of gray worms under its delicate covering of meningeal membrane. The meninges did not appear in any way unusual, which argued against infection. Neither did Dvorak see any signs of epidural bleeding.

The brain would have to be removed for closer inspection. He picked up the scalpel and worked quickly, severing optic nerves and blood vessels. As he reached deeper, to free the brain from the spinal cord, he felt a sharp bite of pain.

At once he withdrew his hand and stared at the cut glove. "Shit," he muttered and crossed to the sink.

"What happened?" said Lisa.

"Cut myself."

"Are you bleeding?"

Dvorak ripped off the gloves and examined his left middle finger. A fine line of blood welled up along the razor-thin laceration. "Scalpel went right through both gloves. Shit, shit, *shit*." He grabbed a bottle of Betadine from the counter and squirted a stream of disinfectant on his finger. "Die, buggers."

131

"He's HIV negative, right?"

"Yeah. Lucky for me," he said, blotting his finger dry. "That shouldn't have happened. I just got careless." Angry at himself now, he regloved and went back to the cadaver. The brain had already been severed of all its connections. Gingerly he scooped it up in both hands, swished it in saline to wash off the blood, and lay the dripping organ on the cutting board. He gave the organ a visual inspection, turning it to examine all the surfaces. The lobes appeared normal, without any masses. He slid the brain into a bucket of Formalin, where it would fix for a week before it was ready to be sliced and mounted on slides. The answers would most likely be found under the microscope.

"Dr. Dvorak?" It was his secretary, Stella, speaking over the intercom.

"Yes?"

"There's a Dr. Carl Wallenberg on the line."

"I'll call him back. I'm in the middle of an autopsy."

"Actually, that's why he insists on talking to you now. He wants the autopsy stopped."

Dvorak straightened. "Why?"

"Maybe you should talk to him yourself."

"Guess I have to take this call," he muttered to Lisa, stripping off his gloves and apron. "Go ahead with the muscle biopsies and liver sections."

"Shouldn't I wait until you talk to him?"

"We've gone this far. Let's finish the tissue sections."

He went to his office to take the call. Even with the door shut, the room was pervaded by the odor of Formalin, carried in on his clothes, his hands. He himself smelled like some preserved specimen, hidden away in this windowless office.

A man in a jar, trapped.

He picked up the phone. "Dr. Wallenberg? This is Dr. Dvorak."

"I believe there's been a misunderstanding. Mr. Parmenter was my patient, and I'm at a complete loss as to why you're performing an autopsy."

"It was requested by one of the doctors at Springer Hospital."

"You mean Dr. Harper?" The sound that came through the line was clearly a snort of disgust. "She wasn't involved with the patient's care. She had no authority to call you."

"According to the record, she did see the patient in the ER."

"That was a week ago. Since then, the patient has been under my care, as well as the care of several subspecialists. None of us felt an autopsy was necessary. And we certainly didn't think it was a case for the medical examiner."

"She led me to believe this was a public health issue."

Again, that snort of disgust. "Dr. Harper's not exactly a reliable source of information. Maybe you haven't heard. Springer Hospital has her under investigation for mistakes she's made in the ER, serious mistakes. She may soon be out of a job, and I wouldn't trust her opinion on anything. Dr. Dvorak, this is a chain-of-command issue. I'm the attending physician, and I'm telling you an autopsy is a waste of your time. And a waste of my taxes."

Dvorak stifled a groan. *I don't want to be dealing with this. I'm a pathologist. I'd rather work with dead bodies than live egos.*

"Also," said Wallenberg, "there's the family. The daughter would be very upset about her father being mutilated. She may even consider legal action."

Slowly Dvorak straightened, his head coming up in puzzlement. "But Dr. Wallenberg, I've spoken to the daughter."

"What?"

"This morning. Mrs. Lacy called to discuss the autopsy. I explained the reasons for it, and she seemed to understand. She didn't argue against it."

133

There was silence on the line. "She must have changed her mind since I spoke to her," said Wallenberg.

"I guess so. At any rate, the autopsy has been done."

"Already?"

"It's been a relatively quiet morning here."

Again there was a pause. When Wallenberg spoke again, his voice was oddly subdued. "The body—it will be returned, complete, to the family?"

"Yes. With all the organs."

Wallenberg cleared his throat. "I suppose that will satisfy them."

Interesting, thought Dvorak as he hung up. *He never asked what I found on autopsy.*

He replayed the conversation in his head. Had he simply been sucked into the petty politics of a suburban hospital? Wallenberg had characterized Dr. Harper as a marginal physician, a woman under scrutiny, perhaps a woman at odds with her colleagues. Was her request for an autopsy merely an attempt to embarrass another physician on the staff?

This morning, he should have exercised a little Machia-vellian reasoning, should have sought out her real agenda. But Dvorak's logic tended toward the concrete. He gathered information from what he could see and touch and smell. A cadaver's secrets are easily laid bare with a knife; human motives remained a mystery to him.

The intercom buzzed. "Dr. Dvorak?" said Stella. "Dr. Toby Harper's on the line. Want me to put her through?"

Dvorak thought it over and decided he was in no mood to talk to a woman who'd already ruined his day. "No," he said.

"What shall I tell her?"

"I've gone home for the day."

"Well, if that's what you really want . . ."

"Stella?"

"Yes?"

"If she calls back again, give her the same answer. I'm not available."

He hung up and returned to the morgue.

Lisa was bent over the cutting board, her scalpel slicing off a section of liver. She looked up as he walked in. "Well?" she asked. "Do we finish the biopsies?"

"Finish them. Then return the organs to the cavity. The family wants it all back."

She made another cut, then paused. "What about the brain? It still needs to be fixed for another week."

He looked at the bucket where Angus Parmenter's brain lay in its bath of Formalin. Then he looked down at his bandaged finger and thought of how the scalpel had sliced through two gloves and into his own flesh.

He said, "We'll keep it. I'll just replace the skull cap and sew the scalp shut." He pulled on a fresh pair of gloves and reached into a drawer for a needle and suture. "They'll never know it's missing."

Toby hung up the telephone in frustration. Had the autopsy been completed or hadn't it? For two days she'd been trying to get through to Daniel Dvorak, but each time his secretary had told her he was not available, and her tone of voice had made it clear that Toby's calls were not welcome.

The oven alarm buzzed. Toby turned off the gas and removed the casserole dish. She was copping out tonight— lasagna from the frozen food section, and a sadly wilted salad. She'd had no chance to shop for groceries and there was no milk left, so she poured two glasses of water and set them on the kitchen table. Her whole life, it seemed, had been reduced to a mad scramble for shortcuts. Frozen dinners and dishes stacked in the sink and wrinkled blouses pulled straight from the dryer. She wondered if her profound weariness was due to some incubating flu virus, or if it was mental exhaustion that was dragging her down. She opened the kitchen door and called out:

"Mom, dinner's ready! Come in and eat."

Ellen emerged from behind a clump of bee balm and obediently shuffled into the kitchen. Toby washed her mother's hands at the sink and sat her down at the table. She tied a napkin around Ellen's neck and slid the plate of lasagna in front of her. She cut the lasagna into bite-size pieces. She did this to the salad as well. She placed a fork in Ellen's hand.

Ellen did not eat but sat waiting and watching her daughter.

Toby sat down with her own plate of food and took a few bites of lasagna. She noticed Ellen wasn't eating. "It's your dinner, Mom. Put it in your mouth."

Ellen slid the empty fork into her mouth and tasted it with great concentration.

"Here. Let me help you." Toby glided Ellen's fork to the plate, scooped up a lasagna noodle, and raised it to Ellen's mouth.

"Pretty good," said Ellen.

"Now take another bite. Go on, Mom."

Ellen looked up as the doorbell rang.

"That must be Bryan already," said Toby, rising from the table. "You keep eating now. Don't wait for me."

She left her mother in the kitchen and went to answer the front door. "You're early."

"I thought I'd help out with dinner," Bryan said as he came into the house. He held out a paper bag. "Ice cream. Your mama does like her strawberry ice cream."

As she took the bag, she noticed Bryan wasn't looking at her; in fact he seemed to be avoiding her gaze, turning his back to her as he removed his jacket and hung it up in the closet. Even when he turned to face her, his eyes were focused elsewhere. "So how're we doing with dinner?" he asked.

"I just sat her down at the table. We're having a little trouble eating today."

"Again?"

"She didn't touch the sandwich I left her. And she looks at the lasagna like it's something from outer space."

"Oh. I can take care of that—"

From the kitchen came a loud crash followed by the clatter of broken china skittering across the floor.

"Oh my God," said Toby as she ran into the kitchen.

A bewildered Ellen stood staring down at the broken casserole dish. Lasagna had splattered all over the floor and against one wall in a shocking spray of cheese and tomato sauce.

"Mom, what are you *doing?*" yelled Toby.

Ellen shook her head and mumbled: "Hot. Didn't know it was hot."

"Christ, *look* at this mess! All this cheese . . ." Toby grabbed the trash can. In rage and frustration she dragged it across the floor to the broken dish. As she knelt down to clean up the ruined meal she realized she was dangerously close to tears. *I'm losing it. Everything in my life is so fucking screwed up. I can't deal with this, too. I just can't.*

"Come on, Ellen sweetie," she heard Bryan say. "Let's have a look at those hands. Oh dear, you're going to need some cold water on that. No no, don't pull away, sweetheart. Let me make them feel better. That's nasty, isn't it?"

Toby looked up. "What is it?"

"Your mama burned her hands."

"Ouch, ouch, *ouch!*" Ellen squealed.

Bryan led Ellen to the sink and ran cold water over her hands. "Isn't that better? Now, we're going to have ice cream after this and that'll make you feel even better. I brought strawberry. Yum yum."

"Yum," murmured Ellen.

Cheeks flushing with shame, Toby watched as Bryan tenderly dabbed Ellen's hands with a towel. Toby hadn't even noticed her mother was hurt. In silence she resumed picking up the pieces of crockery and the lumps of congealing cheese. She sponged up the sauce and wiped down the wall. Then she sat down at the table and watched Bryan coax Ellen into eating the ice cream. His patience, his gentle wheedling, made Toby feel more guilty. It was Bryan who had noticed Ellen's burned hands, Bryan who'd seen to her needs; Toby had seen only the broken dish and the mess on the floor.

Now it was already six-fifteen, time for Toby to get ready for work.

She didn't have the energy to rise from the table. She sat with her hand against her forehead, delaying just a little while longer.

"I have something to tell you," said Bryan. He put down the spoon and gently wiped Ellen's mouth with a napkin. Then he met Toby's gaze. "I'm really sorry about this. It wasn't an easy decision but . . ." He placed the napkin carefully on the table. "I've been offered another position: It's something I can't pass up. Something I've wanted to do for so long. I wasn't *looking* for another job—it just sort of happened."

"*What* happened?"

"I got a call from Twin Pines nursing home, out in Wellesley. They're looking for someone to start up a new recreational art therapy program. Toby, they made me an offer. I couldn't turn it down."

"You didn't say a word about this to me."

"I only got the call yesterday. I had the interview this morning."

"And you took the job, just like that? Without even talking to me?"

"I had to make a decision on the spot. Toby, it's a nine-to-five job. It means I can rejoin the rest of the human race."

"How much are they offering you? I'll pay you more."

"I've already accepted."

"How *much?*"

He cleared his throat. "It's not the money. I don't want you to think that's the reason. It's ... everything combined."

Slowly she sank back. "So I can't make you a better offer."

"No." He looked down at the table. "They want me to start as soon as possible."

"What about my mother? What if I can't find anyone to watch her?"

"I'm sure you will."

"Exactly how much time do I have to find someone?"

"Two weeks."

"Two *weeks?* Do you think I can pull someone out of thin air? It took me months to find *you.*"

"Yes, I know, but—"

"What the hell am I supposed to *do?*" The desperation in her voice seemed to hang like an ugly pall between them.

Slowly he looked up at her, his gaze unexpectedly detached. "I like Ellen. You know that. And I've always given her the best care I could. But Toby, she's not my mother. She's yours."

The simple truth of that statement silenced any response she could have made. *Yes, she is my mother. My responsibility.*

She looked at Ellen and saw that her mother was paying attention to none of this. Ellen had picked up a napkin and was folding it over and over, her forehead wrinkled in concentration.

Toby said, "Do you know anyone who might want the job?"

"I can get you some names," he said. "I know a few people who might be interested."

"I would appreciate it."

They looked at each other across the table, not as

employer and employee this time, but as friends. "Thank
you, Bryan," she said. "For all you've done for us."

In the living room, the clock struck the half hour. Toby
gave a sigh and dragged herself out of the chair.

It was time to go to work.

"Toby, we have to talk."

She looked up from a wheezing three-year-old and saw
Paul Hawkins standing in the exam room doorway. "Can you
wait a minute?" she asked.

"It's pretty urgent."

"Okay, let me give this epinephrine shot and I'll be right
out."

"I'll wait in the staff kitchen."

As Maudeen handed her the vial of epinephrine, Toby saw
the nurse's questioning look. They were both wondering the
same thing: Why was the ER chief here at 10 P.M. on a
Thursday night? He'd been dressed in a suit and tie—not his
usual hospital garb. Already feeling uneasy, Toby drew two-
tenths of a cc of epinephrine into a TB syringe, then forced a
cheerful note into her voice as she said to the child, "We're
going to make your breathing much, much better. You have
to sit very still. This will feel like a bee sting, but it'll be over
quick, okay?"

"Don't wanna bee sting. Don't wanna bee sting."

The child's mother tightened her grip around the boy. "He
hates these shots. Just go ahead and do it."

Toby nodded. Bargaining with a three-year-old was a
hopeless proposition anyway. She injected the drug, eliciting
a shriek that could peel paint off a wall. Just as suddenly, the
screaming was over, and the boy, though still sniffling, was
eyeing the syringe with a covetous look.

"I want it."

"You can have a new one," said Toby, and she handed him
a fresh syringe, minus the needle. "Bathtub fun."

"Gonna give my sister a shot."

The mother rolled her eyes. "She's gonna *love* that."

Already the boy's wheezing seemed to be better, so Toby left Maudeen in charge and went to find Paul in the staff kitchen.

He stood up as she walked in but didn't speak until she'd closed the door.

"We had a hospital board meeting tonight," he said. "It just wrapped up. I thought I should come right over and explain what happened."

"I assume this has to do with Harry Slotkin again."

"That was one of the issues we discussed."

"There were others?"

"The matter of the autopsy came up as well."

"I see. I have a feeling I should sit down for this."

"Maybe we both should."

She took a chair across the dining table from him. "If it was a 'torch Dr. Harper' session, why wasn't I invited for the barbecue?"

Paul sighed. "Toby, you and I could have toughed out the crisis with Harry Slotkin. In fact, so far you're lucky on that case. The Slotkin family isn't talking lawsuit yet. And the negative publicity seems to be over. From what I hear, any fresh news stories were squelched by Brant Hill. And Dr. Wallenberg."

"Why would Wallenberg do me any favors?"

"I guess it wasn't good for Brant Hill, having it known that one of their wealthy residents was wandering around like some street person. You know, they're not your usual Sun City of retirees. Their success depends on their platinum status, on being the best and charging the bucks for it. You can't attract new people if there's any question about the well-being of your clients."

"So Wallenberg was protecting his cash cow and not me."

"Whatever the reason, he helped you out. But now you've

gone and pissed him off. What was going through your head? Calling in the medical examiner? Turning it into a coroner's case?"

"It was the only way to get a diagnosis."

"The man was no longer your patient. An autopsy should have been Wallenberg's decision."

"But he was avoiding the issue. Either he didn't want to know the cause of death or he was afraid to find out. I couldn't think of anything else to do."

"You made him look bad. You made it look like some sort of criminal case."

"I was concerned about the public health issue—"

"This isn't a public health issue. This is a political *mess*. Wallenberg was at the meeting tonight. So were Doug Carey's allies. It was a barbecue all right, and you were the main course. Now Wallenberg's threatening to admit all Brant Hill patients to Lakeside Hospital instead of Springer. Which is going to hurt us. Maybe you don't realize that Brant Hill's just one link in a big chain. They're affiliated with a dozen other nursing homes, and all of them refer their patients to us. Do you have any idea how much money we make on their hip surgeries alone? Add the TURPs, the cataracts, and the hemorrhoids, and you're talking a lot of patients, most of them with supplemental insurance on top of Medicare. We can't afford to lose those referrals. But that's what Wallenberg's threatening."

"All because of the autopsy?"

"He has a pretty good reason to be upset. When you called the ME, you made Wallenberg look incompetent. Or worse. Now we're getting calls from newspapers again. It could be another round of bad publicity."

"Doug Carey's tipping them off. It's just the sneaky kind of thing he'd do."

"Yeah, well, now Wallenberg's pissed that his name could

be dragged into the public eye. The board's pissed that they could lose all their Brant Hill referrals."

"And of course everyone's pissed at me."

"Are you surprised?"

Slowly she let out a breath. "Okay, so you had a barbecue and now I'm a crispy critter."

Paul nodded. "Wallenberg wants your contract terminated. Of course it has to go through me first, since I'm ER chief. I wasn't left with a lot of maneuvering room."

"What did you tell them?"

"That there was a problem firing you." He gave an uneasy laugh. "I used a delaying tactic that you might not approve of. I told them you might fight back by filing a sex discrimination suit. That made them nervous. If there's anything they don't want to deal with, it's a whiny feminist."

"How flattering."

"It was the only thing I could think of."

"Funny. It's something I never would have considered. And *I'm* the woman."

"Remember that sexual harassment suit one of the nurses filed? It dragged on for two years, and Springer ended up paying a fortune in attorney's fees. This was one way I could make them stop and consider their actions. And buy you some time until things cool down." He dragged his fingers through his hair. "Toby, I'm in the hot seat. They're pressuring me to resolve the situation. And I don't want to hurt you, I really don't."

"Are you asking me to resign?"

"No. No, that's not why I'm here."

"What are you asking me to do?"

"I'm thinking maybe you should take a leave of absence for a few weeks. In the meantime, the ME's report will come back. I'm sure it'll show natural causes. That will let Wallenberg off the hook."

"And all will be forgiven."

"I hope so. You're scheduled to go on vacation next month anyway. You could take it now. Extend it by three or four weeks."

For a moment she sat thinking it over, playing a mental game of dominoes. One action produces a result that produces another result. "Who'll fill in for me?" she asked.

"We can pull Joe Severin in to take your shifts. He's only a part-timer now. I'm sure he'd be willing."

She looked straight at Paul. "And I'd never get my job back. Would I?"

"Toby—"

"Wasn't it Doug Carey who brought Severin on staff? Aren't they buddies or something? You're not taking all the personalities into account. If I go on leave, Joe Severin steps right in. I won't have a job to come back to, and you know it."

He said nothing. He just looked at her, his expression unfathomable. For too many years, she had let her attraction for Paul Hawkins obscure the relationship. She'd read more into his smiles, his friendliness, than had really existed. That she realized it only now, at her most vulnerable moment, made the blow even more painful.

She stood up. "I'll take my vacation as scheduled. No earlier."

"Toby, I'm doing what I can to protect you. You have to understand, *my* position isn't secure either. If we lose those Brant Hill referrals, Springer's going to be hurt. And the board will be looking for fall guys."

"I'm not blaming you, Paul. I understand why you're doing this."

"Then why won't you do what I suggest? Take the leave of absence. Your job will still be here."

"Can I have that in writing?"

He was silent.

She turned toward the door. "That's what I thought."

144

9

Molly Picker stood looking at the pay phone, trying to scrape up the courage to pick up the receiver. It was the second visit she'd made to this phone booth today. The first time she hadn't even stepped inside but had turned around and walked away. Now she was standing right in front of the phone and the door was shut behind her, and there was nothing to stop her from making the call.

Her hands shook as she picked up the receiver and dialed.
"Operator."

"I want to make a collect call. To Beaufort, South Carolina."

"Who shall I say is calling?"

"Molly." She gave the number, then leaned back with eyes closed, heart pounding, as the operator put through the call. She heard it ring. Her fear was so intense she thought she might throw up, right there in the booth. *Sweet Jesus, help me.*

"Hello?"

Molly's back snapped straight. It was her mother's voice. "Mama," she blurted out, but then the operator cut in:

"You have a collect call from Molly. Will you accept?"

There was a long silence on the other end.

Please, please, please. Talk to me.

"Ma'am? Will you accept the charges?"

A long sigh, then: "Oh, I guess so."

"Go ahead," said the operator.

"Mama? It's me. I'm calling from Boston."

"So you're still up there."

"Yeah. I been wantin' to call—"

"You need money or something. Is that it?"

"No! No, I'm doin' okay. I'm, uh . . ." Molly cleared her throat. "I'm holdin' my own."

"Well, that's good."

Molly closed her eyes, wishing her mother's voice didn't sound so flat. Wishing this conversation would go the way she'd fantasized it would. That Mama would break down crying and then ask her to come home. But there were no tears in Mama's voice, only that lifeless tone that cut straight to Molly's heart.

"So is there a reason you're calling?"

"Uh . . . no." Molly rubbed a hand across her eyes. "Not really . . ."

"You wanna say something or what?"

"I just—I guess I wanted to say hello."

"Okay. Well, look. I gotta finish cookin' here. If you don't have much more to say—"

"I'm pregnant," whispered Molly.

There was no response.

"Did you hear me? I'm gonna have a baby. Think of it, Mama! I'm hopin' it's a girl, so I can dress her all up like a princess. 'Member how you used to stitch up those dresses for me? I'm gonna get me a sewing machine, learn how to sew." She was laughing now, talking rapidly and desperately

146

through her tears. "But you gotta teach me, Mama, because I never could get it right. Never did learn how to do those blind hems—"

"Is it gonna be colored?"

"What?"

"Is the baby gonna be colored?"

"I don't know—"

"What do you mean, you don't *know?*"

Molly clapped her hand over her mouth to stifle a sob.

"You mean you don't have any idea?" said her mother. "You lost count or what?"

"Mama," whispered Molly. "Mama, it doesn't really matter. It's still my baby."

"Oh, it matters. It matters to people 'round here. What you think they're gonna say? And your daddy—it's gonna kill your daddy."

Someone was rapping on the phone booth door. Molly turned to see a man pointing at his watch, waving at her to get out of the booth. She turned her back on him.

"Mama," she said. "I want to come home."

"You can't come home. Not in your condition."

"Romy's tellin' me to get rid of it, to kill my baby. He's sending me to the doctor today, and I don't know what to do. Mama, I need you to tell me what to do . . ."

Her mother released a weary sigh. Quietly she said: "Maybe it would be for the best."

"What?"

"If you got rid of it."

Molly shook her head in bewilderment. "But it's your *grandbaby*—"

"That's no grandbaby of mine. Not the way you got it."

The man knocked at the door again and yelled at Molly to get off the phone. She pressed her hand over her ear to block out his voice.

"Please," Molly whimpered. "Let me come home."

"Your daddy can't deal with this right now, you know he can't. After the shame you put us through. After I told you and told you what to expect. But you never listen, Molly, you never have."

"I won't cause no more trouble. Romy and me, we're all through. I just want to come home now."

The man was pounding on the booth now, shouting at her to get the fuck off the phone. Desperately Molly braced her back against the door to keep him out.

"Mama?" she said. "Mama?"

The answer came back with a note of triumph. "You made your bed. Now you go lie in it."

Molly stood clutching the receiver to her ear, knowing that her mother had already hung up yet unable to believe the link was broken. *Talk to me. Tell me you're still there. Tell me you'll always be there.*

"Hey, *bitch!* Get off the fucking *phone!*"

Wordlessly she let the receiver drop from her hand. It swung free, clattering against the booth. In a daze she stepped outside, not really seeing the man who was still cussing her out, not hearing a word he said. She just walked away.

Can't go home. Can't go home. Not now, not ever.

She walked without seeing, without feeling her own legs moving, her own feet stumbling in their platform shoes. Her anguish had blocked out all physical sensation.

She never saw Romy coming at her.

The blow struck her under the chin and sent her stumbling against the building. She caught herself on the window bars and clung to the wrought iron to keep from falling. She didn't understand what had just happened; all she knew was that Romy was yelling at her and that her whole head was ringing with pain.

He grabbed her arm and hauled her through the front door. In the foyer, he hit her again. This time she did fall, sprawling onto the steps.

"Where the fuck you been?" he shouted.

"I had—I had things to do—"

"You had an appointment, remember? They want to know why you aren't there."

She swallowed and stared at the step. She didn't dare look him in the face. She only hoped he'd accept a lie. "I forgot," she said.

"What?"

"I said I forgot."

"You are one *dumb* bitch. I told you this morning where you had to be."

"I know."

"You must have shit for brains."

"I got to thinking 'bout other things."

"Well, they're still waiting on you. You get your ass in the car."

She looked up. "But I'm not ready—"

"Ready?" Romy laughed. "All you gotta do is get on the table and spread your legs." He pulled her to her feet and thrust her toward the door. "Go on. They sent you the fuckin' limousine."

She stumbled outside onto the sidewalk.

A black car was parked at the curb, waiting for her. She could barely make out the driver's silhouette through the tinted glass.

"Go on, get in."

"Romy, I don't feel so good. I don't want to do this."

"Don't mess with me. Just get in the car." He opened the door, shoved her into the backseat, and slammed the door shut.

The car pulled away from the curb.

"Hey!" she said to the driver. "I want to get out!" There was a barrier of Plexiglas between her and the front seat. She pounded on it, trying to get his attention, but he didn't react. She looked at the tiny speaker mounted in the partition and suddenly felt a chill of recognition. She remembered this car. She had ridden in it once before.

"Hello?" she said. "Do I know you?"

The driver didn't even turn his head.

She sat back against the leather seat. The same car. The same driver. She remembered that blond, almost silvery hair. The last time, when he had driven her to Dorchester, there had been another man waiting for her, a man in a green mask. And there had been a table with straps.

Her chill turned to panic. She glanced ahead and saw that an intersection was coming up. The last one, before the expressway turnoff. She stared at the traffic light, praying: *Turn red. Turn red!*

Another car cut in front of them. Molly lurched forward as her driver slammed on the brakes. Behind them horns blared and traffic screeched to a halt.

Molly shoved open the door and leaped out of the car.

The driver yelled: "Get back here! You get back here *now!*"

She darted between two idling cars and scrambled to the sidewalk, her platform shoes clacking on the pavement. Goddamn heels almost tripped her up. She recovered her balance and began running down the street.

"Hey!"

Molly glanced back and was startled to see that the blond man had left his car parked near the curb and was chasing her on foot, dodging through a river of honking traffic.

She ran, a clumsy, clacking gait, crippled by her shoes. At the end of the block she glanced back.

The driver was gaining.

Why won't he leave me alone?

She reacted with the automatic response of prey—she fled.

Darting right, she turned onto a narrow street and struggled up the bumpy brick sidewalk leading up Beacon Hill.

Only a block of running uphill and she was out of breath. And her calves ached—these damn shoes.

She looked back.

The driver was scrambling up the hill in pursuit.

Fresh panic sent Molly scrambling faster. She turned left, then right, worming deeper into the maze of Beacon Hill. She didn't stop to look back; she knew he was there.

By now her feet were bruised from the shoes and stinging with fresh blisters. *I can't outrun him.*

Rounding another corner, she spotted a taxi idling at the curb. She made a dash for it.

The driver glanced up in surprise as Molly threw herself into the backseat and pulled the door shut.

"Hey! I'm not available," he snapped.

"Just go. *Go!*"

"I'm waiting for a fare. Get out of my cab."

"Someone's after me. Please, can't you drive around the block?"

"I'm not driving nowhere. Get out or I radio for a cop."

Cautiously Molly lifted her head and peered out the window.

Her pursuer was standing only a few yards away, his gaze scanning the street.

At once she dropped back down to the floor. "It's him," she whispered.

"I don't give a shit who it is. I'm calling a cop."

"Okay. Go ahead! For once in my life I could *use* a fucking cop."

She heard him reach for the radio mike, then heard him mutter "Shit!" as he racked it again.

"You gonna call one or what?"

"I don't want to talk to no cops. Why can't you just get out like I'm telling you?"

"Why can't you drive around the block?"

"Okay, *okay.*" With a grunt of resignation he let out the

parking brake and pulled away from the curb. "So who's the guy?"

"He was driving me someplace I didn't want to go. So I bailed out."

"Driving you where?"

"I don't know."

"You know what? I don't want to know either. I don't want to know nothing 'bout your messed-up life. I just want you outta my cab." He swerved to a stop. "Now get *out*."

"Is the guy around?"

"We're on Cambridge Street. I brought you a few blocks over. He's way the other side."

She lifted her head and took a quick look. There were plenty of people around, but no sign of her pursuer. "Maybe I'll pay you sometime," she said and stepped out of the cab.

"Maybe I'll fly to the moon."

Quickly she walked, first down Cambridge, then onto Sudbury. She didn't stop until she was deep in the maze of streets in the North End.

There she found a cemetery with a public bench in front. COPP'S BURYING GROUND, the sign said. She sat down and took off her shoes. Her blisters were raw, her toes bruised purple. She was too tired to walk even another block, so she just sat there in her bare feet watching tourists wander by with their Freedom Trail brochures, all of them enjoying a surprisingly mild October afternoon.

I can't go back to my room. I can't go back for my clothes. Romy sees me, he'll kill me.

It was almost four o'clock, and she was hungry; she hadn't eaten anything except grapefruit juice and two strawberry doughnuts for breakfast. The delicious smells from an Italian restaurant across the street were driving her crazy. She looked in her purse but saw only a few dollars inside. She'd hidden more money back in her room; somehow she'd have to get it without Romy seeing her.

152

She put her shoes back on, wincing at the pain. Then she hobbled up the street to a pay phone. *Please do this for me, Sophie,* she thought. *For once, please be nice to me.*

Sophie answered, her voice low and cautious. "Yeah?"

"It's me. I need you to go into my room—"

"No way. Romy's going fucking nuts around here."

"I need my money. Please get it for me, and I'll be outta there. You won't have to see me again."

"I'm not going anywhere near your room. Romy's in there right now, tearing things apart. There's not gonna be nothing left."

Molly sagged against the phone booth.

"Look, just stay away. Don't come back here."

"But I don't know where to go!" Molly's voice suddenly shattered into sobs. In despair, she curled up against the booth, her hair falling over her eyes, the strands wet with tears. "I don't have anyplace to go . . ."

There was a silence. Then Sophie said, "Hey, Titless? Listen to me. I think I know someone who might help you out. It'd have to be for just a few nights. Then you're on your own again. Hey, are you listening?"

Molly took a deep breath. "Yeah."

"It's over on Charter Street. There's this bakery on the corner with a boarding house next door. She's got a room on the second floor."

"Who?"

"Just ask for Annie."

"You're one of Romy's girls. Aren't you?"

The woman stared out over the door chain, and through the narrow opening, Molly could make out only half her face—curlicue bangs of brilliant red hair, a blue eye smudged with a dark circle of fatigue.

"Sophie told me to come," said Molly. "She said you might have room for me—"

"Sophie should've asked me first."

"Please—can't I sleep here—just for tonight?" Shivering, Molly wrapped her arms around her shoulders and glanced up and down the dark hallway. "I don't have anywhere to go. I'll be real quiet. You won't even know I'm here."

"What'd you do to piss off Romy?"

"Nothin'."

The woman started to shut the door.

"Wait!" cried Molly. "Okay, okay. I guess I *did* piss him off. I didn't want to see that doctor again . . ."

Slowly the door cracked open. The red-haired woman's gaze shifted downward, to Molly's waist. She said nothing.

"I'm so tired," whispered Molly. "Can I just sleep on your floor? Please, just for tonight."

The door swung shut.

Molly gave a soft whimper of despair. Then she heard the chain rattle free and the door swung open again. The woman stood in full view, her belly swollen under a flowered print dress. "Come in," she said.

Molly entered the apartment. At once the woman shut the door and refastened the chain.

For a moment they looked at each other. Then Molly's gaze dropped to the other woman's belly.

The woman saw Molly staring, and she gave a shrug. "I'm not fat. It's a baby."

Molly nodded and placed her hands on her own gently rounded abdomen. "I've got one too."

"I spent twenty-two years looking after old people. Worked at four boarding homes in New Jersey. So I know 'bout how to keep them out of trouble." The woman pointed to the résumé lying on Toby's kitchen table. "I been at this a long time."

"Yes, I can see you have," said Toby, scanning the work history of Mrs. Ida Bogart. The pages reeked of cigarette smoke. So did the woman, who had carried the stench in on her baggy clothes and infected the whole kitchen with the smell. *Why am I going through the motions?* Toby wondered. *I don't want this woman in my house. I don't want her anywhere near my mother.*

She lay the pages down on the table and forced herself to smile at Ida Bogart. "I'll keep your résumé on file until I make a decision."

"You need someone right away, don't you? That's what the ad said."

"I'm still looking at applicants."

"Mind my asking if you got many?"

"Several."

"Not many people want to work nights. I never had a problem with it."

Toby stood up, a clear signal that the interview was over. She herded the woman out of the kitchen and down the hallway. "I'll keep your name under consideration. Thank you for coming, Mrs. Bogart." She practically pushed the woman out of the house and closed the front door. Then she stood with her back propped against it, as though to barricade her home from any more Mrs. Bogarts. *Six more days,* she thought. *How will I find someone in six days?*

In the kitchen, the phone rang.

It was her sister calling. "So how are the interviews going?" Vickie asked.

"They're not going anywhere."

"I thought you got responses to the ad."

"One who's a chain-smoker, two who barely understand English, and one who made me want to lock up the liquor. Vickie, this isn't working. I can't leave Mom with any of these people. You're going to have to keep her at your house at night until we can find someone."

"She wanders, Toby. She might turn on the stove while we're sleeping. I have my kids to think of."

"She never turns on the stove. And she usually sleeps all night."

"What about the temp agency?"

"It would only be a short-term solution. I can't have new faces coming in and out all the time. It would confuse Mom."

"At least it'd be some sort of solution. It's gotten to the point where it's either that or a nursing home."

"No way. No nursing home."

Vickie sighed. "It was just a suggestion. I'm thinking of you, too. I wish there was more I could do . . ."

But there isn't, thought Toby. Vickie already had two children greedily vying for attention. To force Ellen on their family would be one more burden on an already overwhelmed Vickie.

Toby crossed to the kitchen window and looked out at the garden. Her mother was standing by the toolshed, holding a leaf rake. Ellen didn't seem to remember what to do with a rake, and she kept scraping the teeth across the brick path.

"How many other applicants are you interviewing?" asked Vickie.

"Two."

"Do their résumés look okay?"

"They look fine. But they *all* look fine on paper. It's only when you meet them face-to-face that you smell the booze."

"Oh, it can't be that bad, Toby. You're too negative about the whole process."

"*You* come and interview them. The next one should be here any minute—" She turned at the sound of the doorbell. "That must be him."

"I'm coming over right now."

Toby hung up and went to answer the front door.

On the porch stood an elderly man, face drawn and gray, shoulders slumped forward. "I'm here about the job," was all he managed to get out before he was seized by a fit of coughing.

156

Toby hurried him inside and sat him down on the sofa. She brought him a glass of water and watched while he hacked, cleared his throat, and hacked some more. Just a leftover cold, he told her in fits and starts. Over the worst of it now, only this bronchitis hanging on. Didn't interfere with his ability to do a job, no sir. He'd worked while much sicker than this, had worked all his life, since he was sixteen years old.

Toby listened, more out of pity than interest, her gaze fixed on the résumé lying on the coffee table. Wallace Dugan, sixty-one years old. She knew she was not going to hire him, had known it from the instant she'd seen him, but she didn't have the heart to cut him short. So she sat in passive silence, listening to how he had come to this sad point in his life. How badly he needed the job. How hard it was for a man his age.

He was still sitting on her sofa when Vickie arrived. She walked into the living room, saw the man, and halted.

"This is my sister," said Toby. "And this is Wallace Dugan. He's applying for the job."

Wallace stood up to shake Vickie's hand but quickly sank back down again, seized by a new fit of coughing.

"Toby, can I talk to you for a minute?" said Vickie, and she turned and walked into the kitchen.

Toby followed her, closing the door behind her.

"What's wrong with that man?" whispered Vickie. "He looks like he's got cancer. Or TB."

"Bronchitis, he says."

"You're not thinking of *hiring* him, are you?"

"He's the best applicant so far."

"You're kidding. Please tell me you're kidding."

Toby sighed. "Unfortunately, I'm not. You didn't see the others."

"They were worse than *him?*"

"At least he seems like a nice man."

"Oh, sure. And when he keels over, Mom's going to do CPR?"

"Vickie, I'm not going to hire him."

"Then why don't we send him on his way, before he croaks in your living room?"

The doorbell rang.

"Jesus," said Toby, and she pushed out of the kitchen. She shot an apologetic glance at Wallace Dugan as she walked past him, but he had his head bent over a handkerchief, coughing again. She opened the front door.

A petite woman smiled at her. She was in her midthirties, with trim brown hair in a Princess Di cut. Her blouse and slacks appeared neatly pressed. "Dr. Harper? I'm sorry if I'm early. I wanted to make sure I could find your house." She extended her hand. "I'm Jane Nolan."

"Come in. I'm still talking to another applicant, but—"

"I can interview her," cut in Vickie, pushing forward to shake Jane Nolan's hand. "I'm Dr. Harper's sister. Why don't we go talk in the kitchen?" Vickie looked at Toby. "In the meantime, why don't you finish up with Mr. Dugan?" In a whisper, she added: "Just get *rid* of him."

Wallace Dugan already knew the verdict. When Toby walked back into the living room, she found him gazing down at the coffee table with a look of defeat. His résumé lay before him, three pages chronicling forty-five years of labor. A chronicle that had most likely reached its end.

They chatted a moment longer, more out of politeness than necessity. They would never meet again; they both knew it. When at last he walked out of her house, Toby closed the door with a sense of relief. Pity, after all, did not get the job done.

She went into the kitchen.

Vickie was alone in the room, gazing out the doorway. "Look," she said.

Outside, in the garden, Ellen shuffled along the brick path.

At her side was Jane Nolan, nodding as Ellen pointed to one plant, than another. Jane was like a small, swift bird, alert to every move her companion made. Ellen halted and frowned at something near her feet. She bent down to pick it up—a garden claw. Now she turned it around in her hands, as though searching for some clue to its purpose.

"Now what did you find there?" asked Jane.

Ellen held up the claw. "This thing. A brush." At once Ellen seemed to know that was the wrong word and she shook her head. "No, it's not a brush. It's—you know—you know."

"For the flowers, right?" prompted Jane. "A claw, to loosen up the dirt."

"Yes." Ellen beamed. "A claw."

"Let's put it in a safe place, where it won't get lost. And you won't accidentally step on it." Jane took the claw and set it in the wheelbarrow. She looked up and, seeing Toby, smiled and waved. Then she took Ellen's arm, and the two of them continued along the path and vanished around the corner of the house.

Toby felt an invisible burden seem to tumble from her shoulders. She looked at her sister. "What do you think?"

"Her résumé looks good. And she has excellent references from three different nursing homes. We'll have to go up on the hourly rate, since she's an LPN. But I'd say she's worth it."

"Mom seems to like her. That's the most important thing."

Vickie gave a sigh of satisfaction. Mission accomplished. Vickie the efficient. "There," she said, shutting the back door. "That wasn't so hard."

Another day, another dollar. Another corpse.

Daniel Dvorak stepped back from the autopsy table and stripped off his gloves. "There you have it, Roy. Penetrating wound to the left upper quadrant, laceration of the spleen resulting in massive hemorrhage. Definitely not natural causes. No surprises." He tossed the gloves into the contaminated rubbish bin and looked at Detective Sheehan.

Sheehan was still standing by the table, but his gaze wasn't on the hollowed-out body cavity. No, Sheehan was making moo eyes at Dvorak's assistant, Lisa. How romantic. Romeo and Juliet meeting over a corpse.

Dvorak shook his head and went to wash his hands in the sink. In the mirror he glimpsed the progress of the incipient romance. Detective Sheehan standing a little straighter, tucking in his gut. Lisa laughing, flicking back her blond bangs. Even in the autopsy room, nature will have its way.

Even when one of the parties is a married, middle-aged, overweight cop.

If Sheehan wants to play lover boy to a pair of blue eyes, it's none of my business, thought Dvorak as he calmly dried off his hands. But I should warn him he's not the first cop whose hormones got tweaked down here. Autopsies had become surprisingly popular events lately, and it wasn't because of the corpses.

"I'll be in my office," Dvorak said, and he walked out of the lab.

Twenty minutes later Sheehan knocked at Dvorak's office door and came in, wearing the sheepishly happy face of a man who's been acting foolish, knows it, knows everyone else knows it, but doesn't care.

Dvorak decided he didn't care, either. He went to his file cabinet, took out a folder, and handed it to Sheehan. "There's that final tox report you wanted. You need anything else?"

"Uh, yeah. The prelim on that baby."

"Consistent with SIDS."

Sheehan pulled out a cigarette and lit up. "That's what I thought."

"Mind putting that out?"

"Huh?"

"It's a smoke-free building."

"Your office too?"

"The smell hangs around."

Sheehan laughed. "In your line of work, Doc, you can hardly complain about smells." But he put out the cigarette, crushing it on the coffee saucer that Dvorak slid across to him. "You know, that Lisa's a nice girl."

Dvorak said nothing, figuring that silence was safer.

"She got a boyfriend?" asked Sheehan.

"I wouldn't know."

"You mean you never asked?"

"No."

"Not even curious?"

"I'm curious about a lot of things. But that's not one of them." Dvorak paused. "By the way, how're the wife and kids?"

A pause. "They're fine."

"So things're good at home?"

"Yeah. Sure."

Dvorak nodded gravely. "Then you're a lucky man."

Face reddening, Sheehan stared down at the tox report. Cops see too much death, thought Dvorak, and they run around grabbing at all the highs in life they can get. Sheehan was struggling, a smart guy, a basically decent guy, dealing with the first glimpse of middle age in his mirror.

Lisa chose that moment to walk into the office, carrying two trays of microscope slides. She flashed Sheehan a smile and seemed taken aback when he simply looked away.

"Which slides are these?" asked Dvorak.

"Top tray's liver and lung sections from Joseph Odette. Bottom tray has brain sections from Parmenter." Lisa stole another glance at Sheehan, then pulled her dignity back together again. In a businesslike tone she said: "You just wanted H and E and PAS stains on the brain, right?"

"Did you do Congo-Red?"

"That's in there too. Just in case." She turned and walked out, pride intact.

After a moment, Sheehan left as well, a temporarily chastened Romeo.

Dvorak brought the trays of new slides back to the lab and turned on his microscope. The first slide was of Joey Odette's lung. Smoker, he thought, focusing on the alveoli. No surprise; he'd already recognized the emphysematous changes at autopsy. He flipped through a few more lung sections, then moved onto the liver slides. Cirrhosis and fatty infiltration. A boozer, too. Had Joey Odette not shot himself in the head, either his liver or his lungs would have failed him eventually. There are many ways to commit suicide.

He dictated his findings, then set aside the Odette slides and reached for the next tray.

The first slide of Angus Parmenter's brain appeared through the lens. The microscopic exam of brain sections was a routine part of the autopsy. This slide showed a section of cerebral cortex, stained a hot pink with periodic-acid-Schiff. He focused, and the field came sharply into view. For a full ten seconds he stared through the eyepiece, trying to make sense of what he was seeing.

Artifact, he thought. That must be the problem. A distortion of tissue from the fixing or staining process.

He took out the slide and put in another. Again he focused.

Again, everything looked all wrong. Instead of a uniform field of neuronal tissue stippled with occasional purple nuclei, this looked like pink and white froth. There were vacuoles everywhere, as though the brain matter had been eaten away by microsopic moths.

Slowly he lifted his head from the eyepieces. Then he looked down at his finger—the finger he'd cut with the scalpel. The laceration was healed now, but he could still see the fine line on the skin, where the wound had recently closed. *I was working with the brain when it happened. I've been exposed.*

The diagnosis would have to be confirmed. A neuropathologist consulted, electron microscopy performed, the clinical record reviewed. He should not be planning his own funeral quite yet.

His hands were sweating. He turned off the microscope and released a deep breath. Then he picked up the telephone.

It took his secretary only a moment to locate Toby Harper's number in Newton. The phone rang six times before it was answered by an irritated "Hello?"

"Dr. Harper? This is Dan Dvorak at the ME's office. Is this a good time to talk?"

"I've been trying to reach you all week."

"I know," he admitted. And could think of no excuse to give her.

"Do you have a diagnosis on Mr. Parmenter?" she asked.

"That's why I'm calling. I need some more medical history from you."

"You have his hospital record, don't you?"

"Yes, but I wanted to talk to you about what you saw in the ER. I'm still trying to interpret the histology. What I need is a better clinical picture."

Over the line, he heard what sounded like water running from a faucet, and then Toby called out: "No, turn it off! Turn it off, the water's getting all over the floor!" The phone clattered down and there were running footsteps. She came back on the line. "Look, this isn't a good time for me right now. Can we discuss this in person?"

He hesitated. "I suppose that's a better idea. This afternoon?"

"Well, it's my night off, but I have to make arrangements for a sitter. What time do you leave work?"

"I'll stay as late as I need to."

"Okay, I'll try to get there by six. Where are you located?"

"Seven twenty Albany Street, across from City Hospital. It'll be after hours, so the front door will be locked. Park around in back."

"I'm still not sure what this is all about, Dr. Dvorak."

"You'll understand," he said. "After you see the slides."

10

It was nearly six-thirty when Toby pulled into the parking lot behind the two-story brick building at 720 Albany Street. She drove past three identical vans, each labeled on the side with COMMONWEALTH OF MASSACHUSETTS, CHIEF MEDICAL EXAMINER, and she parked in a stall near the building's rear door. The rain, which had threatened all day, was finally beginning to fall in a gentle sprinkling that silvered the gloom. It was late October, and darkness fell so early these days; already she missed the long warm twilights of summer. The building looked like a crypt walled in by red brick.

She stepped out of the car and walked across the lot, head bent under the rain. Just as she reached the rear entrance, the door swung open. Her head snapped up in surprise.

A man was standing in the doorway, his tall frame silhouetted against the hall light. "Dr. Harper?"

"Yes."

"I'm Dan Dvorak. They usually lock the doors by six, so I was watching for your arrival. Come in."

She stepped into the building and wiped the rain from her eyes. Blinking against the light, she focused on Dvorak's face, reconciling the mental image she'd formed from his telephone voice with the imposing man who stood before her. He was about as old as she'd expected, in his midforties, his black hair generously streaked with silver and tousled, as though he'd been nervously running his fingers through it. His eyes, an intense blue, were so deeply set they seemed to gaze at her from dark hollows. Though he did manage a small smile, she sensed it was forced; it flickered only briefly but attractively across his lips, and then was gone, replaced by an expression she could not quite fathom. Anxiety, perhaps. Worry.

"Most everyone's gone home for the day," he said. "So it really is as quiet as a morgue in here right now."

"I tried to get here as soon as I could, but I had to make arrangements with the sitter."

"You have children, then?"

"No, the sitter's for my mother. I don't like to leave her alone."

They took the stairs up, Dvorak slightly in the lead, white lab coat flapping at long legs. "I'm sorry to ask you here on such short notice."

"You've been refusing all my calls, and then suddenly you *have* to talk to me tonight. Why?"

"I need your clinical opinion."

"I'm not a pathologist. You're the one who did the autopsy."

"But you examined him while he was still alive."

He pushed through the stairwell door onto the second floor and started up the hall, moving with such nervous energy that Toby had to trot to keep up.

"There was a neurologist consulting on the case," she said. "Did you talk to him?"

"He didn't perform his exam until after the patient became comatose. By then there were few signs and symptoms to go on. Other than coma."

"What about Wallenberg? He was the attending physician."

"Wallenberg maintains it was a stroke."

"Well, was it?"

"No." He opened a door and flipped on the wall switch. It was an office furnished with a utilitarian steel desk, chairs, and a filing cabinet. The office of a thoroughly organized man, thought Toby, looking at the neatly stacked papers, at the textbooks lined up on the shelf. The only personal touch to the office was an obviously neglected fern perched on the filing cabinet, and a photo on the desk. A teenage boy, shaggy-haired and squinting into the sunlight as he held up a prize trout. The boy's face was a clone of Dvorak's. She sat down in a chair by the desk.

"Would you like some coffee?" he asked.

"I'd rather have some information. What, exactly, *did* you find on autopsy?"

"On gross exam, nothing."

"No evidence of a stroke?"

"Neither thrombotic nor hemorrhagic."

"What about the heart? The coronaries?"

"Patent. In fact, I've never seen such a clean left anterior descending artery in a man his age. No evidence of infarction, fresh or otherwise. It wasn't a cardiac death." He sat down behind the desk, his gaze so intense on hers she had to force herself to maintain eye contact.

"Toxicology?"

"It's been only a week. The preliminary screen shows diazepam and Dilantin. Both were given in the hospital to treat seizures." He leaned forward. "Why did you insist on the autopsy?"

"I told you. He was the second patient I'd seen with that presentation of symptoms. I wanted a diagnosis."

"Tell me the symptoms again. Everything you remember."

She found it difficult to concentrate while those blue eyes were so intently focused on her face. She sat back, shifting her gaze to the stack of papers on his desk. She cleared her throat. "Confusion," she said. "They both came into the ER disoriented to time and place."

"Tell me first about Mr. Parmenter."

She nodded. "The ambulance brought him in after his daughter found him stumbling around at home. He didn't recognize her or his own granddaughters. From what I gathered, he was having visual hallucinations. Thought he could fly. When I examined him, I didn't find any evidence of trauma. Neurologically, the only localizing sign seemed to be an abnormal finger-to-nose test. I thought at first it might be a cerebellar stroke. But there were other symptoms I couldn't explain."

"Such as?"

"He seemed to have some visual distortion. He had trouble judging how far away I was standing." She paused, frowning. "Oh. That explains the midgets."

"Excuse me?"

"He complained about midgets being in his house. I guess he was referring to his granddaughters. They're about ten years old."

"Okay, so he had distorted vision and cerebellar signs."

"And there were seizures."

"Yes, I saw you mentioned them in your ER notes." He reached for a folder on his desk and opened it. She saw it was a photocopy of the patient's Springer Hospital record. "You described a focal seizure of the right upper extremity."

"The seizures recurred on and off during his hospitalization, despite anticonvulsants. That's what the nurses told me."

He flipped through the chart. "Wallenberg hardly mentions them. But I do see an order sheet here, for Dilantin. Which he signed." He looked up at her. "Obviously, you're correct about the seizures."

Why wouldn't I be? she thought with sudden irritation. Now she was the one who leaned forward. "Why don't you just tell me which diagnosis you're fishing for?"

"I don't want to influence your memory of the case. I need your unbiased recollection."

"Being straight with me would save us both a lot of time."

"Are you pressed for time?"

"This is my night off, Dr. Dvorak. I could be home doing other things right now."

He regarded her for a moment in silence. Then he sat back and released a heavy sigh. "Look, I'm sorry for being evasive, but this has shaken me up quite a bit."

"Why?"

"I think we're dealing with an infectious agent."

"Bacterial? Viral?"

"Neither."

She frowned at him. "What else is there? Are we talking parasites?"

He rose to his feet. "Why don't you come down to the lab? I'll show you the slides."

They rode the elevator to the basement and stepped out into a deserted hallway. It was after seven now. She knew there had to be someone else on duty in the morgue, but at that moment, walking along the silent corridor, it seemed that she and Dvorak were utterly alone in the building. He led her through a doorway and flipped on the wall switch.

Fluorescent panels flickered on, the harsh light reflecting off gleaming surfaces. She saw a refrigerator, stainless steel sinks, a countertop with quantitative analysis equipment and a computer terminal. Lined up on a shelf were jars of human organs, suspended in preservative. The faint tang of Formalin hung in the air.

He crossed to one of the microscopes and flipped on the switch. It had a teaching eyepiece; they could both examine the field at the same time. He put a slide under the lens and sat down while he focused. "Take a look."

She pulled up a stool. Bending her head close to his, she peered into the twin eyepiece. What she saw looked like white bubbles in a sea of pink.

"It's been a long time since I took histology," she admitted. "Give me a hint."

"Okay. Can you identify the tissue we're looking at?"

She flushed with embarrassment. If only she *could* rattle off the answer. Instead she was painfully aware of her ignorance. And of the silence stretching between them. With her face pressed to the eyepiece, she said: "I hate to admit it, but no, I can't identify this."

"It's no reflection on your training, Dr. Harper. This slide is so abnormal the tissue *is* hard to recognize. What we're looking at is a slide of Angus Parmenter's cerebral cortex, PAS stained. The pink is background neuropil, with the nuclei stained purple."

"What are all those vacuoles?"

"That was exactly my question. Normal cortex doesn't have all those tiny holes."

"Weird. It looks like my pink kitchen sponge."

He didn't respond. Puzzled, she raised her head and saw that he was looking at her. "Dr. Dvorak?"

"You saw it right away," he murmured.

"What?"

"That's exactly what it looks like. *A pink sponge.*" He sat back and rubbed his hand over his eyes. Under the harsh lab lights, she saw the lines of fatigue in his face, the shadow of dark beard. "I think we're dealing with a spongiform encephalopathy," he said.

"You mean like Creutzfeldt-Jakob disease?"

He nodded. "It would account for the pathologic changes

on the slide. As well as the clinical picture. The mental deterioration. Visual distortion. Myoclonic jerks."

"So they weren't focal seizures?"

"No. I think what you saw was startle myoclonus. Violently repetitive spasms, set off by a loud noise. It can't be controlled with Dilantin."

"Isn't Creutzfeldt-Jakob extremely rare?"

"One in a million. It tends to strike the elderly on a sporadic basis."

"But there *are* clusters of cases. Last year, in England—"

"You're thinking of mad cow disease. That seems to be a variant of Creutzfeldt-Jakob. Maybe it's the same disease, we're not really sure. The English victims got infected by eating beef with the bovine spongiform strain. That was a rare outbreak, and it hasn't been seen since."

Her gaze shifted back to the microscope. Softly she said, "Is it possible we have a cluster *here?* Angus Parmenter wasn't the first patient I saw with those symptoms. Harry Slotkin was. He came in weeks before Parmenter did, with the same presentation. Confusion, visual distortion."

"Those are nonspecific signs. You'd need an autopsy to confirm it."

"That's not possible with Mr. Slotkin. He's still missing."

"Then there's no way to make the diagnosis."

"They both lived in the same residential complex. They could've been exposed to the same pathogen."

"You don't catch CJD the way you catch the common cold. It's transmitted by a prion. An abnormal cellular protein. It requires direct tissue exposure. A corneal transplant, for instance."

"Those people in England caught it from eating beef. Couldn't it happen here? They could have shared a meal—"

"The American herd is clean. We don't have mad cow disease."

"How do we know that for certain?" She was intrigued

171

now, feverishly pursuing this new line of thought. She remembered that night in the ER, when Harry had come in. Recalled the clang of the steel basin crashing to the floor, and then the sound of Harry's leg rubbing against the gurney. "We have two men from the same housing complex. Presenting with the same symptoms."

"Confusion isn't specific enough."

"Harry Slotkin had what I *thought* were focal seizures. Now I realize it might have been startle myoclonus."

"I need a body to autopsy. I can't diagnose Harry Slotkin without brain tissue."

"Well, how certain are you of Angus Parmenter's diagnosis?"

"I've sent the slides to a neuropathologist for confirmation. He'll examine the sections under electron microscopy. The results may take a few days." Quietly he added: "I'm just hoping I'm wrong."

She studied him and realized she was seeing more than weariness in his face. What she saw was fear.

"I cut myself," he said. "During the autopsy. While I was removing the brain." He shook his head, gave a strangely ironic laugh. "I've cut open a thousand skulls. Worked on bodies with HIV, hepatitis, even rabies. But I've never cut myself. Then I get Angus Parmenter on the table, and it looks like natural causes. A weeklong hospital stay, no evidence of infection. And what do I do? I cut my finger. While I'm working on the goddamn *brain*."

"The diagnosis isn't confirmed. It could be artifact. Maybe the slides weren't prepared correctly."

"That's what I keep hoping." He stared at the microscope, as though regarding his mortal enemy. "I had my hands around the brain. I couldn't have chosen a worse time to nick myself."

"It doesn't mean you're infected. Your chances of actually getting the disease have to be extremely small."

172

"But still there. The chance is still there." He looked at her, and she couldn't contradict him. Nor could she offer any false reassurance. Silence, at least, was honest.

He turned off the microscope lamp. "It has a long incubation period. So it will be a year, two years until I know. Even at five years, I'll still be wondering. Waiting for the first signs. At least it's a relatively painless end. You start with dementia. Visual distortion, maybe hallucinations. Then you progress to delirium. And finally you slip into a coma . . ." He gave a weary shrug. "I guess it beats dying of cancer."

"I'm sorry," she murmured. "I feel responsible . . ."

"Why?"

"I insisted on the autopsy. I put you in a hazardous position."

"I put myself in that position. We both do, Dr. Harper. It comes with the job. You work in the ER, someone coughs on you, you catch TB. Or you stick yourself with a needle and you get hepatitis or AIDS." He removed the slide and set it in a tray. Then he pulled a plastic cover over the microscope. "There are hazards to every job, just like there are hazards to getting up in the morning. Driving to work, walking to the mailbox. Boarding a plane." He looked at her. "The surprise isn't that we die. The surprise is how and when we die."

"There could be some way to stop the infection at this stage. Maybe a shot of immunoglobulin—"

"Doesn't work. I checked the literature."

"Have you discussed it with your doctor?"

"I haven't mentioned this to anyone yet."

"Not even your family?"

"There's just my son, Patrick, and he's only fourteen. At that age, he's got enough things to worry about."

She remembered the photo on the desk, the shaggy-haired boy holding up his prize trout. Dvorak was right; a boy of fourteen was too young to be confronted with a parent's mortality.

"So what are you going to do?" she asked.

"Make sure my life insurance is paid up. And hope for the best." He stood up and reached for the light switch. "There's nothing more I can do."

Robbie Brace answered the door wearing a Red Sox T-shirt and ratty sweatpants. "Dr. Harper," he said. "You got here quick."

"Thanks for seeing me."

"Yeah, well, you're not exactly catching us at our finest hour. Bedtime, you know. Lots of whining and bargaining going on."

Toby stepped in the front door. Somewhere upstairs, a child was screaming. Not a distressed scream, but an angry one, accompanied by the sound of stamping feet and the crash of something hard hitting the floor.

"We are three years old and learning the meaning of power," explained Brace. "Man, don't you just love parenthood?" He latched the front door and led her up a hallway, toward the living room. Once again she was impressed by how big he was, his arms so muscular they could not hang straight from his shoulders. She sat down on a couch, and he settled into a well-worn recliner.

Upstairs the screaming continued, hoarser and punctuated by loud, dramatic snuffles. There was also a woman's voice speaking, calm but determined.

"It's the clash of the titans," said Brace, glancing upward. "My wife, she stands a lot tougher than I do. Me, I just roll over and play dead." He looked at Toby and his smile faded. "So what's this about Angus Parmenter?"

"I've just come from the ME's office. They have a preliminary diagnosis: Creutzfeldt-Jakob disease."

Brace gave an amazed shake of his head. "Are they sure?"

"It still needs confirmation by a neuropathologist. But the

symptoms do match the diagnosis. Not just for Parmenter. For Harry Slotkin as well."

"Two cases of CJD? That's sort of like having lightning strike twice. How could you possibly confirm it?"

"Okay, we can't confirm Harry's case because there's no body. But what if two residents from Brant Hill did have CJD? It makes you wonder if there's a common source of infection." She leaned forward. "You told me Harry had a clean bill of health on his outpatient record."

"That's right."

"Did he have any surgery in the past five years? A corneal transplant, for instance?"

"I don't remember seeing anything like that in the record. I guess you could catch CJD that way."

"It's been reported." She paused. "There's another way it can be transmitted. By injections of human growth hormone."

"So?"

"You told me Brant Hill's doing studies on hormone injections in the elderly. You said your patients have shown improvement in muscle mass and strength. Is it possible you're injecting tainted growth hormone?"

"Growth hormone doesn't come from cadaver brains anymore. It's manufactured."

"What if Brant Hill is using an old supply? Growth hormone infected with CJD?"

"The old growth hormone's been off the market for a long time. And Wallenberg's been using this protocol for years, ever since he was at the Rosslyn Institute. I've never heard of a case of CJD in any of his patients."

"I'm not familiar with the Rosslyn Institute. What is that?"

"Center for geriatric research, in Connecticut. Wallenberg worked as a research fellow there for a few years, before he came to Brant Hill. Check out the geriatric literature—you'll find a number of studies originating at Rosslyn. And half a dozen papers with Wallenberg's name as author. He's the guru of hormone replacement."

"I didn't know that."

"You'd have to be in geriatrics to know that." He rose from the chair, disappeared into an adjoining room, and came back out with some papers, which he set down on the coffee table in front of Toby. On top was a photocopied article from *Journal of the American Geriatrics Society*, 1992. There were three authors listed, and the first name was Wallenberg's. The title of the article was: "Beyond the Hayflick Limit: Extending Longevity at the Cellular Level."

"It's research at its most basic," said Brace. "Taking a cell's maximum life span—the Hayflick Limit—and trying to prolong it with hormonal manipulation. If you accept the idea that our senescence and death is a cellular process, then you want to work toward prolonging cell life."

"But a certain amount of cell death is necessary for health."

"Sure. We shed dead cells all the time, in our mucous membranes and our skin. But we regenerate those. What we don't regenerate are cells like bone marrow and brain and other vital organs. They grow old and die. And we die as a result."

"And with this hormonal manipulation?"

"That's the point of the study. Which hormones—or combination of hormones—prolong cell life span? Wallenberg's been researching this since 1990. And he's finding some promising results."

She looked up at him. "That old man in the nursing home—the one who put up such a good fight?"

Brace nodded. "He probably has the muscle mass and strength of a much younger man. Unfortunately, Alzheimer's has messed up his brain. Hormones can't help that."

"Which hormones are we talking about? You mentioned a combination."

"The accepted research shows promise for growth hormone, DHEA, melatonin, and testosterone. I think Wallenberg's current protocol involves various proportions of those hormones, plus maybe a few others."

"You're not certain?"

"I'm not involved with the protocol. I take care of only their nursing home patients. Hey, it's all pie in the sky right now. No one knows what works. All we know is, our pituitaries stop producing certain hormones as we get older. Maybe the fountain of youth is some pituitary hormone we haven't discovered yet."

"So Wallenberg's giving replacement injections." She laughed. "Literally a shot in the dark."

"It might work. Seems to me Brant Hill's got some pretty healthy-looking eighty-year-olds zipping around on that golf course."

"They're also wealthy, they exercise, and they live a carefree life."

"Yeah, well, who knows? Maybe the best predictor of longevity is a healthy bank account."

Toby flipped through the research article, then lay it on the coffee table. Once again she looked at the publication date. "He's been doing hormone injections since 1990, with no recorded case of CJD?"

"The protocol ran four years at Rosslyn. Then he came to Brant Hill and resumed the studies."

"Why did he leave Rosslyn?"

Brace laughed. "Why do you suppose?"

"Money."

"Hey, it's the reason I came to Brant Hill. Nice paycheck, no hassles with insurance companies. And patients who actually listen to my advice." He paused. "In Wallenberg's case, I hear there were other things going on. Last geriatrics conference I attended, there was some gossip circulating.

177

About Wallenberg and a female research associate at Rosslyn."

"Oh. If it's not money, it's sex."

"What else is there?"

She thought of Carl Wallenberg in his tuxedo, the young lion with amber eyes, and she could easily imagine him being the object of female desire. "So he had an affair with a research associate," she said. "That's not particularly shocking."

"It is if there are three people involved."

"Wallenberg, the woman, and who else?"

"Another M.D. at Rosslyn, a man. I understand things got pretty tense between them, and all three of them resigned. Wallenberg came to Brant Hill and resumed his research. Anyway, that makes it a full six years he's been injecting hormones, with no catastrophic side effects."

"And no cases of CJD."

"None reported. Try again, Dr. Harper."

"Okay, let's look at other ways these two men might've gotten infected. A surgical procedure. Something relatively minor, like a corneal transplant. You might have overlooked that history in their outpatient charts."

Brace made an exasperated sound. "Why are you hung up on this, anyway? Patients die on me all the time, and I don't obsess over it."

Sighing, she sank back on the couch. "I know it doesn't change things. I know Harry's probably dead. But if he *did* have Creutzfeldt-Jakob, then he was already dying when I saw him. And nothing I did could have saved him." She looked at Brace. "Maybe I wouldn't feel so responsible for his death."

"So it's guilt, is it?"

She nodded. "And a certain amount of self-interest. The lawyer representing Harry's son is already taking depositions from the ER staff. I don't think there's any way I *can* avoid a lawsuit. But if I could prove Harry already *had* a fatal illness when I saw him—"

"Then the damages wouldn't seem so severe in court."

She nodded. And felt ashamed. *Your dad was already dying, Mr. Slotkin. What's the big deal?*

"We don't know Harry's dead," said Brace.

"He's been missing for a month. What else would he be? It's just a matter of finding his body."

Upstairs, the crying had stopped, the battle finally won. The silence only accentuated their uneasy lapse in conversation. Footsteps creaked down the stairs, and a woman appeared. She was a redhead, so fair-skinned her face seemed translucent in the glow of the living room lamp.

"My wife, Greta," said Brace. "And this is Dr. Toby Harper. Toby just dropped by for some shop talk."

"I'm sorry about all the screaming," said Greta. "It's our daily tantrum. Tell me again, Robbie. Why *did* we have a kid?"

"To pass on the gift of our superior DNA. Trouble is, babe, she got *your* temper."

Greta sat down on the armrest next to her husband. "That's called *determination.* Not temper."

"Yeah, well, whatever you call it, it's hard on the ears." He patted his wife on the knee. "Toby's an ER doc over at Springer Hospital. She's the one who stitched up my face."

"Oh." Greta nodded in appreciation. "You did a very nice job. He'll hardly have a scar." She suddenly frowned at the coffee table. "Robbie, I hope you offered our guest something to drink. Shall I put on some tea?"

"No, babe, that's all right," said Robbie. "We're all finished here."

I guess that's my signal to leave, thought Toby. Reluctantly she stood up.

So did Robbie. He gave his wife a quick kiss and said, "This won't take long. I'm just running over to the clinic."

Then he turned to Toby, who was looking at him in surprise. "You want to see those outpatient records, don't you?" he asked.

"Yes. Of course."

"Then I'll meet you there. Brant Hill."

11

"I knew you were gonna keep bugging me about this," said Robbie as he unlocked the front door to the Brant Hill Clinic building. "*Check this out, check that out.* Man, I figured I'd just let you see the damn charts for yourself, so you'd know I wasn't holding out on you." They walked into the building and the front door slammed shut behind them, setting off echoes down the empty hallway. He turned right, and unlocked a door labeled: MEDICAL RECORDS.

Toby flipped on the lights and blinked in surprise at six aisles of filing cabinets. "Alphabetical?" she asked.

"Yeah. *A*s are that way, *Z*s the other way. I'll find Slotkin's chart, you find Parmenter."

Toby headed toward the *P*s. "I can't believe how many records you have. Does Brant Hill really have this many patients?"

"No. This is central records storage for all of Orcutt Health's nursing homes."

"Is that like a conglomerate?"

"Yeah. We're their flagship facility."

"So how many nursing homes do they run?"

"A dozen, I think. We all share billing and referral services."

Toby found the cabinet for the *P*s and thumbed through the charts. "I can't find it," she said.

"I found Slotkin's."

"Well where's Parmenter?"

Brace reappeared in her aisle. "Oh, I forgot. He's deceased, so they probably moved that file to the inactives." He walked to a set of cabinets at the back of the room. A moment later he closed the drawer. "Must've been culled. I can't find it. Why don't you just concentrate on Harry's chart? Look it over to your heart's content and prove to yourself I haven't missed anything."

She sat down at an empty desk and opened Harry Slotkin's file. It was organized in a problem-oriented format, with Current Illnesses listed on the first page. She saw nothing surprising here: benign prostatic hypertrophy. Chronic back pain. Mild hearing loss secondary to otosclerosis. All the expected ravages of old age.

She flipped to the past medical history. Again, it was a typical list: Appendectomy, age thirty-five. Transurethral resection of the prostate, age sixty-eight. Cataract surgery, age seventy. Harry Slotkin had been, for the most part, a healthy man.

She turned to the clinic visits record, which contained the doctors' notes. Most were routine checkups, signed by Dr. Wallenberg, with an occasional subspecialist note by Dr. Bartell, a urologist. Toby turned the pages until she paused over an entry dated two years before. She could barely decipher the doctor's name.

"Who wrote this?" she asked. "The signature looks like a *Y* something."

Brace squinted at the illegible handwriting. "Beats me."

"You don't recognize the name?"

He shook his head. "Occasionally we get outside docs coming in for specialty clinics. What's the visit for?"

"I think it says 'deviated nasal septum.' Must be ENT."

"There's an ENT specialist named Greeley here in Newton. That signature must be a *G*, not a *Y*."

She knew the name. Greeley occasionally consulted in the Springer ER.

She turned to the lab section, where Harry's most recent blood counts and chemistries were recorded on a computer printout. All were in the normal ranges.

"Pretty good hemoglobin for a guy his age," she noted. "Fifteen's better than mine." She turned to the next page and paused, frowning at a printout with the letterhead: *Newton Diagnostics.* "Wow, you guys don't believe in cost control, do you? Look at all these labs. Radioimmunoassays for thyroid hormone, growth hormone, prolactin, melatonin, ACTH. The list goes on and on." She flipped to the next page. "And on. The panel was done a year ago, and three months ago as well. Some lab in Newton is raking it in."

"That's the panel Wallenberg orders on all his hormone-injection patients."

"But the hormone protocol's not mentioned anywhere in this chart."

Brace fell silent for a moment. "It does seem strange, doesn't it? To be ordering all these tests if Harry wasn't on the protocol."

"Maybe Brant Hill's padding the pockets of Newton Diagnostics. This patient's endocrine panel probably cost a few thousand dollars."

"Did Wallenberg order it?"

"Doesn't say on the lab report."

"Look at the order sheets. Cross-check the dates."

She flipped to the section labeled: Physician's Orders. The sheets were carbon copies of the doctors' handwritten orders, each signed and dated.

"Okay, the first endocrine panel was ordered by Wallenberg. The second panel was ordered by that guy with the bad handwriting. Dr. Greeley—if that's who this is."

"Why would an ENT order an endocrine panel?"

She scanned the rest of the order sheets. "Here's that signature again, dated almost two years ago. He ordered preop Valium and six A.M. van transport to Howarth Surgical Associates in Wellesley."

"Preop for what?"

"I think this says 'Deviated nasal septum.'" Sighing, she closed the chart. "That wasn't very helpful, was it?"

"So can we get out of here? Greta's probably getting pissed at me about now."

Ruefully she handed back the chart. "Sorry for dragging you out here tonight."

"Yeah, well, I can't believe I went along with it. You don't really need to look at Parmenter's record, do you?"

"If you can find it for me."

He stuffed Harry Slotkin's chart in the cabinet and slid the drawer shut with a bang. "To tell you the truth, Harper, it's not high on my list of priorities."

A light was burning in the living room. As Toby pulled into the driveway next to Jane Nolan's Saab, she saw the warm glow through the curtains, saw the silhouette of a woman standing in the window. It was a reassuring sight, that vigilant figure peering out at the darkness. It told her someone was home, someone was keeping watch.

Toby let herself in the front door and walked into the living room. "I'm back."

Jane Nolan had turned from the window to gather up her

magazines. On the sofa, a *National Enquirer* lay open to a spread on "Shocking Psychic Predictions." Quickly Jane scooped it up and turned to Toby with an embarrassed smile. "My intellectual stimulation for the night. I know I'm supposed to be improving my mind with serious reading. But honestly"—she held up the tabloid—"I can't resist anything with Daniel Day-Lewis on the cover."

"Neither can I," admitted Toby. They both laughed, a comfortable acknowledgment that among women, some fantasies are universal.

"How did the evening go?" asked Toby.

"Very well." Jane turned and quickly straightened the sofa cushions. "We had dinner at seven, and she pretty much devoured everything. Then I gave her a bubble bath. I guess I shouldn't have, though," she added ruefully.

"Why? What happened?"

"She had such a good time she refused to get out. I had to drain the tub first."

"I don't think I've ever given Mom a bubble bath."

"Oh, it's really funny to watch! She puts the foam on her head and blows it all over. You should've seen the mess on the floor. It's like watching a kid play. Which, in a way, she is."

Toby sighed. "And the kid is getting younger every day."

"But she's such a *nice* kid. I've worked with so many Alzheimer's patients who aren't nice. Who just get *mean* as they get older. I don't think your mother will."

"No, she won't." Toby smiled. "She never was."

Jane picked up the rest of her magazines, and Daniel Day-Lewis disappeared into her backpack. There was a *Modern Bride* in the stack as well. The magazine of dreamers, thought Toby. According to Jane's résumé, she was single. At thirty-five, Jane seemed like so many other women Toby knew, unattached but hopeful. Anxious but not yet desperate. Women for whom images of dark-haired movie idols would have to suffice until a flesh-and-blood man came into their lives. If one appeared at all.

They walked to the front door.

"So you think everything went well," said Toby.

"Oh, yes. Ellen and I will get along just fine." Jane opened the door and stopped. "I almost forgot. Your sister called. And there was a call from some man at the ME's office. He said he'd call back."

"Dr. Dvorak? Did he say what he wanted?"

"No. I told him you'd be home later." She smiled and gave a wave. "Good night."

Toby latched the front door and went to the bedroom to call her sister.

"I thought it was your night off," said Vickie.

"It is."

"I was surprised when Jane answered."

"I asked her to watch Mom for a few hours. You know, I *do* enjoy having one night out every six months."

Vickie sighed. "You're pissed at me again. Aren't you?"

"No, I'm not."

"Yes you are. Toby, I *know* you're getting stuck with Mom. I know it doesn't seem fair. But what am I supposed to do? I've got these kids driving me crazy. I have a job, and I still end up with most of the housework. I feel like I'm barely treading water."

"Vickie, is this a contest? Who's suffering the most?"

"You have no idea what it's like trying to deal with kids."

"No, I guess I don't."

There was a long pause. And Toby thought: *I have no idea because I never got the chance.* But she couldn't blame that on Vickie. It was ambition that had kept Toby focused so squarely on her career. Four years of medical school, three years of residency. There'd been no time for romance. And then Ellen's memory had deteriorated, and Toby had gradually assumed responsibility for her mother's affairs. It had not been planned. It was not a path she'd deliberately chosen. It was simply the way her life had turned out.

She had no right to be angry at her sister.

"Look, can you come for dinner on Sunday?" asked Vickie.

"I'm working that night."

"I can never keep your schedule straight. Is it still four nights on, three nights off?"

"Most of the time. I'll be off Monday and Tuesday next week."

"Oh, God. Neither of those nights will work for us. Monday's open house at school. And Tuesday is Hannah's piano recital."

Toby said nothing, merely waited for Vickie to finish her usual litany of how full her calendar was, how difficult to coordinate the schedules of four different people. Hannah and Gabe were so busy these days, like all kids, filling up every spare moment of their childhoods with music lessons, gymnastics, swimming, computer classes. It was drive them here, drive them there, and by the end of the day, Vickie didn't know which end was up.

"It's all right," Toby finally interrupted. "Why don't we try for another day?"

"I really *did* want you to come over."

"Yes, I know. I'm off the second weekend of November."

"Oh, I'll put that down. First let me make sure it's okay with the troops. I'll call you back next week, okay?"

"Fine. Good night, Vickie." Toby hung up and wearily ran her hand through her hair. *Too busy, too busy. We can't even find the time to mend our bridges.* She went down the hall to her mother's room and peeked in the door.

By the soft glow of the night-light, Toby could see that Ellen was asleep. She looked childlike in her bed, her lips slightly parted, her face smooth and unworried. There were times, like this one, when Toby glimpsed the ghost of the little girl that once was Ellen, when she could picture the child with Ellen's face and Ellen's fears. What became of that child? Did she retreat, to become entombed in all the numbing layers of adulthood? Was she reemerging only now, at the end of life, as those same layers peeled away?

She touched her mother's forehead, brushing aside her tendrils of gray hair. Stirring, Ellen opened her eyes and regarded Toby with a look of confusion.

"It's just me, Mom," said Toby. "Go back to sleep."

"Is the stove turned off?"

"Yes, Mom. And the doors are locked. Good night." She gave Ellen a kiss and left the room.

She decided not to go to bed yet. No sense confusing her circadian rhythm—in another twenty-four hours she'd be back on the night shift. She poured herself a glass of brandy and carried it into the living room. She turned on the stereo and slipped in a Mendelssohn CD. A single violin sang out, pure and mournful. It was Ellen's favorite concerto, and now it was Toby's as well.

At the peak of a crescendo, the phone rang. She turned down the music and reached for the receiver.

It was Dvorak. "I'm sorry to call so late," he said.

"It's all right. I just got home a little while ago." She settled back on the sofa cushions, the brandy glass in hand. "I heard you tried to reach me earlier."

"I spoke to your housekeeper." He paused. In the background, she could hear opera music playing on his end. *Don Giovanni.* Here we are, she thought, two unattached people, each of us sitting at home, keeping company with our stereos. He said, "You were going to check the history on those Brant Hill patients. I was wondering if you'd learned anything more."

"I saw Harry Slotkin's chart. There was no surgical exposure to Creutzfeldt-Jakob."

"And the hormone injections?"

188

"None. I don't think he was on the protocol. At least, it wasn't mentioned in his chart."

"What about Parmenter?"

"We couldn't locate his record. So I don't know about surgical exposure. You might ask Dr. Wallenberg tomorrow."

He said nothing. She realized that *Don Giovanni* was no longer playing, that Dvorak was sitting in silence.

"I wish I could tell you more," she said. "This waiting around for a diagnosis must be awful."

"I've had more enjoyable evenings," he admitted. "I've discovered that life insurance policies make very dull reading."

"Oh, no. That's not how you spent your evening, was it?"

"The bottle of wine helped."

She gave a sympathetic murmur. "Brandy is what I generally recommend after a bad day. In fact, I'm holding a glass of it right now." She paused, and added recklessly: "You know, I'll be awake all night. I always am. You're welcome to come over and have a glass with me."

When he didn't answer right away, she closed her eyes, thinking: *God, why did I say that? Why do I sound so desperate for company?*

"Thank you, but I wouldn't be much fun tonight," he said. "Another time, maybe."

"Yes. Another time. Good night." As she hung up, she thought, *And what was I expecting?* That he'd drive right over, that they'd spend the night together gazing into each other's eyes?

She sighed and restarted the Mendelssohn concerto. As the violin played, she sipped her brandy and counted the hours until dawn.

12

James Bigelow was tired of funerals. He had attended so many of them in the last few years, and lately they had become more and more frequent, like an accelerating drumbeat marking the passage of time. That so many of his friends had died was to be expected; at seventy-six years old, he had already outlived most of them. Now death was catching up with him as well. He could sense its stalking footsteps, could envision, quite clearly, his own stiff form lying in the open coffin, face powdered, hair combed, gray woolen suit neatly pressed and buttoned. This very same crowd filing by, silently paying their last respects. The fact it was Angus Parmenter and not Bigelow lying in the coffin was merely a matter of timing. Another month, another year, and it would be his coffin on display in this funeral parlor. The journey comes to an end for all of us.

The line moved forward; so did Bigelow. He came to a

stop beside the coffin and gazed down at his friend. *Even you were not immortal, Angus.*

He moved past, headed up the center aisle, and took a seat in the fourth row. From there he watched the procession of familiar faces from Brant Hill. There was Angus's neighbor Anna Valentine, who had recklessly pursued him with phone calls and casseroles. There were golfing buddies from the club, and couples from the wine-tasting circle, and musicians from the Brant Hill amateur band.

Where was Phil Dorr?

Bigelow scanned the room, looking for Phil, knowing he should be here. Only three days ago, they had shared a few drinks at the club, had spoken in hushed tones about their old poker buddies, Angus and Harry and Stan Mackie. All three of them gone now, and only Phil and Bigelow remaining. A game of poker with just two of them didn't seem worth the effort, Phil had said. He'd been planning to slip a deck of cards into Angus's coffin, a sort of going-away gift for the great poker table in the sky. Would the family mind? he'd wondered. Would they think it undignified to have such a cheap token tucked in with the satin lining? They'd shared a sad laugh about that, another round of tonic water. Hell, Phil had said, he'd do it anyway; Angus would appreciate the gesture.

But Phil had not shown up today with his deck of cards.

Anna Valentine edged into his row and sat down in the chair next to him. Her face was thickly powdered, grotesquely so, every fine wrinkle emphasized by the attempt to camouflage her age. Another hungry widow; he was surrounded by them. Normally he would have avoided striking up a conversation with her, for fear of stirring up mistaken notions of affection in her one-track mind, but at the moment there was no one else close enough to talk to.

Leaning toward her, he murmured: "Where's Phil?"

191

She looked at him, as though surprised he'd spoken to her. "What?"

"Phil Dorr. He was supposed to be here."

"I think he's not feeling well."

"What's wrong with him?"

"I don't know. He begged off the theater trip two nights ago. Said his eyes were bothering him."

"He didn't tell me."

"He only noticed it last week. He was going to see the doctor about it." She gave a deep sigh and gazed straight ahead, at the coffin. "It's terrible, isn't it, how everything's falling apart. Our eyes, our hips, our hearing. I realized today that my voice has changed. I hadn't noticed. I saw the video-tape of our trip to Faneuil Hall, and I couldn't believe how old I sounded. I don't *feel* old, Jimmy. I don't recognize myself in the mirror anymore. . . ." Again she sighed. A tear slid down her cheek, carving a trail through that dusting of face powder. She wiped it away, leaving a chalky smear.

Phil's eyes were bothering him.

Bigelow sat thinking about this as the line of mourners filed past the coffin, as chairs creaked and voices murmured around him: *"Remember when Angus . . ." "Can't believe he's gone . . ." "Said it was some kind of stroke . . ." "No, that's not what I heard . . ."*

Abruptly Bigelow rose to his feet.

"Aren't you staying for the service?" asked Anna.

"I—I have to go talk to someone," he said and squeezed past her, into the aisle. He thought he heard her calling after him, but he didn't glance back; he headed straight out the front door.

He drove first to Phil's cottage, which was only a few houses away from his. The door was locked; no one answered the bell. Bigelow stood on the porch peering in through the window, but all he could see was the foyer with the little cherry wood table and the brass umbrella holder.

192

There was a single shoe lying on the floor—that struck him as odd. Wrong. Phil was so persnickety about orderliness.

Walking back out through the garden gate, he noticed the mailbox was full. That, too, was unlike Phil.

His eyes were bothering him.

Bigelow climbed back in his car and drove the winding half mile to the Brant Hill Clinic. By the time he walked up to the receptionist's window, his palms were sweating, his pulse hammering.

The woman didn't notice he was there—she was too busy yammering on the phone.

He rapped at the window. "I have to see Dr. Wallenberg."

"I'll be right with you," she answered.

He watched with surging frustration as she turned away from him and began typing on the keyboard as she talked on the phone, something about insurance copayments and authorization numbers.

"This is important!" he said. "I have to know what happened to Phil Dorr."

"Sir, I'm on the telephone."

"Phil's sick too, isn't he? He's having trouble with his eyes."

"You'll have to talk to his doctor."

"Then let me see Dr. Wallenberg."

"He's at lunch right now."

"When will he get back? *When?*"

"Sir, you really do have to calm down—"

He reached in through the window and stabbed the disconnect button on her phone. *"I have to see Wallenberg!"*

She pushed her chair back from the window, retreating beyond his reach. Two other women suddenly appeared from the file room. They were all staring at him, at the crazy man ranting in their waiting room.

A door opened and one of the doctors appeared. A big

black man, he towered over Bigelow. His name tag said: ROBERT BRACE, M.D.

"Sir, what seems to be the problem?"

"I have to see Wallenberg."

"He's out of the building at the moment."

"Then *you* tell me what happened to Phil."

"Who?"

"You know! Phil Dorr! They said he's sick—something wrong with his eyes. Is he in the hospital?"

"Sir, why don't you have a seat while the ladies check the files for—"

"I don't want to sit down! I just want to know if he's got the same thing Angus had. The same thing Stan Mackie had."

The front door opened and a woman patient walked in. She froze, stared at Bigelow's flushed face, sensing at once that some crisis was under way.

"Why don't we talk in my office?" said Dr. Brace, his voice low and gentle. He reached out toward Bigelow. "It's just up the hall."

Bigelow gazed at the doctor's broad hand, the surprisingly pale palm across which a lifeline traced thick and black. He looked up at Dr. Brace. "I just want to know," he said softly.

"Know what, sir?"

"Am I going to get sick like the others?"

The doctor shook his head—not an answer to the question, but an expression of bewilderment. "Why would you get sick?"

"They said there was no risk—they said the procedure was safe. But then Mackie got sick, and—"

"Sir, I don't know Mr. Mackie."

Bigelow looked at the receptionist. "You remember Stan Mackie. Tell me you remember Stan."

"Of course, Mr. Bigelow," she answered. "We were so sorry when he passed on."

"Now Phil's gone too, isn't he? I'm the only one left."

"Sir?" It was one of the other clerks, calling through the window. "I just checked Mr. Dorr's chart. He's not sick."

"Why didn't he go to Angus's funeral? He was supposed to be there!"

"Mr. Dorr had to leave town for a family emergency. He asked for his medical records to be transferred to his new doctor in La Jolla."

"What?"

"That's what it says here." She held up the chart, with a note clipped to the cover. "The authorization's dated yesterday. It says 'Patient has moved due to family emergency—will not be returning. Transfer all records to Brant Hill West, La Jolla, California.'"

Bigelow moved to the window and stared at the signature on the authorization: *Carl Wallenberg, M.D.*

"Sir?" It was the doctor, his hand resting on Bigelow's shoulder. "I'm sure you'll be hearing from your friend soon. It sounds like he got called away."

"But how can he have a family emergency?" Bigelow said softly.

"Maybe someone got sick. Someone died."

"Phil doesn't *have* a family."

Dr. Brace was staring at him now. So were the women in the office. He could see them standing behind the glass window, like spectators gazing into a zoo enclosure.

"Something's wrong here," said Bigelow. "You're not telling me, are you?"

"We can talk about it," said the doctor.

"I want to see Dr. Wallenberg."

"He's at lunch. But you can talk to me, Mr.—"

"Bigelow. James Bigelow."

Dr. Brace opened the door to the clinic hallway. "Why don't we go to my office, Mr. Bigelow? You can tell me everything."

195

Bigelow stared at the long white corridor that stretched beyond the doorway. "No," he said, and he backed away. "No, never mind—"

He fled the building.

Robbie Brace knocked on the door and stepped into Carl Wallenberg's office. The room, like the man, showed snooty good taste. Brace wasn't up on fancy furniture brands, but even he could spot quality. The massive desk was made of some warm and exotically reddish wood he didn't recognize. The art hanging on the walls was that fartsy-abstract stuff for which one usually paid a fortune. Through the window, behind Wallenberg's back, was a view of the setting sun. The light glared in, forming a halo around the man's head and shoulders. *Jesus H. Wallenberg,* thought Brace as he stood before the desk.

Wallenberg looked up from his papers. "Yes, Robbie?" *Robbie. Not Dr. Brace. Guess we know who's in charge here.*

Brace said, "Do you remember a patient named Stan Mackie?"

Against the backlight, Wallenberg's expression was unreadable. Slowly he leaned back in his chair, eliciting the rich creak of leather. "How did Stan Mackie's name come up?"

"From one of your patients, James Bigelow. You do know Mr. Bigelow?"

"Yes, of course. He was one of the first patients on my panel here. One of the first to move into Brant Hill."

"Well, Mr. Bigelow was over in the clinic this afternoon, very upset. I'm not sure I got a coherent story out of him. He kept ranting about all his friends getting sick, wondering whether he'd be next. He mentioned Mr. Mackie's name."

"That would be Dr. Mackie."

"He was a physician?"

Wallenberg gestured to a chair. "Why don't you have a

seat, Robbie? It's hard to discuss this with you when you're towering over me."

Brace sat down. He realized at once it was a tactical error; he had lost his advantage of height, and they were facing each other directly across the desk. Now Wallenberg held all the advantages. Seniority. Race. A better tailor.

"What was Mr. Bigelow talking about?" asked Brace. "He seemed terrified of getting sick."

"I haven't the faintest idea."

"He mentioned some sort of procedure that he and his friends had."

Wallenberg shook his head. "Maybe he meant the hormone protocol? The weekly injections?"

"I don't know."

"If he did, he's worrying needlessly. There's nothing revolutionary about our protocol. You know that."

"So Mr. Bigelow and his friends *were* getting hormone injections?"

"Yes. It was one of the reasons they came to Brant Hill. For the benefits of our cutting-edge research."

"Interesting you should use the term *cutting edge*. Mr. Bigelow didn't say anything about injections. He specifically used the term *procedure*. Like some sort of surgery."

"No, no. He hasn't had any surgery. In fact, the only time I recall him needing a surgeon was to get a nasal polyp removed. It was benign, of course."

"Well, what about that hormone protocol, then? Have there been *any* serious side effects?"

"None."

"So there's no chance it caused Angus Parmenter's death?"

"The diagnosis hasn't been determined yet."

"It was Creutzfeldt-Jakob disease. That's what Dr. Harper told me."

Wallenberg went very still, and Brace suddenly realized

197

he shouldn't have mentioned Toby Harper's name. Shouldn't have revealed any contact with her.

"Well," said Wallenberg quietly. "It does explain the patient's symptoms."

"What about Mr. Bigelow's concerns? That his other friends had the same illness?"

Wallenberg shook his head. "You know, it's hard for our patients to accept the fact they've reached the end of their life spans. Angus Parmenter was eighty-two. Senescence and death are what happen to all of us."

"How did Dr. Mackie die?"

Wallenberg paused. "That was a particularly upsetting event. Dr. Mackie had a psychotic break. He jumped out of a window at Wicklin Hospital."

"Jesus."

"It stunned us all. He was a surgeon, and a very good one, too. Never retired from the OR, even at the age of seventy-four. He worked right up until the day of his . . . accident."

"Was an autopsy done?"

"The cause was clearly from trauma."

"Yes, but was an autopsy done?"

"I don't know. He was under the care of surgeons at Wicklin. He died about a week after the fall." He regarded Robbie with a thoughtful gaze. "You seem bothered by all this."

"I guess it's because Mr. Bigelow was so upset. There's one more name he mentioned, another friend who's fallen ill. A Phillip Dorr."

"Mr. Dorr's fine. He moved to Brant Hill West, in La Jolla. I just received his signed authorization to transfer his records." He shuffled through the files on his desk and finally produced a sheet of paper. "Here's his fax from California."

Brace glanced at the sheet, and saw Phillip Dorr's signature at the bottom. "So he's not sick."

"I saw Mr. Dorr in clinic a few days ago, for a routine checkup."

"And?"

Wallenberg looked straight at him. "He was in perfect health."

Back at his own desk, Brace finished up the day's medical charts and dictations. At six-thirty, he finally shut off the microcassette recorder and looked down at his newly cleared desk. He found himself staring at the name he'd scrawled on the back of a lab report: *Dr. Stanley Mackie.* The incident that afternoon in the clinic still bothered him. He thought of the other names James Bigelow had mentioned: *Angus Parmenter. Phillip Dorr.* That two of those three men were now dead was not in itself alarming. All of them were elderly; all of them had reached their statistically apportioned life spans.

But old age was not in itself a cause of death.

Today he'd seen fear in James Bigelow's eyes, real fear, and he could not quite shake off his uneasiness.

He picked up the phone and called Greta, telling her he'd be home late because he had to make a stop at Wicklin Hospital. Then he packed up his briefcase and left the office.

By now the clinic was deserted, the corridor lit by only one fluorescent panel at the end of the hall. As he walked beneath it, he heard a faint humming and looked up to see the shadow of an insect trapped behind the opaque plastic, wings fluttering against its own doom. He flipped off the wall switch. The hallway went dark, but he could still hear the humming overhead, the frantic thrashing of wings.

He walked out of the building, into a damp and wind-blown night.

His Toyota was the only car left in the clinic lot. Parked beneath the sulfurous glow of a security lamp, it looked more black than green, like the shiny carapace of a beetle.

He paused to fish the car keys from his pocket. Then he gazed up at the lit windows of the nursing facility, at the unmoving silhouettes of patients in their rooms, the flicker of TV screens barely watched. He was gripped by a sudden and profound depression. What he was seeing, in those windows, was the end of life. A shadowbox of his own future.

He slid into his car and drove out of the lot, but he could not leave behind that sense of depression. It clung to him like cold mist on his skin. *I should have chosen pediatrics,* he thought. Babies. Beginnings. Growing, not decaying flesh. But in medical school he'd been advised that the future of medical practice lay in geriatrics, with baby boomers gone gray, a vast army of them, marching toward senility, sucking up medical resources along the way. Ninety percent of the health care dollar was spent on sustaining a person's last year of life. That's where the money would flow; that's where doctors would make their livings.

Robbie Brace, a practical man, had chosen a practical field. Oh, but how it depressed him.

As he drove toward Wicklin Hospital, he considered what his life would be like had he chosen pediatrics. He thought of his own daughter, and remembered his joy at looking into her wrinkled newborn face as she'd wailed in fury in the delivery room. He remembered the exhaustion of 2 A.M. feedings, the smell of talcum powder and sour milk, the silky baby skin in a warm bath. In so many ways, infants were like very old people. They needed to be bathed and fed and dressed. They needed their diapers changed. They could neither walk nor talk. They lived only at the mercy of people who cared about them.

It was seven-thirty when he reached Wicklin, a small community hospital just inside the Boston City limits. He pulled on his white coat, made sure his name tag with ROBERT BRACE, M.D. was clipped on, and walked into the building. He didn't have hospital privileges here, nor did he have the authority to request any of their medical charts; he was gambling that no one would bother to question him.

In the medical records department, he filled out a request form for Stanley Mackie's chart and handed the slip to the clerk, a petite blond. She glanced at his name tag and hesitated, no doubt realizing he was not on their staff.

"I'm from Brant Hill Clinic," he said. "This patient was one of ours."

She brought him the chart, and he carried it to an empty desk and sat down. Across the chart cover was written in black marker: *Deceased.* He opened the file and looked at the first page, listing the identifying data: name, birth date, Social Security number. The address caught his eye at once: 101 Titwillow Lane, Newton, MA.

It was a Brant Hill address.

He turned to the next page. The record covered only a single hospitalization—the one in which Stanley Mackie had died. With a growing sense of dismay he read the admitting surgeon's dictated history and physical, dated March ninth.

> 74-year-old previously healthy white male physician admitted with massive head trauma via ER after falling from fourth-floor window. Just prior to accident, patient had been scrubbed and gowned and was performing a routine appendectomy. According to OR nurses, Dr. Mackie displayed marked tremors of both hands. Without explanation, he proceeded to resect several feet of normal-appearing small bowel, resulting in massive hemorrhage and death. When the OR staff attempted to pull him away from the table, he slashed the anesthesiologist's jugular vein, then fled the OR.

Witnesses in the hallway saw him dive headfirst through window. He was found in the parking lot, unresponsive and bleeding from multiple lacerations.

After being intubated and stabilized in the ER, patient was admitted to trauma service with multiple skull fractures as well as probable spinal compression fractures. . . .

The physical exam had been recorded in typically terse surgical style, a rapid rundown of the patient's injuries and neurologic findings. Lacerated scalp and face. Open fractures of the parietal and coronal bones with extrusion of gray matter. A blown pupil on the right. No spontaneous respirations, no response to painful stimuli. The patient's injuries, thought Brace, were consistent with a headfirst landing in the parking lot.

Flipping further, he saw the surgeon's note: "X-ray report: spinal compression fractures C6, C7, T8." That, too, indicated a headfirst landing with the force of the fall transmitted straight down the spinal column.

Stanley Mackie's hospital course was a weeklong deterioration of multiple organ systems. Comatose and on a ventilator, he never reawakened. First his kidneys shut down, probably due to the shock of his injuries. Then he developed pneumonia and his BP dropped out twice, causing a bowel infarct. Finally, seven days after his plunge through the fourth-story window, his heart went into arrest.

He flipped to the back of the chart, where the lab results were filed. There were seven days' worth of computer printouts, a running log of electrolytes and blood chemistries, cell counts, and urinalyses. He kept turning pages, scanning thousands of dollars' worth of lab tests done on a man whose death had been, from the very first day, inevitable.

He paused at a lab report marked: *Pathology*.

Liver (postmortem):

Gross appearance: Weight: 1600 gm., pale, pinpoint surface areas of acute hemorrhage. No evidence chronic fibrotic changes.

Microscopic: On H and E stain, there are scattered areas of poorly stained mummified hepatocytes. This is consistent with focal coagulative necrosis, probably secondary to ischemia.

Brace turned the page and found a blood count report, out of sequence. He turned another page, and found himself staring at the back cover. There were no pages left.

He flipped toward the front of the record, searching for other postmortem reports, but could find only the page describing the liver. This didn't make sense. Why would Pathology do a postmortem on a single organ? Where were the reports for lungs, the heart, the brain?

He asked at the desk if there were more files for Stanley Mackie.

"That's the only one," said the clerk.

"But some of the Pathology reports are missing."

"You can check directly with Path. They keep copies of all their reports."

The Pathology Department, located in the basement, was a low-ceilinged warren of rooms, the walls painted white and decorated with lushly photographed travel posters. Mist over the Serengeti. A rainbow arching above Kauai. An island of mangroves in a turquoise sea. A radio was playing soft rock music. The lone technician at work in that room seemed absurdly cheerful, considering the nature of her job. She herself was another bright splash of color, with rouged cheeks and eyelids powdered a sparkly green.

"I'm trying to locate an autopsy report done back in March," said Brace. "It's not in the patient's file. Medical Records suggested I check with you."

"What was the patient's name?"

"Stanley Mackie."

The technician shook her head as she crossed to a filing cabinet. "He was such a nice man. We all felt awful about that."

"You knew him?"

"The surgeons always come down to check Path reports on their patients. We got to know Dr. Mackie pretty well." She pulled open a drawer and began thumbing through files. "He bought us our department coffeemaker for Christmas. We call it the Mackie Memorial Mr. Coffee." She straightened and stood frowning at the open drawer. "That's frustrating."

"What?"

"I can't find it." She closed the drawer. "I'm sure an autopsy was done on Dr. Mackie."

"Could it be misfiled? Under *S* for *Stanley?*"

She opened a different drawer, searched the files, then closed it again. She turned as another technician entered the lab. "Hey, Tim, have you seen the autopsy report for Dr. Mackie?"

"Wasn't that done way back?"

"It was early this year."

"Then it should still be in the files." He set a tray of slides on the countertop. "Try checking Herman."

"Why didn't I think of Herman?" she sighed, and crossed the lab into one of the offices.

Brace followed her. "Who's Herman?"

"He's not a *who* but a *what.*" She flipped on the lights, revealing a desk with a personal computer. "That's Herman. It's Dr. Seibert's pet project."

"What does Herman do?"

"He—it—is supposed to make retrospective studies a snap. Say you want to know how many perinatal deaths involved mothers who smoked. You type in the keywords *smoker* and *perinatal* and you'll get a list of relevant patients who've been autopsied."

"So all your autopsy data's in there?"

"Some of it. Dr. Seibert started inputting our data only two months ago. He's a long way from finishing." She sat down at the keyboard, typed in the name Mackie, Stanley, and clicked on Search.

A new screen appeared with identifying data. It was Stanley Mackie's autopsy report.

The technician vacated the seat. "It's all yours."

Brace sat down in front of the computer. According to the data on the screen, this report had been input six weeks ago; the actual file must have been lost since then. He hit Page Down and began to read.

The report described the body's gross appearance at postmortem: the multiple IV lines, the shaved head, the incision marks on the scalp left by the neurosurgeon's blade. The report continued with a description of the internal organs. The lungs were congested and swollen with inflammation. The heart showed a fresh infarct. The brain had multiple areas of hemorrhage. The findings at gross examination were consistent with the surgeons' diagnosis: massive head trauma with bilateral pneumonia. The fresh myocardial infarct had probably been the terminal event.

He clicked to the microscopic reports and found a summary of the same page he'd seen in the medical record, describing the liver. In addition there were reports that had not appeared in the medical record—microscopics of the liver, the heart, the lungs. No surprises, he thought. The man fell headfirst onto the pavement, he crushed his skull, and the neurologic trauma led to multiple organ failure.

He clicked to the microscopic report on the brain, and his eyes suddenly focused on a sentence buried within the description of traumatic injuries:

" . . . variable vacuolation in the background neuropil.

Some neuronal loss and reactive astrocytosis with kuru plaques, Congo-red positive, as seen in cerebellar sections."

At once he clicked to the last page and his gaze flew down to the final diagnoses:

1. Multiple intracerebral hemorrhages secondary to trauma.
2. Preexisting Creutzfeldt-Jakob disease.

In the parking lot, Robbie Brace sat in his car, wondering what he should do next. Whether he should do anything next. He weighed all the possible consequences of his actions. This would be a devastating blow to Brant Hill's reputation. Surely the media would pick this up, and there'd be screaming headlines: RITZ AND DEATH. MONEY BUYS MAD COW DISEASE.

He'd be out of a job.

You can't stay silent, man. Toby Harper is right. We have a deadly outbreak on our hands, and we don't know the source. The hormone injections? The food?

He reached under the seat for his cellular phone. He was still carrying Toby Harper's card; he punched in her home phone number.

A woman answered, "Harper residence."

"This is Dr. Brace from Brant Hill. May I speak to Toby Harper?"

"She's not here, but I can take a message. What's your number?"

"I'm in my car right now. Just tell her she was right. Tell her we've got a second case of CJD."

"Excuse me?"

"She'll know what it means." Headlights flickered in his rearview mirror. He turned and saw that a car was slowly moving along the next row. "What time's she getting home?" he asked.

"She's at work right now—"

"Oh. Then I'll swing by Springer Hospital. Never mind about the message." He disconnected, slid the phone under the seat, and started the car. As he pulled out of the driveway, he noticed those same headlights moving toward the parking lot exit. He quickly lost sight of them in the busy flow of traffic.

It was a half hour drive to Springer Hospital. By the time he turned into the parking lot, he'd developed a headache from hunger. He pulled into a stall in the visitors' area. With the engine off, he sat for a moment in his car, massaging his temples. It was just a mild headache, but it reminded him he hadn't eaten since breakfast. He'd stay only a few minutes, just long enough to tell her what he'd learned, and then he'd let *her* carry the ball from there. All he wanted to do now was go home, eat supper. Play with his little girl.

He climbed out of the car, locked it, and started toward the ER entrance. He'd taken only a few steps when he heard the growl of a car behind him. Turning, he squinted at the slowly approaching headlights. The car came to a stop beside him. He heard the electric hum of the driver's window as it rolled down.

A man with hair so blond it looked silvery under the parking lot light smiled at him. "I think I'm lost."

"Where you trying to get to?" asked Brace.

"Irving Street."

"You're nowhere near it." Brace took a step toward the open car window. "You'll have to go back out to the road, turn right, and drive about four or five—"

The *pop, pop* took him by surprise. So did the punch in the chest.

Brace jerked away, startled by the unprovoked blow. He touched his hand to his chest, where the pain was just beginning to assert itself, and found he could not draw in a deep breath. Warmth seeped from his shirt and dribbled onto his fingers. He looked down and saw that his hand was wet and glistening with dark liquid.

There was another *pop*, another punch in the chest.

Brace staggered. He tried to regain his footing, but his legs seemed to fold up beneath him. He dropped to his knees and saw the streetlamp begin to waver like water.

The last bullet slammed into his back.

He collapsed with his face pressed against the cold pavement, the gravel biting into his cheek. The car drove off, the purr of its engine fading into the night. He could feel his life spilling away in a hot stream. He pressed his hand to his chest, trying to stanch the flow, but the strength had left his arm. All he could manage was a feeble clasp.

God, not here, he thought. *Not now.*

He began to crawl toward the ER doors, at the same time trying to maintain pressure on his chest wound, but with every beat of his heart, he felt more heat gush out. He tried to keep his gaze fixed on the sign: EMERGENCY, brightly lit in red, but his vision kept going out of focus, and the word began to waver like seeping blood.

The glass doors of the ER were straight ahead. Suddenly a figure appeared from that warm rectangle of light. It came to a halt only a few feet away. Desperately Brace reached out and whispered: "Help me. Please."

He heard the woman yell: "There's a man bleeding out here! I need assistance STAT!"

And then he heard footsteps running toward him.

13

"Get a third IV in!" yelled Toby. "Sixteen gauge! Ringer's lactate, wide open—"

"Lab says O-negative blood's on its way."

"Where the hell is Carey?"

"He was just in the hospital," said Maudeen. "I'll page him again."

Toby pulled on a pair of sterile gloves and reached for the scalpel. Under the bright trauma room lights, Brace's face was glistening with sweat and fear. He stared up at her, his eyes wide above the hissing oxygen mask, his breaths coming in short, desperate puffs. The bandage over his chest was slowly seeping with red again. A nurse-anesthetist, called down from the obstetrics ward, was already preparing to intubate.

"Robbie, I'm going to put in a chest tube," said Toby. "You're getting a tension pneumothorax." She saw him give a quick nod of comprehension, saw his jaw tighten in antici-pation of more pain. But he didn't even flinch as her blade sliced through the skin above his rib; a subcutaneous injec-tion of Xylocaine had already numbed the nerve endings. Toby heard a rush of escaping air and knew she was now in the chest cavity. She also knew she'd been correct; the bullet had punctured a lung, and with each breath Robbie took, air was leaking from the ruptured lung into the pleural space, building up enough pressure to shift the heart and great ves-sels, compressing whatever pulmonary tissue was still intact.

She slipped her finger through the incision to widen it, then slipped in the clear plastic chest tube. Val connected the other end to low-pressure suction. Immediately a stream of bright red shot into the tube and collected in the drain reser-voir.

Toby and Val glanced at each other, both of them sharing the same thought: *He's bleeding into his chest—and fast.*

She looked at Robbie's face and saw he was watching her, that he'd registered her look of dismay.

"It's . . . not good," he whispered.

She squeezed his shoulder. "You're doing fine, Robbie. The surgeon'll be here any minute."

"Cold. Feel so cold . . ."

Maudeen threw a blanket over him.

"Where's that O-neg blood?" called Toby.

"Just arrived. I'll hang it now—"

"Toby," whispered Val. "Systolic's down to eighty-five."

"Come on, come on. Let's pour in that blood!"

The door sprang open and Doug Carey walked it. "What've you got here?" he snapped.

"Gunshot wounds to chest and back," said Toby. "Three bullets show up on X ray, but I counted four entry holes. Tension pneumothorax. And that"—she pointed to the chest tube reservoir, where 100 cc's of blood had already accumulated—"that's just in the last few minutes. Systolic's slipping."

Carey glanced at the X ray hanging on the light box. "Let's crack the chest," he said.

"We'd need a full cardiac team—maybe bypass—"

"Can't wait. Have to stop the bleeding *now*." He looked straight at Toby, and she felt the old dislike welling up inside her. Doug Carey was a bastard, but right now she needed him. Robbie Brace needed him.

Toby nodded to the nurse-anesthetist. "Go ahead and intubate. We'll get him prepped. Val, open that thoracotomy tray . . ."

As everyone scurried around the room in preparation, the anesthetist drew a dose of Etomidate into a syringe. The drug would render Robbie fully unconscious for the intubation.

Toby loosened Robbie's oxygen mask and saw that he was gazing up, his eyes focused desperately on hers. So many times before she had seen terror in a patient's eyes and had forced herself to suppress her own emotions, to concentrate on her job. This time, though, she could not ignore the fear in her patient's eyes. This was a man she knew, a man she'd grown to like.

"Everything will be all right," she said. "You have to believe me. I won't let *anything* go wrong." Gently she cradled his face between her hands and smiled.

"Counting . . . on you . . . Harper," he murmured.

She nodded. "You do that, Robbie. Now, are you ready to go to sleep?"

"Wake me . . . when it's over . . ."

"It'll seem like no time at all." She nodded to the anesthetist, who injected the Etomidate into the IV line. "Go to sleep, Robbie. That's it. I'll be right here when you wake up . . ."

His gaze remained focused on her. She would be the last image he'd register, the last face he'd see. She watched as consciousness faded from his eyes, as his muscles slowly went slack and his eyelids drifted shut.

I won't let anything go wrong.

She removed the oxygen mask. At once the anesthetist tipped Robbie's head back and slid the laryngoscope blade into the throat. It took her only seconds to identify the vocal cords, to thread the ET tube into the trachea. Then the oxygen was connected and the tube taped into place. The ventilator would take over now, breathing for him, forcing into his lungs a precise mixture of oxygen and halothane.

I won't let anything go wrong.

Toby released a tense breath of her own. Then she quickly gowned up. She knew they were breaking sterile conditions left and right, but it couldn't be helped. No time to scrub— she snapped on gloves and moved to the table.

She stood right across from Doug Carey. The patient's chest had been hastily painted with Betadine and sterile drapes were laid over the operative site.

Carey made his incision, a single clean slice down the sternum. There was no time to be elegant; the blood pressure was falling—down to seventy systolic with three big-bore IVs pouring in saline and whole blood. Toby had witnessed emergency thoracotomies before, and the brutality of it never failed to appall her. She watched with a twinge of nausea as Carey wielded the saw, as the sternum was split in a mist of bone dust and flying blood.

"Shit," said Carey, looking into the chest cavity. "There's at least a liter of blood in here. Suction! Hand me some sterile towels!"

The gurgle of the suction catheter was so loud Toby could barely hear the *beep-beep* of Robbie's heartbeat on the cardiac monitor. As Val suctioned, Maudeen ripped open the sterile seal on a bundle of towels. Carey stuffed one into the chest cavity. When he pulled it out, it was sopping red. He tossed it on the floor, thrust in another towel. Again it came out soaked with blood.

"Okay. Okay, I think I see where it's coming from. Looks like the ascending aorta—leaking fast. Toby, I need more exposure . . ."

The suction catheter was still gurgling. Though most of the blood had been cleared out, a steady stream of it was spilling out of the aorta.

"I don't see a bullet," said Carey. He glanced at the X ray, then stared into the open chest. "There's the leak, but where's the fucking bullet?"

"Can't you just patch it?"

"It could still be lodged somewhere in the aortic wall. We patch and close, another hole could rip open later." He reached for the needle clamp and sutures. "Okay, let's shut off this leak first. Then we'll look around . . ."

Toby retracted the lung while Carey worked. He sewed quickly, his suture needle nipping in and out of the aortic wall. As he tied off and the bleeding stopped, everyone in the room gave a simultaneous sigh of relief.

"BP?" he called out.

"Holding at seventy-five," said Val.

"Keep that O-neg going in. We got more units?"

"On the way."

"Okay." Carey took a breath. "Let's see what else we got in here . . ." He suctioned off the pooled blood, clearing the field for easier inspection. Then, gently applying traction for a better view, he took a sponge and dabbed along the aorta.

Suddenly his hands froze. "Fuck," he said. "The bullet—"

"What?"

"It's right here! It's almost through the opposite wall!" He started to withdraw his hand.

A fountain of blood suddenly exploded upward, splattering them both in the face.

"*No!*" cried Toby.

213

Panicked, Carey grabbed a clamp off the tray and reached in through the rushing blood, but he was working blind, groping in a shimmering sea of red. It spilled out of the thorax and soaked into Toby's gown.

"Can't stop it—feels like he's got a rip along the whole fucking wall—"

"Clamp it! Can't you clamp it?"

"Clamp *what?* The aorta's shredded—"

The cardiac monitor squealed. The anesthetist said: "Asystole! We've got asystole!"

Toby's gaze shot to the screen. The heart tracing had gone flat.

She reached into that hot pool of blood and grasped the heart. She squeezed, once, twice, her hand taking over for Robbie's heartbeat.

"Don't!' said Carey. "You're only making him bleed out!"

"He's in arrest—"

"You can't change that."

"Then what the fuck do we *do?*"

The monitor was still squealing. Carey looked down at the open chest. At the glistening pool of red. Since Toby had ceased cardiac massage, the fountaining had stopped. There was only the slow drip, drip of blood spilling out of the open thorax onto the floor.

"It's over," he said. Quietly he stepped away from the body. His gown was saturated to the waist. "There was nothing to sew up, Toby. The whole aorta was dissecting. It just blew apart."

Toby looked at Robbie's face. His eyelids were partly open, his jaw slack. The ventilator was still cycling, automatically blowing air into a dead body.

The anesthetist flipped off the switch. Silence fell over the room.

Toby lay her hand on Robbie's shoulder. Through the sterile drapes, his flesh felt solid, and still warm.

214

I won't let anything go wrong.

"I'm sorry," she whispered. "I'm so sorry . . ."

The police showed up before Robbie's wife did. Within minutes of their arrival, the first two patrolmen had secured the crime scene and were busy cordoning off half the parking lot. By the time Greta Brace hurried into the ER, the parking lot was already awash in the flashing lights of half a dozen police cars from both the Newton and the Boston PD. Toby was standing by the front desk talking to one of the detectives when she spotted Greta stepping through the ER doors, her red hair in windblown disarray. The waiting area was filled with cops, plus a few bewildered ER patients, and Greta sobbed and cursed as she pushed her way across the room.

"Where is he?" she cried.

Toby broke off her conversation with the detective and crossed toward Greta. "I'm so sorry—"

"Where is he?"

"He's still in the trauma room. Greta, no! Don't go back there yet. Give us some time to—"

"He's my husband. I have to see him."

"Greta—"

But the other woman pushed past her and headed into the treatment area with Toby in pursuit. Greta didn't know which way to go; she zigzagged back and forth, frantically searching the rooms. At last she spotted the door labeled: TRAUMA. She pushed straight into the room.

Toby was right behind her. Dr. Daniel Dvorak, gowned and gloved, looked up from the body as the two women entered. Robbie lay undraped, his chest gaping open, his face slack with death.

"No," said Greta, and her voice rose from a moan to a high, keening wail. *"No . . ."*

Toby reached for her arm and tried to lead her out of the

room, but Greta shook her off and stumbled to her husband's side. She cradled his face in her hands, kissed his eyes, his forehead. The ET tube was still in place, the tip of it protruding from his mouth. She tried to unpeel the tape, to remove the offending piece of plastic.

Daniel Dvorak put his hand on hers to stop her. "I'm sorry," he said quietly. "It has to remain."

"I want this thing out of my husband's throat!"

"It has to stay for now. I'll remove it when I finish my exam."

"Who the fuck are *you?*"

"I'm the medical examiner. Dr. Dvorak." He looked at the homicide detective, who'd just stepped into the trauma room.

"Mrs. Brace?" said the cop. "I'm Detective Sheehan. Why don't you and I go someplace quiet. Where we can sit down."

Greta didn't move. She stood murmuring softly, cradling Robbie's face in her hands, her expression hidden behind that fountain of red hair.

"We need your help, Mrs. Brace, to find out what happened." Gently the cop touched her shoulder. "Let's go sit in another room. Where we can talk."

At last she allowed herself to be led away from the table. At the doorway she halted and looked at her husband.

"I'll be right back, Robbie," she said. Then she walked slowly out of the room.

Toby and Dvorak were left alone. "I didn't realize you were here," she said.

"I arrived about ten minutes ago. With so many people out there, you probably missed me in the crowd."

She looked at Robbie, wondering if his flesh was still warm. "I wish we could just shut down the ER. I wish I could go home. But patients keep walking in. With their stomachaches and their sniffles. And their goddamn piddly complaints . . ." Her vision suddenly blurred with tears. She wiped her face and turned toward the door.

"Toby?"

She halted, not answering. Not looking back.

"I need to talk to you. About what happened tonight."

"I've already spoken to half a dozen cops. No one on the staff saw what happened. We found him in the parking lot. He was crawling toward the building . . ."

"Do you agree with Dr. Carey that death resulted from aortic exsanguination?"

She took a breath and reluctantly turned to face him. "Whatever Dr. Carey says."

"What do you remember about the surgery?"

"There was . . . a small nick in the aorta. He patched it up. But then we saw the bullet . . . had passed through . . . there was an intimal tear. An aortic dissection. Then the wall blew open . . ." She swallowed and looked away. "It was a nightmare."

He said nothing.

"I *knew* him," she whispered. "I'd been to his house. I'd met his wife. Oh Jesus." She pushed out of the room.

The only refuge she could find was the doctor's sleeping quarters. She closed the door behind her and sat down on the bed, crying, rocking back and forth. She didn't even hear the knock on the door.

Dvorak came quietly into the room. He'd stripped off the gown and gloves, and now he stood by the bed, unsure of what to say.

"Are you all right?" he finally asked.

"No. I am not all right."

"I'm sorry about the questions. I had to ask them."

"You were so fucking cold-blooded about it."

"I needed to know, Toby. We can't help Dr. Brace, not now. But we can find the answers. We owe it to him."

She dropped her face in her hands and struggled to regain

control, to stop crying. Her tears felt all the more humiliating because *he* was standing there, watching her. She heard the chair give a squeak as he sat down. When at last she managed to raise her head, she found herself looking straight into his eyes.

"I didn't realize you and the victim were acquainted," he said.

"He's not *the victim*. His name was Robbie."

"Okay. Robbie." He hesitated. "Were you good friends?"

"No. Not . . . not *good* friends."

"You seem to be taking this pretty hard."

"And you don't understand. Do you?"

"Not entirely."

She took a breath and slowly released it. "It catches up with us, you know. Most of the time, when we lose a patient, we can deal with it. Then there'll be a child. Or someone we know. And suddenly we realize we can't handle it at all . . ." She wiped her hand across her eyes. "I have to get back to work. There must be patients waiting out there—"

He grasped her hand. "Toby, if it makes a difference to you, I don't think there's anything you could have done to save him. The damage to his aorta was devastating."

She looked down at his hand, feeling faintly surprised that he was still touching her. He, too, seemed taken aback by that spontaneous contact, and he quickly released her wrist. They sat in silence for a moment.

"This hits too close to home," she said. Hugging herself, she found her gaze drawn, once again, to his. "I walk through that parking lot every evening. So do all the nurses. If this was a robbery attempt, any one of us would have made an easier target."

"Have there been other attacks at Springer?"

"Only one I can think of. A few years ago—a nurse was raped. But this isn't like downtown Boston. We don't worry about our safety here."

"Monsters live in the suburbs too."

The knock on the door startled them both. Toby opened the door to find Detective Sheehan.

"Dr. Harper, I need to ask you a few questions," he said and stepped inside, shutting the door behind him. The room suddenly seemed very crowded. "I just spoke to Mrs. Brace. She thinks her husband might have come here to see *you*."

Toby shook her head. "Why?"

"That's what we're wondering. He called her around six-thirty and told her he was driving to Wicklin Hospital, and that he'd be home late."

"Did he go to Wicklin?"

"We're checking that now. What we don't know is why he ended up *here*. Do you know?"

She shook her head.

"When was the last time you saw Dr. Brace?"

"Last night."

Sheehan's eyebrow twitched upward. "He came to Springer?"

"No. I went to his house. He helped me look up a medical record."

"You got together to look at medical records?"

"Yes." She looked at Dvorak. "It was right after I saw *you*. You'd just told me Angus Parmenter's diagnosis. I wondered about Harry Slotkin—whether he had Creutzfeldt-Jakob disease as well. So Robbie and I looked up Slotkin's outpatient record."

"*What* disease?" interjected Sheehan.

"Creutzfeldt-Jakob. It's a fatal brain infection."

"Okay. So you and Dr. Brace got together last night. And then what?"

"We drove to Brant Hill. We looked at the medical chart. Then we both went home."

"You didn't stop somewhere? He didn't go to your house?"

"No. I got home around ten-thirty, alone. He didn't call

me afterward, and I didn't call him. So I don't know why he'd come to see me tonight."

There was a knock. *How many more people can fit in this room?* wondered Toby as she opened the door.

It was Val. "We've got a guy with left-sided weakness and slurred speech. BP's two fifty over one thirty. He's in room two."

Toby glanced back at Sheehan. "I don't have anything more to tell you, Detective. Now if you'll excuse me, I have patients to see."

At eight o'clock the next morning, Toby pulled into her driveway next to Jane's dark blue Saab and turned off the engine. She was too exhausted to climb out of the car and deal with Ellen just yet, so she sat for a moment, staring out at the dead leaves blowing across the lawn. It had been one of the worst nights of her life, first Robbie's death, and then a succession of seriously ill patients—a stroke, a myocardial infarction, and a case of end-stage emphysema so critical the patient had required intubation. Added to that was the general sense of confusion from all those cops milling about with their chattering walkie-talkies. Was it a full moon last night? she wondered. Some crazy juxtaposition of the planets that had blown chaos into her ER? And then there'd been Detective Sheehan, ambushing her at every opportunity to ask *just one more* question.

A gust of wind buffeted the car. With the heater turned off, she was starting to feel cold. It was the chill that finally drove her out of the car and into the house.

She was greeted by the smell of coffee and the pleasant clatter of chinaware from the kitchen. "I'm home," she called out, and hung her jacket in the closet.

Jane appeared in the kitchen doorway, her smile warm and welcoming. "I've just made a pot—would you like a cup?"

"I would, but I won't be able to sleep."

"Oh, it's decaf. I figured you wouldn't want the real thing."

Toby smiled. "In that case, thanks. I'd love a cup."

Pale morning light shone in through the window as they sat at the kitchen table, drinking their coffee. Ellen wasn't awake yet, and Toby felt almost guilty about how glad she was for the reprieve, how much she was enjoying this moment of peace. She leaned back and inhaled the steam rising from her cup. "This is heaven."

"Actually, it's only a cup of Colombian roast."

"Yes, but I didn't have to grind it. I didn't have to pour it. And I can just sit here and actually drink it."

Jane shook her head in sympathy. "It sounds like you had a bad night."

"It was so bad I don't even want to talk about it." Toby set the cup down and rubbed her face. "And how was your night?"

"A little chaotic. Your mother had trouble going to sleep. She was up and down, up and down, wandering the house."

"Oh no. Why?"

"She told me she had to go pick you up at school. So she searched all over for the car keys."

"She hasn't driven a car in years. I have no idea why she'd start looking for car keys now."

"Well, it seemed really important to her that you not be kept waiting at school. She was worried you might be cold." Jane smiled. "When I asked her how old you were, she said you were eleven."

Eleven, thought Toby. *That was the year Dad died. The year everything fell on Mom's shoulders.*

Jane rose from the table and washed her cup in the sink. "Anyway, I gave her a bath last night, so you needn't bother with that. And we had a big snack at midnight. I expect she'll stay in bed for a while. Maybe all day." She set her cup on the dashboard and turned to look at Toby. "She must have been a wonderful mother."

"She was," Toby murmured.

"Then you're lucky. Luckier than I was . . ." Jane's gaze shifted sadly to the floor. "But we can't all have the parents we want, can we?" She took a breath, as though to say something else, then simply smiled and reached for her purse. "I'll see you tomorrow night."

Toby heard her walk out of the house, shutting the front door behind her. Without Jane's presence, the kitchen seemed empty. Lifeless. She rose from the kitchen table and walked up the hall to her mother's room. Peeking inside, she saw that Ellen was sleeping. Quietly Toby entered the room and sat down on the bed.

"Mom?"

Ellen rolled onto her back. Slowly her eyes opened and focused on Toby.

"Mom, are you feeling all right?"

"Tired," Ellen murmured. "I'm tired today."

Toby lay her hand on Ellen's forehead. No fever. She brushed a strand of silver hair away from her mother's eyes. "You're not sick?"

"I just want to sleep."

"Okay." Toby dropped a kiss on Ellen's cheek. "You sleep, then. I'm going to bed too."

"Good night."

Toby walked out, leaving Ellen's door open. She decided to leave her own bedroom door open, so she'd be able to hear if her mother called out. She took a shower and changed into a T-shirt, her usual sleeping attire. As she sat down on the bed, the phone rang.

She picked it up. "Hello?"

A man's voice, vaguely familiar, said: "May I ask who I'm speaking to?"

Taken aback by the man's rudeness, she answered: "If you don't know who you're calling, sir, I can't help you. Good-bye."

"Wait. This is Detective Sheehan, Boston PD. I'm just try-ing to find out whose number this is."

"Detective Sheehan? This is Toby Harper."

"Dr. *Harper?*"

"Yes. You've dialed my home phone number. Didn't you know that?"

There was a silence. "No."

"Well, how did you get this number?"

"Redial."

"What?"

"There was a cell phone under the seat in Dr. Brace's car. I found it just a few minutes ago, and I punched in redial." Sheehan paused. "You were the last person he called."

It took a half hour for Vickie to arrive at the house to watch Ellen, and another forty minutes for Toby to fight her way through morning traffic into Boston. By the time she'd sat through another questioning session with Detective Sheehan, she was tired and edgy enough to bite the head off the first person who crossed her. What she should have done was driven straight home and climbed into bed.

Instead she used her car phone to call Vickie and tell her she had one more stop to make.

"Mom doesn't look too well," said Vickie. "What's going on with her?"

"She was fine yesterday," said Toby.

"Well, she threw up a while ago. I got her to drink some juice, and I think she's a little better now. But she just wants to sleep."

"Does she have any other complaints?"

"Mainly the upset stomach. I think you should take her to a doctor."

"I am a doctor."

"Well, of course *you* know best," said Vickie.

Toby hung up, irritated with her sister and vaguely trou-

223

bled by the report of Ellen's illness. Just some gastrointestinal bug, she thought. Mom will bounce back in a few days.

She left the police station and drove directly to 720 Albany Street. The ME's office.

Dvorak seemed to sense her ugly mood at once. Politely he ushered her into his office, poured her a cup of coffee, and set it down in front of her without asking if she wanted it. She did; she needed the caffeine.

She took a few quick gulps and then met his gaze head-on. "I want to know why Sheehan's fixated on me. Why he's harassing me."

"Is he?"

"I just wasted the last hour with him. Look, I don't know *why* Robbie called my house. I wasn't home last night—my mother's sitter took the call. I just found out about it."

"Did the sitter know why Brace called?"

"She didn't understand the message. He told her he was driving to the hospital to see me, so she didn't bother to tell me about it. Believe me, Dan, there was nothing going on between Robbie and me. No romance, no sex, no nothing. We were barely friends."

"Yet you seemed extremely upset about his death."

"Upset? Robbie bled out in front of me! I had his blood all over my hands, my arms. I had my fingers around his heart, trying to keep it going, trying to keep him alive. Why the fuck *wouldn't* I be upset?" She took a breath, fighting back tears. "But you don't work with living people, so you wouldn't know. You just get the corpses."

He said nothing. The silence seemed to magnify the anguish, the rage of her last words.

She sank back in the chair and covered her face with her hand.

"You're right," he said quietly. "I wouldn't know. I don't have to watch people die in front of me. And maybe that's why I chose the field I did. So I wouldn't have to watch."

She raised her head but didn't feel like meeting his gaze. So she stared at a corner of his desk. "I don't suppose you've done the autopsy yet."

"We did it this morning. There were no unexpected findings."

She nodded, still not looking at him.

"And Mr. Parmenter? Did the neuropathologist confirm the diagnosis?"

"It was Creutzfeldt-Jakob disease." He said it without inflection, without a hint of the personal devastation that diagnosis must have wreaked.

She looked at him, her attention suddenly focused on Dvorak's crisis, on his fears. She could see he hadn't been sleeping well; his eyes seemed sunken, feverish.

"It's just something I'll have to live with," he said. "The possibility of getting sick. Not knowing if I'll live another two years or forty years. I keep telling myself, I could walk outside and get hit by a bus. That's the way life is. Just surviving another day comes with its own risk." He straightened, as though trying to shake off the gloom. Then, unexpectedly, he smiled. "Not that I live such a thrilling life."

"Still, I hope it's a long one."

They both stood up and shook hands, a gesture that felt too formal for friends. While their relationship had not quite passed over into friendship, that was the direction in which she felt it moving. In which she wanted it to move. Now, as she looked at him, she felt confused by her sudden attraction to him, by her response to the warmth of his grasp.

He said, "The night before last, you invited me over for a glass of brandy."

"Yes."

"I didn't take you up on it because I—well, I was still in a state of shock about the diagnosis. I would have ruined the evening for both of us."

She remembered how she'd spent that night, sitting alone

225

and depressed on the sofa, leafing through medical journals while gloomy Mendelssohn played on the stereo. *You could hardly have ruined that evening,* she thought.

"Anyway," he said, "I wondered if I could reciprocate. It's almost noon. I've been here all morning, and suddenly I can't wait to get out of this damn building. If you're free—if I could interest you—"

"You mean . . . now?"

She hadn't expected this. She looked at him for a moment, thinking how much she'd wanted this to happen, yet afraid that she was reading too much into the invitation.

He seemed to interpret her hesitation as reluctance. "I'm sorry, I guess it's pretty short notice. Maybe another time."

"No. I mean, yes. Now is fine," she said quickly.

"It is?"

"On one condition. If you don't mind."

He cocked his head, uncertain what to expect.

"Could we sit in the park?" she asked wistfully. "I know it's a little brisk outside, but I haven't seen the sun in a week. And I'd really love to feel it on my face right now."

"You know what? So would I." He grinned. "Let me get my coat."

14

They sat with scarves draped around their necks, huddling close together on a park bench while they ate steaming slices of pizza straight from the take-out box. The topping was Thai chicken with peanut sauce—the surprising first choice of both of them. "Great minds think alike," Dvorak had said, laughing, as they'd walked beneath leafless trees to this bench beside the pond. Though the wind was cold, the sun shone down from a bright, clear sky.

This isn't the same man, Toby thought, looking up at Dvorak's face, his hair ruffled, his cheeks ruddy from the wind. Take him out of that depressing building, away from his corpses, and he becomes someone entirely different. Someone with laughing eyes. She wondered if *she* looked different, as well. The wind had tossed her hair in all directions, and she was making a mess of her hands with the pizza, but at that moment she felt more attractive than she had in a long time. Perhaps it was because of the way he looked at her; the most potent of beautifiers, she thought, is to be smiled at by a desirable man.

She turned her face upward, savoring the brightness of the day. "I'd almost forgotten how nice it is to feel the sun."

"Has it been that long since you've seen it?"

"It feels like weeks. First we had all that rain. And then the few sunny days we did have, I slept right through them."

"So why did you choose the night shift, anyway?"

She finished off the last bite of pizza and fastidiously wiped the sauce from her hands. "It didn't start off as a choice, really. When I finished my ER residency, that was the only time slot I could get at Springer. At first, it made a lot of sense. The ER gets quiet after midnight, and sometimes I'd manage to catch a few hours of sleep. Then I'd go home, take a long nap, and have the rest of the day to play." She shook her head at the memory. "That was ten years ago. When you're in your twenties, you can get by on a lot less sleep."

"Middle age is hell."

"Middle age? Speak for yourself, buster."

He laughed, his eyes narrowed against the sunlight. "So now it's ten years later and you're an old lady in her, what? Thirties? Yet you're still working the graveyard shift."

"It got to feel pretty comfortable, after a while. Working with the same nurses. People I could trust." She sighed. "Then my mom's Alzheimer's got worse. And it seemed important for me to be home during the day. To do things for her. So now I hire someone to sleep at my house at night. And then I get home from work in the morning and take over."

"Sounds like you're burning the candle at both ends."

She shrugged. "There's not much choice, is there? Really, I'm lucky. At least I can afford to hire help and keep working, unlike so many other women. And my mother—even at

228

her most exasperating—she never stops being . . ." She paused, searching for the one word that would describe Ellen's essence. "Kind," she said. "My mother has always, always been kind."

Their eyes met. She shivered as a biting wind swept across the pond and rattled the bare branches overhead.

"I have a feeling you're very much like your mother," he said.

"Kind? No. I wish I was." She looked across the pond, where ripples danced. "I think I'm too impatient. Too intense to be kind."

"Well, you are intense, Dr. Harper. I knew that from the first conversation we had. And I can see every emotion playing right across your face."

"Scary, isn't it?"

"Probably healthy for the soul. At least you let it all out. Frankly, I could use some of your intensity."

She admitted, ruefully, "I could use some of your reserve."

The last slice of pizza was gone. They threw the box in the rubbish bin and began to walk. Dvorak seemed not to notice the cold; he moved with easy, long-limbed grace, his coat unbuttoned, his scarf trailing like an afterthought over his shoulder.

"I don't think I've ever met a pathologist who wasn't reserved," she said. "Are you all such good poker players?"

"Meaning, do we all have personalities bordering on the comatose?"

"Well, the ones I know seem so quiet. But also competent, as if they know all the answers."

"We do."

She looked at his deadpan face and laughed. "It's a good act, Dan. You have me convinced."

"Actually, they teach you that in pathology residency.

How to look intelligent. The ones who flunk out become surgeons."

She tossed back her head and laughed harder.

"It's true, though, what you say," he admitted. "The quiet ones go into pathology. It attracts people who like working in basements. Who feel more comfortable looking into microscopes than talking to live people."

"Is that true for you?"

"I'd have to say yes. I'm not very adept with people. Which probably explains my divorce."

They walked for a moment in silence. The wind had dragged a few clouds overhead, and they moved through intermittent patches of shadow, then sunlight.

"Was she a doctor, too?" asked Toby.

"Another pathologist. Very brilliant, but also very reserved. I didn't even notice there was anything wrong between us. Not until she left me. I guess that proves we were both pretty good poker players."

"Which doesn't work very well in a marriage, I imagine."

"No, it didn't." He suddenly halted and glanced down at his belt. "Someone's paging me," he said, frowning at the beeper readout.

"There's a pay phone right over there."

As Dvorak made his call, Toby stood outside the phone booth, eyes closed as she drank in a brief moment of sunshine between passing clouds. A moment of pleasure in just being alive. She was scarcely listening to Dvorak's conversation. Only when she heard the words *Brant Hill* did she suddenly turn and look at him through the Plexiglas.

He hung up and came out of the booth.

"What?" she said. "It's about Robbie, isn't it?"

He nodded. "That was Detective Sheehan. He's been over at Wicklin Hospital, interviewing the staff. They told him Dr. Brace was there yesterday evening. He visited Medical

Records and Pathology, inquiring about an old file on a Brant Hill resident. A man named Stanley Mackie."

She shook her head. "I've never heard the name."

"According to Wicklin, Mackie died this past March of head injuries from a fall. What Sheehan found interesting was the diagnosis found on autopsy. A disease he remembered hearing about only last night."

Overhead, the sun vanished behind a cloud. In the sudden pall, Dvorak's face looked gray. Distant.

"It was Creutzfeldt-Jakob disease."

From the window of the twentieth-floor conference room, Carl Wallenberg could see the ornate dome of the old Boston State House, and beyond that, the trees of the Common, their branches skeletal under a hard blue sky. So this is the view the suits enjoy, he thought. While the rest of us do the real work out in Newton, keeping Brant Hill's clients alive and well, Kenneth Foley and his staff of accountants sit in this plush downtown office and keep Brant Hill's money alive and well. And growing, by leaps and bounds. *Foley's Armani clones,* thought Wallenberg, looking at the other people sitting around the table. Wallenberg remembered their names and titles only vaguely. The man in the blue pinstripes was a senior vice president; the snooty redheaded woman was a financial officer. Except for Wallenberg and Russ Hardaway, the corporate attorney, this was a gathering of glorified pencil pushers.

A secretary brought in a carafe of coffee, gracefully poured it into five bone china cups, and set the cups down on the table, along with the crystal sugar bowl and creamer. No messy paper sugar packets at this meeting. She paused, waiting discreetly for any further instructions from Foley. There were none. The five people seated at the table waited until the secretary withdrew, closing the door behind her.

Then Kenneth Foley, Brant Hill's CEO, spoke. "This

231

morning, I got another call from Dr. Harper. Once again, she reminded me that Brant Hill isn't doing its job. That more of our residents may be getting sick. This could turn into a far more serious problem than I thought." He looked around the table, and his gaze settled on Wallenberg. "Carl, you assured me this issue was resolved."

"It *is* resolved," said Wallenberg. "I've discussed it with Dr. Dvorak. And I've met with the people from Public Health. We all agree now that there's no reason for alarm. Our dining facility is in total compliance with regulations. Our water supply comes off the municipal line. And those hormone injections everyone got so excited about—we have documentation to prove they're from recent lot numbers. Perfectly safe. Dr. Dvorak is convinced these cases are purely coincidental. 'Statistical cluster' is the scientific term for it."

"You're sure both Public Health and the ME's office are satisfied, then?"

"Yes. They've agreed not to make any public disclosure, since there's no cause for alarm."

"Yet Dr. Harper knows about this. We need to know how to respond to her questions. Because if she knows about it, the public will soon know about it as well."

"Have there been inquiries from the media?" asked Hardaway.

"So far, none. But there may be unwanted attention coming our way." Foley refocused on Wallenberg. "So tell us again, Carl, that we have nothing to worry about with this disease."

"You have nothing to worry about," said Wallenberg. "I'm telling you, these two cases are unrelated. Coincidences happen."

"If more cases turn up, it won't seem like just a coincidence," said Hardaway. "It will turn into a PR disaster, because it'll look like we didn't bother to pursue the problem."

"That's why Dr. Harper's call worries me," said Foley. "Essentially, she's put us on notice that she knows. And that she's watching us."

Hardaway said, "This makes it sound like a threat."

"It is a threat," said the financial officer. "Our shares climbed another three points this morning. But what'll happen if investors hear our residents are dying—and we did nothing to stop it?"

"But there's nothing to *stop,*" said Wallenberg. "This is pure hysteria, with no basis in fact."

"Dr. Harper sounded quite rational to me," said Foley.

Wallenberg snorted. "That's the problem. She sounds rational, even when she's not."

"What's she after, anyway?" asked the financial officer. "Money, attention? There's got to be a motive we can address here. Did you get any hint of it when you spoke to her this morning, Ken?"

Foley said, quietly: "I think this is really about Dr. Brace. And the unfortunate timing of his death."

At the mention of Robbie Brace, everyone fell momentarily silent and looked down at the table. No one wanted to talk of the dead.

"She and Dr. Brace were acquainted," said Foley.

"Maybe more than just acquainted," added Wallenberg with a note of disgust.

"Whatever their relationship," said Foley, "Dr. Brace's death has upset her enough to inspire these questions. And she seems to have the inside track on his murder investigation. Somehow she knew about Dr. Mackie's diagnosis. She knew he lived at Brant Hill. None of this was released to the public."

"I know how she found out," said Wallenberg. "The ME's office. She had lunch with Dr. Dvorak."

"Where did you hear that?"

"I hear things."

"Shit," said the financial officer. Leave it to the only woman in the group to utter the first four-letter word. "Then she has names and facts she could leak. So much for the three-point stock gain."

Foley leaned forward, his gaze hard on Wallenberg. "Carl, you're the medical director. So far we've deferred to your judgment. But if you're wrong, if one other patient comes down with this disease, it could kill all our expansion plans. Hell, it could wreck what we already have."

Wallenberg had to suppress the irritation in his voice. He managed to sound perfectly calm and perfectly confident, which he was. "I'll say it a third time. I'll say it a dozen times if I have to. This is not an epidemic. The disease is not going to turn up in any more of our residents. If it does, I'll hand over my goddamn stock options."

"You're that certain?"

"I'm that certain."

Foley leaned back with a look of relief.

"Then all we have to worry about," said the financial officer, "is Dr. Harper's big mouth. Which, unfortunately, could do us a lot of damage, even if nothing she says can be proved."

No one spoke for a moment as they all considered the options.

Wallenberg said, "I think we should just ignore her. Don't take her calls, don't give her any validation. Eventually she'll hurt her own credibility."

"In the meantime she hurts *us*," said the financial officer. "Isn't there some . . . pressure we can bring to bear? Her job, for instance. I thought the Springer board was pushing for termination."

"They tried," said Wallenberg. "But that ER chief dug in his heels, and they backed down. Temporarily, at least."

"What about your friend, the surgeon? I thought he had her termination sewn up."

Wallenberg shook his head. "Dr. Carey's like every other surgeon I know. Too damn overconfident."

The financial officer gave a sigh of impatience. "All right, so how *do* we handle her?"

Foley looked at Wallenberg. "Maybe Carl's right," he said. "Let's not do anything at all. She's already fighting to keep her job, and I think she's losing that battle. We'll let her self-destruct."

"With a little help, maybe?" the financial officer suggested softly.

"I doubt that'll be necessary," said Wallenberg. "Believe me, Toby Harper is her own worst enemy."

From the other side of the freshly dug grave, Toby spotted him, his head slightly bowed, his gaze cast downward at the coffin. Robbie's coffin. Even without the mantle of his white coat, Dr. Wallenberg looked every inch the part of the compassionate and godly physician. What ungodly thoughts does he hide? Toby wondered. The small gathering of doctors and administrators from Brant Hill all seemed to wear the identical expression, as though they'd donned the same rubber masks of mourning. Who among them had truly been Robbie's friend? She could not tell by looking at their faces.

Wallenberg seemed to sense that he was being watched, and he raised his head and looked at Toby. For a moment they stared at each other. Then he looked away.

A cold wind swept the gathering, tumbling dead leaves into the trench. Robbie's daughter began to wail in Greta's arms, not sobs of grief, but frustration at being confined too long among adults. Greta set her daughter down, and the girl was off in a flash, giggling as she weaved through the jungle of grown-up legs.

The minister could not compete with a laughing child.

With a look of resignation he cut short his final words and closed his Bible. As the mourners began to file toward the widow, Toby lost sight of Wallenberg. Only as she circled around to the other side of the trench did she spot him walking away toward the parked cars.

She followed him. She had to call out his name twice before he finally stopped and turned to look at her.

"I've been trying to reach you for almost a week," she said. "Your secretary never puts me through."

"I've been busy with a number of matters."

"May we talk now?"

"It's not a good time, Dr. Harper."

"When *is* a good time?"

He didn't answer. Instead he turned and walked away.

She followed him. "Brant Hill has had two documented cases of Creutzfeldt-Jakob," she said. "Angus Parmenter and Stanley Mackie."

"Dr. Mackie died from a fall."

"He also had CJD. Which is probably why he jumped out that window in the first place."

"You're talking about an untreatable illness. Am I supposed to feel somehow negligent about this?"

"Two cases in one year—"

"Statistical cluster. This is a large population base, Dr. Harper. One can expect several such cases in the greater Boston area. Those two men just happened to reside in the same neighborhood."

"What if this is a more infectious strain of prion? You could have new cases incubating right now at Brant Hill."

He turned to her, his expression so ugly she retreated a step. "You listen to me, Dr. Harper. People buy into Brant Hill because they want a life free of worries, free of fears. They've worked hard all their lives, and they deserve the luxury. They can afford it. They know they'll get the best medical care in the world. They do not need to hear some crackpot theory about a killer brain disease in their food."

"Is that all you're concerned about? Your patients' ease of mind?"

"Ease of mind is what they pay for. If they lose trust in us, they'll start packing up and selling out. It would turn Brant Hill into a ghost town."

"I'm not trying to tear down Brant Hill. I just think you should be monitoring your residents for symptoms."

"Think of the panic *that* would cause. Our food is safe. Our hormones come from reputable drug companies. Even the Public Health Department agrees there's no reason to be monitoring any symptoms. So stop trying to scare our residents, Dr. Harper. Or you'll find an attorney knocking at your door." He turned and began to walk away.

"What about Robbie Brace?" she blurted out.

"What about him?"

"I find it very disturbing that he was killed right after he learned about Mackie's diagnosis." There, she had said it. She had come right out and voiced her suspicions, and she fully expected Wallenberg to lash back in defense.

Instead, he turned and looked at her with an eerily unruffled smile. "Yes, I hear you've been pushing that angle on the police. But they've dropped the theory because they can find no evidence whatsoever of any connection." He paused. "By the way, they asked me a number of questions about *you.*"

"The police? What questions?"

"Whether I was aware of any relationship between you and Dr. Brace? Did I know he'd brought you into our clinic building late at night?" The smile deepened until it looked more like a snarl. "I find it fascinating, the sexual attraction you women have for black men."

Toby's chin jerked up in startled rage. She stepped toward him, her fury propelling her forward. "Goddamn you. You have no right to say that about him."

"Is everything all right, Carl?" a voice said.

Toby turned sharply to see a man, tall and almost completely bald, standing nearby. He was the same elegantly dressed man who'd stood beside Wallenberg during the graveside services. He was staring at her with some trepidation, and she realized her face was flushed with rage, her hands bunched into fists.

"I couldn't help overhearing," the man said. "Would you like me to call someone, Carl?"

"There's no problem here, Gideon. Dr. Harper was just feeling a bit"—again, that nasty, satisfied smile—"*distraught* over Robbie's death."

You bastard, thought Toby.

"We have a board meeting in half an hour," said the bald man.

"I haven't forgotten." Wallenberg looked at Toby, and in his eyes she saw the glint of triumph. He had pushed her over the edge, had made her lose her temper, and this man named Gideon had witnessed it. Wallenberg was the one in control, not her, and he was communicating that fact by his smile.

"I'll see you at the meeting," said the bald man. And with a last, concerned glance at Toby, he walked away.

"I think there's nothing more to discuss," said Wallenberg, and he too started to leave.

"Only until the next case of CJD shows up," she said.

He turned and gave her one last, pitying look. "Dr. Harper, can I give you some advice?"

"What advice?"

"Get a life."

I have a life, thought Toby as she angrily gulped coffee in the ER staff room. *Goddammit, I do have a life.* Maybe it was not the life she'd visualized as a young doctor in training, not the life she would have chosen. But sometimes one

238

could not choose, sometimes one was handed difficult circumstances. Duties, obligations.

Ellen.

Toby drained her coffee and poured another, hot and black. It was like tossing more acid into her stomach, but she desperately needed the caffeine. Robbie's funeral had cut into her usual sleep schedule, and she had managed to catch only a few hours of rest before coming to work last evening. It was now six in the morning and she was functioning purely on automatic reflexes and occasional bursts of primitive emotion. Anger. Frustration. She was feeling both at the moment, knowing that even when this shift was over, when she finally did walk out the hospital doors in an hour and a half, it would be to walk into another set of responsibilities and worries.

Get a life, he'd said. And this was the life she happened to have, the one that had been placed on her shoulders.

Yesterday evening, as she'd gotten dressed for work, she'd looked in the mirror and realized some of her hairs were not blond, but white. When had that happened? When had she passed over from youth into the frontiers of middle age? Even though no one else would have noticed those hairs, she had plucked them out, knowing they would grow back just as white. Dead melanocytes don't regenerate. There is no fountain of youth.

At seven-thirty, she finally stepped out the ER doors and paused to inhale a breath of morning air. Air that didn't smell of rubbing alcohol and disinfectant and stale coffee. It looked like it would be a fair day. Already the mist was thinning, revealing faint patches of blue sky. It made her feel better, just to see that. She had the next four days off to catch up on her sleep. And next month, she had two weeks' vacation scheduled. Maybe she could leave Ellen with Vickie, make it a real vacation. A hotel on a beach. Cold drinks and hot sand. Perhaps even a fling at romance. It had been a long time since she'd slept with a man. She'd hoped it would happen with Dvorak. She'd been thinking about him a lot lately, in ways that could bring an unexpected flush to her cheeks. Since their one and only lunch, they'd spoken on the phone twice, but their conflicting schedules made it hard to meet.

And the last time they'd talked, he'd sounded distant. Distracted. *Have I scared him off so quickly, then?*

She forced Dvorak out of her mind. It was back to thinking about fantasy men and tropical destinations.

She crossed the parking lot and got into her car. *I'll call Vickie this afternoon,* she thought as she drove home. *If she can't or won't watch Mom, then I'll hire someone for the week.* To hell with the cost. For years Toby had faithfully set aside money for her retirement. It was time to start spending it now, enjoying it now.

She turned onto her street and felt her heart suddenly do a flip-flop of panic.

An ambulance and a police car were parked in front of her house.

Before she could turn into her own driveway, the ambulance drove off with lights flashing and sped away down the street. Toby parked the car and ran into the house.

There was a uniformed cop standing in her living room, writing in a spiral notebook.

"What happened?" said Toby.

The cop looked at her. "Your name, Ma'am?"

"This is my house. What are you doing here? Where's my mother?"

"They just took her to Springer Hospital."

"Was there an accident?"

Jane's voice said, "There was no accident."

Toby turned to see Jane standing in the kitchen doorway. "I couldn't wake her up," said Jane. "So I called the ambulance."

"You couldn't *wake* her? Did she respond at all?"

240

"She couldn't seem to move. Or speak." Jane and the policeman exchanged glances, a look that Toby couldn't interpret. Only then did the question occur to her: *Why was a policeman in her house?*

She was wasting time here. She turned to leave, to follow the ambulance to Springer.

"Ma'am?" the cop said. "If you'll wait, someone'll be here to talk to you—"

Toby ignored him and walked out of the house.

By the time she pulled into the Springer Hospital parking lot, she'd already imagined the worst. A heart attack. A stroke. Ellen comatose and on a ventilator.

One of the day shift nurses met her at the front desk. "Dr. Harper—"

"Where's my mother? An ambulance was bringing her in."

"She's in room two. We're stabilizing her now. Wait, don't go in yet—"

Toby pushed past the front desk and opened the door to room two.

Ellen's face was hidden from view by the crowd of medical personnel working around the gurney. Paul Hawkins had just finished intubating. A nurse was hanging a fresh IV bottle, another was juggling blood tubes.

"What happened?" said Toby.

Paul glanced up. "Toby, can you wait outside?"

"What happened?"

"She just stopped breathing. We had severe bradycardia, but the pulse is back up—"

"An MI?"

"Can't see it on EKG. We're still waiting for cardiac enzyme results."

"Oh my God. Oh my God . . ." Toby squeezed forward to the gurney and took her mother's hand. "Mom, it's me."

Ellen didn't open her eyes, but her hand moved, as though to pull away.

241

TESS GERRITSEN

"Mom, it's going to be all right. They're going to take good care of you."

Now Ellen's other hand began to move, thrashing against the mattress. A nurse quickly snatched Ellen's wrist and looped a restraint around it. The sight of that frail hand trapped and struggling against the cloth cuff was more than Toby could bear. "Does it have to be so tight?" she snapped. "You've already made a bruise—"

"We'll lose the IV."

"You're cutting off her circulation!"

"Toby," said Paul, "I want you to wait outside. We've got everything under control."

"Mom doesn't know any of you—"

"You're not letting us do our job. You have to *leave*."

Toby took a step back from the gurney and saw that they were all looking at her. She realized Paul was right; she was getting in the way, making it difficult for them to make the necessary decisions. When she was the physician in charge of a critical case, she never allowed the patient's family to remain in the room. Neither should Paul.

She said, softly, "I'll be outside," and she walked out.

In the hallway, a man was waiting for her. Early forties, unsmiling. A monk's haircut. "Dr. Harper?" he said.

"Yes."

Something about the way he approached her, the way he seemed to be sizing her up, told her this was a cop. He confirmed it by showing her his badge. "Detective Alpren. May I ask you about your mother?"

"I want to ask *you* a few questions. Why was a cop in my house? Who called you people?"

"Ms. Nolan did."

"Why would she call the police for a medical emergency?"

Detective Alpren pointed toward an empty exam room. "Let's step in there," he said.

Bewildered, she followed Alpren into the room. He closed the door.

"How long has your mother been ill?" he asked.

"Are you referring to her Alzheimer's?"

"I mean her current illness. The reason she's here right now."

Toby shook her head. "I don't even know what's wrong with her yet . . ."

"Does she have any chronic illnesses other than the Alzheimer's?"

"Why are you asking me these questions?"

"I understand your mother's been ill for the last week. Lethargy. Nausea."

"She's seemed a little tired. I assumed it was a virus. Some sort of gastrointestinal upset—"

"A virus, Dr. Harper? That's not what Ms. Nolan thinks."

She stared at him, not understanding any of this. "What did Jane tell you? You said she called you—"

"Yes."

"I'd like to talk to her. Where is she?"

He ignored the question. "Ms. Nolan mentioned certain injuries. She said your mother complained about burns on her hands."

"They healed weeks ago. I told Jane what happened."

"And the bruises on her thigh? How did she get those?"

"What bruises? I'm not aware of any bruises."

"Ms. Nolan says she asked you about them two days ago. That you couldn't explain them."

"What?"

"Can you explain the bruises?"

"I want to know why the hell she's saying these things," said Toby. "Where is she?"

Alpern studied her for a moment. Then he shook his head. "Given the circumstances, Dr. Harper," he said, "Ms. Nolan doesn't wish to be contacted."

* * *

After the CT scan, Ellen was admitted to a bed in the medical ICU, and Toby was allowed to visit her again. The first thing she did was peel back the sheets and look for the bruises. There were four of them, small, irregular blotches on the outer left thigh. She stared at them in disbelief, silently railing at herself for being so blind. How and when did this happen? Did Ellen injure herself? Or were those the marks left by someone else's hand, repeatedly pinching that fragile skin? She covered her mother's legs with the sheet and for a long time stood gripping the siderail in silent fury, trying not to let rage cloud her judgment. But she couldn't suppress the thought: *If Jane did this, I'm going to kill her.*

There was a tap on the window, and Vickie came in. She didn't say anything as she took her place across from Toby.

"She's in a coma," said Toby. "They just did the head scan. It appears she's had a massive intracerebral bleed. Nothing they can drain. We just have to watch. And wait."

Vickie remained silent.

"Everything's been so crazy this morning," said Toby. "They noticed bruises on Mom's thigh. Jane's telling the police I did it. She's actually got them thinking—"

"Yes, she told me."

Toby stared at her, dismayed by the flatness of her sister's voice. "Vickie—"

"Last week, I *told* you Mom was sick. I told you she was throwing up. But you didn't seem at all concerned."

"I thought it was a virus—"

"You never took her to a doctor, did you?" Vickie looked at her as though studying a creature she'd never seen before. "I didn't tell you, but Jane called me yesterday. She asked me not to mention it to you. But she was worried."

"What did she say? Vickie, *what did she say?*"

"She said . . ." Vickie released a shaky breath. "She said she was concerned about what was happening. When she

244

first took the job, she noticed bruises on Mom's arms, as if she'd been grabbed. Shaken around. Those bruises faded, but then this week, new ones appeared, on the thighs. Did you see them?"

"Jane's been the one bathing her every day—"

"So you didn't see them? You don't even know about them?"

"She never asked *me* about them!"

"And the burns? What about the burns on Mom's hands?"

"That happened weeks ago! Mom picked up a hot dish from the stove."

"So there *was* a burn."

"It was an accident! Bryan was there when it happened."

"Are you saying Bryan's responsible?"

"No. No, that's not what I'm saying—"

"Then who is responsible, Toby?"

The two sisters stared at each other across Ellen's sleeping form.

"I'm your sister," said Toby. "You know me. How can you believe a complete stranger?"

"I don't know." Vickie ran her hand through her hair. "I don't know what to believe. I just want you to tell me what really happened. I know Mom's hard to deal with. She's worse than a child sometimes, and it's not easy to—"

"What do *you* know about it? You've never offered to help."

"I have a family."

"Mom *is* family. Something your husband and kids can't seem to grasp."

Vickie's chin lifted. "You're turning it into another one of your guilt trips, the way you always do. Who suffers the most, who's most deserving of sainthood. Saint Toby."

"Don't."

"So when did you lose your temper? When did you finally crack and start hitting her?"

Toby jerked back, too shocked to speak, too angry to trust anything she *did* say.

Vickie's mouth was trembling. Her eyes filling with tears, she said, "Oh, God. I didn't mean that."

Toby turned and walked out of the cubicle. She didn't stop until she'd left the building and crossed the parking lot to her car.

The first place she drove was to Jane Nolan's house. She had her address book in her purse, and she looked up the entry for Jane. It was in Brookline, east of Springer Hospital.

A four-mile drive brought her to the address, a green-shingled duplex on a sterile, treeless street. There were planters on the front porch with hard-baked soil and a few dying weeds. The curtains were closed over the windows, shutting off all view of the interior.

Toby rang the bell. No one answered. She knocked, then pounded on the door. *Open up, damn you. Tell me why you're doing this to me!*

"Jane!" she yelled.

The next-door neighbor's door opened and a woman cautiously poked her head out.

"I'm looking for Jane Nolan," said Toby.

"Well stop pounding. She's not there."

"When will she be back?"

"Who're you?"

"I just want to know when Jane will be back."

"How should I know? I haven't seen her in days." The woman shut the door.

Toby felt like hurling a rock through Jane's window. She gave the door one last pound of her fist, then got back into her car.

That's when it all crashed down on her. Ellen in a coma. Vickie turning into a spiteful stranger. She rocked forward and struggled not to cry, not to shatter. It was the blare of her own car horn that snapped her back up. She'd leaned too heavily on the steering wheel. A mailman, passing by on the street, stopped to stare at her.

She drove away. *Where do I go? Where do I go?*

She headed for Bryan's house. He would back her up. He had been there the day Ellen burned her hand; he'd be her character witness, the one person who knew how devoted she'd been to Ellen.

But Bryan wasn't home; he'd be at work until four-thirty, according to his companion, Noel, who answered the door. Would Toby like to come in for coffee? A drink? *You look like you need to sit down.*

What he meant was she looked like hell.

She refused the offer. For want of any other destination, she drove home.

The police car was gone. Three of her neighbors stood conversing on the sidewalk in front of her house. As Toby's car approached, they turned and stared at her. By the time she pulled into her driveway, they had walked off in three different directions. Cowards. Why didn't they just ask her to her face if she'd beaten up her own mother?

She stormed into the house and slammed the door shut.

Silence. No Ellen. No one wandering in the garden, no one watching the morning cartoons.

She sat down on the couch and dropped her head in her hands.

15

"Mine's a baby girl," said Annie, her fingers skimming over the bedcovers, caressing her belly. "I want her to be a girl, 'cause I wouldn't know what to do with a boy. Wouldn't know how to make him turn out right. Hardly meet a man these days who's turned out right."

They were lying side by side in the darkness on Annie's bed. The only light was the glow of the streetlamp outside the window. Every so often there'd be moving fragments of light from a passing car, and Molly would catch a glimpse of Annie's face, head resting on the pillow as she serenely gazed up at the ceiling. It was warm in the bed with Annie. They had put on fresh sheets today, had sat together in the laundromat giggling and leafing through old magazines while the linens had spun round and round in the dryer. Now whenever Molly turned, she smelled that clean scent of laundry soap. And Annie's scent as well.

"How can you tell if it's a girl?" asked Molly.

"Well, a doctor can tell for sure."

"Did you see a doctor?"

"I didn't want to go back to *that* one. Didn't like that place."

"So how do you know it *is* a girl?"

Annie's hands began to move over her abdomen again. "I just know. This nurse I met, she told me that when a mother gets to feeling like that, a real strong feeling, she's never wrong. This one's a girl."

"I don't have no feeling 'bout mine."

"Maybe it's too early for yours, Molly."

"I don't have no feeling 'bout it one way or the other. See, it doesn't seem like a person yet. It seems like just a lot of fat poochin' out here. Shouldn't I be feeling love or somethin'? I mean, isn't that what's supposed to happen?" She turned and looked at Annie's face, silhouetted against the window's glow.

"You must feel something for it," said Annie softly. "Why else would you be keeping it?"

"I don't know."

Molly felt Annie's hand reach for hers under the covers. They lay with fingers entwined, their breathing in perfect synchrony.

"I don't know what I'm doing or why I'm doing it," said Molly. "I kind of got all mixed up. And then, when Romy knocked me around, I got so pissed at him I wasn't gonna do nothin' he told me to do. So I didn't go to that place." She paused and looked at Annie again. "How do they do it?"

"Do what?"

"Get rid of it?"

Annie shuddered. "I only had it done once. Last year, when Romy sent me to that place. Had these people all dressed in blue. Wouldn't talk to me, just told me to get on the table and shut up. They gave me something to breathe, and after that, I just remember waking up. All skinny again. Empty . . ."

"Was it a girl?"

Annie sighed. "I don't know. They put me in the car and sent me back to him." Annie released Molly's hand, and her withdrawal seemed more than just physical. She had retreated into some private compartment. A place for just her and her baby.

"Molly," said Annie, after a long silence. "You know you can't stay here much longer." The words, spoken so softly, delivered a stunning blow.

Molly turned on her side to face Annie. "What did I do wrong? Tell me what I did wrong."

"Nothing. It just can't keep going on this way."

"Why not? I'll do more. I'll do whatever you—"

"Molly, I said you could stay for a few days. It's been over two weeks. Honey, I like you and all, but Mr. Lorenzo, he came up to see me today. Complained that I had someone living here with me. Says that's not in our rental agreement. So I can't let you stay. It's small enough, with you and me here. When my baby comes—"

"That won't be for another month."

"Molly." Annie's voice had steadied. Turned unyielding. "You have to find your own place to live. I can't keep you here."

Molly turned her back to Annie. *I thought we could be a family: You and your baby. Me and mine. No men, no assholes.*

"Molly? You okay?"

"I'm fine."

"You understand, don't you?"

Molly gave a weary shrug of one shoulder. "I guess."

"It's not like right away. You can take a few days, figure out where you're going. Maybe you could try calling your mama again."

"Yeah."

"She's bound to take you back. She's your mama."

When there was no reply, Annie reached over and slung an arm around Molly's waist. The warmth of the other woman's body, the other woman's swollen belly pressing against her back, filled Molly with such a sense of longing that she couldn't resist the impulse. Turning to face Annie, she wrapped her arms around Annie's waist and pulled her close, felt their bellies press together like ripening fruit. And suddenly she wished that *she* was in Annie's womb, that *she* was the child who would find its home in Annie's arms.

"Let me stay," she whispered. "Please let me stay."

Firmly Annie pushed away Molly's hands. "You can't. I'm sorry, Molly, *but you can't.*" She turned and scooted to the far side of the bed. "Now good night."

Molly lay very still. *What did I say? What did I do wrong? Please, I'll do whatever you want me to do. Just tell me what it is!* She knew Annie was not sleeping; the darkness between them was too charged with tension. She sensed that Annie was coiled up as tightly as she was.

But neither one of them spoke.

The sound of groaning awakened her. At first Molly was confused by the last shreds of her dream. A baby floating in a pond, making strange noises. Frog noises. Then she opened her eyes, and it was still night and she was in Annie's bed. A light was shining under the bathroom door.

"Annie?" she said but heard no answer.

She rolled over and closed her eyes, trying to shut out that disturbing sliver of light.

A thump jolted her fully awake.

She sat up and squinted at the bathroom. "Annie?" Hearing no reply, she climbed out of bed and went to knock on the door. "Are you okay?" She turned the knob and pushed, but the door wouldn't open; something was block-

251

ing it. She pushed harder and felt the barrier give way slightly, allowing the door to open. She peered through the crack, at first not understanding what she saw.

A rivulet of blood on the floor.

"Annie!" she cried. Pushing with all her strength, she finally managed to open the door wide enough to squeeze through. She found Annie crumpled in the corner, her shoulder wedged against the door, her cheap nightgown gathered above her waist. Blood was splattered across the toilet seat, and the water in the bowl was a silky crimson. A warm stream suddenly gushed out from between Annie's thighs and lapped at Molly's bare toes.

In horror, she backed away and collided with the sink.

Oh God, oh God, oh God.

Though Annie wasn't moving, her belly was; it was squirming, the bare skin bunching into a tight ball of flesh.

More blood gushed out, streaming across the linoleum. The warmth of the blood trickled around her chilled feet, shaking Molly out of her trance. She forced herself to step through the crimson pool, to cross to Annie's coiled-up body. She had to move her out from behind the door. She grasped Annie's arm and pulled, but her feet kept slipping in the blood. Annie made a noise, a high, soft whine, like the hiss of air escaping from a balloon. Molly pulled harder, finally managing to drag Annie a few feet across the linoleum. Now she placed her feet against the door jamb and, using that as an anchor, heaved at Annie's body.

Annie slid out of the bathroom.

She grabbed both arms now and pulled her completely through the doorway. Then she turned on the bedroom lights.

Annie was still breathing, but her eyes were rolled back, and her face was white.

Molly ran out of the flat and down the stairs. She pounded on the door of the ground-floor apartment. *"Help me!"* she cried. "Please, help me!" No one answered.

She ran out of the building, to the pay telephone on the street, and dialed 911.

"Emergency operator."

"I need an ambulance! She's bleeding—"

"Your name and address?"

"My name's Molly Picker. I don't know the address. I think I'm on Charter Street—"

"What's the cross street?"

"I can't see it! She's going to die—"

"Do you know the nearest address number?"

Molly turned and frantically scanned the building. "1076! I see a 1076."

"Where is the victim? What is her condition?"

"She's in the upstairs apartment—she's bleeding all over the floor—"

"Ma'am, I'm dispatching an ambulance now. If you'll wait on the line—"

Fuck this, thought Molly. She left the phone hanging and ran back into the building.

Annie was lying where she'd left her on the bedroom floor. Her eyes were open but unfocused and glassy.

"Please, you have to stay awake." Molly grasped Annie's hand, but there was no answering squeeze. No warmth at all. She stared at the chest, saw it expand in a shallow breath. *Keep breathing. Please keep breathing.*

Then another movement caught her eye. Annie's abdomen seemed to swell upward, as though some alien creature inside her body was straining to burst free. A gush of blood spilled out from between her thighs.

So did something else. Something pink.

The baby.

Molly knelt between Annie's knees and eased the thighs apart. Fresh blood, mixed with water, dribbled out around the protruding arm. At least Molly *thought* it was an arm.

Then she saw there were no fingers, no hand, just that glistening pink flipper writhing slowly back and forth.

There was another contraction, a final gush of blood and fluid as the flipper slid out, followed by the rest of the body. Molly jerked backward, shrieking.

It was not a baby.

But it was alive and moving, the two flippers writhing in agonal struggles. It had no other limbs, just those two pink stubs waving from a single mass of raw flesh attached to an umbilical cord. She could see clumps of hair, coarse and black, a protruding tooth, and a single eye, unblinking, lashless. Blue. The flippers were thrashing, and the whole organism began to move with almost purposeful direction, like an amoeba swimming in a pool of blood.

Sobbing, Molly scrambled on hands and knees as far away as she could get. She pressed herself into a corner and watched in disbelief as the thing struggled to live. The paddle-arms began to twitch in erratic seizurelike spasms. The body had ceased its amoebic gliding and was only quivering now. When at last the flippers fell still, and the flesh stopped twitching, that eye was still open and staring at her.

Another gush of blood, and the placenta slid out.

Molly buried her face against her knees and curled into a ball.

As though from a great distance, she heard a whining sound. Then, a moment later, someone was banging at the door.

"Paramedics! Hello? Did someone call an ambulance?"

"Help her," whispered Molly. In a sob, louder: "Help her!"

The door opened and two uniformed men burst into the flat. They stared at Annie's body, and then their gazes followed the glistening trail of blood leading from between her thighs.

"Holy shit," one of them said. "What the hell is *that* thing?"

The other man knelt beside Annie. "She's not breathing. Ambubag—"

There was a whoosh as one of the men squeezed air through a mask into Annie's lungs.

"No pulse. I'm not getting a pulse."

"Okay, go! One-one thousand, two-one thousand . . ."

Molly watched them, but none of it seemed real to her. It was a movie, a TV show. It was not Annie but an actress playing dead. The needle was not really going into her arm. The blood on the floor was ketchup. And the thing—the thing lying a few feet away from her . . .

"Still not getting a pulse—"

"Flatline EKG."

"Pupils?"

"Fixed."

"Shit, don't stop."

A radio crackled. "City Hospital."

"This is Unit Nineteen," said the paramedic. "We have a white female in her twenties, looks like massive vaginal hemorrhage—possible abortion attempt. Blood looks fresh. No respirations, no pulse, pupils fixed and midposition. We have an IV line, Ringer's lactate. Flatline on EKG. We are now doing CPR, without response. Should we call it?"

"Not yet."

"But she's flatline—"

"Stabilize and transport."

The paramedic shut off the radio and looked at his partner. "Stabilize *what?*"

"Just get her tubed and moved."

"What about the . . . thing?"

"Hell, I'm not *touching* that."

Molly was still watching that TV show with ketchup blood. She saw the tube go down actress-Annie's throat. Saw the actor-paramedics lift her onto a rolling stretcher and continue pumping on her chest.

One of the men glanced at Molly. "We're taking her to City Hospital," he said. "What's the patient's name?"

"What?"

"Her name!"

"Annie. I don't know her last name."

"Look, don't leave the apartment. Did you hear me? You have to stay right here."

"Why?"

"The police will be coming to talk to you. Don't leave."

"Annie—what about Annie?"

"You check with City Hospital later. She'll be there."

Molly listened to them carry the stretcher down the stairs. She heard the wheels clatter out the front door, and the single whoop of the siren as the ambulance pulled away.

The police will be here to talk to you.

The words finally sank in. She didn't want to talk to the police. They would ask for her name and then they would find out she'd been arrested last year for soliciting a cop. Romy had bailed her out, had given her a few good slaps for being such an idiot.

The police will say it's my fault. Somehow, this will all be my fault.

She rose, shaking, to her feet. The *thing* was still lying there, still glistening, but the blue eye had turned dry and dull. She stepped around it, avoiding the puddles of blood, and crossed to the dresser. There was money in the top drawer—Annie's money—but Annie wouldn't be needing it now. That much Molly had understood from the paramedics. Annie was dead.

She pulled out a wad of twenty-dollar bills. Then she quickly dressed in Annie's clothes, a pair of stretch pants with an elastic belly, a giant T-shirt with *Oh, Baby!* printed across the chest. Black sneakers. She pulled on Annie's giant raincoat, stuffed the cash in her purse, and fled the apartment.

She was on the other side of the street when she saw the

police car pull up in front of the building, its blue dome light twirling. Two cops entered the building. Seconds later, she saw their silhouettes move past Annie's upstairs window.

They were looking at the *thing*. Wondering what it was.

One of the cops crossed to the window and glanced outside.

Molly slipped around the corner and began to run. She kept running until she was out of breath, until she was stumbling. She ducked into a doorway and sank onto the front step. Her heart was skipping; she could feel it flutter in her throat.

The sky was starting to get light.

She huddled on that front stoop until morning came and a man emerged through the front door and told her to move on. So she did.

A few blocks away, she stopped at a pay phone to call City Hospital. "I want to find out about my friend," she said. "An ambulance brought her in."

"Your friend's name?"

"Annie. They took her from the apartment—they said she wasn't breathing—"

"May I ask if you're a relative?"

"No, I'm just—I mean—"

Molly froze, staring at a police car driving by. It seemed to slow down as it passed Molly, then continued up the street.

"Hello, Ma'am? Could I have your name?"

Molly hung up. The police car had turned the corner and was now out of sight.

She left the phone booth and swiftly walked away.

Detective Roy Sheehan settled his ample behind onto the stool next to Dvorak's lab bench and asked: "Okay, so what's a prion?"

Dvorak looked up from the microscope, refocusing his eyes on the cop. "What?"

"I just been talking to your girl, Lisa."

Of course you have, thought Dvorak. Despite Dvorak's advice, Sheehan had been making regular visits to the morgue for several days now, his real purpose not to view dead bodies but to ogle a live one.

"Real smart girl, by the way," said Sheehan. "Anyway, she says this Creutzfeldt-Jakob thing—am I saying it right—it's caused by something called a prion."

"That's correct."

"So can people catch it? Is it, like, floating around in the air?"

Dvorak looked down at his finger, where the cut had recently healed. "You can't *catch it* in the usual sense."

"Toby Harper's saying there's an epidemic in the making."

Dvorak shook his head. "I've spoken to both CDC and the Department of Public Health. They say there's no reason for concern. That hormone protocol Wallenberg's testing is perfectly safe. And Public Health can't find any violations at the Brant Hill facility."

"So why's Dr. Harper up in arms against Brant Hill?"

Dvorak paused. Reluctantly he said, "She's under a lot of pressure right now. She faces a possible lawsuit over that patient of hers who vanished. And Dr. Brace's death shook her up pretty badly. When everything goes wrong in our lives, it's natural to look around for someone—or something—to blame." He reached for a different slide and inserted it under the lens. "I think Toby's been stressed out for a very long time."

"You heard what happened to her mother?"

Again Dvorak hesitated. "Yes," he said quietly. "Toby called me yesterday."

"She did? You two are still talking?"

"Why shouldn't we? She needs a friend right now, Roy."

"There may be criminal charges filed. Alpren says it looks

like elder abuse. The nanny blames Dr. Harper. Dr. Harper blames the nanny."

Dvorak bent his head back to the microscope. "The mother had an intracerebral bleed. That's not necessarily abuse. It doesn't make either one of them a granny basher."

"But there are bruises on the legs."

"The elderly often bruise themselves. Their vision's not so good. They run into coffee tables."

Sheehan grunted. "You're sure doing your best to defend her."

"I'm giving her the benefit of the doubt."

"But she *is* wrong about this so-called epidemic?"

"Yes, she's wrong about that. Catching CJD isn't like catching the flu. It's transmitted in only a few specific ways."

"Like eating mad cows?"

"The U.S. herd doesn't have mad cow disease."

"But people here *do* come down with the human version."

"Creutzfeldt-Jakob occurs in one in a million people, with no obvious history of exposure."

Both men glanced up as the object of Sheehan's affection strolled into the lab, flashed them both a smile, and bent over to open a small specimen refrigerator. Sheehan stared, transfixed by that luscious rear-end view. Only when Lisa straightened and walked out again did Sheehan seem able to draw another breath.

"Is that natural?" he murmured.

"Is what natural?"

"That hair. Is she a real blond?"

"I really wouldn't know," said Dvorak, and he focused his gaze back on the microscope slide.

"There's one way to find out, you know," said Sheehan.

"Ask her?"

"You check out the hair no one sees."

Dvorak leaned back and squeezed the bridge of his nose. "Did you have something else to ask me, Roy?"

"Oh. Oh, yeah. I've heard about viruses, and I've heard about bacteria. But what the hell's a prion?"

Resignedly Dvorak turned off the microscope lamp. "A prion," he said, "isn't what we'd normally call a living thing. Unlike a virus, it has neither DNA nor RNA. In other words, it has no genetic material—or what we *think* of as genetic material. It's an abnormal cellular protein. It can transform the host's proteins into the same abnormal form."

"But it can't be caught like the flu."

"No. It has to be introduced by direct tissue exposure, like brain or spinal cord implants. Or by extractions from neural tissue, like growth hormone. For example, you can catch it from contaminated brain electrodes."

"Those English people got it from eating beef."

"Okay, it's also possible to catch it by eating infected meat. That's how cannibals get it."

Sheehan's eyebrows shot up. "Now *this* starts to get interesting. What's this about cannibals?"

"Roy, this is completely irrelevant—"

"No, I wanna hear this. What about cannibals?"

Dvorak sighed. "There've been villages in New Guinea where eating human flesh is part of a sacred ritual. The only people who caught CJD were the women and children."

"Why only women and kids?"

"The men got the choicest cuts—the meat of the corpse. The muscle. The women and kids had to be satisfied with the parts no one else wanted. The brain." He watched for a disgusted reaction on Sheehan's face, but the cop only leaned closer. In some ways, he was like a cannibal himself, eager to devour the most appalling morsels of information.

"So eating a human brain would do it," said Sheehan.

"An infected human brain."

"Can you tell it's infected by looking at it?"

"No, it's a microscopic diagnosis. And this is a stupid conversation."

"It's the big city, Doc. Weirder stuff happens. We get reports of vampires, werewolves—"

"People who *think* they're werewolves."

"Who knows? All this crazy cult shit going on these days."

"I hardly think there's some cannibalistic cult at Brant Hill."

Sheehan glanced down as his beeper went off. "Excuse me," he said and left to make the call.

Now I can finally get some work done, thought Dvorak.

A moment later, though, Sheehan returned. "I'm headed out to the North End. Think maybe you should come see this one."

"What is it? A homicide?"

"They're not sure." Sheehan paused. "They're not even sure it's human."

16

The smell of blood, cloying and metallic, had wafted even into the hallway. Dvorak nodded to the patrolman standing watch, ducked under the police tape, and stepped into the flat. Sheehan and his partner, Jack Moore, were already inside, as was the CSU crew. Moore was squatting by something near the corner. Dvorak didn't cross toward him right away but held back near the doorway, his gaze carefully scanning the floor.

It was yellow and white linoleum, in a pattern of random squares with a ratty throw rug by the bed. Blood was still drying on the floor near the bathroom—a great deal of blood. There were smear marks, as though something had been dragged across the floor, as well as a confusing collage of bloody shoeprints. He also saw the distinct imprints of bare feet, small ones, tracking toward the dresser, then fading out.

He looked at the walls and saw no arterial splatter. In fact, there was very little splatter at all, just that congealing lake. Whoever had bled in this room had done so while lying quietly on the floor, and not in a panicked frenzy.

"Doc," said Moore. "Come and look at this."

"You got shots of these footprints already?"

"Yeah, those are from the EMTs. It's all been photographed and videotaped. Just step around that way. Watch out for that set of footprints there."

Dvorak stepped carefully around the imprints of the bare feet and circled around to where Moore and Sheehan were squatting.

"What do you think?" said Moore, moving aside to let Dvorak see what lay on the floor.

"*Jesus.*"

"That was our reaction, too. So what *is* it?"

Dvorak didn't know what to say. Slowly he dropped down for a closer look.

His first impression was that it was a leftover Halloween gag, a one-eyed, flesh-colored monster fashioned from rubber and nightmares. Then he saw the streaks of blood drying on its surface, and the fragment of attached placenta, connected by an umbilical cord. This *thing* was not made of rubber, but flesh.

He pulled on a pair of gloves and gingerly touched the surface of the Thing. It felt like real skin—cold, but yielding. The single eye was a pale blue, with a rudimentary flap of skin for an eyelid, but no lashes. Below it were two small holes, like nostrils, then an open cleft. The mouth? He could scarcely identify any normal anatomy on this lump of flesh. Tufts of hair sprang out at crazy angles. And—dear God—was that a tooth poking out by the flipper?

He recalled a tumor he'd once seen removed from a woman's abdomen. A teratoma. It had been the result of an ovum gone crazy, turning into a cancer made up of wildly differentiating cells. The tumor had had teeth and tufts of hair connected in a ball of skin.

Suddenly he focused on the pattern of dried blood on the floor, on the irregular smear leading from the larger pool, and the umbilical cord, stretched out straight. The realization of what he was looking at made him pull his hand away in horror.

"Shit," he said. "It *moved.*"

"I didn't see it move," said Moore.

"Not now. *Before.* It left that trail." He pointed to the flip-flop pattern of blood.

"You mean—it was actually *alive?*"

"It seems to be more than just a random collection of cells. It has rudimentary limbs. It moves, so it has some sort of skeletal structure and muscle attachments."

"And an eye," murmured Sheehan. "A fucking cyclops. And it's looking at me."

Dvorak glanced at Moore. "So what's the story here? How did you get involved?"

"EMTs notified us. Ambulance was dispatched here around five A.M., after a female called in a medical emergency. They found a woman bleeding on the floor over there. There's a lot more blood in the bathroom, in the toilet bowl."

"Bleeding from where?"

"The vagina, I guess. They didn't know whether to call it an unattended birth. Or an attempted abortion." Moore looked down at the thing with flippers. "I mean, do you call that a *baby?* Or just part of a baby?"

"I think it's multiple congenital malformations. But I've never seen anything like it."

"Yeah, well, I hope I never see another one. Can you imagine what it'd be like, to be Daddy in the delivery room? And to see *that* come out? It'd give me a fucking coronary."

"What happened to the victim?"

"The woman was DOA at City Hospital, which makes her

an ME case. We think her name is Annie Parini—at least, that's the name the neighbors know her by."

"What about the other female? The one who made the call?"

"She skipped out before the first patrol car arrived. EMTs said she looked pretty young. Teenager. The name she gave to the emergency operator was Molly Picker."

Dvorak crossed to the bathroom doorway and looked inside. He saw more blood, splattered across the toilet and the shower tiles. A lake of it on the floor. "I need to talk to the girl."

"You think she contributed to the death?"

"I just want to know what she saw. What she knows about the victim." He turned and frowned at the Thing. "If Annie Parini was taking some drug—and if it caused *that*—then we're dealing with a devastating new teratogen."

"Could a drug do that?"

"I've never seen a malformation this severe. I'll send it out for genetic analysis. In the meantime, I'd really like to talk to this Molly Picker. If that's her name."

"We've got fingerprints. She left them all over the place." He pointed to one bloody set on the bathroom doorframe, another set on the wall near the Thing. "We'll confirm the name."

"Find her for me. Don't scare her—I just want to talk to her."

"What about Annie Parini?" asked Sheehan. "You gonna do a post on her?"

Dvorak looked down at the blood on the floor. And he nodded. "I'll see you both in the morgue."

The body on the autopsy table was now nothing but a hollowed-out cavity, gutted of its organs. Throughout the autopsy, Detectives Sheehan and Moore had said very little. Judging by the pallor of their faces, both cops would rather be just about anywhere else. What made this victim more upsetting than usual was her age and her sex. A woman this young should not be lying on an autopsy table.

Dvorak had worked with a minimum of conversation, reserving his comments for the tape recorder. Heart and lungs unremarkable. The stomach empty. Liver and pancreas of normal size and appearance. All in all, a youthful, undiseased body.

He turned his attention to the enlarged uterus, which had been removed in one piece and was lying on the cutting board under a bright light. He slit it open, through the myometrial and endometrial layers, to reveal the cavity.

"We have our answer."

Both cops reluctantly stepped closer.

"Abortion?" asked Moore.

"Not what I'm seeing here. There's no uterine perforation. No evidence of instrumentation. In the old days, before *Roe vs. Wade,* the back room abortionists would usually insert some sort of catheter through the cervix to dilate it, and then leave packing or a tampon to hold the catheter in place. But there's nothing here."

"Could she have passed it? Flushed it down the john?"

"Possibly. But I don't think that's what happened." He touched a probe to a mass of bloody tissue. "That's a placental fragment that didn't completely separate from the uterus. It's called placenta accreta. It would account for the bleeding."

"Is that, like, an unusual condition?"

"Not all that unusual. What makes this one especially dangerous was the fact the placenta implanted itself in the lower uterus. That can lead to premature labor. Massive hemorrhage."

"So we've got a natural death here."

"I would say so." Dvorak straightened. "She probably had pain and went into the bathroom, thinking she had to move her bowels. Bled into the toilet bowl, got dizzy, fell on the bathroom floor. Lord knows how long she was lying there before anyone noticed."

"That makes it easier for us," said Sheehan gratefully, stepping away from the cutting board. "No homicide."

"I still need to talk to the other female in the apartment. Those fetal abnormalities were unlike anything I've seen. I don't like the idea of some new teratogenic drug floating around on the streets."

"We got a hit on the name Molly Picker," said Sheehan. "Arrested last year for soliciting. Bailed out by a guy we assume was her pimp. We'll talk to him—he probably knows where to find her."

"Don't scare her, okay? I just need some history on this victim."

"If we don't scare her just a little," said Sheehan, "she may not talk at all."

Romy had had a shitty day, and now it was turning into a shitty night. He paced the street corner at Montgomery and Canton, trying to stay warm. Should've grabbed a jacket on the way out, he thought, but the sun hadn't yet gone down when he'd left the apartment, and he hadn't counted on this wind, knifing between the buildings. Nor had he counted on waiting around this long.

Fuck it. If they wanted to talk, they could come see him on *his* territory.

He left the street corner and began to walk with his shoulders hunched forward, his hands thrust in his jeans pockets for warmth. He'd gone only half a block when he realized a car had pulled over beside him.

"Mr. Bell?" the man said through the crack in the tinted window.

Romy glowered at the car. "You're late, man."

"I would have come earlier, except for the traffic."

"Yeah, right. Well, fuck off." He turned and kept walking.

"Mr. Bell, we need to talk about this little problem."

"I got nothing to say."

"It's in your best interests to step into the car. If you want to keep doing business with us." There was a pause. "And if you want to get paid."

Romy stopped and stared up the street, the wind lashing his face, the chill cutting straight through his silk shirt.

"It's warm in here, Mr. Bell. I'll take you home afterward."

"What the fuck," muttered Romy, and he stepped into the rear of the car. As he settled back for the ride, his attention was focused more on the plush interior than on the man sitting in the driver's seat. As usual, it was the guy with the white-blond hair, the guy who never looked at Romy.

"You need to find that girl."

Romy gave an irritated grunt. "I don't need to do nothing till you pay me."

"She should have been delivered to us two weeks ago."

"Yeah, well, she wasn't one of my most cooperative bitches, you know? I'll get you some others."

"Annie Parini was found dead this morning. Did you know that?"

Romy stared at him. "Who offed her?"

"Nobody. It was a natural death. Nevertheless, the body went to the authorities."

"So?"

"So they already have their hands on one specimen. We can't let them find another. The girl has to be brought in."

"I don't know where she is. I been looking."

"You know her better than anyone else does. You have contacts on the street, don't you? Find her before she goes into labor."

"She's still got time."

"The pregnancy was never meant to go to term. We have no idea if it will last a full nine months."

"You mean she could pop it any time?"

"We don't know."

Romy laughed and looked out the window as the buildings glided by. "Man, you guys crack me up. You're way behind on this. They already come by, asking about her."

"Who?"

"Police. Dropped by this afternoon, wanting to know where she was."

The man went silent for a moment. In the rearview mirror, Romy glimpsed a flash of panic in the man's face. *Molly Wolly,* he thought, *you got 'em scared.*

"It'll be worth it to you," the man said.

"You want her whole? Or in Reese's Pieces?"

"We want her alive. We need her alive."

"Alive's harder."

"Ten. On delivery."

"Twenty-five, half now, or fuck it." Romy reached for the door handle.

"All right. Twenty-five."

Romy felt like laughing. These guys were scared shitless, and all because of stupid Molly Wolly. She wasn't worth twenty-five thousand. In his humble opinion, she wasn't worth twenty-five cents.

"Can you deliver?" the man asked.

"Maybe."

"If you can't, I'm going to have some very unhappy investors. So *find* her." He handed Romy an envelope. "There'll be more."

Glancing inside, Romy caught a flash of fifty-dollar bills. It was a start.

The car pulled over at Upton and Tremont—Romy's home turf. He hated to leave those nice leather seats, to step out into the slicing wind. He waved the envelope. "What about the rest?"

"On delivery. You can deliver?"

String him along, thought Romy. *Make it sound harder*

than it really is. Maybe the price will go up. He said, "I'll see what I can do," and he climbed out and watched the car drive away. *Scared. The man looks scared.*

The envelope felt nice and thick; Romy stuffed it in his jeans pocket.

Better hide, Molly Wolly, he thought. *Ready or not, here I come.*

Bryan invited her into the house and offered her a glass of wine. It was the first time Toby had been inside his home. She felt uneasy about it, not because of the unconventional nature of Bryan's household, which consisted of two men, happily mated to each other. Rather, it was because she realized, as she sat on the couch in his living room, that she had never really spent time with Bryan as a friend. He had come into her home to care for her mother, had fed Ellen, bathed her. In return, Toby had written him a check every two weeks, *pay to the order of.* Friendship had never been part of the job description.

And why not? she wondered as Bryan set down a napkin and a glass of white wine on the coffee table in front of her. Why had the simple act of writing a check every two weeks made real friendship between them so impossible?

She sat sipping the wine and feeling guilty about never having made the effort. And embarrassed that only now, when she truly needed him, had she even thought to set foot in his house.

He sat down across from her, and a moment passed. They sipped wine, fussed with damp napkins. The lampshades threw arching shadows on the cathedral ceiling. On the wall across from Toby hung a black and white photo of Bryan and Noel on a crescent of beach, their arms slung around each other's shoulders. They wore the smiles of two men who knew how to enjoy life. A knack Toby had never picked up.

Bryan said, "I guess you know the Newton police have already talked to me."

"I gave them your name. I thought you could back me up. They seem to think I'm the daughter from hell." She set down her wineglass and looked at him. "Bryan, you know I'd never hurt my mother."

"And that's what I told them."

"Do you think they believed you?"

"I don't know."

"What did they ask?"

He paused to take a sip, and she recognized it as his way of delaying an answer.

"They asked about medications," he finally said. "They wanted to know if Ellen was taking any prescription drugs. And they asked about the burn on her hands."

"You explained what happened?"

"I repeated it several times. They didn't seem to like my answer. What is going on, Toby?"

She sank back, drawing both hands through her hair. "It's Jane Nolan. I don't know why she's doing this to me . . ."

"Doing what to you?"

"It's the only way I can explain it. Jane comes into my home, and she seems like a—a gift from heaven. She's bright, she's kind. She's perfect. She sweeps in and fixes my life for me. Then everything goes wrong. *Everything.* And Jane is telling the police it's my fault. It's almost as if she *meant* to ruin my life."

"Toby, this sounds so bizarre—"

"People *are* bizarre. They do crazy things to get attention. I keep telling the police she's the one they should focus on. The one they should arrest. But they're not doing anything."

"I don't think attacking Jane Nolan is in your best interests."

"She's attacking *me.* She's accused me of trying to hurt my own mother. Why call the police? Why didn't she just ask *me* about the burn on Mom's hands? And why pull Vickie into this? She's turned my own sister against me."

"For what reason?"

"I don't know why! She's *crazy*."

She saw Bryan avert his gaze, and she realized that *she* was the one who sounded ill, the one who needed psychiatric help.

"I've gone over this again and again in my head, trying to understand how it happened," she said. "How I could have *let* it happen. I didn't look at Jane as carefully as I should have."

"Don't hog all the blame, Toby. Didn't Vickie help make the choice?"

"Yes, but she's so superficial about these things. It was really my responsibility. After you quit, I was in a panic. You gave me so little time to find . . ." She paused, a thought suddenly occurring to her. *That's why Jane came into my life. Because Bryan quit.*

"I would have given you more notice," he said. "But they wanted me to start immediately."

"Why did they choose *you*, Bryan?"

"What?"

"You said you weren't *looking* for a new job. Then suddenly you were hired. How did that happen?"

"They called me."

"Who did?"

"Twin Pines Nursing Home. They wanted a recreational art therapist. They knew I'd been a nurse's aide. And they knew I was an artist. That I had paintings for sale in three galleries."

"How did they know?"

He shrugged. "I guess someone gave them my name."

And hired you away from me, she thought. *Leaving me scrambling for a replacement.*

She left Bryan's house with more unanswered questions than when she'd arrived.

She drove to Springer Hospital to check on her mother.

It was 10 P.M. and visiting hours were already over, but no one stopped her from entering Ellen's ICU cubicle. The lights had been dimmed, and Ellen lay in semidarkness. Toby sat down by the bed and listened to the cycling of the ventilator. On the oscilloscope above the bed, a neon green line traced the rhythm of Ellen's heart. The nurse's clipboard hung at the foot of the bed. Toby reached for it and turned on the small reading light to scan the most recent entries.

> *1545: skin warm, dry; no response to painful stimuli.*
> *1715: daughter Vickie in to see her.*
> *1903: vitals stable; still unresponsive.*

She flipped to the next sheet and saw the most recent entry:

> *2030: lab tech here to draw blood for 7-dehydroxy-*
> *warfarin screen.*

At once she left the cubicle and crossed to the nurses' station. "Who ordered this test?" she asked, handing the clipboard to the ward clerk. "The hydroxywarfarin screen?"

"This is on Mrs. Harper?"

"Yes, on my mother."

The ward clerk pulled Ellen's medical chart from the rack and turned to the order sheets. "Dr. Steinglass did."

Toby picked up the telephone and dialed. It rang twice. Dr. Steinglass barely got out his "hello" when Toby snapped:

"Bob, why did you order a warfarin screen on my mother? Do you have reason to think she's been given Coumadin? Or rat poison?"

"It was . . . because of the bruises. And that intracerebral bleed. I told you her prothrombin time came back severely prolonged—"

"Yesterday you said you thought it might be due to liver inflammation."

"The PT was too abnormal. Hepatitis wouldn't explain it."

"So why the warfarin screen? She hasn't been getting warfarin."

There was a long silence. "They asked me to order the test," Steinglass said at last.

"Who?"

"The police. They told me to call the medical examiner for advice. He suggested the warfarin screen."

"Who did you talk to? Which doctor?"

"It was a Dr. Dvorak."

Barely awake, Dvorak fumbled in the darkness for the phone, finally picking it up on the fourth ring. "Hello?"

"Why, Dan? Why are you doing this?"

"Toby?"

"I thought we were friends. Now I find out you're on the other side. I don't understand how I could have been so wrong about you."

"Listen to me, Toby—"

"No, you listen to *me!*" Her voice cracked. A sob spilled out, but was ruthlessly choked back. "I didn't hurt my mother. I didn't poison her. If anyone hurt her, it was Jane Nolan."

"No one's saying you did anything wrong. I'm not saying it."

"Then why didn't you tell me you're checking her blood for warfarin? Why are you doing this behind my back? If you have information that she's been poisoned, you should have talked to *me.* Told *me.* Not slipped in this test while I wasn't looking."

"I tried to call you earlier, to explain, but you weren't home."

"I've been at the hospital. Where else would I be?"

"Okay, I guess I should have tried calling you at Springer. I'm sorry."

"Sorry doesn't cut it. Not when you're working behind my back."

"That's not how it happened. I got a call from Detective Alpren. He said your mother's clotting times came back abnormal. He asked me what could cause that and would I talk to her doctor about it. A screen for warfarin is just the next logical step."

"Logical." She gave a bitter laugh. "Yes, that sounds like you."

"Toby, there are half a dozen other reasons why her clotting times might be abnormal. A warfarin screen is part of the workup. The police asked for my advice, and I gave it. It's my job."

She said nothing for a moment, but he could hear her shaky exhalation, and he knew she was struggling not to cry.

"Toby?"

"I suppose it'll also be your job to testify against me in court."

"It won't come to that."

"If it did. If it *did* come to that."

"Jesus, Toby." He sighed in exasperation. "I'm *not* going to answer that question."

"Never mind," she said just before she hung up. "You already did."

Detective Alpren had eyes like a marmoset's—bright, inquisitive, quick to pick up details. He couldn't seem to stand in one spot for more than a minute, had paced back and forth in the autopsy lab, and when not pacing, would rock from foot to foot. The dead body on the table interested him not at all; it was Dvorak he'd come to see, and for ten minutes he'd been waiting impatiently for the autopsy to end.

At last, Dvorak shut off his cassette recorder, and Alpren said, "Now can we talk about it?"

"Go ahead," said Dvorak, not looking up from the table, his gaze still contemplating the corpse. It was a young man's, the torso hollowed out from neck to pubis. Inside we are all the same, he thought as he looked at the empty cavity. We're just identical sets of organs, packaged in various shades of skin. He picked up a needle and suture and began to sew the cavity shut, taking deep bites of flesh with his needle. There was no need to be elegant; this was merely a cleanup task, to prepare the body for transfer to the mortuary. A job Lisa normally performed.

Alpren, oblivious to the gruesome needlework, stepped up to the table. "The test came back," he said. "That—what do you call it? RHPLC?"

"Rapid high-performance liquid chromotography."

"Right. Anyway, the hospital lab just called me. The test is positive."

Dvorak momentarily froze. He forced himself to keep stitching, to close the skin over the empty cavity. Had Alpren noticed? he wondered.

"So what does that mean?"

Dvorak kept his gaze tightly focused on the task. "The RHPLC is a screening test for the presence of 7-hydroxy-warfarin."

"Which is?"

"A metabolite of warfarin."

"Which is?"

Dvorak tied a knot and reached for another length of suture. "A drug that affects normal clotting. It can lead to excessive bruising. Bleeding."

"Into the brain? Like Mrs. Harper?"

Dvorak paused. "Yes. It may explain the bruises on her legs as well."

"So that's why you suggested the test."

"Dr. Steinglass told me about the abnormal prothrombin time. Warfarin poisoning is on the differential diagnosis."

Alpren was busy scribbling notes as he asked the next question. "And how do you get this drug, warfarin?"

"It can be found in certain rat poisons."

"Makes them bleed to death?"

"It takes some time to be effective. But eventually they hemorrhage internally."

"Pleasant image. Where else can you get warfarin?"

Again Dvorak paused. He didn't want to be having this conversation, didn't want to be considering the possibilities. "It can be given as a prescription medication called Coumadin. For use as a blood thinner."

"Only by prescription?"

"Yes."

"So you'd need a doctor to order it, and a pharmacy to fill it."

"That's right."

The pen was scribbling faster. "That gives me something to work on."

"What?"

"Area pharmacies. Who's had Coumadin prescribed for them and which doctors ordered it."

"It's not that unusual a prescription. You'd find a number of doctors ordering it."

"I'm screening for one particular name. Dr. Harper's."

Dvorak set down the needle holder and looked at Alpren. "Why focus solely on her? What about the mother's care-giver?"

"Jane Nolan has a spotless record. We've checked with her last three employers. And remember, *she* was the one who called us and raised the question of abuse."

"To cover her own ass, maybe?"

"Look at it from Dr. Harper's point of view. She's a nice-looking woman, but no husband, no family of her own. Probably never even dates. She's trapped with a senile old mother who refuses to die. Then she starts screwing up at work and the stress builds."

"Leading to attempted murder?" Dvorak shook his head.

"Number one rule: look at the family first."

Dvorak tied the final knot on the corpse and snipped the suture.

Glancing at the stitched torso, Alpren gave a grunt of disgust. "Jesus. Frankenstein."

"It'll all be hidden under a dress suit. Even a beggar is allowed to look distinguished in his coffin." Dvorak stripped off the gown and gloves and washed his hands in the sink. "What about accidental poisoning?" he said. "The mother has Alzheimer's. There's no telling what she may have put in her mouth. There could be rat poison in the house."

"Which the daughter conveniently left out for old Mom to find. Right."

Dvorak just kept washing his hands.

"I find it interesting that Dr. Harper now refuses to talk to me without her attorney," said Alpren.

"That's not suspicious. That's smart."

"Still, it makes you wonder."

Dvorak dried his hands, not looking at Alpren, not really daring to. *I shouldn't be commenting on this investigation,* he thought. *I'm not detached enough. I don't have the heart to build a criminal case against Toby Harper.* Yet that's what he *should* be doing, what his job required of him. Examine the evidence. Draw the logical conclusions.

He didn't like what the evidence was telling him.

Clearly the old woman had been poisoned, but whether by accident or by intention was impossible to determine at this point. He could not believe Toby was responsible. Or was he simply refusing to believe? Had he lost his objectivity simply because he was attracted to her?

All last night he'd fought the urge to call her back. Twice he had even picked up the phone but then had hung up, reminding himself he could not discuss the evidence with a possible suspect. Then this morning, *she* had tried calling *him.* He'd used his secretary as a barrier, had asked her to screen out Toby's calls. He felt sick about it, but he had little choice. As friendless and vulnerable as Toby was right now, he could offer no comfort to her.

After Alpren left, Dvorak retreated to the lab next door. Boxes of tissue slides were stacked up on the countertop, waiting to be interpreted. It was quiet, solitary work, and he was grateful for it. For an hour he sat hunched over his microscope, the world shut out, the silence broken only by the occasional clink of glass slides. The hermit in his cell, shut off from the rest of the world. Normally he enjoyed working in isolation, but today he felt miserable and unable to concentrate.

He looked down at his finger, where the scalpel nick had healed, leaving a tiny scar. It was a reminder of his own mortality, of the seemingly trivial events that can lead to catastrophe. Stepping off a curb too soon. Catching an earlier plane flight. Smoking one last cigarette before bed. The specter of death is always watching, waiting for its chance. He gazed at the scar, and he imagined his own neurons imploding even now, driven to self-destruction by a horde of alien prions.

There was nothing to be done about it, nothing that could be done except to wait and watch for the signs. A year, two years at the most. Then he'd be home free. He'd have his life back.

He closed the slide box and stared at the blank wall in front of him. *When did I truly have a life?*

He wondered if it wasn't already too late to start one.

279

. He was forty-five, his ex-wife was happily remarried, and his only son had already made the leap to independence. Dvorak's last vacation six months ago had been taken alone, a driving tour through Ireland, pub to pub, enjoying the occasional human contact, however brief and superficial. He had not considered himself a man in need of companionship until he'd arrived one evening in a small village in the west and found that the only pub was closed. Standing on that deserted road, in a place where no one knew his name, he had felt such deep and unexpected despair that he had climbed into his car and driven straight to Dublin.

He could feel that same despair coming on now as he stared at the wall.

The intercom buzzed. Startled, he rose to his feet and picked up the phone. "Yes?"

"You have two calls. On line one's Toby Harper. Do you want me to keep brushing her off?"

It took all his willpower to say, "Tell her I'm unavailable. Indefinitely."

"The other call is Detective Sheehan, line two."

Dvorak punched the button for line two. "Roy?"

"We have some follow-up on that dead baby. Or whatever it was," said Sheehan. "You know that young female who called for the ambulance?"

"Molly Picker?"

"Yeah. We found her."

17

"I'm sorry, but Dr. Dvorak is unable to take your call."

Toby hung up and glanced in frustration at her watch. She'd been trying to reach Dvorak all day. Every call had been refused. She knew the police were building some kind of case against her, and if she could just talk to Dvorak, she might convince him, as a friend, to reveal what the evidence was.

But he wouldn't accept her calls.

She left the ICU nurses' station and crossed to her mother's cubicle. She stood outside the window, watching Ellen's chest rise and fall. The coma had deepened, and Ellen had no spontaneous respirations. The last CT scan had shown the hemorrhage had extended, and there was now a question of a pontine bleed as well. A nurse was at the bedside, adjusting the IV infusion rate. Sensing she was being watched, the nurse turned to the window and saw Toby. Too quickly, she looked away again. That lack of acknowledgment, of even a courteous nod, spoke volumes. The staff no longer trusted Toby. Nobody did.

She left the hospital and got into her car but didn't start the engine. She didn't know where to go. Home was out of the question—too empty, too silent. It was four o'clock, not time yet for dinner, even if she had an appetite. Her body's circadian rhythm was askew, still in transition to a daytime schedule, and she never knew when hunger or fatigue would strike. She knew only that her mind was fuzzy, that nothing felt right. And that her life, once so well ordered, was now totally and irretrievably screwed up.

She opened her purse and took out Jane Nolan's résumé. She'd been carrying it around, intending to call all four of Jane's former employers for more information, any hint that their "perfect" nurse was not so perfect. She'd already spoken to three nursing directors over the phone, and all had given Jane glowing evaluations.

You pulled one over on them. But I know the truth.

The one employer she hadn't spoken to was Wayside Nursing Home. The address was only a few miles away.

She started the car.

"We'd welcome Jane back in a heartbeat," said Doris Macon, the nursing supervisor. "Of all our nurses, she was the one our patients seemed to love the most."

It was suppertime at Wayside Nursing Home, and the meal cart had just rattled into the dining room. Patients in various states of awareness sat at the four long tables, saying little. The only voices in the room were those of the staff as they set down the trays: *There's your supper, dear. Do you need help with that napkin? Let me cut your meat for you . . .*

Doris surveyed the gathering of gray heads and said, "They get so fond of particular nurses, you know. A familiar voice, a friendly face, it means everything to them. When a nurse leaves, some of our patients actually go into mourning. They don't all have families, so we become their families."

"And Jane was good with them?"

"Absolutely. If you're thinking of hiring her, you're lucky to have such a wonderful applicant. We were so sorry when she left us to take that job with Orcutt Health."

"Orcutt? I didn't see that on her résumé."

"I know she worked for them at least a year after she left us."

Toby unfolded Jane's résumé. "It's not here. After you, she lists Garden Grove Nursing Home."

"Oh, that's part of the Orcutt chain. It's a group of nursing homes, owned by the same corporation. If you work for Orcutt, you can be assigned to any one of their facilities."

"How many do they have?"

"A dozen? I'm not sure. But they're one of our biggest competitors."

Orcutt, thought Toby. Why did the name sound familiar?

"I didn't realize Jane was back in Massachusetts looking for a job," said Doris. "I'm sorry she didn't call us."

Toby refocused her attention on Doris. "She left the state?"

"A few months ago, she sent us a postcard from Arizona, telling us she'd gotten married. Living the life of leisure now. That's the last I heard. I guess she's moved back." Doris looked curiously at Toby. "If you're thinking of hiring her, why don't you just talk to her? She'll explain the résumé."

"I'm double-checking," lied Toby. "I'm thinking of hiring her, but something about her makes me uncomfortable. It's for my mother, who really can't fend for herself. I have to be careful."

"Well, I can vouch for Jane. She was wonderful with our patients." Doris moved to one of the dining tables, where she rested a hand on an elderly woman's shoulder. "Miriam, dear. You remember Jane, don't you?"

The woman smiled, a spoonful of mashed potatoes hovering at her dentureless mouth. "Is she coming back?"

"No, dear. I just want you to tell this lady whether you liked Jane or not."

"I *love* Janey. She hasn't been to see me in a long time."

"Jane's been away, dear."

"And the baby! I wonder how big the baby is. Tell her to come back."

Doris straightened and looked at Toby. "I'd call that a pretty good recommendation."

Back in her car, Toby sat staring at the dashboard in frustration. Why did no one recognize the truth? Jane's former patients loved her. Her ex-employers loved her. She was a dear woman, a saint.

And I've become the devil.

She reached for the ignition and was about to turn the key when she suddenly remembered where she'd heard the name Orcutt.

From Robbie Brace. That night, in the medical records room at Brant Hill, he had told her their building served as central records storage for Orcutt Health's other nursing homes.

She got out of the car and went back into the building.

Doris Macon was in the nurses' station, taking off order sheets. She looked up, obviously surprised to see Toby had returned.

"I have another question," said Toby. "That woman in the dining room. She said something about a baby. Did Jane have a child?"

"A daughter. Why?"

"She never said anything about . . ." Toby paused, her thoughts scattering in a dozen different directions at once. Had the baby since died? Had there ever been a child? Or had Jane simply not bothered to mention the fact she had a daughter?

Doris was looking at her with a puzzled expression. "Excuse me, but is this relevant to your hiring her?"

Why was a baby never mentioned? Toby suddenly straightened. "What does Jane look like?"

"Didn't you interview her? You've seen her yourself—"

"What does she look like?"

Taken aback by Toby's sharp tone, Doris stared at her for a moment. "She—uh—she's quite average-looking. Nothing particularly unusual about her."

"How tall is she? What color's her hair?"

Doris rose to her feet. "We have group photos of our staff. We take one every year. I can point her out to you." She led Toby to the hallway, where a series of framed photos were hanging, each one labeled with the date it was taken. The series went back to 1981—presumably the year Wayside Nursing Home opened. Doris paused in front of the color photo from two years before and scanned the faces.

"There," she said, pointing to a woman in a white uniform. "That's Jane."

Toby stared at the face in the photograph. The woman was standing at the far left edge of the group, her pudgy face smiling, her uniform top a shapeless tent over a massively obese body.

Toby shook her head. "That's not her."

"Oh, but I can assure you," said Doris. "And so can our patients. That is definitely Jane Nolan."

"We picked the girl up over in the North End," said the patrolman. "Witnesses saw some guy slapping her around, trying to drag her into a car. She was screaming her bloody head off, and they stepped in to help. We were the first officers on the scene. Found the girl sitting on the curb with a cut lip and a black eye. She gave her name as Molly Picker."

"Who was the guy beating up on her?" asked Dvorak.

"Her pimp, I guess. She wouldn't tell us. And the guy left the scene."

"Where's the girl now?"

"Sitting in the cruiser. Didn't want to come in here. Doesn't want to talk to anyone. All she wants is back out on the street."

"So the pimp can rough her up again?"

"She's not big in the IQ department."

Dvorak sighed as they walked out the front entrance to Albany Street. He wasn't optimistic about this interview. A sullen teenager, probably uneducated as well, was a poor source for a medical history. The girl wasn't under arrest, and she could walk out any time, but she probably didn't know that. He was certainly not going to enlighten her, not until he had a chance to pick her brains. What brains she had.

The patrolman pointed to the cruiser, where his partner was waiting in the front seat. In the backseat was a girl with stringy brown hair and a cut lip. She sat huddled under a giant raincoat. She was clutching a cheap patent leather purse in her lap.

The cop opened the back door. "Why don't you step on out, miss? This is Dr. Dvorak. He'd like to speak to you."

"Don't need no doctor."

"He's with the medical examiner's office."

"Don't need no exam neither."

Dvorak leaned in and smiled at the girl. "Hi, Molly. We're going inside to talk. It's cold out here, don't you think?"

"Wouldn't be if you'd shut the door."

"I can wait all day. We can talk now, or we can talk at midnight. It's up to you." He stood looking in at her, waiting to see how long it would take her to get tired of being stared at. All three men were watching her, the two cops and Dvorak, no one saying a thing.

Molly took a deep breath and let it out in a snort of frustration. "You got a bathroom?" she said.

"Of course."

"I gotta go real bad."

Dvorak stepped aside. "I'll show you the way."

She struggled out of the patrol car, the oversize raincoat dragging after her like a giant cape. Only when she straightened did Dvorak suddenly focus on the girl's abdomen. She was pregnant. At least six months, he estimated.

The girl noticed the direction of his gaze. "Yeah, so I'm knocked up," she snapped. "So what?"

"I think we should get you inside. Pregnant ladies need to sit down."

She flashed him a *That's a joke, right?* look and walked into the building.

"Nice girl," grunted the cop. "You want us to hang around?"

"You can leave. I'll just put her in a taxi when I'm done."

Dvorak found the girl waiting for him just inside the door.

"So where's the bathroom?" she said.

"There's one upstairs, next to my office."

"Well come *on*. I gotta pee."

She didn't say anything as they rode the elevator; judging by the look of concentration on her face, all her attention was focused on her bladder. He waited for her outside the staff rest room. She took her time, emerging ten minutes later, smelling of soap. She'd washed her face, and the swollen lip seemed to stand out alarmingly purple against that white face.

He led her into his office and shut the door. "Sit down, Molly."

"This gonna take long?"

"It depends on whether you help me out. Whether you know anything." Again he gestured to the chair.

Sullenly she sat down, pulling the raincoat around her like a protective mantle. Her bottom lip stuck out, bruised and stubborn.

He stood with the back of his thighs against the desk, looking down at her. "Two days ago you made an emergency call. The operator recorded your voice requesting an ambulance."

"Didn't know it was a crime to call an ambulance."

"When the team got there, they found a woman had bled to death. You were in the apartment with her. What happened, Molly?"

She said nothing. Her head drooped, the lank hair spilling across her face.

"I'm not saying you did anything wrong. I just need to know."

The girl wouldn't look at him. Bringing her arms up, she hugged herself and began to rock in the chair. "Wasn't my fault," she whispered.

"I know that."

"I wanna go. Can't I just go?"

"No, Molly. We need to talk first. Can you look at me?"

She wouldn't. She kept her head down, as though meeting his gaze would somehow signify a defeat.

"Why don't you want to talk?"

"Why should I? I don't know you."

"You don't have to be afraid of me. I'm not a cop, I'm a doctor."

His words had the opposite effect of what he'd intended. She shrank deeper into her chair and shuddered. He could not figure out this girl. She was an alien species to him. All teenagers were. He was unsure how to proceed.

His desk intercom buzzed.

"Dr. Toby Harper's here," said his secretary.

"I'm unavailable."

"I don't think she's going to leave. She insists on going upstairs to see you."

"Look, I really can't talk to her right now."

"Should I have her wait?"

He sighed. "All right. Have her wait. But it may be a while."

Dvorak turned back to Molly Picker, his irritation more acute than ever. He had one female demanding to talk to him, and another female refusing to say a word.

"Molly," he said, "I need to know about your friend, Annie. The woman who died. Was she using any drugs? Was she taking any medications?"

The girl gave another shudder and curled into a ball.

"This is very important. The woman had a severely deformed fetus. I need to know what she was exposed to. It could be vital information for other pregnant women as well. Molly?"

The girl began to shake. At first Dvorak did not understand what was happening. He thought she was cold, shivering. Then she toppled forward and her head slammed against the floor. Her limbs began to jerk, her whole body wracked by convulsions.

Dvorak knelt down beside her and frantically tried to loosen the raincoat, which had bunched up around her neck, but her limbs were flailing with superhuman strength. At last he got the collar open. She was still seizing, her face a shocking purple, her eyes rolled back. *What do I do now? I'm a pathologist, not an ER doctor . . .*

He sprang to his feet and hit the intercom button. "I need Dr. Harper! Send her up *now!*"

"But I thought you said—"

"I have a medical emergency!"

He turned his attention to Molly. The girl's flailing had stopped, but her face was still a deep red, and a lump was forming on her forehead, where she'd bumped the floor.

Don't let her aspirate. Turn her on her side.

Remembered lessons from his medical school years were finally filtering through his panic. He dropped down beside the girl and quickly rolled her onto her left side, her face slightly downward. If she vomited, her gastric contents would not spill into her lungs. He felt her pulse—it was rapid, but strong. And she was still breathing.

Okay. Okay, we've got an airway. We've got respirations. And we've got circulation. What am I forgetting?

The office door opened. He glanced up as Toby Harper stepped into the room. Her gaze fell at once to the girl, and she knelt down.

"What happened?"

"She had some sort of seizure—"

"Any medical history? Epileptic?"

"I don't know. She's got a pulse and she's breathing."

Toby glanced at the bruise. "When did she hit her head?"

"After the seizure started."

Toby pulled open the raincoat to expose the girl's torso. There was a one-beat pause, then a dismayed: "She's pregnant."

"Yeah. I don't know how far along she is."

"Do you know *anything* about her?"

"She has a police record. Prostitution. Her pimp roughed her up today. That's all I know."

"You have a medical bag?" asked Toby.

"In my desk drawer—"

"Get it."

The girl was groaning, moving her head.

While Toby rummaged in the bag for instruments, Dvorak eased the girl's arm out of the raincoat sleeve. She opened her eyes and looked at him. At once she began to struggle, pulling away from his grasp.

"It's all right," he said. "Take it easy—"

"Let her go," ordered Toby. "She's post-ictal and confused. You're scaring her."

Dvorak released the pitifully thin arm and backed away.

"Okay, honey," murmured Toby. "Look at me. I'm right here."

The girl shifted her gaze to Toby's face, hovering above hers. "Mama," she said.

Toby spoke slowly and softly. "I'm not going to hurt you. I just want to shine a little light in your eyes. All right?" The girl kept staring at her, as though in wonder. Toby turned a penlight beam at the girl's pupils. "Equal and reactive. And she's moving all her limbs." Toby reached for the blood pressure cuff. The girl made a feeble whimper of protest as the cuff squeezed her arm, but she kept her gaze on Toby and seemed to be comforted.

Toby frowned as the sphygmomanometer needle slowly pulsed downward. Quickly she released the pressure and peeled off the cuff. "She needs to be admitted."

"Boston City's right across the street."

"Let's get her to their ER. Her pressure's two-ten over one-thirty, and she's pregnant. I think that explains the seizure."

"Eclampsia?"

Toby gave a quick nod and closed the black bag. "Can you carry her?"

Dvorak bent down and gathered the girl in his arms. Despite her pregnancy, she felt frail, weightless. Or maybe he was too pumped up on adrenaline to feel the burden. With Toby leading the way, opening doors for him, they made it out the building's front entrance to Albany Street.

Wind whipped between the buildings, stinging their faces with grit as they crossed the street. The girl struggled in his arms, and with her raincoat lashing his legs, her hair flying in his face, Dvorak stumbled onto the opposite curb and up the ramp to the ER entrance. The double doors slid open.

Behind the admitting window, a male triage nurse looked up and saw the girl in Dvorak's arms. "What happened?"

It was Toby who answered, stepping up to the window and

opening Molly Picker's cheap little purse for ID. "Pregnant girl with seizures, now post-ictal. BP two-ten over one-thirty."

At once the triage nurse understood, and he called for a gurney.

The stab of a needle jolted Molly fully awake. She thrashed, fighting to free herself from the hands holding her down, but there were too many of them, all trapping her, torturing her. She could not remember how she'd arrived in this terrible place, nor did she know what she'd done wrong to deserve this punishment. *I'm sorry, whatever I did wrong, I'm sorry. Please stop hurting me.*

"Shit, I blew the vein! Toss me another eighteen gauge—"

"Try the other arm. Looks like a nice vein there."

"You have to hold her down. She keeps yanking around here."

"Is that a seizure?"

"No, she's fighting us—"

Hands trapped her face; a voice commanded, "Miss, you have to hold still! We need to get the IV in!"

Molly's panicked gaze focused on the face staring down at her. It was a man dressed in blue. A stethoscope was looped like a snake around his neck. A man with angry eyes.

"She's still out of it," he said. "Just get the IV in."

Another pair of hands grasped her arm, trapping it against the mattress. Molly tried to jerk free, but the hands only squeezed tighter, pinching and twisting her skin. Again the needle stabbed. Molly shrieked.

"Okay, it's in! Get it connected. Come on, come on."

"How fast a drip?"

"TKO it for now. I want five milligrams Hydralazine IV. Let's hang some mag sulfate. And get those bloods drawn."

"Doc, a chest pain just rolled in the door."

"Why the fuck won't they leave me alone?"

Another needle, another lance of pain. Molly bucked against the gurney. Something crashed and shattered on the floor.

"Goddamn it, she won't lie still!"

"Can't we sedate her?"

"No, we need to follow mental status. Talk her down."

"I've tried."

"Get that woman back in here. The one who brought her in. Maybe she can calm her down."

Molly twisted against the restraints, her head aching, pounding with every new explosion of sound. The rapid-fire voices, the clang of metal cabinets slamming shut.

Go away, go away, go away.

Then a voice called to her, and she felt a hand settle gently on her hair.

"Molly, it's me. Dr. Harper. It's all right. Everything is all right."

Molly focused on the woman's face, a face she recognized, though she couldn't remember where she'd seen it before. She knew only that it was a face unassociated with pain. Those calm eyes spoke to her of safety.

"You need to lie very still, Molly. I know it hurts, all these needles. But they're trying to help you."

"I'm sorry," whispered Molly.

"For what?"

"For whatever I did that was bad. I don't remember."

The woman smiled. "You didn't do anything bad. Now they're going to poke you, all right? A little stick."

Molly closed her eyes and stifled a whimper as a needle pierced her arm.

"There, that's a good girl. It's all over now. No more needles."

"You promise?"

A pause. "I can't promise that. But from now on, no one

will poke you without warning you first, okay? I'll tell them that."

Molly reached for the woman's hand. "Don't leave me . . ."

"You'll be fine. These people are taking good care of you."

"But I don't know *them*." She looked straight at the woman, who finally nodded.

"I'll stay as long as I can."

Someone else was speaking now; the woman turned to listen, then looked back down at Molly.

"We need to know about your health. Do you have a doctor?"

"No."

"Take any medicines?"

"No. Uh, yeah. They're in my purse."

Molly heard the woman unsnap the patent leather clutch, heard the clatter of pills in a bottle. "These, Molly?"

"Yeah. I take one when my stomach gets upset."

"There's no pharmacy label on this bottle. Where did you get it from?"

"Romy. A friend. He gave the pills to me."

"Okay, what about allergies? Are you allergic to anything?"

"Strawberries." Molly sighed. "And I like strawberries so much . . ."

Another voice intruded: "Dr. Harper, the ultrasound tech is here."

Molly heard the rattle of machinery being rolled into the room, and her gaze shot sideways. "What are they gonna do? They gonna poke me again?"

"It won't hurt. It's just an ultrasound test, Molly. They need to check your baby. They're going to use sound waves to look at it."

"I don't want the test. Can't they just leave me alone?"

"I'm sorry, but it has to be done. To see if the baby's all right. How big it is and how developed it is. You had a seizure today, in Dr. Dvorak's office. You know what a seizure is?"

"Like a fit."

"That's right. You had a fit. You were unconscious and your body was shaking all over. That's very dangerous. You need to stay in the hospital so they can get your blood pressure under control. And to see if there's any way to save the baby."

"Is something wrong with it?"

"Your pregnancy is the reason you had the seizure, the reason your blood pressure is high."

"I don't want any more tests. Tell them I want to leave—"

"Listen to me, Molly." Dr. Harper's voice was quiet but firm. "Your condition can be fatal."

Molly was silent. She stared at the other woman's face and saw the unflinching truth in her eyes.

Dr. Harper nodded to the technician. "Go ahead and do the sonogram. I'll wait outside."

"No," said Molly. "Stay with me." She held out her hand in a silent plea.

After a hesitation, Toby once again grasped Molly's hand and sat down on the stool by the gurney.

The technician draped a modesty sheet over Molly's thighs and pubic hair, then raised the hospital gown, baring the patient's swollen abdomen. "This'll be a little chilly," he said as he squeezed out a gob of clear gel onto her skin. "This stuff makes the sound waves easier to read."

"It won't hurt? You promise it won't hurt?"

"Not a bit." He held up a squarish device that fit neatly into his hand. "I'm going to rub the edge of this thing over your stomach, okay? And we can see the images on this screen here."

"You can see my baby?"

"That's right. Watch." He dabbed the handheld device in the gob of gel, then placed it on her skin.

"That tickles," said Molly.

"But it doesn't hurt, does it? Admit it doesn't hurt."

"No, it doesn't."

"So now you just relax and watch the show, okay?" Slowly he slid the device across her abdomen, his gaze focused on the monitor. Molly, too, watched the screen and saw a jumble of shadows flicker past. Where was the baby? She'd expected to see a real picture, like a photograph, not just a bunch of gray blots.

"Where is it?" she said.

The technician didn't answer. Molly looked at him and saw that he was staring at the monitor, his expression frozen.

"Do you see it?" asked Molly.

The technician cleared his throat. "Let me just finish the test."

"Is it a boy or a girl? Can you tell?"

"No. No, I can't . . ." He slid the device first in one direction, then another, his gaze focused on the images flickering across the screen.

Nothing but blips of gray, thought Molly. There was one larger blob surrounded by smaller blobs. She looked at Dr. Harper. "Do *you* see it?"

Her question was met with silence. Dr. Harper kept glancing back and forth between the screen and the technician. Neither one of them were looking at Molly. Neither one of them said a word.

"Why aren't you talking to me?" whispered Molly. "What's wrong?"

"Just hold still, hon."

"Something's wrong, isn't it?"

Dr. Harper squeezed her hand. "Don't move."

At last the technician straightened and wiped the gel off

Molly's abdomen. "I'm going to show the film to one of our doctors, okay? You just rest."

"But *she's* a doctor," said Molly, looking at Dr. Harper.

"I'm not trained to read this. It takes a specialist."

"Well what *did* you see? Is something wrong?"

Dr. Harper and the technician exchanged glances.

And the technician said, "I don't know."

18

"Freeze that frame," said Dr. Sibley. He took off his glasses and stared at the monitor, his attention transfixed by the sonogram image. For a moment there was only silence in the room. Then Sibley murmured, "What the hell is that . . ."

"What do you see?" asked Toby.

"I don't know. I honestly don't know what I'm looking at." Sibley turned to the ultrasound technician. "This shadow here is what you're referring to?"

"Yes, sir. That mass right there. I didn't know what it was."

"Is it fetal tissue?" asked Toby.

"I can't tell." He nodded to the technician. "Okay, unfreeze it. Let's see the rest."

As shadows flickered across the monitor, Sibley bent even closer. "There's alternating density of tissue, both solid and cystic."

"It looks like a head," said Toby.

"Yes, it has a vaguely cranial shape. And see that calcification?"

"A tooth?"

"That's what I think it is." Sibley paused as the view shifted to a new field. "Where's the thorax?" he murmured. "I don't see a thorax."

"But it has teeth?"

"A single tooth." Sibley sat frozen, watching the interplay of light and shadow on the monitor. "Limbs," he said softly. "One there, and one there. Solid appendages. But no thorax . . ." Slowly he sat back and put on his glasses. "It's not a fetus. It's a tumor."

"Are you certain?" asked Toby.

"It's a ball of tissue. Primitive germ cells gone crazy, manufacturing teeth, maybe hair. It has no heart, no lungs."

"But there's a placenta."

"Yes. The patient's body *thinks* it's pregnant, and it's nurturing that tumor, helping it gain mass. I suspect this is a type of teratoma. Those tumors are known to form all sorts of bizarre structures, from teeth to hormone-producing glands."

"Then it's not a congenital malformation."

"No. It's disorganized tissue. A hunk of meat. It should be removed from the patient as soon as—" Suddenly Sibley jerked backward, his gaze sharp on the screen. "Run that back! Do it!" he snapped to the technician.

"What did you see?"

"Just run it back!"

The monitor went blank for a moment, then lit up again in a replay of images.

"This is impossible," said Sibley.

"What?"

"*It moved.*" He looked at the technician. "Did you manipulate the abdomen?"

"No."

"Well *look* at that. The appendage—see how it shifts position?"

"I didn't touch the abdomen."

"Then the patient must have shifted position. A tumor doesn't move on its own."

"It's not a tumor," said Dvorak.

Everyone turned to look at him. He had been so quiet Toby had not realized he'd entered the room and was now standing behind her. Slowly he moved toward the monitor, his gaze fixed on the freeze-frame image. "It does move. It has arms. It has an eye. It has teeth. Maybe it can even think . . ."

Sibley snorted. "That's ridiculous. How could you possibly know that?"

"Because I've seen one just like it." Dvorak turned and looked at them, his expression stunned. "I have to make a phone call."

In the darkness of Molly's room, Toby could see the red light on the IVAC machine blinking on and off, silent confirmation that the medication was dripping into the patient's vein. Toby let the door swing shut, and she settled into a chair by the bed. There she sat and listened to the sound of the girl's breathing. The red IVAC light blinked a hypnotic rhythm. Toby allowed her limbs to relax and her mind to drift for the first time all day. She had just called Springer Hospital to check on her mother's condition and had been assured there were no changes. *At this moment, in a different bed, in a different hospital,* she thought, *my mother is sleeping while the red light of her IVAC pulses, like this girl's, in the darkness.*

Toby glanced at her watch and wondered when Dvorak would return. Earlier tonight, she'd tried to tell him about Jane Nolan and had been frustrated by his obvious reluctance to hear her out. He'd had so many distractions as well—the crisis with Molly. His beeper going off. And then he had left, to meet someone in the hospital lobby.

She settled back in the chair and was considering a short nap when Molly's voice suddenly said, through the gloom: "I'm cold."

Toby straightened. "I didn't realize you were awake."

"I've been lying here. Thinking . . ."

"Let me find you a blanket. Can I turn on the light?"

"Okay."

Toby switched on the bedside lamp, and the girl recoiled from the sudden glare. The bruise on her forehead was black against the pallor of her face. Her hair looked like dirty streaks across the pillow.

On the shelf in the closet, Toby found an extra hospital blanket. She shook it out and spread it over the girl's bed. Then she turned off the lamp and felt her way back to the chair.

"Thank you," whispered Molly.

They shared the darkness, neither one speaking, the silence both calming and comfortable for them both.

Molly said, "My baby's not normal. Is she?"

Toby hesitated. Decided that the kindest answer was the truth. "No, Molly," she said. "It's not normal."

"What does it look like?"

"It's difficult to say. The sonogram's not like a regular picture. It's not easy to interpret."

Molly considered this in silence. Toby steeled herself for more questions, wondering just how graphic she should be. *Your baby isn't even human. It has no heart, no lungs, no torso. It's nothing but a frightening ball of flesh and teeth.*

To Toby's relief, the girl didn't pursue the issue. Perhaps she was afraid to hear the whole truth, the whole horror of what was now growing in her womb.

Toby leaned forward. "Molly, I've been talking to Dr.

Dvorak. He says there was a woman—someone you knew—who also had an abnormal child."

"Annie."

"That was her name?"

"Yes." Molly sighed. Though darkness hid the girl's face, Toby could hear the weariness in that sigh, an exhaustion that was more than physical.

Toby's gaze focused on the vague shadow that formed the girl's face. Her vision was adjusting to the darkness, and she could just make out the gleam of her eyes. "Dr. Dvorak is concerned that you and Annie may have been exposed to the same toxin. Something that caused both your babies to be abnormal. Is that possible?"

"What do you mean . . . toxin?"

"Some kind of drug or poison. Did you and Annie take anything? Pills? Injections?"

"Just the pills I told you about. The ones Romy gave me."

"This Romy, did he give you any other drugs? Anything illegal?"

"No. I didn't do that stuff, you know? I never saw Annie do it, either."

"How well did you know her?"

"Not very well. She let me stay with her for a few weeks."

"You were together only a few weeks?"

"I just needed a place to sleep."

Toby gave a sigh of frustration. "Then this doesn't add up."

"What do you mean?"

"Whatever caused the abnormalities in your babies happened very early in pregnancy. During the first three months."

"I didn't know Annie then."

"When did you find out you were pregnant?"

The girl thought it over. In the lull of conversation, they heard the squeak of a medication cart being wheeled down the hall, and the murmur of nurses.

"It was in the summer. I was sick."

"Did you see a doctor?"

A pause. Toby saw the white blanket ripple, as though moved by a shudder. "No."

"But you knew you were pregnant?"

"I could tell. I mean, it wasn't hard to see, after a while. Romy told me he'd take care of it."

"What do you mean by *take care of it?*"

"Get rid of it. Then I got to thinking how nice it'd be to hold a baby. To play with it. Have it call me Mama . . ." The sheets rustled as the girl's arms moved beneath the blankets, caressing her belly. Her unborn child.

Only it was not a child.

"Molly? Who is the father?"

There was another sigh, this one wearier. "I don't know."

"Could it be your friend Romy?"

"He's not my friend. He's my pimp."

Toby said nothing.

"You know about me, don't you? What I do? What I been doing . . ." Molly rolled over in bed, turning her back to Toby. Her voice was now faint, as though it came from a great distance. "You get used to it. You learn not to think about it too much. You can't think about it. It's like your mind sort of fuzzes out, you know? Sort of drifts someplace else. And what's going on down there between your legs, it's not really happening to *you* . . ." She gave a self-deprecating laugh. "It's an interesting life."

"It's not a healthy life."

"Yeah. Well."

"How old are you?"

"Sixteen. I'm sixteen."

"You're from the South, aren't you?"

"Yes, Ma'am."

"How did you get all the way up here to Boston?"

A long sigh. "Romy brought me. He was down in Beaufort, staying with some friends. Had this way about him, you know? These real dark eyes. Never saw a white boy with eyes that dark before. Treated me so nice . . ." She cleared her throat, and Toby heard the rustle of the sheet as Molly brought it up to wipe her face. The IV tube dangled, silvery, over the bed.

"I take it he wasn't so nice to you after he brought you to Boston."

"No, Ma'am. He wasn't."

"Why didn't you go home, Molly? You can always go home."

There was no answer. Only by the shuddering of the bed did Toby realize the girl was sobbing. Molly herself made no sound; it was as though her grief was trapped in a jar, her cries inaudible to anyone but her.

"I can help you go home. If all you need is the money to get there—"

"I can't." The answer was barely a whisper. The girl rolled into a tight lump under the covers. Toby became aware of a soft keening, the sound of Molly's grief at last escaping from the vacuum of the jar. "I can't. I can't . . ."

"Molly."

"They don't want me back."

Toby reached out to touch her and could almost feel the girl's pain seeping through the blanket.

There was a knock, and the door opened.

"Can I talk to you, Toby?" said Dvorak.

"Right now?"

"I think you should come out and hear this." He hesitated, and glanced at Molly's bed. "It's about the sonogram."

Toby murmured to the girl, "I'll be back." She followed Dvorak into the hall and closed the door behind her.

"Did she tell you anything?" he asked.

"Nothing that sheds any light on this."

"I'll try talking to her later."

"I don't think you'll get anything. She doesn't seem to

trust men, and the reason's pretty clear. Anyway, there are too many factors that can cause fetal abnormalities. The girl can't pinpoint anything."

"This is more than just a fetal abnormality."

"How do you know?"

He gestured toward a small conference room at the end of the hall. "I want you to meet someone. She can explain it better than I can."

Dvorak had said *she*, but as Toby walked into the room, the person she saw sitting in front of the video monitor looked more like a man from behind—steel gray hair, closely cropped. Broad shoulders in a tan Oxford shirt. Cigarette smoke forming a drifting wreath above the squarish head. On the monitor, the sonogram of Molly Picker's womb was slowly replaying.

"I thought you gave up the cigarettes," said Dvorak.

The person swiveled around, and Toby saw that it *was* a woman sitting in the chair. She was in her early sixties, her blue eyes startlingly direct, her plain features unadorned by even a hint of makeup. The offending cigarette was mounted in an ivory holder, which she wielded with comfortable elegance.

"It's my one and only vice, Daniel," the woman said. "I refuse to give it up."

"I guess the scotch doesn't count."

"Scotch is not a vice. It's a tonic." The woman turned to Toby and regarded her with a raised eyebrow.

"This is Dr. Toby Harper," said Dvorak. "And this is Dr. Alexandra Marx. Dr. Marx is a developmental geneticist at Boston University. One of my professors from medical school."

"A *very* long time ago," said Dr. Marx. She reached out to shake Toby's hand, a gesture one didn't expect from another woman, but one which seemed perfectly natural coming from Alex Marx. "I've been replaying the sonogram. What do we know about this girl?"

"I just spoke to her," said Toby. "She's sixteen. A prostitute. She doesn't know who the father is. And she denies any history of exposure to toxins. The only med she was taking was that bottle of pills."

Dvorak said, "I checked with the hospital pharmacist. He identified the code stamped on the tablets. Prochlorperazine." He looked at Dr. Marx. "They're usually prescribed for nausea. There's no evidence they cause fetal abnormalities. So we can't blame this on the pills."

"How did the pimp get his hands on a prescription drug?" asked Toby.

"You can get anything on the streets these days. Maybe she's not telling you about all the other drugs she's taking."

"No, I believe her."

"How far along is the pregnancy?"

"Based on her recall, maybe five or six months."

"So we're looking at what should be a second trimester fetus." Dr. Marx swiveled around to face the monitor. "There's definitely a placenta. There's amniotic fluid. And I believe that's an umbilical cord I see here." Dr. Marx leaned forward, studying the images flickering across the monitor. "I think you're right, Daniel. This is not a tumor."

"So it's a fetal abnormality?" asked Toby.

"No."

"What else *is* there?"

"Something in between."

"A tumor *and* a fetus? How is that possible?"

Dr. Marx took a drag from her cigarette and exhaled a cloud of smoke. "It's a brave new world."

"All you've got is a sonogram. A bunch of gray shadows. Dr. Sibley, the radiologist, thinks this is a tumor."

"Dr. Sibley has never seen one of these before."

"And you have?"

"Ask Daniel."

Toby looked at Dvorak. "What's she talking about?"

He said, "The woman who died giving birth—Annie Parini—I sent her fetus to Dr. Marx for genetic analysis."

"I've done only preliminary studies," said Dr. Marx. "We've done the tissue sections and staining. It will take months to complete the DNA analysis. But based purely on the histology of the ... thing, I have a few theories." Dr. Marx turned her chair around to face Toby. "Sit down, Dr. Harper. Let's talk about fruit flies."

What on earth is this leading up to? Toby wondered as she sank into a chair at the conference table. Dvorak, too, sat down. Dr. Marx, at the head of the table, regarded them with the severe demeanor of a professor confronting two remedial students. "Have you heard about the studies coming out of the University of Basel using *Drosophila melanogaster*? The common fruit fly?"

"Which research are you talking about?" said Toby.

"It had to do with ectopic eyes. Scientists have already identified a master gene that activates the entire cascade of twenty-five hundred genes needed to form a fruit fly's eye. The gene is called "eyeless" because when it's missing, the fly is born without any eyes. The Swiss scientists managed to activate the "eyeless" gene in various parts of the fly embryo. With fascinating results. Eyes popped up in bizarre places. On wings, on knees, on antennae. Fourteen eyes grew on *one* fly! And this was merely from the activation of a *single gene*." Dr. Marx paused to stub out her cigarette. She inserted a fresh one into the ivory holder.

"I don't see the relevance of fruit fly research to this situation," said Toby.

"I'm getting to that," said Dr. Marx, lighting up. She inhaled and leaned back with a satisfied sigh. "Let's leap across species lines now. To mice."

"I still don't see the relevance."

"I'm trying to start off on a very elementary level here. You and Daniel aren't developmental biologists. You probably aren't aware of the advances that have occurred since you left medical school."

"Well, that's true," admitted Toby. "It's hard enough keeping up with clinical medicine."

"Then let me catch you up. Briefly." Dr. Marx tapped off a cigarette ash. "I was talking about mice. Specifically, mice pituitary glands. Now, the pituitary is crucial to a newborn mouse's survival. There's a reason they call it 'the master gland.' All those hormones it produces regulate everything from growth to reproduction to body temperature. It secretes hormones whose purpose we don't know. Hormones we haven't even identified. Mice born without a pituitary die within twenty-four hours—that's how vital the gland is.

"And here's where the research comes in. At NIH, they're studying the pituitary's embryonic development. They know that all the different cells that form the gland arise from a single primordium. Precursor cells. But what induces those precursor cells to *make* a pituitary gland?" She looked back and forth at her two remedial students.

"A gene?" ventured Toby.

"Naturally. It all gets back to DNA. Life's building block."

"Which gene?" asked Dvorak.

"In the mouse, it's Lhx3. An LIM homobox gene."

He laughed. "That's perfectly clear."

"I don't expect you to completely understand it, Daniel. I just want you to grasp the concept here. Which is that there are master genes that make primoridal cells develop in certain ways. A master gene to make an eye, another to make a limb, another to make a pituitary gland."

"All right," said Dvorak. "I think we understand that much. Sort of."

Dr. Marx smiled. "Then the next concept should be easy for you. I want you to combine these two pieces of research

308

and consider what they mean *together.* A master gene that kicks off the formation of a pituitary gland. And a fruit fly born with fourteen eyes." She looked at Toby, then at Dvorak. "Do you see what I'm getting at?"

"No," said Toby.

"No," said Dvorak, almost simultaneously.

Dr. Marx sighed. "All right. Let me just tell you what I found on tissue section. I dissected that specimen Daniel sent to me—what he thought was a malformed fetus. I'd never seen anything like it, and I've examined thousands of congenital abnormalities. Now, the human genome is made up of a hundred thousand genes. This *thing* appears to possess only a fraction of the normal genome. And what was present was greatly disrupted. Something catastrophic happened to that entire genome. The result? It's as if you took apart a fetus and then tried to reconstitute it in no particular order. Arms, teeth, cerebrum, all lumped together."

Toby felt queasy. She looked at Dvorak and saw that he had paled. The image conjured up by Dr. Marx sickened them both.

"It wouldn't survive. Would it?" asked Toby.

"Of course not. Its cells were kept alive purely by placental circulation. It was using the mother as its nutrient source. It was a parasite, if you will. But then, all fetuses are parasites."

"I never thought of it that way," murmured Toby.

"Well, they are. Mother is the host. Her lungs oxygenate the blood, her food intake provides glucose and protein. This particular parasite—this thing—could stay alive only as long as it remained in the womb, connected to the mother's circulation. Within moments of being expelled, its cells began to die." Dr. Marx paused, her gaze drifting upward to the rising coil of cigarette smoke. "It was not, in any way, an independent organism."

"If it's not a fetus, what *would* you call this thing?" asked Toby.

"I'm not sure. We prepared multiple sections of tissue. The slides were stained and examined by myself as well as by a pathologist in my department. We both concurred. One particular type of tissue appeared again and again, in organized clusters of cells. Oh, there were other tissues as well—muscle and cartilage, for instance, even an eye. But those seemed random. What was organized, and well differentiated, was the repetitive cell clusters. Glandular tissue we haven't yet identified. Identical clusters, all apparently in the midgestational stage." She paused. "This thing, in short, looked like a tissue factory."

Dvorak shook his head. "I'm sorry, but this sounds pretty crazy."

"Why? It's been done in a lab. We can make eyes grow on fruit fly wings! We can turn on or turn off a pituitary master gene! If it can happen in a lab, it can happen in nature. Somehow, in this girl, human embryonic cells developed multiple copies of the same gene. It meant, of course, that the embryo didn't differentiate properly. So there are no legs, there's no torso. What's growing instead are these specific cell clusters."

"What could cause this abnormality?" asked Toby.

"Outside of the lab? Something devastating. A teratogenic agent we've never seen before."

"But Molly doesn't remember any exposure. I asked her several times—" Toby paused, her gaze swerving toward the door.

Someone was screaming.

"It's Molly!" said Toby, and she shot to her feet. Dvorak was right on her heels as she pushed out of the room and sprinted down the hallway. By the time she reached Molly's room, a nurse was already at the bedside, trying to calm the girl.

"What happened?" asked Toby.

"She says someone was in her room," the nurse said.

"He was standing right here by the bed!" said Molly. "He knows I'm here. He followed me—"

"Who?"

"Romy."

"The lights were off," the nurse calmly pointed out. "You could have been dreaming."

"He *talked* to me!"

"I didn't see anyone," said the nurse. "And my desk is right around the corner—"

The slam of a door echoed in the hallway.

Dr. Marx poked her head in the room. "I just saw a man run into the stairwell."

"Call Security," Dvorak said to the nurse. "Have them check the lower levels."

Toby was right behind Dvorak as he ran into the hall. "Dan, where are you going?"

He pushed through the stairwell door.

"Let Security handle this!" She followed him into the stairwell.

Somewhere below, Dvorak's footsteps pounded down concrete steps.

She started down after him, tentatively at first, then picked up her pace as determination took hold. She was angry now, at Dvorak for this insanely reckless pursuit, and at Romy—if it *was* Romy—for daring to pursue the girl into the sanctuary of a hospital. How had he tracked her down? Did he follow them from Dvorak's office?

She picked up her pace, flying past the second-floor landing. She heard a door bang open, then slam shut again.

"Dan!" she yelled. No answer.

At last she hit the first floor, pushed through the door, and emerged next to the ER loading platform facing Albany

Street. The blacktop was glistening with rain. She squinted as wind gusted at her face, lifting the tang of wet pavement.

Off to her left, through a soft drizzle, a silhouette appeared. It was Dvorak. He halted beneath a streetlamp, glancing left, then right.

She jogged up the sidewalk to join him. "Where did he go?"

"I caught a glimpse of him in the stairwell. Lost him right after he left the building."

"You're sure he *did* leave the building?"

"Yes. He's got to be around here somewhere." Dvorak started across the street, toward the hospital power plant.

The squeal of tires made them both swing around.

The van came straight at them, barreling out of the darkness.

Toby froze.

It was Dvorak who shoved her sideways, who sent her tumbling, scraping across blacktop.

The van roared past, taillights fading away down Albany Street.

As she struggled back to her feet, she found Dvorak already reaching for her arm, steadying her as he helped her back to the sidewalk. The impact of her fall was just beginning to register as pain, first as a vague throbbing in her knees, then the sting of nerve endings scraped raw. They stood beneath the streetlight, both of them too shaken at first to speak.

Dvorak said, "I'm sorry I shoved you so hard. Are you all right?"

"Just a little banged up." She glanced up the street, in the direction the vehicle had just vanished. "Did you get the license number?"

"No. I didn't get a look at the driver, either. It all happened so·fast—I was trying to get *you* out of the way."

They both turned as an ambulance pulled up to the ER loading dock, lights flashing. Somewhere in the distance, the wail of a second ambulance was drawing closer.

"It's going to be chaos in that ER," said Dvorak. "I've got a first aid kit in my office. Let's go there and clean up your knees."

With Dvorak holding her by the arm, she limped across the street, the pain worsening with every step. By the time they'd made it upstairs to his office, she was dreading the first dab of antiseptic.

He moved aside his papers and sat her down on the desk, next to the photo of his fisherman son. The smell of rubbing alcohol and iodine rose up from the open first aid kit. Crouching in front of her, he moistened a cotton ball with peroxide and gently dabbed the abrasion.

She gave a start of pain.

"Sorry," he said, glancing up. "There's no way to do this without hurting you."

"I'm such a wimp," she muttered, clutching the edge of the desk. "Go ahead, just do it."

He continued dabbing her knees, one hand resting on her thigh, the other gently cleaning off dirt and gravel. As he worked, she focused on his head, bent in concentration, his dark hair close enough to ruffle with her hands. His breath felt warm against her skin. *At last I have him alone,* she thought. *No crises, no distractions. This may be my only chance to make him listen. To make him believe me.*

She said, "You think I hurt my mother, don't you? That's why you won't talk to me. Why you've avoided my calls."

He said nothing, just reached for another ball of cotton.

"I'm being set up, Dan. They're using my mother to get back at me. And you're helping them, without even listening to my side."

"I've been listening to you, Toby." He'd finished cleaning her abrasions. Now he took out a roll of adhesive tape and began tearing off strips of it, taping squares of gauze on her knees.

"Then why won't you tell me if you believe me?"

"What I think you should do," he said, "is talk to your attorney. Lay it all out, everything you know. And let him discuss it with Alpren."

"I don't trust Alpren."

"And you think you can trust me?" He looked up at her.

"I don't know!" She exhaled, her shoulders drooping forward as she realized it was hopeless, trying to make him *care.* "I did talk to Alpren, this afternoon," she said. "I told him what I told you. That Brant Hill's getting back at me. They're trying to ruin me."

"Why would they bother?"

"Somehow I've scared them. I've done something, said something to make them feel threatened."

"You have to stop blaming Brant Hill as the source of all your problems."

"But now I have proof."

He shook his head. "Toby, I *want* to believe you. But I don't see how your mother's condition is connected to Brant Hill."

"*Listen* to me. Please."

He snapped the first aid kit shut. "All right. All right, I'm listening."

"The woman I hired to take care of my mother isn't who she says she is. Today I spoke to someone who worked with Jane Nolan years ago—the *real* Jane Nolan."

"As opposed to what?"

"The fake one. The one I hired. They're completely different people. I'll get Vickie to back me up."

He remained silent, closed off, his gaze focused stubbornly on the first aid kit.

"I saw a photograph, Dan. The real Jane was about a hundred pounds overweight. That's not the woman I hired."

"Then she's lost weight. Isn't that possible?"

"There's more. Two years ago, the real Jane worked for a nursing home run by the Orcutt Health chain. I just learned that Orcutt is part of an umbrella corporation—owned by

Brant Hill. If Jane was Brant Hill's employee, then they had her résumé in their files. They'd know she left Massachusetts. It'd be easy for them to slip another woman into my house under Jane's name. With Jane's credentials. If I hadn't seen that photograph, I *never* would have guessed the truth."

He said nothing, but his gaze had lifted to hers now. *At last he's listening to me. At last he's considering my side of it.*

"Have you told all this to Alpren?" he asked.

"Yes. I told him that all he had to do was talk to the *real* Jane Nolan. The problem is, no one knows where she's living or what her married name is. I've tried to track her down, but I can't even find out if she's still in the country. Obviously Brant Hill chose someone they knew would be hard to find. If she's even still alive."

"Social Security records?"

"I suggested that to Alpren. But if Jane's not currently employed, it could take weeks to track her down. I'm not sure Alpren wants to put out the effort. Since he doesn't believe me in the first place."

Dvorak rose to his feet. He stood looking at her for a moment, as though seeing her, really *seeing* her, for the first time. He nodded. "For what it's worth, I'll talk to him."

"Thank you, Dan." She gave a sigh, the tension leaving her body in one exhilarating rush. "Thank you."

He held out his hand to help her off the desk. She grasped his arm and allowed him to steady her as she rose to her feet. Still holding on to him she looked up and met his gaze.

That's all it took, that meeting of gazes. She felt his other hand come up to touch her face, his fingers slowly gliding down her cheek. And she saw, in his eyes, the same longing she felt.

The first kiss was too brief, merely a brushing of each other's lips. A timid first meeting. His arm wrapped around behind her back, drawing her closer. She gave a murmur of pleasure as their lips met again, and then again. She swayed

315

backward, and her hips bumped against the desk. He kept kissing her, matching her whimpers with murmurs of his own. She tipped backward, falling onto the desk, pulling him down with her. Papers scattered everywhere. He trapped her face in his hands, his mouth seeking hers in deeper exploration. She reached out to grasp his waist and instead knocked something away.

Glass shattered.

They both gave a start and looked at each other, their breathing hard and fast. Their faces flushed at the same time. He pulled away, helping her back to her feet.

The photo of Dvorak's son had landed facedown on the floor.

"Oh no," murmured Toby, looking at the broken glass. "I'm sorry, Dan."

"No problem. All it needs is a new frame." Kneeling down, he gathered up the pieces of glass and dropped them in the rubbish can. He stood up, and his face flushed again as he looked at her. "Toby, I . . . didn't expect . . ."

"I didn't, either—"

"But I'm not sorry it happened."

"You're not?"

He paused, as though reconsidering the truth of that last statement. He said again, firmly: "I'm not sorry at all."

They stared at each other for a moment.

Then she smiled and pressed her lips to his. "You know what?" she whispered. "Neither am I."

They held hands as they walked back across Albany Street to the hospital. Toby was moving in a daze, her bruises and scrapes now forgotten, her attention focused instead on the man holding her hand. In the elevator they kissed again, were still kissing when the door slid open.

They stepped out just as a crash cart rattled by, wheeled by a panicked-looking nurse.

Now what? thought Toby.

The nurse with the cart rounded the corner and vanished into the next hallway. An announcement crackled over the public address system:

"Code Blue, room three eleven . . ."

Toby and Dvorak glanced at each other in alarm.

"Isn't that Molly's room?" she asked.

"I don't remember—"

He was in the lead as they chased the nurse around the corner. Toby, her knees stiff from the bandages, couldn't keep up with him. He halted outside one of the rooms and stared into the doorway. "It's not Molly," he said as Toby caught up. "It's the patient next door."

Toby glanced past him and caught a glimpse of chaos.

Dr. Marx was performing CPR. A scrub-suited resident barked out orders as a nurse scuffled through the drawers of the crash cart. The patient was almost lost from view in the press of personnel; all Toby could see through the crowd was one gaunt foot, anonymous, sexless, lying exposed on the sheet.

"They don't need us," murmured Dvorak.

Toby nodded. She turned to Molly's room. Knocking softly, she opened the door.

Inside, the lights were on. The bed was empty.

Her gaze shot to the bathroom, also empty. She looked at the bed again and suddenly realized the IV pole was there, the plastic tube dangling free, the end still attached to the intravenous catheter. A small pool of dextrose and water glistened on the floor.

"Where is she?" said Dvorak.

Toby crossed to the closet and opened the door. Molly's clothes were gone.

She ran back into the hall and poked her head into Room 311, where the code was still in progress.

"Molly Picker's left the hospital!" said Toby.

The charge nurse glanced up, obviously overwhelmed. "I can't leave now! Call Security."

Dvorak pulled Toby out of the room. "Let's check the lobby."

They ran back to the elevator.

Downstairs, they found a security guard manning the front entrance.

"We're looking for a girl," said Dvorak. "About sixteen—long brown hair, wearing a raincoat. Did you see her leave?"

"I think she walked out a few minutes ago."

"Which way did she head?"

"I don't know. She just walked out that front door. I didn't watch where she was going."

Toby stepped out the lobby entrance, and rain gusted at her face. The wet pavement stretched like a glistening ribbon.

"It's only been a few minutes," said Dvorak. "She can't have gotten very far."

"Let's take my car," said Toby. "I've got a phone in there."

Their first swing around the block turned up no glimpse of Molly. They drove without speaking, both of them scanning the sidewalks as the windshield wipers squeaked back and forth.

On their second circle around the block, Dvorak said, "We should call the police."

"They'll scare her off. If she sees a cop, she'll run."

"She's *already* running."

"Are you surprised? She's afraid of that Romy guy. She was a sitting duck in the hospital."

"We could've arranged for police protection."

"She doesn't trust the police, Dan."

Toby circled the block one more time then decided to widen the search. Slowly she drove northeast along Harrison Street. If the girl was seeking the safety of crowds, this was the direction she'd take—toward the busy streets of Chinatown.

Twenty minutes later, she finally pulled over to the curb. "This isn't working. The girl doesn't want to be found."

"I think it's time to call the police," said Dvorak.

"To arrest her?"

"You'd agree she's a danger to herself, wouldn't you?"

After a pause, Toby nodded. "With that blood pressure, she could have another seizure. A stroke."

"Enough said." Dvorak picked up the car phone.

As he made the call, Toby stared out the window and thought about the misery of trudging through that rain, icy water seeping into your shoes, trickling under your collar. She thought about her own relative comfort here in the car. Leather seats. Warm air whispering out of the heater.

Sixteen. Could I have survived the streets at sixteen?

And the girl was pregnant, with a blood pressure lethal as a time bomb.

Outside, the rain began to fall harder.

19

Four blocks away, in an alley behind an Indian restaurant, Molly Picker huddled inside a cardboard box. Every so often, she caught a whiff of cooking smells—strange, spicy scents she could not identify but that made her mouth water. Then the wind would shift and she'd smell the nearby Dumpster instead and would gag on the stench of rotting food.

Her stomach veering between hunger and nausea, she hugged herself tighter. Rain had seeped into the box, and it was beginning to sag, collapsing onto her shoulders in a mantle of soggy cardboard.

The back door of the Indian restaurant opened and Molly blinked as light spilled into the alley. A man with a turban came out, lugging two trash bags, which he carried to the Dumpster. He lifted the metal lid, tossed the trash inside, and let the lid slam back down again.

Molly sneezed.

She knew from his abrupt silence that the man had heard her. Slowly his silhouette appeared at the box opening, the turbaned head frighteningly enormous. He stared at her and she at him.

"I'm hungry," she said.

She saw him glance toward the kitchen, then he nodded.

"You wait," he said, and went back inside.

A moment later he reemerged with a warm napkin-wrapped bundle. Inside was bread, fragrant and soft as a pillow.

"You go now," he said, but not unkindly. Rather than a command, it was a gentle suggestion. "You cannot stay here."

"I don't have anywhere to go."

"You wish me to call someone?"

"There's nobody to call."

He glanced up at the sky. The rain had eased to a slow drizzle, and his brown face gleamed with moisture. "I cannot bring you inside," he said. "There is a church three blocks from here. They have beds for people when it is cold."

"Which church?"

He shrugged, as if one Christian church was the same as another. "You go on that street. You will see it."

Shivering, her limbs stiff from the box, she rose to her feet. "Thank you," she murmured.

He didn't answer. Before she'd even made it out of the alley, she heard the door shut as he went back into the restaurant.

It began to rain again.

She headed in the direction the man had told her to go, devouring the bread as she walked. She could not remember tasting bread so wonderful; it was like eating clouds. Someday, she thought, someday, I'll pay him back for being nice to me. She always remembered the people who'd been nice to her; she kept a list in her head. The woman at the liquor store who'd given her a day-old hot dog. The man in the turban. And that Dr. Harper. None of them had a reason to be nice to Molly Picker, but they had been. They were her personal saints, her angels.

She thought of how nice it would be someday to have money. To slip a bundle of cash in an envelope and hand it to that man in the turban. Maybe he would be old by then. She would stick a note inside: *Thanks for the bread.* He would not remember her, of course. But she would remember him.

I won't forget. I'll never forget.

She came to a halt, her gaze focused on the building across the street. Beneath the large white cross were the words: MISSION SHELTER. WELCOME. Over the doorway a light shone, warm and inviting.

Molly stood momentarily transfixed by the vision of that light glowing in the drizzle, beckoning her to come out of the darkness. She felt a strange sense of happiness as she stepped off the curb and started across the street.

A voice called out: "Molly?"

She froze. Her panicked gaze darted toward the sound. It was a woman's voice, and it came from a van parked near the church.

"Molly Picker?" the woman called. "I want to help you."

Molly took a step backward, on the verge of fleeing.

"Come here. I can take you to a warm place. A safe place. Won't you get in the van?"

Molly shook her head. Slowly she backed away, her attention focused so completely on the woman that she didn't hear the footsteps closing in behind her.

A hand clapped over her mouth, muffling her scream, yanking her head back with such force her neck felt as if it would snap. She smelled him, then—Romy, his aftershave gaggingly sweet.

"Guess who, Molly Wolly?" he murmured. "I been chasing after you all fucking afternoon."

Squirming, fighting, she was dragged across the street.

The van door slid open and another pair of hands hauled her inside and shoved her to the floor, where her wrists and ankles were quickly bound with tape.

The van lurched forward, screeching away from the curb. As they passed under a streetlight, Molly caught a glimpse of the woman sitting a few feet away—a small woman with quick eyes and short dark hair. She lay her hand on Molly's swollen abdomen and gave a soft sigh of satisfaction, her smile like the rictus of a corpse.

"We should go back," said Dvorak. "We're not going to find her."

They had been driving in circles for an hour, had scanned every street in the neighborhood at least twice. Now they sat in her parked car, too weary to converse, their breath fogging the windows. Outside, the rain had finally stopped and puddles glistened in the road. *I hope she's safe,* thought Toby. *I hope she's somewhere warm and dry.*

"She knows the streets," said Dvorak. "She'll know enough to find shelter." He reached over and squeezed her hand. They studied each other in the dark, both of them tired, but neither one quite ready to end the night.

He leaned toward her and had just touched his lips to hers when his pager went off.

"That could be about Molly," she said.

He picked up her car phone. A moment later he hung up and sighed. "It's not about Molly. But it does put an end to our evening."

"Is it back to work for you?"

"Unfortunately. Could you drop me off? I need to get to an address right up this street."

"What about your car?"

"I'll catch a ride back in the morgue van."

She started the engine. They drove north, toward Chinatown, along streets wet and shimmering with the multicolored reflections of city lights.

Dvorak said: "There—it's up ahead."

She'd already spotted the flashing lights. Three Boston police cruisers were parked at haphazard angles by the curb outside a Chinese restaurant. A white morgue van with COMMONWEALTH OF MASSACHUSETTS stenciled on the side was backing into Knapp Street.

She pulled to a stop behind one of the cruisers, and Dvorak stepped out.

"If you hear any news about Molly, will you call me?" she said.

"I will." He gave her a smile, a wave, and walked toward the barrier of crime tape. A patrolman recognized him and waved him through.

Toby reached for the gearshift but then left it in park and sat back for a moment, watching the crowd that had gathered on the street. Even at midnight, the ranks of the curious had assembled. There was a bizarre frivolity in the air, two men slapping palms, women laughing. Only the cops looked grim.

Dvorak was standing just beyond the crime tape, conversing with a man in plainclothes. A detective. The man pointed toward an alley, then flipped through a notebook as he talked. Dvorak nodded, his gaze scanning the ground. Now the detective said something that made Dvorak glance up with a look of surprise. At that moment he seemed to notice that Toby was still parked. The detective stared as Dvorak abruptly walked away from him, ducked under the tape, and crossed back to Toby's car.

She rolled down the window. "I just wanted to watch for a moment," she said. "I guess I'm as morbidly curious as the rest of these people. It's a strange crowd."

"Yeah, it's always a strange crowd."

"What happened in the alley?"

He leaned into the window. Quietly he said, "They found a body. The ID says his name's Romulus Bell."

She responded with a blank look.

"He goes by the name of Romy," said Dvorak. "It's Molly Picker's pimp."

The body was sprawled on the pavement, almost hidden behind a parked blue Taurus. The left arm was bent under the body, the right was flung out, as if pointing toward the restaurant at the end of the alley. An execution, thought Dvorak, eyeing the bullet's entry wound in the corpse's right temple.

"No witnesses," said Detective Scarpino. One of the older cops, close to retirement, he was famous for his bad hairpieces. Tonight, the pelt looked as if it had been slapped on backward in haste. "Body was spotted about eleven-thirty by a couple coming out of that Chinese restaurant. That's their car." Scarpino pointed to the blue Taurus. "The upstairs tenant came into the alley to toss out some trash around ten o'clock or so, didn't see the body, so we're guessing it happened after ten. ID was in the victim's wallet. One of the patrolmen recognized the name. He'd talked to the victim yesterday, when he asked him about that girl you were looking for."

"Bell was seen at Boston City Hospital around nine o'clock tonight."

"Who saw him there?"

"The girl, Molly Picker. He came into her hospital room." Dvorak pulled on a pair of latex gloves and bent down for a closer look at the corpse. The victim was in his early thirties, a slim man with straight black hair pomaded into an Elvis helmet. His skin was still warm; the arm that lay stretched out was tanned and muscular.

"If you'll excuse me for saying so, Doc, it just doesn't look right."

"What doesn't?"

"You driving around with that doctor."

325

Dvorak straightened and turned to face Scarpino. "Excuse me?"

"She's under active investigation. The word I hear is, her mother's not going to make it."

"What else have you heard?"

Scarpino paused, glancing up the alley at the crowd. "That there's new evidence being developed. Alpren's guys are checking pharmacies around town. He's chasing something solid. If the mother dies, it goes to Homicide, and that makes this look *real* awkward. You and her, driving up to a crime scene together."

Dvorak stripped off his gloves, suddenly furious at Scarpino. The hours he'd just spent with Toby Harper made him doubt she was capable of violence, much less violence against her own mother.

"Shit, there are reporters standing right over there," said Scarpino. "They all recognize you. And soon they'll know Dr. Harper's face as well. They'll remember seeing you two together and pow! Fucking front page."

He's right, thought Dvorak. Which made him only angrier.

"It just doesn't look right," Scarpino said, emphasizing every word.

"She hasn't been charged with a crime."

"Not yet. You talk to Alpren."

"Look, can we focus on this case?"

"Yeah, sure." Scarpino threw a disgusted look at the corpse of Romulus Bell. "I just thought I'd pass on a little advice, Doc. Guy like you doesn't need that kind of trouble. A woman who beats up on her own mother—"

"Scarpino, do me a favor."

"Yeah?"

"Mind your own fucking business."

Toby slept in Ellen's bed that night. After driving home from that garish scene in Chinatown, she'd walked into her house and felt she was entering an airless, silent chamber. She felt walled away. Buried.

In her own bedroom, she turned on the radio to a late-night classical station, playing it loudly enough to hear even in the shower. She desperately needed music, voices—anything.

By the time she came out of the bathroom, drying her wet hair with a towel, the music had sputtered to static. She turned it off. In the abrupt silence, she felt Ellen's absence as acutely as a physical pain.

She went down the hall, to her mother's room.

She didn't turn on the light but simply stood in the semi-darkness, inhaling Ellen's scent, faintly sweet, like the summer flowers she so lovingly tended. Roses and lavender.

She opened the closet and randomly touched one of the dresses hanging there. Just by its texture she recognized it: her mother's linen summer shift, a dress so old that Toby could remember Ellen having worn it to Vickie's college graduation. And here it was, still hanging in the closet with all the other dresses Ellen had kept through the years. *When was the last time I took you shopping? I can't remember. I can't remember the last time I bought you a dress . . .*

She closed the closet door and sat down on the bed. She had changed the sheets several days ago, in hopeful anticipation of her mother's eventual return home. Now she almost wished she hadn't done so; all traces of her mother had been stripped away with the sheets, and now the bed smelled blandly of laundry soap. She lay down, thinking of the nights Ellen had occupied this same space. Wondering if the air itself had somehow been imprinted with the shadow of her presence.

She closed her eyes, inhaled deeply. And fell asleep.

Vickie's call awakened her at eight the next morning. It took eight rings before Toby managed to stumble to her own bedroom to pick up the phone. Half-drugged by sleep, she could barely focus on what her sister was trying to tell her.

"A decision has to be made, but I can't do it myself, Toby. It's just too much on my shoulders."

"What decision?"

"Mom's ventilator." Vickie cleared her throat. "They're talking about turning it off."

"No." Toby came fully awake. *"No."*

"They did the second EEG and they said it's just as—"

"I'm coming in. Don't let them touch a thing. Do you hear me, Vickie? Don't let them touch one goddamn thing."

Forty-five minutes later, she walked into the ICU at Springer Hospital. Vickie was standing in Ellen's cubicle; so was Dr. Steinglass. Toby went straight to her mother's side and, bending down, whispered: "I'm here, Mom. I'm right here."

"The second EEG was done this morning," said Dr. Steinglass. "There's no activity. The new pontine hemorrhage was devastating. She has no spontaneous respirations, no—"

"I don't think we should talk about this in the room," said Toby.

"I realize it's not easy to accept," said Steinglass. "But your mother can't comprehend anything we're saying right now."

"I'm not going to discuss this. Not in here," said Toby, and she walked out of the cubicle.

In the small ICU conference room, they sat at the table, Toby grim and silent, Vickie on the verge of tears. Dr. Steinglass, whom Toby thought of as competent but detached, looked uncomfortable in his new role of family crisis counselor.

"I'm sorry to raise this issue," he said. "But it really does need to be addressed. It's been four days now, and we've seen no improvement. Both EEG's show no activity. The hemorrhage was massive, and there's no brain function left. The ventilator is just ... prolonging the situation." He paused. "I do believe it would be the kindest thing to do."

Vickie looked at her sister, then back at Steinglass. "If you really think there's no chance . . ."

"He doesn't know," said Toby. "No one does."

"But she's suffering," said Vickie. "That tube in her throat—all those needles—"

"I don't want the ventilator shut off yet."

"I'm only thinking about what Mom would want."

"It's not your decision. You're not the one who takes care of her."

Vickie shrank back in her chair, eyes wide with hurt.

Toby dropped her head in her hands. "Oh God, I'm sorry. I didn't mean to say that."

"I think you did mean to say it." Vickie rose from her chair. "All right, *you* make the decision, then. Since you seem to think *you're* the only one who loves her." Vickie walked out.

After a moment, so did Dr. Steinglass.

Toby remained in the room with her head bowed, shaking with self-disgust and anger. At herself. At the woman who'd called herself Jane Nolan. *If I could just find you. If I could have just one goddamn moment alone with you.*

By that afternoon, she'd run out of both anger and adrenaline. She didn't have the energy to try reaching Dvorak again; she didn't feel like talking to anyone right now. In a chair by Ellen's bed, she leaned back and closed her eyes, but she could not shut out the image of her mother lying only a few feet away. With every whoosh of the ventilator bellows, she could picture quite clearly her mother's chest rising and falling. The lungs filling with air. The oxygen-rich blood streaming from the pulmonary alveoli to the heart, and then to the brain, where it would circulate, useless and unneeded.

She heard someone enter the cubicle, and she opened her eyes to see Dr. Steinglass standing at the foot of Ellen's bed.

"Toby," he said quietly. "I know it's hard for you. Nevertheless, we have to make the decision."

"I'm not ready."

"We're faced with a difficult situation here. The ICU beds are all full. If an MI comes in, we're going to need space." He paused. "We'll keep her on the ventilator until you make your decision. But you understand the position we're in."

She said nothing. She only gazed at Ellen, thinking: *How frail she looks. Every day she seems to shrink even smaller.*

"Toby?"

She looked at Dr. Steinglass. "I need a little longer. I need to be certain."

"I could have the neurologist speak to you."

"I don't need another opinion."

"Maybe you do. Maybe—"

"Please, can't you just leave me *alone?*"

Dr. Steinglass took a step back, surprised by the anger in her voice. Beyond the doorway of the cubicle, several nurses were staring.

"I'm sorry," said Toby. "Give me some time. I need time. One more day." She picked up her purse and walked out of the ICU, acutely aware, with every step she took, that the nurses were watching her.

Where do I go now? she wondered as she stepped into the elevator. *How do I fight back when I'm being attacked from all sides?*

The opposition had grown too many tentacles. Detective Alpren. Jane Nolan. Her old nemesis Doug Carey.

And Wallenberg. First she had embarrassed him by requesting that autopsy. Then she'd raised troubling questions about his two Creutzfeldt-Jakob patients. She'd made an enemy, certainly, but as far as she could tell, she'd caused him no serious damage.

So why has Brant Hill worked so hard to discredit me? What are they trying to hide?

The elevator stopped on the second floor to admit a pair of billing clerks just getting off work. Toby glanced at her watch and saw it was already past five; the weekend had officially begun. She caught a glimpse of the administrative hallway and suddenly had a thought.

She squeezed out of the elevator and walked up the hall to the medical library. The door was still unlocked, but the library was deserted for the day. She went to the reference computer and turned on the power.

The Medline search screen came on.

Under "author's name" she typed in: Wallenberg, Carl.

The titles of five articles appeared, listed in reverse chronological order. The most recent one was three years old, and it had appeared in *Cell Transplant:* "Vascularization after Cell-Suspension Neural Grafts in Rats." There were two co-authors also credited, Gideon Yarborough, M.D., and Monica Trammell, Ph.D.

She was about to scroll down to the next article listing when her gaze paused on that name, Gideon Yarborough. She remembered the bald man at Robbie's funeral, tall and elegantly dressed, who had tried to intercede when she and Wallenberg were arguing. Wallenberg had called the man *Gideon.*

She went to the reference desk and pulled the *Directory of Medical Specialists* from the shelf. She found the name listed under the section for surgical specialists:

Yarborough, Gideon. Neurosurgery.
B.A. Biology, Dartmouth. M.D. Yale University.
Residency: Hartford Hospital, General Surgery; Peter Bent Brigham, Neurosurgery. Board Certified: 1988.
Postgraduate Fellowship: Rosslyn Institute for Research in Aging, Greenwich, Connecticut.
Currently practicing: Wellesley, Massachusetts, Howarth Surgical Associates.

The Rosslyn Institute. It was the same research facility where Wallenberg had once worked. Robbie Brace had said Wallenberg left Rosslyn after a falling-out with one of his fellow researchers over a woman. A romantic triangle.

Had Yarborough been the other man?

She carried the *Directory of Medical Specialists* back to the Medline computer, and this time she typed in Yarborough under "author's name."

Several articles appeared, among them the one she'd already noted from *Cell Transplant*. She scrolled down to the first article published, dated six years ago, and read the abstract. It described experiments using rat fetal brain tissue fragments, broken up into individual cells by the enzyme trypsin, and then injected into the brains of adult rats. The transplanted cells had thrived and formed functioning colonies, complete with newly grown blood vessels.

A chill had begun to creep up her spine.

She clicked on the next article, from *Journal of Experimental Neurobiology*. Yarborough's co-authors were names she didn't recognize. The title was: "Morpho-functional Integration of Transplanted Embryonic Brain Tissue in Rats." There was no abstract attached.

She scrolled up to the next article titles:

"Mechanisms of Fetal Graft Communication with Host Brain in Rats."

"Optional Gestational Stage for Harvest of Fetal Rat Brain Cells."

"Cryopreservation of Fetal Rat Brain Grafts." An abstract was attached to this one. "After cryopreservation in liquid nitrogen for ninety days, fetal mesencephalic brain cells showed significantly decreased survival as compared to fresh cells. For optimal graft survival, immediate transplant of freshly harvested fetal brain tissue is mandatory."

She stared at that last phrase: *Freshly harvested fetal brain tissue.*

By now the chill had spread all the way up to the nape of her neck.

She clicked on the most recent article, dated three years ago: "Transplantation of Fetal Pituitary Grafts in Elderly Monkeys: Implications for Prolongation of Natural Life Spans." The authors were Yarborough, Wallenberg, and Monica Trammell, Ph.D.

It was the last article they'd published; soon after, Wallenberg and his research partners had left Rosslyn. Was it their controversial research that had forced them out?

She rose and went to the library telephone. Her heart was racing as she dialed Dvorak's home phone number. The phone kept ringing, unanswered. She glanced up at the wall clock and saw it was five-forty-five. The answering machine clicked on, and then came a recording: *This is Dan. Please leave your name and number . . .*

"Dan, pick up," said Toby. "*Please* pick up." She paused, hoping to hear a live voice, but no one came on. "Dan, I'm in the Springer medical library, extension two five seven. There's something here on Medline you have to see. Please, *please* call me back right—"

The library door opened.

Toby turned to see the evening security guard poking his head into the room. He looked just as startled to see her as she was to see him.

"Ma'am, I have to lock up for the night."

"I'm making a phone call."

"You can finish the call. I'll wait."

In frustration she simply hung up and walked out of the library. Only as she pushed into the stairwell did she remember she'd left the computer on.

Sitting in the parking lot, she used her car phone to call Dvorak's direct line in the medical examiner's office. Again, a recording came on. She hung up without leaving another message.

With a violent twist of the ignition she started the car and pulled out of the parking lot. Driving purely by habit, she headed toward home, her mind focused on what she'd just read on the Medline computer. Neural grafts. Fetal brain cells. Prolongation of the natural life span.

So this was the research Wallenberg had been working on at Rosslyn. His associate had been Gideon Yarborough, a neurosurgeon who now practiced in nearby Wellesley. . . .

She turned into a gas station, ran inside, and asked the cashier for the Wellesley telephone directory.

In the Yellow Pages, under *Physicians,* she found what she was looking for:

> Howarth Surgical Associates
> A multispecialty group
> 1388 Eisley Street

Howarth. It was a name she'd remembered seeing in Harry Slotkin's medical record. When Robbie had brought her to Brant Hill to look at Harry's chart, they'd seen the name in the M.D. order sheet:

Preop Valium and six A.M. van transport to Howarth Surgical Associates.

She got back in her car and drove toward Wellesley.

By the time she reached the Howarth building, she was starting to put it all together, in a way that made horrifying sense.

She parked across the street from the building and gazed through the gloom at the nondescript two-story structure. It was heavily cloaked by shrubbery, with a small parking lot in front that was currently empty of cars. The upstairs windows were dark; downstairs, the entryway and reception area were lit but no movement could be seen inside.

Toby got out of the car and crossed the street to the front

entrance. The doors were locked. On the window were stenciled the doctors' names:

Merle Lamm, M.D., Obstetrics and Gynecology
Lawrence Remington, M.D., General Surgery
Gideon Yarborough, M.D., Neurosurgery

Interesting, she thought. Harry Slotkin had been sent here from Brant Hill, supposedly for a deviated nasal septum. Yet none of these doctors was an ear, nose, and throat specialist.

From somewhere in the building came the faint whine of machinery. A furnace? A generator? She couldn't identify the sound.

She circled around to the side of the building, but dense shrubbery hid any view through the windows. The low whine suddenly shut off, leaving absolute silence. She rounded the corner and found a small paved lot at the rear of the building. Three cars were parked there.

One of them was a dark blue Saab. *Jane Nolan's.*

The building's rear entrance was locked.

Toby returned to her car and picked up the phone. Again she tried calling Dvorak on his direct office line. She didn't really expect him to answer and was startled when his voice came on with a brisk: "Hello?"

Her words came out in a rush. "Dan, I know what Wallenberg's been doing. I know how his patients are getting infected—"

"Toby, listen to me. You have to call your attorney at once."

"They're not injecting hormones. They're transplanting pituitary cells from fetal brains! But something's gone wrong. Somehow they transmitted CJD. Now they're trying to cover it up—trying to hide the disaster before it becomes public—"

"*Listen* to me! You're in trouble."

"What?"

"I just spoke to Alpren." He paused. Quietly he said, "They've issued a warrant for your arrest."

For a moment she said nothing but simply stared at the building across the street. One step ahead, she thought. They're always one step ahead of me.

"This is what I think you should do," he said. "Call your attorney. Ask him to accompany you to the police station, Berkley Street headquarters. The case has been transferred there."

"Why?"

"Because of your mother's . . . condition."

Homicide was what he meant. It would soon be considered a homicide.

"Don't make Alpren arrest you at home," said Dvorak. "It'll just turn into a shark-feeding for the media. Come in voluntarily, as soon as you can."

"Why did they issue the warrant? Why now?"

"They have new evidence."

"What evidence?"

"Toby, just come in. I can meet you first, and we'll come in together."

"I'm not going anywhere until I know what his evidence is."

Dvorak hesitated. "A pharmacist near your home says he filled a prescription for your mother. Sixty tablets of Coumadin. He says you called in the prescription by telephone."

"That's a lie."

"I'm only telling you what the pharmacist said."

"How does he know I made the call? It could have been another woman, claiming to be me. It could have been Jane. He wouldn't know."

"Toby, we'll straighten it out, I promise. Right now your best move is to come in. Voluntarily, and without delay."

"And then what? I spend the night in jail?"

"If you don't come in, it could be months in jail."

"I didn't hurt my mother."

"Then come in and tell it to Alpren. The longer you wait, the guiltier you'll seem. I'm here for you. Please, just come in."

She felt too defeated to say a word, and too tired to consider all the tasks that now had to be done. Call an attorney. Talk to Vickie. Arrange for bills to be paid, the house to be watched over, the car to be picked up. And money—she would have to transfer money from her retirement savings. Attorneys were expensive . . .

"Toby, do you understand what you need to do?"

"Yes," she whispered.

"I'm going to leave my office now. Where would you like to meet me?"

"The police station. Tell Alpren I'm coming in. Tell him not to send anyone to my house."

"Whatever you wish. I'll be waiting for you."

She hung up, her fingers numb from clutching the receiver. So now the storm finally breaks, she thought. She sat preparing herself for the ordeal to follow. Fingerprints. Mug shots. Reporters. If only she could slink away somewhere and gather up her strength. But there was no time now; the police were expecting her.

She reached for the ignition and was about to turn the key when she glimpsed the flicker of headlights. Looking sideways, she saw Jane's Saab pull out of the Howarth driveway.

By the time Toby got her Mercedes turned around, the Saab had already glided out of sight around the corner. Frantic she'd lose it, she swerved around the corner. The Saab's rear lights came into view. At once Toby eased up on the gas, letting her quarry pull ahead just far enough to stay in sight. At the next intersection, it turned left.

Seconds later, so did Toby.

The Saab headed west, winding its way into the tonier sections of Wellesley. It wasn't Jane at the wheel, but a man; she could see his head silhouetted against the glare of oncoming headlights. Completely focused on her quarry, Toby caught only glimpses of the neighborhood: iron gates and tall hedges and lights shining from many-windowed houses. The Saab picked up speed, the taillights receding into the night. A truck pulled onto the road from a cross street and slipped between Toby and the Saab.

In frustration, Toby blew her horn.

The truck slowed down and veered right. She shot past it, finally pulling in front of it.

The road ahead was empty.

Cursing, she scanned the darkness for a glimpse of tail-lights. She spotted them fading off to the right. The Saab had turned onto a private drive and was weaving through a dense stand of trees.

She slammed on the brakes and swerved onto the same road. Heart pounding, she braked to a stop and gave herself time to steady her nerves and allow her pulse to slow down. The Saab's taillights vanished beyond the trees, but she was no longer worried about losing it; this road seemed to be the only way on and off the property.

A mailbox was mounted at the entrance, the red flag up. She stepped out of the car and looked inside the box. There were two envelopes inside, utility payments. The name Trammell was on the return address.

She got back in her car and took a deep breath. With the headlights off, guided only by her parking lights, she drove slowly down the road. It wound through the trees in a gentle downhill grade. She rode the brakes all the way, letting the car glide at a crawl along sharp curves that were barely visible in the dim glow of the parking lights. The road seemed endless as it wound past thickets of evergreens. She could not see what lay at the end of the road; all she could make out was intermittent twinkles of light through the branches. Moving deeper into the lair of the enemy, she thought. Yet she didn't turn back; she was forced onward by all the pain and rage of these past few weeks. Robbie's death. Soon Ellen's, as well. *Get a life,* Wallenberg had sneered at her.

This is my life now. All that's left of it.

The road widened to a driveway. She pulled off to the side, her tires skidding across pine needles, and turned off the engine.

A mansion loomed ahead in the darkness. The upstairs windows were lit, and a woman's silhouette glided past one of them, then back again in agitated pacing. Toby recognized the profile.

Jane. Did she live here?

Toby gazed up at the massive roofline, which blotted out her view of half the stars in the sky. She could make out four chimneys, as well as the gleam of third-story windows. Was Jane a guest here? Or merely an employee?

A light-haired man appeared in the upstairs window—the driver of Jane's Saab. They spoke to each other. He glanced at his watch, then made a how-should-I-know? gesture with his arms. Now Jane seemed even more agitated, perhaps angry. She crossed the room and picked up a telephone.

Toby fished a penlight out of her medical bag and stepped out of her car.

The Saab was parked near the front porch. She wanted to find out who owned it, who Jane was working for. She crossed to the Saab and shone her penlight through the car window. The interior was clean, not even a stray scrap of paper in sight. She tried the passenger door and found it unlocked. In the glove compartment were the car's registration papers, made out to a Richard Trammell. She popped open the trunk lock and circled around to the rear of the car. Leaning forward, she played her penlight on the trunk's interior.

From behind her came the snap of twigs, the rustle of something moving through the underbrush. A low, threatening growl.

Toby whirled and saw the gleam of teeth as the Doberman sprang.

The force of its attack sent her sprawling. Instinctively she brought up her hands to protect her throat. The dog's jaws clamped down on her forearm, its teeth sinking straight to the bone. She screamed, flailing at him, but the Doberman would not release her. It began to whip its head back and forth, teeth ripping at flesh. Blinded by pain, she gripped the dog by the throat with her free hand and tried to choke it into releasing her, but its teeth seemed permanently embedded in her arm. Only when she clawed at its eyes did the dog give a yelp and release her.

She rolled free and scrambled back to her feet, blood streaming down her arm, and ran toward her car.

Again the Doberman lunged.

It slammed into her back, knocking her to her knees. This time its jaws caught only her shirt, teeth shredding fabric. She flung off the animal and heard it collide with the Saab. Too soon the Doberman was back on its feet and coiling for the third attack.

A man shouted, *"Down!"*

Toby staggered to her feet but never made it to the safety of her car. This time it was a pair of human hands that captured her and slammed her facedown against the hood of the Saab.

The Doberman was barking wildly, demanding to be allowed to make its kill.

Toby twisted and tried to squirm free. The last thing she saw was the flashlight beam, tracing an arc through the night. The blow caught her in the temple, flinging her sideways. She felt herself falling, tumbling into blackness.

* * *

Cold. It was very cold.

As though surfacing through icy waters, she drifted back toward consciousness. At first she couldn't feel her limbs; she had no sense of where they were, or even if they were still attached to her body.

A door thudded shut, releasing a strangely metallic series of echoes. The sound seemed to ring like a bell in Toby's head. She groaned and rolled onto her side. The floor felt like ice. Curling into a ball, she lay shivering as she struggled to think, to make her limbs respond. Her arm was hurting now, the pain gnawing its way through her numbness. She opened her eyes and winced as light pierced her retinas.

There was blood on her shirt. The sight of it shocked her fully awake. She focused on her shredded sleeve, soaked red.

The Doberman.

As the memory of those jaws flooded back, so did the pain, returning with such intensity she felt herself slipping back toward unconsciousness. She fought to stay awake. Rocking onto her back, she collided with a table leg. Something fell loose and swung above her head. She looked up and saw a naked arm hanging over the edge of the table, its fingers dangling just above her face.

Gasping, she rolled away and scrambled to her knees. The light-headedness lasted only a few seconds, then cleared as the image came shockingly into focus.

There was a body on the table, covered by a plastic drape. Only the arm was visible, the skin a bluish white under the fluorescent lights.

Toby rose to her feet. She was still dizzy and had to reach out to a countertop to steady herself. She refocused on the body and saw there was another table in the room, with another plastic-draped form. A blast of refrigerated air rumbled from a vent. Slowly she took stock of her surroundings—the windowless walls, the heavy steel door—and she realized where she was. The foul odor alone should have told her.

It was a cold room, for the storage of corpses.

Focusing again on the dangling arm, she approached the table and pulled aside the drape.

The man was elderly, his dark brown hair showing silver roots. A bad dye job. His eyelids were open, revealing glazed blue eyes. She peeled back the rest of the drape and saw that the nude body was unmarred by any obvious injuries. The only bruises were on his arm, and she recognized them as the aftermath of IVs. Tucked between his ankles was a manila folder with a name written on the cover: James R. Bigelow. She opened it and saw it was a medical record of the man's last week of life.

The first entry was dated November 1.

Subject observed to be clumsy during breakfast— poured milk on plate instead of cup—responded with look of confusion when asked if he needed help. Patient escorted to clinic for further eval.

On exam, mild tremors. Positive cerebellar findings. No other localizing signs.

Permanent transfer sequence initiated.

The note was unsigned.

She struggled to understand what she was reading, but her headache made every word a challenge. What did that last entry mean? Permanent transfer sequence?

She flipped forward, through the next few entries, to November 3.

Patient unable to walk without assistance. EEG results nonspecific. Tremors worse, cerebellar signs more pronounced. CT scan shows pituitary enlargement, no acute changes.

November 4:

*Disoriented times two. Episode of startle myoclonus.
Cerebellar function continues to deteriorate. All labs
remain normal.*

Then, the final entry, on November 7.

*Patient in four-point restraints. Incontinent bowel and
bladder. Twenty-four-hour IV fluids and sedation.
Terminal stages. Autopsy to follow.*

She lay the chart down on the man's bare thighs. For a
moment she gazed at the body with strangely clinical
detachment, noting the silver hairs on the chest, the wrinkles
on the abdomen, the limp penis in its nest of wiry hair. Had
he known the risks? she wondered. Had it occurred to him
that trying to live forever would exact its costs?

The old are feeding on the young.

She swayed against the table, vision blurring from the
pain throbbing in her head. It took her a moment to refocus
her eyes. When she did, her gaze shifted to the other corpse.

She left the first table and went to stand beside the second
body, still concealed beneath its drape. She drew away the
shroud. Though she'd steeled herself, she was not prepared
for the horror of what lay on that table.

The man's corpse had been flayed open, the rib cage and
abdomen cleanly sliced down the center and spread apart,
revealing a jumble of internal organs. Whoever had autopsied the corpse had removed the organs, then replaced them
again with no concern for proper anatomy.

She backed away as nausea assailed her. The odor of this
corpse told her it had been dead longer than the first one.

She forced herself to step back toward it, to look at the
plastic ID wristband. The name Phillip Dorr had been writ-

343

ten in black marker. She saw no medical record, no documentation of the man's illness.

She forced herself to look at the face. It was another elderly man, eyebrows streaked with gray, the face strangely collapsed like a rubber mask. She noticed only than that the scalp had been slit behind the ear. The flap had sagged, exposing a pearly arc of skull. Gently she tugged on the hair, gingerly peeling the scalp forward.

The top of the cranium fell off and clattered onto the floor. She gave a cry and jerked away.

The skull gaped open like an empty bowl. There was nothing inside; the brain had been removed.

"She'll be here," said Dvorak, watching Alpren tap a pencil on the desk. "Just be patient."

Detective Alpren looked at his watch. "It's been two hours. I think you screwed up, Doc. You shouldn't have told her."

"And you shouldn't jump to conclusions. This arrest warrant is premature. You haven't finished the preliminary investigation."

"Yeah, I'm supposed to waste my time searching for the *real* Jane Nolan? I'd rather arrest the *real* Dr. Harper. If we can even find her now."

"Give her a chance to walk in here on her own. Maybe she's waiting for her attorney. Maybe she went home to square things away."

"She didn't go home. We sent a cruiser there half an hour ago. I think Dr. Harper's put pedal to the metal and skipped

345

town. Right now she's probably a hundred miles away, thinking about ditching the car."

Dvorak stared at the clock on the wall. He could not picture Toby Harper as a fugitive; she didn't seem like a woman who'd run, but someone who'd turn and fight back. Now he had to question his instincts, had to rethink everything he knew, or thought he knew about her.

Clearly Alpren took some measure of satisfaction from all this. Dvorak the M.D. had screwed up; this time the cop had proved a better judge of character. Dvorak sat in silence, anger balling up in his stomach, anger at Alpren for his smugness, at Toby for betraying his trust.

Alpren answered a ringing telephone. When he put it down again, he had a glitter in his eyes, hard and self-satisfied. "They found her Mercedes."

"Where?"

"Logan Airport. She left it parked in the passenger loading zone. Guess she was in a hurry to catch a plane." He stood up. "No reason to hang around any longer, Doc. She's not coming in."

Dvorak drove home with his radio turned off, the silence only fueling his agitation. She ran, he thought, and there was only one explanation for it: a guilty conscience, and the certainty of punishment. Yet certain details continued to trouble him. He played out the sequence of actions that a fleeing Toby would have taken. She'd driven to Logan, where she'd abandoned her car in the loading zone, hurried into the terminal, and boarded a plane, destination unknown.

But this was not logical. Leaving a car in the loading zone was simply flagging attention to it. Anyone attempting a discreet escape would have parked their car in one of the crowded satellite lots, where it might go unnoticed for days.

So she didn't board a plane. Alpren might think she was

346

that stupid, but Dvorak knew better. The detective was wasting his time, checking the flights out of Logan.

She must be fleeing some other way.

When Dvorak walked in his front door, he headed straight for the telephone. He was angry now, stung by Toby's betrayal, and by his own stupidity. He picked up the receiver to call Alpren, then put it down again when he noticed his answering machine was blinking. He hit Play.

The electronic voice gave the message time as five forty-five. Toby's voice came on:

"I'm in the Springer medical library, extension two five seven. There's something here on Medline you have to see. Please, *please* call me back right . . ."

The last time they'd spoken was around seven-thirty, so this phone message had preceded their final conversation. He remembered she'd been trying to tell him something, that he'd cut her off before she could explain what she'd found.

Springer medical library . . . something here on Medline you have to see. Please, please call me back . . .

The pain came on like a fist crushing her abdomen, squeezing so tight it choked off any groan. Eyes closed, teeth gritted, Molly closed her hands into fists and strained against the wrist straps. Only when the contraction had ended did she release a whimper of relief. She had not expected child-birth to be so silent. She had imagined herself screaming, and loudly too, had assumed that pain was a noisy affair. But when it came, when she felt the first ripples of another contraction, and then the seizing up of her womb, she bore it without uttering a sound, wanting not to scream but simply to curl up and hide in the dark.

But *they* would not leave her alone.

There were two of them, both dressed in blue surgical gowns, only their eyes visible in the narrow gap between mask and cap. A man and a woman. Neither one spoke to

Molly; to them, she was an object, a dumb animal on the table, her thighs spread, her legs strapped on elevated leg rests.

At last the contraction eased, and as the haze of pain cleared, Molly became aware, once again, of her surroundings. The lights, like three blinding suns shining overhead. The hard gleam of the IV pole. The plastic tube that had been threaded into her vein.

"Please," she said. "It hurts. It hurts so much . . ."

They ignored her. The woman's attention was focused on the bottle dripping into the IV, the man's on Molly's parted thighs. Had he worn even the vaguest expression of lust, Molly would have felt some measure of control, some measure of power. But she saw no desire in his gaze.

Another contraction began to build. She jerked on the wrist straps, straining to curl up on her side, pain suddenly translating to fury. Enraged, she jerked back and forth, and the table shook with the rattle of steel.

"The IV's not going to last," said the woman. "Can't we put her under?"

The man answered: "We'll lose the contractions. No anesthesia."

"Let me *go!*" screamed Molly.

"I don't want to put up with this noise," said the woman.

"Then dial up the Pitocin and let's get the goddamn thing expelled." He bent forward, his gloved fingers probing between Molly's thighs.

"Let . . . me . . . go!" gasped Molly, her voice suddenly dying as the wave of pain broke and washed over her. The insertion of the man's fingers at that moment intensified the agony, and she closed her eyes, tears trickling down her face.

"Cervix is fully dilated," the man said. "Almost there."

Molly's head lurched forward, and she gave an anguished grunt.

"Good, she's bearing down. Do it. Come on, girl. Push."

Molly forced out the words: "Fuck you."

"Push, goddamn it, or we'll have to get it out some other way."

"Fuck you, fuck you, fuck you . . ."

The woman slapped Molly across the face, the blow so brutal Molly's head snapped sideways. For a few seconds she lay stunned and mute, her cheek ringing, her vision dimmed. The pain of the contraction faded away. She felt hot liquid seep from her vagina, heard it drip, drip onto the paper drape beneath her buttocks. Then her vision cleared and she focused again on the man. And realized that what she saw in his face was expectation. Impatience.

They are waiting to take my baby.

"Increase the Pitocin," said the man. "Let's finish this."

The woman flicked up the dial on the IV, and a moment later, Molly felt another contraction begin to build, this one accelerating so fast and so hard it shocked her by its violence. Her head lifted off the table, face straining toward her chest as she pushed. Blood gushed from between her legs; she heard it splatter the surgical drape.

"Push. Come on, *push!*" the woman commanded.

The pain crescendoed to unbearable heights. Molly gasped in a deep breath, and again strained. Her vision blackened. New pain suddenly exploded in her head. She heard herself cry out, but the sound was foreign to her, like the shriek of a dying animal.

"That's it. Come on, come on . . . ," said the man.

She pushed one last time, and felt the agony between her legs suddenly give way to the pain of tearing flesh.

And then, mercifully, it was over.

Groggy, clammy with sweat, she could neither move nor utter a sound. Perhaps she fell asleep—she wasn't sure. She knew only that time had passed and there was movement in the room. The sound of splashing water, a cabinet clanging shut. It took great effort, but slowly she opened her eyes.

At first the glare of light was all she saw, the trio of bright suns shining directly overhead. Then she focused on the blurred image of the man, standing near her opened thighs, and on what he was holding in his hands.

It had hair, coarse black tufts of it clotted with blood. The flesh was pink and formless, like a clump of butchered meat lying limp in the man's gloved hands. It moved. Only a quiver at first, then a violent shudder, the flesh balling up, the hair stiffening like the fur of a startled cat.

"Primitive muscle function," said the man. "And we still have rudimentary follicular and dentate structures. Haven't eliminated the appendages yet, either."

"Saline bath's ready."

"Are we all set up next door?"

"Our patient's positioned on the table. We just need the tissue."

"Let me get a weight on this." The man rose and lay the clump of flesh on a table scale not far from Molly's head.

Molly stared. A single eye, lidless, soulless, stared back at her.

Her scream shattered into a thousand piercing echoes. Again and again she screamed, her horror swelling with the sound of her own voice.

"We have to shut her up!" the woman said. "The patient might hear it!"

The man clapped a rubber mask over Molly's mouth and nose, and Molly caught a whiff of noxious gas. She jerked her face away. He grabbed her by the jaw and tried to force her to hold still, to breathe in the fumes. Molly caught the man's little finger in her teeth and bit down like a panicked animal. The man shrieked.

A blow slammed into Molly's temple with such force a hundred bright lights seemed to explode in her head.

"Bitch! Fucking bitch!" the man gasped.

"My God, your finger—"

"The syringe. Get the syringe!"

"What?"

"The potassium. Do it *now.*"

Slowly Molly opened her eyes. She saw the woman standing over her, holding a syringe and needle. She saw the needle pierce the rubber dam on the IV line.

What felt like a line of fire slowly burned its way up Molly's arm. In pain, she cried out and tried to pull free, but the strap held her wrist in place.

"All of it," the man snapped. "Give her the whole fucking thing."

The woman nodded. She squeezed down on the syringe.

The count was extraordinary. Embedded in swirls of fetal brain tissue were at least thirty-three separate pituitary glands, more than any previous embryonic implant had produced. The cells appeared healthy and disease free under the microscope, and the girl's blood tests had all been normal. They could not allow any infections to be transmitted. They had made that mistake with their first group of recipients, when they'd used intact fetuses harvested from the hired wombs of women in a poor Mexican village. A village where the cattle were already dying.

This tissue had been grown from a genetically altered embryo started in his own lab. He knew it was clean.

Dr. Gideon Yarborough dissected out three of the glands and dropped them into a vial of trypsin warmed to thirty-seven degrees Centigrade. The rest of the fetus—if one could call the clump of flesh a fetus—was rinsed and placed in a jar of buffered Hanks' balanced salt solution. It bobbed in the liquid, and the blue eye surfaced, staring up at him. There was no functioning brain behind that eye, and no soul, nevertheless it gave Yarborough the willies. He covered the jar and set it aside. Later, he would harvest the remaining pituitaries.

It was a valuable crop; there would be enough to implant ten patients.

Twenty minutes had passed.

He rinsed the vial containing the three pituitaries with salt solution. By now the trypsin had broken up the tissue and turbid liquid swirled in the vial, which no longer contained solid pituitaries but individual cells in suspension. The building blocks of a new master gland. Gently he aspirated the suspension into a syringe, then he carried it into the next room, where his assistant was waiting for him.

The patient, lightly sedated with Valium, lay on the table. A seventy-eight-year-old man in satisfactory health who'd been feeling his age. Who wanted his youth back and was willing to pay for it, willing to endure a minor measure of discomfort for a chance at rejuvenation.

Now the man lay with his head aligned in a Todd-Wells stereotaxic frame, his skull fixed in place. The amplified image taken by an X-ray tube was projected onto a fifteen-inch television. On the screen was a view of the sella turcica, the small bony well containing the patient's aging pituitary gland.

Yarborough sprayed a local anesthetic into the man's right nostril and swabbed it with cocaine solution. Then he inserted a long needle up the right nostril and injected more anesthetic into the mucous membrane.

The patient gave a murmur of discomfort.

"I'm just numbing up the area, Mr. Luft. You're doing fine." He handed the syringe of anesthetic to his assistant.

And picked up the drill.

It had a simple twist bit, almost needle-fine. He inserted this up the nostril. With the image on the screen to guide him, Yarborough began to drill through bone, the bit whining through the floor of the sphenoid bone. As it broke through the other side, piercing the dura propria, the membrane lining the pituitary, the patient gave a sharp cry, his muscles tensing.

"It's all right, Mr. Luft. That's the worst part of it. The pain should last only a few seconds."

As he predicted, the patient slowly relaxed, his discomfort passing. Piercing the dura always caused that brief jolt of pain in the forehead. It did not worry Yarborough.

His assistant handed him the syringe containing the cell suspension.

Through the newly drilled hole in the sphenoid bone, Yarborough introduced the needle tip. Gently he injected the syringe contents into the sella turcica. He pictured the cells swirling into their new home, growing, multiplying into healthy new colonies. Cell factories pumping out the hormones of a young brain. Hormones Mr. Luft himself could no longer produce.

He withdrew the needle. There was no bleeding; a good, clean procedure.

"It went perfectly fine," he told the patient. "Now we're going to remove the head frame. We'll have you lie here for a half hour or so while we watch your blood pressure."

"That's it?"

"It's all done. You sailed through with flying colors." He nodded to his assistant. "I'll stay and watch him. I'll call the van when he's ready to go back to Brant Hill."

"What do we do about . . ." His assistant glanced toward the door. Toward the other room.

Yarborough stripped off his gloves. "I'll take care of that too, Monica. You go back to the house and deal with the other problem."

The thermometer on the wall registered thirty-five degrees Fahrenheit.

Toby huddled in a corner, her knees bent to her chest, a plastic sheet draped over her shoulders. It was a corpse's shroud, and the smell of Formalin permeated the fabric. At first it had repelled her, and she had felt nauseated by the thought of stripping the sheet off one of the dead bodies for her own use. But then she'd started shaking from the cold and she knew she had no choice. It was the only way to conserve body heat.

But it wasn't enough to keep her alive. Hours had passed, and her hands and feet had lost all feeling. At least her arm had stopped aching. But she was having trouble thinking, her mental processes slowed to the point where she could not focus on anything except staying awake.

Soon, though, she lost the will to manage even that.

Gradually her head sagged to the floor and her limbs fell limp. Twice she shook herself awake and found she was lying on her side and that the lights were still shining. After that, she slept.

And dreamed. Not in images, but in sounds. There were two people speaking—a man and Jane Nolan—their voices distorted, metallic. She felt herself floating through black liquid, felt a welcome rush of warmth against her face.

Then she was falling.

She jerked awake to find herself lying on her side in darkness. There was a carpet beneath her cheek. A faint blade of light cut through the shadows and a door squealed shut. She tried to move but found she could not; her hands were bound together behind her back. Her feet felt numb and useless. She heard another door shut, and then the sound of a car engine starting up.

A man said, "Shouldn't you latch the gate?"

The answering voice was Jane Nolan's: "I've tied up the dog. He won't get out. Let's just go."

They began to drive up a bumpy road. The road from the house, thought Toby. Where were they taking her?

A sudden jolt of the van slammed her left shoulder against the floor, and she almost cried out in pain. She was lying on her injured arm, and the merciful numbness from the cold room was now wearing off. With a burst of effort she twisted and managed to roll onto her back, but she now found herself wedged up against something cold and rubbery. Light had begun to filter through the darkness from streetlamps and passing cars. She turned her head to see what she had bumped up against and found herself staring into the face of one of the corpses.

Toby's shocked gasp drew the attention of her captors. The man said, "Hey, she's awake."

"Just keep driving," said Jane. "I'll tape her mouth." She unbuckled her seat belt and crawled to the rear of the van. There she knelt beside Toby and fumbled in the semidarkness with a roll of surgical tape. "Didn't think we'd have to hear from you again."

Toby strained to free her hands but could not loosen the bonds. "My mother—you hurt my mother—"

"It's your fault, you know," said Jane, peeling off a strip of tape. "So obsessed, Dr. Harper. Too busy worrying about a few old men. You didn't even notice what was going on in your own home." She slapped the tape over Toby's mouth and said, in mock disgust: "And you call yourself a good daughter."

Bitch, thought Toby. *You murdering bitch.*

Jane clucked as she peeled off a second strip of tape. "I didn't *want* to hurt your mother. I was only there to keep an eye on you. Find out how far you were pushing it. But then Robbie Brace called your house that night, and everything got completely out of hand . . ." She slapped a second strip of tape over Toby's mouth. "Then it was too late for you to have an accident. Too late to shut you up. People are so willing to believe the dead." She tore off a final piece of tape and pressed it across Toby's face, ear to ear. "But will they believe a woman who'd hurt her own mother? I don't think so." She gazed down at Toby for a moment, as though evaluating her handiwork. In the van's semidarkness, cut only by the occasional gleam of passing headlights, Jane's eyes seemed to take on a glow of their own. How many times had Ellen awakened to find those same eyes staring down at her? *I should have known. I should have sensed the evil in my home.*

The van made an abrupt turn, and Jane reached out to steady herself.

No, her name is not Jane, thought Toby with sudden comprehension. *Her name is Monica Trammell.* Wallenberg's associate at the Rosslyn Institute.

The van swayed as it moved down a winding drive. The pavement gave way to the unevenness of a dirt road, and Toby could feel the old man's corpse bouncing against her, his flesh clapping against hers. They braked to a stop, and the side door slid open.

A man stood silhouetted against the moonless sky. "Gideon's not here yet," the man said. It was Carl Wallenberg's voice.

The woman climbed out of the van. "He has to be here for this. We all have to be here."

"The patient needed stabilizing. Gideon's staying with him."

"We can't do this without him. This time the responsibility has to be shared, Carl. All of us equally. Richard and I have done too much already."

"I don't want to do this."

"You have to. Is the hole dug?"

The answer came out a sigh: "Yes."

"Then let's finish it." The woman turned to the driver, who'd already climbed out of the van. "Get them out, Richard."

The driver grabbed Toby's bound feet and dragged her halfway out. As Wallenberg took hold of her shoulders, Toby squirmed.

He almost dropped her. "Jesus Christ! She's still *alive*."

"Just move her," said Monica.

"My God, do we have to to it this way?"

"I didn't bring the syringes. This way is bloodless. I don't want any evidence splattered around."

Wallenberg took a few deep breaths, then once again grasped Toby's shoulders. The two men swung her from the van and carried her through the night. At first Toby had no idea where they were bringing her. She knew only that the ground was uneven, that the men were having trouble navigating in the darkness. She caught glimpses of Richard Trammell's head, his hair white-blond under the moonlight, then she saw sky and the shadow of a construction crane arching across the field of stars. Turning her head, she noticed lights shining through the filter of a fence, and she recognized the building in the distance: the Brant Hill nursing facility. They were carrying her into the foundation pit of another new building.

Wallenberg stumbled and lost his grip on Toby's shoulders. She fell, her head thudding to the dirt so hard it slammed her jaws together. Pain sliced her tongue, and she tasted blood, felt it pooling in her mouth.

"Jesus," Wallenberg muttered.

"Carl," said Monica, her voice flat and metallic. "Just get it over with."

"Fuck this. *You* do it!"

"No, it's your turn. This time *your* hands get dirty. And Gideon does too. Now finish it."

Wallenberg took a deep breath. Once again Toby was lifted and carried, squirming, into the pit. The two men came to a stop. Toby looked straight up into Wallenberg's face, but she could not see his expression against the moonlit sky. She saw only a dark oval, a fluttering of windblown hair as he swung her sideways, then released her.

Though she'd steeled herself for the landing, the sudden

impact slammed the breath from her lungs. For a moment she saw only blackness. Gradually her vision returned. She saw a bowl of stars suspended above her and realized she was lying at the bottom of a hole. A sprinkling of dirt tumbled in from the side, stinging her eyes. She jerked her head sideways and felt gravel against her cheek.

The two men walked away. *Now,* she thought. *My one and only chance.* She fought to free herself, twisting one way, then another, dirt spilling on top of her as she thrashed against the wall of the pit. No good; her wrists and ankles were too tightly bound, and her struggles only resulted in making her hands numb. But one corner of the tape had begun to peel off her cheek. She rubbed her face against the gravel, scraping her skin raw as more of the tape lifted away.

Hurry. Hurry.

She was coughing and choking on clouds of dust. Another inch of tape peeled off, freeing her lips. She took a breath and screamed.

A figure appeared above the pit, staring down at her. "No one can hear you," said Monica. "It's quite a deep hole. Tomorrow it'll be gone, smoothed over. Tomorrow they pour the gravel. Then the foundation." She turned as the men reappeared, carrying one of the corpses. They threw it in, and it landed beside Toby, the man's head thudding against her shoulder. She recoiled against the far side of the pit, and fresh dirt sprinkled onto her face.

So this is how it ends. Three skeletons in a hole. A concrete slab to seal us in.

The men left to get the second corpse.

Again Toby screamed for help, but her voice seemed lost in that deep pit.

Monica crouched at the side of the hole, staring down. "It's a cold night. Everyone's closed their windows. They can't hear a thing, you know."

Toby screamed again.

Monica dropped a handful of dirt on her face. Coughing, Toby twisted sideways and found herself staring at the corpse. Monica was right. No one was listening; no one would hear her.

The men returned, both breathing heavily from exertion. They threw the last body into the pit.

It landed on top of Toby, the shroud flapping across her face, covering it. She could barely move under the weight of the corpse, but she could hear voices above her, and the sound of a shovel scraping through dirt.

The first scoop of soil fell into the pit. It landed on Toby's legs. She tried to shake it off, but then another shovelful fell, and another.

"Wait for Gideon," said Monica. "He has to be part of this."

"He'll be here to finish up. Let's just get it over with," said her husband. He grunted, and a fresh load of dirt fell onto the top corpse, soil trickling onto Toby's hair. Again she tried to move under the corpse's weight. The shroud slipped down, uncovering her eyes. She stared straight up at the three figures standing around the pit. They seemed to sense that she was watching them, and they fell momentarily silent.

Monica said, "All right. Fill it in now."

Toby cried out, "No!" but her voice was muffled by the fabric. By the weight of the corpse.

Dirt tumbled down. She blinked against the sting of grit. Another shovel of earth fell onto her hair, then more dirt, rivers of it spilling around her body, covering her limbs. She struggled to move, but the corpse, and the steadily falling soil, trapped her in place. She heard her own heartbeat roaring in her ears, heard gasps of air rushing through her lungs. She caught one final glimpse of stars as she burrowed her face under the cover of the shroud.

Then her head was buried, and she saw no light at all.

21

It was his turn to wield the shovel.

Carl Wallenberg's hands were shaking as he gripped the handle and scooped up the first bladeful of earth. He paused at the edge of the pit, staring down into its darkness, thinking about the woman, still alive. Heart still beating, blood still pumping. A million neurons firing off in the panicked throes of death. Beneath that blanket of soil, she was dying.

He threw his load of dirt into the pit and scooped up another. He heard Monica's murmur of approval, and silently he cursed her for forcing him into this appalling act. This was the last evidence to be disposed of, the last two corpses to be covered up from an experiment gone horrifyingly wrong.

We should have been more careful with the donors. We should have screened the fetal material for more than just

360

bacteria and viruses. We never considered the possibility of prions.

But Yarborough had been in a rush to implant the cells. The tissue had to be fresh, he'd insisted. The cell suspensions had to be implanted within seven days of harvest or they would not survive in the brains of the new hosts. They would not colonize. And then there'd been that long waiting list of eager recipients, three dozen men and women who'd paid their deposits, who were clamoring for their second chance at youth. Risk free, they'd been assured. And it was, in truth, a benign procedure: a local anesthetic, the X-ray guided injection of fetal pituitary cells into the brain, and weeks later, the slow rejuvenation of the master gland. He and Gideon had done it dozens of times, without complications, right up until Rosslyn had shut down the project on moral grounds. If not for the necessity of using aborted human fetuses, the procedure would have been hailed as a medical breakthrough. A fountain of youth, distilled from the brains of the unborn and unwanted.

A breakthrough, yes. But one that would be forever shunned because of the politics.

He paused, breathing hard, his sweat already chilling his skin. The hole was nearly filled. By now the woman's lungs would be choking with dust, her brain cells starved of oxygen. The heart pumping its last desperate beats. He disliked Toby Harper, he agreed she needed to be silenced, but he wished her a merciful death, one that would not haunt him in the years to come.

He had never intended to kill anyone.

A few fetuses had been sacrificed, true, but only at the beginning. Now they were using cloned tissue, scarcely human at all, implanted and nurtured in wombs. He did not feel guilty about the tissue's source. Neither did his patients feel any qualms; they simply *wanted* it, and they were willing to pay for it. As long as Brant Hill knew nothing about it, his work would go on, and the private flow of money would continue.

But then Mackie had died, followed by the others. Now it wasn't just the money he could lose; it was his position, his reputation. His future.

Is it worth committing murder for?

Even as he continued to shovel dirt into the rapidly filling hole, he was painfully aware that the woman below was dying. *But then, we are all dying. Some of us more horribly than others.*

He set the shovel down. He was going to be sick.

"More dirt. Make it level," said Monica. "It has to blend in. We can't have the construction crew noticing."

"You do it." He thrust the shovel toward her. "I've done enough."

She took the shovel and studied him for a moment. "Yes, I suppose you have," she finally said. "And now you're in just as deep as Richard and me." She paused, her shoe on the shovel, and prepared to scoop up another bladeful of soil.

"There's Yarborough," said Richard.

Wallenberg turned and saw headlights approaching. Yarborough's black Lincoln bounced onto the dirt road and braked to a stop at the construction fence. The driver's door opened and slammed shut again.

A bright light came on, its beam flooding the construction pit. Wallenberg stumbled backward, shielding his eyes from the sudden glare. He heard the frantic grinding of other tires over gravel, then heard two more cars doors slam shut, and the sound of running footsteps.

He squinted as the silhouettes suddenly appeared before the floodlights. *Not Yarborough,* he thought. *Who are you?*

Two men walked toward them.

Fresh air flooded her lungs, so cold it seared her throat. She gasped in another breath, and another, wheezing in air between coughs. Something was pressed against her face, and she fought to escape it, thrashing out at the hands trapping her head. She heard voices, too many voices to keep track of, all of them talking at once.

"Get that oxygen back on her!"

"She's fighting—"

"Hey, I need a pair of hands here! I can't get the IV in."

She twisted, clawing blindly. There was a light shining in the distance, and she fought to tear her way through the darkness, to reach the light before it vanished. But her arms felt paralyzed; something was pressing them down. The air she breathed in smelled of rubber.

"Toby—stop fighting us!" She felt a hand grasp hers as though to drag her from the darkness.

A black curtain suddenly seemed to tear apart before her eyes and she surfaced into a stream of light. She saw faces staring down at her. Saw more lights now, blue and red, dancing in a circle. *Beautiful,* she thought. *The colors—so very beautiful.* Static crackled in the night. A police radio.

"Doc, you'd better come and see this," one of the cops said.

Dvorak didn't respond; his gaze was focused on the ambulance, taillights shuddering as the vehicle drove up the dirt road, bearing Toby to Springer Hospital. She should not be alone tonight, he thought. I should be with her; it's where I want to be. Where I want to stay.

He turned to the cop and realized his legs were not quite steady, that in fact he was still shaking. The night had taken on a crazy neon quality. All the cruisers, all the lights. And there were onlookers gathered outside the construction fence—the expected crime scene groupies, but this was an older crowd, residents of Brant Hill who'd heard the multiple sirens and, curious, had wandered out into the night still dressed in their bathrobes. They stood in a solemn line, staring through the mesh of the fence into the foundation pit, where the two bodies had been uncovered and now lay exposed on the dirt.

"Detective Sheehan's waiting for you up there," the cop said. "He's the only one who's touched it."

"Touched what?"

"The body."

"Another one?"

"I'm afraid so."

Dvorak followed the cop out of the foundation pit, both of them stumbling their way up to the fence.

"It was in the trunk of the car," the cop panted as he climbed.

"Which car?"

"Dr. Yarborough's Lincoln. The one we followed here from the Howarth building. Looks like he was bringing a last-minute addition to the burial. We sure didn't expect to see *that* when we popped open his trunk."

They walked past the gathering of elderly onlookers and crossed to Yarborough's car, parked by the fence. Detective Sheehan was standing beside the open trunk. "Tonight they come in threes," he said.

Dvorak shook his head. "I'm not sure I can handle much more of this tonight."

"You feeling okay, Doc?"

Dvorak paused, thinking about the night that lay ahead. About the hours it would take him to reach Toby's bedside. The delay could not be helped; this he had to do.

He took a pair of latex gloves from his pocket. "Let's get on with this," he said and looked into the trunk.

Sheehan trained his flashlight beam on the face of the corpse.

For a moment Dvorak could not say a word. He stood gazing at the girl's face, at the bruise marring that fragile skin, at the gray eyes, open and soulless. Once there had been a soul there; once he had seen it, shining brightly. *Where are you now?* he wondered. *Somewhere good, I hope. Somewhere warm and kind and safe.*

He reached down and, gently, closed Molly Picker's eyes.

The sound of nurses laughing in the hallway roused Dvorak from a fitful sleep. He opened his eyes and saw daylight shining in the window. He was sitting in a chair by Toby's hospital bed. She was still asleep, her breathing slow and steady, her cheeks flushed. Most of the dirt had been wiped away from her face last night, but he could still see a few grains of sand sparkling in her hair.

He rose and stretched, trying to work the kinks out of his neck. At last a sunny day, he thought, staring out the window. Only the smallest wisp of a cloud drifted in the sky.

Behind him, a voice murmured: "I had the worst nightmare."

Turning, he met Toby's gaze. She held out her hand to him. He took it warmly in his and sat down beside her.

"But I didn't dream it, did I?" she said.

"No. I'm afraid it was all too real."

She lay silent for a moment, frowning, as though trying to gather all her fragments of memory into one comprehensible whole.

"We found their medical records," said Dvorak.

She looked at him, her eyes questioning.

"They kept data on all the brain implants. Seventy-nine files, stored in the basement of the Howarth building. Patient names, operative notes, follow-up head scans."

"They were compiling data?"

He nodded. "To back up their claims of success. By the look of it, the implants did have benefits."

"And hazards too," she added softly.

"Yes. There was a cluster of patients early last year, when Wallenberg was still using aborted fetuses. Five men received their implants from the same pooled fetal cells.

365

They were all infected at the same time. It took a year for the first one to come down with symptoms."

"Dr. Mackie?"

He nodded.

"You said there were seventy-nine files. What about all the other patients?"

"Alive and well. And thriving. Which presents a moral dilemma. What if this treatment really does work?"

By her troubled expression, he knew she shared his concerns. *How far do we go to prolong life? How much of our humanity do we sacrifice?*

She said, suddenly, "I know where to find Harry Slotkin." She looked at him with startling clarity in her eyes. "Brant Hill—the new nursing home wing. A few weeks ago, they poured the foundation."

"Yes, Wallenberg told us."

"Wallenberg did?"

"They're at each others' throats now. Wallenberg and Gideon against the Trammells. It's a race to pin the blame. Right now, the Trammells seem to be in the worst trouble."

Toby paused, gathering the courage to ask the next question. "Robbie?"

"It was Richard Trammell. The gun was registered to him. We expect ballistics will confirm it."

She nodded, absorbing the painful information in silence. He saw tears flash in her eyes and decided he would wait to tell her about Molly. This was not the time to burden her with yet more tragedy.

There was a knock on the door, and Vickie stepped into the room. She looked paler than she had last night, when Dvorak had seen her visiting Toby. Paler and strangely afraid. She paused a few feet away from the bed, as though reluctant to approach.

Dvorak stood up. "I think I'll leave you two alone," he said.

"No. Please," said Vickie. "You don't have to go."

"I'm not going anywhere." He bent down and gave Toby a kiss. "But I will wait outside." He straightened and crossed to the door.

There he paused.

Glancing back, he saw Vickie suddenly break free of some invisible restraint. In three swift steps she crossed to the bed and took Toby into her arms.

Dvorak brushed his hand across his eyes. And quietly left the room.

Two Days Later

The ventilator delivered its twenty breaths per minute, each whoosh followed by a sigh, the deflation of ribs and chest wall. Toby had found the rhythm soothing as she combed her mother's hair and bathed her limbs and torso, the washcloth gliding across landmarks she had come to know so well. The star-shaped patch of pigment on the left arm. The biopsy scar on the breast. The arthritic finger, bent in a shepherd's crook. But this scar on the knee—how did Ellen get it? Toby wondered. It looked like a very old scar, well healed, almost invisible, its origins lost in the forgotten reaches of her mother's childhood. Gazing at it under the bright lights of the ICU cubicle, she thought: All these years Mom has had this scar, and I never noticed it until now.

"Toby?"

She turned and saw Dvorak standing in the cubicle doorway. Perhaps he'd been there for some time; she hadn't noticed his arrival. That was simply Dvorak's way. In the day and a half she'd been hospitalized, Toby would awaken and think she was alone. Then she'd turn her head and see that he was still sitting in her room, silent and unnoticed, watching over her. As he was doing now.

"Your sister's just arrived," he said. "Dr. Steinglass is on his way upstairs."

Toby looked down at her mother. Ellen's hair was splayed across the pillow. It looked not like the hair of an old woman but the luxurious mane of a young girl, bright as windblown sheets of silver. Toby bent down and touched her lips to Ellen's forehead.

"Good night, Mom," she whispered, and walked out of the cubicle.

On the other side of the viewing window, she took her place beside Vickie. Dvorak stood behind them, his presence felt though unseen. Through the glass they watched Dr. Steinglass enter the cubicle and cross to the ventilator. He glanced at Toby, a silent question in his eyes.

She nodded.

He turned off the ventilator.

Ellen's chest fell still. Ten seconds passed in silence.

Vickie reached for Toby's hand, held on tight.

Ellen's chest remained motionless.

Now her heart was slowing. First a pause. A stumbled beat. Then, at last, the final stillness.

From the moment we're born, death is our final destination, thought Toby. *Only the date and time of our arrival is unknown.*

For Ellen, the journey was completed at two-fifteen, on this afternoon in late autumn.

For Daniel Dvorak, death might come in two years or in forty years. It might be heralded by the tremor of his hand, or arrive without warning in the night while his grandchildren sleep in the next room. He would learn to cope with that uncertainty, as people coped with all the other uncertainties of life.

And for the rest of us?

Toby pressed her hand against the glass and felt her own pulse, warm and strong, in her fingertips. *I've already died once,* she thought.

This was a brand-new journey.

References

Berny, P. J., Buronfosse, T., and Lorgue, G., "Anticoagulant Poisoning in Animals," *Journal of Analytical Toxicology*, Nov.–Dec. 1995; 19 (7): 576–80.

Boer, G. J., "Ethical Guidelines for the Use of Human Embryonic or Fetal Tissue for Experimental and Clinical Neurotransplantation and Research," *Journal of Neurology*, Dec. 1994; 242 (1): 1–13.

Carey, Benedict, "Hooked on Youth," *Health*, Nov.–Dec. 1995; 68–74.

Hainline, Bryan E., Padilla, Lillie-Mae, et al., "Fetal Tissue Derived from Spontaneous Pregnancy Losses Is Insufficient for Human Transplantation," *Obstetrics and Gynecology*, April 1995: 85 (4): 619–24.

Halder, G., Callaerts, P., and Gehring, W. J., "Induction of Ectopic Eyes by Targeted Expression of the Eyeless Gene in Drosophila," *Science*, Mar. 24, 1995; 267 (5205): 1788–92.

Hayflick, L., and Moorhead, P. S., "The Cell Biology of

REFERENCES

Human Aging," *New England Journal of Medicine,* Dec. 2, 1976; 295 (23): 1302–8.

O'Brien, Claire, "Mad Cow Disease: Scant Data Cause Widespread Concern," *Science,* March 29, 1996; 271 (5257): 1798.

Prusiner, Stanley, "The Prion Diseases," *Scientific American,* Jan. 1995; 272 (1): 48–57.

Rosenstein, J. M., "Why Do Neural Transplants Survive?" *Experimental Neurology,* May 1995: 133 (1): 1–6.

Roush, Wade, "Smart Genes Use Many Cues to Set Cell Fate," *Science,* May 3, 1966; 272 (5262): 652–53.

Sheng, Hui, Zhadanov, Alexander, et al., "Specification of Pituitary Cell Lineages by the LIM Homeobox Gene Lhx3," *Science,* May 1996; 272 (5264): 1004–7.

Vinogradova, O. S., "Some Factors Controlling Morpho-Functional Integration of the Transplanted Embryonic Brain Tissue," *Zhurnal Vysshei Nervnoi Deiatelnosti Imeni I.P. Pavlova* (Moscow), May–June 1994; 44 (3): 414–30.

Weinstein, P. R., and Wilson, C. B., "Stereotaxic Hypophysectomy," *Youmans Neurological Surgery,* vol. 6, Julian Youmans, Ed., 3rd ed., Philadelphia: Saunders, 1990.